MR AMERICAN

GEORGE MACDONALD FRASER had already written six of
the Flashman novels and established a worldwide reputation as a humorist who was also a considerable scholar
of the Victorian era when he published *Mr American*. Like
The Pyrates, it stands outside any series – although not
altogether, for Harry Flashman has a considerable sup-
porting role. The ninth and latest volume of Flashman
Papers (all available as Fontana paperbacks) is *Flashman
and the Mountain of Light*: it convinced Kingsley Amis that
the author possesses a "good deal more narrative power
than Kipling". He has also delighted thousands of readers
round the world with three volumes of stories about
Private McAuslan, thoughtfully described as "the biggest
walking disaster to hit the British Army since Ancient
Pistol".

George MacDonald Fraser served both in the Border
Regiment in Burma during the war and in the Gordon
Highlanders. He has worked on newspapers in Britain and
Canada and was deputy editor of the *Glasgow Herald*.

George MacDonald Fraser

MR AMERICAN

HARVILL
An Imprint of HarperCollins*Publishers*

First published in Great Britain in 1980 by Collins
This edition first issued in 1992
by Harvill
an imprint of HarperCollins*Publishers*
77/85 Fulham Palace Road,
Hammersmith, London W6 8JB

9 8 7 6 5 4 3

Acknowledgement is due and gratefully given to Peter Newboldt
for permission to quote from Sir Henry Newboldt's
"The Fighting Temeraire"; and to B. Feldman & Co. Ltd.
for permission to quote from "Everybody's Doing It (Now)"
and from "It's a Long Way to Tipperary";
and to Herman Davewski Publishing Co.
for permission to quote from "Goodbye Dolly Gray".

The Author asserts the moral right to be
identified as the author of this work

A catalogue record for this book is
available from the British Library

ISBN 0 00 271235 0

Phototypeset in Linotron Ehrhardt by
Intype, London

**Printed and bound in Great Britain by
Hartnolls Limited, Bodmin, Cornwall**

Part One

1

Inspector Griffin came down to the landing-stage on a raw autumn morning to see the *Mauretania* berthing. It was part of his job; there was always someone from the detective department on hand when the American liners docked, but for Inspector Griffin it was a pleasure, too. He loved the bustle of the wharf at dawn, and the sight of the huge iron ship edging gently into the quay, the busy little tugs, the squealing whistles, the propellor churning the yellow Mersey into dirty foam; he even enjoyed the bite of the wind and the cold drizzle which was causing his colleague, young Constable Murphy, to hunch his collar round his chin as he stamped his feet on the wet flags. To Murphy it was just another tedious chore; he wiped his nose and glowered at the low clouds over the river.

"Won't be worth their while takin' off at Doncaster this afternoon," he observed glumly, and Inspector Griffin understood. Constable Murphy was a flying enthusiast, like most of the population these days; since M. Blériot had come winging ghost-like out of the Channel mist a few weeks before, the first man to fly from France into England in a crazy contraption that looked like an overgrown kite, the country seemed to have gone flying daft, Inspector Griffin reflected. He didn't like it; perhaps he was getting old and conservative, but the thought that a man could fly in a few minutes across England's last line of defence – and from France, of all places – made him uneasy. It wasn't natural, and it wasn't safe. And what use would the Royal Navy be, if Frogs and Germans and God knew what other breed of foreigners could soar unscathed over their heads?

"Farman an' Cody's goin' to be at Doncaster," said Murphy, with relish. "First flyin' meetin' on British soil, by gum! Wouldn't I like to be there? Cody flew from London to Manchester the other day, over the railway tracks, special markers they had on the ground to guide him – an' they say Farman's been up six hundred feet, an' can go higher yet." He shuddered deliciously and wiped his nose again. "Think of it, sir! Just them tiny machines, an' – "

7

Females, football and flying, Griffin reflected irritably, that was all these young fellows thought about. The gangways were down, and the first passengers were picking their way gingerly down to the quay, shepherded by the *Mauretania*'s stewards, but Murphy, who should have been casting a professional eye over them, was plainly miles away in the sky above Doncaster, performing aerobatics with Cody and Farman and his other heroes.

"Cody's goin' to become naturalized British, they reckon," he went on. "If he lives long enough – there was a crash at Paris t'other day, fellow broke his neck, shocking risks they take – "

"Thought you were more interested in Everton," said Griffin, vainly trying to stem the flood. "Aren't they playing Liverpool this afternoon?"

"Gah, they'll get beat, them," said Murphy derisively. "Play football, that lot? They dunno what football is – you should have been up in Glasgow the other day, sir, my Saturday off. Glasgow versus Sheffield, that was something. See that McMenemy, an' Quinn – bloody marvellous! We don't see nothing like 'em, down here. Now, Quinn, he – "

I was a fool to mention it, thought Griffin, and a bigger fool for being so soft. Any right-minded inspector would have shut up the garrulous Murphy with a look, but he wasn't a bad lad and Griffin had a liking for him. Irish though – mind you, who wasn't, in Liverpool these days? Griffin the Welshman had strong views about immigrants and while the Micks were undeniably fellow-Britons there were still a damned sight too many of them about.

"Come on," he said, "they're coming ashore," and the two officers moved off into the long, dingy Customs shed where the officials were waiting with their watchful eyes and pieces of chalk among the mounds of baggage, to deal soft-voiced with the first passengers who were congregating at the tables.

This was what Griffin liked. The faces, the clothes, the voices – above all the voices. Many years before, Inspector Griffin had been a strapping young constable in the North-west Mounted Police; it was where his career had begun, and he had never lost his affection for the North American accent – even the harsh nasal Yankee voice which was so often heard in that shed awoke memories for him; he had that vague privileged feeling of kinship that one feels for foreigners in whose country one has lived. Not that Canada was foreign, of course, quite the opposite; neither were Americans, really – he scanned the faces beyond the tables with an interest that was only part-professional, indulging in his habitual speculation. Who were they? Where were they from? What would they be doing in England? How many of them were rascals? One or two, in his experience, but nothing serious this trip, or Delgado in New York would have telegraphed. He'd never met Delgado, and knew him only as a name at the end of cables and occasional official reports – Delgado would know him in the same way. Wonder what he was like? – sounded like an Italian name, maybe. Good policeman, anyway, whatever he was; it was Delgado's tip that had helped them nail that German forger in Leeds a year ago.

"Do I look as though I am carrying more than half a pint of spirits?" A mountainous lady in an expensive sealskin coat and a mountainous English accent was glaring at a Customs man. "Spirits, indeed! I never heard of such – "

"Perfumes are spirits, madam," said the Customs man quietly. "Have you any perfume, madam?"

"Of course I have. A normal quantity, and certainly not half a pint – "

"And chocolates, madam? Confections of any kind?"

"Chocolates?"

"Sweets are dutiable, madam. Any American candies, or bonbons – "

"What arrant nonsense!" The lady turned indignantly to the pale young companion at her side. "Have we any sweets, Evelyn? Dangerous, highly contraband sweets whose introduction into England will unbalance the Budget?"

Griffin smiled, but his eyes were elsewhere, running over a small, stout man waiting his turn at the next table, politely allowing a lady to go first, smiling affably and tapping his fingers on the handle of his valise. Three or four bottles of brandy in there for a start, thought Griffin. That was not strictly speaking any of his business, but the stout little man could easily be a sharp. Griffin sauntered closer to listen to the voice.

" . . . one bottle of bourbon, open, and a half pound of cigars, nothing else, officer." It was an American voice, sharp and eager, perhaps a little too conciliatory. "Oh, and I have a copy of one of Mr Conan Doyle – I beg your pardon, *Sir* Arthur Conan Doyle's novels,

9

printed in America. I know that English copyrighted books are liable to confiscation, but I assure you it's the only one I've got."

" – an' anyway, Liverpool'll win by two clear goals, easy," Constable Murphy was saying. "Want me to keep an eye on that one, sir?"

Griffin turned away, surveying the other passengers. Rich, influential, upper-class, most of them, as one would expect aboard the *Mauretania*. Well-fed faces, substantial broadcloths and tweeds on the men, furs on the ladies, fox stoles and sealskins, diamond pins, gold watch-chains, a profusion of expensive rings and brooches – a pickpocket's paradise, if any of the local dips had had the nerve to invade the area between the quay and Riverside Station, well-policed as it was. About half were American visitors, about half returning Britons; the voices mingled in a babble round the Customs tables. "Anything to declare . . . ? Well, I don't know how many cigars make a pound, officer. . . . I have this silk scarf, but it's a present for my mother, don't you know . . . if you'll open the large trunk, please, sir . . . but it's an *engagement* ring – this is my fiancé – surely you won't charge on that? . . . anything to declare, madam?"

All the usual little lies, the half-hearted deceptions, the unnecessary anxieties, thought Griffin. But nothing really to excite his official interest. He noted that the mountainous lady was preparing to erupt as her nervous companion clumsily unbuckled the straps of a suitcase and twitteringly guided and hindered the Customs man as he plunged into the mass of female clothing within.

"One would think one were a criminal, or a passenger to New York!" exclaimed the large lady indignantly, her feather hat quivering with affront. "It is bad enough to have one's belongings turned out wholesale in front of half the population of America, but in England – really!" Plainly the lady had suffered, on her arrival at New York, at the hands of the minions of "Lucky" Loeb, the Customs Chief, whose private war against smuggling had caused considerable indignation and sundry spluttering letters to the *New York Times*; Griffin seemed to remember that even a steamship line's director had had to turn out his pockets. But now the Customs man was delving and bringing forth a large bottle of gin, and the lady was going bright purple and demanding of the shrinking Evelyn how *that* had got there?

"Serve the old trout right," observed Murphy coarsely, and Inspector Griffin privately agreed. Nothing much here, though; he glanced again at the little stout man, who was bustling off crying "Thank you, thank you, sir!" to the Customs man, and was preparing to speak to Murphy, when his eye fell on a face at the table beyond.

A man was stepping forward to take his place at the table, pausing momentarily to make way for two pretty, giggling American girls who were gathering up their cases; they had succeeded in wheedling more than their allowance of perfume past a grey-haired and indulgent official, and were tripping off to find a porter. One of them shot a quick, appraising glance at the man who was stepping aside, received a grave touch of the hat-brim in return, and whispered, tittering to her companion; she was what Murphy would have called a peach, a lissom little blonde whose bobbing curls and tight-skirted bottom drew an approving sigh from the constable as he watched her clicking off on her high heels, showing a tantalising glimpse of silken ankle; a nudge from Griffin brought him back to earth.

"That one at the far table. All right, turn this way and tell me about him."

Murphy glanced at the man for a couple of seconds and turned obediently to face Griffin; he only slightly resented his superior's habit of playing classroom games by way of instruction in police routine.

"American," he said confidently, "thirty to thirty-five, not more. Six foot one, maybe two, between twelve an' thirteen stone, well built on the lean side, black moustache, no whiskers, could do with a hair-cut, thin features, sunburned, wearing a bowler, brown, an' a tweed cape, dark suit, no rings, plain pin, watch-chain as might be gold but might just as easy be brass, not carryin' a stick, but with a big green valise – "

"Yes, yes, boy," said Griffin. "But what *about* him? Turn and have another look."

Murphy shrugged and glanced round at the man, who was watching the Customs official go through his valise; he looked ordinary enough to Murphy; not quite so well-dressed as most of the passengers, perhaps, a trifle more – bohemian was the word that might have occurred to Murphy if he had known it, but it would have been wide of the mark. Quiet-looking chap, very attentive to what the Customs man said, nodding seriously and thanking the official as he restrapped the valise and turned his attention to the battered trunk which lay beside the table. Murphy frowned and shrugged again.

"That's all, sir; don't see anything out o' the way. He's no crook, that's certain; not so – well, smooth as most, but otherwise . . ." He

11

shook his head. "Quiet chap, I'd say; you know, a bit soft-like, in his manner – for a Yankee, any roads."

The Customs man was bending over the trunk, chalk in hand, and the American was stooping beside him, apparently reassuring him about the contents. Griffin strained his ears, and felt a slight thrill of satisfaction when the passenger spoke. All he said was: "No, no I don't believe I have any of those. Guess I'd know if I did, all right. Thank you, thanks very much."

The voice fitted, Griffin thought. That soft, husky drawl, so different from the nasal rasp of the Eastern seaboard; it was a voice from the Plains, the kind he remembered from the Saskatchewan prairie. North Central United States, then, or thereabouts; it was an accent which Griffin, with his sympathetic Welsh ear, could have listened to all day; a voice from out yonder.

"Have I missed anything, sir?" Murphy was wondering.

Just about everything that matters, thought Griffin, but since he couldn't blame Murphy for failing to recognize something he had never seen before, all he said was: "No, boy, you had him summed up nice for description. He isn't sunburned, though; he's weather-beaten. There's a difference. Tell you what, Constable Murphy – that little stout chap who went through a minute since. See if he gets on the London train, will you? If he doesn't, get his address."

He was not particularly interested in the little stout man, but he wanted to study this other one at leisure. Not that there was anything really remarkable about him, but he was out of the run of the normal transatlantic traffic. A Westerner, and not a townsman, either. Griffin studied the tall, rangy figure in its slightly incongruous cape and new bowler; good features, behind the black moustache that turned down slightly at the corners of the mouth, quite a fine face, like a scholar's, even, thought Griffin, although this patently wasn't a scholar. Soft-like, Murphy had thought, and Griffin could excuse him for the mistake; there was a gentleness, almost a diffidence, about the face and the man's whole bearing, as though he were ready to apologise for being there. But he wasn't soft; oh no, thought Griffin, you're not soft – but nobody will realize it until the moment when they wish they hadn't misjudged you.

The Inspector smiled. How long ago was it now? – twenty-four years, nearly twenty-five since the day that sometimes came back to him in bad dreams. The tangled clearing at Duck Lake, the reek of powder smoke and the crash of firing, the shrill yells of the Metis sharpshooters and the whooping of Big Bear's Crees as they closed in through the woods on the battered circle of red coats among the carts and slaughtered horses. The Army Colt jumping in his fist as he fired over the shelter of his saddle, and then the scorching pain in his left arm, and himself pawing at the feathered arrow in his blood-soaked sleeve, crying great tears of pain, until the man next to him had crawled across to snap the shaft off short and thrust the arrow-head agonisingly through Griffin's arm and out the other side. He remembered the man's face; the same wide-spaced grey eyes, the lean features and straight jaw under the broad-brimmed hat, and the soft, almost apologetic voice: "Easy does it, Mountie. Just lie there, head down – okay?" Why, he might have been this fellow's father, for looks. MacPherson, his name had been, a big, gangling scout in buckskin – but then, there had been hundreds like him, all through that campaign; tall, quiet men who said little, and that to the point, courteous in manner, pensive, rather lonely men.

And the wounded bewildered young constable in the red tunic was now Inspector Lloyd Griffin, of the Liverpool force, dressed in authority and drab overcoat, heavier about the jowls and waist, and instead of the trees and war-whoops by Duck Lake there was the echoing Customs shed and the respectable passengers and staff going about their business quietly and orderly in the civilised centre of England's second city, and it was no buckskin man but a soberly-dressed American who was nodding to the Customs man and looking about for a porter.

Griffin sauntered closer and cast an eye at the label on the battered trunk. It read "M. J. Franklin, Adelphi Hotel, Liverpool, England." Well, he hadn't expected to see the name MacPherson, anyhow. Just because this boy was from the same stable, so to speak, of the same breed and the same neck of the woods, give or take a thousand miles or so, meant nothing. Inspector Griffin shook himself almost irritably. That was all long ago, and things had changed; this was the twentieth century, and the wild days were well gone now, except in the memories of old hands like himself. But for a moment there, the sight of that . . . that *type*, working on his Celtic imagination, had taken him back. Well, of course, men didn't change, even if times did. And this one still seemed out of place, somehow, in grimy old Liverpool. In quiet old England, come to that.

He watched M. J. Franklin trying to catch a porter's eye and not succeeding. No, decidedly he wasn't a city-dweller. A farmer, perhaps?

13

No, that wasn't right. A surveyor, then, or an engineer. Most probably something like that, with his sundowner complexion. And what was he doing in England? Any one of a thousand perfectly ordinary things – Inspector Griffin chided himself to remember that men came and went with startling speed from the ends of the earth nowadays, on all sorts of errands; the old conventions that tied a man to his place were going, and it was becoming one world indeed. Bloody Frogs flying the Channel, for example.

"He got on the London train, second class, his name's Kruger, and he travels for a New Jersey typewriter manufacturer." Constable Murphy was back, reporting with every sign of self-satisfaction. "An' he'll be staying at Peterson's Hotel, Baker Street."

"Very good, Constable Murphy," said Griffin, and since it would never do for Murphy to think he was impressed, he added: "And the little Yankee charmer with the blonde curls, then? Where was *she* going?"

"Maidstone, to visit her aunt," said Murphy, grinning. "Well, she was having trouble finding a seat, and a policeman's meant to be helpful, isn't he?"

"She must be uncommon helpless if she can't find a seat on a train that's never half-full," said Griffin drily. He was still observing Mr Franklin's unavailing attempts to summon a porter. On impulse the Inspector whistled, short and sharp, half a dozen porters looked round, and a jerk of his head directed their attention to Franklin's trunk. In a moment it was on a barrow and being rolled out of the shed; Franklin, who had heard the whistle, raised an acknowledging finger to the Inspector.

"Much obliged to you, sir," he said, and strode off after his trunk, valise in hand, open cape flapping. Griffin watched the rangy figure out of sight, and sighed. So much for his romantic imagination, he decided. Still . . .

"Duck out o' water," said Murphy carelessly, following his chief's glance.

"Yes," said Inspector Griffin, turning away. "Yes, constable, you're probably right."

*

Once outside the Customs shed, Mr Franklin paused to examine the railway timetable board; there were, he saw, five companies competing to carry him to London on Monday. After some deliberation, he

14

decided on the London and North-western, which undertook to convey him to Euston in something over four hours, via Crewe and Rugby, for 29 shillings first-class. Just under six dollars, in fact. It was the fastest train, not that that could matter to a man who had not taken the special vestibuled boat-train for Atlantic passengers which was even now pulling out of Riverside Station with a shrilling of steam.

His porter was waiting at the cab rank, and on his inquiring whether the gentleman wished to travel by taxi or horse cab, Mr Franklin fixed him with a thoughtful grey eye and asked what the fare might be.

"Cab's a shillin' a mile, taxi's sixpence a half-mile an' twopence every sixth of a mile after that," replied the porter.

"And how far is the Adelphi Hotel?" asked Mr Franklin.

This innocent question caused some consternation among the taxi-men and cab drivers; some thought it would be about a mile, if not slightly more, but there was a school of thought that held it was a bare mile by the shortest route. No one knew for certain, and finally the porter, a practical man who wanted to get back to the Customs shed for another client, settled the matter by spitting and declaring emphatically:

"It'll cost you a shillin', anyways."

Mr Franklin nodded judiciously, indicated a horse-cab, and then paid the porter. He seemed to be having some difficulty with the massive British copper coins, to which he was plainly unaccustomed, and the tiny silver "doll's-eye" threepence which he eventually bestowed; the porter sighed and reflected that this was a damned queer Yank; most of them scattered their money like water.

This was not lost on the cabby, who mentally abandoned the notion of suggesting that he take his passenger by way of Rodney Street – which would have added at least sixpence to the fare – there to gaze on Number 62, the birthplace of the late Mr Gladstone. Americans, in his experience, loved to see the sights, and would exclaim at the Grand Old Man's childhood home and add as much as a shilling to the tip. An even better bet was the house in Brunswick Street where Nathaniel Hawthorne had kept his office as U.S. Consul in the middle of the previous century, but somehow, the cabby reflected morosely, this particular American didn't look as though he'd be interested in the author of *Tanglewood* and *The Scarlet Letter* either.

The cab drew out of the quayside gates and up the long pier to the main street at the top, where the electric trams clanged and rumbled and a slow-moving stream of traffic, most of it horse-drawn, but with the occasional motor here and there, slowed the cab to a walk. The cabby noted that his fare was sitting forward, surveying the scene with the air of a man who is intent on drinking everything in, but giving no sign of whether he found it pleasing or otherwise. For the cabby's money, central Liverpool was not an inspiring sight in any weather, with its bustling pavements and dirty over-crowded streets, and he was genuinely startled when after some little distance his passenger called out sharply to him to hold on. He was staring intently down the street which they were crossing, a long, grimy thoroughfare of chandlers" shops and warehouses; he was smiling, the wondering cabby noticed, in a strange, faraway fashion, as though seeing something that wasn't there at all. He was humming, too, gently under his breath, as he surveyed the long seedy stretch of ugly buildings and cobbles on which the rain was beginning to fall.

"You want to go down there, sir?" the cabby inquired. "Takes us oot o' the road to the Adelphi, like."

"No," said Mr Franklin. "Just looking." He nodded at the street-sign, a plaque fixed high on the corner building. "Paradise Street." And then to the cabby's astonishment he laughed and sat back, quoting to himself in an absent-minded way:

> As I was walking down Paradise Street,
> Way-hay, blow the man down.
> Thirty miles out from Liverpool town,
> Gimme some time to blow the man down.

That had been Tracy's song, Tracy the Irishman who had been a sailor. And there was Paradise Street itself, come on all unexpected, and nothing like the picture the song had conjured up when Tracy sang it, far from the sea. What had he imagined? Waving palms, blue water, sandy shores – and here were the cold grey stones of Liverpool's sailortown. Very unexpected – but then England was sure to be full of unexpected, unimagined things. He became aware that the cabby, twisted round on his box, was viewing him with some concern; Mr Franklin nodded and gestured him to drive on.

A funny monkey, the driver decided; American interest in things English was, he knew from experience, liable to be eccentric, but Paradise Street . . . ? Was this bloke one of those who might be enthused by a view of St George's Hall, that startling showpiece of

16

Liverpudlian architecture which they would see towards the end of their journey? Or if he didn't care for mock Graeco-Roman temples five hundred feet long, would he respond to some useful information on the subject of the Walker Fine Art Gallery, with its striking sketch by Tintoretto and its portrait of Margaret de Valois, possibly by Holbein but more probably school of J. Clouet? The cabby, who had done his homework carefully for the benefit of tourists, stole another look at his fare's impassive bronzed face and decided regretfully that he wouldn't. Putting all hope of a substantial tip out of his head, he drove on to the Adelphi Hotel.

Here, he was rewarded with his shilling fare and another carefully-selected silver threepence, and Mr Franklin was escorted by porters into the luxurious marble and red plush interior of the lobby. He paused to survey the elegant little staircase leading to the main lounge, the mixed throng of affluent transit guests and local, no-nonsense business men in sober suits and watch-chains, the quiet efficiency of the Adelphi's numerous hall staff – and was surveyed in his turn by the Irish head porter, who was as great an expert in his way as Inspector Griffin. No stick, no gloves, well-worn boots, and a decid-edly colonial look to his clothing, the porter thought; his first ques-tion'll be the price of a room.

"How much do you charge," asked Mr Franklin quietly, "for a single room?"

"Four shillings and upwards, sir," replied the porter. "That's eighty cents in your own money," and he favoured Mr Franklin with an avuncular smile, being one who had relatives in Philadelphia himself. "Just off the boat, sir? You'll be ready for a bite of breakfast, then. In the coffee-room, sir; the gentlemen's cloak-room is to your right. And the name, sir? Frank-lin, very good. Of –?"

"Ah . . . United States."

"First-rate, sir. The boy will take up your luggage. You'll be staying . . . two nights, sir. I see. Now, when you've breakfasted, if there's any assistance I can give, you just inquire at my desk. Not at all, sir." And as Mr Franklin hesitated, as though wondering whether to reach into his waistcoat pocket for another threepence, the porter generously solved the problem for him by turning to attend to an angular English lady, changing in that instant from a warm and genial father-figure into the respectfully impersonal butler to whom her ladyship was accustomed.

Mr Franklin left his cape and hat in the cloak-room, warily exam-

17

ined the array of flacons of lavender water, Hammam's Bouquet, Mennen's toilet powder, and Eno's Fruit Salts laid out for exterior and internal refreshment, and compromised by washing his hands. He should have stayed over in New York, at the Belmont or the Clarendon, to get the feel of these places, but the city had been bursting at the seams for the Hudson-Fulton festivities celebrating the three hundredth anniversary of the former's discovery of Manhattan, and the hundredth of the latter's steam navigation; consequently, there had been no rooms to be had. Besides, he had had a vague desire to come fresh to England from where he had been; an odd ambition which he would have had difficulty in defining.

He ate an excellent breakfast in the cosy coffee-room, sitting at a little window table and watching the constant stream of traffic and pedestrians in the street outside. He deliberately ate slowly, conscious of a mounting feeling of excitement – which he found strange in himself, for he was not normally an excitable man. Then he returned to the lobby, and questioned the attentive porter.

"Guide books to London and East Anglia, sir? Sure, now I can get those for you. And a large-scale map of the county of Norfolk?" The porter's eyebrows rose a fraction. "You'll want the ordnance survey – yes, I dare say I can get that, too. It may take an hour or so, but if you're going out . . . you are, for a look at the town. Capital, sir."

Mr Franklin thanked him, and set off to tour the city on foot, content to walk at random, watching and listening, standing on street corners to observe the passing crowds, trying to accustom his ear to the strange, soft mumbling accent of the Liverpudlians, observing the magisterial police on traffic duty, spending five minutes listening to an altercation between a stout woman and a street trader, riding on an electric tram and on the famous overhead railway, and generally presenting the appearance of an interested wanderer absorbing the sights and sounds around him.

He lunched in a public house off soup and sandwiches, washed down by a pint of heavy dark beer which he found rather cloyingly sweet, spent another couple of hours in apparently aimless strolling, and returned to the Adelphi as dusk was falling. There he dined, and after calculating that the five shillings, or one dollar, which the dinner cost, still left him with a comfortable balance from the ten dollars which, the *Mauretania*'s purser had assured him, was all that a first-class traveller need spend per day in England, retired to his room.

Here the guide books which the porter had obtained were waiting

18

for him, but he ignored them in favour of the large ordnance survey map of Norfolk, which he spread out on the bed and began to examine with close attention. For half an hour he pored over it, the dark face intent as he traced over the fine print and symbols denoting such detailed items as railway cuttings, plantations, marshes, forest paths, churches with spires (and with towers), historic sites, and the like, and the quaint, pastoral place-names, Attleborough, Sheringham, Swaffham, Methwold, and Castle Lancing.

Mr Franklin smiled, and lay down on the bed, and for another half-hour he was quite still, stretched out, hands behind his head, the dark grey eyes staring up at the ceiling, the gentle mouth beneath the black moustache slightly open. An onlooker would have thought he was asleep, but presently he came swiftly to his feet, and went purposefully to the work of undressing and preparing himself for bed.

He unpacked his few toilet articles from his valise, took off his jacket, removed the money-belt round his waist and methodically counted its contents – one hundred and ninety-eight gold sovereigns, which was a considerable sum, even for a transatlantic passenger, and had caused the American Express clerk in New York to purse his lips doubtfully when Mr Franklin, changing his dollars, had insisted on carrying so much on his person. If Inspector Griffin, or the Irish head porter, had been privileged to peep into Mr Franklin's room they, too, might have been mildly surprised. But they would not have thought anything particularly out of the way until the moment when Mr Franklin, having stood for several minutes contemplating his battered trunk where it stood against the wall, gave way apparently to a sudden impulse, and unbuckled the straps which secured it. Even then there was nothing strange in his behaviour, or in the way he paused, glancing round the room with its homely fittings, the shaded light, the marble wash-stand with its bowl and ewer, the floral wall-paper and patterned carpet, the little notice informing guests of meal-times and fire precautions; nor even in the way he meditatively touched the linen pillow and embroidered bed-spread, like a man reassuring himself of his surroundings, before he turned to the trunk again and threw back the lid.

At that point they might have taken notice, for the contents of Mr Franklin's trunk were, to say the least, slightly unusual for a guest in a Liverpool hotel. Not that there was anything about them to excite Inspector Griffin's professional attention; there was no contraband, no illicit goods, nothing to which, in those easygoing days, even a law

19

officer could have taken exception, although he might have made a mental note that Mr Franklin was a man of unusual background and, possibly, behaviour.

The principal object in the trunk, taking up most of its space, was a saddle – but the kind of saddle that would have made an English hunting squire rub his eyes and exclaim with disgust. It was what the Mexicans call a *charro* saddle, heavily ornamented and studded with metal-work, very high both before and behind, and therefore a sure recipe (in the eyes of the English squire) for a broken pelvis if its owner were unwise enough to use it over hedges. There was also a blanket, of Indian pattern, neatly folded, and a heavy canvas slicker, or cape; a very worn and stained wideawake hat, a pair of heavy leather gauntlets, a pair of battered boots in sore need of repair, a large drinking mug of cheap metal, and several packets of papers done up in oil-skin.

Mr Franklin, squatting in front of the trunk in his long underwear – he had discarded his newly-bought nightshirt on the first day of his voyage – handled each item in turn, very carefully, running his long fingers over their surfaces, caressingly almost as a man will handle old things which are familiar friends. He spun the big rowels on the spurred boots and put them back, smiling a little, rapped his knuckle on the mug, balanced the packets of papers in his hands, and restored them to their places. There were half a dozen books in the trunk; he leafed through them slowly – *Old Mortality, Oliver Twist, Humphrey Clinker*, Baedeker's *Guide to England*, the 1897 edition; the poetical works of Wordsworth, George Borrow's *Lavengro, Huckleberry Finn*, the complete works of Shakespeare.

He read the fly-leaf on the Shakespeare, although he knew the inscription off by heart, the spidery writing in faded ink: "To Luke Franklin, in the earnest hope that he may find profit, pleasure, and peace of mind in its pages, from his affectionate father". The signature was "Jno. Franklin, 1858". His grandfather's gift to his own father; he could hear the old man's voice reading from it – Luke Franklin had loved best of all to recite Falstaff's part, chuckling over the grosser jests, rolling Shakespeare's rich periods over his tongue . . . "when I was of thy years I was not an eagle's talon in the waist; I could have crept me into any alderman's thumb ring." He had wondered what an alderman was, and Luke Franklin had told him, on a soft and starry summer night when they camped on the road to El Paso; he had been just a boy then, lying staring into the fire, listening

20

while his father explained that it was a corruption of "eolderman", an old English word – "it's the same as elder, an elder man, an alderman, who is a kind of city councilman back in England. They still have them there." His father had resumed his reading aloud, and the boy had gone to sleep, to awake in the pearly dawn, beside a dead fire, with his father still croaking away through the Battle of Shrewsbury, oblivious of time and place, lost in the magic of the play.

Mr Franklin sighed. Shakespeare and he had travelled some long roads since then, into some strange places. There had been the time in the silver camp when he had read *Othello* to a group of amusement-starved miners, and old Davis, his partner, had burst out: "Why, that damnfool nigger! Couldn't he have asked around? Couldn't he *see* they were makin' a jackass out of him?" Or the night in Hole-in-the-Wall when he had lent the book to Cassidy, the last man on earth who might have been expected to appreciate the Swan of Avon, but he had studied away at it, the broad, beefy face frowning as he spelled out the words, and Franklin had caught the whispered mutter: "Before these eyes take themselves to slumber, I'll do good service, or lie in the ground for it, aye, or go to death. But I'll pay it as valorously as I may. That will I surely do." Yes, Cassidy might never have heard of Harfleur or the Salic Law, but he could understand that kind of talk, all right. Wonder where he was now? Where were any of them, for that matter?

Well, he was here, in Liverpool, Lancashire County, England, quarter of the way round the world from Hole-in-the-Wall, or El Paso, or the Tonopah diggings, or the Nebraska farm that he could barely remember. Already it seemed far away, that other world, in mind as well as distance. Only the instinct of the wanderer, whose home and effects travelled with him, whose whole being could be contained in one old trunk, had prompted him to hold on to all these relics – not the books, but the trail gear. Why hadn't he abandoned it? Habit? Sentiment, perhaps? Insurance? Mr Franklin had to admit that he did not know.

He replaced the books, paused, and then reached under the saddle and drew out the belt with its scabbards and the two .44 Remingtons; he unsheathed them and weighed them in his hand, one after the other, the light catching the long slim silver barrels. Like the Shakespeare, they had belonged to his father; like the Shakespeare, they were rather old and out of date; but again, he told himself, like the Shakespeare they would probably outlast most modern innovations.

21

He rolled the cylinders, listening to the soft oily clicks of the mechanism; then he frowned, broke open the chambers, and carefully shook the little brass shells out into his palm. Loaded pistols in Liverpool were as incongruous as . . . as Shakespeare in Hole-in-the-Wall.

Dropping the cartridges into an old cloth, he knotted it and stowed it under the saddle with the empty pistols. Then he closed the trunk, buckled its straps securely, looked round the room again, rolled into bed, and turned out the light.

2

Mr Franklin travelled down to London on the Monday afternoon; noting that the railway company hedged its bets by giving the journey time as "from four to five and a half hours" he armed himself with every paper and periodical that the head porter could find and walked the short distance to Lime Street with his luggage borne behind him on the hotel barrow. Here he resisted the offer of a five-guinea book of rail tickets for 1000 miles-worth of first-class travel, buying only a single, and found himself an empty carriage, rather dusty and redolent of stale cigar smoke and Victorian grandeur.

For the first few miles there was nothing to see except the smoke-grimed roofs of Liverpool under heavy rain; Mr Franklin wondered why so much downpour didn't have the effect of cleaning the city, and concluded that the rain was probably as dirty as the buildings. He turned at last to his newspapers, and settled himself comfortably to discover what England, the great mother of Empire, was concerning herself with that week-end; it seemed to him essential, if he was to accustom himself to his new surroundings.

The news was mixed and, to him, confusing. Mr Cody had crashed his aeroplane at Doncaster on Saturday and had emerged from the wreckage congratulating himself on his amazing good luck; further evidence of the flying mania was contained in a report of a race at Clapton Ladies Swimming Club, in which the fair competitors had taken the water equipped with model flying machines. There were columns about the Budget which had been introduced months before, but was still exciting heated debate, although it was all Greek to Mr Franklin – he noted a prominent advertisement on a facing page strongly recommending him to write to an insurance company for advice on how to provide against Mr Lloyd George's new death duties. Jack Johnson, the highly unpopular black boxing champion, who had recently delighted the sporting public by his failure to defeat a rising young British heavyweight named Victor McLaglen, had somewhat restored his laurels by knocking out the formidable Stanley Ketchell in nine rounds; a French scientist, M. Flammarion, was proposing to harness the internal heat of the earth as a source of energy, Mr Bernard Shaw had made a witty speech on photography as an art form, and a Plymouth Rock hen had had its broken leg set at the London Hospital.

On the lighter side, questions had been asked in the House of Commons about the forcible feeding of suffragettes; the German army were reported to be buying flying torpedoes from Sweden, and El Roghi, a pretender to the Moroccan throne, had been exhibited in an iron cage at Fez and subsequently executed. Spain was at war with the Riffians.

Having brought himself abreast of current events, Mr Franklin studied the advertising pages. Here he was invited to subscribe to Cuban Telephones, Val d'Or Rubber, and Brazilian Railways; his custom was also solicited for Mexican Hair Renewer, Poudre d'Amour, Dr Deimel's celebrated porous undergarments, and the new chocolate "massolettes" costing a penny-farthing each and containing "ten million beneficent microbes" guaranteed to kill all pernicious germs and ensure perfect health if taken twice daily.

For his intellectual nourishment he was offered H. G. Wells" latest novel, *Anna Veronica*, E. Phillips Oppenheim's *Mr Marx's Secret* and a sensational new work entitled *All At Sea: a novel of Life and Love on a Liner*, by none other than Lily Langtry, whose outstanding attractions, displayed in an accompanying photograph, suggested to Mr Franklin that she was liable to outsell Mr Wells and Mr Oppenheim on appearance alone, whatever her prose was like. Her most serious competitor was obviously the Countess of Cardigan, whose *Recollections* promised a feast of scandal and included (according to the reviewer) "at least two stories which should *not* have been printed".

Mr Franklin betrayed his sad literary taste by laying the reviews aside unfinished, and taking up a recent back number of *The Strand* which the porter had particularly recommended, since it contained a new story by Conan Doyle which he judged would be to Mr Franklin's taste. And it might have been, for it was a spirited piece about a young prize-fighter hired by a vengeful beauty to beat up her brute of a husband, the Lord of Falconbridge, but the train had now left the grubby environs of Liverpool, and Mr Franklin was more interested in his first view of the English countryside. A glance at Baedeker informed him that he was passing through that fertile country famous for Cheshire cheese, and that the Welsh hills might be seen to the right, and like any dutiful tourist he sat looking out on the green fields and neat hedgerows, thinking how small and tidy and well-ordered they looked, like a little model toyland that a giant might have laid out for his children to play with.

Whether he enjoyed the prospect it would have been difficult for an onlooker to say, for he sat impassively surveying it, with his eyes far away, the dark face reflected in the carriage window, and did not even stir for the best part of an hour, when the spires of Lichfield came into view. The birthplace of Dr Johnson, the scene (at the George Hotel) of the "Beaux' Stratagem", according to Baedeker, but any philosophic reflections which this information might have inspired were interrupted by the arrival in his carriage, when the train had halted, of a beautifully-dressed old gentleman with a glossy top hat, an impressive white moustache spreading over his claret-enriched cheeks, and a copy of *The Times* in his hand.

He greeted Mr Franklin with a resounding "Good afternoon to you", spread an enormous white handkerchief on the opposite corner seat, and carefully lowered himself on to it, remarking:

"The condition of modern trains is absolutely damnable. Dust an inch thick, haven't been cleaned since the Jubilee by the look of them, might as well travel in a coal-cart. I should have gone on the Midland, but there isn't a dam' thing to choose between 'em, I dare say. Why the devil can't they have de luxe trains, like the Continentals, eh? No wonder traffic's falling off – but it's all of a piece, of course. Everything's running down, as I expect you've noticed."

Gathering that a reply was called for, Mr Franklin considered his informant steadily and confessed that he was not in a position to make comparisons, since he was new to the country.

"Indeed?" said the old gentleman, and gave him back an equally steady stare. "An American. I see." He considered this. "Well, filthy as they are, I suppose our trains could be worse. No doubt the French railways aren't a whit better, if one comes right down to it, which I for one have no intention of ever doing. I've no experience of your American system, of course, but I believe it's quite extensive."

Mr Franklin, watching the platforms slide by as the train pulled out, said he believed it was, and the old gentleman shook out his *Times* and remarked that he didn't suppose railways would last much longer anyway, what with these damned motor cars, to say nothing of aeroplanes; one thing was certain, that the combination of infernal machines would certainly mean the end of decent horsemanship, and did Mr Franklin ride? Mr Franklin admitted that he did.

"Hunt?" inquired the old gentleman, hopefully.

"Occasionally."

"Where, would you tell me?"

"Colorado, mostly."

The old gentleman looked doubtful. "Didn't know they had hounds there." He frowned. "What d'you hunt?"

"Bear," said Mr Franklin, and after a look of surprise the old gentleman laughed heartily and said, of course, he meant *game*, big game. Well, that was another matter; he had done something in the bear line himself, in India, and enjoyed it, in moderation, not like these damned Germans, who according to the shooting correspondent of *The Field* were going off to Spitzbergen and Greenland and slaughtering every bear in sight, which was just about what you would expect.

"If you're hoping to shoot in England, I'm afraid you won't find much sport, though," he went on. "Bad year for grouse, you know. Too few birds. Nesting badly, as they're bound to, of course, considering the way they're over-driven. No one seems to know how to look after a moor these days; like everything else, going to the dogs. Sport especially – why, in my young days, if anyone had suggested to me that an American polo team – yes, sir, your own Yankee riders – could come over here and open our eyes to the game, well, I should have laughed at him. But that's what they've done, sir – saw it myself, at Hurlingham. It's this new technique – meeting the ball. Magnificent! Changed the whole game. Well, you remember what it used to be – when the ball was coming at your goal, what did you do, eh?"

Mr Franklin considered this gravely, but the question was fortunately rhetorical.

"You swung round, sir," cried the old gentleman, "and you hit an orthodox back-hander. But not your fellows – no, they come to meet the ball, head-on, and damn the risk of missing at the gallop! Splendid! Mind you, there were those who didn't care for it, thought it too chancy – but that's our trouble. Hide-bound. Timorous. I was all for it, myself. If we won't change, won't show some enterprise, where shall we be? Polo's no different from anything else, I'd have thought. But we seem to have lost the spirit, you see." He sighed, shaking his head, and since Mr Franklin offered no consolation, the old gentleman

26

presently retired into his paper, leaving the American to continue gazing out of the window at the rainy green country speeding past.

He was not allowed to continue his silent contemplation for long, however; the old gentleman discovered a news item about the defence budget, and drew Mr Franklin's attention to the deplorable fact that the British Army seemed to be non-existent and was receiving only £27 million for maintenance against £38 million that the Germans were spending.

"And already they spend half as much on their navy as we do ourselves – depend upon it, they're greedy for empire, and we'll find ourselves face to face with them before very long. It's this damned Liberal Government – I take it you don't have a Liberal Party in America? Well, you can thank God for it. I must say your chap Roosevelt seems quite admirable – I'd love to see Asquith at the head of the Rough Riders, I don't think!" The old gentleman laughed derisively. "Fool seems to think it will be time enough to arm when we have the Kaiser at our throats! Immortal ass! But what can anyone look for in a party that seems bent on our ruin, helping the blasted Socialists to get on their feet – they'll find that that's a plant they've nourished to their own undoing, one of these fine days, let me tell you. In the meantime, they curry favour with the masses with their old age pensions, and use the country's parlous lack of defence as an excuse for bleeding us dry. But of course you know about the Budget . . ."

If Mr Franklin had been wise he would have said, untruthfully, yes, that he knew all about the Budget, but since he kept a polite silence his indignant informant took the opportunity to dilate on the iniquities of Mr Lloyd George, the Liberal Chancellor, who, aided and abetted by "young Churchill", of whom the old gentleman had expected better things, was proposing to increase death duties by one-third, raise income tax to one shilling and twopence in the pound, tax undeveloped land and unearned increases in land values, and generally subject the country to a flood of legislation which any right-thinking person could see was downright communistic.

"The Lords will throw it out, I imagine – which is what the little snake is after, of course. He wants them to provoke a crisis, and break 'em. God knows where it will end – in the ruin of the property-owning class, undoubtedly, and then heaven help us. You don't have a House of Lords in America. Well, you may be right; ours have their hearts in the right place, but they're damned short of intelligence. No

27

match for the Welsh Wizard, anyway." And the old gentleman retired glumly to his paper, emerging only once more to remark on the controversy about the North Pole; personally he doubted whether either Dr Cook or Commander Peary had reached it, and much good it would do anyone if they had. Thereafter he fell asleep, snoring peacefully in his corner with the fine white moustache fluttering gently with his breathing; Mr Franklin, absorbed in his own thoughts, continued to gaze out silently on the passing scene, watching the shadows of the trees lengthening in the hazy October afternoon.

It was dark when they reached London at last, after the full five-and-a-half hours conceded by the railway company, the train clanking slowly through mile after mile of suburbs with their yellow-flaring windows, of dark deserted warehouses and factories, of long wet streets with their flickering lights, of black roofs and viaducts – that same prospect which another newly-arrived American, Henry James, had found so ugly but delightful a generation before. Possibly Mr Franklin was meditating that this was the greatest city that the world had ever seen, the most important capital of earth since ancient Rome, the heart of an empire dominating a quarter of the globe – fourteen miles long by ten miles wide, and housing more than seven million people, half as many again as New York: if so, he gave no sign of it, thought the old gentleman, who had wakened silently and was watching him through half-open eyes. Interesting face, for all its impassivity, purposeful and yet curiously innocent, with those steady eyes that obviously saw everything and yet gave away nothing. Difficult chap to know, probably; not over-given to opinion, but he'd speak his mind succinctly when he had to. Not a city man, obviously – Colorado, of course, he'd said as much. Tough customer? No, that wasn't right – not with that almost gentle mouth and those long, slender hands. Not weak, though, by any means. And like Inspector Griffin and the Adelphi porter, the old gentleman wondered idly who he might be, and what brought him to England. Interesting bird.

"Give me a call if you feel like a week-end's shooting." As the train rolled slowly into Euston, and they gathered up their hand-luggage, the old gentleman drew a card from his waist-pocket. "Turf Club will always find me. Can't promise you any bear or bison, but partridge is better than nothing, eh? Good evening to you."

And to his astonishment, the old gentleman was rewarded first by a lift of the brows as Mr Franklin took the card, and then by a surprisingly bright, almost embarrassed smile.

28

"Thank you, sir. That's most companionable of you."

Extraordinary word to use, thought the old gentleman, as he left the carriage; American, of course; rather pleasant. Hadn't exchanged cards, or even given his name. Still, Colorado . . . different conventions.

Mr Franklin left the station in a taxi, having made his customary comparison of fares and been astonished to find that the motor was fourpence a mile cheaper than the horse. He had never, in fact, ridden in an automobile before; possibly he felt it was more in keeping with the metropolitan atmosphere. The Cockney cabby, having weighed up his fare with an expert eye, asked where he would like to go, and received the disconcerting reply: "The best hotel convenient to Chancery Lane."

"You mean – any 'otel, sir? Well, now, there's the Savoy, in the Strand, which is about the best in London, but just a bit farver on, there's the noo Waldorf, which is first-class, an' on'y arf the price. Closer to Chancery Lane, an' all, or there's – "

"The Waldorf," said Mr Franklin, "will do."

"Right you are, sir. First time in London, sir? Ah, an' from America, very nice. Then we could go round by White'all, if you like, not far aht the way, an' let you see a few o' the sights . . ."

And taking his fare's nod for consent, the cabby cranked his machine into life and set off, shouting above the roar of his engine and the traffic, in his role as self-appointed guide. It was, he knew, an exciting ride for a stranger, and from experience he could guess to a nicety what the American made of it. First, that the streets were the most crowded he'd ever seen in his life, with the big omnibuses, taxis and cars, the two-wheel hansoms and the growlers, and the astonishing number of cyclists, including ladies, even at this time of day, weaving expertly through the traffic in their hobble skirts and hats tied down with scarves; second, that the noise, to which the cabby added with his running fire of incomprehensible comment, was deafening; third, that the buildings seemed uncommonly close together, and the streets far too narrow for their volume of traffic. That was what they always said – so when you'd given them their fill of jammed pavements, brilliantly-lit shop fronts, cursing drivers, and honking horns, and topped it off with a mild altercation with a helmeted policeman, just for local colour – then you wheeled them suddenly into one of the great majestic squares, with its tall buildings and towering trees above the central square of green, where the couples sauntered under the strings of lights, and it was possible for the taxi to crawl slowly along the inner pavement, to give the passenger the best view of the laughing girls tripping by on the arms of their top-hatted young men, with an organ-grinder going strong on the corner, and the constant stream of pleasure-seekers round the entrances of the brilliantly-lit hotels. The cabby thanked God for London's squares – depending what you wanted you could give 'em beautiful lamp-lit peace, with the throb of the metropolis muffled by the magnificence of the trees, or all the bustle and glitter of the richest city in the world, or the dignified quiet of the residential squares with their opulent fronts and the carriages waiting patiently and perhaps a glimpse of a liveried footman pacing swiftly with a message from one great mansion to another. Variety, that was what they wanted – provided it wasn't raining.

This particular Yank wasn't like some of 'em, though; the cabby was used to an incessant yammer of nasal question, with demands for Buckingham Palace, but this bloke just sat sober and quiet, taking it in – judging to a nicety, the cabby decided to limit his diversionary route to Trafalgar Square and the Embankment, after first exposing his fare to the bedlam of St Martin's Lane, where the theatres were going in, and he could feast his eyes on everything from ladies glittering with diamonds and swathed in furs, sailing in stately fashion up the steps with their opera-cloaked escorts, to the raucous Cockney boys and girls of the gallery crowds, dressed in their raffish best, cackling like jackdaws, or the stage-door johnnies with their capes and tiles rakishly tilted, monocles a-gleam for the expensively painted and coiffured beauties sauntering in pairs – hard to tell 'em apart from the duchesses, the cabby always thought, even when they were plying their trade after the show at the Empire Promenade in Leicester Square. He said as much to Mr Franklin, who nodded gravely.

"Trafalgar Square," said the cabby presently, and watched curiously as his fare surveyed the famous lions around the sparkling fountain and the immense pillar of Lord Nelson's monument; oh, well, thought the cabby, you can't please everyone, but we'll startle even this one in a minute. Which he did by driving down Whitehall, wheeling out on to the Embankment, and stopping sharply; it was a cunning move, to confront the unwary suddenly with the magnificent sweep of Thames, and beyond it the great electric-jewelled pile of the Houses of Parliament, with the massive structure of Big Ben towering over all, framed against the glowing night sky. It never failed to win excited gasps, especially if the cabby was clever enough to time his run down Whitehall just as the chimes were beginning; well, why not, he thought; that's England, after all, in everyone's imagination.

Mr Franklin did not gasp, but sat while eight o'clock struck, the great notes booming across the water like an imperial benediction; then he nodded slowly, which the cabby rightly guessed was the equivalent of three cheers followed by an ecstatic swoon. He must have been impressed, for when they got to the Waldorf he paid the cabby's three shillings without a murmur, and even added a three-penny tip.

It was as he was turning away from the taxi that the American found himself face to face with a young woman; he stepped politely aside, she stepped with him, he moved again, raising a hand in apology, only to find her still blocking his way. Baffled, Mr Franklin stopped, and the young woman pulled what looked like a small maga-zine from a sheaf under her arm, and thrust it at him, announcing:

"This is a copy of the *Englishwoman*, the official journal of the suffragette movement. Will you please buy it, and support the cause of women's rights?"

And while Mr Franklin still hesitated the young woman turned her head and announced loudly: "Votes for women! Support the cause of women's suffrage! Votes for women!" Then to Mr Franklin: "Six-pence, please!"

Like her first announcement, it was a command rather than a request, and Mr Franklin paused with his hand half-way to his pocket, to study this peremptory young lady. One glance was enough to tell him that her voice was exactly in character; she was tall and command-ing and entirely assured, and the hazel eyes that looked at him from beneath the brim of her stylish broad-brimmed hat were as clear and direct as his own. They were wide-set beneath a broad brow; the nose, like the face, was a shade too long for beauty, but she was undeniably handsome – really very handsome indeed, he decided, with that wide, generous mouth and perfect complexion. The expen-sive sealskin coat effectively concealed her figure, but Franklin could guess it was beautiful; the grace with which she moved and stood proclaimed it. He caught a drift of perfume, and possibly it was mere male susceptibility that made him not only draw a sixpence from his fob, but favour her with a longer speech than he had addressed to anyone since landing in England.

"Sixpence is a good deal of money for a paper that I never heard

31

of. I mayn't like it, you know; can you tell me any good reason why I should?"

He got a question back in return – plainly it was a stock one. "Do you think that you alone are entitled to the vote? Simply because you are a man? Votes for women!"

"But I'm not entitled to the vote – not in this country, at any rate. I'm tolerably certain of that."

The young lady frowned irritably. "You're an American," she said, almost indignantly, and raised her voice again for the benefit of passers-by. "Our leader, Mrs Pankhurst, is in America at this moment, spreading our message among our American sisters, and among those American men who have the intelligence and decency to listen." She turned her attention directly to Mr Franklin once more – really quite unusually handsome, he decided. "Are you one of those – or perhaps you believe that the land of the free is free for men only?"

"In my experience it's free only to those who can afford to pay for it," he said smiling, but the lady was not there to be amused.

"Spare us your transatlantic humour, please! Will you buy a paper or will you not? Votes for women!"

"Before such persuasive salesmanship, I reckon I can't refuse," he said, holding out his sixpence. "Or should it be saleswomanship? I don't – "

A presence loomed up at his elbow, heavy, whiskered, and officially bowler-hatted. In a deep patient voice it addressed the lady: "Now then, miss, please to move along. You're annoying this gentleman . . ."

"Oh, but she's not, really," said Mr Franklin, and the lady shot him a glance before directing a withering stare at the plain-clothesman.

"I am entitled to sell our newspaper in the street, like any other vendor." She might have been addressing a poor relation whom she disliked. "If you are a policeman, be good enough to give me your name, rank, and number, since you are not wearing a uniform."

"Sergeant Corbett, Metropolitan Police, B Division, and I must ask you to move along at once, miss – "

"And I am not 'miss'," said the young woman loudly. "If you must address me by title, I am 'my lady'. "

The illogicality of this retort from a suffragette passed Mr Franklin by for the moment, but he was naturally intrigued, not having encountered nobility before. She looked expensive, but otherwise quite normal. The policeman blinked, but made a good recovery.

"That's as may be," he said. "You're not wearing a uniform either. And entitled to sell you may be, but you're not entitled to cause an obstruction, which is what you're doing."

It was true; a small group had formed on the already crowded Aldwych pavement, some amused, but most of the men, Mr Franklin noted, either contemptuous or hostile. Aware of her audience, the suffragette raised her voice again.

"Another example of police harassment! You are interfering with a public right! I am breaking no law, and you are deliberately seeking to provoke – "

"You're creating a public nuisance," said the sergeant brusquely. "Now you move along, or – "

"Move me along if you dare! I will not be bullied! Votes for women!"

"Really, sergeant, I wasn't being bothered a bit," Mr Franklin was beginning.

"Be quiet!" snapped the young lady, and to the sergeant: "Arrest me, if I have done wrong! If the peaceful distribution of literature has become a crime in England, let us see you punish it! Votes for women! End the tyranny of forced feeding! Votes for – "

"That'll do!" shouted the sergeant, who was plainly reluctant to try the physical conclusions which this violent female was obviously bent on provoking. "I'll warn you just once more – "

"Freedom and equality among the sexes!" cried the lady triumphantly.

"Officer, may I say a word?" interposed Mr Franklin, and the unaccustomed accent, in the gentle drawl which Inspector Griffin had found so attractive, caused the sergeant to hesitate, and even the flashing young lady, her sheaf of papers brandished to assist denunciation, paused in full flood. "This is probably my fault," Mr Franklin explained. "The young . . . her ladyship, that is, asked me to buy a paper – very civilly, I'm sure – and I asked her what it was about. She still hasn't told me," he went on, with a slight bow in her direction, "and I'd like to know. Really, I would. So I just wish to say to her, with your permission, that if she would do me the honour of accompanying me into my hotel there, I'd be charmed to continue our discussion in a less public place."

It was not, perhaps, the happiest way of putting it, but it might have passed if the cabby, a gleeful spectator, had not supplied his own ribald interpretation, with a raucous guffaw; someone in the crowd sniggered, and a voice chortled: "I'll bet he will, too!" The lady, either genuinely indignant, or seizing another opportunity to take offence, flushed to her handsome cheekbones; then she went pale, a look of utter scorn came into her fine eyes, and before the sergeant could interfere she had exclaimed: "You insolent blackguard!" and slapped Mr Franklin resoundingly across the face.

The onlookers gasped. "Right!" roared the sergeant, lunging ponderously. "That's assault!" His hand went out, but before it could grip her arm his own wrist was caught in sinewy fingers.

"I'm sorry," said Mr Franklin quietly. He inclined his head towards the lady, who was preparing to resist arrest. "I meant no offence, and I beg the lady's pardon. She misunderstood me – but that's a woman's privilege, wouldn't you say, sergeant?" He released the policeman's hand, and smiled into her speechless glare. "You know – like hitting someone, without the risk of being hit back." He held out the sixpence. "Now, may I buy a copy of your ladyship's paper, please? If I can't have the privilege of your personal explanation, I can always read about it."

There was a pause, and someone in the crowd murmured sympathetically – though on whose behalf it was difficult to say. The sergeant hesitated. Not so, however, the militant scion of the aristocracy, who could see herself being baulked of martyrdom by this odiously placatory colonial. She drew herself up with that icy dignity which only generations of aristocratic breeding and nursery teas can produce.

"You can have the bloody lot for nothing!" she snapped, throwing the bundle of papers at him, and before the sergeant could react to this further outrage against public order, she had turned on her heel with a swirl of expensive fur and vanished into the crowd.

"Here!" exclaimed the sergeant, and half-started to follow her, but thought better of it: arresting suffragettes was no fun at the best of times, and he honestly doubted his capacity to handle that one without considerable loss of dignity and possibly some tufts of hair as well. He turned reprovingly to Mr Franklin. "That's what you get for being tolerant! You shouldn't encourage 'em, sir; they're a dam' nuisance. She'll be smashin' shop windows with a hammer tomorrow, like as not. Vicious little hooligans. She didn't cut your face, sir? Some of 'em ain't above using brass knuckles."

Mr Franklin, who had been gazing thoughtfully along the pavement where the lady had disappeared, became aware of his questioner. "No

34

– no, I'm fine. Curious, though." He frowned. "I thought they liked to fight it out. She didn't. I wonder why?"

The sergeant gave him a hard stare, shrugged, and moved off heavily along the pavement. Mr Franklin stood for a moment, sighed, shook his head, pocketed his sixpence, stooped to pick up one of the fallen papers, folded it, and walked into the Waldorf Hotel.

3

At an hour when most of the Waldorf's guests were still asleep, or, if they were unusually energetic, were thinking of ringing for their early morning tea, Mr Franklin was striding briskly east along Fleet Street. It would have interested that student of men and appearances, Inspector Griffin of Liverpool, to note that the clothes which had seemed a trifle incongruous among the *Mauretania*'s conservative passengers, were in no way out of place in cosmopolitan London, E.C.; but then as now, one would have had to be an eccentric dresser indeed to attract even a second glance in the English capital, which had seen everything. The inspector might also have noticed a difference in the American's manner; the slightly hesitant interest of the tourist had gone, and Mr Franklin no longer lingered on corners or spent time glancing about him; it was as though the anonymity which the great city confers on visitors had somehow reassured him. Also, he walked like a man who is going somewhere, which a London tourist seldom does. Now and then he would refer to a pocket map and glance at a street sign, but he never asked his way.

His first call was at the American Express Company's office at 84 Queen Street, and Inspector Griffin might have been mildly surprised by the deference with which he was received there, once he had given his name and satisfactory proofs of identification – unusually conclusive proofs, as it happened. It was the manager's private office for Mr Franklin, a comfortable chair, the offer of a cigar, and the exclusive attention of the manager in person, with his deputy standing by. Mr Franklin stated his requirements – and at that point Inspector Griffin's jaw would have dropped as far as the manager's did.

"Fifty thousand pounds?" said the manager, staring. "In gold?"

Mr Franklin nodded.

"But," said the manager, blinking. "But . . . but . . . I don't quite understand . . ."

"New York handled the transfer, surely. They told me everything would be in order."

36

"Oh, certainly, certainly!" The manager hastened to reassure him. "Your account is perfectly in order – no question about that. Your credit is . . . well, I don't have to tell you, sir. But . . . gold. That's rather – unexpected, sir. And such a vast sum . . . an enormous sum."

"You've got it, though?"

"Got it? Why . . . why, yes . . . that's to say, I can get it." The manager shot a look at his assistant, and found his own astonishment mirrored on the other's face. "But we're not used . . . that is, it would take an hour or two . . . the banks . . . so forth. We don't hold such a sum on the premises, you understand." He hesitated. "You would want it in . . . sovereigns?"

"Or eagles. I don't mind. Just so it's gold."

"I see," said the manager, although plainly he didn't do anything of the kind. "Well, now . . ." He frowned at his blotter and pulled his lip, "Uh . . . Mr Franklin . . . forgive me, but it's an unusual request – most unusual. I mean, we like to help our customers every way we can – especially a fellow-American like yourself, you understand. We try to advise, if . . . what I mean is, if you want it in gold, fine – but if you'll excuse my saying so, it's a hell of a lot of hard cash, when I could arrange for a cheque, or a letter of credit, for any amount you like, at any bank in Great Britain." He paused hopefully, meeting the steady grey eyes across the desk. "I mean, if you would care to give me some idea, you know . . . what you needed the money for . . ." He waited, looking helpful.

"To dispose of," said Mr Franklin amiably, and there was a long silence, in which manager and deputy stared at him baffled. Finally the manager said:

"Well, sir, you're the customer. I'll get you the money, but . . . well, let's see . . ." He scribbled hastily, calculating. "Fifty by ten by a hundred . . . holy smoke, there's enough to fill a suitcase, supposing you could lift it – it'll weigh about half a ton!"

"Not nearly," said Mr Franklin, rising. "When shall I call back for it?"

He left a bewildered and vaguely alarmed American Express office behind him, and there was close re-examination of the credentials he had presented, and anxious consultation between the two officials.

"Could we stall him and cable New York?" wondered the deputy.

"No point," said the manager. "They can't tell us anything we don't know already. There's his letter, with McCall's signature on it – and I know McCall's fist like I know my own. He's given us his

37

thumbprint, and it checks; his description fits, he has the numbers right . . . New York couldn't add a damned thing short of a reference from Teddy Roosevelt."

"But – gold?"

"Why not? If you're as rich as this bird – hell, he's probably Carnegie's nephew. Get me Coutts', will you?"

And such is the efficiency of the admirable American Express organization that when Mr Franklin returned shortly after eleven o'clock he found waiting for him four heavy leather handbags, their flaps open to reveal a tight-packed mass of dull gold coin in each, a manager in a state of bursting curiosity, a deputy still full of dark suspicions, and two burly civilians in hard hats. These, the manager explained, were ex-police officers who would escort Mr Franklin and his treasure to . . . wherever he wished to go.

"Oh, they won't be necessary," said Mr Franklin. He handled a few coins from one of the bags, nodded, and replaced them. "If you could have a cab called, though, perhaps they'd be good enough to put the bags aboard." And while the goggling deputy called a cab, Mr Franklin signed the receipt, and watched the burly pair hefting out the bags with some difficulty, while the manager drummed his fingers.

"Mr Franklin," he said solemnly. "Are you absolutely sure you know what you're doing? I mean – well, dammit all, sir – that's no way to treat money!"

Mr Franklin looked at him. "I know exactly how to treat money," he said. "And I know what I'm doing. Do you?"

"How's that? Do I – ?" The manager took a deep breath. "Yes, Mr Franklin, I do," he said with some dignity. He thought of the letter, the proofs . . . I hope to God I do, he thought.

"That's fine then," said Mr Franklin. "I'm obliged to you, sir; you've been most helpful."

Boarding his taxi, he waited until the ex-policemen and the nervously hovering deputy had reluctantly retired, and only gave the driver his destination when the cab was under way. But it was not an address: merely a street corner a half-mile away. There he swung his four bags out on to the pavement, paid off the taxi, waited until it had disappeared, hailed a passing hansom, reloaded his precious cargo, and drove to the Chancery Lane Safe Deposit. (It is a sad reflection on human nature that the taxi he had dismissed returned immediately to the American Express Company office, as the deputy

38

had privately instructed the driver to do, and there was momentary blind panic when it was understood that Mr Franklin had disappeared with quarter of a million dollars' worth of ready money, no one knew whither. There was frantic re-examination of the credentials, and the manager finally concluded that they were as watertight as he had originally supposed. Even so, he re-examined them several times during the course of the day, and the deputy did not sleep well for a week.)

At the Safe Deposit the well-respected manager, Mr Evans, personally rented to Mr Franklin a private strong room for five guineas per annum. For an additional guinea he was given one of the company's reliable safes, into which the bags were packed; the safe was then man-handled into the strong-room, securely locked, and Mr Franklin presented with the key.

After such an important morning's work he might have been forgiven for relaxing and basking in the reflection of treasure stored up upon earth, but he showed no such inclination. After a brisk bite at a public house he was afoot again by noon, to the biggest estate agent's he could find; the senior partner, whom he asked to see in person, was engaged, and Mr Franklin spent the time of waiting in acquainting himself with the town and country properties advertised on the office walls.

There was to be had, he noted, in the reasonably fashionable area of Cadogan Square, S.W.1, a Gentleman's Apartment comprising a Full Ground Floor; Mr Franklin stood absorbed by the catalogue of luxury – the fitments and furnishings by Liberty, the crockery by Doulton with which the kitchen and pantry were stocked, the fine master-bedroom with its private dressing-room and bathroom, the cosy panelled study, the opulent drawing-room with its Afghan carpeting and French chandelier, the elegant breakfast-room with furniture by Chippendale, the spare bedroom and second bathroom, the servants" room at the back, the excellent storage space, the polished cedar floors, the embossed wallpaper, the newly-installed silent flush toilets from Stoke-on-Trent, the electric lighting throughout at 1,000 candlepower for a penny, the patent boiler ensuring constant hot water . . . and all for the moderate sum of £200, a mere thousand dollars, per annum . . .

. . . Twelve cents a night for twelve square feet of Yancy's shack in the Tonopah diggings and a place at the communal table, bring your own grub.

39

Fifteen cents if your space was against the wall – old Davis had rated a wall space, being over sixty, with Franklin on his unguarded side so that Yancy's clientele couldn't come creeping in the night to untie the blanket lashed around the old boy's ankles and remove the precious poke from beneath it. One thing about London, S.W.1, you probably didn't need to sleep with your goods tied to your legs. Twenty-seven cents a night all told, more than they could afford, but the old fellow's chest couldn't take the weather any longer; just a week in the mud under the tarpaulins would have curled him up for keeps – and even if it hadn't, it would have left him unfit to dig on the ledges. And life without the ability to dig his stint wouldn't have been worth living to Davis – "Hell, boy, I'm just an old gopher; 'less I'm grubbin' up the dirt I feel all deprived like. I shifted so much shit offn Mother Earth, she's got a permanent tilt. Seen 'em all – Comstock, Australie, Cripple Creek, Sierra Madre, Klondyke – ten thousand dollars Jocky Patterson an' me took into Dawson City, nuggets an' dust, an' the little bastard lost the whole dam' pile in a stud game while I was drunk. Never did touch liquor since, 'cept for medicinal purposes . . ." And his old croaking voice had trailed into sleep, gradually murmuring into gentle snores in Yancy's mouldy, flea-ridden, sweat-stinking shack, packed with scratching bodies, wet and filthy, and the Mex came slithering like a rattler, eyes glinting in the moonlight from the window, hand out towards old Davis's blanket until Franklin's Remington was thrust into his face, the muzzle resting on the olive cheek, and the eyes widened in terror, with gasping breath as the hammer clicked back: "Si, si . . . campadre!" Si, si, campadre, your greasy dago ass, stir a finger and I'll blow your black head off! Vamos! Twelve cents a night for the privilege of lying awake against verminous thieves while old Davis babbled in his sleep in that leaky shed under the Big Smokies – and fifty dollars a night at the Bella Union after they came down singing together from the mountains with their saddle-bags plump with silver, soaking off the grime of months in their own private bath-tub, with French champagne being poured over old Davis's matted grey locks by a squealing twenty-dollar whore, and the waiter feeding the old rascal cream cakes as he wallowed in the tub, yelling at the girls to get in beside him 'cos he was the richest son-of-a-rich-bitch and he was going to blow the whole danged pile in one riotous night and die in the morning, see if he wasn't, and Franklin sitting on the tin trunk that held their goods, the Remingtons handy beneath his jacket and an eye on the waiters and bar-flies and raddled strumpets who abetted old Davis's hooting celebrations and drunken staggerings – the wreckage of their private room had cost them a mint in damages, on top of the fifty-dollar rent for that single carousing night . . .

Two hundred pounds a year in Cadogan Square, cheaper than the Bella Union, dearer than Nancy's, and with silent flush toilets from Stoke-on-Trent thrown in . . .

"A most desirable property, sir." The senior partner was murmuring at his elbow; perhaps he would care to see over it that afternoon? One of the assistants would be most happy to . . . ah, the gentleman had something else in mind. Quite so – and Mr Franklin was borne off to the inner sanctum where he and the senior partner spent an hour in earnest discussion. Mr Franklin's requirements were specific – unusually so, and while the result of their talk seemed to satisfy him, it is a fact that he left the senior partner in a state of some mystification, blended with satisfaction at the cheque which his visitor had paid over, sight unseen.

Mr Franklin's next call took him to the West End, and the discreet offices of one of those exclusive domestic agencies which specialised in supplying personal servants to the nobility and the more ancient *nouveaux riches*. Here Mr Franklin beat his own record for upsetting managers, for while he had caused concern at the American Express, and bewilderment at the estate agent's, he caused in Mr Pride, director of the domestic agency, something close to outrage.

"You wish to engage a personal attendant," said Mr Pride, faintly, "for one afternoon only? *One* afternoon?"

"Yes," said Mr Franklin.

"My dear sir," said Mr Pride, recovering his normally austere composure, "I am afraid that is quite impossible. Indeed," he went, on turning his cold eye-glass on this peculiar person and deciding, after a distasteful survey of his eccentric tweed cape (a disgusting garment, in Mr Pride's opinion) that he might carry his refusal a stage farther in reproof – "indeed, I do not recollect ever to have heard of such a thing. There are, I believe, agencies which undertake to engage staff for limited periods and . . . ah . . . what I understand are called special engagements – " he said it in a way that suggested longshoremen being recruited to help out at carnivals "– but we . . . ah . . . do not."

Mr Franklin nodded sympathetically. "The commission isn't worth it, I suppose. However, in this case I can assure you it will be."

Mr Pride's eye-glass quivered as though it had been struck, but he mastered his emotion. Pointless to try to explain to this eccentric that managing an exclusive domestic agency, which dealt with clients even

41

more sensitive and highly-strung than their noble employers, called for the combined qualities of a theatre manager, a sergeant-major, and a racehorse trainer; financial consideration was the least of it to one who, like Mr Pride, had had to contend with hysterical butlers, psychotic nannies, and on one never-to-be-forgotten occasion, a Highland head stalker who had tried to assassinate an Indian potentate because he was teetotal. He contented himself now by saying icily:

"Our personnel come to us in the hope of permanent employment, or at the very least, extended engagements. I may say that we have on our books three individuals whose families have served in the same establishments – the very highest establishments – since the eighteenth century."

He had no sooner said it than Mr Pride was uncomfortably aware that it sounded like defensive boasting, stung out of him by this person's gross mention of "commission'; he was, however, gratified at the admiration it produced.

"The eighteenth century? You don't say!"

Mr Pride smiled frostily. "So you see, Mr . . . ah . . . Franklin, that we can hardly – "

"With a record like that, it ought to be easy to fix up a first-class valet for just one afternoon. For the right price, of course."

"I have tried to indicate that it is out of the question," said Mr Pride with asperity. "We could not consider it."

"Could one of your clients, though?" asked Mr Franklin. "For five pounds an hour, say. Or whatever you think would be reasonable."

He regarded Mr Pride innocently, and Mr Pride, on the brink of a crushing retort, suddenly hesitated. He looked again at his visitor and wondered. You could never tell with Americans; this one, in spite of his outlandish attire and uncivilized ideas, had an indefinable air about him – it couldn't be breeding, of course, so it was probably money, and yet, Mr Pride admitted reluctantly, he could not truly be described as vulgar. Perhaps he had been a trifle hasty in rejecting Mr Franklin's peculiar request; after all, it would be foolish to offend one who might, just possibly, prove against all the signs to be a lucrative customer if properly handled. And Mr Pride had to confess it to himself – he was curious. A valet – for one afternoon? It was, when he came to think of it, intriguing.

"It is most unusual," he said at length. "Most unusual. And frankly, I cannot guarantee that any of our clients would be agreeable . . . however, it is just possible that there may be one . . ." Samson, he

42

was thinking, was in his servants' waiting-room at the moment, and Samson, in addition to being A1 starred on Mr Pride's list, was also in need of a new employer, his previous master having recently fled the country rather than face certain conviction for indecent assault on the Newcastle Express. Of course, Mr Pride would have no difficulty in placing Samson in a new situation; he had just the viscount in mind for him, in fact – but in the meantime Samson would be the very man to satisfy Mr Pride's curiosity about his American visitor.

He rang a bell, and within five minutes Samson, a stocky, sober and impassive man of middle-age who looked more like a retired cavalry trooper (which he was) than one of the best gentlemen's gentlemen in London (which he also was), had agreed, without a flicker of expression on his craggy face, to place his unrivalled expertise at Mr Franklin's disposal for the rest of the afternoon. Mr Franklin was gratified, and was plainly on the point of asking Mr Pride, how much? when the director airily waved him aside – the agency were privileged to assist in such a trivial matter, and would not dream of charging, leaving it to Mr Franklin to make his own arrangement with Mr Samson. Mr Pride, in fact, had come full circle and decided that if he was going to humour this strange American, he might as well do it properly. What, he wondered, as the pair took their leave, could be behind it?

The answer, could he have overheard it on the pavement outside, was disappointingly mundane. Mr Franklin wanted to buy clothes and equipment suitable for his new surroundings, and he was prepared to pay handsomely for the best advice on the matter. He explained as much to Samson, and the latter accepted the information with judicious gravity. Mr Franklin had a vague feeling that if he had suggested they should rob the Bank of England, Samson would have received it with the same courteous detachment and asked: "And will there be anything further, sir?" As it was, he merely asked: "Both for town and country wear, sir? Then we had better begin with Lewin's."

At this exclusive establishment they bought shirts, and more shirts, and Mr Franklin was initiated into the mysteries of stiff fronts and rolled collars, for evening and day wear respectively, after which they passed on to socks, in the fashionable shades of tobacco, Leander, Wedgwood and crushed strawberry, with black lace silk for the evenings; the grey ties known as "whitewash" they also added to their store, with a selection of new Mayfair pins, and when a zealous assistant attempted to demonstrate the latest treble knot, Samson patiently took the tie from him and tied it with such swift precision that the assistant abased himself as before a high priest.

With Mr Franklin's body linen attended to they repaired to Lobb's for boots, a matter in which Mr Franklin needed little assistance. They then considered suits, and on Mr Franklin's supposing that they should visit Savile Row, for which he had read advertisements in the newspapers, Samson pursed his lips, observed, "I don't think we need to, hardly, sir," and conducted him to a small, dim establishment off Oxford Street where an unhappy-looking little Jewish tailor, whom Samson addressed as Zeke, provided Mr Franklin with two immaculate morning dress suits, two evening dress suits, with white weskits and ties, two tweed suits, a magnificent Norfolk jacket and breeches, two lounge suits, all off the peg, and for a total of less than £100.

Mr Franklin was both delighted and doubtful. "Are these as good as we'd get at the fashionable shops?"

"Better," said Samson briskly. "Most gentlemen can't buy off the peg, sir, and wouldn't if they could, because they feel bound to patronise the fashionable tailors. Not necessary, sir. Zeke can cut with any man in London – you'll have to shorten the sleeves on the Norfolk, Zeke, and bring in the waist on the morning coats. Have them all round at the Waldorf by six, mind. Now, sir, spats, top hats, cane, great-coat, opera cloak, caps, everyday hat – not a bowler for you, sir, I think. You'll feel more at home in something more wideawake, I dare say, like Mr Andrew Lang. Very stylish, the broad brim, but only for travellers and literary men."

"And which am I?" wondered Mr Franklin aloud, as he surveyed the growing stack of clothing on Zeke's table with some misgivings. Samson, without a flicker of a smile, replied gravely: "I'm sure you enjoy good literature very much, sir. Plain grey in the spats, I think."

The fact was, Mr Franklin was half-regretting his recruitment of an expert in the matter of clothing. It had been an impulse – since he could afford the best, why not make sure that the best was what he got? But he had thought of what, to him, was a full outfit – a couple of suits, coat, hat, and boots, and here he was being kitted out with an opulence that would have embarrassed a railroad tycoon. The trouble was that every purchase seemed to call for some undreamed-of-accessories; it wasn't the expense he minded, so much as the extravagance – but there was nothing to be done about it now. Piker was a word that Mr Franklin had been brought up to despise; besides, this Samson undoubtedly knew his business, and it would have been a shame to spoil his fun.

In fact, Samson was enjoying himself immensely, in his restrained way. He had never had the opportunity, despite his great experience, of outfitting a gentleman entire before, and this one was a pleasure to equip. Too long and lean for true elegance, perhaps, but splendid shoulders, trim waist, and excellent bearing: Samson the soldier liked a man to look like a man, and not a tailor's dummy, and he went to work accordingly, undeterred by the growing unease which he sensed in Mr Franklin's manner. He could guess its source, and wisely did not let it trouble him. His professional pride apart, he liked this big American with his frontier face and diffident manner, and he was going to see him right. So when the last garment had been bought, he bore Mr Franklin off to Drews of Piccadilly for a full set of oxhide luggage, and finally to a Bond Street jewellers for a rolled gold cigarette case, silver and diamond links and studs, and the thinnest of platinum watch-chains set with tiny pearls. By this time Mr Franklin was totally silent; never mind, thought Samson, you're the best-dressed man in London this minute – or will be when you've put them on. And having weighed his man up precisely, he was not in the least surprised, as they drove back to Aldwych in a four-wheeler loaded with packages, when Mr Franklin broke the silence by saying suddenly:

"I imagine you think I'm all kinds of fool – buying all this sort of stuff?"

Samson looked straight to his front. "I'd think you would be ill-advised to continue in your present garments, sir," he said, and Mr Franklin digested this.

"You know what I mean, Samson. It isn't – well, it isn't my style, and you know it. Is it, now?"

Samson turned to look at him, his bright blue eyes without expression. "It's as much your style as anybody's, sir. The clothes you've bought look extremely well on you. And that's a professional opinion, sir."

"Well," said Mr Franklin, looking out at the bustling Aldwych traffic, "I guess that's why I asked you along."

"I'm glad you did, sir. It's been a pleasure." He preceded Mr Franklin from the cab at the Waldorf, and when they were both on the pavement he added: "You'll be dining out this evening, sir. A theatre, perhaps. I'll look back in a couple of hours and help you

45

dress. Many gentlemen dress themselves, of course, but with new clothes, sir, it's advisable to have a second opinion, I always think, in case of any last-minute adjustments, sir."

He knew perfectly well that Mr Franklin had not given a thought to dining out, let alone the theatre; a sandwich in his room while he glowered uneasily at his new-bought finery would be more like it. Samson was not going to permit that if he could help it; why this quiet American had engaged him in the first place, and allowed Samson to provide him with the trappings of the fashionable metropolis, he did not bother to speculate, but since he had, Samson's professional ethic demanded that the job be seen through. So having refreshed himself with a pie and a pint of beer at a St Clement's tavern, he returned to the Waldorf at seven prompt and proceeded to attire his client for the evening.

Mr Franklin submitted with a good-natured tolerance behind which there obviously lay a deal of self-consciousness; the statutory uniform of dress tails with white tie and weskit he bore without too much unease, but at the cloak, hat and cane he rebelled.

"No." He shook his head. "I don't need them. I don't need a stick."

"For the theatre, sir – "

"Who says I'm going to the theatre? I could go in my street clothes, couldn't I?"

Samson's raised brows suggested that he could go in a diving suit if he wished, but he merely said:

"Then for dining out, sir . . ."

"I don't have to dine out, either. I can get supper downstairs."

"Of course, sir." Samson allowed a moment of neutral silence while Mr Franklin glowered at his patent-leather shoes. "Shall I return your evening dress to the wardrobe, sir?"

Mr Franklin regarded him steadily, prepared to speak, changed his mind, breathed through his nose, and finally squared his shoulders, Sydney Carton leaving the tumbril.

"No," he said heavily. "Let's put the damned things on."

"Thank you, sir," said Samson. "The cane, sir – and the cloak. If it feels more comfortable, why not carry the hat, sir?" It sounded like a concession; in fact he was a trifle uneasy about the length of his client's hair. He stepped back, contemplating his handiwork, mentally comparing the tweeded colonial of the afternoon with the imposing and even elegant gentleman who now confronted him; quite striking, really, with that bronzed face, and the slightly raffish hair and moustache seemed to enhance the splendour of his dress. Samson made a mental note to recommend a barber of his acquaintance. "Very passable, sir," he said, and indicated the pier glass.

Mr Franklin looked, stared, and said softly: "I'll be damned." He was not a vain man, Samson knew, but he stood frowning at his image for a full minute before adding: "You tricked me into this, you know. I didn't exactly . . . oh, well, never mind." He turned to the dressing table, took up his money belt, and carefully counted out thirty sovereigns. "I'm obliged to you, Samson. You've given me more than I bargained for, and I'm not sure it isn't more than I care for. But I asked for it, I guess." He handed over the coins.

"Thank you very much indeed, sir." Samson flicked an invisible speck of dust from the lapel. "I have dressed several gentlemen in their first evening attire, sir. Invariably they were reluctant to put it on – but not nearly so reluctant as they were later to take it off. It grows on one, sir." He paused. "Did I understand, sir, from what Mr Pride said, that it is not your intention to engage an attendant?"

Mr Franklin had been sneaking another glance at the long mirror. "How's that? No – no, I'm not."

"I quite understand, sir. However, if you should contemplate such a course in the future, sir, I should be happy to be considered. If you thought me suitable, sir, of course."

Mr Franklin looked sharply to see if he was being mocked, and saw he was not. "I'll be damned!" he said again, and fingered his moustache thoughtfully. "Look – Samson. You don't know the first thing about me – except," and he jerked his thumb at the mirror in a gesture which made Samson wince, "except that the party there is a fraud, by your lights. Now – isn't that so?"

"I don't know, sir," said Samson evenly. "And, if you'll pardon the liberty, I don't think you know either. The cloak just a trifle back off the right shoulder, sir. Very good. I've known frauds, sir, and gentlemen, and some that were both, and some that were neither. I've even known some Americans. Will there be anything else, sir? Then if I might suggest, sir, Monico's is very pleasant for dinner; if you were to ask for Maurice, and mention my name – Thomas Samson, sir, he would see you had a good table. Or the Cavendish, in Jermyn Street; Miss Lewis knows me, and it's quieter." He had taken up his own hat and coat. "I hope you have a pleasant evening, sir. Good night, sir."

Mr Franklin pondered him thoughtfully, and then held out his hand. Samson shook it, let himself out quickly and efficiently, and left Mr Franklin frowning at his own reflection.

4

The great theatrical attraction of London in that week, or in that autumn for that matter, was undoubtedly *The Whip*, a drama of racing and high society which in addition to a highly sensational plot also offered the astonishing spectacles of a rail crash, a pack of hounds on stage, and a thrilling horse race. Unfortunately, as the Waldorf's porter informed Mr Franklin, it had been booked out for weeks ahead; however, he was able to provide a synopsis from an evening paper of alternative entertainments, and Mr Franklin, having concluded that since Samson had decked him out for the theatre, he might as well go, studied it as his hansom drove west along the Strand.

To his disappointment, there was no Shakespeare available. The only performance of his father's favourite author he had ever seen had been under canvas at the Tonopah diggings, when a travelling production of *Hamlet* had been broken up by a crowd of miners outraged at the prince's cavalier treatment of Ophelia. He would have liked to see Falstaff in the flesh, for his father's sake; the alternatives were not immediately inviting. Mrs Patrick Campbell in *False Gods*, and a new play badly entitled *Smith*, by Mr Somerset Maugham, did not sound interesting; he hesitated over an Arabian Nights comedy, *The Brass Bottle*, by F. Anstey, passed on to *Making a Gentleman*, the story of a retired pickle-maker aspiring to a place in society, decided it was a thought too close to home for comfort, and considered *The Great Divide*, a drama about three men in the backwoods gambling for possession of a girl. Understandably, it did not attract him, and he was left to choose between Miss Lily Elsie in *The Dollar Princess*, and a variety bill at the Oxford.

On the cab driver's recommendation he settled for the latter, and sat gravely in the middle of an uproarious audience who revelled in the drolleries of a sad-looking man in a bowler hat called George Robey; Mr Franklin found the accent and topicalities equally confusing. The popularity of the other star attraction on the bill he found much easier to understand; the fish-netted thighs and voluptuous figure of Miss Marie Lloyd, swaying suggestively across the stage, brought uproar and a chorus of whistles which almost drowned out her stentorian rendering of "Yip-aye-addy-aye-ai". She followed it with a ballad whose unabashed ribaldry was rapturously received; Mr Franklin, although not shocked, was mildly surprised that London should accept gleefully innuendoes which would have been regarded as out of place in some saloons he had known. What interested him most, however, was the tumultuous enthusiasm which greeted the rendering of a song, apparently an old favourite, anent the German Emperor and his naval ambitions:

> His friends assert he wouldn't hurt a fly.
> But he's building ships of war
> What does he want 'em for?
> They'll all be ours by and by!

It was by two young writers unknown to Mr Franklin, an American named Kern and an Englishman called Wodehouse; hearing the chorus taken up by the audience with patriotic abandon, he recalled the dire prophecies of his companion of the railway train.

When the show had thundered to its brassy finale, Mr Franklin made his way to the theatre steps and paused among the dispersing, high-spirited audience, wondering, for the first time since he had come to England, what he should do next. He had spent a busy day; he had, thanks to Samson, experienced a London theatre, and been slightly surfeited by brilliant lights, heady, swinging music, and half-understood jokes and choruses; now he had time on his hands. As he hesitated on the steps, he felt perhaps just a touch of what every stranger to London, in any age, must feel: that consciousness of being alone in the multitude. It did not trouble him; he was only a little tired, but content, and presently he would feel hungry. Until then, he would walk and take in the sights, and at that he set off along the pavement, hat and cane in one hand, stepping briskly – to the chagrin of several bright-eyed and exotically-dressed ladies skirmishing in the foyer, who had simultaneously noted his diamond and silver studs, his hesitation, and his solitary condition, and had been sauntering purposefully towards him from various directions. Disappointed, they wheeled away gracefully like high-heeled, feathered galleons, while Mr Franklin, unaware of his escape, walked on where his feet led him, taking in the sights and sounds and wondering vaguely where he was, exactly.

It seemed to him, as he walked, that this section of London was one vast theatre – everywhere there were canopies with their myriad electric bulbs, names in lights, huge posters, and audiences escaping into the open air, laughing and surging out in quest of cabs and taxis. To escape the crowds, he turned into a less-congested side street, and found himself confronting a stout little old woman, surrounded by flower baskets, soliciting his custom.

"Posy fer the lady, sir. Boo-kays an' posies. W'ite 'eather fer luck, sir. Buy a posy."

Instinctively he reached for a coin, smiling; he did not want flowers, but he was in that relaxed, easy state which is easily imposed on. As it happened, the coin he held out was a florin, and before he knew it he was grasping a massive bunch of blooms, and the grateful vendor was calling down luck, blessings, and good health on his head. He was on the point of suggesting an exchange for something smaller, but another customer had arrived, so Mr Franklin shrugged ruefully and walked on, examining his trophy, vaguely aware that just ahead of him, in that unpromising side-street, with its dust-bins and littered gutters, some activity was taking place round a lighted doorway.

His glance took in several couples, men dressed like himself, each with a girl on his arm, laughing and chattering as they moved away towards the main street; he was abreast of the doorway when a young woman came tripping out and almost collided with him. Mr Franklin stepped back, starting to apologize; the young woman looked right and left and straight at him; her glance went to the flowers in his hand, she smiled radiantly, then looked more closely at the bouquet, and regarded him with astonishment.

"Where did you get those, then?" she demanded.

"I beg your pardon?" Mr Franklin, nonplussed, looked from her to the flowers. "Why – from the old woman – along there."

"You never!" She found it incredible. "Well, you're a fine one, I must say!"

For a moment Mr Franklin, recalling his encounter with the suffragette the previous night, wondered if all Englishwomen were mad, or at least eccentric. This one looked sane enough – not only sane, in fact, but beautiful. Or if not beautiful, perhaps, then quite strikingly pretty. She was small, with bright blonde hair piled on top of her neat little head to give her added height; the face beneath was a perfect

51

oval with pert nose, dimpled chin, and vivid blue eyes – one of them unfortunately had a slight squint, and Mr Franklin instinctively dropped his glance, taking in instead the hour-glass figure in the glittering white evening dress beneath the fur cape. Altogether, she was something of a vision in that grimy back street – a slightly professional vision, though, with her carefully made-up complexion and bosom rather over-exposed even by the generous Edwardian standard.

"You buy flowers from a florist, dear," she said, regarding him with something between laughter and indignation, "not from street-hawkers. Not for me, anyway."

Mr Franklin stiffened. "I'm afraid you've made a mistake," he said. "I didn't buy flowers for – "

"Here!" exclaimed the young woman. "Aren't you from Box 2A?"

"No," said Mr Franklin firmly. "I'm not. Not lately."

"This isn't your card?" And she held up a rectangle of pasteboard on which some message, indecipherable in that faint light, was scrawled. He shook his head.

"Well!" she exclaimed in some vexation. "I was sure you were him. Where the hell is he, then?"

Mr Franklin automatically looked round; certain there was no one else waiting. Behind her two other girls, in the same theatrical finery, were emerging from the doorway. For the first time he realized that the light overhead shone from within an iron frame reading "Stage Door", and understanding dawned.

"Oh, damn!" said the blonde. "Another one with cold feet! Honestly, it makes you sick. They get all feverish, watching you on stage, and then at the last minute they remember mama, all worried about her wandering boy, and leave you flat." She pouted, tore up the card, shrugged, and regarded Mr Franklin ruefully. "Who were you waiting for, then – Elsie, is it? She'll be out in a minute. I say, Glad," she said over her shoulder, "he isn't from 2A after all."

"Shame." Glad, a dark, languorous beauty, looked Mr Franklin up and down regretfully. "Elsie has all the luck. "Night, Pip." She and her companion sauntered off, and Mr Franklin, conscious that he was at a rather ridiculous disadvantage, was about to withdraw with what dignity he could, when the small blonde snorted indignantly.

"Of all the rotten tricks! D'you know, I haven't been stood up since I was in the chorus? *Brewster's Millions*, that was – and just as well, really; I think he was married – "

"I'm afraid – "

" 'Course, in the chorus, you learn to expect it – now and then. But when you get out in front – well, when you have a solo, and if you've got any kind of figure at all – and I have, no mistake about it – well, you don't get billings as 'The Pocket Venus' if you haven't, do you? Huh! Of all the disky beasts! Blow him – whoever he was. I could have done with dinner at the Troc., too," she added wistfully. "Hold on, I'll see what's keeping Elsie. Won't be a sec."

"Just a minute!" Mr Franklin spoke sharply, and the blonde checked, startled. "I'm sorry, there's been a misunderstanding. I'm not waiting for Elsie. In fact, I'm not waiting for anyone. I bought these flowers by chance – "

"You're an American," said the blonde, smiling brilliantly. "Well, I never!"

"I'm sorry if you were disappointed," Franklin went on. "But you see – "

"Hold on a shake." She was considering him, head on one side. She descended the step, still smiling, but with less animation than before. "I think you *are* the fellow from 2A, aren't you? And you *did* send round the card, asking me to dinner at the Troc., didn't you?"

"I assure you – "

"And then you saw me, close to. And I've got a squint. Wasn't that it?" There was a curl of bitterness at the corner of the pretty mouth. "It's my damned squint, isn't it?"

Mr Franklin stood for a moment in silence. He was a level-tempered man, but he had found the last few minutes uncomfortable. He had felt momentarily bewildered, and then slightly foolish, and he was not used to either. The fact that the situation should have been amusing, or that most men would have seen it as an opportunity to further acquaintance with this unusually attractive girl, only increased his natural reserve. And now it was not amusing at all. He found himself at a loss, holding a bunch of flowers (something he had not done since childhood, if then) being reproached by a creature who was apparently preparing to feel aggrieved, through no fault of his. It was new to him, and he must take thought how to deal with it.

"No," he said at last. "You're quite wrong. I wasn't waiting for you, or anyone. I said so. And I didn't even notice if you had . . . a squint," he lied. "I still don't. And if I did, it wouldn't make any difference – if I had been waiting for you, I mean." For Mr Franklin, this was positively garrulous, but in this novel and disturbing situation

53

he felt that frontier chivalry demanded something more. "You're a remarkably beautiful girl, and anyone who saw you on the stage would be even more . . . impressed, when he met you. I'm sorry your friend didn't turn up."

He stepped back, intending to say good-night and go, but the blonde was regarding him with quizzical amusement.

"My," she said, "you aren't half solemn. Look, it's all right, really. If you're waiting for Elsie, I'll be gone in a – "

"I am not waiting for Elsie," said Mr Franklin emphatically.

"Well, the flowers, I mean . . . it looks odd. And if you *are* the chap from Box 2A – well, I don't mean about the squint, but some fellows really do get quite nervous, you know, and change – "

"And I'm not from Box 2A. I've never even been in this theatre – "

"You mean you haven't seen me singing 'Boiled Beef and Carrots'? That's my number, you know – a bit vulgar, but if you've got a shape for tights, why, that's what they give you – and it hasn't done Marie Lloyd any harm, has it? Are you married – is that it?" she asked speculatively.

"No," said Mr Franklin patiently, "I'm not."

"Well, then, that's all right!" she said cheerfully. "Neither am I. And here we are – I've been stood up, and I'm starving – and you're an American visitor, from the wild and woolly west, seeing the sights of London – you are, aren't you? Well, then, you can't go home to . . . to New York, or wherever it is, and say you missed the chance of taking a musical comedy star to supper in a fashionable restaurant – I don't know about the Troc., though – I had a bad oyster there last time – but there's the Cri.; no, that's getting a bit common. Or there's Gatti's, that would do." She smiled winningly at the silent American. "Well – don't look so worried! It's only a dinner – and it's your own fault, anyway, promenading outside stage doors with bunches of flowers – a likely story! Give 'em here," and she took the bunch of flowers, surveyed them critically, and dropped them on the pavement. "Now, then," she put a gloved hand on Mr Franklin's arm. "Where you going to take me?"

Mr Franklin understood that he was being made the victim of a most practised opportunist, but there was little that he could do about it – or, on reflection, that he wanted to do about it. She was a remarkably good-looking girl, and with all his reserve, he was human. However, it was not in him to capitulate informally; he looked down at her, the dark face thoughtful, and finally nodded.

54

"Very well. May I take you to supper, Miss . . . ?"

"Delys. Miss Priscilla Delys, of the *Folies Satire*," and she dropped him a little mock curtsey. "Enchanted to accept your gracious invitation, Mr . . . ?"

"Franklin. Mark J. Franklin." He found himself smiling down at her.

"Why have all Americans got a middle initial? You know, like Hiram J. Crinkle? Mind you, I'm one to talk – it's not really Delys – it's Sidebotham, but when you sing numbers like 'Boiled Beef and Carrots'" you need all the style you can get. Priscilla's real, though – Pip, for short. Come on, let's get a taxi."

Without any clear idea of how he got there, Mr Franklin found himself on the main street again, surveying the post-theatre bedlam in the vain hope of spotting an empty cab. But Miss Delys was equal to the occasion; she stepped daintily to the edge of the pavement, removed a glove, inserted two fingers in her mouth, and let out a piercing whistle, followed by a shrill cry of "Oi, Clarence!" A taxi swung into the kerb as though by magic, Miss Delys smiled right and left as heads turned, some obviously in recognition, said "Monico's, Ginger," to the driver, and seated herself regally, followed by a diffident but grateful Mr Franklin.

He was still collecting his thoughts as they sped towards the restaurant, which was just as well, since Pip Delys talked non-stop. He learned, in short order, of her career in the chorus of *Brewster's Millions*, of her brief sojourn at the Gaiety, and of her emergence as third principal at the *Folies Satire*, where she hoped for even greater things, " 'cos Jenny Slater, who's second, is sure to go into panto somewhere this season, as principal boy – she's got the thighs for it, you see, like sides of bacon – an' Elsie Chappell can't last much longer – stuck-up cow, just 'cos she started in the chorus at the Savoy – well, I mean, that was back before the Flood, practically, not that she hasn't got a good voice, 'cos she has, but she's getting on – must be thirty if she's a day, and dances like an ostrich." Miss Delys giggled happily, and Mr Franklin took the opportunity to wonder if thirty was so old, after all.

"Well, I'm twenty-three," said Pip seriously. "Twenty-three, professionally, that is. I'm twenty, really, but I've been in the business five years, and you daren't tell 'em you're just fifteen, you see. Anyway, I've always been plump enough, but I'm small, that's the trouble – you've got to be tall, really, to be a principal – but I make up for it with bounce and bubble – that's what Mr Edwardes used to say. Here we are – the Monico. All right, Ginger – " she tapped the driver on the shoulder – "double or quits."

The driver, who was elderly and had no vestige of hair, ginger or otherwise, sighed heavily and glanced at Mr Franklin, who was producing change. Pip snatched a coin from him, spun it and clapped it deftly on her gloved wrist. " 'Eads," said the driver hopefully, and she crowed with delight. "Too bad, Ginge – it's tails. Better luck next time," and she skipped out onto the stained velvet carpet which covered the Monico pavement, leaving Mr Franklin to present a tip which more than covered the lost fare.

Within, Monico's was a glaze of crystal and gilt, with a small covey of flunkeys greeting Miss Delys by name, removing her wrap, and bowing obsequiously to Mr Franklin. It was at this point he recalled a name, supplied by Samson, and felt himself obliged to mention it.

"I'd like to speak to Maurice," he told the nearest minion, a small Italian who looked puzzled and repeated: "Morris, sir? Ah – Morrees, but of course." Pip raised a questioning brow.

"What's that, then? I thought you were a stranger. Never mind, Renzo – table for two on the balcony, for champagne, and a supperroom afterwards." To Mr Franklin she went on archly: "How d'you know the head-waiter's name, straight from the backwoods? I can see you'll need an eye kept on you – flowers at the stage door, too. Well, well! You're a dark horse."

He explained, as they were conducted to their table by the balcony rail, that the name had been learned accidentally, but Pip was too occupied to listen; she was making her entrance, keeping an eye cocked and a profile turned for theatrical managers, calling and waving brightly to acquaintances, keeping up a running fire of comment while the champagne was poured, and pausing only to take an appraising sip.

"Not bad for a tanner a glass," was her verdict, and Mr Franklin, who had tasted French champagne for the first time on the *Mauretania*, would not have presumed to argue. Privately, he thought it an overrated drink, but he was content to sip while his companion prattled, and watch the well-dressed throng in the dining room below.

"Thin house tonight," was how Pip described it. " 'Course, it's early yet; there'll be more later." Mr Franklin remarked that so far as he could see, every table was full, and Pip clicked impatiently.

"I mean *real* people, silly – celebrities. They're nobodies – " and

56

she dismissed the assembly with an airy wave. "Let's see, though –
there's one or two – see, over there, that dark lady with the pearls,
beside the chap with whiskers? Mrs Pat Campbell, that is – you've
heard of her. They reckon she's a great actress – in all them grisly
plays by Henry Gibson, or whatever his name is. She's got a new play
now, at Her Majesty's, but I heard tell it was a stinker. *False Gods*, I
ask you!" Pip rolled her eyes and pronounced in a strangled contralto:
" 'Desmond, our ways must part – forevah! Yah touch defiles me!'
Honest, that's the sort of thing they put on – well, how can that run
against revues and variety and niggers singing in the bioscope?"

She drained her glass, and twitched at the sleeve of a passing waiter.
"Menus, Dodger – I'm peckish." She suddenly put her forearms on
the table and leaned across towards him, smiling impishly, but with
a hint of apology. "I'm sorry – I'm dead common, aren't I? Chivvying
waiters and taxi-drivers, shouting out and making an exhibition of
myself. Aren't you ashamed? Sorry you came? But it's the way I'm
made – and being in the show business, you see. I'm just a Cockney
sparrow – well, you can tell by the accent. And I squint, too."

Mr Franklin was spared a gallant denial by the arrival of the menus,
imposing documents of several pages in ornate script, most of it in
French. Pip seized on hers with satisfaction.

"Oysters! Say a couple of dozen between us? I love oysters – prob'ly
comes of having a father in the fish business."

"He keeps a shop?" said Mr Franklin, idly scanning his menu.

"He had a barrow. Jellied eels and whelks – but you won't know
about those, I guess. He's retired now. Rheumatism – and rum, too,
if you ask me. Poor old Dad. Here – " she suddenly lowered her
menu and regarded him seriously " – you all right for a fiver, are
you?"

"I beg your pardon?"

"Have you got five quid? – let's see, that's twenty-five dollars, your
money. 'Cos that's what this'll cost you, including our private room.
Well, we could eat out here, but nobody does who's anybody in
the theatre – and then we could get away for three quid, if you're
stretched."

"If your standing in the theatre is at stake," said Mr Franklin
gravely, "I think I could manage five pounds without embarrassment."

"You're sure?" The pretty face under the blonde tresses was earnest, and Mr Franklin found himself liking this girl a great deal. " 'Cos
if you're not – we can go dutch, you know. That's fifty-fifty. Oh, stop

grinning like that – " Mr Franklin realized that he had been smiling at her with pure pleasure. "Just for that, I'll have the consommé, the salmon stuffed with shrimps in champagne sauce – let's see, the veal cutlets, the pheasant – and we'll see about pudding after. That'll take care of your fiver, all right . . . "

Five pounds at the Monico . . . ten cents at Yancy's if you hadn't any grub of your own to bring . . . eggs at a dollar apiece when the boom was at its height at Tonopah . . . the Indian girl baking bread at Hole-in-the-Wall, and Sundance Harry Longbaugh burning his fingers on the crust . . . tortillas and flapjacks, and his father frying bacon and corn that morning after the Battle of Shrewsbury on the El Paso road . . . "No beef this trip, son . . . 'I am a great eater of beef, and I believe it does harm to my wit' " . . . the old man saying grace over the frying-pan . . . salmon and shrimps in champagne sauce . . . that steak and fried onions at the Bella Union, with the tin plate on his knees as he sat on the trunk watching the door, looking over a balcony rail just like this one, but instead of the orderly parties of diners in their evening finery, eating off china and crystal and snowy cloths, with waiters hovering – instead of that, the huge crowded bar-room of the big bonanza time, with bearded, booted miners capering on the tables with the sluts, yelling and sprawling and smashing furniture while the fiddlers on the stage scraped out, "Hurrah, boys, hurrah!" and the long bar was three-deep with drinkers, awash with beer and red-eye, while he finished his steak, touching the hilt of his Remington every so often as his eyes ranged over the inferno of celebration, looking for the Kid and his gang, and old Davis snoring drunk on the bed with his britches round his ankles . . . and he had sat through that thundering, boozing, carousing night on the tin trunk, drinking coffee with his back to the wall, shaking his head at the brown girl with smoky eyes in the red silk dress, and she had tossed her head and spat in disappointment and left him to his determined vigil in the brawling, bawling Bella Union, with a fortune in silver six inches beneath his pants-seat . . . .

"You haven't heard a word I've been saying, have you?" Pip was laughing at him across the table. "Where *were* you? Renzo wants to know if you want Bordeaux or Burgundy – unless you want to carry on with the bubbly?"

Of course they continued with the champagne, and as they ate their splendid dinner in the velvet-lined little private cabinet on the second floor, Mr Franklin wondered if it was the working of the wine that made him enjoy himself more and more with each passing minute.

No, to be fair, he decided, it was Pip herself; she was merry and animated and full of gossip, about the theatre, and herself, and her eccentric parents and their large family, who appeared to live on laughter and a portion of her earnings, and about London, which was all the world to her, and her ambitions, which consisted simply of being the Queen of Musical Comedy some day, and strutting the boards of the West End, singing the latest rude songs, having hosts of admirers waiting at the stage door, preferably in carriages with crests – and marrying one of the richest and most noble of them? wondered Mr Franklin.

"No," said Pip, and sighed. "I'm not the kind they marry. Oh, plenty from the chorus finish up as My Lady – they say half the heirs to the Lords married Gaiety Girls, and it's not far wrong. But I *like* the theatre, you see – couldn't be happy away from it, and all the noise and chat and fun. I couldn't give that up. Can't see me in a stately home, dishing out tea – not while there's curtains going up and orchestras playing my cue." She laughed. "I'm just a shameless, painted hussy of the variety stage – common as dirt and glad of it. You have to be, if you want to get to the top of my trade – look at Marie Lloyd, she's no lady, but she'll be topping the bill until she drops, no matter how fat she gets. Maybe I've got a little of what she's got – not just the voice, and the figure, and the cheek, but – well, you know, it's how you put it over. If I've got it, then I'll go on until I drop, too – and if I haven't, I'll prob'ly finish up married to some sobersides in Ealing, if I'm lucky, with six kids and a couple of maids." She chuckled happily. "Sing 'em 'Boiled Beef and Carrots'" at the church social, too. Meantime, I'm enjoying myself, so who cares? Anyway," and she stretched a hand across and patted Mr Franklin on the arm, "I'm fed up talking about me, and you must be, too. What about you, Mr American? You've just sat all evening, very polite and quiet, listening to me gassing on and on and on, and you haven't said a word about little ole New York, or Redskins, or anything." She pushed her plate aside, put her elbows on the table, cupped her chin in her hands, and smiled eagerly. "I'm listening."

It took him by surprise – but what was even more surprising was that he found himself responding. Later, he was to reflect that in all his life he had hardly ever talked about himself – certainly not to a stranger, and that stranger a woman. Perhaps it was the novelty or, he was prepared to admit, that he was under the spell of that lively beauty hanging on his every word. It did not occur to him that Miss

Pip Delys, the professional performer, could be as skilled a listener as she was a prattler. In any event, he found himself talking – about half-remembered Nebraska, and about the time of wandering, with his itinerant schoolmaster father, from one small settlement to another – "I don't even remember their names, just the wall-paper in the rooming-houses where we stayed; one or two of them didn't have wallpaper" – and later, the brief years as ranch-hand, railroad ganger, timber-jack, miner, and transient on the dwindling frontier; it was a fairly bald recital, and far from satisfying Pip's curiosity, which was evidently well-grounded in comic papers and Colonel Cody's Wild West Show.

"Weren't you ever a cowboy, with them hearth-rug things on your legs? Didn't you have to fight Indians, or rustlers? You must have had a six-gun, surely . . .?"

"Yes, I was a cowboy," he said, smiling. "Anyway, I worked with cattle – it isn't all that fun. No, I didn't fight Indians, or rustlers – there aren't really many of them about, nowadays. A six-shooter? Yes – mostly for scaring prairie dogs." There was no point in telling her of that night of waiting at the Bella Union for the Kid and his cronies. But it was in his mind when she asked her next question.

"Outlaws? Now, why on earth should I know any such people? D'you think America's peopled by bandits and pistoleers? You've been reading dime novels."

"Well, you can't say there aren't any!" said Pip indignantly. "I mean, it didn't get called the Wild West for nothing, did it? Why, I don't suppose we've had an outlaw in England since . . . oh, since Robin Hood. I just thought – if you'd been a cowboy – "

"That I might have been a road agent myself, on the side? Texas Tommy, with pistols stuck in a crimson sash and a big sombrero?"

This sent her into peals of delight. "Course not! Though you could look the part, you know – you really could! Specially when you come all over grim and thoughtful – like when you were thinking, faraway, down on the balcony. Made me all goose-pimply." She shuddered deliciously. "You might have been planning to rob the stage to Cactus Gulch, or – "

"You've got a real theatrical imagination, I'll say that for you." He shook his head. "If you must know, I've seen outlaws, one or two – and they look pretty much like anyone else, only a bit more in need of a bath. Matter of fact, my old mining partner, Pop Davis – he'd been outside the law in his time, I guess. But you wouldn't have thought much of *him* – looked just like any old tramp. He was all right, though. Good partner."

"But the other ones," she insisted. "You said one or two – what were they like?"

"Oh, just ordinary fellows; nothing very romantic, I'm afraid. And yet – I don't know. You'd have liked Big Ben Kilpatrick, I guess – very tall, good-looking; and Cassidy, too – he must have been the politest brigand that ever was, and quite presentable when shaved. Ever hear of them?" She shook her head, wistfully. "Well, they're the best I can do for you – and I couldn't claim more than nodding acquaintance. Old Davis and I stayed with them once for a spell, at a place called Hole-in-the-Wall; he'd once been teamed up with one of Kilpatrick's gang – "

"Hole-in-the-Wall! You're making it up!"

"That's what it was called. And they called themselves the Wild Bunch, if you like. Not so wild, either; they'd robbed a train or two, I guess, but didn't make much of it. Pretty harmless outlaws, I reckon." He picked up the menu. "Most of them. Anyway, what are you going to eat for dessert?"

"Oh, never mind that! I want to hear about the Bad Bunch – and the ones who weren't pretty harmless!"

"Well, you're not going to – or you'll wind up with the idea that I'm some sort of crook myself. And I'm not."

"No, you're not," said Pip, dutifully consulting her menu. "You're a very respectable cowboy, visiting England, wearing silver and diamond cuff-links and studs, and dining in a swish restaurant, as visiting cowboys always do." She stole a glance at him over the top of the menu. "I'm real cheeky, aren't I? And it's none of my business, is it? All right, I'll keep quiet."

"I doubt it," said Mr Franklin drily. "I'd just like you to understand that this dinner is not going to be paid for out of the loot from the ... the Cactus Gulch stage-coach. You're eating the result of a lot of hard, dirty, very ordinary digging in the earth, and an old man's crazy hunch, and a great deal of luck. Now, what – "

"Ooh!" Her eyes were wide. "You mean you struck it rich!"

"Crepes Suzette," read Mr Franklin. "Bombe Caligula, whatever that is; Poire Belle Hélène; Macedoine à la duchesse – "

"Mean thing! I just wondered ... right-ho, then, I'll have trifle and a double helping of whipped cream. But you might tell a fellow ... "

61

But Mr Franklin felt he had said enough for one evening, and when Pip had worked her way through a mountainous trifle, and coffee was served, their talk returned to normal channels – in other words, the theatre, and the possibility that she might play Dandini in the forthcoming Gaiety pantomime, but then she might find herself replaced at the Folies, and it was a good billet, with excellent prospects, but Dandini would pay at least an extra pound a week ... Mr Franklin smoked a cigar, and nodded attentively, and presently, when the waiter presented the bill, Pip rose and stretched and sauntered in behind the crimson curtain which screened off a small alcove at the back of the supper-room. Mr Franklin paid, and added a handsome tip, and smoked for a few moments more before he began to wonder idly what she was doing. At that moment there came a soft whistle from behind the curtain; he rose, slightly startled, and going across, pulled the curtain aside. There he stopped, stock-still.

The third principal of the *Folies Satire* had piled her clothing neatly on a chair, all except her stockings, and was reclining on a large couch which filled most of the alcove, observing herself with approval in a large overhead mirror, and humming softly. She glanced at Mr Franklin, smiled brightly, and asked:

"Did you bolt the door?"

"My God," said Mr Franklin, and then paused. He turned away, put his cigar in an ash-tray, and returned to the alcove, looking down at her.

"Pip," he said, "you don't have to, you know."

Pip stopped in the act of smoothing her stockings. "Course I don't," she said, and winked at him. "But I'd rather. Here," and she patted the couch beside her, "come and sit down. You make me feel all girlish, standing there."

Mr Franklin frowned. Then, in response to her outstretched hand, he came to the couch and sat down, looking at her steadily.

"I don't," he began, and paused before adding: "I just brought you out to supper, Pip."

"No, you didn't," said Pip. "I brought you. And it wasn't just for supper, Mr American." She slipped her arms round his neck and pulled his face down to hers, parting her lips and flickering her tongue at him. "You don't get off that lightly." She kissed him, slowly at first, then very deeply and lingeringly before drawing her lips away. "Are you looking at my damned squint again?"

A rather dazed Mr Franklin shook his head. "Good," murmured

Pip, "now you'd really better go and bolt the door, so we won't have any distractions. I want to enjoy myself."

Which she did, so far as Mr Franklin could judge, for the next twenty minutes, at the end of which time she lay very still, panting moistly into the pillow until she had recovered her breath, when she observed that *that* was better than working, or standing in the rain.

"Aren't you glad you bought that bunch of flowers, then?" she added, and Mr Franklin admitted, huskily, that it had been a most fortunate chance. She nodded happily, running her fingers idly up and down his naked back while she studied her reflection overhead.

"I'm losing weight . . . I think. Here, any more of that champagne left? Oh, good, I need it, I can tell you! Talk about the Wild Bunch – you're a bit wild yourself, aren't you, though? Hey – you're not getting dressed! The idea!"

In fact, it was after two o'clock in the morning before Pip sighed regretfully that she supposed they had better call it a night, because Renzo would be wanting to get to bed, and a relieved but contented Mr Franklin agreed. He was, to tell the truth, rather shaken, and not a little puzzled by the events of the evening, as appeared when they were preparing to leave the supper-room, and Pip was making final, invisible adjustments to a coiffure which had miraculously remained undisturbed through all the hectic activity in the alcove. Mr Franklin in the background, was contemplating his hat and gloves thoughtfully; Pip observed him in her hand-mirror.

"Don't reach for your note-case, or I might get offended," she said and as his head came up she turned, smiling, and shook her head at him. "You were going to, weren't you?"

Mr Franklin cleared his throat. "I wasn't certain."

"You don't give money to actresses," said Pip, gravely, and kissed him on the nose, giggling at his perplexity. "Don't you understand, darling? – I do it 'cos I like doing it. With the right one. Girls enjoy it, too, you know, spite of what you hear. You didn't stand a chance, from the minute I saw you outside the stage door, you poor silly! No, you're not, either – you're a nice American, and it's been a beautiful evening, and I just wish it could have gone on and on."

"So do I," said Mr Franklin. "Perhaps another – "

"Careful," said Pip. "It might get to be a habit." She frowned, and dropped her voice: "You don't have to, you know," and they both laughed. Then she threw her arms round his neck and kissed him again, stretching up on tip-toe before subsiding breathlessly. "That's enough of that – Renzo's got to get to bed sometime."

They went down to the street through the restaurant, where the lights had been turned down, and Pip called " 'Night, Renzo" to the darkened dining-room. Mr Franklin hailed a growler, and they clopped slowly down to Chelsea, where Pip had a room. "Next rise I get, it'll be Belgravia, and chance it," she confided. "Mind you, many more dinners like tonight, and I'll get so tubby I'll be bloody lucky if I can afford Poplar."

Mr Franklin thought for a moment, and asked: "Aren't there lots of dinners like tonight's?" She turned to look at him in the dimness of the cab, and he heard her chuckle.

"Lots of dinners," she said. "All the time. But not many like tonight. So you needn't be jealous."

He handed her out on the corner. "I don't know how to thank you," he was beginning. "I mean, I wish I could express my appreciation . . ."

"Oh, you know," she shrugged. "Diamond bracelet to the stage door – couple of emerald earrings. Any little trinket your lordship happens to have lying around spare." She giggled again and pecked his cheek. "Don't be so soft. Tell you what – pay your money at the box-office some night and watch my solo. Then you'll have done your bit." Her gloved hand touched his cheek. " 'Night, Mr American."

Her heels clicked on the pavement, the white figure faded into the gloom, humming happily:

> Boiled beef an' carrots,
> Boiled beef an' carrots!
> That's the stuff for your derby kell . . .

Mr Franklin sighed, climbed into the growler, and was driven back to the Waldorf.

5

He left London on the following morning. A four-wheeler was engaged to remove from the hotel the two handsome Eureka trunks containing the clothing purchased the previous day, as well as the battered old case with which Mr Franklin had arrived, and his valise; these were despatched to St Pancras, while the gentleman himself took a cab by way of Bond Street.

Here, at the exclusive jewellers which he had patronized the previous day, Mr Franklin stated his requirements; the manager, who had seen him coming, smoothly set aside the assistant dealing with him – he personally would see to it that nothing too inexpensive was laid before a customer who paid cash for pearl and platinum watchchains.

"A bracelet, perhaps, sir. For the wrist?"

"I had thought a necklace," ventured Mr Franklin. "For the . . . chest. That is – the neck, of course."

"Of course, sir. Diamond, emerald – ruby perhaps. May I ask, sir, if the recipient is dark or fair?"

"Oh, fair. Very fair – quite blonde."

"The sapphires, perhaps. It is a matter of personal taste. Diamonds, of course – " the manager smiled " – complexion is immaterial."

"How about pearls? You know, a strand – a substantial strand. These collars one sees . . ."

The manager was too well-trained ever to lick his lips, but his smile became a positive beam.

"The perfect compromise, sir. Pearls – with a diamond cluster and clasp." He snapped his fingers, and presently Mr Franklin found himself blinking at a triple collar of magnificent pearls, gripped in their centre with a heart-shaped design of twinkling stones; he visualized it round Pip's neck, beneath the beautiful dimpled chin, imagining her squeals of delight when she tried it on.

"That'll do," he said without hesitation, "I'll take it," and two fashionable ladies examining rings at a nearby counter paused in

65

stricken silence at the sight of the lean, brown-faced man weighing the brilliant trinket before dropping it on its velvet cushion. Speculative whispers were exchanged, a lorgnette was raised, and Mr Franklin was carefully examined, while he produced his cigarette case, selected a cigarette, remembered where he was, and returned it to its place. The manager made amiably deprecating noises, and asked:

"I trust the case gives satisfaction, sir?"

"What – oh, yes." Mr Franklin restored it to his pocket. "Haven't lost a cigarette yet."

In this atmosphere of good will the pearl necklace was bestowed in its velvet case, wrapped, and tied, and the manager inquired if the account should be forwarded to Mr Franklin's address; the attentive ladies, busily examining their rings again, were disappointed when he replied: "No, I'll pay now."

The manager bowed, a slip of paper was presented, and Mr Franklin gripped the counter firmly and coughed, once. He should, he realized, have inquired about prices first – but his hesitation was only momentary. He could not recall an evening in his life that he had enjoyed so much, or any single human being whom he had liked so well; he had only to think of Pip's fresh young face smiling at him across the table to find himself smiling, too, and producing his note-case. It occurred to him, too, that visible signs of affluence probably assisted a stage career – and if that career faltered, well, expensive jewellery was realizable.

His note-case required reinforcement from his money-belt – a sight which slightly embarrassed even the manager, and brought the lorgnette into play again. "Ah," murmured one lady, "Australian, undoubtedly," and on being asked by her companion how she knew, replied: "His accent, of course." They watched intently while Mr Franklin, having paid, wrote out a plain card; he simply addressed it: "Miss Priscilla Delys, *Folies Satire*", without enclosure, and asked the manager to see it delivered to the appropriate theatre – no, he told that astonished gentleman, he didn't know which one it was.

None of which escaped the ladies, who concluded that Mr Franklin was either an unusually forgetful individual intent on marriage, or a foreign maniac – probably both; as he swung out of the shop their eyes followed him with some wonder and genteel regret.

He caught the eleven o'clock train to Ely via Cambridge with barely a minute to spare, and spent two and a half hours alternately glancing at the paper and out of the carriage windows at the passing fenland;

it was not a cheering prospect, but by the time Ely was reached, and he had changed to the Norwich line, Mr Franklin was in, for him, a positively animated state – from sitting quietly enough, he now leaned forward, hands on knees, to stare out of the window; he shifted position at least three times during the many local halts, and by the time Lakenheath was reached he was actually drumming his fingers on the arm-rest. Beyond Brandon he let down the window; by Thetford he was leaning out the better to see ahead, and at the next stop, where he alighted, he positively hurried along the platform and in his excitement bestowed a shilling instead of the usual threepence on the porter who unloaded his baggage.

But if Mr Franklin was now disposed to haste, he soon discovered that Norfolk was not. The station was a tiny one, and it took half an hour to summon an ancient gig, driven by an urchin of perhaps nine years, and drawn by a horse possibly twice as old. Mr Franklin gave the lad his destination and resigned himself to patience as they creaked off at a slow walk.

Fortunately it was a glorious autumn afternoon, and their way ran through broad meadows and occasional woodland, the brown and yellow tints mellow in the sunlight. Mr Franklin drank it in with a silent eagerness, as though he would have imprinted every leaf and hedge and thicket on his mind; if he did not display visible impatience, he was certainly breathing rather more quickly than usual, and at each bend in the road he would gaze eagerly ahead. At last, after two hours, they topped a gentle rise, and beyond it a village nestled among woods in the hazy afternoon; a scatter of cottages round a little triangular green; a dusty street winding in front of a small inn; a pond, mud-fringed, a pump and a horse-trough; on the farther side, a lych-gate and the square tower of a Norman church rising among elms and yews.

"Cassel Lancin'," said the urchin stolidly, and Mr Franklin took a deep breath and let it out slowly.

"Castle Lancing," he repeated. "Well, now." He smiled and shook his head. "Think of that. All right, Jehu, let's go."

They creaked up the main street, past the mean cottages where one or two poorly-dressed women started at them from the low doorways, and a few children played in the dust of the unpaved street; there seemed to be no one else about, except for a working-man on a bench outside the Apple Tree, who favoured them with a blank stare. Across the green was a small shop with bottle-glass windows and the name "A. Laker" above the door; a dog lay drowsing in the threshold.

They halted outside the inn, and Mr Franklin asked if the man could direct him to Lancing Manor. The man stared in silence for a moment, and then, in a broad drawl which Mr Franklin found surprisingly easy to understand, said:

" 'Arf a mile down the road." His eyes roved over Mr Franklin and the bags in the gig, and he added: "Ain't nobody 'ome."

Mr Franklin thanked him, and they drove on, through the village and along a winding way between high hedges, until they came to a pair of lichened stone gate-posts under the trees, and two large rusty gates chained and padlocked. Mr Franklin got down, took a bunch of keys from his pocket, and after some exertion, unlocked the gates and pushed them open. The narrow drive was high with weeds and rank grass, so he ordered the boy to help him down with his baggage in the gateway; he would not need the gig any longer, he said, and presented the urchin with half a crown.

The boy considered the coin, and then looked at Mr Franklin, standing beside the trunks and valise, and at the tree-shaded pathway. He addressed his passenger for the second time in two hours.

"Ain't nobody 'ome," he said, echoing the labourer, and Mr Franklin smiled.

"There is now," he said, and with a nod to the staring boy, walked up the drive. He was aware that his heart was beating as he pushed his feet through the rustling grass, and that he was walking unduly quickly; then he rounded a bend under the trees, and stopped suddenly as a house came into view. For a full minute he stood looking at it. Then:

"I must have been out of my mind," he said aloud. Then he took off his hat and looked around him. Finally he said: "No, I wasn't, either," and walked towards the house.

Mr Franklin had no romantic notions of what a manor ought to look like, so where another might have expected mullioned windows, crenellations, and half-timbering, he accepted without a second thought the solid, unpretentious Georgian structure which could hardly have been over a hundred and fifty years old. It was, in fact, rather a fine house, built on an Elizabethan site, its shuttered windows precisely spaced on either side of a massive, pillared porch. The broad gravel sweep before it was sadly overgrown, and the lawn to his right was a tangle of rank grass and fox-gloves, but even he could see that the structure was sound and the roof good, and the beeches and chestnuts which surrounded it on three sides were nothing short of magnificent. "Beautifully matured grounds of nearly two acres", the estate agent had said; sure enough, thought Mr Franklin, it's mature.

There was a little fountain in the middle of the gravel sweep, lichened and full of leaves, and two heavy stone seats, one on either side of the porch. Mr Franklin paused with his back to the front door, surveying the tangle of sweep, lawn and drive and the trees which screened him from the road; the air was full of the still hum of the late autumn afternoon, broken only by the occasional murmur of pigeons behind the house. His hand was shaking as he fumbled the key into the big lock.

Inside it was cool and dim, and slightly chill from a year's emptiness. The hall was surprisingly spacious, with a stairway curving gracefully upwards, and doors opening on either side into the main reception rooms. "A delightful Georgian residence, charming woodland situation, three reception, four bed, bathroom with patent water-heater, panelled hall and lounge, expensively fitted, every convenience, kitchen garden . . ." Well, here it was, and the agent had been as good as his word; it was an admirable house and would plainly have been snapped up long ago if it had been more convenient for the outside world. But the agent understood that Mr Franklin was not concerned with that; quite the contrary, in fact.

The American made his way from room to room, taking his time. It was larger than he had expected, for the agent had made nothing of the servants' quarters, which consisted of two small rooms at the back, off the low, flagged kitchen. There was running water – cut off for the moment – but no electricity, of course, and no gas. Behind the house was the promised kitchen garden, and a small orchard, heavy with the famous Norfolk apples. Mr Franklin picked a couple and ate them as he surveyed the small coach house and stabling for two horses. All was overgrown, but not seriously; the timber stood at a good distance from the house itself, and all was enclosed by a stout ivy-covered wall.

Mr Franklin returned inside, having hauled his baggage up from the front gate, and stood in the hall, finishing his second apple, glancing round in the satisfaction of possession. It was strange, unreal almost, but it filled him with a quiet content; he took off his hat and was about to hang it on the newel post when he stopped himself, smiling, and laid it instead on the settle which stood to one side of the empty fireplace. When in England, he thought . . . and I am in England, in Castle Lancing and the County of Norfolk, and it's been a long, long haul. Three hundred years, give or take a little, and who'd ever have thought it? Long way from Tonopah, but a sight easier to come back from than it must have been to get to.

Mr Franklin ranged his baggage beside the settle, picked up his hat again, and left the house.

By that time, of course, every soul in the village of Castle Lancing, pop. 167, knew that there was a new occupant at the manor. The carrier's boy, refreshing himself at the Apple Tree from Mr Franklin's half-crown, had spread the word of the arrival, and opined that he was a big-game hunter and definitely not from Norfolk – Lincoln, maybe. He was silent, and rich, from the cut of his duds, but by the look of his bags he'd come a powerful long way. This was sensation, and by the time Mr Franklin, in his eccentrically broad-brimmed hat and dark suit, had reached the village green, Castle Lancing was fairly agog. Curious eyes watched from the doorways, children were hushed, the labourers on the bench outside the Apple Tree suspended their pints and observed in silence the rangy figure swinging up the dusty street, and the landlord cuffed the carrier's boy and remarked derisively:

"He's never from bloody Lincolnshire. He's furrin."

Mr Franklin was observed to go into the village shop, and five minutes later the news was winging that he had bought a loaf, two tines of corned beef, butter, coffee, a tin of pears, half a dozen boxes of matches, and a tin of paraffin, which he had asked to have left at the manor's back door. The proprietress, Mrs Laker, had been quite overcome, not least by the fact that the newcomer had made his purchases with a sovereign, dismissing the change and politely asking her to credit it to his account. The prospect of trade thus opened up caused her to sit down, panting, and observing to Mrs Wood, from the dairy, that she'd never been so took aback in her life, and if Mrs Wood was wise, she'd see there was a pint of milk at the manor's door, too.

Meanwhile, the Apple Tree had been stricken to silence by Mr Franklin's arrival and request for a glass of beer. Surprised grunts had greeted his "good evening" as he passed the labourers' bench, and as he stood in the little tap-room, sipping his drink and surveying the collection of horse-brasses behind the bar, the landlord, Mr Herbert, polished glasses with unusual energy, chivvied away those of his offspring who were peering at the prodigy from the back parlour, and maintained a painful silence. Gradually, with heavy nonchalance, the occupants of the bench drifted within and sat down, and after a decent interval began to converse quietly among themselves. Mr Franklin ordered a second glass of beer, and conversation died. He drank it, slowly, but otherwise quite normally, and the muted talk began again, until he turned round, smiled amiably at the small gathering, and asked if anyone would care for a drink.

At this, one startled drinker dropped his tankard, another sent his pint down the wrong way and had to be slapped on the back, and there was some confusion until an ancient, beady-eyed in a corner, licked his lips and told the ceiling that he didn't mind if he had a pint of bitter. This was provided, the ancient bobbed his head over the foam, grinned a gap-toothed grin, said "Good 'ealth," and drank audibly. The others stirred, wondering if they too should accept the stranger's bounty, and then Mr Franklin observed, to the room at large:

"I just moved in at the manor house."

There was a moment's pause, and then the ancient said: "Ar. We know that," and buried his face in his pot. For the rest, half a dozen pairs of eyes avoided Mr Franklin's; the landlord made indistinct noises.

"I was wondering," said Mr Franklin, "if any of you could tell me how I turn the water on. Nothing comes out of the taps, and I'm afraid the agent didn't remember to tell me."

Further silence, muttered consultation, and then the landlord observed that there would be a stop-cock. The ancient agreed; there always was a stop-cock, where there was taps, like. Someone else remarked that Jim Hanway had done odd jobs at the manor, when Mr Dawson was there; Jim'd know. Mr Franklin's hopes rose, only to be dashed by the recollection of another patron that Jim had moved over to East Harling last February.

"Las' March," said the ancient, emerging from his beer.

"No, t'weren't. Febr'y, 'e moved."

"March fust," cried the ancient. "Fust day o' March. His lease were up. Oi know. March fust it was."

At this the other speaker stared coldly at the ancient and said flatly: "It was Febr'y. An' *Oi* know."

"You know bugger-all," said the ancient, and emptied his tankard with relish. He beamed at Franklin. "Thank'ee, sir. That was foine. March fust."

The landlord interposed with a reminder that the gentleman wanted his water turned on, no matter what month Jim Hanway had moved, and silence fell again, until a young labourer said there ought to be a key, for the stop-cock, like, and it'd be round the back o' the house, likely. Mr Franklin acknowledged this; he would look in the outbuildings.

"Stop-cock won't be round the back, though," observed the ancient. "Mains water runs by the road; stop-cock'll be at front. Grown over, an' all," he added with satisfaction, as he hopped off his stool and laid his tankard on the bar. "In all that grass, somewheres." He sighed.

"Would you care for another drink, Mr – " said Franklin, smiling.

"Jake," said the ancient, beaming. "Wouldn't mind, thank'ee very much."

"No, you won't mind, you ole soak," said the man who had disputed with him. "Mind 'im, sir; there's a 'ole inside 'im, an' it ain't got no bottom."

There was a general laugh at this, and Mr Franklin took the opportunity to repeat his invitation; this time the tankards came forward en masse, and while they were being filled he said to Jake:

"My name's Franklin. Mark Franklin," and held out his hand. Jake regarded it a moment, carefully wiped his gnarled fingers on his jacket, and inserted what felt like a large, worn claw gingerly into Mr Franklin's palm. "Jake," he said again. "Thank'ee, sir; thanks very much."

Mr Franklin nodded and glanced at the man who had disputed with Jake, a burly, middle-aged labourer with a square, ruddy face and thinning hair. The man hesitated and then said, "Jack Prior", and took the American's hand. Thereafter, in quick succession, came the others, with large, rough hands that touched Mr Franklin's very gently; flushed faces and grey eyes that slid diffidently away from his. He guessed that introductions were not the norm, at short notice, that anything like social ceremony embarrassed these men, but that because he was an affable stranger, they were making a concession to him. Also, presumably, they had no objection to free drink. He was not to know that no occupant of the manor within living memory had set foot in the Apple Tree; nor did he know that if he had introduced himself in similar company two hundred miles farther north, there would have been no answering acceptance. He did not know England, or the English, then.

The tankards were filled and lifted; Jack Prior said, "All the best, sir," and the others murmured assent; Mr Franklin prepared to answer questions. But none came. In the saloons that he knew, he would have been asked where he came from, how long he planned to stay, what brought him here; he would have responded laconically, as seemed proper. But here, where he had gone out of his way to make himself known, had taken for him the unprecedented step of familiarity – here they drank in shy silence, avoiding his eye and each other's, moving restlessly like cattle in a pen, and trying to appear unconcerned. Mr Franklin knew there was no hostility; he was sensitive enough to recognize embarrassment, but why it should be there he had no idea. Finally, having finished his own drink, he nodded pleasantly, preparing to take his leave; there was a shuffling of feet, almost in relief, it seemed to him, and then Prior suddenly said:

"Franklin." He was frowning thoughtfully. "There's a Franklin over'n the Lye Cottage, at Lancin' End. Old Bessie Reeve – 'er name was Franklin, warn't it, afore she married?"

In spite of himself Mr Franklin exclaimed: "You don't say?"

"Oi do say," replied Prior seriously. "That was her name. Franklin. Same's yours." He looked round, nodding emphatically. "Franklin. She's the only one hereabouts, though."

Jake cackled. "Ain't bin round the churchyard lately, 'ave you? Plenty Franklins there." He wagged his head, grinning, and drained his glass noisily.

The landlord caught Mr Franklin's eye. "Used to be a biggish family, sir, in the old days. None left now. Wait, though – ain't there Franklins over at Hingham?" His question hung unanswered in the silence, and Mr Franklin waited hopefully. The silence continued, and finally he broke it himself, indicating to the landlord that another round would be welcome. The tankards were thrust forward again and withdrawn, replenished; there were salutary murmurs in his direction, but beyond that nothing audible except the occasional gurgle and sigh as another gallon of home-brewed descended to its several resting-places. Mr Franklin decided that Prior's brief conversational flight had probably exhausted the Apple Tree's store of small talk as far as he was concerned, so he drained his glass, not without some effort, and remarked that he must be getting along.

Again he sensed the relieved shuffling, but even as he straightened

73

his coat and prepared to nod to the landlord, Prior took a deep breath and said:

"You'll have another, first – sir? On me, like." Mr Franklin hesitated. With three pints of home-brewed inside him, backing and filling, he felt he had as much as he wanted to carry, and more. It was on the tip of his tongue to decline politely. Then he saw that Prior was standing rather straight, with sweat on his red forehead, and knew that the invitation had been made with considerable effort. Instinctively he sensed that Prior, while a labourer like his fellows, was perhaps of some standing in that humble company, and was in a curious way asserting his dignity; for Prior's credit, it would be right to accept.

"Thank you, Mr Prior," he said. "That's kind of you."

"Jack," said Mr Prior, and laid his coppers carefully on the counter; his glass and Mr Franklin's only were refilled, although Jake ostentatiously drained his few remaining drops, waited hopefully, sighed, and finally announced that he'd better be off to find that stop-cock afore the light went; all growed over, it'd be. Mr Franklin protested, but Jake hopped away, making ancient noises, leaving the American to pledge Prior and attempt his fourth pint of the dark, soapy liquor which seemed to be filling every corner of his abdominal cavity, and possibly running down into his legs as well.

Finally it was done, and Mr Franklin was able to bid the Apple Tree good evening, and escape from that hot, musty atmosphere, apparently compounded of cow's breath and old clothes; he was to grow to recognize it as the distinctive scent of the English farmhand. He was feeling decidedly bloated, but otherwise at peace with mankind; his feet seemed slightly farther away from the rest of his body than usual, and it took longer to place them one in front of the other, but he was in no hurry to get home on this balmy evening – for one thing, home was half a mile away, and if there was one thing he was certain of, in his slightly soporific condition, it was that he was going to have to shed some of his alcoholic burden somewhere, somehow, before he got there.

A dusty and deserted side-turning off the main street caught his eye; it wound between large, untidy, and concealing hedges, so Mr Franklin followed it with casual deliberateness, and two minutes later was shoulder deep in a thicket at the roadside, leaning his head against a branch and solemnly examining a spider's web at close range, grunting contentedly as his troubles poured away into the rank grass,

74

and his lower torso began to feel normal again. Thereafter he took a turn farther up the by-road, and presently found himself regarding an ancient lych-gate set in a mossy wall, and there beyond it, half-hidden by the great yews that lined the wall, the square weathered tower of the village church.

Mr Franklin surveyed it, balancing carefully. What was it his father had said, about some old English king bringing yew-trees from Europe, planting them in every churchyard in England so that the country should never be short of the material on which its army depended – the yew wood that made the great long-bows with which the English peasantry had humbled the armoured might of their nation's enemies.

"Dam' good idea," said Mr Franklin approvingly, staring at the massive, ugly black trunks, their shadows falling on the trim grass among the lichened tombstones. "Bully for you, king." He passed through the gate with its little steep roof, swayed slightly, and leaned on the nearest tree for support, feeling a trifle dizzy. For the moment he was content to rest there; the evening air was warm and tranquil, and he listened to its quiet stirring while he studied the ruddy stone pile of the old church bathed in sunset; from there his attention turned to the gnarled bark under his hand – and an echo was sounding in his mind, assisted by four pints of October ale, an echo from somewhere in memory – the El Paso road? Hole-in-the-Wall? Cassidy's slow, deliberate murmur . . . "and you, good yeomen, whose limbs were made in England, be copy now to men of grosser blood, and teach them how to war . . ."

He disremembered which battle that had been, but he wondered idly if any of its bows had come from this churchyard, or if any of the people who had been there were perhaps now here – under those old gravestones, dark and crooked on the level turf, and decidedly the ale must have been at work on his imagination, for he was suddenly aware of a voice at his elbow, high-pitched and pleasant, and it was saying:

"Well, we aren't Stoke Poges, you know, but I suppose the lines are appropriate for all that. The rude forefathers of the hamlet . . . well, I imagine they don't come much ruder than ours. How d'ye do?"

Mr Franklin realized that he was sitting down, on one of the flat, raised tombs, and was being surveyed by a stout, baldish man in spectacles, with wisps of silvery hair fluttering over his ears; he was an untidy man, with a flannel shirt open at the neck, a huge tweed jacket which fitted where it touched, and knickerbockers insecurely fastened above elderly stockings. He had a sheaf of papers under his arm and a look of whimsical inquiry on his carelessly-shaven face. Mr Franklin made a partially successful effort to rise and beg the newcomer's pardon.

"Not at all. I should apologize for breaking in on your . . . ah, reverie. But when I hear Grey's Elegy, in an American accent . . ." The short-sighted eyes peered and twinkled.

"Was I reciting?" Mr Franklin made a mental note to steer clear of Norfolk beer in future. "I guess I must have been ready to drop off. I'm sorry."

"I'm not. Very proper thing to do. Quite natural. Where else should one recite Grey's Elegy? Apart form Stoke Poges, of course. Forgive me, but I was correct, wasn't I? You are American?"

"Yes, sir. I – "

"I wouldn't inquire, but we see very few visitors, you know, much less transatlantic ones. Not much to attract tourists to our rural retreat, I'm afraid – unless you are interested in runes. We have rather a fine example of one of the stones just inside the doorway there – in fact, while I was at Cambridge I was privileged to assist in deciphering it – curiously enough, it was a learned gentleman from one of your universities – Yale, in fact – who finally made the translation. Splendid scholar; splendid. It was really quite interesting," went on the stout man, "because the inscription reads: 'Lanca wrote this rune on this stone". And of course, this place is called Castle Lancing – well, Lancing means Lanca's people, so we have the mystery of a stone engraved by a Norseman, Lanca, possibly as early as the ninth century, and our church is only twelfth century. Curious, isn't it? Or perhaps," said the stout man anxiously, "you aren't interested in runes?"

Mr Franklin had recovered himself by now. "I might be," he ventured, "if I knew what they were."

"Teutonic engraving – adaptation of Roman letters to permit them to be carved in stone – Anglo-Saxon, Danish, that sort of thing," said the stout man. "But I'm so sorry – you must think me extremely rude, breaking in on you . . . only – " and he suddenly beamed in a way which made him look about ten years old " – one doesn't often hear Grey being quoted aloud in one's churchyard."

"I'm the intruder," said Mr Franklin. "Is this – I mean, are you the . . . the clergyman?"

"Heavens, no!" The stout man laughed. "I'm simply a pest who infests the vestry, like death-watch beetle – which we haven't got, thank God, not yet, touch wood. Parish records, that sort of thing. No – our vicar is a much more useful member of the community, I'm happy to say." He smiled on Mr Franklin. "Are you staying in the neighbourhood?"

"You could say that," admitted Mr Franklin. "I just bought Lancing Manor."

"Good God!" said the stout man distinctly, and dropped his papers. Mr Franklin helped him gather them up. "You've bought . . . the manor? Well, I never! Well, I'm damned! I do beg your pardon." He adjusted his spectacles, combed his scanty hair with his fingers, and stared at Mr Franklin. "Well," he said at length, "that is an extraordinary thing. Of course, after Dawson left, one assumed . . . still, it is unexpected . . . goodness me . . ."

"Not unpleasantly so, I hope?" said Mr Franklin.

"My dear fellow!" The stout man looked alarmed. "I assure you – quite the contrary, absolutely. Splendid news. By God," he added, emphatically, "I'd sooner we had someone in Lancing Manor who quotes Grey in churchyards than . . . than – well, you know what it is, some awful people buy country property nowadays. Men in loud checked bags and women with Pekinese voices. Drive about in motors, take the local people into service and don't know how to treat 'em, try to pretend they're gentry, simply shocking." The stout man paused for breath. "Damned motors."

"I won't be buying a motor," said Mr Franklin.

"Ha!" exclaimed the stout man, and beamed. "No, I don't imagine they'd be your style. You look much too sensible. But, I say – we're neighbours, you know. Well, I live over at Mays Cottage – " he waved vaguely. "Retired, you understand, after forty years lecturing on the sixteenth century to precocious loafers who only want to waste their parents" money on drink, amusement, and young women. No," added the stout man seriously, "that's not fair. Some of 'em did want to learn about the Tudors, God knows why. However, I'm Geoffrey Thornhill, I'm delighted to welcome you to Castle Lancing, and what on earth induced you to buy the manor? I'm all ears."

Mr Franklin frowned, glanced round the churchyard in some perplexity, and sighed. "It's a long story," he said.

"Of course it is! Here, sit down – " Thornhill indicated the flat tomb. "There, now. By the way, you'll get used to me. The villagers think I'm mad, and may be right; I talk compulsively, can't mind my own business, am undoubtedly eccentric, but can easily be managed by anyone who'll simply say 'Shut up, Thornhill'. Right-ho?" His expression invited Mr Franklin to discourse.

"Well . . ." the American began, and stopped. His head was feeling clearer than it had done a few moments earlier, clear enough for him to be aware that he had not quite been in control of his tongue, and to realize that he had not meant to say to anyone what he was on the point of saying to this perfect stranger. But why not, he was thinking. I'm here now, and there's no secret, anyway; this is the end of the line, and this fellow'll find it all out, anyway, for what it's worth. He looked out through the yew-trees to the meadow beyond the village, where the dying sun was casting a pale haze over the fading green.

"Well, my name's Mark Franklin, and I'm an American, as you guessed. And I – " he hesitated. "Well, I guess you could say I've come back." He stopped, frowning, and after a moment Thornhill said:

"Back? To England? Ah, you were born here?"

"No," Mr Franklin smiled. "But my family came from England, and – "

"Franklin, of course. Not a common name, but not uncommon, either, meaning – "

"A free-born landholder, but not of noble blood," quoted Mr Franklin. "That's what my father used to say – and the dictionary bears him out. From what they tell me down at the tavern, there's quite a few Franklins around here." He gestured at the gravestones.

"At the tav –, ah, the pub. Why, yes, there are Franklins in the old registers, and certainly the name is on some of the graves – but, of course, I daresay you'd find it in most English church records. Your people may not be East Anglian – unless they emigrated recently and you can establish from your own knowledge that they came from a certain area, it would be difficult to – "

"My people," said Mr Franklin, "left the village of Castle Lancing in the year sixteen-hundred-and-forty-two. That much I do know – and not much besides, except that the man who left, with his wife and children, was called Matthew Franklin, and every descendant since has been named after one of the four gospel-writers. Where they've been in between . . ." He shrugged. "Grandfather was from Ohio, father from Kansas, but farther back is anybody's guess. Only one thing's sure, because it was in grandfather's bible – which got lost in the war; farm in Kansas got burned – and that was that the first American in our family was Matthew, and he came out of Castle Lancing when they made the place too hot for him. Dad used to say old Matthew was a king's man, and that the local sentiment was pretty Republican round that time . . ." He laughed and shook his head, while Thornhill bounced up and down, making apoplectic noises which eventually spilled out in a flood of excited words.

"But . . . but . . . but . . . good God! Well, I'm blessed! You mean you've – you've come back to the very village! But that's splendid! Well, I'm damned! That is ab-so-lutely splendid, my dear chap! I never heard the like! After all these years – these generations – these centuries . . ." Thornhill gaped and beamed. "I mean – well, I suppose most of us here have a vague notion where our families hail from – well, my own lot claimed that they were Normans called Tournelle, but since my own grandfather was a swineherd from Dumfriesshire, I imagine that the village of Thornhill in that county supplies a more plausible clue – it was my aunt, actually, who tried to pretend to the Norman nonsense – foolish old woman, snob to the eyebrows, of course . . . but, my goodness, to be able to walk back, after nearly three hundred years, into your ancestors" own place! Dear me! And there can't be any doubt, you see – the parish registers will show Matthew – it was Matthew, wasn't it? – and his parentage . . . I mean, you've got the date – 1642 – Civil War, King and Parliament – yes, it fits, your father was perfectly right, this was very strong Parliamentarian country, yes, indeed, and anyone of royalist sympathies might well clear out . . . well, I say!"

Mr Franklin became aware that he was being regarded with something like reverence; Thornhill took off his glasses, polished them on a huge handkerchief, replaced them, and viewed the American with delight.

"This is absolutely first-rate! I'm more delighted than I can say! I must calm down, I really must . . ." He puffed and shook his head. "Steady, Thornhill, steady . . . but this is my hobby, you see – well, more my passion, I suppose – I told you I was an enthusiast for parish records – and to find you . . ." he regarded Mr Franklin with a possessiveness that was positively gloating, as though he were some rare species of butterfly " – why, it's as though you had walked straight off the page of one of my birth-ledgers – a Franklin of Castle Lancing – " He sprang up suddenly. "But what are we sitting here for – my dear fellow – where's that blasted key . . ." He rummaged in his pocket, sending its contents broadcast. "We must look – at once! They're on the vestry shelves – we can find Matthew, and . . . and . . . oh, damn!" He struck his forehead a resounding slap. "The lamp's empty, and it's getting dark. But we can get some oil from the shop – it'll only take a moment – " His voice trailed off as he caught sight of Mr Franklin's expression, and his face fell. "But perhaps you don't feel like . . . I mean, I could probably track old Matthew down in an hour or two, if you'd care to . . ."

He looked so much like a wistful little boy that Mr Franklin almost agreed; in fact, he had felt his own excitement rising in tune with Thornhill's enthusiasm. But he was suddenly aware that daylight was fading, and the air was getting chilly; also, Norfolk beer and a brief sleep the previous night had left him feeling suddenly bone-weary, and the tombstone on which he was sitting felt uncommonly cold and hard.

"Well . . . " he insisted, reluctant to damp the other's evident eagerness. "I know it must sound downright ungrateful – and real disrespectful to my great-great-however-many-greats-grandfather and all, but – "

"My dear chap!" Thornhill was all contrition. "How thoughtless of me! Of course you must be quite used up – journey, travelling, only this minute here – I am most frightfully sorry! That's my trouble, of course – off in a burst of sparks like a damned rocket! Like one of your prospectors, what? Tell you what – I'll see you down the road now, but I'll be up here first thing, and I'll have old Matthew pinned to the floor by lunch-time, you'll see! What a splendid thing! The vicar will be delighted. Well, the whole village will be – the wanderer returns, and all that . . ." He took Mr Franklin's arm and was steering him towards the lych-gate, when he gave a sudden galvanized start, and stood quivering. "My God! I think – yes, I'm almost sure . . . here, it'll only take a second . . ."

And seizing Mr Franklin's wrist, he dragged him off towards the church, and round to the side-wall, puffing through the twilight and muttering, ". . . certain I saw one . . . somewhere along here – yes, against the wall there! Come on – you'll see . . ."

There was a row of old tombstones, piled shoulder to shoulder against the church wall, and Thornhill threw himself on them like a terrier, peering at the lichen-encrusted surfaces, muttering and swearing while Mr Franklin waited slightly nonplussed. "No . . . no . . . dammit all . . . nothing but bloody Quayles and Plowrights . . . bred

80

like rabbits ... no ... oh, blast! ..." He crouched from stone to stone, vituperating in an aggrieved whisper, and then suddenly gave an absolute squeal of delight.

"Franklin! Look – come here! Look at that! Damn this dark!" It was almost too dim to see in the gathering gloom at the foot of the wall; Thornhill struck a match, and by its light Mr Franklin found himself looking at a smooth sandstone on which were the faint, spidery letters of an old inscription.

"I knew it! I knew there was one here!" Thornhill's voice was shaking with excitement. "Look, don't you see?" And as he pronounced the letters, Mr Franklin could just make them out:

"J-o-h-a-n-n-e-s F-r-a-n ... then two blank spaces where the letters are worn away ... then i-n. Johannes Franklin – with two squiggly bits afterwards which are probably the letters 'u' and 's' – Latin style, you see. Johannes Franklinus. John Franklin. And see here ..." His finger traced underneath the name: "Obit 1599 – plain as a pikestaff!" The match went out, but Mr Franklin could see the spectacles gleaming in the dusk.

"That," said Thornhill quietly, "is quite probably your great-great-great-great-great-great-grandfather, give or take a 'great' or two. Buried somewhere within a few yards of us. I'll go over this with a fine toothcomb tomorrow, but ... well, as your countrymen say – isn't that something? It's just a matter of establishing who Matthew's parents were – if his father's called John, and the date of death fits – well, there you are."

Mr Franklin stood up; suddenly he felt cold. It was almost dark now; a moth fluttered past him in the dusk; there were a few stars out in the dim vault of the sky. He suddenly felt utterly unreal, standing there by the church wall, in this strange village – where was it? What was he doing here? Maybe he was asleep, and it was only happening in a dream.

Then he was aware that Thornhill, a bulky indistinct figure in the gloom, was holding out his hand. Automatically he took it, and felt his hand shaken firmly.

"Welcome home," said Thornhill quietly.

He muttered something by way of thanks, but still the feeling of unreality persisted. But what was it that was unreal? Himself? His being here? No, it wasn't that – it wasn't the crowded facts of the past few days, either – the liner, and Liverpool, and the railroad journey, and the Waldorf Hotel, and Pip's blonde softness in his hands, and the glitter and noise of Monico's, or the smelly stuffiness of the inn down the road – it was none of that: that was all real enough. Was it the time before, then – the other world he had come from? But he was still Mark Franklin the miner, the ranchhand, the wanderer, wasn't he? Or was that some other person, someone he'd once known? Had he changed into someone else? That couldn't be, not with just coming to a new place; only this place wasn't new. It was old, and whether he stayed or whether he went away, it would remain, in his mind, and there would remain, too, the sense of belonging to it – where did he belong, if not here? There was no one spot anywhere else on earth that he *belonged* to. Here, in this place he'd never seen until today, he had a house, where his belongings were – and within a few yards of him, under the grass, there were the bones of people who, if they could have come back to life, and could have known all that had happened in three hundred years, would have looked at him and thought, why, that is the son of Luke, who was the son of John, who was the child of Matthew's people who went to the New World in the time of the Great Rebellion, the King's War. But they were ghosts, from a long time ago – and yet, his own father was a ghost, too, from only a little closer in time. He had no kin, no one anywhere, who was really any closer than those old bones – and everyone had the old bones of kinsfolk, *somewhere*. But he knew where his were – they were *here*. Johannes Franklinus had walked down this same road where he was walking now, with Thornhill prattling at his elbow.

". . . time to settle in, at first, bound to. Very quiet, of course, but friendly – anyway, you can be sure that I'm going to be busy tomorrow – and for as long as need be, hounding old Matthew out of his dusty obscurity. There's a thought, eh – while all your people have been crossing the Atlantic, and building log-huts, and fighting Redskins – and the damned British, too – and each other, and driving wagons, and 'going West, young man' – why, all that time, that page with old Matthew's name on it has been enclosed in that book on that shelf in that same vestry, letting the world pass by for a few centuries, just waiting – for you to come and look at him! Strange thought, isn't it?"

They came out of the side-road into the village's main street. There were lights in a few of the houses, and from the Apple Tree; voices drifted across from the knot of men who were walking slowly, arguing, from the pub's door. As they turned past the village shop, the proprietress was at the door; she came hesitantly forward, and Mr Franklin paused.

"Just to let you know, sir, that I put some sugar in with your order, in case you'd forgot," Mrs Laker explained. "Just so you know to look for it."

"Well, thank you, I had forgotten." Mr Franklin smiled and touched his hat; Thornhill, watching, reflected that in ten years of getting groceries from Mrs Laker he had never been so favoured; if he forgot he went without and that was that.

"And Mrs Wood here – " there was a figure bobbing nervously, dabbing her nose with a handkerchief, at Mrs Laker's elbow, "she put you down a pint of milk."

"That was most thoughtful, Mrs Wood," said Mr Franklin. "And it's Mrs . . . Laker, isn't it? Ladies, you're very kind. I guess when I get squared away I'll discover what my requirements are."

"Ooh," whispered Mrs Wood, impressed. "Squared away – I never!"

"Well, my dear chap, I can see you're in good hands," said Thornhill. "What we would do without Mrs Laker, I can't think . . . I wonder, Mrs Laker, if I could trouble you for some paraffin." He glanced apologetically at Mr Franklin. "It's no use – I must have a shot at Matthew tonight – shan't sleep otherwise. No, no, my dear fellow, you get some rest – I'll look along some time, or if you've a moment, you know where I'll be, at the church. Mrs Laker, you are a ministering angel." He accepted his paraffin gratefully, and wondered if he would have got it so readily if this imposing American in his long black coat and astonishing hat had not been present, dazzling the senses of the good wives of Castle Lancing.

And not only the good wives, it appeared. As Mr Franklin was preparing to take his leave, a small boy, who in common with his associates, had been observing Mr Franklin from a distance, was heard to exclaim that the Yankee hadn't got a six-shooter, so there. Mrs Wood squeaked indignantly, and Mrs Laker exclaimed: "Sauce! You get out home, Tommy Marsh, or I'll get your mother! The idea!"

"Well 'e 'asn't!" cried the impudent urchin, while his friends giggled in the shadows by the shop's light, and Mr Franklin half-turned in their direction.

"I never carry it at night, Tommy. I do all my shooting in the daytime. Except for Indians and cattle rustlers, of course."

At which Mrs Wood and Mrs Laker exclaimed with astonishment,

Mr Franklin bade them good-night with another touch of his hat, thanked Thornhill warmly for his welcome, and turned as another voice said: "Goodnight, Mr Franklin, sir." It was Prior, with his cronies from the Apple Tree – and why, wondered Mr Franklin, as he strode down his homeward road, was it such a good thing that he had been able to recall Prior's Christian name, and respond with "Goodnight, Jack; good-night all"? It pleased him – and suddenly, as he paused outside the manor's rusty gates, he felt an overwhelming, warm content; a great happiness of fulfilment, of a kind that he could remember only rarely – after the Sunday School prize, at Omaha, when he'd been all of six years old, and his father had led him away afterwards by the hand, smiling down at him; outside the Home-steaders' Bank in Carson City, when he had made the big deposit, and walked across to the Star and Garter saloon for a beer – and yes, just last night, lying joyously content with Pip's breast in his hand, blowing playfully at the blonde tendrils of hair across his face. Such different kinds of placid happiness – and now he was feeling it again, as he walked up the drive, brushing his feet through the grass and weeds, feeling for his key – and checking only momentarily as a dim figure rose from one of the stone seats and hailed him in a beer-roughened croak.

"I foun' the stop-cock, sir – down yonder by the path. All growed over like anythin' – but I got the key on her all right. So water'll be runnin' right enough, whenever you turn the tap. If I coulda gotten in, I'd 'a lit the boiler like, to warm 'er up." He sniffed complacently. "But I couldn't get in. All locked up."

"Why, Jake, that was very considerate." Mr Franklin felt in his waistcoat pocket, and found a guinea. "I'm much obliged to you."

"A'right, now," said Jake. "Say, though, there's some weeds aroun', tough, ain't there? Like an old swamp, I reckon?"

"Think you could get rid of them?" wondered Mr Franklin, and fingered the guinea aside in his pocket, searching out two half-crowns instead. Despite his euphoria, caution told him that if he overpaid Jake the first time he would regret it. Jake assured him volubly that he would tackle the weeds first thing, and make a right proper job of them.

"Well, not too early; I'd like to sleep a long time tonight," said Mr Franklin, and when Jake had expressed rapture over his five shillings and hopped away into the dark, promising prodigies of service, the new owner of Lancing Manor let himself into the dim, empty hall.

He stood in the darkness, looking round at the half-seen shadows, feeling the tiredness wash over him. He ignored his trunks, but unbuckled his valise, drew out his blanket, and made a bed by simply spreading it before the empty fireplace. He folded his clothes on the settle, made his valise into a pillow, and stretched out, rolling the blanket round him. For a few moments he lay, looking up at the shadowy ceiling, while he thought of the worn stone up in the church-yard, and of his father, and of dim figures that he could not recognize, although he knew they had once existed.

"Well," said Mr Franklin aloud. "We're back." Then he was fast asleep, in Castle Lancing.

6

Mr Franklin's arrival at the Manor was something of a nine-day wonder in the neighbourhood. Not only was he foreign, and slightly exotic with his sunbrowned complexion and lanky striding gait, he was also a mystery, and Castle Lancing enjoyed a mystery as much as the next village. Speculation had a field day: as a result of his playful answer to Tommy Marsh it was quickly understood that he had killed a man in the bush, and was in hiding with a price on his head; there followed the rumour that he was the bastard offspring of a Duke, come home to claim his inheritance (this, doubtless, sprang from a chance remark of Thornhill's anent the American genealogy); finally, the obvious deduction was made that he was extremely rich, and that he intended to buy half Norfolk and reverse the country's agricultural decline with go-ahead Yankee schemes; this was a popular theory because it was at least comforting in an area which was watching with anxiety the absorption of small holdings into larger farms, and where landlord-hatred was an article of faith.

So interest ran high at the activity observed round the Manor; gangs of workmen arrived from as far away as Norwich to re-gravel the drive, point and sand the stonework, paint the timber, repair the plumbing, and carry out internal improvements to the decoration; local labourers, mysteriously recruited by Jake, who lost no opportunity of establishing his unofficial stewardship and special relationship with the owner, cleared acres of weed and rubbish from the grounds, relaid the flower-bed and repaired the borders; there was a coming and going of pantechnicons and drays with furniture from Norwich – and on two sensational occasions, from London itself – with men in aprons heaving in beds, chairs, sofas, curtains, and mysterious packing-cases whose contents could only be guessed at; for one full day a magnificent new bath, with gleaming taps and a shower attachment of strange pipes and faucets, lay on the gravel before the house, and in Mr Franklin's absence the entire population of the district came to marvel, and to be kept at a respectful distance by the ubiquitous Jake. All was bustle and concern, great quantities of ale were drunk by the toilers – for Mr Franklin had been prodigal in his provision for the refreshment of his helpers, and the Apple Tree was threatened by drought as the result of its traffic down the Manor road – and it was agreed that the Yankee must have a power of money. The young men spat and exclaimed in respectful envy; the young women and wives were unstinting in their admiration; the gaffers agreed that no good would come of it; and Jake, ensconced on his stool at the inn, cackled knowingly and implied that they had seen nothing yet; let them wait until the Yankee squire – the title dropped into place inevitably with ownership of the Manor House – really went to work (with Jake's guidance, be it understood). Then they'd see.

Yet Mr Franklin was a disappointment, after the first excitement of his arrival had died down. He kept very much to the Manor, supervising installations in the house itself, occasionally inspecting the work out of doors, stating his requirements civilly but briefly; he knew what he wanted, and that was that. He employed no personal servants, which gave rise to much wonder – who cooked and washed the dishes and kept the house, for one thing? His laundry went to Thetford, his bodily provisions were ordered regularly from Mrs Laker and the dairy, and that seemed to satisfy him. Once or twice he appeared in the Apple Tree, but while he was courteous and affable, he was not communicative, and a natural shyness among the villagers prevented inquiry. Word of his arrival had naturally spread to the more important houses in the district, such as they were, and while there was mild curiosity there was a natural tendency to let the newcomer settle in; the largest estate-owner was an absentee landlord who lived in London most of the year, leaving the management of his estate to a steward whose duties excluded social niceties; the vicar, an amiable elderly soul who studied birds, met Mr Franklin once, and promptly forgot who he was, to the chagrin of the vicar's wife, who had wished to invite the American to tea but hesitated to do so on such erratic acquaintance.

It followed that initially Mr Franklin's sole contact with Castle Lancing society – excepting his commerce with the working class – was the eccentric Thornhill, who was himself something of a recluse. They had a brief period of intimacy while Thornhill was busily scavenging the parish records on the American's behalf: Matthew was duly identified, as was his wife, who proved to have the baptismal name Jezebel – an unprecedented and impossible thing, in Thornhill's view, but there it was, and how to explain it he could not imagine. Johannes Franklinus of the gravestone proved to be Matthew's uncle, and Thornhill had no difficulty in tracing the family, and its association with Castle Lancing, back to the Black Death, where the parish records began.

But their relations, though cordial, did not blossom into friendship. Thornhill visited the Manor once or twice, and received al fresco refreshment; he gave Mr Franklin a bachelor supper at his own cosy, deplorably untidy cottage, amidst a litter of books and papers, but although the Burgundy was excellent, and the American was enthusiastic over Thornhill's researches, they discovered, once the topic of the ancient Franklins had been exhausted, that they had no especial common interest. Mr Franklin was prepared to talk, within limits, about the United States; Thornhill was prepared to talk, without limits, about everything, but he did it with only half his mind, the other half being firmly rooted in that exciting misty area between the accession of Edward III and the Reformation. The truth was that, unless his interest was aroused on his own subject, as it had briefly been in Mr Franklin's case, Thornhill's garrulity was a nervous habit; he really preferred talking to himself, which he frequently did, thus provoking cries of "Loony!" from the coarser young spirits of the village.

So they remained amiable acquaintances, meeting occasionally in Mrs Laker's or the street, Thornhill pouring out a torrent of small-talk, and Mr Franklin nodding gravely and occasionally observing "Just so". And gradually Castle Lancing's interest dwindled, as such interests do; Mr Franklin remained an object of remark, slightly mysterious – but a mystery has to manifest itself mysteriously if it is to claim much attention, and Mr Franklin remained undeniably normal; a minor sensation in September, he was old news by October – and that suited him very well, apparently. He was content, it seemed, to merge into the background of Castle Lancing, far from the great world, and to forget about it, at least for a season. But, although he did not suspect it as he went about placidly improving and perfecting his house, watching the apples wrinkle and wither in his orchard, and the leaves fall to carpet his garden in brown and gold – although he was far from suspecting it in his sought-out rustic solitude, the great world was not prepared to forget him.

It was a raw October day that Mr Franklin unstabled the hack hired from a farrier in Thetford, hitched it expertly to his small trap, and set out on the fifteen-mile journey to the village of West Walsham. He had seen an advertisement in the local paper offering for sale seventy-five feet of Japanese oak panelling, and since his own hall had struck him as being in need of lightening, he had decided to drive over to the country house where the panelling was on view. It was, he admitted to himself, a fairly thin excuse for the journey; he had no real notion of what Japanese oak looked like, but he had not been abroad for a fortnight, and the prospect of a ramble along the back-roads of Norfolk was attractive. Thornhill had recommended a drive by Wayland Woods – the very wood, he assured an amused Mr Franklin, where the Babes of the famous legend had been abandoned by their wicked uncle, whose house at Griston was still to be seen. So the trap carried a large and well-filled picnic hamper, and Mr Franklin bowled off not caring a great deal whether he reached his destination or not.

He ambled very much at random, roughly in what he believed was the West Walsham direction, guiding himself by the orange ball of the sun which shone dimly through the autumn mist, content to admire the golden woods and the pale green meadows on his way. There was an invigorating nip in the air, a damp cosiness about the countryside with its heavy brown earth and dripping hedges, which he found strangely pleasant; in the far distance he caught once or twice the sound of many dogs barking, and wondered what so large a pack could be doing. It was all very peaceful and English, he told himself, and he was enjoying it – was he turning into a Limey, he wondered, smiling at the thought. Even after a few weeks he was aware that his appearance had probably changed a little; the trim tweeds he was wearing, the shooting-hat and gaiters, were all right in the Norfolk character; he laughed aloud and said "Squire!", shaking his head – how the roughnecks at Tonopah or the barkeeps at the Bella Union would have laughed at that. He didn't care; it suited him.

He came out of his pleasant daydream to the realization that he had no idea where he was, and that it must be getting close to noon. He chucked the reins, the hack roused itself to a gentle trot, and they came over a rise and down a gentle slop to a bridge among the thickets where, on a clear space by the roadside, a large Mercedes motor-car was parked. It was an imposing machine, with five passengers that he could see: a lady and gentleman seated on camp-chairs by the road-side, having lunch, with another woman in the car, what looked like a servant attending to the tiny camp-table before the diners, and an undoubted chauffeur busying himself at the back of the car. It occurred to Mr Franklin that where there was a chauffeur there would certainly be a map; he slowed to a halt beside the car and raised his hat.

"Good day," he said. "I wonder if you could tell me if I'm on the right road for West Walsham?"

The gentleman appeared not to have heard him; at least, he did not take his attention from the heaped plate on his lap. He was a stout, elderly man, clad in a heavy caped coat and plaid trousers, with a cap pulled down over his brows, and he appeared to be enjoying his lunch immensely. Mr Franklin glanced at the lady, and immediately forgot all about the male half of the dining party; she had looked up in surprise at his question, and he found himself looking into a face that was quite breath-takingly beautiful. Bright green eyes and auburn hair were a startling enough combination, with that perfect complexion, but there was a liveliness about her expression, and in the sudden brilliant smile which she bestowed on him, that prompted Mr Franklin to bow in his seat as he repeated his question.

"West Walsham?"

The lady glanced at her companion, who carefully wiped his grizzled beard on a napkin before shaking his head.

"Couldn't say, I'm afraid. Don't know where *we* are, for that matter." And he gave a deep, hearty chuckle.

"Perhaps Stamper knows," said the lady, and turned to repeat the question to the chauffeur, who consulted a map. He seemed to be having some difficulty, and the lady presently rose to help him; the long heavy motoring-coat could not conceal the grace of her movements, and Mr Franklin was charmed as he watched the lovely face intent on the map which the chauffeur spread on the motor's bonnet, and the tiny gloved hand tracing on it. The stout old gentleman, having reluctantly surrendered his empty plate to the servant, was now contemplating an unlit cigar; no one else was saying a word, and Mr Franklin politely removed his attention from the beautiful map-reader and remarked that it was a fine day for a picnic.

The old gentleman seemed surprised at this. The grizzled beard and heavy moustache were turned on Mr Franklin; small bright eyes regarded him for several seconds, taking in his clothing, his horse and trap, his person, and (Mr Franklin felt) his standing and moral character. The old gentleman spoke.

"Yes," he said, and placed the cigar in his mouth. The servant lighted it, and the old gentleman puffed irritably for a few seconds, and then turned to address the lady and chauffeur. "Can't you find it?"

The lady laughed, intent on the map. "That can't be it, Stamper – that's miles away." She raised her head. "Stamper's found a *North* Walsham, but it's at the other end of the county."

The old gentleman considered, puffing thoughtfully. "Then look at this end," he said. "Towards the west. That's where it'll be – wouldn't you say?" he added to Mr Franklin.

"Please," said Mr Franklin, "I'm putting you to a great deal of trouble, and – "

"It's no trouble," said the lady, "we shall find it in a moment. Come along, Stamper – you take that side and I'll take this . . ."

The old gentleman sighed, and Mr Franklin sat through an uncomfortable minute, wishing he had passed by without inquiry, while the lady and chauffeur were joined by the second lady from the car; they continued the search, murmuring over the map, but West Walsham proved as elusive as ever, and Mr Franklin was on the point of asking them to desist when the old gentleman said suddenly:

"Had lunch?"

"I beg your pardon – no, no thank you," said Mr Franklin hurriedly. "Thank you very much, but I'm . . . ah, lunching farther on."

The old gentleman grunted, smoked busily, and then said:

"Have a glass of wine, anyway, while you're waiting." And before he could protest, Mr Franklin found himself being presented with a glass by the ever-ready servant. He raised it to the old gentleman, searching for the right words.

"Why thank you, sir. Your very good health, and – " he bowed towards the group round the map " – and your daughter's, too."

Why he assumed that the beautiful lady was the old gentleman's daughter he could not have said; they could hardly be man and wife, and the relationship seemed a reasonable supposition. That he was wrong, offensively wrong, was evident immediately; at his words the murmur of voices over the map stopped dead, and the old gentleman stared at him with his face going crimson. Surprise and anger showed in the little bright eyes staring at Mr Franklin; then the eyes closed as their owner began to wheeze loudly – to his relief Mr Franklin realized that the old gentleman was laughing, and laughing with abandon, heaving precariously on his camp-chair, and finally going into a coughing-fit which brought the beautiful lady to his side. She bent

91

over him, an arm about his heavy shoulders, as the coughing fit subsided and the old gentleman found his voice again.

"Don't fuss at me!" he said. "There, that's better – that's better." He would have resumed his cigar, but the lady gave him a reproachful look, and with a sigh he tossed it away. "Well – have you found the place yet?"

"I'm afraid not." The lady gave Mr Franklin an apologetic look. "Really, we are hopeless navigators."

"Well, I hope Stamper can at least find the way to Oxton," said the old gentleman. He cleared his throat heavily and addressed Mr Franklin. "And that you find your West wherever-it-is, Mr . . . ?"

"Franklin," said the American, and the old gentleman reached for his own wine-glass and drained it, his gesture inviting Franklin to accompany him.

"You're an American, aren't you?" said the old gentleman; now that he had got over his coughing, he had a surprisingly deep, gruff voice, pronouncing his "r's" with heavy deliberation. "Yes – I told you he was, when we saw him driving down, didn't I? Always tell an American with horses. Well, good day to you, sir," and the old gentleman nodded to Mr Franklin as the servant helped him to rise, the lady taking his arm. She smiled pleasantly as Mr Franklin got down to put his empty glass on the table.

"I do wish we could have helped you," she said.

"I'm just sorry for putting you to so much trouble," said Mr Franklin. "You've been very kind. And I thank you for a glass of excellent wine, Mr . . . ?"

"Eh?" The old gentleman squared his broad shoulders and the little eyes met Mr Franklin's again. "Oh . . . Lancaster. Glad to have seen you, Mr Franklin."

He stumped off towards the car, the lady moving gracefully beside him. Mr Franklin mounted his trap again, shook the reins, and set off; he glanced back once, and saw that the old gentleman was being settled into his seat by the chauffeur, who was wrapping a rug round his legs. The lady waved gaily to Mr Franklin, and then he was over the bridge and out of sight, puzzling over the unpredictable behaviour of the English gentry: there had been a moment there when the old fellow had looked ready to burst, but he seemed a decent enough sort. And what a green-eyed beauty she had been; Mr Franklin wondered if Englishwomen were really more handsome than any others, or if there was something in the English air that was making him more susceptible.

A mile or two farther on he stopped for his own picnic on a slight rise from which he had a good view of the misty country round, except to his right, where a high hedge obscured a stretch of ploughed land. He unpacked from the hamper some cold cuts and salad and cheese, as well as a bottle of Bernkastler, a wine for which he had conceived a loyalty, if not perhaps a liking exactly, on the voyage from New York; it was, in fact, the first wine he had ever tasted. He spread his old slicker on the damp grass at the roadside, and fell to, munching contentedly and taking in the scenery.

From somewhere across the ploughed land the sound of the barking dogs came again, closer than before, and this time the distant sound of human voices, sharply interrupted by the unmistakeable note of a horn. Mr Franklin stopped eating to listen; the distant voices were shouting, and there was that dull drumming sound which he knew so well, of galloping horses; the baying of the dogs rose clamorously – they must be in the ploughed field beyond the hedge by now, and Mr Franklin was just rising to have a look when something small and frantic burst suddenly through the hedge, there was a reddish blur streaking across the road, swerving to avoid the startled Mr Franklin, then leaping an astonishing height and actually striking the side of the trap with a slight thud. It happened in the twinkling of an eye; the small creature tumbled over the side of the trap in a flurry of bushy tail, fell into a picnic basket – and the lid which Mr Franklin had carelessly left open, fell abruptly, the patent catch clicked shut, and the invader was trapped. The basket jerked and shook, to an accompaniment of squeaks within; Mr Franklin stood astonished, a drumstick in one hand and a glass in the other – and then over and through the hedge came what seemed to be a torrent of dogs, brown and white brutes with long tails and floppy ears, baying and squealing and surging round the trap, threatening to overturn it in their eagerness to get at the basket. The din was deafening, the trap shuddered under the impact of canine bodies struggling against its sides, and the hack, which Mr Franklin had fortunately turned loose to graze, neighed wildly and clattered off down the road.

Mr Franklin considered the situation; it was new to him, but he was not a man given to acting without thinking, except in truly mortal situations; dealing with a swarming pack of excited dogs was outside his scope, and he was relieved at the abrupt appearance of a wiry

93

little man who looked like a jockey in a large red coat, and who fell on the dogs with a long-lashed whip and a tongue to match. There was shouting and cheering from the hedge; riders were trying to find a way through, and now from gates some distance down the road on either side they came clattering on to the road – men in red or black, with top hats, caps, and crops, converging on the trap, where the wiry little man was thrashing at the squealing dogs, swearing shrilly in a jargon which Mr Franklin did not recognize. But the appearance of the new arrivals was at least familiar from prints in books and on saloon walls; this, he concluded, was a fox-hunt.

"What the blazes is happening, Jarvie?" "What is it?" "Where away, then?" "I say, Jarvie, what's happened?" The riders were reining in round the trap, the frustrated pack, the belabouring huntsman, and the innocent Mr Franklin, with a clamour of inquiry; a burly young man with a heavy moustache was to the fore, flourishing a heavy riding crop.

"Good God, Jarvie, what are the hounds doing?" he demanded, and the sweating little man, having beaten a way through the yelping mass, was springing nimbly into the trap and surveying the jerking picnic basket with astonishment.

"I . . . I dunno, milord. Why, bloody 'ell – I think it's gone to ground in this 'ere basket!"

Cries of astonishment and laughter; Mr Franklin noted that a couple of ladies were among the hunters who were pressing forward to see. One horse stamped perilously close to him, and he had to step back, catching at the hedge to prevent his falling.

"What's that? In the basket? Good God!" exclaimed the burly young man. "Well, I'm damned! Heave it out then, Jarvie – sling it on to the road, man!"

"I think it's locked, milord," said Jarvie, eyeing the basket.

"Then break the dam' thing open, can't you? Throw it down!"

Mr Franklin was conscious of a slight irritation. It was not only the brutality of the burly young man's tone, proclaiming as it did an obvious disregard for anyone and anything that got in his way; nor was it the threatened destruction of his property. What ruffled Mr Franklin's spirit was the fact that no one, especially the burly young man, had even noticed him or apparently given a thought to who the owner of the trap and basket might be. On the contrary, he had been forced into the hedge, and was still in some danger of being trampled as the riders pressed their horses forward round the trap, chattering excitedly.

"In the basket?" "Good lord, it can't be!" "Open it up, then Jarvie." "Come on, man!" Jarvie stood perplexed, and was just stooping to the basket when Mr Franklin succeeded in forcing himself between the hedge and the nearest rider, and approached the trap.

"Just a moment," he said, and the chatting subsided slightly. The riders regarded him with some surprise, and the young man demanded:

"Who are you?"

It was said impatiently, and Mr Franklin found himself disliking the young man. His face was beefy, his moustache was aggressive, and his eyes were staring with that unpleasant arrogant hostility which Mr Franklin had already noted in a certain type of Englishman. He hadn't put a name to it, but it was the look of a nature that would rather be rude than not, and took satisfaction in displaying contempt for outsiders, and putting them in their place.

"I'm the owner of the basket. And the trap. And the horse – wherever it is," said Mr Franklin quietly, and a lady laughed among the hunters. The young man stared at Mr Franklin blankly, and then directed his attention to Jarvie again.

"Come on, Jarvie!" he snapped, slapping his crop, and as Jarvie stooped obediently Mr Franklin lost his temper completely. There was no outward sign of this; he simply laid a hand on the side of the trap and said:

"Don't touch that basket, Jarvie. And get out of the rig, will you – now."

Jarvie looked, and stopped abruptly, his hands coming away from the basket. He was conscious of a lean brown face and two cold steady eyes staring into his, and what he thought he saw in them took him aback. Still, he hesitated, and then the quiet voice said:

"Step down, Jarvie."

And to his own astonishment, Jarvie found himself stepping down into the road, while exclamations of surprise and bewilderment came from the onlookers.

"Thank you," said Mr Franklin, and came round to Jarvie's side of the trap, where the hounds, subdued and fretful by now, were whining round the huntsman's boots. It was echoed by a murmur of discontent from the hunt. "What the deuce?" grumbled one stringy old gentleman with a puce complexion, and a stout woman said:

95

"Really!" At this the burly young man, momentarily rendered speechless by his huntsman's apparent defection, swung down from his saddle and strode towards the trap. Mr Franklin moved to confront him, and the young man stopped, his face flushed with fury.

"What the devil d'you mean by . . . by impeding the hunt?" he demanded.

"What do you mean," responded Mr Franklin, "by interrupting my dinner and invading my property?"

"His *dinner*," exclaimed a female voice. "Did you hear?" And: "Property?" demanded the stringy man. "What property? Stuff and nonsense!"

"As I said, it *is* my trap, and my basket," said Mr Franklin, and the murmur rose to a growl, although one or two of the hunt, struck by the comic side of the situation, laughed. Among them was an angel-faced young lady in a bowler hat with her hair tied back in a large black bow; it seemed to him that her laughter particularly stung the burly young man, who was standing glowering uncertainly.

"Dammit, sir, this is dam' ridiculous," exclaimed a fat man whose complexion matched his coat. "You've got the dam' fox in the dam' basket! What? You – you can't steal a dam' fox, dammit!"

"I'm not stealing anything," said Mr Franklin abruptly; his temper was still high. "The fox arrived uninvited – "

"Well, then, let the dam' thing go!" exclaimed the stringy man. "Good God, never heard the like in all my life!" He glared suspiciously at Mr Franklin. "Are you some kind of blasted Yankee crank, or what?"

"Shove him out of the way, Frank," shouted a voice, and the burly young man came a step closer to Mr Franklin; plainly he was measuring the American's breadth of shoulder and general potential in a roadside brawl, for he demanded: "Are you going to stand out of the way?"

"No," said Mr Franklin with a coolness he was far from feeling, "and if you lay a hand on anything that belongs to me, I'll not only sue you under whatever laws you have in England, I'll also beat the living daylights out of you."

At this, slight pandemonium broke out; someone suggested getting the police, the young man clenched his fists, Mr Franklin braced himself, but before the young man could do anything rash he was set aside by a blond young giant who grinned amiably at Mr Franklin, tossed his hat away, and cried: "That's the ticket! Want a turn-up, do you, Yankee! Come on, then, here we are!"

"Arthur, stop it!" cried the girl with the black bow, but Arthur shook his head, his eyes laughing as he watched Franklin. "No, no, Peg, you mind your own business. If this chap's ready to fight for his fox, good luck to him! Eh, Yankee?"

"If you like," said Mr Franklin slowly, and at this point another of the huntsmen urged his horse forward; an elderly, intelligent-looking man with a distinct air of authority.

"Stop this dam' nonsense," he said. "Arthur, don't be a fool! And you, sir, what are you driving at? Are you bent on making mischief – you've no right to . . . to make away with that fox, and you know it!"

"I haven't even touched the fox," said Mr Franklin. "And I dare say I'd have felt obliged to let him loose five minutes ago – if someone had just troubled to ask me politely."

"Politely!" echoed the stringy man in disbelief, and the fat man said the fellow was mad. But the intelligent-looking man stared hard at Mr Franklin and then said: "Come sir, this is foolish. It's not our fault if the creature went to ground in your basket – "

"Not mine, either," said Mr Franklin. "I didn't chase him there."

There were cries of derision at this, and then the angel-faced girl with the bow called out mischievously: "If I say, 'Please, sir, may we have our fox back?'" will you let him go?"

"Too late, Peg, too late!" cried Arthur, grinning. "Isn't it, Yank?"

"This is a dam' farce!" cried the fat man. "Dammit, this is meant to be a dam' hunt, isn't it?"

Mr Franklin surveyed the faces in front of him; Arthur, gleefully ready for a fight, the burly man Frank scowling, most of the mounted men plainly annoyed, the angelic girl watching speculatively; one or two of the others grinning. He was dimly aware of the sound of a motor engine approaching.

"All right, then," he said, nodding to the girl. "I'll let the fox out – and your dogs can pull him apart. Is that what you want?"

She stiffened, and twitched a hand at her modishly-fitting black riding skirt; a spot of colour showed on her cheek.

"I said 'if I asked'," she said. "Well, I'm not."

"Good for you, Peg!" said Arthur. "Come on, Yankee – either cough up or put them up." And he assumed a boxing pose, while exclamations of disgust and anger rose again, only to die away very suddenly, and Mr Franklin was aware that the huntsmen were reining back, removing their hats, and making respectful gestures towards the road behind him. He turned, and saw that the large Mercedes motor had pulled up a few yards off; the stout old bearded gentleman and the green-eyed lady were staring at him with astonishment.

"You," said the bearded gentleman loudly. "I thought you were going to West . . . West – where was it, Alice?"

"Walsham," said the green-eyed lady. Her lively glance was taking in the scene, sensing that something extremely odd was taking place. "I rather fancy that Mr Franklin has met with some unexpected delay."

One of the hunt, an extremely bald and ugly man, had hurried to the motor, hat in hand, and was speaking rapidly to the bearded gentleman, whose comments as he listened were distinctly audible. "What? What? I don't believe it, Soveral! In where, d'you say? His picnic basket?" And then he began to laugh again, his little eyes shut as he wheezed in helpless mirth – and Mr Franklin noted that the hunt were echoing his laughter, but in a most forced and wary way. It was extremely odd – but then the whole ridiculous incident was odd; Mr Franklin wondered if he were dreaming, but now the bearded gentleman's laughter had subsided, and he was beckoning, and possibly because he sensed that the bearded man was someone of consequence, or out of politeness, Mr Franklin moved up to the motor.

"Tell me," said the bearded gentleman, and his small eyes were twinkling with delight. "Were you thinking of adding the fox to your lunch?"

There was a roar of laughter at this, and Mr Franklin smiled. "No, Mr Lancaster," he said. "But I wasn't chasing him. I don't know what these ladies and gentlemen intended by him."

"Ha!" cried Mr Lancaster, and chuckled. "But they want him back, you know. Can't interfere with a hunt, eh?"

"Well, sir, all they have to do is ask. But for some reason they don't seem to want to – they seem to prefer to smash up a man's things, without so much as a by your leave. We don't reckon much to that, where I come from. Anyway – I don't know your English law, but I'd imagine the fox belongs to whoever's property it's on, and it's on mine this minute, no question." Mr Franklin paused for breath; he was not used to long speeches, but although his temper had cooled by now, the memory of the man Frank's boorish behaviour rankled. Besides, Mr Lancaster looked like a good man to explain things to, after the heated and inconsiderate attitude of the hunters. "And anyway, this is the King's highway, I reckon – "

To his astonishment the green-eyed lady clapped her gloved hands with delight, someone tittered, and the bald, ugly man shot a nervous glance at Mr Lancaster, who was regarding Mr Franklin with unmixed amusement.

"You think that, do you?" said Mr Lancaster, and in that moment a frightful suspicion dawned on Mr Franklin, and was immediately transformed into a certainty; he stared at the neat grey beard, the heavy face with the cap set rakishly above it, the burly figure, and above all the bright little eyes in the sleepy, pouched cheeks. There were copper coins in his pocket bearing that face, and child of the Great Republic though he was Mr Franklin experienced a chill shock in his stomach and a momentary weakness at the knees.

"Well, then?" said Mr Lancaster calmly.

"Well, then," echoed Mr Franklin, somewhat confused. "I guess it is your majesty's fox."

"No doubt of that," said the King, and laughed again. His glance, twinkling maliciously, strayed from Mr Franklin to the assembled hunt. "Going to have a report of this in *The Field*, Clayton, are you? Splendid headline: 'Gone to earth in a picnic basket!' " He guffawed at his own wit, the huntsmen laughed with hollow enthusiasm, and the green-eyed Alice smiled at Mr Franklin.

" 'American gentleman's unexpected luncheon guest'," she suggested.

"Tell you what, Clayton," said the King, and Mr Franklin became aware that the intelligent-looking man was at his elbow, smiling respectfully at majesty. "If you don't want this in the penny papers, I suggest you invite Mr . . . ah, Franklin, isn't it? – to dinner. Swear him to silence, eh? Have Miss Peggy persuade him," and the little eyes warmed as they regarded the angel-faced girl, who bowed in the saddle.

"A pleasure, sir," said Clayton, looking as though it would be anything but.

"Capital," said the King. "See you this evening, Franklin. Play bridge do you? – of course, all Americans do. All right, Stamper," he gestured to the chauffeur, but even as the car was moving off, the royal memory was stirred. "Wait, though – what about the fox, Franklin?"

"At the moment, he is detained at your majesty's pleasure," said Mr Franklin, startling himself by his own readiness.

"Give him time off for good behaviour, then," said the King, and as the car moved off he called over his shoulder: "Provided he *has* behaved himself, in among your smoked salmon and foie gras!" His deep laugh sounded as the royal car passed on, the hunt bowing in their saddles respectfully. Mr Franklin found himself being considered by an interested group, in which Clayton, Miss Peggy, the large grinning Arthur, and the bald ugly man were prominent.

"Well, well, old Ted's in a better temper than I've ever seen him," said Arthur, retrieving the hat he had thrown aside. "How'd you like to be court jester, Yankee?"

"That will do, Arthur!" said Clayton sharply, and turned to Mr Franklin. "My name is Clayton, sir, how do you do? I seem to recall your name – are you by any chance the gentleman who has recently bought Lancing Manor?"

"Yes, Mr Clayton."

"Ah – Sir Charles Clayton, in fact. My dear, may I present Mr Franklin – my daughter. The Marquis de Soveral – " at this the ugly man inclined his head " – and my son, Arthur." Clayton glanced round; the burly young man Frank was standing some distance off, in no good humour. "Lord Lacy, who is a neighbour of yours – Mr Franklin." The American nodded, Lacy continued to glare. These civilities concluded, Mr Franklin felt that a word of explanation was in order.

"May I say, Sir Charles," he began "that I had no intention of kidnapping your fox. It just came flying – "

"Not at all," said Clayton, and Mr Franklin had the impression that he had said something indecent. "I think we may forget the fox. Jarvie! Will you be good enough to take the basket and release the animal – at a safe distance from hounds. The hunt," he went on with dissatisfaction, "is at an end."

"Better say 'please' Jarvie, or Mr Franklin will certainly flatten you," called Arthur cheerfully.

"Stop it, Arthur," said Peggy. "You can think yourself lucky Mr Franklin didn't flatten *you*. Are you always so kind to animals?" she went on, innocently, and Mr Franklin had the impression that he was being flirted with, on very brief acquaintance. He was human enough to be pleased; she looked distinctly fetching, in her cute little mannish bowler, and the dark habit setting off her graceful figure. He noted approvingly that she sat side-saddle with unconscious ease. And apart from her obvious attractions, he was prepared to like her for her pert

100

cheerfulness – her brother, too, for that matter, even if Father seemed a bit of a cool stick.

"We shall be delighted if you will give us the pleasure of your company at dinner, Mr Franklin," Clayton was saying, and it flashed across the American's mind that he was in a position to cause acute alarm in the Clayton family if he chose to decline the invitation – had anyone, he wondered, refused to dine with the King of England? Probably not – and he was certainly not going to be the first. He murmured his acceptance, was informed that Oxton Hall was a mere six miles from Castle Lancing, and that dinner would be at 8.30.

"And please, try to make the King laugh as much as you did this afternoon," said Peggy. "Tell him American jokes, or something."

"Otherwise the curse of the Claytons will descend on you," said Arthur.

"Until this evening, then," said their father, effectively cutting off his children's indiscretions, and as the men remounted, Peggy waved gaily, and the party trotted off down the road after the rest of the hunt, Mr Franklin found his arm taken by the saturnine Marquis de Soveral, who proceeded to examine him carefully, but with extreme courtesy, as to his background, antecedents, politics, and ability to play bridge – the last of which concerned Mr Franklin somewhat, since his card repertoire was confined to pinochle, poker, black jack, and a little whist; of bridge he knew no more than he had picked up idly watching other passengers on the voyage from America.

"Dear me," said de Soveral, "that is a pity, since his majesty obviously intends that you should play. However, no doubt dear Mrs Keppel will see you through. Remember, only, that his majesty likes to win. And he is very easily bored, which is why – I say it without the least desire to offend, my dear fellow – you will be something of a godsend. You are new, you see – which is why I am finding out all I can about you." The dark eyes twinkled shrewdly, and it occurred to Mr Franklin that the Marquis de Soveral, with his forbidding looks and bristling dark moustache, was nobody's fool. "Officially, you understand, I am the Minister of Portugal at the Court of St James's, but I occupy the much more exalted position of confidant to his majesty, and he will certainly want to know all about you when I return to Oxton Hall. That, of course, is what a diplomat is for. Evening dress, of course – ah, what more? You will be expected to stay the night, so I urge you to bring the necessary changes. You have a man – no? I shall arrange that. Might I presume to suggest that you

101

bring a small gift for Mrs Keppel – the lady in the car with his majesty. It is not necessary, of course, but it would delight her, and what delights her pleases his majesty. She is a truly charming person, in every way, and keeps his majesty amused. You will not, of course, flirt with her – it would greatly embarrass her, and his majesty would be most offended. I merely mention it because she is so extremely attractive. For the rest, if you are in doubt at any time, catch my eye. And when his majesty says 'No bid,' and lays his cards flat on the table, do not, I implore you, if you are his partner, bid yourself – not unless you have a certain slam in your hand. Ah, I see Jarvie has recovered your horse. Well, Mr Franklin, it has been a great pleasure meeting you – to tell you the truth – " and the Marquis bared his teeth in a bandit smile " – I was delighted at your disruption of this afternoon's hunt. So, I gathered, was his majesty. It is good for these squires to be reminded that the pursuit of the unfortunate fox is not quite a sacred ritual. I look forward to this evening."

He swung gracefully into the saddle and cantered off with a flourish of his hat, leaving an astonished, slightly bewildered, but also rather elated American staring after him. Then, and not until then, did Mr Franklin realize that he was still holding in his left hand a half-eaten chicken leg; he stared at it in consternation, and then, being a practical man, finished it.

7

At eight o'clock precisely by Mr Franklin's fine gold half-hunter his trap drew up at the gates of Oxton Hall. For the hundredth time he touched his silk hat, stopped himself from fidgetting with the tie which he had adjusted before his mirror with meticulous care, glanced up the drive to the lights of the long, low rambling house among the trees, listened to the coughing roar of motor-cars moving on its carriage sweep, and murmured, "Uh-huh". He was aware that his neck was prickling under his collar, and his hands were sweating inside his evening gloves. He felt slightly sick.

"Now remember," said Thornhill. "Spades, hearts, diamonds, clubs – in that order. 'Solomon has delightful crockery.' Four of a major suit makes a game, or five of a minor. Three no-trump makes game also. Otherwise it's just like whist, more or less, God help you."

"Thank you," said Mr Franklin. "Start with the outside cutlery and work inwards. Right. Got that. My God, I don't think I washed my face – did I? Of all the – "

"Yes, you did," said Thornhill gently, "after you put on your right sock. I distinctly remember. My dear chap, there is absolutely nothing to worry about – there are probably fifty people in there all fretting about their dresses and their hair and their finger-nails and the awful possibility that they may break wind accidentally in the royal presence, and not one of 'em looks as well as you do, take my word for it. Poor old Clayton – not two beans to rub together, and no hostess except that idiot flapper of a daughter, and the whole damned royal circus eating him out of house and home – how he'll pay for it, heaven alone knows. And having to put up with the county riff-raff as well – atrocious people – and going mad at the thought that his cook's liable to poison the King-Emperor! So you see – *you* have nothing to be alarmed about. Just watch the rest of 'em having silent hysterics; gloat, and enjoy yourself."

"Yes," said Mr Franklin. "All the same – "

"Nonsense," said Thornhill firmly. "All right, Jack," and as Mr

Prior, coachman for the evening, snapped the reins, the trap moved smartly up the drive.

"I don't know how to thank you," said Mr Franklin. He had arrived at Thornhill's door at about five o'clock, wearing an anxious frown, with the news that he was bidden to dine with royalty, and thereafter events had passed in a frantic mist. For perhaps the first time in his life, Mr Franklin admitted, he had been off balance and at a loss; the sudden social horror of his situation had come to him while he was driving back from the hunt – he had realized that his brief acquaintance with England had left him helpless in the face of the ordeal that awaited him; he had no notion of how royalty dined, or what might be expected of him as a guest; for all he knew it might be a banquet with gold plate and footmen in old-fashioned wigs – visions, which he knew were pure fantasy, of an enthroned monarch with people kneeling before him, had flashed across his disordered mind, and he had heard the voice of the town-crier thundering: "Mr Mark Franklin of the United States of America!" while a glittering throng of lords and ladies turned to regard him with amused disdain. At this point he had remembered Thornhill, and decided to appeal to him – and the dishevelled don, after his first bewilderment, had moved calmly and precisely, guiding Mr Franklin back to the manor, explaining that a country-house dinner for the King would be no more formal than a meal in a fashionable restaurant, that the American's manners and bearing were perfectly equal to it ("damned sight better than most of 'em, moneyed bumpkins and decayed gentry'), and that provided he took care with his dress and behaved naturally, he had nothing to fear.

This had been vastly reassuring – still, it had seemed ridiculously unreal as he dressed himself in full evening rig of white tie and tails (thank God for the expert taste and guidance of Thomas Samson, valet extraordinary – that had been money well spent) while Thornhill had ferreted about finding studs and shoes and discoursing at large of the monarch's personality, of bridge and billiards, of evening charades and party games, and anything else that Mr Franklin might conceivably find it useful to know.

"Never met our sovereign lord myself," Thornhill had said. "Remember he came to college to open a new building once; looked bored to tears, poor old thing; can't blame him. They say he's genial, but a stickler for dress – " at this point Mr Franklin, adjusting his stiff-front shirt with ponderous care, had thrust his pearl and diamond pin into his thumb " – but you're all right there, at any rate. Beautiful duds, my dear fellow." He surveyed Mr Franklin with approval. "Just call him 'sir', be respectfully polite, and you're home and dry."

Then there had been the problem of a driver – Mr Franklin felt that the less exertion he had on the six-mile journey to Oxton, the better his collar and cuffs would like it, and he guessed that to entrust Thornhill with the reins would mean a short sharp trip to the nearest ditch. They had driven to the Apple Tree at night-fall, Thornhill had gone in and negotiated while Mr Franklin sat in the trap in the darkened village street wondering whatever had induced him to leave Nevada, and presently a crowd of astonished villagers had emerged to gape, with Jack Prior masterfully shouldering his way through them and mounting the trap with no more than a nod to its occupant. And now they were rolling up the drive to Oxton Hall, and Prior was stopping at a discreet distance from the motor-cars, three or four of them parked on the carriage-sweep with their engineers making their way round to the servants' entrance.

"Got the thingummy for Mrs Keppel? Good for you – in you go then, old man." Thornhill beamed through the dusk. "Don't eat too much, and spades, hearts, diamonds, clubs, remember? Right-ho, Jack."

Mr Franklin watched them drive away, took a firm grip of his small parcel, squared his shoulders, and marched up the steps to be received by an elderly butler, who took his hat, case, cloak, and name, in that order. And he was just glancing apprehensively at an open door across the hall, from which loud voices and laughter were drifting when the daughter of the house, resplendent in what looked like lilac satin, emerged rapidly from a door beneath the stairs, paused for breath, and cried out in relief at the sight of Mr Franklin.

"Thank heavens you've come! We thought you'd missed your way, and Kingie's been asking for you – full of foxy jokes . . . " Peggy rolled her eyes. "Father has been bearing up manfully, poor old soul. It's been an absolute frost, you know – the old Teddy Bear got his feet wet, and there were no ginger biscuits at tea – well, how was *I* to know that they're practically a drug with him? – but fortunately Jinks Smith slipped on the stairs and fell all the way down, and *that* put our gracious King in a good temper again – Arthur says Jinks did it on purpose – you're looking at my hair, what's the matter with it?"

"I beg your pardon – why, nothing at all." Mr Franklin had been noticing two things; one was that her hair, which he had thought fair,

105

was a very pale auburn, so that piled up and around her face it looked like a monstrous halo; the other, that the angel face had just a hint of petulance around the small cupid's mouth, as though a beautiful seraph had grown impatient of posing in Botticelli's studio. "Your hair's beautiful, Miss Clayton."

"Oh, my, how formal!" She pulled a face. "I'm Peggy, you're Mark, and no nonsense. 'Miss Clayton' – you'd think I was a governess, or somebody's aunt. But come on – the King's in there, so do your stuff."

She took him by the arm, guiding him towards the door, stopping en route to make minute adjustments to her hair and the shoulders of her dress before the hall mirror. Mr Franklin remarked that there seemed to be a great many guests, and was disillusioned.

"Oh, the house is bursting with Arthur's disky friends – we've got about twenty for the week-end, but don't you worry, they're well out of the way in the west wing. Can't have them ragging and racketting in court circles, so there's just about a dozen for dinner. Everyone else takes pot-luck in the old nursery." Peggy twitched doubtfully at her neck-line. "Too much, too little – d'you think? Oh, it'll do – Kingie's stopped leering, anyway. Now, then."

Clayton himself met them at the drawing-room door, with evident relief; Soveral was smiling at his elbow, and to Mr Franklin's surprise the packet he had brought for Mrs Keppel was twitched surreptitiously from his hand. There seemed to be about a dozen people in the room, in evening clothes – there was the King, portly but immaculate, seated by the fire, puffing on a cigarette, with Mrs Keppel at his elbow, a Junoesque figure in crimson, with diamonds in her hair and sparkling on her celebrated bosom; Soveral was attracting her attention. Mr Franklin recognised some of the faces from the hunt – the stringy man, the stout man of whom he thought as "Colonel Dammit", the scowling Lacy, various ladies, but none of them comparable with Peggy or Mrs Keppel. Beside him he was aware that Peggy was bobbing a slight curtsey; he forced himself to make a forward inclination which might pass for a bow if a bow was in order and wouldn't be noticed if it was not. Then the small eyes were on him, and the other guests were willing him magnetically towards the fireplace.

"Ah, Franklin. Good evening to you." Majesty was nodding. "Brought any more foxes?" There was polite laughter, and the King went on: "Now, you're American – you can tell us – what do they say over there about votes for women?"

106

He isn't smiling, thought Mr Franklin, but he's looking affable. Everyone else was watching him, the men attentive, the women with frozen smiles, and he sensed the nervous under-current of the pre-prandial drawing-room. What to say? – he suddenly remembered the militant young lady outside the Waldorf.

"Well, sir, that depends." His voice was unnaturally loud, and he made a conscious effort to speak normally. "If they're single men, I guess they know better than to say anything – and if they're married men, they don't get much chance."

In that moment he knew how a comedian feels when his first joke draws a roar from the pit; in fact, he was astonished that his fairly feeble response made the King chuckle, the ladies titter, and the gentlemen laugh aloud. God, he thought, do they expect me to be the droll Yankee? Well, I can't do it – and at that moment he was rescued by an exclamation of delight from Mrs Keppel; she was turning from Soveral to stoop so that the King could examine the open box in her hands: Mr Franklin felt a tremor of anxiety at having his present submitted for the royal inspection.

"Look what Mr Franklin has brought me! Oh, they're simply beautiful! How very, very kind of you, Mr Franklin!" The green eyes were glowing with genuine delight as she glanced up at him. "They're silver – how absolutely gorgeous!"

"What on earth are they?" demanded the King.

"They're spurs, sir," Mr Franklin explained. "Mexican spurs – the kind the *vaqueros* use – Mexican cattlemen, that is."

He reflected that he hadn't hesitated a moment that evening when, remembering Soveral's suggestion of a gift, he had hit on the notion of presenting his spurs to Mrs Keppel. They were silver, in fact, and he had spent twenty minutes, between shaving and putting on his shirt, in polishing them fiercely in the kitchen. They had come from that small collection of personal belongings in his valise, because somehow he had felt that a present with the giver's brand of ownership on it was better than anything bought – and he had been in no position to buy anything, anyway; Laker's stores and the Castle Lancing dairy carrying only a limited supply of trinkets for the *haut monde*, as Thornhill remarked.

"Extraordinary things." The King had lifted one of the spurs from the box, and was spinning its big rowel which tinkled musically as it moved. "Care to go hunting in those, Arlesdon?"

"Rather not, sir. Bit conspicuous, I fancy." There were murmurs of agreement, and Colonel Dammit remarked that they were barbarous-lookin' things; Peggy said:

"Aren't they dreadfully cruel – to the horse, I mean?"

"Not as cruel as the ones you were wearing today," said Mr Franklin. "Those big rowels are blunt; they won't even dent a horse's hide."

"Well, I shall certainly wear them, and they will make beautiful knick-knacks of decoration," said Mrs Keppel, smiling warmly at Mr Franklin. The King was watching him curiously.

"You've been in Mexico? What were you doing there?"

Mr Franklin paused, in that distinguished little assembly, and then said with a smile: "Well, sir, I was what they call 'on the prod'; just moving from place to place, doing this and that; punching cattle – that's driving them, you know – "

"I know," said the King. "But you're not a cow-hand."

"Why, no, sir. Most of the time, when my partner and I could raise the stake, we went prospecting – mining for silver, gold, in the sierras."

"Extraordinary. A miner forty-niner, eh?" The King sat back in his chair. "May I have one of your cigarettes?"

Mr Franklin realized that quite unconsciously he had drawn his case from his pocket, and was turning it between his fingers. He hastened to open it; the King took the case and examined its contents.

"What's this? 'Colonel Bogey'? Don't know them." He put one between his lips, closed the case and examined it, before returning it.

"And then – you struck it rich? Isn't that the expression?" He looked directly at Mr Franklin while Mrs Keppel lighted the cigarette for him.

"Not too badly, sir. We paid for our trip."

"And for a trip to England?" The King puffed, coughed, and peered at the cigarette.

"Why, yes, sir. My family was English, a long time back."

"Yes – Soveral was telling me you've brought a house. Now, most of our American visitors 'do' the sights, buy up Bond Street, take all the best shooting, and marry into the House of Lords." The King coughed and chuckled. "Can't blame the peers – marrying rich Americans is about all they'll be able to do if Mr Lloyd George has his way. Eh, Halford? But – " to Mr Franklin again " – you mean to stay, I gather?"

"I believe so, sir."

"Remarkable." The King coughed again, and regarded his cigarette. "Alice, you may stop rebuking me; I shall never smoke cigarettes again."

"Never, sir!" Mrs Keppel made a pretty grimace of mock surprise. "I can't believe that!"

"True, though." The King replaced his cigarette, wheezing. "I shall cease smoking cigarettes, and smoke only 'Colonel Bogeys'. I'm not sure what they are, but they're certainly not cigarettes. Eh, Franklin?"

Mr Franklin smiled apologetically amidst the polite laughter, and the King went on:

"Do any hunting in Mexico?"

"Hardly, sir. But I have hunted in the Rocky Mountains."

"Someone got a grizzly bear in his luncheon basket that time, did he?" The little eyes screwed up in royal mirth, the others applauded dutifully, and his majesty went on to say that that reminded him, what about dinner?

Sir Charles Clayton had been turning anxious glances towards the door for five minutes; Peggy had vanished, presumably to see what was happening in the kitchen. At this reminder Sir Charles looked wretched and muttered an apology, Mrs Keppel covered the embarrassed silence with a bright remark, and the King sat back, grumbling quietly. Mr Franklin, from his place by the mantelpiece, observed the looks that were being exchanged among the guests, marvelled inwardly at the curious atmosphere which, he supposed, must surround royalty even in this democratic age, and decided it was nothing to do with him. Should he offer the King another cigarette? – probably better not; the portly figure had disgruntlement written in every line of it now, and even Mrs Keppel was looking anxious. Clayton, who had aged five years in as many minutes, muttered another apology and fled from the room; there were a few muted whispers, a stifled laugh, and a growl from the King. The minutes ticked by; Mr Franklin wondered if he should offer conversation, but was restrained by a vague sense that one didn't speak in the presence of royalty until spoken to. He made the most of his time by examining the King surreptitiously: how old was he? Around seventy, and in some ways he looked it; the beard was grey, although the moustache was still dark, but the face was heavily-veined and high living had puffed up the fat round eyes which, Mr Franklin reflected, were probably small and shrewd in a King, but in a commoner might well have been described as piggy. Powerful build, though, and vigorous enough apart from that cough; in the silence he could hear the asthmatic rustle – old man Davis had sounded just the same; come to think of it, if you put a red undervest on Edward VII, and a battered old hat, he'd pass for a Tonopah silver-hog anywhere. What would Davis have thought if he could see his partner now, hob-nobbing with royalty; what would his ghost be saying if it were at Mr Franklin's shoulder . . . ?

"That the King? *The* King? King of England? Well, goddamighty! Looks a likely old feller, don't he? Knows a few songs an' stories, I bet. And that she-male coo-in' over him? Say, wherever did you see a pair o' paps like those? Ain't those the real arttickles, them; and ain't she the finest piece of meat you ever saw in a skirt? Why, the dirty old goat, she's wasted on him! Say, wouldn't I like to squire *her* to the Bella Union, though, an' get her playful on whisky-punch? Yessir, she'd be a real playful lady . . ."

Mr Franklin became suddenly aware that the King was looking at him – God, had he been thinking aloud? But in fact his majesty was merely examining him speculatively; there was even a twinkle in his pouchy eyes. Presumably some happy thought had momentarily banished his sulky impatience for dinner.

" 'On the prod', was it? Curious expression. Not the same thing as 'on the dodge,' though, I fancy?"

"No, sir. No, not at all," said Mr Franklin, and despite himself he felt a tiny prickle on his spine. It occurred to him that in their brief conversation King Edward had probably found out more about him in two minutes than most people could have discovered in two years, and was even making a little humorous speculation. No, he hadn't been on the dodge; not really – not until now, at any rate. And this tubby old gentleman had sensed it. It occurred to Mr Franklin that possibly being a king, and presumably spending a lifetime among statesmen and diplomats and ministers, probably did nothing to blunt a man's native shrewdness; he was certainly nobody's fool, this one. Fortunately Mr Franklin was spared any further embarrassing inquisition by the announcement of dinner, at which royalty heaved up gratefully, and even beamed at the slightly flustered Peggy.

"Trouble below stairs?" inquired the King playfully, as he took her arm, and Peggy admitted that the cook had had a little trouble with the ptarmigan.

"Oh," said the King. "Ptarmigan." It was said with a weight of gloom which caused Mrs Keppel to raise her eyebrows; to Mr Franklin's surprise she offered her arm to him, and he found himself pacing

110

behind the King with the King's mistress for his escort, while she enthused again about his gift of spurs. She had, in fact, been rather sorry for Mr Franklin, cut off and presumably out of his depth during the royal sulk, and exerted herself to put him at his ease – and the effect of Alice Keppel, when she set herself to charm, was such that Mr Franklin took his seat at dinner feeling quite ashamed at himself for allowing old Davis's lewd thoughts to run through his mind.

Dinner, to his relief, was far less of an ordeal than he had expected. It was served at an enormous round table in what even Mr Franklin recognized as being a rather shabby dining-room; with frontier insight he guessed that the silver and crockery had probably been hired from Norwich or even London for the occasion; it was rather too splendid for its surroundings. He was seated about halfway round from the King, who was flanked by Mrs Keppel and another lady; Peggy, as hostess, sat approximately opposite the royal chair, next to Mr Franklin. To his surprise, she exhibited none of the nervousness that he would have expected; her slight disorder immediately before dinner, she explained to him sotto voce over the soup, had been the result of what she described as a flaming row with that bloody cook, and the bitch could pack her traps in the morning. Mr Franklin considered this gravely, and remarked that the soup was extremely good.

"D'you think so? Well, I'm glad someone's pleased. Frankly, I don't give a damn if the whole meal's inedible." Peggy sipped at her spoon and leaned forward, smiling brightly, to answer Lord Arlesdon, seated farther round the table. "I mean, it's all just too horrid-ino for words, isn't it?" she went on to Mr Franklin. "Why did he have to come here for the night, when he could have stayed with the Albemarles, or at Elveden? It would have been bad enough, even if Mummy had still been alive, but as it is . . . well, I'm not up to playing mother-hen, and I don't care who knows it." She laid down her spoon and pulled a face. "Poor old Daddy – how he's suffering!"

Sir Charles was certainly showing signs of strain, Mr Franklin reflected. He was sitting beside Mrs Keppel, smiling mechanically as she talked, but every few seconds his eye would stray towards the King, who had finished his soup and was studying the empty plate with deep melancholy, crumbling a roll. Sir Charles bit his lip and turned back to Mrs Keppel, but by now she was talking to a slight, vacant-looking man across the table.

"That's Jinks Smith, the royal whipping-boy," murmured Peggy in answer to Mr Franklin's inquiry. "And beside father is Lady Topping,

111

and then Lord Arlesdon, who'll be a duke some day and is supposed to be a prize catch, and then that distinguished American – what's his name? Franklin, of course – and then Miss Peggy Clayton, who is going mad trying to catch the butler's eye – oh thank goodness he's noticed, so with any luck we'll get the pâté before midnight. Then the Marquis de Soveral you know, and Halford, who's the King's equerry, and Mrs Jensen, and Ponsonby, and Smith and Viscountess Dalston. Cosy, isn't it? The seating is all wrong – that'll be another fault, no doubt – far too few ladies, and several distinguished gentlemen are not dining – do you know why? Simply because there isn't room – so the Honourable George Keppel for one isn't here, nor Lord Dalston, and if it weren't for Daddy's sake I wouldn't be either. It . . . it makes one feel so small – knowing that things aren't up to scratch, and that Halford and Ponsonby will be looking at each other later and sighing ever so wearily." Peggy stabbed moodily at her pâté as though it, too, had sighed. "Arthur's well out of it – lucky dog. He and the others will be having a jolly good time in the nursery." She sighed. "Oh, who cares?"

Mr Franklin was not certain whether to take these confidences as a compliment or not; he guessed she would have gone to the stake rather than make them to one of her English acquaintances, but presumably he, not being of that charmed circle, and therefore unimportant, was a suitable recipient. But he could guess that for all her pretended indifference, the strain of preparing for the King's visit, of minor crises about ginger biscuits and ptarmigan, of anxiety about being thought "not up to scratch", of imagining arch looks and raised eyebrows, must be considerable even on this self-confident young beauty; it all mattered, in her world.

"I'm sorry your brother isn't here," he said. "Perhaps I'll see him later on, though?"

Peggy giggled. "He'll probably want to fight you again, if you do. I think he was awfully disappointed that you wouldn't square up to him this afternoon."

"I can imagine. And I'd guess he's a pretty useful scrapper, too."

"Oh, he was Universities Heavy-weight Champion – before he went to Sandhurst." She smiled mischievously. "So perhaps it's just as well you didn't take him on."

But Mr Franklin was not to be drawn. "Yes, just as well, I guess. For one thing, he seems like a nice fellow. And I make it a rule never to fight a nice fellow in front of his sister."

"Why ever not?"

"Well, if he beats you, she won't admire you – and if you beat him, she won't like you."

But Peggy was not to be drawn either. She smiled and sipped her white wine. "I take it your rule applies only with brothers and sisters. If it had been Frank Lacy?"

"Who? Oh, 'milord", the polite one. No, I guess I wouldn't have minded too much if he'd become violent – for a moment this afternoon I thought he was going to."

"You mean you hoped he was going to. I was watching, remember – do you know, Jarvie said you looked ready to do murder?" She laughed cheerfully. "Were you?"

"Not quite." He glanced round the table. "Where is he, by the way? – he looked like the kind who would get fitted in somehow."

"Oh, he was – until the King invited you to dinner. You're occupying his place, you know." She eyed him with amusement. "He wasn't very pleased, I can tell you."

Mr Franklin studied her thoughtfully. "No, he wouldn't be. Would this be . . . his usual place?"

"He thinks it ought to be," said Peggy carelessly. "And what Frank thinks ought to be – well, ought to be, you know." She shrugged. "I don't mind in the least, I may say. Do him good to have his nose out of joint for a change – Frank thinks he owns the earth, as well as half the county."

"I see." Mr Franklin nodded pensively, and found himself glancing across at Sir Charles. "Not two beans to rub together," Thornhill had said, and it was confirmed by what he had seen. Good-looking daughter, wealthy young landowner showing interest – uh-huh. No wonder Sir Charles's enforced invitation had been chilly. But his daughter didn't seem to mind; Mr Franklin imagined that she was not the kind to be a dutiful child unless it suited her, or that she would find a nature like Lord Lacy's to be entirely to her taste. He turned to look at her; she was catching the butler's eye, and fish was coming to replace the pâté. She met Mr Franklin's look and sighed.

"Let us pray for the success of poached salmon," she said solemnly. "Cook wanted trout, but I overruled her, and it would be just like her to ruin it. Oh, well, if Kingie doesn't like it, he doesn't like it, and that's that."

Mr Franklin considered his fish, and took a sip of his wine. "You don't care for entertaining too much?"

113

"Not this sort – well, who would? It's like having a particularly bad-tempered baby on one's hands. Oh, I know he can be jolly enough, but he sulks so much, and shows how bored he is, and the people who traipse about after him are the giddy limit. Mrs Keppel's a darling, and the Marquis is a pet . . ." She turned to Soveral and said: "I'm just telling Mr Franklin how divvy you are, marquis. Aren't you flattered?"

Soveral laughed and bowed. "Alas, I am far too fierce-looking, and far too grown-up to be 'divvy' any longer, Miss Peggy. Don't you agree, Mr Franklin?"

"I might if I knew what divvy meant," said Mr Franklin, and was promptly informed by his hostess that it was short for divine. "I don't know what we'd do without the Marquis and La Keppel, anyway," Peggy went on. "But isn't it ghastly, so many people having to kow-tow and scrape and butter up, just to keep one odious old man from being thoroughly ill-natured all the time?"

Mr Franklin stole a glance at the table, but everyone was talking animatedly, presumably to compensate for the royal silence, and Peggy's indiscretions went unheard. "Well, he doesn't seem too bad, you know," he said. "I guess when I'm his age I'll be pretty cranky, too." Privately, he thought on short acquaintance that his majesty had probably had too much of his own way all his life, but no doubt that went with kingship, he decided. The King, after a mouthful of his fish, had laid down his fork and was muttering to Mrs Keppel, who preserved her bland smile in the face of what was obviously a royal complaint.

"Wait till he's had the ptarmigan pie, and he'll wish he'd eaten his fish," remarked Peggy. "Did you ever see anything so disagreeable? I mean, honestly, even if the fish is rotten, would you sit mumping like that if you had Alice beside you, positively slaving to cheer you up?"

"I hope not. I'd try not to, anyway."

"I think she's a gorgeous creature," said Peggy, looking across the table. "And one of those lucky people who are even nicer than they look."

He smiled at her. "You don't need to be jealous, you know. She's not the prettiest girl in this room."

"Oh, come off it!" Peggy glanced at him sidelong, and her mouth took on the tiny sneer which he had noticed in the hall, but she looked

114

pleased nonetheless. "Every woman would be jealous of looking like that, including yours truly. Anyway, look where it's got her."

"Is that such a happy position? I wonder what Mr Keppel thinks about it."

She turned to stare at him, and the little sneer seemed to him even more marked; at that, he decided, that angel face was still something that Mrs Keppel, for all her beauty, might have envied.

"Don't tell me you're shocked? A Puritan Uncle Sam? Really!" She shrugged. "Well, I suppose he feels quite honoured, don't you?"

"I can't imagine it. Can't see that any man would be. In fact, I feel sorry for him. And for Mrs Keppel. Don't you? I mean, would . . ." He realized what he had been going to say, and stopped. "I beg your pardon. I . . ."

"You were going to say, 'would I, if I were Mrs Keppel', weren't you?" He was slightly shocked to see that she was regarding him with amusement. She glanced across the table. "It's a dreadful thought. Still, if I were her age, I suppose I might. I don't know."

Mr Franklin felt decidedly uncomfortable. He was far from being a prude, by his own lights, but that had nothing to do with it. What he disliked was what seemed to him a deliberate display of cynicism, assumed by this lovely young woman presumably because it was the smart, advanced thing to do; it was so much part of the hard, artificial atmosphere which he could feel round that dinner-table, and it annoyed him quite unreasonably. How old was she? Nineteen, perhaps twenty, and she was trying to pretend that she held the views and values of the women who made up the royal circle – well, he didn't know what they were like, but he could guess. Peggy was so obviously not their sort, and he felt somehow demeaned that she should try to convince him that she was. Still, she was young, and no doubt it was natural enough that she should want to appear worldly; it couldn't be easy for a young girl, having to play hostess to the smartest set in the world for a week-end. Mr Franklin began to eat his ptarmigan pie. It was awful, and automatically he glanced towards the King, to see how it was being received there. Sure enough, his majesty was looking displeased; his pie was untouched, and he was staring round the table, frowning.

"Thirteen," said the King suddenly; he said it loudly, and everyone stopped talking. "Thirteen," he repeated, and then to Mrs Keppel: "Alice, there are thirteen of us at dinner."

"Oh, dear," said Mrs Keppel brightly. "I never noticed. Well . . ."

115

The King muttered irritably, picked up his fork, glared at his ptarmigan pie, put down his fork, and pulled his napkin away fretfully. "I don't *like* having thirteen at dinner," he exclaimed petulantly. "Don't people know that?"

There was dead silence round the table, broken by a sharp clatter as one of the servants at the buffet dropped a spoon. Everyone was looking at the table-cloth, except for Sir Charles, who was gazing in consternation at his daughter. Mr Franklin raised his glass and stole a sidelong glance at her; she was looking straight ahead, her face pale. Mr Franklin was beginning to wonder if he had heard right; was the King seriously objecting because the guests made up an unlucky number? Evidently he was, for Mrs Keppel suddenly said, looking across at Peggy:

"Perhaps we could have another place set, my dear? If your brother would join us? Then we should be fourteen, and . . ." She made a gesture that combined apology, appeal, and whimsicality all in one, but the King was growling beside her, apparently indicating that his dinner was spoiled.

"Oh, stop it, Alice. It doesn't matter."

"Oh, but it does! I feel ever so uncomfortable myself when there are thirteen."

"Unlucky," said one of the men helpfully. "Thirteen."

"I'll send for Arthur," Peggy was beginning, and Mr Franklin could hear the trembling snap in her voice; careful, King, he thought, or you're liable to get a plateful of ptarmigan pie where you won't like it. He suddenly wanted to laugh aloud; it was too foolish for words, but although there was a variety of expressions on the faces round the table, astonishment was not among them. Sir Charles, who had been so cool and precise and assured this afternoon, was literally pulling at his collar, and preparing to get to his feet, but he was forestalled from an unexpected quarter.

The insignificant-looking Smith was rising. "No, no, not necessary; I've a much better idea." He bowed towards the King. "With your permission, sir, I'll take my dinner over there, on that corner table. Then there'll only be twelve, what?"

"Shall I join you, Jinks?" said Soveral quickly, and Mrs Keppel, laughing, cried: "No, no, Jinks, it's too silly!" but Smith was on his feet, beckoning one of the servants, telling him to mind and not spill his glass, indicating the corner table, and people were laughing as though at some excellent joke. Mr Franklin sat stupefied, watching

116

Smith bustling about, directing the servants, until they had transferred his place to the small table by the buffet, and he had seated himself, pulling comical faces, holding his knife and fork like a caricature of a hungry small boy, and then waving to Peggy and calling: "Toodle-oo, old thing! It's ever so jolly over here!"

The King had slewed round in his chair to look at him. "Jinks," he said, "you're an ass."

"Of course, sir!" cried Smith. "Here, where's my ptarmigan pie?"

"You can have mine, if you like," said the King, and taking up his plate he placed it on the floor beside his chair. "Come on, Fido!" he snapped his fingers. "Come, boy! There's a good doggie!"

Smith said "Woof! woof!", and Mr Franklin almost expected him to drop on all fours and crawl across the floor, but at that moment the King turned back to the table. He was laughing, and of course the table was laughing, too, including Peggy. Mr Franklin suddenly realized that his own features were twisted into an expression of mirth – he hurriedly took a drink, and plunged into conversation with Lord Arlesdon. What he said, he had no idea, but it occurred to him later that his lordship was almost certainly not listening. What Mr Franklin was thinking was, I don't believe this, but I know it's happening. Presently he took stock of the table again; the flow of conversation had resumed, the King was actually eating heartily and talking loudly to Mrs Keppel while he shovelled away at his plate, Peggy was laughing at something that Soveral was saying – and over by the buffet Smith was clamouring for another helping, and being treated to various sallies from the male guests on that side of the table. Mr Franklin continued his meal, determined not to meet anyone's eye.

"You see what I mean?" murmured Peggy quietly. "Do you know what I think I should do, if it weren't for Daddy? I think," she went on dreamily, "that when the ices came I should take one and smear it all over his fat, ugly, piggy, nasty little face. Wouldn't that be splendid?"

"Don't they put you in the Tower for that sort of thing?" wondered Mr Franklin.

"They put you on the front page of the *Express*," said Peggy. "Ah, well, daydreams, daydreams. However, he seems happy enough for the moment, the old beast." The King's deep laugh boomed across the table, and a moment later Peggy was laughing animatedly with Mrs Keppel, and calling across a gay inquiry to the distant Smith –

a fatuity about his not wanting an ice since he was dining in Siberia, which provoked a royal chuckle.

His majesty was equally affable when the time came for the ladies to rise, bowing to Peggy as they withdrew and complimenting her on a capital dinner, absolutely capital; she in turn bestowed on him a dazzling smile and curtsied magnificently in the doorway with a rustle of skirts and a gleam of white shoulders and bosom as she sank beneath the approving monarchial eye. As the door closed the gentlemen moved in to those seats nearest the King's, Mr Franklin making haste to follow. But when Smith would have joined them, he was waved away by the royal hand.

"No, no, Fido; dirty little doggies don't sit round for their port. Here, come to heel – come on, there's a good boy." He took up a decanter and saucer, turning his chair and stooping with difficulty to fill the saucer at his feet. "Now then, Fido," the King beckoned with the cigar which Ponsonby had lit for him, while the others crowded round his chair, "come and get drinkies, there's a good dog! Come on!"

Smith dropped obediently on all fours, and scuttled across the carpet making joyful barking noises. As he began to lap up the port, his face in the saucer, the King gravely tilted the decanter and poured its contents over the courtier's head. There were roars of laughter as Smith shook himself like a retriever, splashing port broadcast, the King crying out in disgust and protesting boisterously that he was a dirty dog, and not fit to be in a gentleman's dining-room. Then, good humour at its height, Soveral chuckling genially while his dark eyes strayed watchfully, Sir Charles wearing a fixed grin, and the rest chortling loudly at Smith's discomfiture, they settled down to their cigars and conversation. Smith was permitted to take a seat, amidst much boorish banter and shoving, and was soon deep in animated talk with his neighbour, oblivious of the sticky, plastered condition of his hair, and the wine which continued to trickle down his face on to his soaked shirt-front. Mr Franklin contemplated the wine-sodden figure, the pallid face, and the nervous, unnaturally bright eyes which occasionally met his own only to slide quickly away – and wondered.

They were not long over their port. The banalities of conversation soon bored even the King, who presently heaved himself up and led the way to the drawing-room, where the ladies were assembled. Here his majesty took a fresh cigar, coughed resoundingly and announced: "Bridge. All right, Soveral? And let's see – Alice, are you ready?

That's three – " and as he surveyed the company Mr Franklin was conscious of a tremor in his stomach. With luck one of the others . . . "No, no, Halford, I haven't forgotten – you trumped my queen last week. Where's our American friend? Ah, there you are, Franklin – come on!"

He stumped across to the card-table in the alcove where packs and pads were already laid out; Mr Franklin preserved an unmoved countenance, despite a grimace and commiserating wave from Peggy across the room, and followed. As he pulled out a chair for Mrs Keppel, and Soveral moved to join them, the King flicked over the top four cards – "Alice, Soveral, Franklin, and the head that wears the crown – uneasily, too, since I've got you as partner, Alice. Come along, then – England versus the United States and Portugal, what? Stakes – no, none of your two penny whist stakes, Soveral – " he nudged the Marquis ostentatiously – "heavens, your partner's a silver millionaire, and you can pay up out of diplomatic funds! Shilling a point, eh?" He beamed genially over his cigar while Mrs Keppel cut and Soveral dealt, and the game began.

For Mr Franklin it was a disconcerting experience. He had a reasonable knowledge of whist, picked up in the parlours of those dimly-remembered Western school-houses where he and his father had sometimes played with a local doctor and his wife, or it might have been a parson and his sister – but that was a long time ago. Thanks to Thornhill he knew that the principle of bridge was to bid for tricks, and he kept trying to remember the little mnemonic about suit seniority: "Solomon has . . ." What did Solomon have – some kind of crockery – spades, heart, something, and clubs; well, it must be diamonds, then . . . He arranged his cards carefully, conscious of the heavy bulk of the King at his right elbow, the heavy asthmatic wheezing, and a subtle mixture of cigar smoke and pomade; to his left, even more distracting, was the perfumed beauty of Mrs Keppel, which at a range of two feet was positively overpowering; whatever he did, he must not allow his glance to rest on the white splendour of her superb bust, which was difficult, since it seemed to project alluringly halfway across the table. He shifted his legs, accidentally touched her shoe, muttered an apology, received a sweet smile of reassurance, and heard the King mutter: "If you must kick someone, Alice, kick me – right shin for major suits, left for minors, remember!" followed by a throaty chuckle.

"Club," said Soveral, and the King promptly said: "A heart," and replaced his cigar, his small eyes turning challengingly in Mr Franklin's direction.

Mr Franklin examined his cards – he had the ace, queen, ten, and two other hearts, the king of clubs, and nothing else. Which, in view of his majesty's bid, was interesting, but to a novice like Mr Franklin, of no particular use; he hesitated a second, and then for no good reason said: "Two clubs," at which Mrs Keppel gave a little fluttering sigh and smiled winningly round the table.

"Well, well, come on, Alice," growled the King. "They've got clubs, we suspect. What have you got to say?"

"Let me see . . ." Mrs Keppel puckered her flawless brow and tapped her lips thoughtfully. "I think . . . one diamond – oh, no, of course, two diamonds. Yes, two diamonds."

"Double two diamonds," said Soveral, to Mr Franklin's total bewilderment – did that mean Soveral was *bidding* diamonds himself? (Thornhill's instruction had not gone the length of doubling.) The King growled cheerfully, and leered across the table.

"Shall I leave you, Alice? Or redouble, eh?" In reply to her squeak of protest he grumbled happily, said "Two hearts," and squinted at Mr Franklin.

"Double two spades," said Mr Franklin, in total confusion.

"You mean double two hearts?" said the King, staring.

"Oh – yes, sir. I'm sorry. I should have said hearts," said Mr Franklin hastily; he had no idea what he should have said, but he was not going to contradict royalty.

"Just so," said the King, frowning. "Two hearts doubled, Alice – but at least we know where the spades are," he added contentedly, puffing at his cigar – his notions of bidding etiquette were evidently informal, when it came to communicating with his own partner. Mrs Keppel surveyed her hand in pretty consternation, while the King grunted impatiently, tapping his cards and puffing audibly.

"I'm not . . . I don't . . . oh, dear!" Mrs Keppel hesitated, and shot a glance of entreaty at the King. "Three . . . hearts?" she wondered. "Really, I . . ."

"About time, too!" exclaimed the King, surveying his hand with satisfaction. "Come on, Soveral!"

"Double three hearts," said the Marquis smoothly, the black eyes smiling across at Mr Franklin, and there was a mutter of alarm from the royal seat. "Double, eh?" The King lifted his cards and frowned at them. "Double, you say. I think you're bluffing, Soveral . . . very well, then, I'll larn you. Re-double!" His cigar jutted out at Franklin in a manner that dared contradiction. "Three hearts, re-doubled. Come on, Alice."

Mrs Keppel toyed nervously with an earring. "Perhaps Mr Franklin would like to bid again?" Her face was a picture of comical despair – not entirely comical – as she laid a hand on Mr Franklin's. "Please, dear Mr Franklin, are you *sure* you wouldn't like to bid again? Just a teeny little bid – to please me?"

"Stop that!" said the King testily. "He doesn't want to bid, so keep your wiles to yourself, and let's see dummy."

Mr Franklin shook his head in apology, and Mrs Keppel gave a great sigh. "Oh, well," she said, and laid down her cards. "God save the King." And added, with a flustered giggle: "And heaven help Mrs Keppel."

"My God!" The King was staring at her cards in disbelief. "And you said . . . three hearts! Are you entirely out of your mind, Alice?"

When Soveral had discreetly nodded to Mr Franklin to start leading, the slaughter commenced. Mrs Keppel's fine diamonds were so much decoration in a hand devoid of trump; it soon became clear that the power lay with Soveral, and the King's hearts, strong in themselves, fell easy prey to Mr Franklin's, lying in ambush for them. It was plainer sailing now to the American, and he collected the tricks as they fell and the King writhed and muttered; at the end of the hand, only five tricks lay before the royal place, and the storm broke over Mrs Keppel's beautiful head.

"And why didn't you double first time round?" demanded the King of Mr Franklin. "Every heart in the pack, dammit, and you said clubs!"

"And thereby informed me of his heart strength," said Soveral quickly. "Correct, partner?" Mr Franklin tried to look knowing, and the King muttered testily that he supposed it was another of these blasted new conventions. But he shot Mr Franklin a look in which respect was equally blended with annoyance and suspicion, before returning to the demolition of Mrs Keppel, who bore it with sweet contrition.

The rubber continued, Mr Franklin playing in a fog as regards the finer points of bidding, but manfully assisting Soveral simply by declaring the strongest suit in his hand when he got the chance, and thereafter leaving the marquis to his fate. Since Soveral was an extremely good bridge player, and their initial disaster had reduced

121

the King and Mrs Keppel to growling recklessness and twittering lunacy respectively, the Soveral-Franklin axis prospered, with the assistance of rather better cards than their opponents. Mr Franklin even developed a psychological trick of his own; when he knew he was going to pass he took his time about it, eventually saying "Pass" in a soft, thoughtful tone which did not deceive Soveral for a minute but filled Mrs Keppel with alarm. The result was that the marquis and the American took the rubber in two straight games, Mr Franklin having to play only one hand, an easy two spades in which he made a couple of over-tricks. The King crashed heavily on a five-diamond bid which emerged from pure frustration and left Mrs Keppel biting her necklace in dismay; his majesty's temper was not improved on the next hand, when she passed in terrified silence after his one-club opener, and they made six.

"And some idiots want to give them the vote!" observed the King acidly as Soveral totted up the score after the first rubber. "Pray notice, my dear Alice, that when Mr Franklin says 'Pass' it does not necessarily mean that his hand is utterly void; he and the Marquis pay heed to each other's bidding, which is the usual practice in this game."

"I know," said Mrs Keppel, "but I am so fearfully stupid, and when Mr Franklin fixes his cards with that baleful stare and says: 'One heart' as though he were going to eat it, I quite lose my wits. Never mind," she added cheerfully, lifting her evening bag, "I shall pay for the rubber – please whisper what we owe you, Marquis, so that I am not too shamed."

"Nonsense!" said the King, and rummaged in his pockets; he pushed sovereigns on to the table. "Can't have our womenfolk stumping up for us," and he even unbent so far as to wink heavily at Mr Franklin, who realized that next to winning his majesty probably enjoyed playfully brow-beating his partner – fairly playfully, at any rate. "Play a bit, do you?" went on the King. "Thought so; I don't quite get the hang of your bidding yet, but it's damned effective, eh, Soveral?"

"Mr Franklin has the American gift – his face tells one nothing," said Soveral blandly; he might have added that his partner's bidding didn't tell him much either, but tactfully forebore. "Shall we cut for partners for the next rubber?"

"Please do," said the King heavily and Mr Franklin prayed that he would not be drawn with his majesty; the cards gave him Mrs Keppel, and the King said: "Thank God for that" gallantly, and changed places with Mr Franklin. "Now, Soveral," he said, lighting a fresh cigar, "let's have no more nonsense; we want some Yankee dollars from the rubber, what?"

But he did not get them in the two rubbers that followed. Mrs Keppel, sparkling at Mr Franklin across the table, ran into a succession of those hands which bridge-players dream about; aces and kings dropped from her dainty fingers at every hand, long runs from the honours down seemed drawn to her as by a magnet, her singletons invariably coincided with Mr Franklin's aces, and when their opponents played a hand her queens were always there over his majesty's knaves and her kings over his queens. Twice when Mr Franklin opened in no trump she took him straight to three, and when her dummies came down – lo, there were the slams ready-made. The King growled and muttered about under-bidding, Soveral sighed and shook his head, Mr Franklin began to enjoy himself, and Mrs Keppel gleefully exclaimed: "What? Is that another rubber to us? Splendid, partner! God bless America!" and raked in her winnings, assuring the King that it was all in the run of the cards.

"Don't be so confounded patronizing, Alice!" snapped the King. "No, Soveral – never mind cutting. We'll stay as we are and break these Klondike sharpers yet." He growled impatiently at the deal, picking up his cards as they were dealt, and exclaiming with disgust at each one. "Whoever saw such rubbish! What's that, Franklin? One no-trump? Oh, lord, they're doing it again!"

Another two rubbers went by, and Mr Franklin began to feel uncomfortable. Bad hands he had seen, in his time, but what his majesty was picking up was past belief; he seemed to have a lean note of everything from seven downward, and Mr Franklin found himself picking up his own hands with a fervent prayer that they might be bad for a change – but no, there was the usual clutch of pictures, with a couple of languid aces among them to round things off; he even resorted to the shameful expedient of passing when he knew he should have bid, to save royalty from further humiliation. But that could be dangerous, too; once he passed a powerful hand only to have to lay it down as dummy for Mrs Keppel; she shot him a quick glance over her cards, and Soveral's silence spoke louder than words, but the King only said: "And how the deuce is one to lead into that? Go on, Soveral, let's get it over with."

It was well past midnight when the fifth rubber ended, and Mrs

123

Keppel artlessly suggested a change of partners; once again, to Mr Franklin's relief, he drew Soveral, and another two rubbers were played, both of them marathons; the cards still favoured Franklin and his partner, but he sensed that Soveral was now deliberately under-playing, skilfully and subtly, and the games ran on endlessly. But still nothing could contrive the King a rubber, and Mr Franklin noticed with interest that as the royal temper grew shorter, so its owner became quieter; he had ceased berating Mrs Keppel, which obviously troubled her, and played his cards with a grim, desperate intensity.

During one of his own dummy hands Mr Franklin took the oppor-tunity to survey the rest of the party. Another bridge game was in progress; Smith and Lady Dalston were playing backgammon; Peggy was turning the pages of a magazine, and Sir Charles was talking to one of the other gentlemen – or rather, he was listening, with half an ear, for his attention was anxiously fixed on the royal table. Presumably he knew the King was losing; his eyes met Mr Franklin's for a moment, and seemed to be saying: "Please, forget about those unpleasantnesses of 1776 and 1812, and do me the great favour of allowing his majesty to win now and then." Mr Franklin would have been glad to; he was not only embarrassed but extremely tired. Did no one go to bed – not even the ladies? He was unaware that protocol demanded that no one should retire until his majesty did, and that the more experienced courtiers were perfectly prepared to be there at four in the morning.

At one point Peggy approached the table to announce that a supper was being served in the dining-room; thank God, thought Mr Frank-lin, at least we can stretch our legs, but to his dismay Mrs Keppel said quietly: "Do you think we might have sandwiches at the table, my dear? – it's such an engrossing game, you see." His majesty was at that point intent on trying to make one diamond, and going down below the nethermost pit in the process; when the sandwiches came he engulfed them steadily without a break in the play; there was a hock to go with them, but the King gruffly demanded whisky and soda. Mr Franklin stirred to ease his long legs, and received a warning glance from Mrs Keppel; the rubber finally petered out with Soveral winning a three-bid in spades which was virtually a laydown.

He'll have to call it a day now, thought Mr Franklin; the King was looking old and tired, his cough was troubling him, and he wheezed and went purple when he exchanged his cigar for a cigarette. Mrs Keppel was prattling carelessly about the next day's programme, in the hope of reminding his majesty that a night's sleep might be in order, but she was far too clever to press the point. The King emerged, coughing and heaving, from the depths of his handkerchief, took a long pull at his glass, and said huskily: "Cut 'em again." Mrs Keppel did so, and this time Mr Franklin drew the King.

And, as is the way with cards, the luck changed in that moment. Not that the hands began to run loyally to the throne, but they evened out, and they became interesting – the occasional freak deal in which three players each had only three suits, or all the strength lay in the hands of two opponents, their partners having rags. Mr Franklin had gradually got the hang of bidding during the evening, and knew enough not to disgrace himself; his play would have caused raised eyebrows in any well-conducted club, but in the slightly eccentric game in which he found himself, it served – just. He and the King squeaked home in the first rubber, to universal satisfaction, and then lost the second by the narrowest of margins; his majesty cursed the luck, but he did it jovially, and even congratulated Mr Franklin on his defence against Soveral's two-no-trump on the last hand – this came as a gratifying surprise to Mr Franklin, who had dutifully followed suit throughout.

"Final rubber," announced the King. "This time, eh, Franklin? Here, let's have another of your – what-d'ye-call-em's? – Colonel Bogeys, will you? Never you mind, Alice, just mind the business of shuffling and leave me alone – and you needn't shuffle the spots off 'em, either. It won't do you a bit of good." He coughed rackingly on the cigarette, mopped his little eyes, and chuckled with satisfaction as he picked up his cards.

He was less satisfied five minutes later, as Soveral totted up a grand slam in spades; on the next hand Mrs Keppel made five clubs having bid only two, which slightly restored the royal temper. "Had the rubber then, if you'd had the courage," he reproved her. "Let off for us, partner. Come along, then, we'll have to fight for it. What d'ye say, old monkey?"

To Mr Franklin's surprise, this was addressed to Soveral – he did not know that the Marquis's unusual ugliness had led to his being christened "the blue monkey", nor did he know, of course, that Soveral disliked it intensely. But he did become aware that a change came over the marquis's play – Mr Franklin had the decided impression that the Portuguese was out to win at last; there were limits, apparently, to leaning over backwards in and for royalty's favour. Mrs Keppel may have sensed it, too; she became nervous in the next hand and badly underbid, but Soveral, playing in earnest, pushed their partnership relentlessly towards game; once he was within two tricks of the rubber, and Mr Franklin, with two cards left, and Soveral's last trump staring up at him, hesitated in his discard – nine of hearts or six of spades? He had no idea of what had gone, but as he prepared to throw down the spade some perverse bell tinkled at the back of his mind and he dropped the heart instead. Soveral sighed, swept up the trick, and led – the four of spades. Mr Franklin played his six, Mrs Keppel squealed as she and the King played rags, and his majesty thumped the table in triumph and cried "Well, held, sir! Oh, well held!" before going off into a coughing fit that had to be relieved by a further application of whisky and water.

"He had 'em counted, Soveral!" the King exulted, and Mr Franklin wished it had been true. Mrs Keppel smiled her congratulations, the cards went round again, and the King clinched the game with a bid in no-trump.

He was thoroughly boisterous now, as they went into the final game, and the other guests, sensing that he was poised for victory at last, came to surround the table at a respectable distance and lend syco- phantic support. The King snapped up each card as it was dealt, his face lengthening as he assembled his hand; he stared hopefully across at Mr Franklin, but Soveral went straight to four clubs and made the contract. Again he and Mrs Keppel stood within a trick of the rubber, and the King was leaning back wearily, gnawing his cigar and staring dyspeptically before him, his momentary good humour banished by the prospect of defeat. Peggy came to stand beside Mr Franklin's chair, and he glanced up at her and smiled; she was looking apprehen- sively towards the King, and suddenly, conscious of his own cramped limbs and slightly aching head, he thought, oh, the blazes with this: why must everyone be on tenterhooks just because one peevy old man isn't getting it all his own way in a stupid game of cards? What does it matter, whether he wins the rubber or not?

He glanced at the people behind the royal chair, the deferential figures, the concerned aristocratic faces, the ladies trying to look brightly attentive, Clayton's worried eyes seeking his daughter's – and with a sudden insight realized that it did matter, to them. In their peculiar world, royal disappointment and ill-temper, with their impli- cations of lost favour, were vitally important. How much face would Clayton lose among his Norfolk neighbours, among the sneering,

126

artificial London "society", if this royal week-end were a failure? How much might it hurt Peggy, for all her brave pretence at indifference? And it could easily depend on whether the King got up from that table a winner – on something as trivial as that. But to them it wasn't trivial – only Soveral, in that courtly assembly, didn't seem to care a damn whether the King was kept sweet or not – couldn't the man see that it mattered to Peggy and Clayton and the others? Or didn't he care? Mr Franklin felt a sudden unreasoning dislike of the marquis, and with it a reckless determination to contrive the King a winning rubber in Soveral's teeth, to send the royal old curmudgeon happy to bed, and do the Claytons a good turn – and if he failed, well, it didn't matter, he was an outsider here anyway. He was sick of this false, uncomfortable, stuffed-shirt atmosphere and pussy-footing deference. With that reckless imp in control he leaned forward, rubbed his hands, and said:

"All right, your majesty, we've gone easy on them long enough, I reckon. This is the hand where we wring 'em out and peg 'em up to dry! Spread 'em around and let's go!"

He heard Peggy gasp, saw the stunned disbelief on the faces round the table, and Mrs Keppel holding her breath at such vulgar familiarity. The King stared, and then his eyes puckered up and he began to heave and cough, laying down the pack and leaning back to guffaw while the shocked faces relaxed and joined in his mirth. When he had recovered and mopped his eyes he shot the American an odd look, half amused and half resentful, and concluded the deal, shaking his head.

"Very good, partner. Let us go, indeed. I trust I have . . . ah, spread them to your satisfaction."

There were relieved faces behind his chair, and Mr Franklin was aware that Peggy's hand had momentarily touched his shoulder, and was now being withdrawn. The King fanned his cards, muttering "Peg 'em up to dry, though!", frowned uncertainly at Mr Franklin, and then announced: "One club."

Soveral said "One spade" quietly, and Mr Franklin surveyed his hand – six hearts to the king, the ace of spades, a singleton diamond, and rags. By his lights, hearts were in order, so he bid two of them, and the King grunted and sat forward. Mrs Keppel, obviously wishing to pass, but uncomfortably aware that her hand was visible to the watchers behind her, smiled nervously and said "Three diamonds."

The King shot her a quick, doubtful look, glanced at his cards, and grinned. "No use, Alice." He leered playfully at her. "Struggling against fate, m'dear. Three hearts."

Soveral studied the score-card, his face impassive. "It's not a game bid, monkey – yet," said his majesty, with a glance at Mr Franklin which was a royal command if ever there was one. Soveral smiled with his mouth and said: "Four diamonds."

There was a strangled noise from his majesty, and an anxious glance at Mr Franklin, who promptly did his duty with a clear conscience, and said: "Four hearts."

"Ha!" said the King, relieved. "Excellent. Very good, Alice, lead away." His glance invited Mr Franklin to gloat with him. "Come along, Alice, come along."

"Pass," said Mrs Keppel, smiling sweetly, the King grunted his satisfaction, and Mr Franklin realized beyond doubt that Mrs Keppel would cheerfully have gone five diamonds in normal circumstances, but had desisted because she knew the King desperately wanted the rubber. Soveral, however, had plainly made the same deduction, for as the King passed he said without hesitation: "Five diamonds."

There was a buzz of astonishment round the table. The King, on the point of laying down his hand as dummy, stared at Soveral in disappointment and deep suspicion. Mr Franklin felt his stomach muscles tighten a fraction. It might be a spoiling bluff – but was it? Looking at his own hand, Soveral could have five diamonds for him . . . on the other hand, the King had supported Mr Franklin's hearts . . . dammit, the old man must have something going . . . but *five*. Mr Franklin took another sip of hock. What the hell, anyway . . .

"Five hearts," he announced and the King's eyes widened in dismay.

"My goodness," said Mrs Keppel, and seemed about to add a light remark, but a glance at the King made her change her mind. He was busily excavating his cards again, breathing heavily, and when she passed he stared anxiously across the table, passing in turn. Soveral lighted a cigarette, musing, and then the ugly face turned to smile thoughtfully at Mr Franklin. "Five hearts?" he said softly, and placed his finger-tips together. "I do believe that you want to . . . wring us out, Mr Franklin. Mmh? Six diamonds." And in that moment the game changed, for Mr Franklin, and he thought: showdown.

"Dealer folds," as Cassidy threw in his cards. "Too many for me," from old Davis, and the greasy cards being pushed away; across the table Kid Curry with his wolf smile and eyes bright through the smoke of the oil lamp,

watching him. "What about you, Mark? Had enough?" The jeering smile,
disdaining him with his pair of kings, an eight, and an ace on the table; in
front of Curry lay two tens and two threes – was there another ten or three
in the hole? On the face of it, two pairs against his one, and Curry might
have a full house – the cagey, greasy bastard with his sly smile, he'd seen
him go the limit on a single pair, and men drum their fingers and throw
in better hands, and Curry with his jeering laugh raking in the pot – and
never failing to face his cards and show the pikers how he'd bluffed them.
But then, he was Kid Curry, the Mad Dog, with the Colt in his armpit
and ready to use on anyone who turned ugly; not even Cassidy, or Long-
baugh, was quicker than the Kid, and everyone knew it. Deaf Charley
throwing in, Jess Linley's watery eyes sliding to his cards and away again
as he too folded. "Had enough, Mark? Why don't you quit, little boy? I got
you licked!" Old Davis's dirty face under the battered hat, his mouth
working: that's our stake, son, that's to take us to Tonopah, don't fool with
Curry, son, it isn't worth it; fold and call it a day. His own voice: "A
hundred, and another hundred," Davis muttering, oh Jesus, that's it, and
the smile freezing on Curry's face, the long silence before he covered and
called, and Franklin turned over his hole card, a second ace – and the
snarling curses as Curry swept his own cards aside and came to his feet,
and Cassidy snapping: "That'll do, kid!" And it had done, too; Curry had
taken his beating and old Davis had scooped in the pot, cackling and
swearing, and Franklin had tried to keep the relief from his face as, under
the table, he quietly uncocked the Remington that he had held trained on
Curry's chair, and slid it back into his boot.

Instead of Kid Curry – the Marquis de Soveral, smiling confidently,
and Mr Franklin, with four to five sure losers in his hand, met the
smile with a composure which he certainly did not feel. If I'd any
sense I'd let you go down the river on your raft of diamonds – but
would it be down the river? Suppose Soveral made it? Suppose
nothing, this was the hand, as Soveral had reminded him, when he'd
vowed to wring the opposition out. The King, slumped in his seat, was
eyeing him morosely; Mrs Keppel was absently fingering a flawless
eyebrow; the faces behind the royal chair were waiting expectantly –
and it crossed his mind, who'd have believed it, here I am, with the
King of England, waiting on my word, and an Ambassador calling the
shot, and the flower of the mighty empire's nobility waiting to see
what the Nevada saddle-tramp is going to do about it. And it was
pure five-card stud training that made him ask for another glass of

hock, while the King writhed and muttered impatiently (the words "double, double, for heaven's sake!" being distinctly audible), and only when the wine was being poured did Mr Franklin say casually: "Six hearts." Smith jerked wine on to his sleeve, and the King stared across in stupefaction.

"D'you know what you're doing?" he demanded. "Six . . . oh lord! Well, I hope you've got "em, that's all! Six . . ." mutter, mutter, mutter.

"Double six hearts," murmured Soveral, and "Re-double," said Mr Franklin, in sheer bravado; he had a sketchy idea of what it would mean to go down, in points, redoubled and vulnerable, but that didn't matter. Money was the least of it to that bearded picture of disgruntled alarm across the table, losing, and Soveral's smoothly apologetic satisfaction, and (worst of all) Mrs Keppel's nervous condolences – that was what he couldn't stand. He was glooming apprehensively over his cards, as Mrs Keppel led the ace of clubs; the King spread the dummy and sat back, staring resentfully at his partner.

Ace and four hearts, king of spades, king of clubs – and one hideous rag of a diamond. They were one down, for certain; Mrs Keppel's ace of clubs took the first trick, Soveral scooped it in, and waited for the inevitable diamond lead that would break the contract. But Mrs Keppel, possibly because she had in her own hand a profusion of diamonds to rival Kimberley and feared that Mr Franklin might be void, led a spade instead; Mr Franklin dropped his ace on it, and then – in the view of Sir Charles, who was standing apprehensively behind his chair – began to thrash his way through trump with reckless abandon. In fact, Mr Franklin, having bid himself into an impossible situation, was simply going down with colours flying; he could not get rid of his diamond loser, and there was nothing for it but to plough on to the bitter end, with occasional sips of hock along the way. The King would not be pleased. Well, it had been interesting meeting royalty, anyway.

He paused, with the last three cards in his hands – two trump and that singleton diamond leering obscenely at him in its nakedness. He knew from Soveral's discards that Mrs Keppel had the ace and king; the problem, more akin to poker than to bridge, was to make her discard them both, and short of wrenching them from her hands he could see no way of doing it.

"Three to get," muttered the King, presumably in case Mr Franklin had not noticed. His majesty had roused slightly from his gloomy

130

apathy, and was regarding the table as a rabbit watches a snake: there were nine tricks in front of the American – perhaps the age of miracles had not passed. His majesty's asthmatic wheezing rustled through the room as Mr Franklin led a heart, and Mrs Keppel dropped her diamond king. Perspiring freely, Mr Franklin led his last heart and smiled hopefully at Mrs Keppel, who frowned pathetically and said: "Oh, dear."

She fingered her cards and bit her lip. "Oh, it is so difficult . . . I never know what to play. And I always get it wrong, you know." The green eyes met Mr Franklin's, and his tiny flickering hope died; they were smiling quizzically – she knew perfectly well he had a diamond, it seemed to him. She toyed with her cards, hesitating – and played the ace of diamonds. The King choked, Soveral sighed, Mr Franklin gathered in the trick, played his nine of diamonds, and Mrs Keppel emitted a most realistic squeal of dismay as she faced her queen of clubs. There was an instant's sensation as Soveral's last card went down – a spade – and the King was roaring with delight, coughing and slapping the table: "Well done, Franklin! Oh, well done indeed! Game and rubber! What, Soveral? Pegged out to dry, hey? Oh, Alice, you foolish girl! The Yankee sharper bluffed you into the wrong discard, didn't he? Oh, my!"

That's what you think, reflected Mr Franklin, as Mrs Keppel feigned pretty confusion and exclaimed: "Oh, I am such a goose! I always get it wrong – if only I would count the cards, but I always forget! Oh, marquis, what must you think?"

What the marquis thought was fairly obvious, at least to Mr Franklin, but of course he gallantly brushed her penitence aside, and said seriously that it must have been an extremely difficult decision; he was not sure that she had not, in theory, been right. Mr Franklin wondered if there was irony in the words, but if there was, the King did not catch it; he called for whisky nightcaps, clapped Mr Franklin on the shoulder and said they must play together again, and twitted Mrs Keppel unmercifully as he led her to the centre of the laughing group at the fireplace. Mr Franklin offered his arm to Peggy.

"Thank goodness you won at last," she said. "I shudder to think what he'd have been like at breakfast if you hadn't. Daddy said he was sure you must go down." She studied him sidelong. "Do you do everything as well as you play bridge?"

"I hope not," said Mr Franklin, and as Soveral joined them, he added: "Mrs Keppel was the one who played well, I thought," and

131

Peggy wondered why Soveral laughed. By the fire the King was being noisily jovial at Mrs Keppel's expense as he sat back, contented, whisky glass in hand, cigar going nicely, and the beautiful Alice, sitting gracefully on the rug by the royal knee, laughed gaily at what she called her own feather-brain; her expression did not change when she met Mr Franklin's eyes, and he wondered, with a momentary revulsion, if it was always like this in the royal circle – the petty deceits and subterfuges to keep the monarch amused, to order events for his satisfaction. Was the King himself deceived, or did he, too, join in the pretence? Perhaps it was the warmth of the room, the smoky atmosphere, the long game, the over-indulgence in hock, but Mr Franklin felt vaguely uncomfortable, even ashamed – not for himself, really, but for being a part of it all. It was so trifling, and yet – he listened to Mrs Keppel's tinkling laugh at one of the King's sallies, and realized that once again he, too, was smiling mechanically and making approving noises. Soveral, score-card in hand, was announcing smoothly that the last rubber had comfortably levelled up his majesty's score over the night, and Mr Franklin received a handful of sovereigns from the marquis and polite applause led by Mrs Keppel, tapping her palm on her wrist and smiling up at him. He bowed and pocketed the coins, reflecting that she probably considered it money well spent, and the game well lost, if it ensured his majesty a happy repose.

8

Finally, it was over; the King, yawning but affable, withdrew, a collective inward sigh was heaved, Sir Charles Clayton was smiling a tired smile of pure relief, and the party drifted out into the hall, the dinner guests to go to their cars, and one or two, like Mr Franklin, to be shown their rooms for the night. He, having arrived late, had not yet had one assigned to him, and Peggy summoned her brother from the other end of the house, whence came a sound of distant revelry; the younger set, it seemed, kept hours just as late as their elders, but probably a good deal more happily.

"You ought to have the chamber of honour," said Arthur, as he led Mr Franklin upstairs. "Peg says you saved the day. Good scout." And he patted the American affectionately on the shoulder. "But this is the best we can do, I'm afraid – " He led the way along a narrow corridor which seemed to lead to the very end of the gloomy upper floor. Mr Franklin noticed that the doors they passed had visiting cards pinned to them; his own, when they reached it, had a sheet of paper marked "Mr Franklin'.

"If you need anything, pull the bell, but don't be surprised if it comes out of the wall," said Arthur cheerfully. "We're rather in need of repair, I'm afraid. Someone'll bring your shaving water in the morning. Good night, old chap."

Repair was about right, thought Mr Franklin, as he prepared to undress; the room was decidedly shabby – much shabbier than he'd have expected from the comfort of the rooms downstairs. Probably the Claytons hadn't had so many guests in living memory, and of course all the attention would be lavished on royalty's apartments. But he remembered the hired cutlery and crockery and wondered again, idly, if old Clayton was perhaps pretty well stretched. None of his business, of course, but they seemed nice folk – Peggy was an uncommonly attractive girl, not just for her seraphic beauty, but for the spirit that lay underneath; she looked like an English rose, but

133

there were some pretty sharp thorns on that shapely stem, or he was much mistaken.

What a strange day it had been – how long since he set off to West Walsham? Eighteen hours? And then the ridiculous fox business, and his frantic preparations with Thornhill, and the dinner, and that astonishing game which he still didn't know how to play properly – and he'd met and talked to the King of England, and shared that intimacy of bridge partnership – that was the odd, unbelievable part, that for a time he had occupied the King's thoughts, and been the object of his attention: he, Mark Franklin, nobody from nowhere. And yet he was just as much somebody as the King was, after all – just not so many people knew him. And he'd sniffed the air of a court, and in its way it was just like the history his father had taught him – about the Caesars, and the Italian tyrants, and Henry VIII, who slapped people in jail because their faces didn't fit, or clipped their heads and ears off. Would he have bid six hearts with Henry VIII sitting over the way? There was a thought, now. He turned down the lamp, rolled into the creaking bed, and felt his head throb and spin as soon as it hit the pillow. He knew he wouldn't sleep easily.

From far off, below him, he could hear the distant murmur of voices, and music, amd muffled laughter; Arthur's friends were still whooping it up down there. No doubt they were at a safe distance from royalty; it was quite a soothing murmur, anyway, and Mr Franklin must have dozed off, for suddenly he was conscious that the voices were sharp and clear and much closer – in the corridor outside his room, feet clattering, and laughter, and the squeal of feminine laughter. "Where's Rhoda? Oh, Jeremy, you utter idiot – well, you'll just have to go back for it!" "Which is my room, then?" "I dunno, can't you read, Daphne?" "I say, Connie, old thing, give us a ciggy." "Oh, lor', look at my dress?" "What is it – custard?" Squeals of laughter, young men's babbling, idiot catch-phrases: "Oh, a divvy party!" "Oh, Jeremy, how too horridino! Take it away!" Squeak, giggle, clatter, at the tops of their shrill voices, doors slamming – Mr Franklin groaned softly and wondered how long it would be before they shut up. After a few moments it subsided, with only occasional cries and laughter muffled by the walls; then whispers and stifled giggling, furtive rustlings as later arrivals hurried along the passage; Mr Franklin dozed again, uneasily . . .

His door opened and closed, feet swiftly crossed the room, and in one instinctive moment he was out of bed before he was even awake, crouched and ready, his hand automatically snaking under his pillow. A lamp was turned up brilliantly, dazzling him, a female voice cooed playfully: "All right, Frankie, here's a little coochy-woochy come to get you!" and Mr Franklin had a horrifying vision of a plump, dark-haired young lady throwing aside her frilly dressing-gown and sprawling naked on the bed he had just left. "Where are . . ." she began, surveying the empty bed, and then her eyes met his, a yard away, and she squealed aloud, putting her knuckles to her mouth. "Oh, my God! You're not Frank! Oh! Oh, my God!"

"I'm Franklin," he said mechanically, and the young lady squealed again and belatedly snatched the sheet up to her chin.

"Oh! Oh, my God! What are you doing here? This is Frank's room! Go away!"

"It's my room!" Mr Franklin crouched, appalled. "Franklin. You've made – "

"What?" The dark eyes stared in panic. "Oh, my God, my God! But the door . . ." She squealed again. "That bloody Jeremy! He's changed the cards! The swine! Oh, God!" She dived completely under the covers. Her voice sounded muffled. "Go away!"

"I can't." Mr Franklin, standing in his nightshirt, observing the heaving sheet with alarm, was at a loss. "This is my room – I . . . I . . . can't just . . . here." He walked round the bed, picked up the discarded flimsy gown, and dropped his voice to a whisper. "Take your . . . your robe, and get out, quick. Before someone comes."

"What?" An eye peeped from beneath the sheet. "You mean you've got someone . . ."

"I don't mean anything of the dam' sort!" hissed Mr Franklin. "Look – take it and vamoose, will you?"

"No! I can't! Oh, God, why don't you go away! If Frank finds out he'll . . ."

"Will you get out of here – please?" whispered Mr Franklin, desperately. "Look, you can't stay here – "

"Damn that rotten little toad Jeremy!" Suddenly her head came out. "My God – I wonder whose name he's put on Frank's door? Here, who are you, anyway?"

"That doesn't really matter!" He was beginning to get thoroughly annoyed. "Will you please go?"

"You're American," said the young lady. "I say, what an utter frost!" She brushed the hair out of her eyes, still keeping the sheet firmly in place. Then, alarmingly, she giggled; Mr Franklin wondered

135

was she going to have hysterics. But she seemed to have regained her composure remarkably.

"That little brute! Of all the mean tricks!" She giggled again, considering Mr Franklin. "You weren't in the crowd downstairs, were you? I'd have seen you – I mean, I'd have noticed you." She nibbled the top of the sheet. "You're rather divvy, really." And she giggled once more, infuriatingly.

Mr Franklin took a deep breath. Then he dropped the dressing-gown on the bed, walked to the door, took hold of the knob, and jerked with his thumb. "Out," he said.

The young lady looked at the robe and tossed her head. "You're not very gallant! I mean, it's not my fault I mistook your rotten room, is it?"

"Out!"

"Well, it isn't! So there's no need to be horrid. I mean, it could happen to anyone." Again the giggle. "It's rather a lark, really – gosh, what would Frank say?" And to his alarm, the young lady snuggled down in the bed. "Anyway, it's awfully comfy here."

Mr Franklin felt the hairs rise on his neck. He was not a prude, and faced with Pip Delys in a similar situation, he had been human enough not to hesitate above a moment. But that had been entirely different: Pip had known precisely what she was doing, and he doubt-ed if this young woman did. This was a silly, feckless, no doubt promiscuous but completely irresponsible little piece of . . . of English upper-class stupidity – or so he supposed. My God, was the country just one great cat-house? Or had he got her wrong? Was she just so dam' stupid that she didn't realize what she was doing? Was she drunk – probably under the influence, slightly, but not so that it mattered. No, she thought it was just a great lark – and since she'd been going to roll in the hay with someone – Frank, whoever he was – well, presumably the next best thing would do. Mr Franklin swore softly, and at that moment there were feet moving in the passage, and a voice was whispering irritably:

"Poppy? Poppy? Where the devil are you?"

There was a muted squeak and giggle from the bed. "Oh, golly – that's Frank!"

"Poppy? Oh, come on! What are you playing at?" The voice was louder, and impatient. "Poppy! Damnation! Poppy!"

"Poppy's killed in South Africa," called a distant male voice, and a girl laughed shrilly. The footsteps paused outside Mr Franklin's

136

door, and he heard a match being struck; a distant door opened and a young voice called: "What on earth's up, Frank? Why the blazes can't you go to bed?"

"Which is Poppy's room?" The questioner was on the other side of the panels, loud and truculent. "Blast! Oh, go to hell, Jeremy!"

Convulsive rustlings came from Mr Franklin's bed; he could hear Poppy giggling hysterically. The young voice was coming closer, laughing: "Oh, leave off, Frank! You're tight, you silly ass! Poppy's fast asleep by . . ."

"Shut up!" Another match scratched, followed by heavy breathing. "What? This is *my* room – but it's not . . . what the hell?"

"Well, if it's *your* room, Poppy's probably in there, don't you think?" The malicious amusement in the young voice was evident, and then abruptly the door was thrust open almost in Mr Franklin's face, and in the bedside light's gleam a large young man in evening dress shirt and trousers stood framed in the doorway. As Mr Franklin had deduced from the voice, it was Frank, Lord Lacy, his acquaintance from the foxhunt.

"What the hell?" Lacy glared at him, blinking in the light. Behind him a fresh-faced young man was doubling up with laughter, and on the other side of the passage another man's head was emerging.

"You!" Lacy stood, his face blank. "Oh! Where's Po—" He broke off, his eyes bulging, as he looked beyond Franklin to the bed. "Christ! Poppy!"

"Take it easy," said Mr Franklin, but Lord Lacy seemed to be having difficulty in taking in anything at all. He stared from the bed where Poppy, eagerly apprehensive, was huddled up bright-eyed, hugging her knees beneath the sheet, to the American.

Mr Franklin spoke quickly. "The young lady mistook my room for yours. The names seem to have got switched." He looked past Lacy at the fresh-faced young man. "She just this minute got here, and was on the point of leaving."

"Leaving?" His lordship gurgled. "Leaving? She bloody well looks like it, doesn't she?" He plunged forward towards the bed before Mr Franklin could stop him. "You dirty little bitch!" he roared, and made a grab at the squealing Poppy who slithered frantically out of the other side screaming: "No, Frank, no! Leave me alone!" She was pulling the sheet with her, but Lacy caught it, dragging it from her grasp. Left naked, Poppy covered her eyes and dived wildly towards the door, Mr Franklin obligingly side-stepped to let her past. She

137

stumbled into the fresh-faced young man, bringing him down, the corridor was suddenly full of staring faces, female shrieks, cries of astonishment, and hurrying feet, and Mr Franklin took his forehead in his hand and swore, with feeling. Someone began to have hysterics, and then he was aware of Arthur, half-dressed, emerging from the confusion. "What on earth's happening?"

Mr Franklin explained rapidly; Arthur glanced quickly from the door-card to the errant Poppy, now huddled in semi-decency in someone else's gown, to Lacy, who was still gaping foolishly at the sheet in his hand, and nodded, grinning. "I see. Just so. Poppy, you half-wit, what the – "

"Twasn't my fault!" Poppy, with several people between her and her bewildered lover, was prepared to enjoy the excitement. She tossed her head. "I wasn't to know, was I? Jeremy, you pig, you changed the cards – I know you did! Beast!"

"What happened?" "Poppy, what on earth?" "The wrong room?" "A likely story!" "Whose room was it?" "Oh, crumbs! Isn't it priceless!" The babble of the bright young things was drowning Poppy's giggling protestations when there was a sudden roar from Lacy. His lordship might be slow on the uptake, but a thought had evidently occurred to him. He turned on Mr Franklin, his face working in rage, and before Arthur could intervene, he flung himself at the American, head down and fists swinging.

Mr Franklin became impatient. He had had a trying day; several things had happened which were outside his experience, and he was not used to being at a loss. It irritated him. Now, however, a problem had arisen with which he was equipped to deal; furthermore, the angry man intent on murdering him was a man for whom he had formed an instinctive dislike. He almost welcomed the opportunity of expressing his own feelings, which he did by side-stepping quickly and hitting Lord Lacy hard on the jaw as he went past, thus diverting him head-first into the wall. But to his surprise the peer merely shook his head, swore luridly, and resumed the attack, so Mr Franklin, who had learned his self-defence in an irregular school, kicked him sharply in the stomach. Lord Lacy doubled up, fell into the corridor, and was profoundly sick.

"Here, you can't do that!" cried Arthur indignantly. "Can't kick a chap!"

Mr Franklin did not reply. He did not feel like discussing the ethics of rough-housing, and with the corridor resonant with cries of disgust,

138

alarm, and – unless his ears deceived him – raucous amusement and excited cries of female glee, it would have been a waste of time. He stood over Arthur, who had dropped to one knee beside the groaning Lacy.

"You'd better get him to bed," said Mr Franklin, shortly. "His own, for preference. And since I'm a guest in your father's house, Mr Clayton, and don't wish to cause him embarrassment, I suggest you tell Mr Lacy – oh, no, *Lord* Lacy – that if he comes near my room again I'll break his goddamned neck. I might – " he paused with his hand on the door " – even kick the chap. Good night."

He closed the door with unnecessary violence, surveying his room and the wreckage of his bed. Outside the babble of voices, giggles, and groans gradually died away, with Arthur supervising the assistance of Lord Lacy to some distant haven. Mr Franklin swore again, pondering on the ways of English house-parties, and the morals of the younger generation, as he restored his bed to some order. Poppy's gown still lay on the floor; he picked it up and marched to the door, intending to throw it up the corridor, which was now presumably empty – but on opening the door he found Poppy herself, fetchingly swathed in her borrowed garment, in earnest whispered conversation with Arthur. They started.

"Your robe," said Mr Franklin, holding it out.

"Oh, thank you," said Poppy brightly. "I say, I *am* sorry – but you see, I wasn't to know – "

"Jeremy had switched cards," said Mr Franklin heavily. "I know."

"He's a horrid little beast," said Poppy, and giggled again. "It was quite fun, though, wasn't it? I say, that was a dreadful thump you gave poor Frank – serve him right for getting in such a wax over nothing. He's a bit of a spoilsport, isn't he?"

"Just a bit," agreed Mr Franklin.

"I'm awfully sorry, old chap," said Arthur. "Our guests don't usually have their rooms invaded, I assure you – oh, shut up, Poppy! It's all your fault, anyway; go on!" He pushed her playfully away, and she tripped up the corridor to the open door of a bedroom. "No harm done, anyway," went on Arthur. "Except to Frank – and he'll be right as rain in the morning. Don't worry about him, by the way. I mean, he won't – "

"No," said Mr Franklin, "I don't think he will."

"No." Arthur laughed. "Gosh, I'm glad the guv'nor didn't hear us, though. Phew! Or Peg. There'd have been hell to pay, I can tell you."

139

"Or the King, I imagine."

"Don't mention it! Oh, shut up, Poppy. I'm coming." He gave Mr Franklin an apologetic grin. " 'Night, old chap."

"Night-night," called Poppy softly, and fluttered a hand at Mr Franklin. She vanished into the bedroom hastily, and Arthur, with another slightly sheepish look at Mr Franklin, shrugged and followed her.

Mr Franklin closed his door, a trifle shaken, and retired to sleep for what remained of the night. But even that was denied him; he was aware of stealthy peregrinations in the corridor, and once all hell broke loose shortly before six – it transpired that Poppy, intent on revenge, had stolen into Jeremy's bedroom, and emptied a jug of cold water over the occupant – or rather, occupants, neither of whom, it turned out, was Jeremy at all. None of which surprised Mr Franklin when he heard about it next day.

That day began for him at the most unsatisfactory hour of eight-thirty, when he had just fallen into a deep sleep; a nondescript person knocked and entered with a can of hot water which he emptied into the wash-stand bowl, pulled back the curtains, and without a by-your-leave turned out Mr Franklin's case and cast a critical eye over his tweed suit.

"Ought to been hung up last night," he observed coldly. "I'm sorry, sir, I shall attend to it while you shave. I would 'ave run you a 'ot bath, sir, but hunfortunately some of the young gentlemen 'ave been playing pranks with the soap and boot-polish, and the bath ain't fit to be used. Disgustin', it is; one of the guests can't even get dressed, covered with muck, 'e is. I don't know; you'd think they'd learn 'em better at their expensive schools. Your tea is on the bedside table, sir. Thank you."

Mr Franklin drank his tea and shaved, and was ready in his underwear when the servant returned with his suit. He thanked the man and asked if the King was in the habit of going down to breakfast.

"It is 'is majesty's custom to break 'is fast with the other guests – at the better country 'ouses, sir," was the astonishing reply, and Mr Franklin paused in pulling on his trousers.

"Not here, you mean?"

"I could not say, sir, not bein' conversant with the routine of this hestablishment."

"But don't you work here?"

"No sir, I do not." The nondescript man stiffened slightly. "I am 'ere on a pro tem basis honly – I am 'appy to say." He hesitated. "I beg your pardon, sir, but would you be a transatlantic gentleman?"

Mr Franklin hid a smile and said that he would be.

"I see, sir. I ask because I would not wish you to be hunder any misappre'ension, or to carry away a false himpression. This is not what I am haccustomed to. Do you know, sir, that I 'ave five other gentlemen to valet besides yourself, and 'alf of them I daren't go into the rooms – " he dropped his voice " – on account of their not bein' alone? Fair scandal it is; I don't know what the country's comin' to – it is not like this at such as the Duke of Devonshire's residence, I can tell you. But nowadays, with 'is majesty bein' so generous of 'is presence, an' very free an' easy about where 'e stays – "

"You work for the King?" Mr Franklin was astonished.

The man smirked. "Very kind of you to think that, sir, but no; I 'ave not 'ad that honner. I am not in regular employ at the moment, but occasional, like now." Mr Franklin noted the bottled nose and slightly shaky hand, and guessed the employ was very occasional. "What I meant to say, sir, was that with 'is majesty bein' so easy, Society 'as enlarged nowadays, an' there is country 'ouses which he honners with 'is presence that wouldn't 'ave smelt so much as 'is equerry's cigar smoke in the old Queen's time, God bless 'er. That is a very fine suit, if I may say so, sir; reg'lar pleasure to lay out. An' the trouble is, sir, they 'aven't got the money nor the dignity, 'arf of 'em. Oh, fine old families, no doubt – but not up to the top mark, you see. An' some rather queer fish, too, that didn't ought to be in Society at all – Jews an' rich foreigners and that like – not Americans, of course, sir, they not bein' foreigners – you know what I mean, though, sir – Eyetalians, an' so forth. Well, what can you expect? Standards go down, and the young people's behaviour is fair shockin'; it's this new music, if you ask me, sir, an' them motor cars. Even the young ladies – well! Young ladies, did I say?" He shook his carefully-pomaded grey head sorrowfully. "It's my belief that 'alf of them goes to the altar knowin' more than their mothers do. But it's the same everywhere, sir, isn't it?" He adjusted Mr Franklin's pocket handkerchief. "Excellent, sir. Now, was there anythin' else, sir?"

"No, thanks. Hadn't you better be seeing to your other . . . er . . . gentlemen?"

" 'Er . . . gentlemen' is about right, sir." The man chuckled beerily. "They can wait their turn, sir – an' get them little hussies out their rooms, an' all, afore I attend to them! I wouldn't neglect a real

141

gennleman like yourself, sir, not on their account. Oh, thank you, sir; most kind of you."

Mr Franklin made his way downstairs thoughtfully, and was rather taken aback to find the King planted before the hall fireplace, smoking a cigar and talking to one of his equerries. He hailed the American genially.

"Morning, Franklin. Sleep well?"

"Very well, thank you, sir," lied Mr Franklin gamely, wondering if he should inquire in kind. The King settled it for him.

"More than I did, then. Draughts seem to follow me about these days. Getting too old for all this gallivanting, sitting up to all hours getting fleeced by Yankee card-sharps, what?" He beamed over his cigar; for all his complaints about draughts, and the fact that he could not have had more than four hours' sleep, he was looking remarkably spruce in his check breeches and jacket, hideously offset by his pink tie; his eye was clear and his face ruddy with health. Mr Franklin wondered how he did it.

"Hardly fleeced, sir," said the equerry, warming Mr Franklin with his smile. "Soveral complains that you and Mr Franklin gave him a very rough passage indeed."

"We'll give him worse than that, you'll see. Eh, Franklin? Now, look," said his majesty, "you'll come down and see us at Sandringham next month – what's the date of that, Halford? Ne'er mind; let Franklin know in good time. We'll have some shooting, and plenty of time for bridge and so on. You'll enjoy it; nothing like this – " and his majesty frowned and waved his cigar at their surroundings with a deprecating gesture that would have given Sir Charles Clayton heart failure. "Small party, good fun – some interesting people for you. You ought to meet them, get to know your way about." The little eyes twinkled kindly, and Mr Franklin was amazed that he could ever have thought this charming old gentleman spoiled or ill-tempered. "We'll have Jackie Fisher down, perhaps Churchill, we'll see. Which reminds me – excuse me, Franklin; no, don't go." The King turned to his aide. "Jackie ought to know that he has to pack up at last; if he wants to do it gracefully, Asquith'll give him a title. But one way or the other, he's got to go. It's up to him. Where the devil," his majesty resumed, "is Alice? Women! Is there any one of 'em who can be on time? Had your breakfast yet, Franklin?"

"No, sir – I shall in a moment." Mr Franklin was looking for

words. "I thank you for inviting me next month; I'll be delighted – "
He wasn't sure that he would be, but it had to be said.

"My dear chap! Now, go and get your breakfast before the wolves
descend. I gather there are young people whom we don't know about."
Mr Franklin nodded gravely. "I shan't see you again," added the
King, "but we look forward to next month."

Mr Franklin had a feeling of being dismissed from audience, and
wondered if he should back across the hall to the dining-room.
Common sense triumphed in a slight bow before he turned away; as
he reached the opposite door the King called: "Oh, Franklin!", adding
in a conspiratorial growl which echoed round the hall: "Don't touch
the haddock. Ghastly."

Thus advised, Mr Franklin went in to breakfast, which in its way
was the biggest ordeal he had struck yet. There were four or five
people round the table – Arlesdon, Lady Dalston, Ponsonby, Smith,
someone else; they called "Good morning!" loudly, and he went on
to help himself from the buffet (Thornhill had briefed him on the
etiquette of country-house breakfast). Being in no condition to attempt
a cooked meal, he ignored the bacon, eggs, ham, kidneys, chops, and
condemned haddock beneath the silver covers, contenting himself
with fruit, toast and coffee, and sliding quietly into a seat beside
Lady Dalston. She smiled automatically and made the usual formal
enquiries before rejoining the conversation at large, which was well
over Mr Franklin's head – some society children's party which was
to take place at the Savoy, shooting at Quiddenham the following
week, the new roller-skating craze. Mr Franklin concentrated on not
crunching his toast, and studied the marmalade dish; once, Lady
Dalston tried to draw him into the conversation by asking if he
intended to visit Scotland before Christmas; she caught him with a
mouthful of toast and apple, and he risked serious injury getting it
down while she regarded him with cool interest; the hoarse "No"
with which he eventually succeeded in answering her seemed a poor
return for her attention.

He was pondering the curious fact that the informality of breakfast
was infinitely more trying than the formality of dinner had been when
they all got up and went out – the King was leaving. Mr Franklin,
cup poised, supposed that etiquette demanded that he should go out,
too, to speed the departing monarch, and then thought, the hell
with it, he can make it without me. So he lingered, in solitary enjoyment, over his toast and coffee, and wished he hadn't, for the King's

departure evidently meant that the house was now free for the younger set, and presently he was invaded by a chattering horde who swarmed round the covers, loaded their plates, shouted and squealed at each other, and turned the quiet morning-room into something like a juvenile picnic.

The fresh-faced Jeremy bounced down beside him, taking him aback by crying: "Morning, Mark, old bean – shove the pepper along, will you?" Poppy followed, bright-eyed and blooming despite the fact, Mr Franklin calculated primly, that she had probably not slept at all. She startled him by kissing him resoundingly on the back of the neck, patting his head, and addressing him as Uncle Sam.

"You don't look half as grim in tweeds," she informed him as she sat down opposite and attacked a large plate of kedgeree. "Does he, Jeremy? Proper old grizzly bear he was last night, too." She bared her teeth across the table. "Hallo, Arthur! Is that the other grizzly bear away – the teddy one? And the bee-yoo-tious Mrs Keppel. Oh, my deah, how ravishing!" She rolled her eyes in affected languor. "You had to play cards with them last night, Mark, didn't you? You poor darling – how disky for you! Did Kingie cheat? Oh, shut up, Madge – stop shoving!" This to a slim and beautiful redhead who had sat down beside her; Poppy cast envious eyes on her flimsy morning dress. "Oh, you grim pig! Is that Worth?"

"Lucile," said the redhead, "and if you get marmalade on it I'll slay you." She glanced across at Mr Franklin, who to his knowledge had never seen her before in his life. "Hullo, Mark dear – can I have one of these cigarettes everyone's talking about? Oh, no, they're not just Colonel Bogeys? How common!" She pealed with laughter. "The King thought they were marvellous, Peggy says; poor old ass never heard of them!"

Arthur sat down beside Poppy, said "Hullo, young pig-face," and ruffled her hair. She pushed at him, upsetting his coffee-cup, and they squabbled like ten-year-olds until he threatened to push bacon down the back of her dress – as though they were in a nursery together, thought Mr Franklin, yet last night they had finished up . . . oh, well. Beside him Jeremy, with his mouth full, was discussing cars with a young man at the other end of the table. The raised voices were lost in the din: " . . . keep your old Panhard rattle-trap! Haven't you seen Tony's Albion? Well, it's his pater's, anyway. Sixteen horse-power, two cylinders, goes uphill like a rocket – and Jack's going to give me a tool in his new Pilain. Six hundred and forty quid – all right if you've got it!"

"Why's he called the octopus?" The redhead was calling across to a girl beside Mr Franklin. "You'll find out if you go to the theatre with him! Ask Poppy – " she turned to whisper, and Poppy choked with laughter. A squeal from the other end of the table drew all attention; a girl was doubled up, laughing and obviously beating off the under-the-table attentions of the boy beside her. "Stop it, Hugh! Oh, now you've made me tear my stocking! You're an absolute blight!" And she struck him angrily on the cheek, to the accompaniment of cheers and light ribaldries.

Children, thought Mr Franklin, grown-up children. It was only now, when he saw them in daylight, that he realized how young they were. It was his first good look at the rising generation of the British upper class, and while he found it rather disturbing, it was fascinating, too. The faces and bodies and appetites of adults, the smart clothes, the confident voices, loud and shrill, sophisticated far beyond their years – and at the same time minds and vocabularies which, so far as he could judge, hadn't progressed much beyond leading-strings. Their manners were appalling, their talk loaded with an amazing, affected slang, they aped the behaviour of their seniors – and yet there was something pathetically innocent about them, too. Innocent and vicious? That didn't make sense – until he looked across at Arthur and Poppy, chuckling together like toddlers, snatching together for the marmalade – and heard that bedroom door closing behind them a few hours before.

It was their cast-iron confidence that impressed him particularly – it went with the good looks, of course, the shared experiences which obviously went back to infancy, the same schools, the same privileged world. How the dickens had he got here? He glanced round, and with a shock realized that the young woman who was sitting next to the girl who had slapped the forward Hugh, and had carried on talking to her neighbour as though nothing were happening, was Peggy. She caught his eye and waved, smiling, calling "Good morning" through the noise, but at that moment Jeremy started a toast-throwing fight with another young man across the table, and Mr Franklin beat a diplomatic retreat to the hall. He was too old and defenceless, he decided.

Seeing that the group who had seen off the King were still chatting on the gravel outside the front door, Mr Franklin turned abruptly

145

down the passage to the back of the house; at the moment he wanted solitude as he had seldom wanted it in his life. The past interminable hours seemed to have been a steady procession of dreadful people, of high-pitched grating voices raised in clipped, confident tones. He could decently get away in an hour or two – for the first time he found himself thinking with real warmth of the tranquillity of Lancing Manor; could it be that he was homesick for it already? It struck him in that moment that Lancing Manor *was* home, more than anywhere else. A place to go back to; most importantly, at the moment, a place where he could be alone.

The passage led him to the kitchen, where a startled cook directed him to the back door, and without hat or stick he strode out through a kitchen garden and into the paddock beyond, following his nose until he had put a safe distance between himself and the house. It was a sunny, misty morning, with the grass wet underfoot, and the very fact of escape from the cloying, nervous atmosphere of the house-party raised his spirits. He kicked contentedly at the piles of damp fallen leaves, breathing in the pure morning air, circling the wood beyond the paddock with his long, easy stride, and coming at last to a fenced track that ran along the wood leading back to the house. He was half-way along it when he saw that a man was standing by the wicket-gate at the far end; it would have looked odd if he had turned back so he carried on, and the figure turned out to be Sir Charles Clayton.

His smile seemed rather warmer than any Mr Franklin had seen from him so far, and he looked a good deal happier than the harassed host of the previous night. Mr Franklin guessed that as soon as the King had been sped on his way, Sir Charles had taken the opportunity of a few minutes alone to let out several deep breaths; he seemed content just to be standing there, surveying a pleasant pastoral scene view, and the narrow, intelligent face turned towards him.

"You like land, Mr Franklin?"

Mr Franklin gave the question his usual careful concentration, and replied: "Yes, I guess so. I don't exactly think of it as land, though. We call it country."

Sir Charles laughed pleasantly, and nodded. "There speaks the new world. When it has been enclosed, and worked and farmed for centuries, it's land; when it is open, unbroken, waiting to be possessed, it's country. Not everyone would appreciate the difference." The grey eyes were interested. "Do you intend to farm at Castle Lancing?"

146

Mr Franklin shook his head. "No, I have the garden round my house – that's all the farm I want."

"Ah. But then, you probably still have business interests in the United States."

Mr Franklin looked across the long meadows to the wooded slopes, and smiled. "I doubt if there's much business, and even less interest, in the claim my partner and I left at Tonopah. You could say I'm in retirement, Sir Charles."

"But – you're still a young man." Sir Charles hesitated, obviously reluctant to pry, but equally obviously interested. "I gathered from Soveral that Norfolk is the county of your ancestors – as it is of mine. But don't you think it might pall; it must be very different from what you've been used to?"

"Perhaps that's what I like about it," said Mr Franklin. He realized that Sir Charles was regarding him with an almost benevolent concern. "I don't know, Sir Charles. I've never stayed long in one place, but right now it suits me. That's all I can say."

"Well, I'm glad to hear it. I've no doubt that the last thing you intend is to rusticate. You'll find something in Norfolk to occupy you." He added thoughtfully: "It's what we need, heaven knows. Young blood. Our own fault, of course; we simply haven't made the best of what we have, or moved with the times." He gestured at the meadows. "Not that I'm a farmer – thirty years in the Army teach you precious little about agriculture – but if I were I'd probably be at my wits" end like the rest of them, what with shortage of labour, repairs, and the rest of it. Shooting rents mayn't be much, but they serve one's turn. But here I am, prosing on like some old Farmer Turvey – I do apologize." He laughed easily. "You must be thoroughly bored with hearing the English talk about England. If I were any sort of host I should be asking after your creature comforts, how you've enjoyed your stay . . . oh, good. Last night wasn't too tiring, then?"

"It was the most astonishing night, I think, that I ever spent in my life," said Mr Franklin, and meant it.

"Well, I suppose very few visitors meet the King, far less have the privilege of partnering him at bridge. Rather an ordeal, wasn't it?" Under the smiling regard of the grey eyes, Mr Franklin recalled that his first impression of Sir Charles had been of cool, calculating intelligence. "Anyway, I thought you came through it extremely well. There's no doubt your presence added to his enjoyment of the visit." That was as near as Sir Charles could decently come to saying that

147

Mr Franklin's victory in the final rubber had prevented the visit from being a complete fiasco. "My daughter and I are very grateful to you. I understand his majesty has asked you to Sandringham next month?"

It was casually said, but Mr Franklin understood clearly that Sir Charles had not been asked, and never expected to be. He murmured a vague reply, and they walked towards the house in silence. Once or twice Mr Franklin had the impression that his host was going to say something, but not until they had reached the edge of the gravel sweep did the baronet pause. Then he said:

"I hadn't meant to mention it – wouldn't ordinarily discuss such a thing with a guest – but in the circumstances I feel I must." He was looking ahead towards the house, the spare, rather severe profile turned to the American. "My son tells me – or rather, having heard some talk, I made him tell me – that there was some unpleasantness in the west wing last night. In the first place I must apologize to you, personally, but that's not what I wished to say. I understand that Lord Lacy was behaving improperly towards one of the . . . female guests, and that you knocked him down. No, there is no need to say anything about it, Mr Franklin; it is a distasteful subject, and the last thing I should wish is to cause you the least embarrassment. That you should have been . . . forced to do what you did is distressing enough, and I am more sorry than I can say that you should have had to punish such behaviour under my roof. I can only assure you that I think your conduct was entirely proper."

Mr Franklin received this in silence, and after a moment Sir Charles went on:

"However, as I said, I think I should not have mentioned the incident but for your own circumstances. You are entitled to an explanation. Lord Lacy has already left the house, and it is not my intention that he shall return. I cannot say that that troubles me unduly, but he was a neighbour, one knew him and received him as one does everyone in the county." Mr Franklin rightly translated this as meaning everyone of a suitable social station. "His father and I were good friends, served in the same regiment. You understand." Sir Charles paused. "Young Lacy and my own children have known each other since the nursery." He paused again. "But I am not prepared to excuse improper conduct, especially when it causes distress to guests in my house – and on this occasion of all occasions, when . . ." Sir Charles obviously found it difficult to put into words his emotions at the thought of royalty being made aware of immoral

148

advances and brawling under his roof. On top of the ptarmigan pie it would have been too much. He turned to look Mr Franklin directly in the eye.

"All this, you may think, is of no immediate concern to you. However, as I think you know, Lord Lacy is a close neighbour of yours at Castle Lancing, and I imagine that you will find him an unpleasant one." He shrugged. "He's influential, of course – on the bench, county council, and so forth – and knowing him, I'd expect him to do you any disservice that lies in his power. You have not only knocked him down, you understand, with all that that implies for a young man in his position, you have also been the indirect cause of his exclusion from a house where he had previously been welcomed, if only for his late father's sake. I can't regret that, from my own point of view; on the other hand, I'm deeply distressed at the thought that it might cause you any . . . difficulty. Especially since you are not only a guest in my house, but also in my country. I'm profoundly sorry." He turned away and paced towards the house, with Mr Franklin keeping step. "That's all I wanted to say, but I felt I must say it, to make things perfectly clear."

You've done that, too, thought Mr Franklin. I've not only given Lacy a sore stomach, I've been the indirect cause of scuppering his chances with your daughter – for which you're only half-thankful. You wouldn't regard him as the ideal son-in-law; on the other hand, he would have been a rich catch. Just so. He chose his reply carefully.

"Well, thank you, sir – but don't be distressed on my account. From what I've seen of Lord Lacy, I'd probably have hit him sooner or later, anyway. I'm just sorry to have been the cause of any . . . trouble to you."

"Quite the contrary," said Sir Charles briskly. "We'll say no more about it. At least I hope that you understand that you are always more than welcome here, and that you will regard us not only as neighbours, but as friends."

It was courteously said, and yet Mr Franklin felt that there was more than formal politeness behind it. He doubted if Sir Charles was normally this forthcoming – of course, it might be that English hospitality dictated extra consideration towards a guest who'd been put to the trouble of rough-housing with furious peers in the middle of the night. He found himself wondering, too, if his host was always as stiffly puritanical as he appeared to have been towards Lacy – was the man entirely unaware that his son's friends habitually behaved like excited rabbits on a spring day?

They reached the house as the remaining guests were preparing to depart, and Mr Franklin remarked that he, too, must be on his way. Would he not stay to luncheon? Sir Charles and the children would be delighted; it would be especially pleasant to have him join the family party . . . Mr Franklin, feeling that if he had much more formal courtesy he would be in danger of breaking down and taking it all at its face value, in which case he'd presumably be at Oxton Hall for the rest of his life, was firm. He must be going. In that case, Arthur would drive him over to Castle Lancing . . .

But when Mr Franklin had collected his bag from the beery servitor in the west wing, it was not Arthur, but Peggy, who was waiting with the family's open Humber at the front door, adjusting her motoring veil in the rear-view mirror, and looking thoroughly efficient in dust-coat and gauntlets.

"I suppose you imagine I'm not fit to drive this thing?" she said, noting Mr Franklin's hesitancy; in fact, he had been thinking exactly that. "Well, Arthur has been in every ditch between here and Norwich, so think yourself lucky. Jump in."

She set off with a great clashing of gears and stamping of the clutch, and so far as he could judge, drove extremely well, if rather fast; he was not used to 20 m.p.h. Conversation was impossible above the coughing roar of the 25 h.p. engine, but after a mere twenty minutes of jolting over the Norfolk back roads, with Mr Franklin clutching his hat in one hand and the car-door in the other, they swung through the gate of Lancing Manor, and Peggy yanked on the brake to bring them to a shuddering stop on the gravel before the front door. Jake emerged as from a trap round the side of the house, peered, and then effaced himself with many a backward glance as Mr Franklin handed the driver down and invited her inside.

"I think that performance calls for a cup of tea," he said, and left her removing her veil and bonnet and shaking out her hair as she surveyed the hall. As he brewed the tea he found himself wondering what she thought of the place – until now he had never considered it as something to show off; what did it look like, anyway? For that matter, if you had a lady visitor, did you serve her tea in the hall, or in the drawing-room? Which, if any, *was* the drawing-room? He frowned; better take the ginger biscuits out of their wrapper, anyway, and put them on a plate – and was there milk at the back door?

(There was.) He surveyed the tray critically, used his handkerchief to dust a shaving out of the new and unused tea service, and carried the tray through to the hall. Peggy was examining the *charro* saddle which occupied a corner near the front door; he still hadn't decided where to put it.

"I'm not really . . . prepared for receiving, I'm afraid," he said.

"It's beautiful," she said. "Simply beautiful. Who arranged everything?"

"Well . . . I did, I guess. With the help of a few magazines . . . people from the shops. Milk and sugar?"

"Just milk, thank you." She glanced round at the set of antique chairs against the panelling; the big refectory table and hall-stand; the Chinese rugs on the well-worn but highly-polished floor; the heavy damask curtains which her feminine eye identified as Liberty's; the hunting prints, small and discreet, near the fireplace. Watching her sidelong as he poured the tea, he said, "I hope you like it. If you do, it isn't my fault. I just saw a few things I liked, and told them to go ahead." He handed her cup, and indicated a seat, but Peggy remained standing, looking round her.

"It's remarkable," she said at last. "What a strange man you are. I'm sorry – I didn't mean that to sound rude. But – well . . . it's unusual, isn't it? I mean, here you are, all alone, in this lovely old house, which you've furnished beautifully – you'll let me see the rest of it, won't you? – and yet . . . well, why? I mean," she added hastily, "you don't seem like the kind of person who would . . . well, do all this, unless you had some . . . well, some good reason for doing it."

"Living in the place is a good reason, isn't it?" He offered her a biscuit.

"Yes, for some people." She took a biscuit and grimaced. "The King ought to have stayed here – you have ginger biscuits. No, what I meant was – someone older, who was retiring, or coming to live with his family – but you're not. You don't seem to belong to this . . . quiet life, d'you see what I mean?"

"What kind of life do you think I belong to?" he wondered.

"Oh, something much more active – something busy. Well, look at that saddle – or the spurs you gave Mrs Keppel. That's the sort of thing I mean – they suit you much better than Chinese rugs."

"Oh? I thought I looked pretty good standing on a Chinese rug."

Peggy laughed. "You know what I mean! You're an out-of-doors man – or a business man, if you like. I mean, if you were living

151

in Town, and this was a country retreat, that would be perfectly understandable. But you haven't got a place in Town, have you? I asked Soveral, you know, and he said you hadn't . . ."

"Well, if that's what he said, you can be sure it's correct. I doubt if that gentleman ever gets things wrong."

"And he said you were not in business, or had any connections in the City – or anything at all. He just didn't know anything about you; nor did anyone else. Well," said Peggy firmly, "that won't do. You can't go about being so mysterious, when everyone wants to know about you. Now can you?"

"I doubt," said Mr Franklin, "if everyone wants to know about me."

"They do, though. Everyone at Oxton kept asking me who you were, and where you came from, and what you were doing here. So I said: 'Why don't you ask him – if it's any of your business", which put them into a huff, naturally."

"Naturally. Some more tea. I'd offer you another ginger biscuit, but I gather you don't go for them. Well, no one came and asked me, so they can't have been all that curious, can they?"

"Oh, stuff!" said Peggy. "I'm curious – as you know perfectly well. No, I'm not, either. Curiosity's vulgar. But I am interested, you know."

Mr Franklin looked at the beautiful, smiling face under its Titian halo as he handed back her cup. "Well, I'm flattered. But I'm not really interesting at all, I'm afraid. Just an ordinary man, doing something quite unremarkable. That's the strange part of it, I guess. If I'd come here making a big noise, doing all sorts of – well, the kinds of things American visitors do, I guess – you know, trying to buy the Houses of Parliament, or the fishing rights on the Thames . . . everyone would say, 'Oh, another mad Yankee', and lose interest – "

"It's not ordinary and unremarkable to pinch people's foxes, and have the King on the verge of apoplexy with the way you play bridge, or have fights in the middle of the night in country houses," said Peggy calmly, looking at him over her cup.

"Oh, you heard about that?"

"Somewhat. Arthur told me. You knocked Frank Lacy down – which you'd been itching to do all day, of course. Nothing wrong with that – although I think you might have chosen a better excuse than Poppy Davenport."

Mr Franklin stirred his tea for a moment. "The only excuse I had

152

was that Lord Lacy came at me like a wounded buffalo," he said. "There was no matter of choice."

"Oh? Arthur seemed to think you were protecting a damsel in distress. Not that I'd describe Poppy as a damsel, exactly, and if she was distressed I imagine it was entirely her own fault. It usually is. She manages to attract a good deal of attention – or notoriety might be a better word."

Mr Franklin felt irritated; cross-examination he could take, placidly, but not when it was accompanied by innuendo. But he said easily:

"I'm not really concerned with Poppy, or with any of the peculiar circle she moves in. And I certainly wouldn't want to protect any of them – I doubt if they need it, or it would do them any good. My only regret about last night is that I gather – from your father – that it's led to an estrangement between him and Lord Lacy. That's a pity – but it wasn't really my fault."

"Oh, come off it! You don't need to be so coy, you know." He looked up in surprise; she was laughing, but the tiny sneer which he had noticed the previous evening was now quite marked. "Poppy was in your room, after all."

"Uninvited – and by mistake. I gather your brother's playful friend Jeremy had changed the cards on the doors. I was putting her out, within half a minute of her arrival, when your friend Lacy came on the scene, and misunderstood what was happening." He paused. "That was all. On the whole, it really seems to me that if anyone has a right to be offended, it's me – but then, I'm not conversant with English country-house manners and customs. Anyway, it doesn't matter."

There was a strained pause, and then Peggy put down her cup and observed: "I could break Arthur's blasted neck!"

"I beg your pardon?"

"Oh, he and his giggling little friends – oafs like Jeremy who think it's just splendid to cause trouble, and little tarts like Poppy who just revel in that sort of thing. You can guess what they make out of it – all the sniggering and sly glances, and whispering: 'I say, did you hear about Poppy and the American, and Frank walked in and caught them? Such a lark!' Ugh! They make me sick!" She looked at Mr Franklin. "But it wasn't like that, was it?"

"It was exactly as I've told you."

I know. I'm awfully sorry. I don't know what you must think . . ." She smiled quickly, and held out a hand to him. "And when I heard

153

that that little beast Poppy had been in the thick of it . . . oh, they make me so tired! Don't think too badly of us."

Mr Franklin took her hand automatically. "I don't think badly – I mean, it's none of my business. I . . . I'm just sorry if it's caused any trouble." He hesitated. "I got the impression from your father that Lacy and you . . . well, that it might have spoiled things . . . "

"There wasn't all that much to spoil," said Peggy carelessly. "Oh, father may have thought there was. Maybe he hoped that Frank and I . . . in fact, I know he did. But . . ." she shrugged. "Oh, Frank's all right, in an ape-like sort of way – but I've never cared for him all that much. Certainly not enough to marry him. So you haven't done me a bad turn, you see." She regarded him calmly. "What's the matter?"

"I'm not quite sure. It's just . . . well, you'll probably think me no end of a stuffed-shirt, but . . . well, the kind of conversation we've just had – I find it sort of . . . unusual."

"Young ladies didn't ought to know about such things – or talk about them?" Amusement sounded in her voice.

"I'm not used to England, I guess. It's still a little strange."

"Our loose ways distress you?" The little sneer was evident again. "I'm not surprised. Don't judge us all by Poppy and Jeremy and Frank Lacy – oh, and Arthur. They're a pretty disky lot – oh, not Arthur, really; he's not a bad sort. A bit of an ass, but . . ." Peggy shrugged. "And I'm sorry if I seemed to be prying – about last night, I mean. But I'm glad I did; it clears the air, don't you think?"

Quite illogically, and for no good reason except that this unusually beautiful girl was standing in front of him, in the dim quiet of his hall, Mr Franklin felt a strong urge to kiss her. It shocked him, momentarily, but once the shock had passed he found that the urge was still there. There was no particular expression in her eyes, but the angelic face was smiling, in the most friendly way, and he had a vague sense that she was waiting for something. It couldn't be that, though; she was a lady, his hostess of the previous evening, who had just driven him home, and graciously accepted tea in his bachelor establishment – he wondered for a moment about the propriety of that, and decided it must be all right, or she wouldn't have done it. He felt uncomfortable about her reference to the Poppy incident – but, after all, she'd been perfectly right to want to know the truth of it, since she was the lady of Oxton Hall, and he'd been relieved to be able to explain it to her. She was uncommonly pretty, though, and . . .

"You said you'd like to see the rest of the house?" he said suddenly.

"If you don't mind," said Peggy. "And I'm still curious – oh, no, we agreed interested was the word, didn't we? – about its owner. You can't put me off the track by talking about last night, you know. Tell me as we go round."

This proved impossible, of course; possibly the woman exists who can listen to someone's life story when there is a newly-furnished house to be examined at the same time, but probably not. Peggy was all agog at Lancing Manor, admiring fittings, decoration, and furniture to the point where Mr Franklin became quite proud of it, and wondered if by some freak of chance he possessed that mysterious thing known as good taste; he was also fairly silent because he knew that he was going to satisfy her curiosity, and since this was against his rather retiring nature, he was not certain how he was going to go about it. He had withstood inquiry pretty well, up to now, even Thornhill's, but it would have been rude to be reticent with this girl; the sense of intimacy that he had felt sitting beside her at dinner the previous night, the shared feeling of being on her side and her father's during the ordeal of the royal visit, the fact that he had, in a curious way, helped to make the visit a success – all that combined to make him feel more at ease in her company than he had felt with anyone since he came to England. Even Pip, in their brief passage of physical love, hadn't been as close as this. She had been different – cheerful, charming, animal, obvious, and simply out to enjoy herself; Peggy was – well, she was a lady, for one thing, and on quite a different plane. (It did not occur to Mr Franklin that in assuming the surroundings, dress, and to some extent the ways of his new environment, he might also have assumed some of its social standards.) Anyway, he knew that he could talk to her as he would not – could not – have talked to Pip.

So when she had seen the house, and they had returned to the hall, and she had pointed to the *charro* saddle and said: "Now tell me, what the man who owns *that*, and can't bear to hide it away out of sight, is doing in this cosy little nook?" he did not laugh. She walked across to kneel in the window-seat beside the saddle, looking out across the drive at the chestnuts dripping in the light rain that had begun to fall; Mr Franklin studied the back of her auburn head and the graceful figure with its arms resting on the sill, and said:

"It's not easy to explain. You see, I know what I'm doing – but I'm not so sure I understand why I'm doing it. Does that make any sense?"

"It may. What *are* you doing?"

"Well, I'm here – living here, but I'm not altogether sure why. My people left this very place – not this house, but this village – more than two centuries ago. Like an awful lot of Americans; but most of us don't know all that much, I suppose, about where we came from; my family, by chance, handed it down: Castle Lancing, in Norfolk County." Peggy caught herself smiling in the window-pane at the odd-sounding American phrase: Norfolk County. "My father talked a lot about England; he was a country schoolmaster, but he was the most educated man, in his own way, that you ever saw. When he talked about a thing – say, about England – it wasn't about how many tons of coal or how many acres under cultivation or what the climate was like – it was about Bosworth Field and the old stories of King Arthur and Wordsworth's poem about daffodils, until you could almost see it all in your imagination. He'd never been here, of course – except, as he used to say, 'in his mind's ship'. I guessed he loved it – or what he thought was it. So I suppose that's what started it; I hoped I'd come home, some day."

"Home?" Peggy frowned. "But home is where you're born – at least the country you're born in."

"Maybe, if you're born *here*. But when you spend your childhood in half a dozen different states, it's not easy to say which is home. I used to see people, in Texas and California, who were settled; the homes they were in were their grandparents" houses; their people had broken the land maybe a hundred years ago. Even when I was quite small, I used to envy them: they had a place to go back to. I'd never stayed in one place more than a few months at a time – then, just when I was getting used to a bed or a chair and a picture on the wall, Dad would move on to another school. It seems, after my mother died, when I was about three years old, he just couldn't bear to settle in one place any more. So he kept moving on . . . and of course I went along. He was still moving, the day he died. We were on the road out of a little place in North Texas – I don't even remember its name – and we were in a horse and buggy. I was driving; I was fourteen. All of a sudden he said: 'Pull up, son', so I pulled up, and he sat, and took off his hat, and fetched two or three deep breaths, and looked at his hands, and said: 'I'll be leaving now, Mark'. Then he closed his eyes and he was dead, with his hat still in his hands."

Peggy said nothing, and after a moment Mr Franklin went on.

"In a way, *he* was the last home I had – wherever he was. Since then, I've been on my own. And I guess the nearest thing I've had to a home has been that old saddle – or a blanket, or a pair of boots. Don't misunderstand me; when I say that, I'm not feeling sorry for myself. There's a lot of advantage to not having a home, except where you hang your hat. No ties, no responsibilities, no crops to gather, no bills to pay, no neighbours to fuss you, no worries about the roof letting in. If you don't like a place, you move on. That's what I did, for ten years."

He paused so long that she turned to look at him, and said: "And then you wanted to settle down?"

He shook his head, smiling. "No, then this old sourdough and I, an old miner called Davis that I'd teamed up with, we struck a line of luck. I'd prospected a little, not much, just paying my way, but old Davis had been in on some of the biggest strikes there were: Comstock, Yukon, Australia. He wasn't a careful man, though – hit paydirt, go on the spree, look for another lode: that was his mark." Mr Franklin laughed quietly. "He was an old reprobate, but I liked him. Maybe I sort of adopted him, having been left an orphan myself; I couldn't say he was a second father to me. My father was everything that old Davis wasn't: decent, well-read, kind, careful. He was all wool and a yard wide, was Dad. Davis – well, he only had one virtue. No, two, for he could smell silver ten miles away. But the great thing about him was, if you were his partner, he'd share his last drop of sweat with you. Fifty-fifty Davis, they used to call him. God, but he smelled something awful – I'm sorry, that's rather an indelicate thing to say."

"Go on", smiled Peggy. "I rather like the sound of your old reprobate."

"Well, the sound of him is perhaps the best part. You sure wouldn't have liked the sight or scent. Anyway, we went to Tonopah together – it's a place you've never heard of, in Nevada. They mine silver in a big way there, nowadays; we went there because there was news of a strike, although Davis wasn't too keen, at first. He was pretty old, and used up, and tired, and he reckoned we'd never raise the grubstake. But we got in a poker game, with some fellows we knew – a pretty rough crowd – and I struck some fair hands, and the long and short of it was we cleaned up enough to get us to the diggings. The fellows in the game laughed at us, and called Davis an old gopher –

that's a burrowing animal out there – and said he'd just be digging his own grave, and that made him mad, and he vowed he'd strike it rich if it was the last thing he did. So the two of us got a mule, and grub, and shovels, and we went to Tonopah.

"We got a claim, and we worked it – and nothing. So we worked another – and nothing. Oh, some were taking plenty out, but not us. We were down to the bare bones, and Davis was sick, and I thought we ought to quit. But no, he had the silver fever on him now, good and proper. 'Let me get on my feet again and take a sniff at the gravel', he used to say; he was croaking under his blanket and shivering so hard his bones rattled. 'I know just where to look', he would say. 'These other dummies don't.' Well, I humoured him along, and when he got better – or rather, less ill – he insisted we dig in the black rock along a place called North Slide. Everyone knew there was nothing there; the claims office almost died laughing when we staked a section. I guessed the old man's mind had given out at last, but I went along, and we registered our forty feet apiece, and then we grubbed away at rock and mud for six weeks, and turned up nothing but a quarter-dollar someone had dropped. And even it was counterfeit.

" 'Davis', I said, 'We're crazy. I'm going to call it a day'. 'Go on, then, quit", said he. 'I'll keep it all to myself, then you'll laugh the t'other side of your face. Young pup, you think it grows on trees?' So I said all right, I'd stick it another couple of days, and we plugged on through the black rock and came on this sticky blue clay that messed up our cradles and stuck to our boots and picks so hard you could barely move around. Filthy stuff, I'd never seen anything like it; neither had Davis, even." Mr Franklin shook his head. "No wonder. It was eighty per cent. pure silver. And the other twenty per cent. was pure gold."

Peggy gasped, her eyes shining, and automatically clapped her hands. "How wonderful! Oh, what a marvellous moment! What did you say? What did he say? Oh, I bet you wanted to dance all over it!"

"I'm afraid not. It doesn't happen like that. We didn't think it was anything, you see; old Davis only had it assayed because he wasn't sure what it was. Then, when the assayers told us that it was the richest reef since the Ophir Mine at Comstock – well, then old Davis just said: 'Oh, my God! We got a whole parcel o' trouble here, Mark – a whole parcel o' trouble'. "

"Whatever did he mean?"

"Well, finding a lode is one thing – getting it out, smelting, stamp-milling, that's another. We hadn't a hope of keeping it dark – especially after Davis insisted on going on the spree with our first big consignment." Mr Franklin smiled ruefully. "He blew most of it inside a week – and of course word got out, and suddenly there were more vultures around than you ever saw. Slickers trying to buy us out, big mining concerns trying to horn in – and they weren't the worst of it." He thought of that night at the Bella Union, sitting with his Remingtons, waiting for the Kid. "Yes – it was trouble. But we got it out, all we wanted. Half a hillside, at more than four thousand dollars a ton. It took us the best part of four years, because we did it all ourselves – just Davis and me. The worst of it was looking after those shipments of silver, getting them to the bank, not daring to go to sleep, hardly, knowing the kind of scalpers who were ready to grab it if you batted an eye. But in the end – there it was. All of it. And old Davis was dead three weeks later, of delirium tremens, mostly."

A sudden gust of rain hit the panes, and Peggy shivered. Mr Franklin looked out at the wet garden, toying with his watch-chain; she wondered if he was seeing old Davis dying, and pictured to herself a funeral in some squalid field outside a mining-town; she had no idea what it could have been like, and envisaged men with lamps in their hats and pick-axes standing round an open grave into which a solid silver coffin was being lowered, while Mr Franklin stood by in his tweeds. But of course she knew it would look nothing like that.

"I'm sorry," she said. "The poor old man – what awful luck! To find a fortune, and then . . . " She shrugged and made a little gesture with her hands.

"He wouldn't want you to feel sorry for him. He had four years of knowing he'd hit the big bonanza – and three weeks of living it up, in his own style, and that made him happy. It meant more to him to swagger around town, sticking his head into each saloon and hollering: 'The drinks are on Davis!', until the whole community was swilling it down at his expense, and he was buying cigars for everyone he met, and throwing money from his hotel window, and bathing in champagne – I've seen him do that, in a hip-bath in the middle of the biggest saloon in the place, with everyone curling up with laughter – that was all he wanted. To be the man who'd made the big strike. It wasn't the money, or any idea of buying things with it, or saving; no, he just wanted *to have done* it, after a lifetime grubbing round the hills. Oh, he died happy, all right. And do you know what his will said? He'd made one, leaving a bar of silver to every saloon in town, to be drunk up by the customers. And for the rest it just said: 'To my partner, Mark Franklin, I leave my hurricane lamp and all my goods'. The 'goods' was all the silver that had been in his share of the mine."

"His lamp? What a strange thing to leave. Why did he do that?"

"He valued that lamp; he'd had it a long time."

"That must be a rather precious possession, I should think," said Peggy.

"I haven't got it," said Mr Franklin. "I gave it to the barkeep at the Bella Union – that was Davis's favourite watering-hole – so that he could hang it up over the main bar, between the chandeliers, and keep it lighted, day and night."

"As a memorial, you mean? That was a jolly good idea," said Peggy warmly. "I should think your old friend would have liked that. I hope the . . . barkeep, did you call him? I hope he keeps it lit."

"The day he doesn't, he loses the Bella Union," said Mr Franklin. "I gave him the place on that condition."

Peggy caught her breath. Something in the casual, matter-of-fact tone, startled her, but she said nothing for a moment, and then asked: "And what did you do after that?"

"Well, nothing much, for a while. There was no point in going on mining, was there, or working around the way I had done? When people strike it rich, what do they do? Go home – but I didn't have one. I knew the West, but I didn't want to buy a spread, or settle there; I didn't know the East. And yet, I found I was tired of being on the move – where was there to move to? What was there to move for? It was all I had ever done, but you know, Peggy – " it was the first time he had used her name in a conversational way, she reflected "– unless you have to move from necessity, to work or to live – why, you find you don't want to move at all. If you have the means to make a home, to settle, then that's what you feel you should do. It was then I thought of England. Of Norfolk, and Castle Lancing. At first I thought I would just visit; then, in London, I went to a real estate man, and there was this house – " he waved a hand at his surroundings " – and it seemed somehow that it had been waiting. So I bought it. And here I am."

Peggy sat thoughtfully, and then shook her head. "And you think that's an ordinary story? I think it's the most exciting thing I've ever heard – and the strangest, too. But . . . wasn't there anyone – no

160

relatives, no friends. No one to . . . well, share your fortune? Most people have *someone*, you know?"

"Not me." He sighed gently. "I don't seem to make friends easily. Perhaps it comes from being alone a long time – and then, after the strike – it's a shocking thing to say, but you get wary, you know. There are so many free-loaders and bar-flies – oh, and some of them look like anything but! Anyway, you tend to be suspicious. That was another reason for coming to England, I think. Here I could be quiet, and no one would know anything about me, or where I came from. And I'll say this for Castle Lancing – they've been very polite, and let me alone. They think I'm an odd fish, I suppose, but we get along just fine. At a distance, anyway. But, as I said, I don't make friends easily."

"That's nonsense! Of course you do!" Peggy stood up, smiling at him. "You're one of the friendliest people I've met! Why, here we are – yesterday we hadn't even met, and today it's as though I'd known you for ages!"

"Maybe it just seems like a long time," he smiled. "It's been a pretty busy twenty-four hours. First the fox, and then the King – and last night wasn't any too easy for you and your father, I know. But I guess the King went away happy, didn't he?"

"Oh, I hope so! He's a sickening old pest, and I wish he'd never come – but naturally I hope he isn't going to go round the country saying how ghastly the Claytons are – when I saw him moping over that awful ptarmigan pie I wanted to curl up and die! Do you really think it went off well, though? I'd like to think it wasn't too bad, for Daddy's sake. He was awfully strung up about it all, poor old dear."

"Not this morning, he wasn't," said Mr Franklin reassuringly. "If ever there was a man with a load off his mind it was Sir Charles Clayton, Esquire."

"Not esquire, you goose! He's a baronet – so he can't be an esquire, too. Oh, I must tell him – he'll love it. Sir Charles Clayton, Esquire. Now, if you'd said that to the King . . . " She laughed outright. "I wonder if he'd have been pleased or shocked? That's the trouble with the old bore . . . you never can tell. But he likes you. No, he really does. Mrs Keppel said this morning that she couldn't remember him taking to anyone so easily. That's why he's asked you to Sandringham." She regarded him gravely. "That's rather a score for you, you know. Only very special people are asked there. It could mean a great deal to you."

161

Mr Franklin frowned. "I don't know about that. Oh, I know it's a great honour – and that's kind of uncomfortable, when I think about it – but it's not the sort of thing I want, exactly . . . "

"Not want? Good lord, listen to the man. Isn't Kingie good enough for you, then?"

"Of course he is – I didn't mean that at all," exclaimed Mr Franklin hastily. "It's just – well, he's the King, isn't he? And . . . I don't mean to sound ungrateful, because you and your father couldn't have been kinder – but last night . . . the dinner, and bridge, and everyone being so genteel around him. Well – it isn't my style. I don't feel I fit in, exactly."

"Oh, you fit. Exactly," said Peggy, regarding him with wry amusement. "Whether you like it or not. If the King likes you – then you're somebody, with a capital S. Heavens, when I think of the people I know, who'd give their right arm for the chance!"

"The chance of what?"

"Oh, really!" The little sneer was back again. "The chance to be known in Society – really known! To be invited to Sandringham, to be talked about as the King's bridge partner – "

"But I can't even *play* bridge!"

"To be one of the inner circle, a friend of Mrs Keppel's, the man who went six hearts against the Blue Monkey, and beat him, who pinched a fox under the King's nose, and made him laugh – "

"I didn't pinch the fox. And I didn't even know it *was* the King."

"All the better, then." She put her head on one side, as though examining him. "Are you really as innocent as you make out? I mean, don't you know that after this people will talk about you, and want to know who the mysterious handsome American millionaire is, and send him invitations, and look for his picture in the Society papers, and . . . and . . . all that sort of thing? Heavens above, why, what you've been telling me, about you making a fortune as a miner – "

"I shouldn't have said that. That was foolishness . . ."

"Well, I hope you don't think it was foolish to tell me! I'm not going to go babbling it about – but if you think that'll stop people from finding out, you've got another think coming. You can be in the social swim – that's what I mean. In fact, you're going to find it very difficult not to be."

"Well, I don't want to be," said Mr Franklin firmly.

"That's too bad," said Peggy, and the Botticelli mouth curled a little at the corner. "Would it surprise you to know that I expect a sudden rush of invitations in the next few weeks – as the lady who was the first hostess to have the newcomer at her dinner table?"

"You don't mean that!"

"Don't I, though?" Her laugh sounded hard in his ears. "You don't know how things work, do you? It's a small world, and it's always eager for novelties. Of course, one doesn't know how long you'll last – but while you do, you'll find that you're quite a focus of attention." She watched him with interest. "Does that disturb you?"

"It hadn't occurred to me. Well, I'm afraid that your . . . people, or Society, or whatever you call 'em, are going to be disappointed. I'm not – that kind."

"If they suspect that, it'll probably intrigue them all the more," said Peggy drily, and then her expression softened into a smile. "Anyway, I hope you don't find it all too much of a bore, or that people make themselves too much of a nuisance." She laid a hand on his arm and said brightly: "If it gets too much, you can always come and take refuge at Oxton Hall. I promise we shan't put you in the west wing next time."

"I might just do that, if you'll have me."

"Then we're not one of the invitations you're determined to refuse?"

"You know darned well you're not," laughed Mr Franklin, and in that moment he was conscious that her hand was still resting on his sleeve, and there was an odd look in her eyes that reminded him of the urge to kiss her, and it seemed the most natural thing in the world to put his hands on either side of her waist, and when she didn't move, it was equally natural to draw her to him and kiss her indeed, gently at first, and then rather more firmly, until her mouth opened just a little under his. That was all; she neither returned his kiss nor tried to move away, and again it seemed only reasonable to put his arms round her to kiss her with greater intensity, and again she accepted it but did not respond one way or the other.

Finally, with natural curiosity, he desisted, to see how she was taking it; her eyes were half-closed, and there was the little smile at the corner of her mouth, that smile which seemed so out of place in the angelic perfection of her face, and yet added to its attraction.

"Don't do that too often," she said quietly. "Or you'll find yourself married before you know it." She kissed him lightly on the lips and moved away, touching a hand to her hair. "I really must be getting back – oh, gosh, look at the car! The seats will be soaking wet! What a goose I am! I never thought about the rain – "

Which changed the subject very neatly: Mr Franklin hastened to get a towel, and mopped the driver's seat while she replaced her hat and veil; fortunately the rain had stopped, and when he had got the seat reasonably dry he handed her up,and received instructions on how to crank the starting-handle to set her on her way. He swung vigorously, the engine coughed and roared at the third attempt, and he was moving round to express his thanks for his visit to Oxton Hall when she called: "Come to lunch tomorrow!" and with a wave was chugging down the drive.

Mr Franklin watched her out of sight, and then went back indoors, where he stood for several minutes, lost in thought. Very pretty little lady, he said to himself. Quite a straight edge to her, underneath, but bright, and lively, and capable – and pretty. No denying that. Graceful and cool and collected; a lot of character. A lady, of course. Very pretty.

Peggy Clayton drove back from Castle Lancing as quickly and expertly as she had come, the Humber roaring round the bends and sending up showers from the puddles which filled the ruts after the rain. Once she was held up by a herd of cattle crossing the road, mooing and lumbering round the car, to the alarm of the elderly cow-whacker, who was used to motorists fretting and swearing, and females who became agitated when cows approached. But the smart young lady was not in the least impatient or perturbed; in fact, when he touched his hat, she smiled at him most pleasantly before driving away.

9

Mr Franklin discovered that he must change his way of life. The realization began to dawn on the following evening, when on returning from Oxton Hall where he had lunched in accordance with Peggy's invitation, he found Jake in a state of high excitement. Three parties, he was told, had called during the afternoon, and in Mr Franklin's absence, had left cards; Jake indicated with an earth-grimed finger the three little rectangles of pasteboard lying on the stone ledge under the bell.

"There wasn't no'un to take 'em, 'cept me – an' they didn't 'alf fancy givin' me cards. 'Put 'em on there, then' says I, an' they didn't like it, but they 'ad to," Jake said smugly, while Mr Franklin examined the cards – Sir Peter Stringer, Major Aldridge, and a Mr Plowright. Who the devil were they? He had a vague notion that Stringer might be the name of the stout huntsman whom he had privately named "Colonel Dammit"; possibly the others had been among the hunt also. Peggy had been right, then; he was being sought after already. He sighed. But what to do? He had no notion of card etiquette, or what notice, if any, he should take of these evidences that he had been called upon. He sought out Thornhill, and was enlightened.

"The neighbourhood is aware of your existence, and that your station in life is above the untouchable. These three gentlemen, possibly accompanied by the frightful women they are married to, have called to pay their respects, and on finding you not at home, have left cards, to show that they've been – and that if anyone has plundered the house in your absence, it wasn't them."

"What should I do?"

"Nothing. Unless you feel like fleeing the country. I should, if I thought there was the remotest chance of meeting Mrs Aldridge."

"You mean they'll come back?"

"Certainly. They want to know you – and to see what your furniture's like, and your wallpaper, and to find out if you have three mad mistresses locked in the attic. Run the rule over you; see if you're fit to be received in society at large." Thornhill's spectacles took on an evil glint. "This is what comes of going six hearts before the face of kings, and roaring about like a social lion."

"I did precious little roaring," said Mr Franklin. "Look here, though, Thornhill – what do they expect of me?"

"When they call on you? Well, to be received, of course – unless your servants tell them you're 'not at home', in which case – "

"Dammit, I don't have servants."

"Neither you do. Well, in that case, you have the delightful opportunity of opening the door yourself and saying that you're not at home. But if you invite them in – which in my view would be extremely rash – then you must regale them with afternoon tea, thinly-sliced bread and butter, cucumber sandwiches, scones, toasted tea-cake, Dundee cake, jam tarts, and conversation. Have some of this gingerbread and a glass of beer," added Thornhill hospitably, thrusting the elements of his evening snack through the litter of his desk. Mr Franklin sat down abruptly.

"The devil you say! But I . . . " It came home to him that he was not equipped to offer afternoon tea, or any other social entertainment, to visitors. It had been different with Peggy, but people who called formally, leaving cards . . . He looked round the cosy squalor of Thornhill's room, with its beer-bottle paperweights, scorched hearth-rug, litter of paper, old clothes, and undusted furniture.

"What," he asked, "do you do when people call?"

"They don't," said Thornhill contentedly, chewing gingerbread. "One couple did, when I first came here, but they took one look at this – " he waved at the scholarly mess around him. "That sickened them. They realised old Thornhill was beyond the pale – all the more so because I ought to have known better, and didn't. No good, Franklin. I ought to employ a housekeeper, at least, and dress decently, and have some yokel keeping my garden in order, and ride to hounds, and pay calls, and be a willing guest at their foul dinner-parties. But I don't and won't. Academic riff-raff, that's what I am, so they let me alone, thank God. Look, I wish you'd have some gingerbread – made it myself, and I can't stand the taste of the bloody stuff. Oh, well, if you won't, you won't." He sighed and took another piece. "But they won't let you get away with my sort of backsliding – not now that you've mingled with the topmost drawer." He wagged his head with morbid satisfaction.

How right he was Mr Franklin discovered a few afternoons later when Sir Peter and Lady Stringer descended on him. He was not entirely unready; afternoon tea, prepared by Mrs Laker, had been waiting under a cloth in the kitchen every day, with the result that on three successive afternoons Jake had been called in to dispose of platefuls of cucumber and tinned crab sandwiches, to the disturbance of his internal economy. On the fourth afternoon, however, the Stringers arrived, and Mr Franklin was able to entertain them suitably. True, there were minor embarrassments; he was helping Jake to clear a blocked drain when they arrived, and on hearing the front bell he thoughtlessly went round to see who was there, and so received his visitors in his shirt-sleeves, befouled to the elbows. Later, having made a hasty toilet, he was listening politely to Lady Stringer's small talk when he realized that he was still wearing his wellington boots. And finally, when it came time for him to bear in the tea, he discovered that he had brewed the pot without any tea-leaves in it.

However, the Stringers appeared to notice none of these things, and were affability itself. They invited him to dine, Sir Peter (who was, in fact, Colonel Dammit), asked him over to shoot, and towards the end of their call Lady Stringer, out of pure kindness for this strange American who was so obviously out of his depth, observed casually: "I believe you have not engaged any servants yet, Mr Franklin? But of course you have been fully occupied settling in. Still, you will want to have made your arrangements before you go to Sandringham; please do let us know if we can be of any help."

The implications of this gave Mr Franklin food for thought. He had realized that at Oxton Hall the other older guests had brought their own servants with them; it now dawned on him that if he was going to visit the King, he would have to take a valet. But he didn't want a valet; he wouldn't know what to do with one. He could hire one, no doubt – there flashed across his mind the memory of the solid, dependable Thomas Samson, who had outfitted him in London. But Samson would only be interested in permanent employment – that wouldn't do, then. Or would it? After all, if people like the Stringers were going to call on him, he ought to have someone opening doors and carrying in tea-trays ... oh, lord, was he being entrapped in their ridiculous social customs already? At that, it would be convenient to have someone keeping house ... why not Samson, if he was available? He'd liked the man, and they'd got on. And he couldn't entertain the idea of some motherly old housekeeper; it would have to be a man or nobody.

167

He brooded over the matter that evening, and other trains of thought developed. The result was that on the following morning he went into Norwich, and visited the town's largest bookshop, where he scouted the shelves in the furtive manner of a visitor to Paris buying pornography, and emerged with a small volume entitled *A Guide to Behaviour and Etiquette in Polite Society*, purportedly written by a Member of the Nobility. Despising himself, but driven by necessity, he took it home to study, and its effect on him was much the same as a nervous hypochondriac experiences on reading a medical text-book.

A brief survey of the book convinced him that it was impossible for any normal human being to endure for five minutes in the fashionable world without committing some gross blunder of protocol which would ensure his ostracism for ever. He had always supposed that his own behaviour was at least tolerable, and he had visited Oxton Hall in the belief that if a man conducted himself naturally and watched his table manners – and Mr Franklin's, instilled in innumerable frontier parlours, would have done credit to a Duke – he could rub by. Not so, according to the Member of the Nobility. He must know how to manage his hat and stick, and what to do with them when visiting a lady; he must know the ritual of card-leaving (Mr Franklin read, with bated breath, that as a foreigner – he was, he supposed, a foreigner – he should signify the fact by folding over one end of his cards); he must know all forms of style and address and precedence, in case he made the ridiculous error of supposing that a doctor of divinity was superior to an army officer of field rank; he must know how to reply to a christening invitation from a baronet's wife, how to address an unmarried lady if he met her in the street with a married lady to whom he hadn't been introduced, at what hours to ride in the Park (wherever the Park was), how to dress for a water-party (a water-party?), how to take leave after luncheon – it was all there, with awful warnings against the solecism of tipping servants at a hunt ball, or smoking while talking to a lady in public, or pronouncing Marjoribanks or Strachan or Ruthven the wrong way; there was even a whole chapter on when and when not to shake hands . . . modes of address, rules even for bowing, walking, riding, and driving . . . "without the strict rules which etiquette imposes, it would be impossible for society to function satisfactorily; no matter what the social stratum, received manners and forms of address and behaviour are absolutely essential . . ."

"Who isn't a lady? Why, goddamn you, you greasy, stinkin' old buzzard, I'll larn you whether I'm a lady or not!" He could hear the shrill voice of the dance-hall girl at Fanny Porter's in Forth Worth, standing there, brassy-haired and strident, her tawdry red satin dress slipping off one shoulder, the paint streaked on her haggard face. "You ain't got a nickel's worth of manners, you lousy old drunk!" And Davis, fuming with liquor and stagger-ing on the stairs, pushing aside Franklin's restraining hand. "I ain't drunk, I ain't stinkin', an' my manners is a dam sight too good for any two-bit hoor! So now! Manners, by Christ! You talk about manners, you poxed-up slut? Go get yourself an Injun, or a Mexican! Don't talk to me!" The girl screaming and hurling a bottle, old Davis tumbling downstairs, bawling, the bouncers moving in and the fight breaking out, the chairs flying, the ornate glass window shattering, himself wrestling with an infuriated miner and going down in the wreckage of the chuckaluck cage, the shrieks and oaths and turmoil – and somehow he was lying half-stunned behind the wreckage of the bar, and the brassy-haired girl was crouching on hands and knees close by, her dress half off and one breast hanging out, mopping her nose and whimpering: "He said I wasn't a lady! Dirty ole bastard!" Her voice rising to a shrill wail. "I am – I am too a lady! I was brought up good – you know I was brought up good, don't you, mister? I got good manners . . . " The wail dying to a drunken sob. " . . . sure I got good manners, huh?" The smell of cheap liquor and cheap scent. "Say, you look like a nice boy . . . a real gentleman – you got good manners, huh? Know how to treat a lady, darlin', won' you treat me . . . ? All right, goddamn you, you're so choosy, go an' git –." For what we are about to receive may the Lord make us truly thankful sit up straight Mark elbows off the table there's a good boy . . . manners maketh man . . . Sundance Harry Longbaugh bowing and pulling back the chair for Etta Place, pretty little Etta the schoolmarm, with her neat dark hair and shy smile, raising her coffee-cup with the finger daintily crooked . . . grimy hands reaching into the communal stew-pot at Hole-in-the-Wall . . . "I am too a lady! I got good manners! . . . "

Mr Franklin sighed and continued to read at random . . . "It would be the height of bad *ton* not to receive callers on an 'at home' day . . . after coffee has been served the gentleman highest in rank shall lead the way to the drawing-room . . . a gentleman should never walk arm-in-arm with a lady out of doors unless she is of an age to require support . . . a young lady may drive a motor-car in the afternoon, but

169

should not drive with a gentleman unless accompanied by a married lady or suitable chaperone . . ."

Mr Franklin muttered an exclamation familiar to the Bella Union saloon, but seldom heard in polite drawing-rooms, and thrust the book aside. What did such rubbish have to do with him? And who minded it? Peggy had driven alone with him, and no one so far as he could see had given a damn about precedence at Oxton Hall – the King always went first and that was that. But one passage in the Member of Nobility's work stuck in his mind: ". . . on visiting a country house, a gentleman shall be accompanied by his manservant; if he does not have one, his host may place one at his disposal, which is not an arrangement favoured in polite circles . . ." If he was going to Sandringham, he'd have to have a man, however much his nature revolted at the idea. And afterwards . . . was it so foolish, the idea of having someone around to run the place, look after things?

On the spur of the moment he sat down and wrote a letter to the austere Mr Pride, of the London domestic agency, with the result that a bare week later the square sturdy figure of Thomas Samson walked up the gravel drive of Lancing Manor, bowler hat on head and well-worn suitcase in hand, and Mr Franklin, observing his approach from an upstairs window, felt a profound relief mingled with a vague regret, as though some virtue had passed away from him. And why should he feel that, the intangible sense of loss, of abandoning something, of surrender almost? It was almost momentary and it passed with Samson's firm handshake, and the friendly steady look in the blue eyes as he returned Mr Franklin's greeting and then glanced round the hall and stairway of the house. "Very pleasant, sir, if I may say so. Shall I prepare some tea?"

The relief was remarkable, and there was no doubt that in the next few weeks life became much easier. Mr Franklin found himself being weaned away, painlessly and without stress, from his normal irregular bachelor habits: meals became a matter of routine, as did his hours; there were fewer small chores to attend to, and yet no less to occupy him. In a strange way Samson's presence seemed to give a purpose to things; as though routine itself were a matter of occupation. Mr Franklin noted this without considering it deeply, and was aware of a security that he had not known before in his time at Lancing Manor. It did not occur to him that what he was feeling was the sense of no longer being alone in this curious world.

And even that world, in the next few weeks, became gradually less alien. Several things happened which drew Mr Franklin closer into the web of local life, not all of them unmixedly pleasant. The first was a visit, proposed by Thornhill, to the old Mrs Bessie Reeve of Lye Cottage, she who had been a Franklin of Castle Lancing before her marriage, and therefore presumably Mr Franklin's distant kinswoman. He called on her not knowing quite what to expect, with Thornhill and the local curate in tow to break the ice, for it was explained that Mrs Reeve was not only old but deaf, and almost senile. Had he thought, Mr Franklin might have imagined a rose-festooned cottage with tiny windows and a thatched roof, tenanted by an apple-cheeked old lady in a mutch and apron, bobbing at the doorway and offering seed cake and elderberry wine in her spotless parlour, with a kettle singing on the hob and a black cat purring before a cheerful fire. The reality was rather different.

Lye Cottage itself was outwardly decent enough, give or take a few missing slates, an apparent absence of paint in the last twenty years, and a garden head-high in nettles. Within, however, it was squalid beyond anything he could have imagined; the smell of damp and poverty hit his nostrils as he ducked his head under the low lintel. With a quick sweep his eyes took in the dim room: the rug with its pattern worn clean away, the rickety table and chair, the empty grate with a pan half-full of stale gruel on the hob, the threadbare sofa with a leg missing. He had a glimpse through a half-open door into a bare kitchen, and then the curate led him through into the bedroom, where a bundle was lying on a low bed in the corner, beneath the window. The walls were peeling, the floor was paved with stone flags; on the window-ledge was a jam-jar containing a few ferns. The bundle stirred as the curate, a hearty young man, shouted "Good morning, Bessie, here's a visitor for you," and with a shock Mr Franklin realized that the bundle was a tiny old woman, incredibly wizened, wrapped in grimy blankets. Two bright eyes peered fearfully up at him, and as the curate introduced him a toothless mouth opened and closed, and the little head nodded under its woollen hood. There was a choking smell of soiled linen mixed with camphor.

"Your name was Franklin, too, Bessie," shouted the curate, adding to Franklin, "I'm afraid you'll have to yell at her." Mr Franklin stooped over the bed and said loudly: "How do you do, Mrs Reeve? I hope we're not disturbing you. I'm very glad to know you. We're from the same family."

"She doesn't hear you," said the curate, and shouted: "His name's

171

Franklin, Bessie! He's from America! He's come to see you! Isn't that nice?"

The little old woman nodded again, and made a noise which might have been an acknowledgement. She reached out a small, claw-like hand to a tea-cup of brown liquid beside her bed.

"It's damned draughty in here," muttered Thornhill.

"What's that, Bessie?" said the curate, picking up the cup she was reaching for. He sniffed. "Good gracious, it's rum! Now, Bessie, you know you shouldn't – "

The old woman made an unhappy noise, reaching. Thornhill said, "Oh, come on, Ralph," and the curate, with a reproachful murmur, handed her the cup. She sipped at it, and nodded.

"It's a great pleasure meeting you," shouted Mr Franklin, and held out his hand. The old woman hastened to protect her rum, shrinking back, and then, realizing no harm was intended, put her free hand into Mr Franklin's palm for a moment. It felt like a few dried sticks.

"She doesn't hear," said the curate, but the old woman nodded and said: "Franklin. Ar," and returned to her rum, watching Mr Franklin over the rim of her cup.

"Doesn't anyone look after her?" asked Mr Franklin quietly, and before the curate could reply the old woman croaked: "No. Here by meself."

"Yes!" shouted the curate. "You're here all alone, aren't you, Bessie? All by yourself, I said. But Mrs Farrar looks after you some- times! MRS FARRAR LOOKS AFTER YOU SOMETIMES, DOESN'T SHE?"

"Ar. Sometimes."

"Yes, the neighbours keep an eye on her," said the curate. "And she has an order for medical attendance from the relieving officer. You get along all right, don't you, Bessie?" he roared, and Mrs Reeve sipped at her rum and nodded.

"She seems to be able to get booze, anyway," muttered Thornhill. "She can't be too badly off."

"She couldn't be much worse off," said Mr Franklin. He hunkered down beside the bed and raised his voice. "How do you cook, Mrs Reeve? How do you . . . eat? Do you get enough to eat?"

The old woman stared at him and nodded. "Turnips," she said.

"You eat turnips?"

"You had some turnip for dinner yesterday, didn't you, Bessie?" said the curate, and added: "Mrs Farrar sees she gets something. The parish does what it can, of course; we make sure she gets sufficient. It's terribly difficult, though; the poor relief doesn't go as far as we'd like."

The old woman, watching them, took another cautious sip at her rum, and then fumbled with her free hand in the recesses of her bedding, bringing out at last what looked like a very old boiled sweet. She put it in her mouth, sucked, and looked at Mr Franklin.

"Don't like the taste," she croaked, and sipped again.

"What of – rum or sweets?" wondered Thornhill.

"Gettin' some soup," said the old woman.

"Yes, that's capital!" shouted the curate. "Mrs Farrar will be bringing some soup presently, won't she?"

"Drop o' spirits," said the old woman, nodding, and set her cup down. She sucked at the sweet, slowly, her bright little eyes on Mr Franklin's. He smiled into the wrinkled old face; under her woollen hood he could see that the tiny head was almost bald, only a few white strands on the pink of her scalp. Her hands on the blanket were like old parchment, the fingers bent by arthritis, the veins standing out blue in relief on the transparent mottled skin.

"Is this your own cottage?" he asked loudly, and after a moment she nodded. "My cottage. Ar." She coughed, and the sweet slipped from her mouth on to the blanket. She fumbled uncertainly for it; Mr Franklin lifted it, and she restored it, sucking gratefully.

"Freehold," she croaked, nodding.

I wonder who our common ancestor was, he thought. And what he'd have thought if he could see the two of us, in Castle Lancing.

"Do you like it here?" he asked. The old woman blinked, looked at the curate, and then whispered: "Ar." She sucked for a moment and then added: "Cold."

"She's right there," said Thornhill. "Just as well she can get her rum. Wonder how she does it?"

"Fuel's very difficult," said the curate.

"Would you like to go to some other house," asked Mr Franklin. "Somewhere warm – where they could look after you?"

There was a sudden flicker of fear in the old eyes. She shook her head. "Not to Norwich," she said.

"She thinks you mean the workhouse," said the curate, and bawled: "No, no, Bessie! Not the workhouse; nothing like that!"

"No rum there, for one thing," murmured Thornhill.

"Not the work'us," said the old woman fearfully. "Stay 'ere."

"All right," said Mr Franklin. "You'll stay here." He got up. "This

173

Mrs Farrar – I'd like her to take on the care of Mrs Reeve on a paying basis – say ten shillings a week, or whatever will recompense her satisfactorily. I want her to provide three meals a day, and clean and look after the place properly. Would she be willing to do that?"

"I should say so!" exclaimed the curate. "Why, you – "

"And I take it Mrs Reeve would have no objection if the house were renovated and made comfortable, properly decorated?"

"I'm sure she wouldn't," said the curate, beaming. "My dear Mr Franklin, this is most remarkably generous!"

Immediately Mr Franklin regretted his impulse; he should have waited until they got outside, and fixed things with the curate quietly. For now the curate was roaring the glad news to Mrs Reeve; he had to shout it several times before it got through, and then she looked in bewilderment at Mr Franklin. Then her eyes strayed round the room.

" 'E wants to buy me 'ouse?"

Mr Franklin was on the point of explaining, and then he thought why not? "Yes," he said. "I'll buy your house, Mrs Reeve. But you go on living here, just as long as you like, you understand?"

The curate added his explanation, and the old woman nodded uncertainly, and then looked at Mr Franklin again. "What for?" she asked.

"Because we're the same family," he said. "We're both Franklins. You're my kin – we're relations, you see. My name's Franklin, too. So we'll keep it in the family."

She nodded uncertainly, and the curate murmured: "I'm afraid she doesn't understand about you. Never mind, she – "

"Ar," said the old woman. "My name wor Franklin." She looked at the American. "You're . . . Franklin?" And she gave a little chuckling laugh. So the curate laughed, too, and Mr Franklin smiled and felt extremely content, and Thornhill remarked that she'd probably cost him a fine bill in rum if he wasn't careful.

Later, Mr Franklin felt a little less pleased with himself. It was an odd, contrary thing, but being conscious of doing a good deed made him uncomfortable; it smacked of charity, and although he could justify it to himself on the score of his kinship with Mrs Reeve – well, a highly probable, distant kinship, anyway – at the same time he felt his spontaneous gesture had been somehow immodest. He didn't want to appear as though he was playing Lord Bountiful, or to have the village thinking that *he* thought he could just go around buying any-

174

thing, and showing off his cash. At the same time, he felt an immense private satisfaction that he had been able to pay back something to . . . to whom? Those ghosts up in the churchyard, perhaps – old Matthew, and John, and Jezebel. His ghosts, and Bessie Reeve's.

There was no way of keeping the affair from the village, of course. The activity round Lye Cottage when the painters, joiners, and others moved in was there for all to see, and Mrs Farrar, after Mr Franklin and the curate had called on her to state their requirements, was thunderstruck with her good fortune and ready to tell her neighbours so. On the whole, Castle Lancing approved; the Yankee squire was ready to look after his own – it remained to be seen if his beneficence would extend even further than his own namesakes, but in the meantime, good for him.

And even outside Castle Lancing Mr Franklin's quixotic gesture was noticed. A few days after his visit to Lye Cottage – indeed, on the very morning when he received from a Thetford solicitor the deed which made him its owner for the princely sum of thirty pounds sterling, duly paid to the solicitor on behalf of Elizabeth Reeve, widow, née Franklin – a caller arrived at Lancing Manor just as Mr Franklin was finishing his breakfast. Samson showed him into the study: a soldierly, abrupt gentleman named Major Blake, very spruce in breeches and jacket.

"I represent the Gower Estate, Mr Franklin. As you will be aware, we hold considerable property in and round this village. You didn't know? You surprise me. However, that is the case." The major crossed one neatly-booted leg over another. "I understand that you have recently purchased Lye Cottage."

"I got the deed only this morning." Mr Franklin tapped the buff envelope on his table, and the major nodded.

"Indeed. I confess to being slightly puzzled, Mr Franklin – even slightly piqued." The major smiled without amusement. "You see, for several years the Gower Estate has been trying, unsuccessfully, to purchase Lye Cottage. The owner, a widow woman, has refused several offers – several generous offers – from us. Perhaps you knew that?"

Mr Franklin shook his head. "This is the first I've heard of it."

"Ah." Major Blake raised his eyebrows in polite surprise. "That being so, we were taken aback to learn that you, a comparative new-comer to the district – if you'll forgive me for saying so – had

175

succeeded where we had failed. May I ask what was your interest in the property?"

The clipped tone, the tilt of the head, touched lightly on Mr Franklin's republican skin. But he replied amicably. "Certainly. May I ask first of all what is your interest – in my interest?"

"Of course. As I said, the Gower Estate owns extensive property in this area. Most of the village, in fact, except for a few properties – your own house here, for example, and half a dozen others. Most of the residents are tenants of the estate, and work on our land. Naturally, for the sake of . . . uniformity, we are interested in adding properties to our present holdings."

"I see." Mr Franklin frowned. "Lye Cottage isn't much of a place, though, surely?"

"In itself, no. In fact, in itself it is virtually worthless." Major Blake's gesture dismissed Lye Cottage. "But it would be useful for its position." He paused, and favoured Mr Franklin with a sour smile. "I am costing my principal money in saying this, I dare say, but Lye Cottage is the one small enclave on the north side of Castle Lancing village which we do *not* own. Without going into detail which would be of little interest to you, I can say that while it remains outside our control, we are unable to proceed with developments from the point of view of Gower Estate – and for the area generally, of course."

"Well," said Mr Franklin, "that certainly explains your interest. Thank you. Mine is simple enough. The old lady, Mrs Reeve, who lives there, is a distant relative of mine. You didn't know? You surprise me. I thought everyone around here knew by now that I'm a returned exile. Anyway, I bought her cottage – it was pretty run down, the old lady was at low water . . . so, I took it over. That's all."

"A generous gesture," said Major Blake. "But I still fail to see why – Mrs Reeve, did you say? – should have accepted your offer when she has repeatedly rejected ours. May I ask what you paid her for it?"

"Thirty pounds for the freehold."

The major frowned. "We offered rather more than that – "

"Yes, but you probably weren't prepared to let her stay in the cottage. I was, you see."

"Ah-h." The major opened his eyes a little wider. "She remains as your tenant, in fact."

"You could say so."

"That explains things," said Major Blake wisely. "Well, that being so, we are rather at your mercy, Mr Franklin. However, we must just

176

grin and bear it, mustn't we?" He smiled knowingly. "I think it will save us time if you state your terms."

"Sorry?"

"How much do you want for Lye Cottage, Mr Franklin?"

Mr Franklin stared in genuine surprise, and then laughed. "I don't want anything for it! I just explained, I bought it so that I could make it fit and comfortable for my old relation to live there. How long that will be, I don't know; a few years, I hope. But for that time, I'm sorry – it's not for sale."

"But surely – one cottage is very like another. Could she not live somewhere else?"

"She doesn't want to. She likes the place." Mr Franklin shook his head. "Believe me, major, I'm no horse trader. If the old lady wanted to move out, I'd let you have it, and welcome. But she doesn't. I agreed that she'd go on living there – in fact, I signed to that effect . . . ." He shook his head, smiling. "So there's no way past it, I'm afraid."

Major Blake pursed his lips. "It might be possible to persuade her, surely?"

"I wouldn't dream of trying," said Mr Franklin, and his smile was a shade less warm.

"You're sure?" The major looked knowing again. "I feel bound to tell you . . . that the Estate is willing to be more than generous as to purchase price. Far more than generous."

Mr Franklin considered him. "Go on."

"Two hundred pounds," said the major impressively, and Mr Franklin whistled.

"Is there oil on that property? You really want it, don't you?" He frowned. "Might I ask . . . this development . . . what's it to be, exactly?"

"That," said the major primly, "I am not at liberty to divulge."

"No? Well, I was only curious. It doesn't make any difference, major. I still can't sell Lye Cottage. I'm sorry."

"You're not serious?" The major's eyes were wide open now. "Really! You won't take two hundred pounds?"

"Not two thousand. As I said, I'm not horse trading."

The major regarded him in silence for a moment, obviously puzzled. Then he sighed, and tapped his chin. "I see. Well, in that case . . ." He hesitated, and then said, in a confidential tone: "Mr Franklin, this is rather difficult, but I'm obliged to ask you. I appreciate your concern for this woman – this Mrs Reeve. Ah – that apart . . . may I ask you, as man to man, you understand, whether your reluctance to sell is in any way connected with the fact that I represent Gower Estate?"

"Gower Estate?" Mr Franklin shook his head in surprise. "Why should it be? I never even heard of them."

He was aware that Major Blake was regarding him with open disbelief, expressed by a rather cynical smile.

"If you say so, of course. But I must say . . . well, the coincidence is remarkable. However, that is nothing to do with me." The major placed his hands on his chair-arms, preparatory to rising. "I'm sorry to have wasted your time, Mr Franklin – "

"Just a moment." Mr Franklin rose behind his desk. "You're way ahead of me, major. What is the remarkable coincidence?"

The major was brisk. "You haven't heard of Gower Estate? You are acquainted with its owner, though. Lord Lacy."

"Lord Lacy? Frank Lacy?"

"His family name is Gower." Major Blake's tone was chilly, but as he looked at Mr Franklin it thawed slightly. "Were you really not aware of that?"

"Not for a minute."

"Oh." The major paused, and looked at the ceiling. "Then in that case, I imagine I owe you an apology."

"You're still ahead of me. Major, would you mind telling me what you're talking about."

The major thought for a moment, choosing his words.

"It is fairly common knowledge that you had a disagreement with his lordship at Oxton Hall. Immediately following that, you purchase a property on which he has had his eye for some years past. That was the coincidence I mentioned just now. It did not appear to be a coincidence to Lord Lacy. He assumed – and I confess it seemed a not unreasonable assumption – that the two events were connected. That – "

"That I bought Lye Cottage just to spite him? He really thought that?"

The major shrugged. "Or to make him pay an exorbitant price for it. That had crossed his mind."

"And a charitable mind it must be, yes, sir!" Mr Franklin laughed, and it was not a pleasant laugh. "Well, I'm damned! He really has a high opinion of me. You can tell him, major, with my compliments, that when I disagree with anyone, I settle it on the square. As I imagined I had settled with Lord Lacy. When I hit somebody, that ends it, for me – I don't go around trying to pick his pocket, too."

"Quite so." Major Blake nodded. "I remind you, Mr Franklin, that I have already tendered my own apology; I'm in no doubt that in buying Lye Cottage you were unaware of his lordship's interest. It's unfortunate, though."

"Yes," said Mr Franklin. "Come to think of it, I guess I can't blame him for being suspicious," he added ruefully. "If I thought it would clear the air – well, I'd like to oblige him, but . . ."

"You'd consider it?"

"I can't, sir. Mrs Reeve has got to stay. I hope Lord Lacy will understand that, and that there's no . . . no personal feeling about it."

"Between ourselves," said Major Blake, "I doubt if he will. It's all very unlucky. However – "

"Look," said Mr Franklin, "the last thing I want is any misunderstanding . . . any bad blood. Suppose I were to explain to him, personally . . ." He caught the major's look. "No, I guess not." He sighed. "Then, as you say – it's very unlucky."

In fact it was the kind of ill-luck which he could bear with fortitude; he was not going to lose any sleep over Lord Lacy. But he did mention the matter to Peggy, on one of those visits to Oxton Hall which were becoming increasingly regular; he thought hard before broaching the subject to her, for he had no wish, he told himself, to make Lacy appear any blacker in her eyes. On the other hand, he did not want it publicly thought that he had acted out of spite towards the peer.

"No one's going to think that for a minute," said Peggy firmly. "They know Frank, and will realize it's just the sort of mean idea that would occur to him. Really, he's the giddy limit! And he sent that odious Blake to try and bribe you into selling the cottage and putting the old woman out?"

"Not exactly. And I didn't find Blake all that odious, actually. Pompous, perhaps, but – "

"He's a tick," said Peggy. "Gives himself huge airs, when everyone knows he was in the Service Corps, or something equally unfashionable – what Daddy calls a baggage-wallah. Only a louse would work for Frank, anyway."

"My, you've really taken a dislike to him – to Lacy, I mean."

"It's nothing new. And after the way he behaved here, and now this suggestion that you were trying to do him the dirty over some silly cottage . . . well, d'you blame me?"

179

"I guess not." They were riding back to Oxton for afternoon tea, pacing along beside the paddock wood. "I can see his side of it, though. We got off to a bad start that day of the hunt, and then the business in the middle of the night when I slapped him down, and now the cottage. He hasn't got many reasons to like me, has he?"

Peggy gave him a sidelong look. "You think those are the worst turns you've done him?"

"You mean there are others I don't know about? Oh – the business of your father showing him the door? Yes, he can blame me for that, too, I suppose."

"Even that's the least of it, so far as he's concerned."

"For Pete's sake! What else have I done?"

"Well," said Peggy, patting her horse's mane and looking carefully straight ahead, "you've been around here a good deal, haven't you? And you can't imagine that Frank doesn't know that. And draws his own sweet conclusions."

"Which are?"

"Don't be so coy, Mark. You know perfectly well what I mean."

"Sure I do," grinned Mr Franklin. "I just want to hear you say it."

"Well, you can jolly well want! Say it yourself, and don't be so confounded smug!"

"All right, then. He thinks I've cut him out with the beautiful Miss Peggy Clayton."

"Silly ass, isn't he?"

"Is he?" His tone was light enough, but his smile was not quite bantering.

"Mm-mh." Peggy frowned, as though over some deep problem. "Let's say that you help to pass the time."

"Oh, well, thank you, Miss Clayton – "

"But Frank certainly *thinks* you've cut him out, so you ought to be duly flattered."

"Oh, but I am, ma'am. I value Lord Lacy's jealousy no end – if he really *is* jealous."

"He is," said Peggy complacently, and as she turned towards him he saw the little crook at the corner of her mouth.

"How do you know?"

"He told me so."

"You mean you've talked with him – since . . . since the King was here?"

"Of course. Any reason why I shouldn't?"

180

"Certainly not. Free country. And he told you he was jealous?"

"Not in as many words, no. He started by telling me what he thought of Daddy, and saying it didn't make the slightest difference to him, and he intended to go on seeing me."

"And?"

"I told him he'd find it easier seeing Poppy – after all, there's so much more of her – and I'd prefer it if he kept as far away from me as possible, since I didn't want to see him. He swore a bit at that, and then said: 'I suppose it's that bloody cowboy?'" I asked him who he meant, and he said: 'You know bloody well who I mean – that cheap Yankee upstart'. "

"I see. Nice turn of phrase he's got. And what did you tell him?"

"To mind his own damned business, and not to make a scene in the middle of Thetford High Street. He lost his temper, so I left him to get on with it. Satisfied?"

"Up to a point," said Mr Franklin. "That's to say, I kind of like the idea of his lordship having a tantrum to himself in the middle of Thetford. Of course, I still don't know whether he was justified or not."

"Gosh, the way men fish for compliments! You'll just have to go on wondering, then, won't you? Or make the effort to find out."

They had reached the stables by now, and as they left their horses with a groom and strolled round to the side-door, Mr Franklin pondered humorously on the simple delights of flirting. It was all very pleasant and casual and civilized; also, it was new to him, and all the more attractive for that.

"Make the effort to find out, eh? What kind of effort would be required, do you suppose?"

"Don't ask me," said Peggy. "You won't know until you make it, will you?"

"That sounds awfully like an invitation." The trivial formulae sounded perfectly meaningless in his ears, but it seemed to be part of the game. Peggy had stopped at the hall-stand in the little back lobby to remove her bowler-hat and survey her hair before the mirror. Her eyes met his in the glass.

"Don't you believe it," she said, and hesitated just those extra two seconds before the mirror which enabled him to step closer. She didn't move, but continued to give exaggerated attention to her hair, patting it and turning her head from side to side, so he made the next conventional move in the game and kissed her lightly on the corner

181

of the mouth. He had not kissed her since the afternoon at Lancing Manor, and assumed that she would accept it much as she had accepted it then, without special reaction, but as something mildly pleasant to do. But this time she went on complacently tittivating her hair; he kissed her again, and she turned, giving him a direct, appraising stare, but neither responding nor moving away. Mr Franklin was slightly intrigued – and in that moment life changed, as it so often does; he sensed it, and was on the point of drawing away, but her lips opened, and it was pure sexual attraction that made him suddenly pull her close and kiss her with considerable force; he was conscious of her body pressed against him, and her mouth working fiercely against his, her arms going round his neck, and his hand closing on her breast. It was not the pleasant game any longer, but something infinitely more primitive and important; she was pressing harder against him – and at that moment there were the sounds of distant footsteps in the main hall round the corner of the passage, and they came apart breathlessly. Peggy took a deep breath, and said quietly: "Yes – you do help to pass the time, don't you?" and slipped past him towards the hall. But she kept hold of his hand, and he followed her, wondering what had happened in that brief few seconds. Whatever it was, things were different.

He was conscious of it in the days that followed, in that raw November when the winter night was falling on that curious golden time which posterity was to call the Edwardian era. It was a coincidence that he could not be aware of: that his own metamorphosis took place at a time when the world itself was approaching a watershed, a change from one great historical age into another. He sensed only the change in himself, without fully understanding it, any more than he fully understood the new life surrounding him.

And he was becoming acclimatized. With Samson in residence at Lancing Manor, regulating the small household as a good engineer runs his engine-room, it was no longer an ordeal if people came to call, as they did; nor was it arduous to enter occasionally into the social life of the neighbourhood, with Samson behind him. He dined out at one house or another perhaps once a week, and found the experience tolerable if not enjoyable. He knew he would never be gregarious, but it was still new enough to be interesting. At Oxton Hall he even rode to hounds once or twice, and found the experience both enlightening and chastening. He went to his first meet with all the confidence of one who had ridden almost as soon as he could walk, and in the expectation of being able to do rather more than hold his own; he came away from it in a respectful awe of horsemen and women whose expertise over rough country, ditch, and hedgerow was matched only by their reckless disregard for life and limb. The experience of turning sensibly away from a fearsome barrier of stakes and brambles only to have a stout, grey-haired old lady come thundering past him and go flying over in style, whooping like a tipsy Cossack, was one which Mr Franklin did not forget in a hurry.

He found he was spending even more time at Oxton than at his own house, and occasionally it troubled him. It was pleasant enough to be treated as one of the family, to ride and dine with them, to squire Peggy to a ball at Arthur's old college in Cambridge, to talk with Sir Charles, to play snooker with Arthur, to have Peggy drive him into Thetford or Norwich in the family motor, to enter into their leisurely activities; at the same time he found himself chafing a little at the very readiness with which they accepted him. He was adjusting to their ways, and they took it for granted that he should; sometimes he felt that he was letting his independence go by default, particularly where Peggy was concerned.

He traced it to that moment in front of the mirror, when in a subtle way their friendly relationship had changed into a deeper intimacy. It was a physical thing as much as anything; it had become perfectly natural for them to take hands, for him to put his arm round her waist, or to play gently with her hair as they sat talking, for Peggy to tap his cheek or lean on his shoulder. And there were those moments when sexual pleasure in each other came so naturally and inevitably, when her mouth would open hungrily under his, and he would fondle and pet her to the point where he knew with certainty that the ultimate fulfilment of love-making was there if he chose to take it. It was difficult to say whether it was innate caution or an old-fashioned, Puritan stream of propriety that restrained him; or it may have been a sense that his enjoyment of her would somehow be spoiled by completion. But even stronger was the instinct that if they became lover and mistress he would have surrendered himself, lost that freedom which he still prized, and given himself as a hostage in this new world.

He knew that with her strong, self-confident nature there went a good streak of possessiveness; he was made especially aware of it as the time for his visit to Sandringham approached. Some weeks had gone by since the King's visit to Oxton Hall, and Mr Franklin had

183

half-hoped (a hope that was oddly mingled with disappointment) that the offhand invitation had been forgotten. Near the end of November, however, a note had arrived from Halford, confirming it; Mr Franklin showed it to Peggy when she came to lunch with him at Lancing Manor.

"Ah, the summons from on high," said Peggy, handing back the note. "How does it feel to be admitted to the elite?"

"You tell me," said Mr Franklin. "You've had him to stay."

"That's no great privilege – in fact, it's a complete nuisance, as you know. The old bore imposes himself on everybody, but he's pretty choosy who he invites back. It'll be a long time before he descends to my level – especially after that ptarmigan pie."

"I'm not so sure that I'm glad that he's descended to mine," said Mr Franklin.

"Oh, stuff! Wild horses wouldn't keep you away, and you know it. Just think – you'll be able to go three no trump with the gorgeous Alice."

"Playing bridge with Mrs Keppel unfortunately means playing bridge with his majesty as well. And that's something I can do without. D'you know I even bought a rule book on the subject? At least if I have to play, I'll know the rules this time."

"There's only one rule where Kingie's concerned – he always wins. But you don't have to be told that. And if you were so foolish as to forget, there are plenty of toadies to remind you – including Mrs K."

"Would you say she was a toady? I thought you liked her."

"Oh, she's all right," said Peggy. "Yes, I like her – and heaven knows what he'd be like if she wasn't there to smooth his feathers. Well, you saw how it was that night. But they're such a sickening crowd, all crawling to him – yes, sir, no, sir, three bags full, sir. I wish – " she went on, and then stopped. Mr Franklin, having seated her at his dining-table, said: "What do you wish?"

"I was going to say – I wish you weren't going."

"Why ever not?"

"I don't know, really – I just hate to think of you with that disky set. Soveral oiling about, and Halford and Ponsonby fawning to the King and being generally obnoxious to everyone else, and Alice fluttering her eye-lashes and simpering at you to conspire to keep the King sweet – ugh!" Peggy made an unladylike grimace, and Mr Franklin waited until Samson had brought their soup and left the room.

184

"I doubt if Mrs Keppel's going to do much simpering in my direction," he said, smiling and shaking his head. Peggy took a mouthful of soup and then said casually:

"Still, I daresay you could stand it if she did. Most men seem to be able to. She's very lovely, of course."

Mr Franklin regarded her with mild interest. "Of course," he agreed. "Isn't that why the King keeps her around?" But Peggy changed the subject, and it was only later that Mr Franklin found himself feeling a slight irritation. Was it possible that she was jealous of Mrs Keppel? The idea was ludicrous, on every count; what irritated him, however, was that Peggy apparently felt the right not only to be jealous, but to let him know it. And yet, let him be honest – he had felt a shadow of discontent across his own mind when she had told him that she had met Frank Lacy, and the shadow was not dispelled by the knowledge that she had told Lacy where to get off – she said. Mr Franklin took stock: was he starting to take Peggy Clayton seriously? It was a disturbing thought – but no, he liked her, that was all, and presumably she liked him. Even casual acquaintances were not immune to little jealousies; everybody was human, after all. He dismissed the matter from his mind, and gave his attention to the forthcoming trip to Sandringham.

10

This, he quickly realized, called for preparations on a grander scale than he had imagined. Although the visit was to last only from Friday to Monday, it was necessary, according to Samson, that he should take nearly all his wardrobe; in addition to evening dress and lounge suits, they must also pack his shooting jacket, tweeds, breeches, and hats to match; shoes for day and evening, stout boots, waterproof spats, mackintosh, cape, and overcoat. Mr Franklin raised a mild objection.

"We aren't going on an expedition to find Peary," he said, and Samson, who in his respectful way was something of a humorist, remarked that they'd need rather less clothing if they were. He wondered if Mr Franklin knew how to skate.

"Skate? No, I don't – you're not going to tell me that the King does?"

"Not so far as I know, sir, but I believe that the younger guests at Sandringham are accustomed to play ice hockey, when the lake is frozen. In this weather, the ice will probably bear."

"Well, they can play without me. Bridge is bad enough, but ice hockey – no, I draw the line there."

In the event, the visit when it came proved to be no ordeal at all, from that point of view. Thanks to Samson, they timed their rail journey from Thetford via Norwich to King's Lynn so that they reached the royal station in mid-afternoon, when a car took them to Sandringham. It was much more modest than Mr Franklin had imagined, and he tasted the informality of the place within a minute of his arrival. As he stood in the pleasant, light-panelled hall waiting to be shown his room, a high-pitched female voice from the open drawing-room instructed the footman to show him in directly, and he found himself in the presence of a most elegant, elderly lady who, with another younger lady, was engrossed in a jigsaw puzzle; without introduction they demanded his assistance, and it was only when he tentatively suggested fitting a piece of cloud into a piece of sky, and realized that the elegant lady was extremely deaf, that it dawned on him that he was doing a jigsaw puzzle with the Queen, with his travelling-cape still over his shoulders and his hat in his hand.

An imperturbable butler presently arrived and belatedly announced him; Mr Franklin made his bow with his piece of cloud poised to fit into place, the Queen rewarded him with a dazzling smile and informed him that the puzzle was a birthday gift from a grandchild, and he was then permitted to escape under the butler's wing, feeling a trifle dazed. In his room he confided to Samson, who was laying out his new subdued herring-bone tweed for tea, that at least the visit had got off to a good start; Samson, who had already undertaken a backstairs scouting operation of his own, briefed his employer on the composition of the house-party.

"Quite small, sir. Their majesties, Mr and Mrs Keppel, the Marquis of Soveral, and one or two others whom you know. The Marquess of Ivegill and his daughter, who was a lady-in-waiting to the Princess of Wales ..."

Mr Franklin, who was human enough still to be contemplating jigsaws and the charming condescension of royalty, heard him with half his attention, and presently, at a quarter to five, made his way downstairs to the drawing-room, marvelling at the number of framed photographs which seemed to cover small tables in every nook and cranny along the way. Sandringham was a remarkably cosy, family sort of place, it seemed to him; even so, he approached the drawing-room cautiously, and was startled, as he paused on the threshold, to hear a rasping masculine voice exclaiming: "Of course, give you half a chance and you'd have the whole dam' navy on the beach, and all of us pensioned off!"

The Queen, he saw, was no longer there, and the speaker was a burly, grey, clean-shaven man in a tightly buttoned jacket with a handkerchief in his sleeve. He was planted four-square before the fire, talking to a fresh-faced, slightly cherubic man of about Mr Franklin's age; they both glanced towards him and then, with the innate ill-breeding of their kind, resumed their conversation as though he did not exist.

"Of course," said the older man aggressively, "now you're rid of me, you think you can do what you bloody well like."

"That's nonsense," said the other. "No one has a higher regard for the navy than I do, and you know it."

"Looks like it, doesn't it? Of course, you army people are all alike.

187

All right; let's see you beat the Germans on your own." He gave a barking laugh. "You'll laugh on the other side then, and be sorry you undercut the navy."

"No one's undercutting your precious navy! But the country can only afford so much, and if you think we can pour all our cash into Dreadnoughts – "

"No such thing! I'm all for economies – of the right sort. But I don't want 'em at the expense of scientific advance and technical improvement . . . Here, did I tell you?" The older man's voice rose in indignation. "Beresford's been putting it about that I'm a half-caste!"

"Good God! Why on earth did he say that?"

" 'Cos I'm in favour of submarines and he isn't, I expect. Anyway, that's what he said . . ."

It seemed to Mr Franklin that he had unwittingly intruded on a private and important discussion, so he drifted slightly south-west and began to study a group of framed photographs with immense interest. It was embarrassing; there appeared to be no one else in the drawing-room, and he was wondering if he should withdraw and come back later when he became aware of volcanic noises from a deep leather arm-chair half-hidden by a large Chinese screen. There was the sound of a newspaper being violently crumpled, a creaking of springs, and elderly arthritic gasps, and then a man emerged from behind the screen. He was extremely old and extremely large; Mr Franklin had an impression of stalwart height, and massive shoulders encased in a beautifully-cut frock coat of antique design, with a flower in its button-hole; above, reared a striking head of silver hair framing a lined, mottled face half-concealed by magnificent flowing white whiskers. It was the face of an aged, inebriated satyr, with a prominent heavily-veined nose and dark, bloodshot eyes which glared past Mr Franklin at the conversing couple, and then back to Mr Franklin again.

"Ha! Bloody rabble!" exclaimed this apparition. "Sailors and politicians. Knew I shouldn't have come." The voice was a deep croak, suddenly raised. "If you two want to talk shop about the blasted navy – which isn't worth a hoot, and never was – why don't you do it in Whitehall? Hey?" Seeing them continue without paying him the least attention, the old gentleman fixed a wicked eye on Mr Franklin. "You're not a sailor. Politician, eh? No? Well, thank God for that. Don't know you, do I?"

Mr Franklin admitted it, and introduced himself.

188

"American, eh? Well, well, now." The old gentleman drew himself up and looked Mr Franklin over with interest. "Where from? Nebraska, eh? My stars, how long is it since I was in Omaha? Thirty-odd years, anyway. Changed, I expect. Know Kansas, do you? No?" The old man chuckled and shook his head, fingering his flowing whiskers. "I was a deputy marshal there, in Abilene, years ago. Before you were born. What d'ye think of that? And it was a dam' sight quieter," he went on, transferring his attention to the two talkers, "than some drawing-rooms I could mention. Can't even conduct a private conversation without some jack-in-office stopping your ears with drivel." He peered malevolently. "Fisher and young Churchill, eh? Oh, God help the nation. Come in here, sir – Franklin, did you say? Come on!" And the old gentleman gestured impatiently and stood aside to admit the American to the space behind the screen. "Company at this end of the house is a dam' sight more entertaining than those two bores – dam' sight better-looking, too. My dear, may I present Mr Franklin, of Nebraska, U.S.A. – my great-niece, Lady Helen Cessford."

To Mr Franklin's surprise, there was a lady sitting on a chaise-longue beside the window; she glanced up with a cool smile, and then stared; Mr Franklin, in the act of bowing, stopped and stared also. The old gentleman, his glittering, blood-shot eye darting from one to other of them, cocked his head.

"Met before, have you?"

Mr Franklin hesitated. He would have recognized that face anywhere, with its broad white brow and proud lines; the rather long nose and generous mouth, the imperious hazel eyes appraising him coldly. The last time – indeed, the only time – he had met their owner, she had been selling a suffragette magazine outside the Waldorf Hotel, and doing her best to get arrested. And now, here she was, in the King's drawing-room. He was wondering what to say when the lady solved the problem for him.

"We have met, but not formally," she said. "How do you do, Mr Franklin?" She did not extend a hand.

"Lady Helen." Mr Franklin completed his bow. "Yes – we met . . . at the Waldorf Hotel, I think it was."

"Aha," said the old gentleman, and Mr Franklin became conscious that he was watching them with some amusement. "Didn't know you behaved informally in hotels so far from the West End, Button."

His grand-niece looked calmly at Mr Franklin. "It was a very brief, chance meeting. On the pavement. I was selling our newspaper."

189

"Oh, that rag!" The old gentleman lowered himself ponderously into his chair and waved Mr Franklin to a seat. "Hope you didn't buy one, my boy."

"I was willing to," said Mr Franklin, "but Lady Helen insisted on giving them away."

The tiniest flush appeared on Lady Helen's cheek, but she said nothing. The old gentleman, who was obviously mentally alert beyond his years, and had a fine nose for mischief, stroked his whiskers and said: "Well, come on, then – don't keep a fellah in suspense. What happened?"

Lady Helen gave him a look, and sighed impatiently. "Must you, uncle? Very well – if we don't tell you, and satisfy your horrid curiosity, you'll only imagine something worse – and probably spread it all over the place. Since you must know, Mr Franklin was impertinent, and I slapped his face. There now, will that do?"

"First-rate!" exclaimed the old gentleman. "And then?"

"Then a policeman tried to arrest me, and Mr Franklin stopped him."

"Did he, by gad? That was handsome of him! Good for you, Franklin! Then what happened?"

"Nothing. I left, and – "

"Nothing?" The old gentleman gazed at Mr Franklin. "You mean you didn't take her to dinner? Good God!"

"I'm afraid I didn't get the chance."

"She was there, wasn't she? Heavens, man, one makes the chance! I don't know what's wrong with you young folk! And you, Button – " the old gentleman grinned wickedly at his great-niece " – why didn't you get yourself arrested, eh? That's what you were after, wasn't it? Didn't you have your handcuffs with you, then? If you'd had your wits about you, you could have shackled yourself to his ankle, and both been carted off to Holloway together!" He leaned back, chuckling to himself, glinting beneath his great brows.

"Great-uncle Harry has such a lively sense of humour," said Lady Helen. "And of course he finds our movement ever so funny. But then, most men do."

"Well, of course I find it funny! Dam" ridiculous. Votes for women!" The old gentleman snorted. "If you'd any sense you'd campaign to have the vote taken away from men – I'd smash a few windows myself if I thought it would keep clowns like Asquith out of Parliament. Anyway, young Button – who bailed you out last time, eh? Wasn't Daddy, was it? No, nor Mr Keir Hardie nor Mr Bernard Shaw! It was odious old Uncle Harry, and don't you forget it."

"You know very well I shan't," said Lady Helen, and to Mr Franklin's surprise she gave her ancient relative a look that was almost affectionate. Strangely, it did not add to her charm, he thought; that handsome, haughty profile was at its best unsmiling. Uncle Harry leaned forward to pat her on the knee. "I'd bail the whole blasted lot out if they were as pretty as you," he said. "But they ain't. Set of ugly old trots. What d'you say, Franklin? You approve of votes for our fair sex – give 'em equal say with men in the running of the country?"

Mr Franklin smiled and shook his head. "I'd rather not be drawn into any arguments, sir, if you don't mind. The last one didn't end too happily, and if I may I'd like to take this opportunity of apologizing to – "

Lady Helen rose abruptly to her feet. "If you will excuse me. I think tea is about to be served." There were sounds of other voices from beyond the screen, and a tinkle of cutlery. With two graceful steps Lady Helen disappeared round the screen, and Uncle Harry shook his great head reproachfully at Mr Franklin.

"You don't know much, do you? Never apologize to 'em in public. Especially when they're like Helen – proud as Lucifer and dam' contrary. She'll make some poor devil the deuce of a wife one of these days. Fine gal, mind you, dam' fine. Reminds me of a female I knew in Russia – oh, years ago, in the Crimea. Sara, her name was. Partial to steam-baths. Got me into no end of bother. Button – Helen – is like that, too. Born to trouble as the sparks fly upward. Got her head full of this suffragette nonsense – well, I don't care, women are as fit to vote as men, any day, for my money. That's why I bailed her out – because she's got ten times the spirit of these other mealy little nursery tarts. Cost me my membership of the United Service Club, bailing her out did." He glared resentfully. "Not that I cared a dam about that – place had gone down scandalously of late . . . well, dammit, the King's a member, and you can't say much worse than that, can you? They'll be letting in nigger clergymen next." Uncle Harry tugged his whiskers and mused on the enormity of life. "But it won't do Button any good, you see, all this votes-for-women stuff. Get her a bad name; not acceptable. Well, it's bad enough for the chit that she's related to *me*, but if she chains herself to many more railings, or chucks acid in pillar-boxes, she'll find herself out in the cold. Bloody nonsense!"

191

Mr Franklin prepared to rise, but Uncle Harry forestalled him with an admonitory finger.

"Mind you, I don't think any the less of her for it, and if I haven't boozed all my fortune away by the time I kick the bucket, she'll get her share. Any women with a figure like that deserves well, although I'm her own grand-uncle that says it. Mind you, they're hell, these good-looking gals with strong characters; you must watch out for them. Take your own country," he went on, settling himself comfortably. "American women are the frozen limit. I remember one – black gal, she was . . . escaped slave, can't think of her name offhand . . . deuce of a dance she led me. Beautiful, but with a will of iron. I got shot in the backside over her, which goes to show you. And there was another I knew, out West – your neck of the woods, perhaps – Powder River country, in '76 – half-Sioux, half-Frog – damme, looked like a woodland nymph, but she saved my life at Greasy Grass . . ."

Mr Franklin was beginning to feel decidedly uncomfortable. From the sounds now coming from beyond the screen, he guessed that afternoon tea was being served; there was a hum of polite voices, and he thought he could make out the King's deep rumble among them. It would be politic to join the party; on the other hand, he hesitated to emerge in the company of this astonishing old eccentric, whose views about his host, for one thing, made it seem amazing that he had been invited to Sandringham at all. But it might be equally embarrassing to stay where he was; Uncle Harry's voice was no dulcet instrument, and sooner or later it seemed likely that his presence, and Mr Franklin's behind the screen, would become known. Should he just get up and go in alone . . . ?

"Mind you, it's our own fault entirely. Take you and Button – I don't suppose your impertinence to her amounted to anything beyond a very proper refusal to buy her awful magazine – oh, and no doubt you forgot to lick her boots, too – she thinks she's God Almighty's aunt, does Button, bless her. But from the sound of it she could have got you hauled off by the bogies . . . well, there you are. What's the matter?" He broke off to glare at Mr Franklin.

"I believe they're having tea," said Mr Franklin. "Perhaps we should – "

"Let 'em! To hell with 'em!" was the rejoinder. "You don't want to go out there, surely? You'll have to talk to that bounder Bertie – " Mr Franklin winced at this indiscreetly loud reference to his majesty " – and eat their vile sandwiches, and stand around like Lord Fauntleroy. Ghastly!" Uncle Harry shuddered at the thought. "Is the Keppel wench there? Fine buttocks she's got. But – tea! I'm eighty-eight next May, and I attribute my longevity to an almost total abstinence from tea. Except the jasmine variety – used to drink that out East . . . there were two little Chink lassies in Singapore, I remember . . ." he shook his lead, leering reminiscently, ". . . and they used to serve jasmine tea afterwards – what, you're going? Well, if anyone asks for me, tell 'em I'm asleep, will you? When you're my age, it's reckoned excusable. Take a pinch at Keppel for me." And with a wink of pure evil, Uncle Harry laid his ravaged head back and closed his eyes.

Mr Franklin made his escape as unostentatiously as possible; fortunately all the guests had assembled, and there were enough people in the room for him to mingle without being noticed. The King and Admiral Fisher were by the fireplace, talking; the Queen, on a sofa nearby, was laughing animatedly with Mrs Keppel, among others; there was Soveral, with Churchill, and there were about a dozen others, ladies and gentlemen, whom Mr Franklin did not know. The King noticed him and called, "Ah, Franklin, glad to see you. Come here." So Mr Franklin found himself being introduced to Fisher, who grinned sympathetically and said: "I see you had the bad luck to catch the eye of our Ancient Mariner – or our Ancient Pistol, I ought to call him. What did you make of him?"

"He's a remarkable man," said Mr Franklin cautiously.

"Remarkable bore," laughed Fisher. "What did he tell you?"

"Well," said Mr Franklin, searching for something that would bear repetition, "he did mention that he had been a peace officer in an American cattle-town, but I wasn't entirely sure whether I should believe him."

"Oh, that's true enough," said Fisher. "Anything he tells you is liable to be true – and the unlikelier it sounds the more true it probably is. He's been everywhere, done everything – amazing old bird."

"Who's that, Jackie?" asked the King.

"General Flashman, sir. Mr Franklin has been having the privilege of his conversation."

"Oh, God, is he here? Can't stand the fellow." The King pulled a face of irritation. "How did he – oh, of course, he would come with the Ivegills." His majesty glanced round apprehensively. "Where is he?"

193

"Behind that screen, sir," explained Mr Franklin. "I'm afraid he . . . dropped off."

"Well, for heaven's sake don't wake him," said his majesty. "The longer he sleeps the better I'll like it."

Fisher smiled. "He's a bit of a penance, but . . . well, when you've charged with the Light Brigade I suppose you're entitled to bore a bit." To Mr Franklin he went on: "He was aide to your President Grant, you know, in the Civil War; fought the Indians, too, with that chap Custer. And served in the Indian Mutiny, Crimea, Zulu War, China, practically everywhere . . ."

"Yes, and don't we all know it," exclaimed the King testily. "Talk about something more congenial, Jackie."

The course of tea-time conversation moved Mr Franklin from group to group; he chatted with the Queen and Soveral, joked about bridge with Mrs Keppel, and finally worked his way to where Lady Helen was presiding at one of the twin silver tea services. She filled his cup, asked how many sugars he took, poured milk, and handed cup and saucer back to him with polite indifference. He stirred his tea and said:

"I like your great-uncle."

She gave him her level look. "Do you really? You must be extremely patient – but then of course you are, aren't you, Mr Franklin?"

He shook his head. "Listening to him doesn't call for any patience. You must be very proud of him, I should think."

"Extremely," said Lady Helen, and at that moment another guest arrived for tea, and Mr Franklin waited until he had gone.

"What I wanted to say, before," he began, "was to apologize for what happened that night outside the hotel. The last thing I wanted to do was to cause you any embarrassment – "

"You didn't. I'm not easily embarrassed."

"I see. But if I caused any offence – "

"Why should you think that?"

"Well, it isn't every night I get hit over the ear by a young lady."

Just for a moment the hazel eyes avoided his, and then she said: "You heard what my great-uncle said – he was right, as usual; he understands people very well. I wanted to be arrested, Mr Franklin. As you probably know, it is one of the ploys we use, in our campaign. I'm afraid you were just . . ." she shrugged ". . . a convenient target. So, you see, it is I who owe you an apology."

"I assure you, Lady Helen, that's quite unnecessary. I'm just sorry the slap was wasted – if that's what you wanted. To get arrested, I mean."

She took her time about replying, and when she did her voice was cold. "I can't see that that need concern you, do you know? If you think it's a joke – as most of your sex do, those who don't oppose us with a cruelty that I should have thought was the very negation of what you call manhood – then I have no more to say to you. If you don't – then I have accepted your apology, and given you mine. Either way that would seem to end the matter."

Her hostility puzzled him. Was it, too, part of the "campaign", he wondered? "Well," he said, "I'm sorry if that's so. But I wasn't treating you as a joke, you know. I merely wanted to apologize, so that . . ." He shrugged, silently.

"So that – what, Mr Franklin?"

"So that at least we wouldn't be at daggers drawn, I guess. We got off to a pretty poor start, didn't we – policemen, and slaps, and all." He smiled down at her. "I'd much rather be friends, wouldn't you?"

"So that you could flirt over the teacups, perhaps? No, thank you."

"Not necessarily. But – would that be such an awful thing?"

"It would be a waste of time." Lady Helen turned, smiling brightly, to take a teacup from Soveral, and Mr Franklin moved away reflecting ruefully that General Flashman was undoubtedly right: he didn't know much about women.

He had enough male vanity, of course, to tell himself that that was not the end of the matter. Some men retire permanently chilled before personalities like Lady Helen Cessford's; others, and Mr Franklin was discovering that he was one of them, merely have their interest piqued; he found himself hoping that she might be placed beside him at dinner, and was disappointed when his partners turned out to be a perfectly charming lady-in-waiting and a most affable Jewish knight whose most striking characteristics were a remarkably hooked nose, a massive black moustache, and a gleaming bald head; his name was Ernest Cassel. Lady Helen was placed near the foot of the table, plainly to keep an eye on her eccentric great-uncle, who had been removed as far from the King as was possible. He sat glittering-eyed, like an elderly and debauched eagle, inbibing heroic quantities of champagne without visible effect, and occasionally making unnerving pronouncements. Over the consommé, he was heard describing, in graphic detail, how a Cheyenne Indian squaw who evidently doted on him had taught him the preparation of soup from buffalo blood, which

195

was highly recommended for its rejuvenative powers; again, the arrival of a dish of fried whitebait stirred a reminiscence of a royal banquet in Madagascar at which the behaviour of the female guests had been unconventional to a degree, and might, he hinted, have been copied with advantage by present company, Mrs Keppel in particular. Fortunately the talk was so loud and general that his observations did not carry beyond his immediate neighbours; they included the Queen, but she was notoriously deaf.

To Mr Franklin the most interesting thing about the meal was the contrast with the last dinner he had had with royalty, at Oxton Hall. The constraint and apprehension of that occasion were entirely absent, and he quickly realized why. Here the King was on his home ground; there was no question of hosts and hostesses falling over themselves to please, or communicating their nervousness to him when things went wrong. No wonder the man was irritable when he found himself in a strange house, Mr Franklin mused, knowing that he was being watched anxiously to see if his chair was comfortable, or the soup was too hot, or the table talk too dull. At Sandringham he was completely at ease, content in the company of people he knew and (General Flashman excepted) liked; if he didn't care for the fish he could say so, without having to feel that he was voicing a complaint that would be recalled with shame for a lifetime; everyone knew him and all his foibles, and there would be no gaffes to throw a pall of embarrassment over the company. It was cosy, and happy, and he could enjoy himself in the certainty that his guests were enjoying themselves, too.

For Mr Franklin there was an additional, vicarious satisfaction in listening to the talk around him. This, too, was of a very different quality from the conversation at Oxton. There, although the topics had meant little to a stranger like himself, they had at least been mundane; here, unless he was much mistaken, great matters beyond the ken of the public were discussed – and discussed with a confidence and freedom which surprised him. He had already heard Admiral Fisher, whom he knew vaguely to be Britain's leading naval authority, and a political stormy petrel, disputing high naval policy with Mr Churchill, a minister of the Crown; which was no doubt very gratifying to a chance visitor, until he reflected that their debate had been conducted with a complete indifference to whoever might be listening, which seemed indiscreet, and even more extraordinary, its tone had been that of two neighbours quarrelling over a garden wall. Was this how the mighty ordered the destiny of nations? Mr Franklin had

196

supposed in his innocence that such matters were weighed in secret by grey-haired senators, all personal differences and prejudices subdued, with decisions slowly emerging only after mature deliberation. Not that Fisher and Churchill had determined to surprise the German High Seas Fleet, exactly, but their attitude and tone had suggested a carefree pragmatism, a casualness almost . . . It was all very unexpected, and startling, in a heady sort of way.

They were at it again, on a different tack; from the table head he caught a reference to the House of Lords – now that was a crisis of high moment, surely? At least, so the newspapers, which he read with an alien's foggy half-interest, led him to believe; weren't the Lords the crux of the impending dissolution of Parliament, and the General Election which would follow early in the New Year? Mr Franklin increased the intensity of his smile at the lady-in-waiting, and attuned his ear to muffle her chatter about the forthcoming Christmas festivities in Mayfair, and catch what the King, wearing a slightly dyspeptic smile, was saying to Fisher:

". . . so I suppose there is a funny side to it. Balfour wanted to know what titles we could give 'em; J. M. Barrie, for example. He seemed to think Lord Pan of Whimsy would be appropriate."

There was a murmur of laughter, and Churchill said: "Lord Never-Never would be more like it."

"Or Lord Darling Hook?" suggested another voice.

"I can see it becoming all the rage among Christmas party games, at this rate," sighed the King. "Balfour had another – what was it? Oh, yes, for Anthony Hope – Lord Rupert of Hentzau!"

There was more laughter, and Mrs Keppel exclaimed: "No – I have it! Lord Buckle of Swash!"

"Surely that ought to be reserved for Stanley Weyman," said Fisher, smiling.

"Oh, he's not important enough, Jackie. Mere boys' stories!"

"Poor old Oscar Wilde thought he was important, though. Wanted to give Weyman's romances to all the convicts in Reading Gaol – required reading for safe-crackers, evidently."

"Imagine thinking of a title for Wilde! No, better not, perhaps. Who else, though?" Churchill frowned in mock concentration. "What about Bernard Shaw?"

"Catch him accepting," said Soveral. "Of course, you'd have to give him the chance to refuse, with immense publicity; he'd never forgive you otherwise."

197

"Call him plain Lord Shaw – with a preliminary 'P', of course.
Lord Pshaw!"

"Or call him Lord Chancellor – he'd be sure to like that!"

Mr Franklin could make nothing of this; he glanced round and
found Cassel's eye on him.

"I feel more provincial every day," confessed Mr Franklin. "What
are they talking about?"

"Titles – for authors raised to the peerage," was the reply. "I can't
imagine that his majesty finds it terribly amusing, though." And indeed
the King was leaning back in his chair, with a slight frown between
his brows, murmuring something to Mrs Keppel as the suggestions
flew back and forth across the table before him.

"Are they going to make some writers peers?"

"I very much doubt it – more's the pity, in a way. If anyone must
be elevated, it might as well be someone who has the wit to write a
novel or a play. What would you think? – suppose it was suggested
that Mark Twain, and – let's see, who else? – oh, Jack London and
Henry James, and that clever chap whose name I never seem to hear
nowadays – Dreiser, Theodore Dreiser. Suppose it was suggested
that they and other American writers should be appointed to the
Senate – in addition to the Senators you already have?"

"I guess there'd be plenty of support for Mark Twain, anyway,"
smiled Mr Franklin. "It's an interesting idea."

"Well, something of the sort might happen here." Cassel sipped
his wine. "You know about the Budget, and all that?"

"I know the Conservatives don't like it, and that the House of
Lords threw it out the other day. And that the House of Commons
are saying the Lords have betrayed the Constitution. And since you
don't have a Constitution – am I right? – it's kind of confusing for
an American cousin."

"Ye-es, it's rather odd, I agree. But the issue's quite simple, really.
The Liberal Government wants that Budget passed, and it's being
suggested that the King should create enough peers – about 500, they
say – which indeed he has the power to do, to ensure a majority for
the government in the House of Lords. It's unprecedented, and leaves
him a nasty choice. If he *does* make all these new lords, he'll infuriate
the Tories, who are his traditional support, and be setting a shocking
precedent – for theoretically any monarch henceforth could make as
many peers as he liked and play fast and loose with Parliament. If he
doesn't create the peers that Asquith wants, on the other hand, he'll

be seen to be frustrating the will of his democratically-elected government, and that's a risky thing to do. Plenty of people might call the whole existence of the monarchy into question. That's why it's being talked of as a crisis. It's the government's own fault, in my opinion – making the monarch a catspaw. A dangerous game. At worst, I suppose it could lead to revolution."

He said it so blandly that for a moment Mr Franklin thought he had misheard. "You don't mean that seriously?"

"Why not? Everyone thinks it could never happen here. They forget that it's happened before. No doubt it came as a terrible shock in 1641, and again in 1776, in your country." Cassel smiled. "I know you think of that as your revolution; it can just as well be described as Britain's second civil war. And the conditions were no more dangerous then than they are now.

Mr Franklin considered his pudding, and saw no political enlightenment therein. "Well, of course, you know, and I don't – but it's pretty hard to believe."

"It always is. You know that your countrymen blame George III for your revolution – and in a way, they're right. He didn't start it. That was the work of idiot ministers in London and, if you'll forgive me for saying it, some fairly seedy political opportunists in Boston. But he could have stopped it. Whatever the King's lawful power, or lack of it, he has the tremendous influence of his position, if he knows how to use it. George III, poor old soul, didn't know how; he didn't know the right moves to make. Edward VII is in a similar position now. Thank God he's wiser than George was – and cleverer. And in his own way, more honest, for he knows what matters. And that isn't government or opposition or Liberals or Tories or peers – but the people of the land. You see, our ridiculous system, our so-called parliamentary democracy – which is a flagrant contradiction in terms, if only people would think about it – our ridiculous system, without any written constitution and so forth, is open to all sorts of abuses. It works – and works probably better than any other form of government yet devised by man – only as long as the people who operate it play fair. And that's something that can't be guaranteed by any law or constitution. And if ever they don't play fair – and many people think they're not playing fair now – then there's only one hope. And he's sitting up there now, being bored stiff by Jackie Fisher on the German Navy. In the end, it's up to him. 'Upon the King', as Shakespeare said."

199

"I didn't realize he had any power in politics," said Mr Franklin. "I thought he was just a figurehead. What do you think he'll do?"

"Wait. And play the political chess game between Liberals and Tories to the best of his not inconsiderable ability. But in the long run he'll try to do what he thinks the ordinary people want – that's what he'll be guided by. Oddly enough, I doubt if the politicos realize that; they think in political terms, and can't see any other. The King can, because in the last resort, it's what he's there for. Figurehead? Oh, yes – but the day any monarch forgets his reason for existence – to be the people's champion, in the face even of Parliament if necessary, then God help us."

Mr Franklin was impressed. It had not occurred to him, from what he had seen, that kingship amounted to much more than a leisurely progress from country house to race meeting to theatre, seeking pleasure, stuffing and swilling, and being fawned upon. What Cassel said caused him to view the monarch in a rather more sympathetic light; he had his troubles, too, and awesome they were indeed – on the other hand, as Mr Franklin glanced up the table he could not help thinking that they sat uncommonly light on the royal shoulders. The King was sitting back, listening to a whisper from Mrs Keppel, a bored, well-fed, contented smile on his pouchy, bearded face. Mr Franklin's puritan soul was vaguely stirred – if *he* had had the creation of 500 peers on his mind, he'd have been striding up and down somewhere, worrying and demanding advice from grey-bearded counsellors. The King, on the other hand, was quite prepared to join in jokes about the subject, or listen to Mrs Keppel's tittle-tattle while fondly contemplating her bosom, and surround himself with admirals and statesmen who discussed great affairs with a carefree abandon. And what they said mattered; what the King thought mattered; what took place round that elegant, well-bred, gossiping dining-table mattered – why, the veriest trivia exchanged among these light minds could have world-wide effects. There was Churchill, leaning across towards Mrs Keppel, coaxing her to choose from a dish of petit-fours ... "the stuffed dates are delicious ... or there are the little German biscuits ..." She was considering, a finger on her cheek – suppose she chose the date, and got her glove sticky, and later in the evening he, Franklin, had to come to her aid with a handkerchief, and the King noticed, and thought irritably that Alice was paying too much damned attention to that Yankee fellow, and Fisher happened to be talking to the King at that moment about naval strategy or something, and the King gave him a snappy answer, and Fisher went back to the Admiralty and said the King wasn't in favour of such-and-such – why, in two years' time the Royal Navy might be building only two submarines instead of twenty, and all because Mrs Keppel had chosen a stuffed date instead of a German biscuit . . .

"No, really, I think I'd rather not. I eat far too much as it is." She was smiling and declining the petit fours, and Churchill was offering the plate to his other neighbour. Mr Franklin felt a sudden relief; the naval crisis was past, for the moment anyway.

Of course, that was ridiculously fanciful, and he chuckled automatically. "What's the joke?" asked Cassel, so Mr Franklin told him. The Jewish knight nodded, smiling. "Well, it's not so ridiculous. That's how human destiny works. Napoleon's father felt amorous one evening, and nine months later Napoleon was born and the shape of the world changed; now, if Napoleon's father had stubbed his toe getting into bed, and quarrelled with Madam Bonaparte in consequence – no Napoleon, no Waterloo, and a different world today. It's the old horse-shoe nail proposition, and there's no guarding against it, or sense in worrying about it. Anyway, I doubt very much if H.M. is going to be greatly influenced by anything said or thought – " his gesture took in the table " – in this company. No one here counts for very much. Oh, Jackie Fisher's the most brilliant sailor we've had since Nelson, and if this country is prepared for any trial by combat that may arise, it will be due to his brilliance and determination; but he's a wild man, and the King regards him as a good friend and no more. Churchill? He's not one of the royal circle – indeed, I'm surprised that he's here – and certainly the King would never turn to him for advice, thank God; a political gadfly, and too clever by a quarter, many people think. No, you won't find many top-weight people round the King; he doesn't care for 'em. Some regret it, but I don't; he's capable of making up his own mind."

"You've got a high opinion of the King, haven't you?"

"High?" Cassel frowned thoughtfully. "He's the best friend I've ever had. Does that imply a high opinion? I know the worst that can be said of him – that he can be selfish, spoiled, petulant, and horribly self-indulgent where his own pleasure and comfort are concerned. Which of us isn't? But our faults aren't under such a merciless light as his; no one notices if you or I pull a face over a cup of coffee. And I know the best of him, too: he's kind, and honest with himself, and

201

he's got common sense. I'd be happy enough if they could put those things on my tombstone."

"So you don't really expect a revolution, then?"

Cassel leaned back and laughed with pure amusement. "No, I can't honestly say that I do. But I don't make the mistake of ruling the possibility out entirely, just because we're in civilized old England in the civilized twentieth century. Revolution doesn't just belong to the ancient past – heavens, there are thousands of people still alive who fought in *your* last rebellion – old Flashman there, for one." He nodded down the table, where the ancient general, his fine whiskers a-bristle, champagne glass at the ready, could be distinctly heard:

". . . so I said to Bismarck – ugly devil he was, tried to put me out of a carriage once, used to shoot rats with a saloon pistol, revolting brute – I said, 'Your trouble, Bismarck, is that you didn't go to a decent public school. So you've got no manners, see?" Frightful bounder, rode foul against me in a steeplechase in Rutland, I remember . . ."

Cassel shook his head. "It's hard to believe, perhaps, that he knew a man who fought in the last revolution in these islands. His own grandfather served against the Jacobites at Culloden. I say served – in fact, according to Flashman, his grandfather ran screaming from the field at the first shot, and didn't stop running till he reached Inverness. Ah, I see the ladies are leaving us."

The port did not circulate very long after the ladies had left, however. General Flashman, rendered even more reminiscent by the champagne he had consumed, joined the group round the King at the table head and launched into a vivid recollection of how his majesty, as a youthful Prince of Wales fifty years before, had been compromised by an actress in Ireland, to the dismay of the other guests and the suppressed fury of the King. To make matters worse, the old man took to calling the King "young Bertie", and an unpleasant scene was prevented only by Soveral's tactful suggestion that they should join the ladies, who would be eager for bridge. The King, glaring thunderously, took the hint and led the way from the dining-room; General Flashman cocked a malevolent eye and observed: "Bridge, eh? Played it in Russia before you lot were born. Game for half-wits," and then fell asleep over the decanter.

A couple of winning rubbers soon restored his majesty to good humour, to the general relief; Mr Franklin partnered him in one of them, and thanks to his study of the game since Oxton, acquitted

202

himself reasonably well. But he was glad when the game broke up early; he had found his attention straying towards Lady Helen, playing backgammon with one of the gentlemen at the other end of the drawing-room, and wished he could have joined her, rather than sit through the tedious business of watching the King make three diamonds or two no trumps. Strange, that what had been an ordeal a few weeks ago should now be a bore; he must be getting unusually blasé. Strange, too, that he hankered to continue his conversation with Lady Helen, who didn't seem to like him much, and was not an outstandingly attractive girl – handsome, yes, and with a fine figure, but not to be compared with Peggy. What was it about her? She was something different, with her revolutionary views, and her challenging, aggressive front – why did he feel that in spite of her assured, even arrogant manner, she was vulnerable in a way that women like Peggy were not? However, no opportunity presented itself of a tête-à-tête between the end of the bridge game and bedtime, since the gentlemen resorted to the billiard room for a communal game of slosh, and on returning for supper at one o'clock, discovered that the Queen had taken advantage of their absence to retire, the other ladies following suit.

In the morning there was a pheasant shoot, which occupied most of the daylight hours, and Mr Franklin found himself, like many an expert before him, in the curious position of excelling at something which interested him hardly at all. He was a good shot, by his own standards, and by those of the Court, a brilliant one, but it was tame work, and a far cry from the hunting he had done at home. Shooting birds with a shotgun was mechanical, repetitive, and wasteful, and to pose in a group at the end of the day, to be photographed behind a mound of feathered carcases, was positively childish.

But it was obviously part of the ritual, and had to be borne – in the moment of posing before the picture was taken, Mr Franklin glanced along at the rest of the group, and was aware of a sudden impatience; there was the King, hat at a rakish angle, cigar poised between his fingers; there were his gentlemen, immaculately tweeded and assured; there was the whole tedious paraphernalia of the day's sport, the guns, the shooting-sticks, the bags, the dogs, and the dead pheasants – had anyone really enjoyed it, he wondered, any more than they enjoyed the bridge games, the endless, trivial gossip, the stilted, mannered routine of afternoon tea, and dressing for dinner, and eating dinner, and watching the King, and listening to the King, and going through the semi-religious forms of behaviour, like participants in some eternal, meaningless minuet, without purpose and without completion? At Oxton it had been a novelty; now, after twenty-four hours of Sandringham, he was regarding it all with something close to revulsion; with insight, he speculated that probably the King himself felt something akin to his own disenchantment, but the King would hardly be able to identify it, since for seventy years he had known nothing else, and was more the prisoner of this unreal merry-go-round than any of his courtiers could ever be.

Home the day after tomorrow, to the peaceful informality of Castle Lancing, thought Mr Franklin, and in the meantime we'll break the monotony by a spirited chat with Lady Helen on the subject of women's rights, or the provocation of policemen, and see if there isn't a more amiable side to her after all.

But in this he was disappointed. When the party returned to the house it was discovered that she and her great-uncle had left unexpectedly. General Flashman, excused the shooting party on the score of his age and presumed infirmity, had belied the latter by beguiling the time indoors with sporting activities of his own. These had included a late breakfast of champagne mixed with brandy, and the pursuit of a personable young between-stairs maid to whom, by report, he had offered the most enthusiastic familiarities. The maid, a nimble girl, had escaped by a short head, but the old warrior's ardent advance had resulted in his losing his footing at the head of the stairs, colliding with a table loaded with photographs of Queen Victoria's German nieces, and coming to rest in the hall with a sprained ankle. In the circumstances his great-niece had thought it best to remove him, and he had been borne protesting to a motor car which had carried them both to King's Lynn. None of which was referred to publicly, of course, the official version being that the General had had one of his feverish turns again – which was true enough, in its way. The full facts were gleaned from the servants" hall by Samson, who reported to an astonished Mr Franklin that there was considerable scandal among the senior staff, but that the maid herself had remarked giggling that the General was a game old devil and couldn't half shift when he wanted to.

"She doesn't seem to realize, sir, that she's fortunate not to have lost her situation, with no character," Samson added. "Very fortunate indeed."

"Why on earth should she? She's the injured party, I'd have thought."

"Quite so, sir. But most employers do not care to retain female servants who have attracted the attention of gentlemen."

Mr Franklin stared. "You mean because she's a pretty girl, and was unlucky enough to come within reach of that dirty old rip, she should lose her job?"

"Well, sir, many household superintendents would feel that she should have been careful to avoid being placed in such a position. I am putting out the lovat suit, sir, and the fawn tie. However, Lady Helen Cessford's intervention made it quite certain that no steps would be taken to give the maid warning, I understand."

"Lady Helen, you say? What's she got to do with it?"

"I imagine her ladyship has had to deal with similar difficulties, sir, where her great-uncle was concerned. And she has strong views on the position of women of whatever class." Samson tucked a handkerchief deftly into Mr Franklin's breast pocket. "I gather from the senior maid that her ladyship sent for the butler and informed him that she would countenance no action against the maid; indeed, she went so far as to hint that if the young woman suffered at all, the matter would find its way into the newspapers. The butler was quite put out, sir, according to the senior maid."

Mr Franklin whistled. "I'll bet he was! My, she's quite a young lady that one, isn't she? She threatened to tell the papers! Yes, I'll believe it."

"Her ladyship is unconventional, sir."

"Unconventional is right. Mind you, with a great-uncle like that, she probably needs to be. I hope the old scoundrel's suitably ashamed of himself – but I doubt it."

"No, sir. Indeed, I gather that when he left the General was only with difficulty restrained from offering the maid a post in his own employ. Her ladyship spoke to him quite sharply, they tell me."

"I can just hear her. You know, Thomas, she's a remarkable girl. I don't know much about suffragettes, but I'd guess it must be pretty difficult for her to keep her place in your polite English society – I've hardly met her, but I've seen her commit breach of the peace and common assault, and come as close as dammit to getting arrested. And now she's threatened to make a public scandal involving the royal family. How long's society going to put up with her?"

"Her father is the Marquess of Ivegill, sir, and greatly respected."

205

"My God, I'd forgotten about him! He's here, isn't he – that slim, frail old stick with the eye-glass? Or has he gone, too?"

"His lordship is still here, sir, I believe."

"Well – what did he have to say about it all? Isn't Flashman his uncle?"

"His late wife's uncle by marriage, I believe, sir. They do not speak, I understand."

"Yes, but dammit, if your late wife's uncle, who is a fellow-guest, tries to act indecently with a royal servant – well, you can't ignore it, can you? Darned embarrassing, I'd call it."

"I doubt if his lordship is aware of the incident, sir, or will notice that his daughter and the General have left the premises."

"Not aware? He was here, wasn't he? He certainly wasn't out with us on the shoot."

"No, sir, he was down at the lake all day, sir. Watching the fish. He is greatly interested in carp, sir, and roach."

Mr Franklin stared at his attendant for a long moment. "I see. He's crazy, is that it?"

"His lordship is a very detached gentleman, sir, so they tell me. I fancy that it is time for afternoon tea, sir; the other guests will be assembling in the drawing-room."

It was a very thoughtful Mr Franklin who absorbed his tea and ginger biscuits that evening, and those thoughts were concentrated on Lady Helen Cessford. A remarkable girl, as he'd said to Samson; what would Peggy have thought of her? Not much, probably – or, rather, too much. They wouldn't have got on: there was too much character on both sides. Both highly attractive girls in their different ways – Peggy was undeniably the more beautiful, but Lady Helen was . . . interesting, and it was going to be a dull Sunday without the possibility of seeing her.

Or her disgraceful great-uncle, for that matter. Now, there was a character, and no mistake: still chasing tweeny maids at the age of eighty-seven, treating old age as an advantage rather than a handicap, obviously. What must it be like to be that ancient, and just not give a dam? Mr Franklin could not envy the General, but as evening passed again with its ritual of dressing and dinner and languid conversation and bridge and more conversation and supper, he found himself half-regretting his own inability to break out of the deadening convention that the royal circle imposed. Not that he wanted to pursue giggling housemaids, or get drunk, or go to sleep over the port, or

206

any of the other unimagined things which the eccentric General might have done – he was the kind who would have wandered off to the kitchens and exchanged drinking reminiscences with the butler, or charmed the cook with recollections of exotic foods eaten at the ends of the earth, or started a five-card school with the under-footmen, or lured Admiral Fisher into some impossible bet over the billiard-table.

Mr Franklin sighed as he realized that it was not in him to do any of these things; he would have been content to pass the evening talking to Lady Helen, or Peggy, or cute little Pip from the *Folies Satire* – was he turning into a squaw man? There had never, somehow, been much time for women until he came to England, and here much of his time seemed to be spent in their company. He must be getting susceptible, and he smiled at the thought, and had to make up a bantering explanation of the smile to Mrs Keppel, who offered him a penny for his thoughts.

Sunday seemed interminable, the high spots being a twenty-minute conversation about San Francisco with Admiral Fisher, whose discourse was a remarkable mixture of breezy anecdotes larded with Biblical quotations, and a game of billiards after tea with Churchill who, it turned out, had an American mother, and appeared fascinated by Mr Franklin's metamorphosis from Western transient into English squire.

"It's all that's going to matter, you know, in the long run – America and England," the young politician told him cheerfully. "It's the hope of the world; the only hope. When the struggle comes – with Germany, with Russia, or whoever it is – China, perhaps, some day, perhaps even France again, as it was in the past, although it isn't fashionable to say that now – but whenever it comes, the great crisis, you won't have long to make up your minds over there. And you'd better pick the right side – you can't stay out, you know. You're too big to be neutral, and in the end you'll find that we're the only friends you've got. I don't say we aren't rivals, because we are – and we may even cut each other's throats in the way of trade and politics and so forth – but when the guns are on the table, and they will be, then for our own sakes the differences must be sunk, and we have to stand together. Otherwise, as one of your eminent statesmen said, we'll assuredly hang separately."

"You think there's going to be a war?" asked Mr Franklin.

"If there isn't, it'll be something new in history. There are always wars, and always will be as long as people have different aims and interests. I expect to be in uniform again within the next ten years. Do you think," said Churchill, squinting along his cue, "that that red will go in the top pocket? I doubt it; have a look."

Mr Franklin obligingly squinted in his turn. "It'll touch the white," he said. "But, you know, quite a lot of people in America might not feel like fighting a British war. Suppose it was against the Germans – there are a lot of German-Americans who might want to take the other side."

"Then they ought to have stayed in Germany. By becoming Americans they've picked their side already. I don't mean there's any moral obligation on them to support us – just that if they're realistic people, with sound common sense, they'll see where their interest – and their children's interest – lies. You're an English country, whether you like it or not, with English ways and English traditions. Don't misunderstand me – I'm not suggesting that you *belong* to us, in any sense whatever, just because we're older, or the mother country; we belong to you just as much. We both come from the same root, and it doesn't matter who came first. Of course, you'll change, as we will. But we must stay together. I think the red *will* go," added Churchill, and struck the cue ball; the red quivered in the jaws of the pocket and stayed out. "Well, it would have gone, if I had hit it properly. Anyway, when the war comes, I hope and pray you'll be on our side."

"I don't know anything about it," confessed Mr Franklin, "except that everyone over here keeps saying that it's going to happen, but somehow it never does. If you're an outsider, like me, you get quite alarmed at first – I remember feeling shocked the first night I was in this country, and heard them singing a song in a music-hall about how they were going to sink the Kaiser's fleet. I thought I'd better book my passage back to the States pretty smart. But three months later I'm used to it, and when I see a story in the papers – as I did a couple of days ago – claiming that your Mr Asquith is deliberately trying to get up a war with Germany to distract attention from your Budget thing – well, I get kind of sceptical, you know?"

Churchill grinned. "I enjoyed that one. I can think of fifty excuses for fighting the Germans, but that was one that hadn't occurred to me – worried me rather: it seemed so far-fetched that for a moment I wondered if it was true. However, I am now reassured. But when it comes – and it will – it will quite likely appear to be over something equally trivial. But the real reasons won't be apparent; they seldom are – "

"What are the real reasons? Go on, tell me – I'm on the outside, you're on the inside, and you know about these things. Why do wars start?"

"That's easy," said Churchill. "Greed. And fear. And both those emotions are concerned with power and money. That's all. And they work away, until some accident – or some contrivance, although people are seldom clever enough to be able to contrive exactly – sets them off into war. Then the justifications – liberty, patriotism, compassion, indignation, religion, even – come into play. But they aren't reasons. Money and power, they're what count."

Mr Franklin replaced his cue in the rack and considered the fresh, rather baby face with its humorous mouth and lively eyes under the balding forehead. Slowly, he said: "I'd have thought those others things you mentioned – liberty, patriotism, and so on – I'd have thought they mattered, too."

"Of course they matter," said Churchill. He stood waiting for Mr Franklin, his hands on his hips, his head thrust forward. "Of course they matter – nothing matters more." He smiled at the American, nodding. "But money and power are what *count*."

He and Fisher left for London that evening, and since the King was slightly indisposed with a cough aggravated by the previous day's shooting, Mr Franklin was spared a final bridge session. He and Samson left on the following morning and reached Castle Lancing late in the afternoon; it was too late to pay a call at Oxton Hall – somehow it seemed the most natural thing in the world to want to see Peggy again and give her the news of his visit to Sandringham, but it would have to wait until tomorrow. But having done nothing for the past three days, or so it seemed, Mr Franklin was not prepared to sit about the house until bed-time; he recalled that it was more than a month since he had last looked in at the Apple Tree, and after Sandringham there was something strangely attractive about the prospect of a large beer in that cosy taproom, with no ginger biscuits or polite trivialities about Town life, where no one would cross an elegantly trousered leg to show an ankle encased in pearl-grey spats, where no one would make a steeple of his fingers and talk with urbanely-arched brows, and where a man could sit down without worrying about soiling the furniture. So it seemed to Mr Franklin in his rather exaggerated relief at getting home; he interrupted Samson's unpacking and said: "Thomas, get your hat, and come on. I'm going to buy you a pint."

For the first time in their acquaintance Samson betrayed genuine surprise. He stood with a pile of Mr Franklin's shirts in his hands and said: "A pint, sir? You mean at the Apple Tree."

"I don't mean at Thetford Town Hall," said Mr Franklin cheerfully. "Let's go."

Samson laid down the shirts on the bed carefully and straightened up. "That's very kind of you, sir. But thank you, I'd rather not."

"Don't tell me you don't like beer," said Mr Franklin, grinning. "You've been up at the pub often enough. Come on, put your jacket on."

Samson hesitated. "It's not that, sir." He seemed to be reaching a decision. "It's just – I don't think we should drink together, sir. Not in the village, at any rate."

"What?" Mr Franklin stared. "Oh, bosh! You mean because you work for me? What's that got to do with it? You're off duty, man! Heavens above – look, I'll tell you something! When I was working in cattle, as a ranchhand, we were on a drive into a big place called Magdalena, and the boss of the whole spread, Big Jim Eliot – a man who owned more acres than the Duke of Devonshire, and a millionaire ten times over – bought *me* a beer at the end of the trail – so why shouldn't I buy you one?"

Samson looked vaguely uncomfortable. "I think it's better we don't, sir."

"Oh, come on! This isn't Sandringham, you know. Are you worried about what the neighbours'll say? Well, I'm not – and it's my responsibility. So put down those shirts and – "

"Not entirely, sir." Samson was frowning. "It's my responsibility, too."

"How d'you mean?"

"Well, sir." Samson was obviously choosing his words with care. "It's like this. I enjoy working for you, sir, very much; I'm very well suited here. And I hope you are, too – "

"You know very well I am. What's that to do with it?"

"Thank you very much, sir. What I mean is – it's still a two-sided arrangement. It has to suit you – and me, if you understand me. And – it's nothing personal, sir, but I wouldn't feel altogether proper if we were to be seen drinking together, in public. You know what I mean?"

"Not exactly," said Mr Franklin. "We're not quite the usual . . . what's it called, master and man couple, are we? At least, I hope we're not." He paused. "Are you trying to say it would be an offence against your professional ethics?"

"In a way, sir. Yes, you could say that. As I say, it's nothing personal. If it was – well, I wouldn't be here in the first place. And I wouldn't tell you straight out why I'm declining your kind offer. I'd make some excuse or other."

Mr Franklin laughed. "Well, that's honest!" He shook his head. "Maybe you're right. You know better than I do about the . . . conventions. But I still don't see why we can't have a beer together . . . Look, suppose you were still in the Army, and I was your . . . company commander or whatever it is. What about it then?"

"That would depend where we were, sir. In Aldershot – no. Out on active service – yes. But a soldier isn't a servant, sir."

"Well – if we were in Magdalena, New Mexico – as I was, with Jim Eliot?"

"If I were one of your cowboys, sir, I'd be happy to accept your offer. If I were with you in the capacity of personal attendant, I wouldn't."

"You know your trouble Thomas – you're a snob."

"Yes, sir. Very much so."

Mr Franklin made his way to the Apple Tree alone, reflecting on the personal and professional pride of Thomas Samson, gentleman's gentleman, and deciding that he liked him very well indeed. And Samson was right, of course; he knew far better than Mr Franklin how to keep the master-servant relationship running smoothly. It was satisfactory to know that it could not only survive the kind of conversation they had just had, but be all the better for it. By God, he thought, that's a real expert. For, when he viewed the matter calmly, it was ludicrous that he, Mark Franklin, should have a valet who waited on him; it was against all his training, and upbringing, and beliefs moral, spiritual, and political. And yet Samson made it seem the most natural thing in the world, and maintained a perfect self-respect at the same time. In his way, quite a remarkable man.

He drank his pint at the Apple Tree, and bought one for Jake, who was perched in his usual place at the end of the bar. Jake had been in something of a huff since Samson's arrival, which had deprived him of his self-appointed stewardship over Lancing Manor, at least as far as the internal arrangements were concerned. Jake continued to fight a delaying action over the grounds and out-houses, jealously watching to see that the newcomer did not encroach on his paths, borders, and lawns; since Samson had no interest in these, and had forgotten more about man-management than Jake would ever know, their relationship was improving gradually, and Jake now came occasionally for his cup of tea to the back-door in the afternoon, like an ancient sparrow accepting crumbs after warily scouting the provider. Now, finding that he had Mr Franklin to himself for the first time in weeks, he waxed garrulous on the condition of the back wall, and the drainage of the kitchen garden, for which he had grandiose plans in the coming year; Mr Franklin heard him out contentedly, and it would have amazed Jake beyond all measure to learn that his patron was actually musing on the fact that Jake's conversation was at once more stimulating and restful than that of his majesty's drawing-room. Afterwards Mr Franklin strolled back to the Manor, and was considering retiring early when there was a knock at the front door. He looked out of his study as Samson answered the door, and was surprised to see Thornhill stepping into the hall.

"They told me in the pub that you were back. I thought I ought to let you know as soon as possible – the curate was round to see me this afternoon, rather distressed." Thornhill shook his head. "It's a damned odd business – they're trying to get old Bessie Reeve out of Lye Cottage."

11

"Now then," said Mr Franklin grimly, "let's just get this straight. I want to be sure I have it right."

They were in the curate's cottage, where Mr Franklin had insisted on going directly after hearing Thornhill's strange tale; they had found the curate on the point of going to bed, and he was now pouring tea with that fussy old-maidishness of which only a very large, virile young Englishman is capable, and summarizing the facts.

About one week previously a very kind gentleman had called on Mrs Reeve, bearing a bottle of rum and the information that another very kind gentleman wished to let her have a cottage in a neighbouring village, if she would move out of her present home. It was very important that she should move, since her ground was needed for some great scheme which would benefit the neighbourbood; she could expect a cash reward if she co-operated. She had accepted the rum but declined the offer, and the kind gentleman had gone away.

The next day, however, another man had called, and he had not been kind. He had brought no rum, and had spoken as though her departure was a foregone conclusion. He had also warned her to say nothing about himself or the kind gentleman to anyone; it would be best if she simply told her present landlord that she did not like the changes at Lye and wished to leave. The man had hinted that it might be unpleasant for her if she said anything more, and old Bessie had been so thoroughly frightened that she mentioned the visits to no one.

Then, two evenings later, the unpleasant man had returned, with a large, rough-looking companion; they had not come to the cottage but had stood beyond the gate, watching. They had still been there at dusk, and Bessie had lain awake all night in an extremity of terror. The next evening she had seen them again, and that night, after dark, she had heard footsteps round the house; they had stopped beneath her window, and she thought she had heard soft, sinister laughter.

"Mrs Farrar found her weeping and cowering under the bedclothes next morning," concluded the curate. "Naturally, she sent for me,

213

and I got the whole disgusting story out of old Bessie, who was in a complete blue funk with it all. Mrs Farrar has stayed with her since, and I've been keeping a look-out after dark."

Mr Franklin had sat motionless during the recital, his eyes on the curate's face. Now he asked carefully: "Was either of the men who called on her a military man, maybe?"

"No, nothing like that. Oh, you mean Major Blake. No, it wasn't him, or anyone local."

"Why should you think I meant Blake?" asked Mr Franklin sharply.

"Common sense, old boy," said Thornhill. "Blake called on you after you bought Lye Cottage, didn't he? And everyone knows Lacy has been trying to buy up that side of the village for ages. You wouldn't sell, though, we hear. So now they've come up with this new ploy, presumably in the hope that Bessie would be scared into leaving without telling you why. I say, Ralph, speaking of Bessie – you wouldn't have anything stronger than tea, would you?"

"In the cupboard," said the curate, who was watching Mr Franklin with slight apprehension. "We haven't told the police, or anything like that – we thought it best to wait till you got back. Besides," the curate's mild blue eyes glinted behind his spectacles, "I was rather hoping the brutes might show up again – I haven't had much exercise lately."

Mr Franklin sat in silence; he was actually working hard to prevent himself seething visibly with rage at the thought of the tiny old woman crouching terrified in the dark, knowing that hulking enemies were lurking outside . . . waiting for the creak of boards, the stealthy footfall, the slow lifting of the latch . . .

"Police can't do anything, anyway," said Thornhill, busily pouring the curate's whisky. "You couldn't press charges, not as it stands. They haven't broken any law."

"Terrifying an old woman nearly to death?" exclaimed the curate. "Menacing her – "

"Prove it. You can see old Bessie in the witness-box, can't you?"

"The police could at least put a man on her gate – "

"To spend all winter guarding Bessie Reeve? Talk sense, Ralph. Anyway, it's odds they won't come back; they've done what they wanted – scared a senile old woman even sillier than she is. Now she can live with her night fears until the polite gentleman calls again by day and suggests she moves out quietly. God!" Thornhill stirred wrathfully in his chair. "I'd like to see the swine flogged to ribbons!"

"But hang it!" protested the curate. "We can't just sit back and do nothing!" Thornhill shrugged, and they both looked at Mr Franklin, who was sitting with his hands clasped, staring narrow-eyed at the table. At last he spoke.

"Oh, there are things we can do. Things I can do, anyway. I can't give old Bessie back her peace of mind for a while – Mrs Farrar will have to bunk down there until the old girl gets over it." He rose and picked up his hat. "But I can make sure she's never troubled again. That's easy."

On that he took his leave, and the curate rescued the last of his whisky and wondered: "What d'you suppose he'll do?"

"Something original, I daresay – like breaking Lacy's neck, with luck. I know, incidentally," went on Thornhill wisely, "why Lacy wants Lye. Oh, we know he always has – but he wants it worse than ever now because friend Franklin's got it. You know they've been at each other's throats already, over at Oxton? No? Well, rumour has it that the fair Miss Clayton is involved – you know how it was with her and Lacy. Well, that's all over, and our stalwart colonial is the favoured beau."

"No!" said the curate. "Well, well, well! She's rather a peach, Peggy Clayton – far too good for a tick like Lacy. I say, d'you really think he sicked those bullies on to frighten Bessie?"

"Who else?" said Thornhill. "Anyway, I'd love to be there when he tries to convince Franklin that he didn't."

But Thornhill would have been puzzled if he could have seen how the American prepared for that momentous confrontation. Gower Estate's office was on Thetford's main street, and Major Blake was to be found there most days, although Lord Lacy's visits were infrequent. Mr Franklin might have been expected to make an appointment to see his lordship; instead, having consulted the lawyer who served him locally, he simply repaired to a modest tea-shop opposite the Gower office, sat down at a little table near the window, and waited for three days. It was eccentric behaviour by the standards of anyone unfamiliar with Mr Franklin's background; for those three days he gave no thought to other business, rising early and driving into Thetford, taking up his station in the tea-shop, sitting patiently until six o'clock, and then driving home. On both Wednesday and Thursday he observed Major Blake arriving and leaving, and the vehicles and pedestrians passing by; he took his meals where he sat, paid no attention to the other customers, and drove the proprietor

215

and waitresses of the tea-shop into a frenzy of speculation. No, he didn't require anything else, thank you; no, he wasn't expecting anyone else to join him. He was just waiting; the proprietor and waitresses retired, baffled, and wondered if they ought to do anything about the tall American gentleman – yes, he was the one from Castle Lancing, that was him all right – who was simply content to sit at the table, stirring his occasional cup of coffee, and looking out at the street with patient indifference. They concluded eventually that he was a loony, and left him alone.

In fact, Mr Franklin was behaving instinctively. He had sat in exactly that way, in other places, waiting, and he saw no reason to adjust his behaviour. A psychologist, had there been such a thing in Thetford, would have found him an object of some interest, and might have speculated on the trance-like attitude which he assumed as he sat back from the window, impassive and relaxed. He would have been intrigued to see the curious images which from time to time crossed the waiting man's mind as he gazed out at the drizzle, the occasional cab and wagon going by, or the motor car coughing and rattling on the wet cobbles, the figures leaning into their umbrellas as they hurried against the rain.

Where had it been – Casper or Cheyenne? He couldn't remember, and yet he could recall the spot on the check table-cloth, and the feel of the hard chairback against his spine, the cramp in his leg rested on the chair opposite, and how every few minutes he had laid his hand on the butt of the Remington, easing it out of the holster and back again. The crowded street through the flyblown window curtains, and the steady, falling rain; the slickered figures at the hitching-rail, the steam rising from the backs of the horses, the crack of whips as the big wagons lumbered by, churning up the rich black mud – and across the street on the boardwalk Harry Tracy, in his long coat and billycock hat, the shotgun under his arm, his head turning ceaselessly as he looked up and down the street. Waiting for the same thing, for different reasons; Tracy knew he was there, and why, but that nothing would happen; not yet. And still there was no sign of Deaf Charley; a dozen times in that long day he had stiffened slightly at the sight of a likely figure drawing rein outside the Morning Star *saloon where Tracy was standing; a dozen times he had relaxed, disappointed and yet relieved, when the figure had not been Deaf Charley. And it had been evening, with the yellow lamps guttering and reflecting through the rain, and his attention had wandered – and then Tracy was talking to a rider at the hitching-rail, and glancing nervously across the street, and the figure was dismounting easily, without haste, cocking his head forward to hear what Tracy said, cupping his ear under the broad-brimmed hat, laughing and turning to survey the street – and that had been Deaf Charley Hanks at last. Dirty and down-at-heel as always, unshaven, shambling in his walk, his thumb resting in his belt beside the big Navy Colt that was the only clean and well-kept thing about him. Should he let them go into the saloon, and walk in on them there, or go straight out now? Tracy was liable to run, but not the other one, not O. C. Hanks, alias Camilla, alias Jones, alias Deaf Charley. He had felt the muscles tightening in his stomach as he fingered the Remington for the hundredth time and stood up, pushing back his chair and dropping his dollar on the table, watching through the window as Tracy backed on to the boardwalk, shotgun cradled, and Hanks settled himself against the hitching-rail, gnawing at a tobacco plug while he watched the street and waited. And now that the moment had come, he felt easy, as he put on his hat and went out to meet Deaf Charley.*

Well, Thetford wasn't Cheyenne – or Casper – thank God, and Deaf Charley Hanks was dead and gone and of no significance anywhere. But the rule that fitted one was just as useful in the other; watch and wait, and by inaction fret the opposition's nerves. So he sipped his coffee, and wondered how long it would be before it became a matter of general remark that the new American from Castle Lancing was sitting, day after day, in the little tea-shop, doing nothing; the wait-resses were whispering about it, and perhaps the word would spread, in such a small place, and people would be puzzled. It was quite amusing, really; it would make Major Blake think, when he heard about it; nothing disturbing, of course, not in peaceful old Norfolk, but unusual, unexpected, and what on earth could he be doing that for? Odd chap – not quite right in the head, perhaps?

Mr Franklin smiled. Three times on the Thursday afternoon Major Blake appeared at the upstairs window of Gower Estate Ltd, looking out into the street with apparent unconcern, glancing up and down with his hands in his pockets, and each time his glance came to rest on the tea-shop window, with its blank glazed face and muslin cur-tains. Mr Franklin's smile grew a little broader, and he ordered another cup of coffee.

It was on the Friday morning that Lord Lacy made his appearance. A fine Daimler drew up outside Gower Estate Ltd shortly before noon, and his lordship went into the office. Mr Franklin paid his bill, and walked the short distance to the premises of Smith, Cross, Newbold, and Wise. Mr Cross apologized to the client he was interviewing, begged to be excused, and followed Mr Franklin to Gower Estate Ltd, where they entered the front office and asked the young clerk if they might see Lord Lacy. At that moment Major Blake appeared at the head of the stairs, looked down, started violently, and disappeared.

"It's in connection with Lye Cottage, at Castle Lancing, in which I understand the estate is interested," said Mr Franklin. "I've already spoken to Major Blake about it, and now I'd value a word with Lord Lacy. I have my legal adviser with me."

That, he thought as the clerk scurried upstairs, should set things moving. Five minutes passed, and he could guess at the frantic speculation that must be ensuing; finally the clerk descended. Would they please step this way?

Lacy was standing by the window, his thumbs in his weskit pockets, scowling out at the rain; Major Blake, behind the desk, performed the greetings and waved them to chairs, Lacy bestowing no more than a curt nod on Mr Franklin in reply to his quiet "Good morning, my lord." Mr Cross seated himself primly, Major Blake clasped his hands on the desk before him and assumed a ruptured smile.

"Well, Mr Franklin, may I say how pleased we are to see you again. Pleased and surprised. I confess I hadn't expected to be talking to you again so soon, about Lye Cottage." He paused. "What can we do for you?"

"I'm a little surprised myself," said Mr Franklin. "I thought our last conversation had settled the matter. But in fact, major, there has been a development. Since we talked, I've been thinking about things, and I've modified my views a little. In fact," he settled back in his chair, "I've come to tell you that I've changed my mind."

Lacy turned abruptly from the window to stare at him; Major Blake's well-cultivated eyebrows rose sharply. It was plain that whatever they had expected, it wasn't this. Lacy's heavy face still wore its habitual scowl, but it was a scowl of astonishment.

"Well," said the major, "I am delighted to hear it. Absolutely delighted." His smile expanded, but cautiously. "May I ask what brought about this . . . ah, change?"

"Several things," said Mr Franklin, and looked from one face to the other, the major's impassive and watchful, Lacy's heavy with suspicion, but with a slight curl of the full lips beneath the bushy moustache. They must surely be wondering incredulously if their

218

pressure on Mrs Reeve had paid off in some unexpected way; Lacy might already be feeling the first stirring of triumph . . .

"You remember, major, that when we talked some time ago, I told you that if Mrs Reeve wanted to leave Lye Cottage, I would let you have it and welcome." He smiled. "I think I added that I wasn't a horse-trader, and that I'd no wish to put a shotgun to your head where the price was concerned." He looked an amiable question at the major.

"Why, yes – yes, indeed," said Blake hastily. "That was what I understood. However – " his eyes strayed quickly towards Lacy and back again " – however, I have no doubt that the offer which I made then . . . ah, still stands." He smiled in his turn. "We are not . . . ah, horse-traders either, Mr Franklin. Do I take it, then, that Mrs Reeve has changed her mind, and is willing to move elsewhere?"

"I haven't spoken to Mrs Reeve," said Mr Franklin. "No, my decision has been reached independently."

This was sufficient to bewilder the major, he observed. With Lacy it was difficult to tell, since his face was not best designed to act as a sensitive mirror of the soul.

"Ah," said the major, uncertainly. "I see. Well – the decision is the important thing, after all, however you may have reached it. I'm sure you have excellent reasons. And I'm sure we can settle matters satisfactorily between us."

"That's what I'm here for," said Mr Franklin. "And Mr Cross, of course. The fact is, I've decided that Mrs Reeve's wishes needn't enter into it. That is the point on which I've changed my mind. I told you at our last meeting that if she was willing to go, I'd sell; I am now telling you that whether she is willing to go or not, whether she dies tomorrow or lives to be a hundred and thirty-five – which I sincerely hope she does – I now have no intention of selling. That, as I say, is how I've changed my mind, and since it represents an important alteration in what I told you at our last meeting, I wanted Lord Lacy to hear it, too, so that there should be no misunderstanding." He paused. "I have discovered another, and important, use for the land after Mrs Reeve is finished with it."

Like all bombshells, it produced a mixed reaction. Major Blake, with his quicker intelligence, may have been half-prepared for something like it; he had been cautious of Mr Franklin's apparent readiness to co-operate. Even so, he was momentarily taken aback; he realized that Mr Franklin had been amusing himself in his quiet way, and his lips hardened into a tight line. Lacy, slower on the uptake, scowled in angry bewilderment.

"You mean you won't sell?" They were the first words he had spoken. "Even if the old woman wants to go? Why not?"

"As I was saying," continued Mr Franklin, "I have another use for the land, eventually. When I was a young man, in the United States, my father and I were entertained, on one occasion, at a village of Arapaho Indians. You may not have heard of them; they're a prairie tribe, and extremely hospitable. I've always remembered their kindness, and wished I could return it. It occurred to me the other day that when, in the fullness of time, Mrs Reeve has gone, and Lye Cottage is untenanted, it would make an ideal hostel for any transient Arapaho Indians who happen to be travelling through this part of Norfolk. So that's what I intend to do with it. Mr Cross here has drawn up a deed of trust, whereby Lye Cottage is secured, in perpetuity, for the use and enjoyment of Arapaho Indians, and no other – "

"What the hell are you talking about?" roared Lacy, his face purple. "Is this your idea of a joke?"

"Certainly not," said Mr Franklin. "Mr Cross has the deed already drawn, and will read it to you – "

"That won't be necessary," snapped Major Blake. "I cannot congratulate you on your sense of humour, sir – "

"There's nothing funny about it," said Mr Franklin seriously. "It's a perfectly genuine document, and to prove my good faith as far as Gower Estate is concerned, Mr Cross has inserted a special clause providing that if, at any time, Gower Estate wishes to purchase the property, it may do so, at current valuation, provided that it obtains the consent of the Arapaho tribe. You'll furnish these gentlemen with a copy of the deed, Mr Cross? And one for the newspapers?"

"Certainly," said Mr Cross, and ducked his head. Mr Franklin rose. "Thank you for your time, major, your lordship. I just wanted you to know exactly where you stood."

Major Blake had risen also, grimly silent; he at least was not prepared to give Mr Franklin the satisfaction of a protest. But Lord Lacy was made of more choleric stuff; it had dawned on him that this Yankee upstart, who had thwarted him painfully, and assaulted him more painfully still, was now trying to make a fool of him, and liable to succeed. He glared from Blake to Mr Franklin, his fists clenched.

"What the hell d'you mean, the newspapers?"

"I'm sure they'll be interested," said Mr Franklin. "I don't imagine they get many stories about Arapaho Indian hostelries in Norfolk."

"Is that what you've been sitting in that bloody tea-shop for three days to tell me?" roared his lordship.

"It's not a bad tea-shop," said Mr Franklin, pulling on his gloves. "I thought the papers might be interested in something else about Lye Cottage, and that is that attempts have been made – I can't imagine who by – to force Mrs Reeve to leave it. Strange visitors trying to threaten and coerce her – "

"What are you insinuating?" demanded the major. "I should advise you to be extremely careful what – "

"I'm being careful," said Mr Franklin. "That's why I've got my legal adviser with me. Of course I know that Gower Estate would have nothing to do with that kind of scandalous action. That goes without saying. But someone's doing it, and if they do it again, I'm not going to waste time proceeding against the hired hands. I'm going to seek out the person unknown who's behind it, and I'm going to see that he ends up in hospital, a very sick man indeed. In fact, he may never ride to hounds again." And he turned his cold eyes on Lord Lacy and very carefully looked him up and down.

It was, as Mr Franklin had calculated, more than his lordship could bear. Lacy gave a snarl of fury and started forward, Major Blake reached out a restraining hand, but it was flung off. Possibly because he had painful recollections, however, his lordship advanced only a couple of steps, and stood glaring at Mr Franklin.

"You impertinent bastard!" he snarled, and Mr Franklin turned an inquiring eye on Mr Cross.

"Is that actionable?"

Mr Cross shook his head reluctantly. "Common abuse."

"You – you bloody Yankee crawler!" Lacy's temper, which he had never troubled to school, suddenly gave way – but not to the point of physical assault. "Don't bloody well think you're going to get away with this – with anything! Because you're not! I know all about you, and how you go worming about at Oxton! You filthy –!" And he added a word which brought a slight flush to Mr Franklin's cheek. He wondered for an instant if Lacy was so lost to shame that he might parade his jealousy by dragging Peggy's name into his tirade, but the furious peer stopped just short of it. "I know what your bloody game is, you lousy tell-tale rat! Well, see how far it gets you! Because I'll take care of you, all right! I'll make you sorry you ever stuck your dirty nose in here! You'll see! Now, get out! Get out of my bloody office!"

Mr Franklin was moved to contempt. To hear a grown man raving like a hysterical schoolboy was bad enough, but the poverty of his lordship's vocabulary made it even worse. But he was dispassionately interested to discover just how intensely Lacy hated him.

"Good day, major," he said to Blake. "Don't trouble to see us out."

"And don't bloody well come back!" shouted Lacy, as they went downstairs. "You sod!"

"Now that might be actionable," said Mr Cross, but Mr Franklin shook his head. "Even if it was, Mr Cross, who wants to take candy from foul-mouthed children?"

He went home to Castle Lancing that afternoon satisfied with his three days' work. He had ensured that Bessie Reeve would be let alone; he had punished, by ridicule to Lacy's face, the mean attempt to drive her from her cottage, and he had discovered how to cause alarm in the enemy camp whenever need arose – all he had to do was go and sit in the tea-shop across the road. That would certainly send Major Blake to the telephone, and Lacy into apoplexy, with any luck.

And that, he decided, was sufficient; his threat to release details of the trust deed to the press had been half in earnest, but on reflection he would keep it to himself. He had given Lacy enough crow to eat for the present; any more would be vindictive. He even refrained from mentioning what had passed in Thetford, when he drove over to Oxton Hall later in the day; when Peggy wanted to know where he had been since his return from Sandringham he simply said that he had had business to attend to, and parried her curiosity by guiding the talk deftly on to the royal weekend party, and what a crashing bore it had been.

"I'll bet it wasn't. You enjoyed every minute of it," she said. "Just watch you trot away if Kingie invites you again."

"Somehow I don't think Kingie will. I was a novelty once, as you kindly remarked, but they've played with me now, and I can be chucked to the back of the cupboard. I didn't win any amazing hands at bridge, and I shot pheasants a great deal too well. And I'm not cut out for the company of the great, I discover; they talk too much about being great, and that makes me feel small."

Of course she wanted to know who had been there, and when

222

he began to tell her about Fisher and Churchill she interrupted impatiently.

"Not them, silly! Who were the ladies? How many fascinating widows did you make love to, and were there any youngest daughters of dukes looking for an American fortune? Did you languish at Mrs Keppel's feet, and – "

"No, she languished at mine, and the King caught us and challenged me to a duel, but I told him he was too old. That's really why I won't be invited back. No, there weren't any fascinating widows, or duke's daughters – there was a suffragette, whose great-uncle got drunk and chased one of the tweenies, and fell downstairs – "

"Oh, shut up!"

"Listen, that is strictly true! Cross my heart," but he could not convince her, and they went in to tea with Sir Charles, making fun of each other while he watched them, smiling over his cup. It was pleasant, and cosy, and as he sat with them round the fire Mr Franklin was conscious of a great ease and content; he felt at home, and as he glanced across at Peggy laughing as she poured the tea, and considered the angel face with its halo of auburn hair, and the supple lines of her figure in the blue velvet afternoon dress, he felt a great hunger for her, and wished that Sir Charles had taken his tea elsewhere.

His reticence in the matter of his interview with Lacy was wasted after all, as he might have known it would be in a rural community one of whose principal industries was the discovery of other people's business. No doubt Major Blake's clerk had had his ear to the keyhole; possibly Major Blake himself was indiscreet; it may even have been that someone in the office of Smith, Cross, Newbold and Wise, aware of the eccentric trust deed whereby Mr Franklin had secured Lye Cottage to the future use and enjoyment of transient aborigines, their heirs and successors forever, breached professional etiquette by gossiping in a Thetford pub – whatever the source, a Norwich newspaper soon heard of it, and a humorous article (and there never were in the history of journalism humorous articles so arch and droll as those of the Edwardian era) appeared under the heading "Redskins at Castle Lancing?"

Of course, all Thetford and district knew what lay behind it; Thetford and district, in fact, fell about laughing. Lord Lacy's car was regularly followed by rude lads on bicycles ululating the most realistic war-whoops, and it was agreed that the Yankee was a very shrewd

223

bird with a wry sense of humour, and him such a quiet and courteous gentleman, too. All of which Mr Franklin was human enough to find mildly gratifying; his one slight regret was that Lacy was now bound to assume that he had carried out his threat and divulged the story out of pure malice.

"He'll never forgive you for this, Mark," said Sir Charles Clayton. "Heaven knows he wasn't much liked before, but this makes him a positive laughing-stock. Arapaho Indians!" His lips twitched with amusement as he laid the paper aside. "Are there such people?"

"Certainly there are; they were a powerful tribe once, very war-like, in spite of their name, which means 'trader'. But they were friendly enough to Dad and me; they looked after us very well."

Sir Charles shook his head, smiling. "You've led an extraordinary life, haven't you? Cowboys, miners, Redskins . . . doesn't Norfolk seem awfully sleepy and prosaic after that?"

"It suits me. I'm beginning to feel at home, I guess; it's been three months now, you know."

"As short a time as that? I must be getting old – I'd have sworn it was longer. You seem to have been one of the family for . . ." Sir Charles broke off, staring into the fire; they were alone in the late afternoon in the big drawing-room at Oxton, waiting for Peggy and Arthur, home from Sandhurst, who had gone into Thetford. It was snowing heavily, but the curtains were still drawn back, and the firelight was flickering in reflection against the panes. Sir Charles went on: "You've become quite a local character, too – with all this Lye Cottage business. That kind of thing can win a lot of good will . . . people like it when a newcomer takes their part. And you're more of a new-come-backer really." Sir Charles smiled. "I'm only sorry there's been this new unpleasantness with Lacy."

"It doesn't add much to the total score," said Mr Franklin. "I just seem to have an unfortunate knack of getting in his way. If it isn't cottages, it's foxes and . . . night encounters."

"Yes." Sir Charles paused, for quite a long moment, and then said, without inflection. "And then of course there is Peggy. You've rather cut him out there."

It occurred to Mr Franklin that Sir Charles himself had done some of the cutting, but he replied evenly: "I guess he thinks so."

Sir Charles sat for another silent moment and then said: "I imagine everyone thinks so. Certainly I can claim to know Peggy as well as anyone does – and I don't merely think it, I know it." He smiled

224

candidly at Mr Franklin. "It's been rather amusing, in a way. Peggy has never been what one would term a wall-flower, and her attitude to young men has hitherto been . . . nonchalant? At least, I've noticed in her a tendency which one often sees in the beautiful, to take admirers – including Lacy – very coolly for granted. But of late I seem to have heard a good deal of 'Mark says' and 'Mark thinks'. I must say," added Sir Charles, with a wry twist to his smile, "that it's rather refreshing to find her paying the slightest attention to anyone else's words or thoughts. She never has to mine, so far as I can remember . . . ah, I think I hear the wanderers returning. Heavens, is that the time already?"

The door opened and Peggy, glowing and bright-eyed from the cold, swept in with Arthur in her wake.

"Are you two sitting in the dark? Men! Never think to close the curtains, do you?" She snapped on the lights, gave Mr Franklin a flashing smile, and began to pull the curtains together. "Gosh, I'm starved! Haven't they brought tea yet? Arthur, give them a shout, will you, the idle things." She slipped down on to her knees by the hearth and spread her hands to the fire. "It's a perfect blizzard out there – I thought we'd stick in a snowdrift. And what have you two been chattering about?"

"You, you'll be gratified to hear," said Sir Charles.

"An improving subject. What did you decide?"

"That you're a pain in the neck," said Arthur, collapsing on to the sofa. "Not a bad-looking pain, but a rotten driver. She insisted on taking the wheel all the way home, and how the poor old buggy survived is a mystery. You must have had a boring conversation."

"Quite the contrary, in fact," said Sir Charles. "You'll be interested to know that the Arapaho Indians – "

"Don't talk about Arapaho Indians!" exclaimed Peggy. "Ever since that article appeared I've been dreading meeting Frank Lacy, in case I burst out laughing!"

"Serve the brute right," said Arthur. "Anyone who sicks on thugs to scare old women deserves all he gets."

"That's something I still find hard to believe," said Sir Charles, frowning. "That Bob Lacy's boy would stoop to such a – "

"Oh, Frank's game for anything," said Arthur. "Remember how he used to blackmail us, Peg, when we were kids? Nothing crude, mind you, but when I broke the dining-room window, Frank managed

225

to hint, ever so delicately, that unless I parted with my new cricket bat, the information might leak out, somehow."

"Frank gets what he wants," said Peggy thoughtfully, staring into the fire. She looked at Mr Franklin. "You're sure he was responsible, Mark?"

"I don't know anyone else who was interested in getting Bessie out of Lye Cottage."

"I suppose not," said Peggy. "Unless Blake did it, without Frank's knowledge."

"Blake's a tick, all right," said Arthur, "but Frank's an even bigger tick. Anyway, Blake wouldn't dare, not on his own responsibility. No, it's just the sort of rotten stunt that Frank would try to pull. You ought to know that, Peg. Why make excuses for him?"

"I'm not making excuses for him. But it's pretty ruthless and cold-blooded, even for him. I mean, I agree he's a bit of a tick, but I don't like to think he's as big a tick as all that."

"The old fire still smoulders," said Arthur solemnly, winking at Mr Franklin. "Although Sir Jasper de Vere, her childhood sweetheart, had proved unworthy of her regard, a lingering fondness pervaded the maiden's – " He rolled over on the couch as his sister began to belabour him with a cushion. He emerged, dishevelled. "She couldn't resist Frank's brutal charm, even when he was in frocks. I could, though. I pasted the little skunk whenever I got the chance – "

"It's a pity someone doesn't paste you," said Peggy, warmly. "You talk too much. Anyway, Frank blacked your eye more that once, and didn't you roar, just? Little blubberer!"

"That's when he was still bigger than I was," protested Arthur, but at that moment the arrival of a maid with tea put a stop to his childhood recollections.

They were a cheerful group round the fire, while the storm thickened outside. At Peggy's request, Arthur now pulled back one of the curtains she had drawn, and they watched the flakes drifting against the windows, climbing up the panes from the corners of the frames.

"It's going to be a white Christmas," said Arthur. "We don't get that many of them – four that I can remember. I know it's four, because Peg and I always used to build a snowman, and I know we've only ever had four snowmen on Christmas Day. Jolly good snowmen, with coal eyes and carrot noses and that old top hat – wonder what ever became of that topper?"

"Did you have white Christmases, Mark?" Peggy wondered, and he laughed.

"Never had anything else – not on the North Plains, anyway. White October clear through to March, usually, and several feet deep, at that. I remember trying to make a snowman, once, but the snow wouldn't stick. Too cold, I guess. Your English snow is probably more civilized."

"Well, this year you'll make your first snowman," said Peggy. "You'll spend Christmas with us, won't you?" And in the face of that invitation, with Arthur seconding and Sir Charles murmuring agreeably, Mr Franklin could hardly decline.

He stayed for dinner, and they played solo whist afterwards, until it was time for him to leave. But by then the snow was so thick, and the drifts even on the drive so deep, that it was obviously out of the question for him to attempt the few miles back to Castle Lancing in his gig. So a spare room was prepared – not in what Arthur called the savage west wing, but in the main part of the house. Sir Charles turned in early, and Arthur tactfully went to play snooker against himself; Mr Franklin and Peggy sat and talked quietly before the fire, sitting on the rug with their backs to the sofa, kissing and petting gently at first, and then kissing more lingeringly, her body pressed against his, his hands caressing her breasts through the smooth velvet. They heard Arthur's whistling in the hall, and drew apart; he came in loudly, challenging Mr Franklin to fifty up before bed, and Peggy bade them good-night and went upstairs, Mr Franklin inwardly cursing the importunate Arthur as his eyes followed the graceful, blue-sheathed figure on the staircase. But when the game was over, and he had gone upstairs, undressed, made his way to the bathroom in his borrowed dressing-gown, and returned, he found the door of his room open and Peggy adjusting the curtains.

"Just seeing it was all snug and cosy," she said, and turned to face him. She was wearing a Japanese gown of gold silk; her hair was still up, framing the perfect face, and he felt he had never seen anything so beautiful or desirable in his life. She was smiling at him, gently, and there was no trace of that little curl on the full lips; with a sudden electric thrill he realized that there was no white lace or frill showing at the collar or cuff or ankle of the clinging gown; no sign of a nightdress, in fact. He closed the door and turned to look at her for a long moment.

"Hello, Mark," she said softly.

227

"Hello, Peggy."

He came to her, and she to him, and they kissed very long and deep; he slipped his hands within the robe and felt the soft smoothness of her body for the first time, and she gave a little laugh of sheer pleasure as he drew her on to the bed. They made love with a slow, intense enjoyment that surprised them both, and afterwards lay in each other's arms, blissfully content, murmuring the usual nonsense which is more clearly intelligible to the initiated than any proposition of logic. He talked of her beauty, and she of his strength, which is as it ought to be; they also announced their infatuation with each other, at not more than fifteen-second intervals, and finally Mr Franklin looked down at her, at the incredible loveliness of the angel face and even more angelic body, and fondled it gently until her eyes narrowed and her lips parted, and in the headiness of the moment it seemed inevitable that he should say:

"You know, we could go on doing this for the rest of our lives."

He knew what he was saying, although he said it recklessly; he knew it was reckless, and all the better for that; he was as happy then as he had ever been in thirty-five years, and he wanted nothing more than that the happiness should continue. And apparently Peggy was of the same mind, for all she said was:

"Let's."

"You know what I'm saying? What we're saying?"

"Mm-mh."

There was a long, but by no means tranquil interval, and when it had passed Mr Franklin lay with her head pillowed on his chest and his hand stroking the silky nakedness of her back and inquired of the ceiling: "D'you think your father will approve?" He received no answer; she was fast asleep. Which told him, when he came to think of it, that his question was irrelevant.

However, Sir Charles did approve, when Mr Franklin raised the matter with him the following morning; indeed, he appeared delighted, and that even before a radiant Peggy was summoned to reassure her father that it was exactly what she had always wanted, and to prove the point by embracing Mr Franklin with an ardour that caused the baronet to turn tactfully away in search of the bell-pull. For there had to be a bottle from the best bin, and Arthur, grinning from ear to ear, had to thump Mr Franklin on the back and state his opinion that this was the best news since Cambridge last won the Boat Race. "I knew it was going to happen the moment I saw him standing in the lane with the fox in his basket, gaping (he was gaping, not the fox) at Peg as though she was Helen of Troy, and *she* was all a-quiver, like jelly in a high wind. Oh, well, that's another cut-glass decanter up the spout – unless you'd prefer a fish-slice."

There was considerable gaiety, and drinking and spilling of champagne, and presently Arthur went to fetch the servants and more bottles, and a positively Pickwickian scene was enacted in the drawing-room, with the maids bobbing in their aprons, and the butler and footman grinning, and Sir Charles proposing the health of what, with rare felicity, he described as the happy couple, Mark Franklin and my daughter Peggy. At which the housekeeper burst into tears, and had to be helped to a chair, and the butler said a few words, couched in terms of unctuous servility, and wishing all happiness and success to our dear young mistress and her intended; it would possibly have been enough to turn Mr Franklin immediately from the prospect of marriage if Peggy had not been beside him looking good enough to eat with a spoon. He managed a few words of reply, which the servants applauded enthusiastically, in the hope of refills, and after these had been poured and disposed of, the loyal retainers trooped off, full of this great sensation, and Sir Charles smiled and nodded and expressed his delight yet again, and Arthur clapped Mr Franklin on the shoulder once more, and Peggy squeezed his hand tight, and Mr Franklin wondered precisely what he had done, and sought reassurance in another glance at the chocolate-box beauty beside him and the feel of her soft young body as he slipped his hand about her waist.

"And when," said Sir Charles, "do you propose to get married?" Peggy said, soon, don't we, Mark, to which Mr Franklin could think of no more appropriate rejoinder than an enthusiastic affirmative. Sir Charles said he wasn't certain what the preliminary formalities were, but quite apart from the business of banns, which the vicar would know all about – unless Peggy wanted a Town wedding? Peggy said of course there would have to be a Town wedding, she didn't want to get married in the depths of the country; all her school friends would expect it to be in London, and Mark would like that anyway, wouldn't you, Mark? But that, said Sir Charles, was looking some way ahead; in the meantime there would have to be an announcement in *The Times* and the other newspapers, that sort of thing; Arthur said that was all right, but the important thing was to see that Peggy's picture got onto the main inside page of the *Sphere* – *that* would spread the news like nothing else, and give the event the prominence it deserved, and the *Sphere* would jump at the chance, because they loved to get good-lookers into the paper, and although he hated to admit it, his sister was a bit of a peach. He would fix it, and see that the *Sphere* and *Illustrated London News* and the society rags got in a mention of the King's recent visit to Oxton, and Mr Franklin's sojourn at Sandringham, and all that rot . . .

It was slightly breathtaking, and Mr Franklin was glad to slip away presently with Peggy, for more embraces and quiet conversation; like most men in his position, he had no desire to think beyond the next few minutes, or to contemplate anything except a pair of eyes, and a nose, and a mouth whose arrangement exercised a fascination which sent odd little shivers up his spine.

That there was another side to the affair did not cross his mind until later that afternoon, when he had torn himself away – with a promise to return for dinner – and driven back through the sunlit snow to Castle Lancing. Once he was alone, he could give serious thought to what he had done; he even pulled up once on the road and asked himself if he was absolutely certain he loved Peggy? After all, he had known her only a matter of weeks; he was in a new country, and many strange things had happened to him in a short time – was he still sane and balanced and sure of his own mind, he who at thirty-five had never been seriously involved with any woman before? Did he really want to spend the rest of his life with Peggy? – what, for that matter, was the rest of his life going to be?

He had no idea – all he knew was that at the moment, he did not want to spend the rest of his life without her. And he could hardly say fairer than that. Besides, he had offered; he couldn't draw back now, even if he'd wanted to, and he could search his soul and tell himself that he didn't. For one thing, he had seen the look in her eyes, and if she didn't love him then he knew nothing – and to have someone love you, that was a remarkable achievement, and you could count yourself lucky.

And there was something fateful about it, perhaps; those vague thoughts about England, land of his fathers, all his life, and the decision, taken he didn't quite know how, to come and see it, and the feeling of inevitability, with his first view of Castle Lancing, and the house, and the old churchyard, and Thornhill crouching beside him peering at the tombs – that this was home, his place, his people, his land. And now an English girl, from the same pasture and the same stock – their sons would be Englishmen, and their daughters

Englishwomen, and that was a strange thought, too. He tried to imagine those people leaving Castle Lancing more than two and a half centuries ago – a dusty road, and perhaps a horse and wagon with their things piled on top; a man in his rough smock and steeple hat, a woman in her long drab skirt and mutch cap, perhaps a child or two, taking the Thetford road, and looking back through the summer haze to the little wooded village that they would never see again. Or perhaps it had been winter, and they had seen it as he saw it now, deep in brilliant white, with the snow heavy on the bare branches and hedges, and the sun like a disc of blood in the pale sky. And beyond those figures, others, in coarse linsey or buckskin, powerful bearded men and worn, strong women, wrinkling up their eyes and looking west, cutting their timber, ploughing their land, rolling their wagons into the endless distance, surviving revolution and civil war and Indian raid and blizzard and storm and drought, just so that one of them could turn homeward again and close the circle – until others would open it again, some day, and the story would continue into other unforeseen chapters. English sons and English daughters – what did he know? What an irony if they should do what he had done, and go back to *their* father's country? He'd be glad – just as those two dusty figures of his imagination, Matthew and Jezebel Franklin, turning for a last look back in the year 1642, would surely rejoice if they could see him now, home again in Castle Lancing, and know that their journey had not been in vain.

Mr Franklin shook the reins and drove on. If he was thinking this way, imagining a future out of a dream of the past, he must be in love with Peggy, since she was an essential, vital part of that future. And he only had to think of her, smiling at him, with those lips slightly parted and that light in her eye, to feel a pleasurable tingling, and a desire to turn back as quickly as might to Oxton and see her again.

In the meantime, there was Lancing Manor, and Samson being told the news, standing impassive for a moment, and then his face breaking into a glad smile.

"May I congratulate you, sir, and wish you very happy – you and Miss Clayton both? A charming young lady, sir, if I may say so."

"You may indeed, Thomas – in fact, you can go round the house saying it as often as you like, and I won't contradict you. I think she's kind of charming myself. Phew!" Mr Franklin stood in the hall and grinned hugely at his servant. "It's been quite a day – quite a day! And I'm going back to Oxton this evening – but you can pack our

231

bags for a few days in London, because never mind getting married – it seems that just getting engaged entails all sorts of coming and going – I've a ring to buy, for one thing – " Mr Franklin was calling over his shoulder as he strode upstairs " – I guess I ought to have had one in advance, but the truth is I didn't realize . . . ." He stopped short of admitting that twenty-four hours ago he had had no idea of getting married – well, it had crossed his mind vaguely, he supposed, a few times over the past couple of months, but nothing definite. "Anyway, Miss Clayton's going up to Town to stay with her aunt for a few days – things to arrange, photograph to be taken for some paper or other, apparently, people to see – you know. We'll stay at a hotel – we'll see which one when we get there."

"I shall send a boy from the village into Thetford with a telegram, sir. Probably you would prefer to stay at Claridge's."

"Would I? What's wrong with the Waldorf?"

"Claridge's, I think, sir, unless you have a preference for the Ritz. May I ask where Miss Clayton's aunt resides?"

"Hold on – Dover Street, was it? I think so – "

"Then Claridge's would be more convenient, sir."

"Whatever you say – you're the authority . . . " Mr Franklin checked on a sudden thought and came out on to the landing. Samson had just arrived at the head of the stairs.

"That's a point," said Mr Franklin, frowning. "Look, Thomas – this won't make any difference to you, will it? It's just occurred to me – you don't have any objection to staying on with me, after I'm married, do you?"

"None in the least, sir. I shall be most happy to continue in your service, if you and Miss Clayton wish it."

It was the gentlest of reminders that Mr Franklin's decisions would no longer be entirely his own; he digested it quickly.

"You needn't have any doubts about that. I'm going to need you more than ever, I should think." He paused as another thought struck him. "Come to that – well, I suppose we'll have to take on other staff, won't we? I don't know what kind of an establishment – well, what do married couples usually have?"

Samson paused before replying. "That depends, sir, entirely on their own wishes and convenience." He might have added that it also depended on their means, but left Mr Franklin to draw that conclusion for himself. "I imagine Miss Clayton, apart from her own maid, will wish to engage the usual servants – a cook, of course, housemaid and

232

parlour maid. But it depends on the size of the establishment – of the house, and whether it is in town or country."

"Holy smoke!" said Mr Franklin. "That's three maids, a cook, and you. That's five." Automatically he glanced round the landing. "There isn't room. Is there? We've got four bedrooms – and the servants' quarters, but they're only big enough for two . . . "

His voice trailed off as it dawned on him that in the euphoria of the morning, to say nothing of the previous night, he had given no thought to the immediate practical considerations of marriage. It had all happened so quickly – in fact, it had happened at one hell of a lick. He'd had no time . . . he had a sudden, irrelevant recollection of looking down at Peggy, smiling drowsily and provocatively up at him, her smooth nakedness joined to his own – it hadn't crossed his mind at that particular moment that an inevitable consequence was going to be a domestic reorganization on a large scale. Where they'd live hadn't even occurred to him – and in that moment he knew that he wasn't going to give up Lancing Manor. Whether they lived there or not, he was going to keep it. Money wasn't a problem, thank God. But it wasn't big enough, that was certain, for the kind of household that Samson was talking about – and a girl in Peggy's station couldn't be expected to do with less. Would she want them to live at Oxton Hall? – no, that was out of the question. It would have to be his house – wherever it was . . . He realized that he was looking at Samson with what must resemble consternation in his eyes, and Samson, as usual, was about five jumps ahead.

"I don't know exactly what the arrangements will be, yet," said Mr Franklin. "It's quite possible that we'll take another house in the neighbourhood. But I'll certainly be keeping this place."

"I'm very pleased to hear that, sir. I feel that this house suits you very well, if I may say so."

"Yes," said Mr Franklin. "I like it, too." Another thought was occurring, and he wasn't sure that he liked it. He aired it in a roundabout way which did not deceive Samson for a moment. "You wouldn't object to living in London, if we decided to set up house there?" That's damned silly, he thought immediately; it sounds as though where we live depends on what he wants. "We haven't settled anything in that way, Miss Clayton and I . . . oh, what the hell, Thomas, I haven't the foggiest idea!" Mr Franklin burst out laughing. "All I know is I've proposed to Miss Clayton, and she's said yes, and I don't know whether we're going to live in Norfolk or Nevada!"

Samson was smiling back. "Nevada would suit me very well, sir, I dare say," he said, "but I think I should prefer Norfolk, on the whole."

"Well, so should I, and I'm darned sure Miss Clayton would – or somewhere not far away. So we'll cross Nevada off our list for a start." He shook his head. "It's quite a business, though. I'm darned glad you're around, I can tell you. Anyway, for the moment we needn't look farther than Claridge's, the day after tomorrow. Oh, and we'll be at Oxton Hall for Christmas." He grinned at Samson. "Our tranquil days are over, Thomas – for the moment, anyway." But if he could have foreseen the circumstances in which he would remind Samson of that jocular phrase, Mr Franklin would not have smiled as he said it.

He had supposed that his few days in London would be fairly unhurried, and like everyone else who visits that city, in any age, he was quite wrong. He had to call at the American Express Company, for he had decided that there was no point in leaving the bulk of his assets in the States; the die was cast, and the time had come, England was where he was going to be, and with fifty thousand pounds snugly locked up in Mr Evans's Chancery Lane Safe Deposit, it was only common sense to transfer the rest of his money to London and put it out in sensible investments. Nothing fancy or speculative; Mr Franklin's pioneer prudence wanted no get-rich-quick schemes; he knew nothing about finance beyond putting his dollar on the counter and picking up his goods, but he understood that there were safe, cautious advisers to be had in the City who would lay his cash out for him in directions which would ensure a modest, certain return in any circumstances short of total revolution. And that, in spite of Cassel's mild misgivings, he could not see happening.

The American Express Company, when he called on it, gave a violent start and then welcomed him with open arms. Plainly the assistant manager still was wary of him; he lurked behind the manager's chair in a manner which suggested that he expected Mr Franklin to ask for a draft payable in the British Crown Jewels; but the manager himself, once he had ascertained that all that was required was a simple credit transfer from New York, and that there was to be no sudden demand for bullion, was all affability and co-operation. Mr Franklin's assets would be deposited with Lloyd's, who in turn would advise him on their profitable disposal. The manager would have dearly liked to know what became of the fifty thousand in gold that Mr Franklin had spirited away that September day, but he could hardly ask, and the client took his leave with the manager concealing his curiosity, and the assistant eyeing his departure apprehensively all the way to the door.

"That's an odd bird," said the manager reflectively. "Isn't he the little Englishman now, though? – why, I didn't recognize him at first."

"I did," said the assistant, darkly. "Carnegie's nephew – huh!"

"Oh, he's sound," said the manager. "And he's darned warm, too – there aren't many better-heeled individuals walking along Queen Street this minute."

"That's it," said the assistant. "He's got no right to be. Why, you said yourself he doesn't know how to treat money."

"When you've got as much as he has," said the manager heavily, "you can treat it how you damned well like. Let's cable McCall and get things moving."

Meanwhile Mr Franklin had called for Peggy at a fashionable photographers, and bore her off to Asprey's for the first important purchase of their partnership. He approached it with a private determination that whichever ring Peggy chose, it should far outweigh in value the jewellery he had bought for Pip; his Puritan soul and sense of fitness would demand no less, and he was resolved to cajole and coax if he had to. To his relief, it was not necessary; what he had thought extravagant, in his provincial ignorance, was evidently commonplace in London society. Peggy examined several trays of rings with critical care, and finally selected a circlet of diamonds which, to his inexpert eye, seemed to consist of stones whose minute size was out of all proportion to the price demanded. However, he was assured by the salesman, and a glowing Peggy, that size was not necessarily a guide to value; on an impulse, he bought her a pair of emerald earrings, which were accepted only after a bright-eyed protest and murmurs about extravagance, while the assistant beamed in his most avuncular fashion.

"Engagement earrings!" said Peggy, turning her head this way and that to admire them. "Mark, you're mad! Whoever heard of such a thing?"

"It's an old Arapaho custom," said Mr Franklin. "Every brave gives his intended squaw a pair of engagement earrings, generally made out of whole buffalo horns."

"They don't!"

"They're going to have to, after this," said Mr Franklin. "And it's going to be mighty tough, because the emerald buffalo is just about extinct." He noticed that the assistance was staring at him in some concern, and thought, careful Franklin, or you're liable to start a whole new bogus zoology. Peggy said there was nothing for it: the *Sphere* would just have to take her picture all over again, with the earrings, and Mr Franklin left the shop walking on a little air. He took her to tea at the Ritz, and was brought back to earth when, drawing off her gloves and settling herself into a corner of the couch, she said quite matter-of-fact:

"Where are we going to live, Mark?"

However, he was not taken aback. "Where would you like to live?" he asked, and Peggy replied without hesitation.

"London. If you don't mind. My friends are here, and while Mummy was alive we used to take a house during the season, in Eaton Place. And it has all the shops, theatres, that sort of thing. I suppose I always imagined that when I got married I would be living in the West End, Belgravia – or Mayfair when I was really day-dreaming." She smiled at him. "But don't worry – I don't want to live in Mayfair. It's too . . . oh, too 'House of Lords' nowadays, and political hostesses, and stuffy and awful and rather vulgar. You're in Brook Street or Curzon Street, everyone sizes everyone else up, and there's the most ghastly competition – do you know what I mean? But if you're in Belgravia, well, it's still absolutely the best, but so much easier, somehow, and younger and smarter. Not so many grisly Duch-esses." She wiggled her eyebrows whimsically, and sighed. "That's what I'd like. But that's just *me*." She sat forward to pour tea. "What about you?"

It was going to be London, then. Did he mind? He tried to visualise the kind of house he had read about, months ago at the estate agents – Cadogan Square, it had been, and he'd been rather attracted by it. How long would he have endured the solitude of Castle Lancing, even if he hadn't been going to get married? Had he intended to settle there? What, indeed, had he intended? He was stirring his cup thoughtfully, and Peggy said: "Oh, dear. Have I said the wrong thing? You tell me where – "

"Far from it." Mr Franklin reached out and took her hand reassur-ingly. "Very far from it. No, if I didn't answer right away it wasn't because I had any doubts about London. I was just wondering – about me, selfishly." He grinned. "You see, Peg – I don't really know, still, why I came to England. Don't misunderstand me; I love it, and I don't want to leave it. But I came here with no clear notion of what I was going to *do* – that's an awful admission for a grown-up man, isn't it? It was a strange business, all right. But the last few days have changed things a lot. Now – I do know what I'm going to do."

She was watching him, expectantly. "What, Mark?"

"I'm going to get married," he said. "That's the important thing. And I don't care where I live, except that it has to be with you. And if you want London – then I want London; it's that simple." He grinned and nodded with that emphatic phrase that was a byword among his countrymen: "Every time!"

"Oh, Mark, are you sure? You're not just – "

"No, I'm not just. I really mean it. How about Cadogan Square?"

"Cadogan Square?" Peggy stared. "Oh . . . well, yes . . . that sort of thing." But not quite, he realized. "But what on earth do you know about it? I didn't know you'd even been there!"

"Haven't. But I read about it – when I first came here. It sounds like the kind of place that would have the sort of house you want – I imagine," said Mr Franklin knowledgeably, "that it would have to accommodate us, and your maid, and my man Thomas – " he glided past the name with slight trepidation, but Peggy did not so much as blink " – and a cook, and two or three maids, or a footman, or something. Wouldn't it?"

"Why – yes!" Peggy was laughing, and he felt a sudden urge to kiss her, and see what the murmuring Quality of the Ritz, politely engulfing their pâté sandwiches and coffee cake, made out of that. "But, Mark, I didn't know that you'd even thought about it. I hadn't, really! Gosh, you're a dark horse!"

"Would we have to have a butler? By God, there's an idea! I'll bet Thomas would be the butlingest butler you ever saw! If he'd do it, that is. Anyway, we can settle all that – " Mr Franklin waved a light-hearted hand. "Is there any more of that tea? And those kind of fishy sandwiches – why d'you suppose they make 'em six to a man-sized bite? Fellow could starve to death in here . . . "

"Oh, Mark!" Peggy shook her head at him, smiling lovingly. "I'm so glad we're getting married. We are, aren't we?"

"That's the way the wise money's going," said Mr Franklin. "At least, I asked this girl – down in Norfolk, you know – God, what a little beauty she is! And she said 'Yes", so unless she's taken up with some other guy in the meantime – there are these smooth Americans who hang around Claridge's and the Ritz – "

"Stop it, idiot! People will look, and I'll start laughing!" She shook her head. "D'you know – you've changed. Ever so much, really. When we first met, you were a terribly serious person – you just looked at one in that quiet, steady way – it was rather frightening, really. D'you know what Father said about you – it was the very first time you were at Oxton, the day the King left? He said, 'I like that chap. He's straight'. And then he said 'He's very dangerous'. I asked him what on earth he meant, and he laughed and said, he didn't mean you *were*, really, but that you could be, that you'd be a bad enemy. I thought he was right, and you were rather sober, and didn't say a great deal, and one couldn't tell what you were thinking at all. Now – well, you're different – at least to me. Jolly, and – " she shrugged, looking for a word. "I don't know – you seem much happier, somehow."

She was right, reflected Mr Franklin. He, who had always been reserved to the point of shyness, had been astonished to find himself of late feeling positively frivolous – at least, it was frivolity by his lights. He had found himself laughing aloud once or twice, or grinning without restraint; he had made occasional jokes, and not of the wry variety, but nonsensical things, which made her laugh. Maybe he was changing. "Or maybe it's just getting engaged to be married," he said. "Ever seen young deer in spring? They prance and tumble and rush around; I guess that's what I'm doing. All right, I'm going to be very serious. Cadogan Square – or wherever it's going to be. Are you quite certain you don't want to live in Mayfair? We can, you know. And I don't want you to think that we can't because of . . . expense, or anything like that. So if secretly you'd rather live around Brook Street or off Piccadilly, just say so. It doesn't make any difference."

Peggy considered this, and then said: "No, I don't want to. The reasons I gave are what I really feel. I'm not a Mayfair person – Daddy isn't . . . well, there are funny levels in Society, and my family has never been in the forefront of the fashionable world. You can mix in among them, without belonging to them, do you see what I mean?" She paused, looking across the room, and when she spoke again it was with an odd expression, half-frown, half-smile, looking at him curiously almost. "Mark – are you awfully rich?"

The old Mr Franklin would have considered this rather solemnly; the new one laughed straight out before settling himself to give a serious answer. "Rich? I don't know what rich is, really. But yes, I think I am – anyway, the thought of keeping *two* houses in Brook Street, if we had to, wouldn't worry me. And one in the country."

"You'll keep Lancing Manor, won't you?"

"Why, yes." He was pleased. "I'd always want to keep that. It's not very big, of course – we couldn't live there – "

"But it will be ideal, if we want to get away to the country for a little while – it's close enough to Oxton to be convenient. And it's a beautiful place. D'you remember the first time you took me there – after the King's awful week-end?" Peggy smiled reminiscently. "I think that was the moment . . ." She let it trail away, and he had to ask what the moment had been.

"I'm not going to make you conceited," said Peggy, becoming mock business-like and putting on her gloves. "Now, just you use some of that fabulous wealth to pay for our tea – I have to be at Aunty Sophy's by half-past five, or she'll have a fit."

12

A few days later Mr Franklin returned to Castle Lancing, for what he felt was a necessary rest. It was a strange thing that he, who could ride thirty miles a day, in bad weather, sleep on the ground, and get up long before first light to punch cattle or dig in rock and mud until dark, and feel no more than pleasantly weary, should find himself bone-tired after a few days spent in nothing more exacting than talking to estate agents – Wilton Crescent, not Cadogan Square, it transpired, was where Peggy had set her heart on living – or opening negotiations with the urbane Mr Pride for domestic staff.

From these discussions, tied as they were to some vaguely-resolved date in the coming spring, Mr Franklin and Peggy gradually began to find their wedding-date settled for them; their decision to take a West Indian cruise as their honeymoon finally determined them, and February 3, 1910 was fixed on. A notice appeared to that effect in the better newspapers, and in the last week before Christmas Mr Franklin, on the point of setting out for Oxton Hall for the holiday, sat in Castle Lancing and contemplated Page Three of the *Sphere*, where Peggy, resplendent in her emerald earrings, sat in maidenly serenity, apparently contemplating, with slightly parted lips, an advertisement for tonic wine on the page opposite. He had actually caught his breath on opening the magazine – was she really that beautiful? No doubt he was biased, but to him she looked like a rather thoughtful angel who might, at any moment, make a caustic remark about God, and then turn aside rebuke by releasing one of those brilliant smiles; who was very conscious of posing for her picture, and was ready to mock herself and the viewer on the point. He'd have to ask the photographer for the original, if not for the caption beneath it. "Miss Peggy Clayton, only daughter of Sir Charles Clayton, of Oxton Hall, Norfolk, whom readers will remember as one of the reigning beauties of last season ..." "... Sir Charles recently had the honour to entertain His Majesty ..." "... Mr Mark Franklin, of Castle Lancing,

Norfolk, who has extensive mining and cattle interests in his native United States."

He smiled at that. What would Jim Eliot have said about his 'cattle interests'? Extensive experience as ground-hog and saddle-tramp was more like it, but one couldn't expect the *Sphere* to say that, even if they'd known it.

Samson and he drove over to Oxton in the late afternoon; the snow had gone, and the countryside was bare and sodden and still. Mr Franklin, jumping down from the passenger's seat to close the great gates, glanced back at the garden and paused with his hand on the wrought-iron latch; it was peaceful and rather melancholy with its stark branches and dripping bushes and damp grass, but how pleasantly familiar now, and how comfortable to look on it and the solid, four-square house, and feel the gentle thrill of ownership. Even when he lived in London, it would still be here. As he turned away he would not have believed the circumstances in which he was to look on it again.

Oxton Hall was full in Christmas week, with Arthur's companions and Peggy's friends chattering their congratulations, and decorations going up, and bustle everywhere, late meals, Sir Charles' routine thrown quite out of gear, raised voices and happy laughter ringing along the old corridors, groups round the piano singing after dinner, or playing party games with a tireless zest which made Mr Franklin wonder if he was getting old. When he was not with Peggy, he found himself gravitating to the company of Sir Charles and his more senior neighbours who dropped in for afternoon tea, or for dinner. Peggy, he noticed, joined in the preliminary merry-making perfunctorily; of course, she was the hostess, and had other things to attend to while the bright young things romped and shouted and gossiped noisily, but he found himself hoping that her tastes were, in fact, rather more sedate and adult than those of her brother and his friends. He hoped it because he had to face squarely the fact that there was a fifteen-year age difference between Peggy and himself, and it would be reassuring to think that she did not have quite as much indefatigable energy for juvenile amusement as her contemporaries.

"Preparing to be a staid and respectable old married woman," she said lightly, when he remarked on it. "I think I stopped being a bright young thing when I was about seven. When I hear them whooping it up I just want to go and lie down." She grimaced as the sound of Poppy, the bedroom peregrinator, shrilled across the hall from the

241

drawing-room, where the piano was being mercilessly hammered to the accompaniment of stamping feet:

Has anybody here seen Kelly?
Kelly from the Isle of Man!

"Has anybody here heard Poppy?" wondered Peggy. "They'd have a job not to. I do hope Arthur gets sick of her soon – or she gets sick of him, and goes back to Frank Lacy. He sent a Christmas card the other day, did you know? 'To Sir Charles Clayton and Family', if you please, and signed 'Lacy'. Of all the fat-headedness – I mean, he's either Frank or nothing, and since he's ceased to be welcome you'd think he'd know better than to send a card at all. I sometimes wonder if he's slightly touched."

"Have you seen him lately?"

"Not since before your great encounter with him and Blake. I've wondered, once or twice, what he thought about us – since the engagement was announced. I half expected to have him over here, roaring at me, but he must have decided to treat the whole thing with lofty disdain. Once upon a time I'd have felt rather peeved, but now I'm just relieved."

Christmas Day, when it came, was the customary mixture of orgy and anti-climax; presents were piled under a tree in the hall, with the younger people squealing and rioting while their elders watched indulgently – Poppy received a rubber hot water-bottle from an anonymous admirer, and belaboured Arthur with it indignantly – huge quantities of turkey and plum pudding were consumed, and remarkable quantities of port drunk; Mr Franklin walked bare-headed through the grounds in the bleak afternoon, smoking a cigar, and feeling at peace with himself and the world. Peggy, taking her duties as chatelaine seriously, and full of preparations for the party that was to follow in the evening, had banished him briefly, and he was content to escape from the hullabaloo for half an hour. He stood at the end of the path, just where he had stood with Sir Charles three months earlier, looking across the misty fields to the far woods, with the orange sun half-hidden behind them, and felt mellow with rather too much port and a great deal too much turkey. He was rather looking forward to the evening, and the party; the younger set's diversion he could join in for a limited period and in moderation, comforted by the knowledge that tomorrow they would mostly have gone, and life

242

would return to something like normal. Whatever normal was going to be; not much more than a month, now, and he'd be married, and cruising in the Caribbean, and from that his thoughts naturally strayed to Peggy as she remained so disturbingly in his imagination, as she had been that night, smiling lazily up at him, sensual and intoxicating. Consequently he was puffing slightly more quickly on his cigar when he was aware of a figure approaching through the dusk, and saw that it was Samson.

He had been across to Castle Lancing for a look-round, and to collect any late mail which might have arrived. There was only one envelope, and Mr Franklin wondered idly as he turned it over why Samson had bothered to bring it to him out here, instead of waiting till he returned to the house. Then he saw the postmark, "Windsor", and when he opened the envelope he understood. It was a Christmas card from the King and Queen; Samson, with his shrewd sense, had guessed that probably no royal card had been sent to the Claytons, and was sparing his master any possible embarrassment. Mr Franklin was both surprised and gratified as he looked at the hand-written wish for a merry Christmas, and was properly impressed by royalty's impeccable taste as he examined the design, which reflected that happy sense of the appropriate for which the British have always been noted. It depicted, in funereal colours, the reception of Sir Tristram by King Arthur at the Round Table, with Sir Lancelot standing by, presumably to render assistance if required, and was, according to the manufacturers, Messrs Raphael Tuck, from a painting in his majesty's possession.

"All quiet at home?" he asked, as they walked back towards the house.

"Yes, sir. I saw Jake, and he says he's keeping an eye on things. But everything's all right," added Samson, who had a quiet humour of his own. "He said there was a gentleman called and inquired for you yesterday, but nothing else."

"Who was it, did he say?"

"No, sir, Jake didn't know him, and he didn't leave a card. Good evening, sir."

As they neared the side-entrance Samson touched his hat and effaced himself towards the back of the house, Mr Franklin slipped the card and envelope into his coat pocket thinking, what about that, a Christmas card from the King, and an observer would probably have noticed a complacent smile as he pushed open the side-door to the passage. Who'd have thought . . . and he stopped dead, his hand on the door-knob.

"Don't be an absolute fool! If that's all you came to say you'd have been better staying away. You can't – "

It was Peggy's voice, harshly interrupted by another that sent the hairs rising on his neck in anger: Lacy's.

"I'm not the one who's behaving like a fool! You are! Thinking about marriage to this – this bloody outsider! You don't know who he is, you don't know the first dam' thing about him, you don't know what the hell you're doing!"

"I know one thing about him!" Peggy's voice was like steel. "And that is that he's a gentleman, which you most obviously are not! And it is none of your business – "

"Of course it's my blasted business! D'you think I'm going to watch you throw yourself away on some Yankee guttersnipe? Some damned hobbledehoy from God knows where? You must have taken leave of your senses! Well, I'm not standing for it, d'you hear? You're not marrying him, and that's that!"

The new Mr Franklin came within an ace of thrusting open the door, striding into the passage to the little cloak-room from which he realized the voices were coming, taking Lord Lacy by the collar, and dragging him out of the house. But the old Mr Franklin stopped him, a hand gripping the half-open door, one thought in his mind: would Peggy want to know that he had been a witness to their argument? She would not. Obviously Lacy had done what she feared he might do, come round "to roar" at her, as she had put it; it might be unpleasant for her, but knowing her as he did Mr Franklin was certain that she would want to get rid of him in her own way, with the least possible embarrassment. If she wanted to tell him about it afterwards – that could be the time for taking Lacy by the neck. The impudent bastard! To come round hectoring at her – maybe she was right, and he was a little mad. He stood, still hesitating, and he would have been far more than human if he had not stayed where he was. He had to, the fellow might turn violent – and Peggy was speaking again, in a lower tone, controlling her rage.

"You had better go at once. Or would you rather I brought Mark, or my father? No, the servants should have the job of throwing you out. Now, will you go, or be kicked out?"

"I'll go when I've . . . when I've said what I've got to say, damn it! And when I've heard some-s-s-some s-sense from you!" Lacy was beginning to stutter in his fury; hearing the hysterical quiver in his voice Mr Franklin braced himself to intervene quickly.

"You're raving," said Peggy curtly. "I advise you to go and put your head under a cold tap. But do it somewhere else."

From the sound of her voice he could tell that she was leaving the cloak-room. Lacy shouted "No!" and his footsteps came after her. "No! Peggy!" Suddenly there was a different tone in his voice; from braying and hectoring it was sounding in anguished entreaty. "Peg, please! Wait! Damnation, woman, will you stand still? I . . . oh, Christ, Peg, I'm sorry! Please listen to me! I didn't mean to yell at you – my God, you're the last person I want to yell at! But I've been half-mad over all this! Can't you see it? I love you, you stupid bitch! Don't you understand me? I love you, Peg!"

"Then you have a most peculiar way of showing it." Peggy's voice was still cold, but not in dismissal.

"Well, what the hell d'you expect? You fling yourself at this bloody hooligan – this nobody! D'you want me to dance at your bloody wedding, and throw confetti, for Christ's sake? When I know it's just bloody spite and mischief, and – "

"You impertinent, insufferable . . . oh!" Peggy's words ended in an explosive sound of outrage. "You actually have the effrontery to suggest that *you* – or any thought of you – has anything to do with my marrying Mark Franklin! Why, you . . . you conceited oaf! You think you're the only person on the face of the earth with the least importance, don't you? You can't conceive that to some people you may simply not matter at all? That some people are not thrown into raptures by fat, ugly, red-faced boors with ridiculous walrus moustaches who have been used to going into screaming tantrums ever since they were three years old, and who think they must always have their own way – "

"Stop it! Stop it, Peg! I'm not bloody well fat! And I'm trying to explain, blast you! If I lose my temper, it's because you won't listen, because you've done this idiotic thing when you know I love you, and always have! And I can't bear to think of you throwing yourself away – "

"Oh, shut up!" snapped Peggy. "Just for once, use your intelligence – if you have any. You're so impossibly selfish, you never even bother to think about other people – "

"I do, Peg! About you, I swear I do!"

"You don't. It never occurs to you that *I* may have wishes, and feelings, does it? You don't seem to realise it's possible that I might not only *not* want to marry you, but that I might want to marry someone else? Of course, I know it's incredible that any woman in her right mind could fail to be won by the outstanding charms of the great Lord Lacy, who not only chases fat trollops all over the place – "

"That's a lie! I didn't – "

"Poppy's a lie, is she? Care to call her in and ask her? She's in the drawing-room, you know. Oh, she doesn't matter. Don't you see, Frank, whatever you may think, I want to marry Mark Franklin? Not you! It may be a dreadful shock, but I don't love you – "

"You do! You did! And, dammit, I love you – "

"All right, so you say! I'm sorry, but you'll just have to get over it. I don't love you, so you may as well pull yourself together and stop behaving like a spoiled child! Now, will you please go – and leave me alone? You'd better go by the side door, unless you want everyone to know what a fool you're making of yourself."

"I will not go by the bloody side door! Please, Peg . . ."

The angry, pleading voice faded up the passage, and Mr Franklin could see in his mind's eye Peggy walking swiftly, head up, and Lacy lumbering behind – in Mr Franklin's imagination he was dressed in hunting pink and flourishing a crop – growling frantic protestations. Well, she'd given him his come-uppance, sure enough, the impudent scut. Given him more of an explanation than he deserved, too; still, they'd known each other since they were children (Mr Franklin felt an unhappy twist of jealousy at the thought), and Peggy undoubtedly knew the best way of handling the brute – better than summoning assistance and creating a nasty public scene. He was glad he'd heard it, and felt no shame about eavesdropping; he'd had the satisfaction of hearing Peggy confirm her own feelings for himself, for one thing – and she'd never know he had overheard, unless she chose to mention the incident herself. He'd perfectly understand if she didn't; better she shouldn't, really . . .

Mr Franklin went in cautiously, and listened. With any luck Peggy, on reaching the hall, would have sailed straight across to the drawing-room, which would be full for afternoon tea; Lacy couldn't follow her there, so presumably he would gnash his teeth for a minute, non-plussed, and then make off through the front door. Several minutes had passed; the coast ought to be clear by now.

Mr Franklin walked up the passage, round the corner, and on to the entrance leading to the hall. Directly opposite, through the half-open drawing-room door, he could see the throng at tea; the sounds of conversation and laughter drifted faintly to him. But there were no sounds to indicate that the hall was occupied, until, just as he reached the entrance, Lacy's voice sounded harshly from the direction of the front door.

" . . . and so I've told her, and I don't see why the devil I shouldn't!"

And pat on its heels, Sir Charles's clipped tones, hard with anger: "There is the door! Use it! Good afternoon!"

Mr Franklin stopped abruptly, just out of sight. Plainly there had been a brief sequel to what he had overheard earlier, the principals being Lacy and Clayton this time. Short, sharp, and conclusive by the sound of it, and not to be improved by his own presence. So he stopped, waiting, expecting to hear some foot-stamping and door-slamming as his lordship took his leave. He would wait where he was until Sir Charles was out of the way, too.

Footsteps came from the back of the hall. Samson was coming out of the servants" door beyond the stairs, glancing towards the front door, and then hesitating as he noticed Mr Franklin patently loitering within the side-corridor. Mr Franklin's hand was already rising to gesture discretion at his servant, when another voice was heard, again from the front door, and Mr Franklin froze in sheer disbelief.

"Oh," it said, in tones of mild surprise. "I'm sorry, gentlemen. Hope I don't intrude. My name's Logan. I understand there's a Mr Mark Franklin staying in this house."

The silence that followed the polite inquiry could have been no more than a second. To Mr Franklin it seemed like a year. And then, involuntarily, he had taken two paces into the hall, to confirm with his own eyes the unbelievable, the impossible, news that the voice had conveyed.

To the left of the front door stood Sir Charles, slim and erect, turning from the newcomer to look in Mr Franklin's direction. To the right of the door, Lord Lacy – not in hunting pink, but in perfectly respectable tweeds – was standing with his fists clenched at his sides, his heavy face set in a furious scowl, glaring uncomprehendingly at the figure on the threshold. It was a small man, thin and wiry, in a long drab coat, holding a well-worn bowler hat across his middle. His face was narrow, and bore a straggling dark moustache; above a high forehead was thin, untidy hair with a wisp falling to his brow; the

247

little man brushed it back and then his eyes fell on Mr Franklin and brightened in recognition.

"Why, and there he is!" The voice was quiet, almost diffident, and unmistakably American. "Hullo, there, Mark."

Mr Franklin stood in silence, aware that Sir Charles was staring at him, waiting for an explanation; he was conscious too of Samson silently hovering at the back of the hall. But all his attention was on the small, shabby figure on the threshold, the mouth with its wry smile beneath the moustache, the bright, dark eyes fixed on his own. It was Lord Lacy who broke the silence, characteristically.

"Another damned Yank!" he snorted. "This will be the bloody best man, no doubt!"

He brushed rudely past the little man, and vanished into the dusk, his boots crunching across the gravel. The little man turned his head curiously to look after him, and then turned back to Mr Franklin.

"Maybe you don't remember me," he said. "Logan. Harvey Logan."

Mr Franklin, outwardly unmoved, was aware that his heart had started to race. His nerves had always been good, but where a sudden physical emergency, an attack, or an impending blow, would have found him reacting instinctively, the sight of the slight, unobtrusive figure of a man who had been dead for several years, and dead many thousand of miles away in another world, seemed to have stiffened his muscles. At last he spoke.

"Yes," he said. "I remember you."

"That's fine," said the little man, and waited, glancing from Mr Franklin to Sir Charles, and then to his bowler hat. Sir Charles, after waiting in vain for Mr Franklin to proceed with the courtesies, said quietly: "Perhaps, Mark, you would care to take Mr . . . Logan into the study. I'll see that they send you in some tea."

He moved aside, with the slightest of inclinations of his head to Logan, who blinked and said: "Why, that's most kind of you, sir. Much obliged, I'm sure." His pleased smile followed Sir Charles across the hall, the drawing-room door closed, Samson had faded into the back of the hall, and Mr Franklin was left alone with his visitor, the length of the hall between them. For a moment neither spoke. Then:

"Well, Mark." Logan came forward a pace or two, slowly, his hands toying with the rim of his bowler. "Long time, uh?" He was surveying Mr Franklin with quiet, curious amusement. Abruptly Mr Franklin

248

came to life, strode to the study door, and threw it open. "In here," he said.

Logan walked slowly across, as though he were rather stiff, and careful in his movements. "I declare you've put on a little weight," he said, and passed into the study. Mr Franklin followed him and closed the door, standing with his back to it. Logan moved into the room, looking round at the comfortable, well-worn leather of the furniture, the water-colours on the walls, the fire glowing in the grate, the crystal vase of hothouse flowers on the polished table, nodding in approval.

"Pleasant room," he said, and bent to sniff the flowers, sighing appreciatively. "Very pleasant. Fine house, too. That would be Sir Charles Clayton, wouldn't it? Thought it was. He looks a real nice gentleman. Very polite. Who was the other bastard?"

"He's a lord. Lord Lacy."

"You don't say!" Logan straightened up from the flowers, and placed his hat on the table. "A lord, eh? Well, now, it's as well I'm not heeled, or I just might have put a shot through the middle of a lord's big black head." He turned towards Mr Franklin, spreading his hands, palms outward. "But I'm not heeled." He smiled. "Guess you're surprised to see me, though?"

"Since when were you called Logan?" said Mr Franklin.

"Since I was born," said Logan amiably.

"Then how come everybody called you Curry?"

"Professional name. Called myself after Big Nose George. Remember him? Oh, no, he'd be a bit before your time, I guess. Yes, I took his name. But then, when I read in the papers a few years ago that Kid Curry had got himself killed over at Glenwood Springs . . . " Logan shrugged and smiled. "Well, I thought: why not? Let him rest in peace. So I just became Harvey Logan again."

"I read about it in the papers, too," said Mr Franklin. "Didn't believe it, much. But if it wasn't you who got killed at Glenwood, who was it?"

"Search me." Seeing Mr Franklin's look, Logan smiled disarmingly. "I mean it, Mark. You know me, I never hold out on things like that. They were a new bunch I was with – and not much, between ourselves." He chuckled reminiscently. "We blew this train at Parachute, Colorado – you never seen such a mess! Why, it almost made Cassidy and Sundance look like professionals! Yes, sir." He shook his head. "Posse got after us, I lit out for Wyoming – next thing I

249

know the Pinkertons are claiming they got Kid Curry. Well, you know what lawmen are like. They get one of the gang, and they want to pretend it's the big fish. Who's going to contradict 'em? Not Harvey Logan. Mind if I sit down?"

"Help yourself," said Mr Franklin, and Logan settled himself in an arm-chair, crossed his legs, carefully hitched the leg of his frayed trousers, and looked about him. "You know, this is really nice. Guess this is one of these English country seats, is it? They live all right, don't they? Yes, sir. They do that. Comfortable fixings, beautiful countryside, peace and quiet. I like it. If a man just had a drink in his fist as well, he'd have nothing to complain of."

Mr Franklin walked to the sideboard, opened a small cupboard, and drew out a whisky decanter and a glass. He poured a stiff measure while Logan watched him bright-eyed, and handed it over.

"It isn't Mount Vernon," he said.

"Well, I'll be!" Logan laughed and stared at him in admiration. "You remembered that! After all these years! You son-of-a-gun!" He took a deep swallow. "Say, it'll do, though. Yes, it will, just about." He shook his head, eyeing Mr Franklin, who stood with his back to the fire. "And you remembered about me and Mount Vernon! You were always a deep one, though, weren't you, Mark? All that education, I guess. You knew a lot. Knew a lot about *me*, didn't you?"

"Enough," said Mr Franklin, and Logan nodded, and drank again.

"You said a minute ago you didn't believe it when you heard I got killed. Why not?"

"Because after that someone held up a bank in Wyoming somewhere, and – "

"Cody – Cody, Wyoming," said Logan, shaking a finger. "Now, that – that was professional. And you tied me to it, did you? You're a smart boy, Mark. Real smart." He coughed suddenly, setting down his glass, his shoulders shaking. "Goddam it!" He coughed rackingly, his sleeve across his mouth, while Mr Franklin watched him impassively. "There! That's better. Phew! I reckon this English climate ain't too kind to the chest, though. Too damp. And that fog in London – why, that's poisonous! How d'you stand it?" Getting no reply he went on: "No, I reckon you can take it well enough. I was just – "

At that moment the door opened, and a maid entered, bearing a large silver tea-tray, which she set on the table near Logan's elbow. He smiled on her benevolently, murmuring appreciatively, and

250

watched with interest while Samson, who had followed the maid silently into the room, addressed Mr Franklin.

"Will there be anything further, sir?" It was a question plainly intended to cover a wide range of possibilities, but no one but Mr Franklin could guess that.

"No, thank you, Thomas, that'll be all. I'll ring if I want you."

"Very good, sir."

As the door closed behind him, Logan slapped his knee in delight. "Why, goddam it! Goddamit to hell! 'Will there be anything further, sir?' 'No, Thomas, you can kiss my ass until further notice!' I wouldn't ha' believed it! He's real! A goddam butler in a goddam tail-coat! And you standing there like you're the Dook o' Crap!" He gazed at Mr Franklin in something like awe, and then regarded the tea service. "And tea in cups, for Chrissakes! All brought in by an itty-bitty-pretty little maid in a starched cap! Well, that beats the band, that does!"

"You want some?" Mr Franklin came to the tray and began to fill a cup.

"What? Tea? Oh, an elegant sufficiency, old fellow – if you please!" Logan bowed from his sitting position, and began to load his plate indiscriminately with sandwiches, cake, brown bread, and tea-cake from the little bain marie. "Say, this is real nice, though! And napkins, too. This is real style." He chuckled, with his mouth full. "Say, what d'you think the old Wild Bunch would say if they could see you and me this minute? Mark Franklin and Kid Curry sitting down to after-noon tea in a stately home of England, with butlers and maids waiting on 'em, and dainty little pats of butter, and a real silver pisspotty tea service! Boy, they'd bug their eyes out of their heads!"

Mr Franklin carried his cup back to the fireplace. "How's Cassidy these days?"

"Butch?" Logan's eyes widened. "Didn't you hear? Why, Butch is dead – just a few months back. Him and Sundance both. Down in South America."

"I heard they went down that way."

"Sure. They were working for this Scotch fellow down there, but then they took off, crazy-like, you know how they were, and bush-whacked a mule train. There was talk of a pay-roll, but if I know Longbaugh and Cassidy they probably got nothing but stirrup-irons and mule-shit. Anyway, they lit out and got boxed in somewhere, and Sundance got killed. They reckon Butch shot himself." Logan shook

251

his head in reproof of loose rumour. "I doubt that. For one thing, the crazy bastard wasn't that good a shot. And it wouldn't be like him – hell, he didn't care all that much."

"He cared about Longbaugh. They were pretty close partners."

"Enough to kill himself?" Logan shook his head doubtfully. "I don't take that, somehow. You mean, if Sundance was dead, Butch wouldn't think life was worth living? Hell, that's tall! Anyway, those *rurales* greasers are just like the Pinkertons – you know they said *I* shot *myself*. Can you imagine that? Ten to one Butch gave up, and they took him prisoner and shot him. Now, that would fit, all right. Kind of fool way you'd expect those two to go. I don't know how they lasted as long as they did."

Mr Franklin hardly heard him. He was remembering the burly, ugly young man with the great wide grin and tousled hair that was forever falling down into his close-set eyes; he could still hear the voice stumbling over Jamy's speech from *Henry V.* " . . . but I'll pay it as valorously as I may, that will I surely do. That is the brief and the long." Now Butch was dead, in South America. And Sundance, with his carefully-parted hair and trim moustache and neat clothes, looking more like a lawyer or a doctor or a shipping magnate (one of the better-class ones), than a *bandido Yanqui*. Why, he looked more like a British member of Parliament than the real thing. Now they were both dead, in South America, and he and Kid Curry were taking afternoon tea in Oxton Hall, Norfolk.

A remarkable fact for which he expected to receive a remarkable explanation, and knowing the Kid it was liable to be an unpleasant one. It had set him back on his heels to see that ghost from the past in the hall; one suspicion had crossed his mind immediately, to be strengthened as soon as he noticed the threadbare but well-brushed clothing, the darned shirt and cheap tie, and the voracious appetite with which Logan had fallen on his food. But all this way . . . and how had he known where to look . . . ?

Logan's plate was clean. He swallowed and reached out to the bain marie for another tea-cake, smeared it liberally with jam, and wolfed it down; then he reached for a piece of cake, caught Mr Franklin's eye, and shrugged in mock apology.

"Hungry, Kid? Have some more tea." Mr Franklin reached for the tea-pot while Logan chewed and made grateful noises before swallowing again. "When did you eat last?"

"Oh, this morning. But I haven't been eating too regular. Nothing like this," and he waved a sandwich. "This is A1 grub, all the trimmings. Wouldn't put much belly in you if you was riding or living rough, but it's mighty welcome." He sighed and wiped his lips, accepting his tea-cup. "Thank you kindly. You're fixed kind of pretty here, Mark."

"Here? Well, it isn't my place, Kid . . . "

"No, I know. Your papa-in-law-that's-to-be. *Sir* Charles Clayton. Nice spread, though; good grazing. Better to farm than anything back in Missouri, I guess. Imagine it'll be yours some day – no, hold on though, there's a son, ain't there? Yes, Arthur Clayton. That's right. Still, you ain't worrying, I'll be bound. That's a handsome property you've got yourself, over at Castle Lancing. I took a look at it yesterday – met your hired hand, that Jake." He chuckled again, "Don't you find one like him hanging around every livery stable and saloon from Denver to the Gulf? Here, though, that's a strange thing – this is the first part of England I could understand what they say? In London, they just whine at you, can't speak English worth a dam, but round these parts – every word. You noticed that, Mark?"

"Yes, I noticed."

"Strange, all right." Logan shook his head over the wonders of dialect. "But that's a good place, Mark. Worth a piece of money. Yes, sir, you're well set up. Going to get married, too – and I got to hand it to you there. That's the prettiest little gal I ever laid eyes on, and I laid eyes on a few." Logan nodded appreciatively, and reached into his inside pocket to draw out a folded sheet of paper; then, to Mr Franklin's astonishment, he fished out a pair of steel-rimmed spectacles, blew on them, rubbed them on his sleeve, set them on his nose, tilted his head well back and squinted at the page. "These glasses don't read worth a piss in the wind! Yes, that's her – Miss Peggy Clayton. Ain't she a real peach of a peach, though! Why, you horny young goat, you!" He leered at the page salaciously: it was the page from the *Sphere*. "Yes, sir, that's bully. I admire your taste. I've got another paper here, too . . . " He rummaged and drew forth another page, rather more tattered. "Yes . . . what's it say? ' . . . among the guests, Lord Somebody . . . Marquis D. Soveral . . . ' No, here's the bit. 'One of the most successful guns in His Majesty's party was Mr Mark Franklin, with seventeen brace'. What's a brace?"

"Two birds."

"You shot birds? How did you do that?"

"Wing-shooting."

"What – with a forty-five?"

For the first time in their interview Mr Franklin smiled. "With a shotgun."

"You shot thirty-four birds with a shotgun – and they put it in the newspapers?"

"It's different over here. It's a . . . a social amusement."

Logan looked over the top of his spectacles, and the sudden glance of the bright eyes took Mr Franklin back with chilling speed to that poker table, the wolf-smile on that face, the Remington butt greasy in his grip under cover of the table-top. But the Kid's smile was amiable enough now; it was difficult to realize that it was the same man, the little tiger, the fast snake of the Wild Bunch. He looked older, almost frail in his spectacles – until the bright eyes fixed you, and then you forgot the frayed clothes, and the ageing look of the skin, and the touch of white in the fading, untidy hair, and automatically you glanced at the hands, the lean brown fingers as supple as ever, and remembered who he had been – and was.

"Must be mighty amusing," said Logan, and replaced his papers inside his coat. "You've seen this picture – of your girl, haven't you? I'll keep it, then" He patted his coat back into place. "That was the King of England you were shooting with," he said, almost accusingly, like a wife casting her husband's boozing cronies in his face.

"That's right."

"Holy damn!" He regarded Mr Franklin with anxious reverence, and then asked possibly the most unexpected question every put about Edward VII. "How does he handle a gun? Good?"

"Pretty fair. Don't ever draw on him if you're a partridge."

"Uh-huh. That's fancy company, though, for a rough-rider from Hole-in-the-Wall. The King, eh? And Lord this and Marquess that – why, even that son-of-a-bitch at the front porch, there, he was a lord, you said. And you're going to marry a Sir's daughter – that doesn't make you a Sir, does it?"

"No."

"Well, anyway. Sir or plain mister, you're in the Upper Ten society now, Mark. Ain't you?"

"That's right, Kid."

"And you're stinking rich. Oh, I know about that. Everyone round your village knows all about the Yankee millionaire. They're downright proud of you, Mark, you know that? Proud as if they'd dug eleven tons of paydirt out of Tonopah themselves! Course, I knew about that before they did – like everybody else in Colorado. They're talking still, and telling bigger lies every day, about the Franklin-Davis Silver Hill – not so many of them know about the Belle Bourche Bank, or the Union Pacific hold-up at Wilcox, though." Logan sat back deep in his chair, and glanced placidly at his host.

Mr Franklin looked at him for a moment, set his cup on the mantelpiece, and moved absently to the table to replace the silver cover on the bain marie. Then he went back to the fireplace and leaned his shoulders on the mantel. But still he said nothing. Logan watched him, then shook his head in reluctant admiration.

"You're a cool boy, though, Mark. I always liked that about you – nobody ever ruffled Franklin, did they? Remember that poker game, with Linley and Davis pissing their britches? You came chest to chest with me then, Mark, and took the pot, didn't you? 'Course, I knew you'd slipped your piece into your boot-top before we sat down – even so, you didn't blink at Kid Curry." Just for a moment, over the top of the spectacles, Mr Franklin saw the mad-dog flicker in the dark eyes before it passed. "And who got me out of Deadwood Jail? – not Cassidy, not Kilpatrick, not the Sundance Kid. Just young Mark Franklin – with that little creeping Jesus holding your horse – what's his name – ?"

"Carver."

"Yes, Carver. But it was you who covered the deputy and broke me out. You know that's twelve years ago? And you're as quiet and composed this minute as you were then – remember? 'Don't try it, Mr Deputy. Just sit still and put your thumbs in your mouth'. And he did like you told him, the same as that goddam butler of yours. Dammit!" In sudden irritation Logan struck the arm of his chair. "You still haven't asked me what I'm here for!"

Mr Franklin gave an inward sigh, but all he said was: "I figured when you were ready, you'd tell me."

"But you wouldn't ask! Not you! That's why I like you, Mark. Why, you didn't even blink out there in the hall just now, with your fine papa-in-law-that's-to-be! You just come in here, and feed me tea and cookies, and pass the goddam muffins or whatever the hell they are, and inquire after Butch and Sundance, and watch me and wait and say no more than a clam on an ice-cake!" Logan stared at him. "Damn it, you're still doing it!"

"Have some more tea if you feel like it," said Mr Franklin, and Logan suddenly began to cough again, rackingly, the frail body

255

shuddering as he held the arms of his chair. The fit passed, he breathed heavily, reached out and poured some milk into his cup, and drank it.

"All right, I'll tell you. When you and Davis made the strike, I was coming to see you – "

"I know that. I was waiting at the Bella Union."

"Yes, but you didn't know why I never got there. A payroll train got in the way, but it went wrong. I was on the dodge for a while, and then there was the Glenwood affair – where you heard I got killed – and then the bank at Cody, and then Mexico, where a fellow got himself shot, and I drew five years in a stinking jail at Sonora, under the name of Allen. When I got out, I came looking for you – last summer. Gone east, everybody said. So I went east, and bummed around New York, where they said you'd gone, and just by the grace of God someone I knew spotted your name on a passenger list for England. So I came to England. I traced you as far as London."

Logan coughed and cleared his throat painfully, dabbing at his eyes. "That beat me – I could have trailed you from Pecos to Powder River with my eyes shut, but not there. I slept in gutters nights, and prowled round hotels by day, asking for anybody called Franklin. If you'd changed your name I'd have been bitched. As it was, I took more shit from snot-nosed English clerks than I ever heard in my whole life before! And then I hit the right one – the Waldorf. Just when my last few cents ran out. I had to hi-jack a fellow in an alley for the fare down here." He nodded, and rubbed his chin. "So I made it."

Mr Franklin stood looking down at the slight body in the arm-chair, wondering, remembering that night at the Bella Union, waiting for the Kid, for the shoot. And now, years later, the Kid had finally arrived – better if he had reached the Bella Union with his pearl-handled Peacemaker against the Remingtons; it would have been more cleanly settled. At last he said:

"All right, Kid. How much?"

Logan looked up at him. "How much for what?"

"For keeping your mouth shut."

For several seconds Logan stared at him, apparently uncomprehending, and then suddenly the dark eyes blazed in anger, in the feral menace that he remembered, and the lips pulled back from the teeth as the small man seemed on the point of launching himself at Mr Franklin's throat. But he held his seat, his hands gripping the arms

256

of the chair, mastering his rage. He let out his breath in a hissing sigh, and relaxed, but not into the quiet, courteous little man of a few minutes ago. This was the Kid he knew, all spite and icy wickedness.

"Well, you son-of-a-bitch." It came out in a whisper, in a tone almost conversational, so devoid of passion as it was. "To keep my mouth shut, eh? You know, Mark, you disappoint me. What the hell d'you think I am? You think I came here to squeeze you? That I'm a blackmailer – the kind that's going to say, 'Pay up, or I tell the world that the rich and respectable Mr Mark Franklin of Castle Wherever-the-hell is a Hole-in-the-Wall gunslick, a Wild Buncher?' Is that what you really thought? That I'd blacken your name to your big English friends – and the King, and them – and that sweet little girl in the paper?" The level of the voice never rose, but the glare of the eyes was unwavering. "You think I'd do that to a friend? To the man that bust me from Deadwood, and stood up with me at Wilcox and Snake Bend and Greentree Creek where we broke banks for coffee and doughnuts – or all those trains Cassidy was so sure had payrolls and never did? The stupid son-of-a-bitch," added Logan, with dispassion-ate irrelevance, "no wonder he got his fool head blown off in South America. D'you think I'd do that to you?"

The restrained fury, as much as the substance of the quiet outburst, gave Mr Franklin pause. There was something here beyond his under-standing, and it made him wary, knowing his man as he did.

"All right, Kid," he said at last, "if I owe you an apology, you have it. But if it isn't money – "

"Oh, it's money, all right." Logan's rage seemed to have vanished as quickly as it had come. "You don't think I sicked my guts up in a lousy tramp steamer all the way to this piss-sodden pimple in the ocean just for the pleasure of seeing your sweet smiling face?" He smiled without particular mirth. "Oh, yes, it's money."

Mr Franklin frowned thoughtfully. "But if you haven't come to squeeze me . . . then . . . what d'you want?"

Logan sat forward in his chair. "I want what's mine, Mark," he said quietly. "I want exactly one-half of everything you've got."

There was a moment's silence, in which Mr Franklin's expression altered by not a fraction; if the unbelievable enormity of the statement disturbed him, there was no sign of it. To an onlooker it would have seemed ludicrous: the small, middle-aged, insignificant man sitting on the front of his chair, his patched boots together, his wiry body inadequate even to his seedy clothes, his cheap spectacles perched down his nose, looking like a Punch cartoon of the poor relation in the opulent surroundings of his betters – unless the onlooker had been aware, as Mr Franklin was, of the cold, furious inner spirit behind the bright eyes. And knowing exactly what he had to deal with, Mr Franklin chose his words and spoke quietly in his turn.

"How do you reckon you are entitled to that?"

"Davis was my partner long before he was yours," said Logan. "We had a bond between us – nothing in writing, nothing legal, just the word of partners. You know all about that. We undertook to share everything we ever got, forever – fifty-fifty, down the middle. So what he got from Tonopah – "

"Davis told me that was a lie. Anyway, a partnership agreement only lasts as long as the partnership, and yours with Davis was long over. He and I were the only ones entitled to anything out of Tonopah, and you know it."

For the first time Mr Franklin was speaking with a cold firmness that matched Logan's own. The small man shook his head.

"No. I'm entitled to half. It'd be a quarter if Davis was still alive – half of his half – but since he's dead I'm his heir. Fifty cents of every dollar from Silver Hill is mine – I don't know how much it was, and I don't care all that much. I'll settle for half a million dollars." He paused and added simply: "It's mine, Mark."

It was remarkable that until the last few moments, their conversation had been marked by artificiality and constraint on both sides – Mr Franklin recovering from the shock of Curry's appearance, taking refuge in wary, impassive silence until the precise purpose of this strange visit emerged; on the other hand, the Kid's quiet, diffident geniality, followed by his sudden icy rage – but now, with the chips finally down, they were talking like two men discussing the weather.

"It won't do, Kid. You had no stake in Tonopah. You've got nothing coming. I'm ready to *give* you ten thousand, as an old friend, to get you home and set you up again. But that's all."

Logan shook his head. "I don't have to get set up again. You don't understand – it isn't for me. Personally, I've no use for it any more. I don't have more than a year or so at the best. You heard me coughing back there? That's the cancer – it's all inside me, eating me away, the doctor says, nothing to stop it. So it's not for me I want the dough. But it's mine by rights, and it'll go where I want it to go – and that's to my brother. He can – "

258

"Your brother died ten years back. Sayles and Charley Siringo got him."

"That was Lonny!" Logan gestured impatiently. "I'm talking about Henry. You didn't know him – he never left Dodson, Missouri, and he's still there, working his ass off for his wife and family. He wasn't like me and Lonny – Henry was the straight one, who never played hooky and won the tickets in Sunday School and stayed out of saloons and cathouses. Respectable, Henry was; a good kid. If anyone can use the money well, he can. I want him to have it."

Mr Franklin offered his cigarette case, but the Kid shook his head, patting his chest. "I could use another snort, though," he said, and Mr Franklin refreshed his glass and then lit himself a cigarette with a taper at the fire.

"Even if I believed you, Kid – and I'm not saying I don't – it doesn't make any difference. You've no claim on anything of mine." He paused, and stared down deliberately at Logan, sitting attentively. "And you've no way of making me part. Just in case you were to change your mind about trying to blackmail me, you ought to remember something. There were never any warrants or posters or rewards out for me; I'm not wanted anywhere. You could talk your head off and no one in the States would give a dam; it wouldn't do me the least bit of harm in England, either – they'd just think it was romantic, supposing they were prepared to accept the word of a convicted felon called Kid Curry who'd go to jail here for extortion before being sent back to the States to get hung. So – "

"I'm not here to squeeze!" There were two flushed patches on Logan's thin cheeks, and his eyes were glittering dangerously. "But if I was, there might be something in the States that they *did* give a dam about, and that's Deaf Charley Hanks, shot in – "

"– shot in self-defence, and half the population of Cheyenne to prove it. Forget that one, Kid. But, of course, you're not here to squeeze."

"No, I'm not here to squeeze."

"So there's an end of it, Kid. I'm offering you ten thousand for old times" sake. You can take it or leave it."

Logan sat quite still, staring over the tops of his glasses. Then he sighed, took the glasses off, and began to polish them. "I had a suspicion this might happen," he said. "Mark – I'm entitled to half. It's better business for you to pay that half, than to end up with nothing."

259

"And how could I end up with nothing, Kid?"

Logan replaced his spectacles. "You've got nothing," he observed, "when you're dead."

There was a soft knock at the study door, and the maid came in. "May I clear away the things, sir?"

"Yes, thank you, Kitty. We've finished," and as she crossed to the table he went on, to Logan: "I know what you mean, of course. But it isn't quite the same here as it is in Colorado or Wyoming. The law doesn't work in quite the same way."

"Oh, I appreciate that." Logan was nodding blandly, and as the maid deftly piled the used dishes on the tray he turned to smile at her and murmur: "Thank you very much. That was delicious, quite delicious." She bobbed and simpered at the kindly old gentleman, and Logan went on: "But I'm sure certain things hold good, just the same here as there. You know what I mean?" The door closed behind the maid. "A forty-five slug travels just as far."

Mr Franklin shook his head. "You're talking like a fool, Kid, but you don't know it. If you were crazy enough to try it, you'd never get away with it. They'd catch you, and they'd hang you — "

"You don't understand, Mark. I'd get away with it – but even if I didn't, it wouldn't matter. I'm a goner in the next two years anyway. That's why it's good business for you to do the square thing by me. If you do – then that's fine. You'll still have more than you'll ever need to live on, with that pretty little girl, and your nice house, and your English friends, and all. If you don't – you're a dead man." He was looking over his spectacles with an expression that was almost benign and it was only in that moment that the full realization of what was happening came home to Mr Franklin, and he felt the first finger of cold fear touch his spine.

It was nonsense, of course. This was England, the land of law and order and strict, inexorable justice. A puny, friendless beggar with nothing but the old clothes he wore, was threatening a respectable citizen with deadly assault unless he allowed himself to be menaced out of a fortune – all that had to be done was call a constable, if so much was even necessary, and have the impudent scoundrel thrown out or given in charge. He probably couldn't be convicted of anything, right now, since it would only be Mr Franklin's word against his – but with all the influence against him he could certainly be hounded out of the country with stern warnings. Better still – could Mr Franklin have him apprehended as Kid Curry, a known and dangerous criminal under sentence of death in the United States, and extradited to the welcoming arms of his own country's law? Rather more difficult, probably, since Kid Curry was officially dead . . . but all these courses were possible, reasonable, and attractive – the only flaw being that long before they could be successfully pursued to a conclusion, Curry would have killed him. Harmless and insignificant, even defenceless, he might look, but no one knew better than Mr Franklin how fatally deceptive that appearance was. Curry had been the quickest and deadliest shot alive in the United States at the turn of the century, a name mentioned respectfully with the Hardins, Thompsons and Hickoks of an earlier generation; Mr Franklin had seen that expertise practised, and with a cold-blooded callousness remarkable even for Hole-in-the-Wall. Perhaps even more to the point, he knew that Curry never promised what he did not perform. It would not matter in the slightest to him that the possibility of murder going unpunished in England was infinitely lower than on the Western frontier, that as a disoriented stranger his hope of escape would be infinitesimal, that he would be hunted by a police whose efficiency was world-famous, and that once marked down his capture and execution would be an almost mathematical certainty. He had said, and he would do. The thought of Curry, Western desperado, prowling the fields and villages of East Anglia with a single-action Colt in pursuit of human prey, was outlandish, but it would certainly happen – unless Mr Franklin capitulated, and that he was not prepared to do.

"What good would it do you – killing me? You wouldn't get a plugged nickel that way, Kid. But what you would get is a rope round your own neck, and that's for certain."

"No more certain than what's going to happen to me anyway. But I'd like to see Henry fixed up first. And believe it or not, I'd like to think of you and that nice English girl living happy ever after. I've got nothing against you, Mark; nothing at all. I just want what's rightly mine. If you won't give it me, I'll just have to take the next best thing. And it doesn't matter what it costs me." He said it blandly, wistfully almost, and then for a split second the eyes were like chips of black ice in the worn face. "And I'll do it, Mark. Before New Year's. So, as I said – it would be good business for you to do me right."

Mr Franklin held his stare, as he had done so many years before, with the cards on the table. "Nothing doing, Kid. There's ten thousand if you want it – not a cent more."

Logan nodded, and glanced reflectively at the fire. "Well, that's

261

settled, then." He said it almost as though it were a weight off his mind. "Maybe I didn't put it to you right . . . if I'd asked you more roundabout, know what I mean? Nobody likes to think he's being bulldozed – he gets on his dignity, feels he can't back down. You wouldn't have to feel that with me, Mark. We knew each other too long."

"That's right," said Mr Franklin. "The same applies to you, Kid. Ten thousand would go a long way. Get you on the boat for one thing."

Logan pocketed his spectacles carefully and got to his feet. "No, thanks." He picked up his hat. "What are you going to do, Mark? Set the law after me? It wouldn't work, you know. They've nothing on me – and I'd get you, just the same."

"Maybe you would," said Mr Franklin. "It's what you came for."

Logan's head turned abruptly. "What was that?"

"I said it's what you came for." Mr Franklin was smiling, and his tone was contemptuous. "You don't fool me, Kid. You never did. You knew I wouldn't pay up. Oh, maybe you thought it was worth a try – but that's not why you came. I didn't just come chest to chest with you, Kid, and take a pot at poker – I did something a lot worse. I struck it rich, and went on striking it, while you were breaking rocks in Sonora, living on prison hash and knowing the best you could hope for when you got out was mooching dimes and robbing whores. You couldn't stand that – not Kid Curry, the big gun of the Wild Bunch. It ate you up in jail, didn't it? I don't know when you figured out that moonshine about old Davis promising you fifty-fifty forever – maybe by now you even believe it. You're crazy enough. But it was me you really wanted – the smart kid who called your bluff, and then found the elephant on the proceeds." He was openly scornful now, looking down from his commanding height. "That stuff about 'I've got nothing against you' and 'D'you think I'd blacken you to your English friends'! You came to England for my hide, Kid, because you hate everything inside it, and you know you're finished, and you'll never leave a score unsettled! You see, I haven't forgotten Winter, and the Norman brothers, and that deputy at Hanging Rock – they were all scores, weren't they? And you settled them. Well, here I am, Kid. Now you can try and settle me. You want another drink before you go?"

He moved unhurriedly over to the sideboard, and turned with the decanter in his hand. Logan had not changed his position, or his expression; if anything he had heard had struck home, he was not showing it.

"I'll settle you, Mark," he said. "Don't you fret about that. No, I won't have another drink."

They looked at each other in silence for a full half-minute, and then Logan said:

"Last chance, Mark."

Mr Franklin replaced the decanter and closed the cupboard. As he did so, the door of the room opened and Peggy paused on the threshold.

"Oh!" She looked from Logan – who bowed – to Mr Franklin. "I hope I'm not interrupting . . . Mark, Daddy wondered if Mr Logan would care to join us for supper? I'm afraid it will be supper – no one feels like dining on Christmas Day, do they? – if Mr Logan doesn't mind . . . ?"

Mr Franklin collected himself. In a day of surprises, what he now found himself doing was the most bizarre of all. "May I present Mr Harvey Logan – my fiancée, Miss Clayton?"

"Charmed, I'm sure." Logan was repeating his bow, in formal, and surprisingly practised style. He beamed at Peggy warmly. "I was just telling Mark I saw your picture in the illustrated papers, Miss Clayton, and thought I'd never seen anything lovelier. Well, it doesn't do you justice."

"Oh, you're far too kind," said Peggy, bestowing on him her most flashing smile. "Will you join us, Mr Logan?"

"Why, that's most kind of you, Miss Clayton." Logan inclined his head courteously. "But I really have to be getting back . . . I've kept your intended away from you and your good people far too long as it is. Talking over old times back home, you know – "

"Oh, what a shame you can't stay." Peggy pouted in polite disappointment. "Are you in England for very long, Mr Logan?"

"No, no, just a few more days. Business, you understand." He followed Peggy into the hall, with Mr Franklin bringing up the rear. Sir Charles, emerging from the drawing-room, approached with his features composed in the appropriate half-smile; it occurred to Mr Franklin that if his caller had been an Indian half-breed or a Christie minstrel, the Claytons' formal reception would probably have been precisely the same. Sir Charles murmured his regrets, and at the same time managed to elicit, with disarming ease, Logan's relationship with Mr Franklin.

263

"You hadn't met for some time, I gather?"

"No, not for . . . oh, six-seven years, Mark?" Logan turned to him for confirmation. "About the time you went into the mining business."

"Were you a 'miner-forty-niner' too, Mr Logan?" asked Peggy.

"No, not really . . . nothing like Mark here." Logan blinked and smiled. "I was in banking . . . and railroads, mostly. But we were associated in one or two little business ventures. Matter of fact, Mark came to my rescue one time, when I'd got in a little too deep, as you might say. Now, sir," Logan turned to Sir Charles, "I deeply appreciate your hospitality – and your charming daughter's. I take my leave of you."

"Can we have you driven to the station?" asked Sir Charles.

"Thank you, no. The walk will do me good. 'Bye, Mark. Sir, and Madam. A merry Christmas and . . . no, I won't say 'Happy New Year's' just yet. Bad luck in advance." He paused on the threshold, pulling his coat about him, smiling at them. Peggy completed the formalities of departure by saying:

"Good-bye. Perhaps we shall see you again."

"I'm afraid not," said Logan, and glanced at Mr Franklin. "Unless just for a second, maybe. Good-bye, good-bye all."

He disappeared beyond the circle of light from the porch lamp and the door closed on him.

"What a strange little chap!" said Peggy. "Whoever was he, Mark?"

"Just an old acquaintance I didn't even recognize," said Mr Franklin, forcing himself to sound easy. "We knew each other – not very well – out in Colorado."

"But how extraordinary he should have turned up here! He looked – well, he looked as though he was rather down on his luck, didn't he?" said Peggy.

"Yes," said Sir Charles, with a sympathetic glance at Mr Franklin. "Not too welcome, my boy? How much did he want?"

Mr Franklin smiled. "No more than I could afford, thank goodness. He'd seen Peggy's picture in the papers, and recognized my name. I guess he thought the chance was too good to miss, especially since it's Christmas."

"Damned nuisance," said Sir Charles. "Taking up your time. At least he had the good sense not to stay to supper."

Peggy looked doubtful. "I'm sure he would have been glad of some supper. Poor little chap. Mark, did you ... ? I mean, if he's in difficulties ... "

"Don't worry, Peggy," said Mr Franklin. "He went away well satisfied."

13

Although no one at Oxton Hall could guess it, Mr Franklin's behaviour for the rest of the evening did him greater credit than anything he had shown in public since his arrival in England. There were no children in the house, but with Arthur and Poppy and the younger set the festivities were strictly of the nursery variety – the innocences of blind man's buff, musical chairs, "sardines", and hide-and-seek being readily adaptable to pursuits which ended with the young ladies emerging flushed and bright-eyed from cupboards and distant nooks of the house, and the young men guiltily smoothing hair and clothing. But at intervals there were less boisterous activities like charades, consequences, and a treasure hunt, in which the older guests joined, and in these no one was more imperturbably genial and carefree than Mr Franklin. When he drew the card which made him detective in the murder game, he conducted his investigation with a concentrated gravity which suggested that he had not a thought on his mind beyond the success of the party; no one, watching the skill with which he trapped Colonel Dammit into contradicting himself as to his whereabouts at the moment of the crime, or reducing Peggy to giggling confusion by his ruthless interrogation on what she had eaten at lunch, would have guessed that only an hour earlier he had heard virtual sentence of death passed on himself. Even Sir Charles, who had shrewdly guessed that Mr Logan had been an unwelcome visitor, never dreamed that he had been more than some reduced old acquaintance on the scrounge; if there had been anything serious on Mr Franklin's mind he could hardly have devoted his thoughts so successfully to the ingenious destruction of Arthur's alibi – for, of course, Arthur was the guilty party, as Mr Franklin had known from the moment that an elaborately tremulous scream from the billiard room had proclaimed that Poppy was the victim. It had taken her a good ten minutes to scream after the lights went out, which told the "detective" all that he needed to know.

Indeed, the only time during the whole evening when Mr Franklin allowed his thoughts to dwell with any force on the fatally dangerous ordeal that lay ahead of him, was in those ten minutes when he and the other guests waited in the darkened house before the "murder" was committed. He had leisure then to think, unseen, standing in the shadows of the hall, with the giggling and rustling and occasional startled squealing of the other players coming out of the dark, sometimes distant, sometimes close, as the nervous ones sought quiet corners, and the extroverts bumped into each other, and the amorous found havens to pant and fondle in. And while the game went on in the safe, comfortably eerie dark of the old creaking house, somewhere in the real dark outside another small figure would be going its purposeful way, to whatever its secret lodging might be, there to open a drawer, or a case, or a parcel, and draw out the pearl-handled Peacemaker (if it still existed), and touch the cylinder, check the chambers, heft the heavy iron in hand, and conjure it out of sight beneath the clothing. And then to stand, probably in candle-light, the bright eyes fixed and steady, considering the where and when . . .

He was mad, of course. It might seem incredible that he had crossed a continent and an ocean to track down his man, determined to kill, wantonly and uselessly, unless he got what he wanted, but then Curry himself had always been incredible. Perhaps all the men of violence were; perhaps he was himself. Really, he had no place here, in this life of order and form and accepted stability – oh, they knew about violence, and life and death, these people, none better, but their civilization was built on a system that kept these things in their proper place and time and occasion. No doubt Sir Charles Clayton, landowner, justice of the peace, pillar of the community, who would express censure if he heard that a neighbour had so much as raised his voice to another, had in another time and place done things, and faced evils and dangers, and known enemies and hardships that would have made the Wild Bunch draw rein and turn on to another road – but that would have been elsewhere, in his other life: such things had no place in his existence as a Norfolk squire.

And he, Mark Franklin, had supposed that he could put *his* other life behind him, and find a new one, and they would remain poles apart, those two existences, and never meet. He had forgotten that there were men like Kid Curry who recognized no divisions or frontiers, who never were even aware that such things existed, who had one set of rules to live by and would apply them indiscriminately. That afternoon, a man had brushed past Curry with an offensive

267

remark, and Curry had observed later that if he had been heeled he might have put a bullet through that man's head. Only someone who knew the Currys of the world, as Mr Franklin did, could know that it had been true. Not a jest, or a boast, but a plain fact. Lord Lacy, if he had been told of a Western desperado who, in a cattle-town, had shot a youth dead for impertinently knocking a cup from his hand (which Mr Franklin remembered vividly) would have believed it; it would have seemed shocking, but not inappropriate, to the time and place. But if Lord Lacy had been told that for a boorish remark at the front door of an English country-house he might himself have been coldly shot dead by a perfect stranger, he would have laughed the idea to scorn. The idea, to put it mildly, would have been out of place. He would not have understood people like Kid Curry. Mr Franklin, understanding, was under no illusions; he knew what would happen, and what he himself must do . . . and at that moment Poppy squealed with superb histrionic fervour in the billiard-room, and he turned the future out of his mind and calmly played his part in the present.

It was all the easier because his mind was made up, and he knew there was nothing to be done for the next twelve hours at least. So he joined in the games, and in the noisy chatter over the buffet supper, and in the songs round the piano afterward, and kissed Peggy a long and happy good-night before the study fire, talking over the party and Christmas generally, but mostly about the busy pleasures ahead after New Year – back to London to see about the house, and the servants, and the countless details of the wedding, and the final arrangements for their honeymoon cruise. Peggy sighed contentedly in his arms, yawning and shivering with weariness, murmuring drowsily until they finally stirred themselves and went their separate ways to bed.

After breakfast next morning most of the guests took their leave; Mr Franklin was to have stayed to lunch, but excused himself on the ground that there were things to attend to at Lancing Manor that he would rather not leave until after New Year, which was going to be such a busy time. He drove himself, with Samson beside him, and if the valet was surprised at the roundabout route they took, he made no comment; it brought them home without going through Castle Lancing village, and when they drew up at the front gate Mr Franklin sat for quite a minute after Samson had opened up, studying the trees and the surrounding hedges before finally driving up to the front

268

door. There he lost no time in entering the house, leaving Samson to put away the horse and trap.

For the rest of the day he stayed indoors, working in his study or bedroom. This consisted largely of sitting in silent contemplation, or of examining the view from various windows in the house, keeping back out of sight from the outside – indeed, it did not look like work at all, but it was, of a specialized and exacting nature. Then, having sent Samson on an errand to the village shop, he went quickly out of the back door and across to the stable, where he closed the door carefully from the inside.

The trap-horse was munching contentedly in its stall; Mr Franklin patted it and talked to it before surveying the stable proper, a draughty apartment perhaps forty feet long, its walls of crude planks fairly badly fitted together. At one end was a rough bench on which lay items of saddlery; on it Mr Franklin laid one of his Remington pistols, and a heavy horn-hilted hunting-knife. He examined the pistol carefully to ensure that it was unloaded, closed it, and weighed it first in his left hand, then in his right; then he spun it dexterously on his forefinger, turned it in his hand, spun it again, and finally thrust it into the waistband of his trousers across his stomach, unsheathed the knife, and took his stand facing the far wall, perhaps thirty feet away. He thought for a moment, changed the position of the pistol at his waist, and resumed his stance, the bare knife hanging loosely from the fingers of his right hand.

A moment he stood, and then sharply whipped back his right hand and threw the knife, like a bowler releasing a ball, underhand. It flew along the stable, turning once, while his right hand jerked the pistol with remarkable speed from his belt and levelled it before his face, covering a spot on the far wall. The knife buried its point in the wall a foot to the right of the spot, and on a slightly higher elevation. Mr Franklin shook his head, retrieved the knife, and tried again.

A dozen times he repeated the exercise, and on four out of the last five tries the knife struck precisely on the spot which his pistol covered. Of course the satisfactory way to do it would have been to throw the knife, draw his pistol and fire, and see if the knife entered the bullet-hole, but he had no wish to wake the echoes of Castle Lancing with revolver-fire. He was satisfied with his practice, and went quickly back to the house with the weapons concealed beneath his jacket.

He spent the evening in his study, with the thick curtains closely drawn, wondering how he could get Samson out of the way. In the end, when the servant brought his supper, Mr Franklin simply told him to catch the morning train to London, and spend some days consulting with Mr Pride about staff for the house in Wilton Crescent; since Peggy herself had already taken care of this, and Samson knew it, the instruction was fairly vague and unconvincing, but it was the best Mr Franklin could manage in the circumstances. Samson accepted it without demur at the time, but when he had returned to his kitchen he stood for some minutes stroking his square chin thoughtfully. Then on an impulse he went upstairs, and came down after a while very slowly, pausing to stare at the study door before returning to his own quarters. Half an hour later he emerged with his usual light, steady step, crossed to the study, knocked and entered.

"I'll remove the tray now, sir."

"Oh . . . thanks, Thomas." Mr Franklin, stretched out in his chair before the fire, roused himself, and yawned. "Yes . . . then get yourself an early night. You can catch the morning train." He expected to hear the tray being lifted; when it was not he turned his head. Samson was standing on the hearth-rug, hands clasped before him, impassive, evidently waiting. "What is it, Thomas?"

"I have been thinking, sir. Perhaps it would be best if I did not go to London."

Mr Franklin stared at him. "Not go? But I want you to."

"I think, sir, that I might be of greater use here."

"I've told you – I can manage perfectly on my own. There's nothing on earth to do, that I can't – "

"I was thinking, sir, of any emergency that might arise." He said it in a perfectly flat, matter-of-fact way, and Mr Franklin slowly sat upright in his chair.

"Thomas, just what are you talking about?"

"The gentleman who called to see you yesterday, sir, at Oxton Hall – Mr Logan." Samson was watching Mr Franklin carefully, and thought he saw the slightest flicker of reaction. "I spoke to Jake in the village today, and there is no doubt he is the person who inquired for you here on Christmas Eve. The carter's boy was in the Apple Tree this evening, sir; as you know, his duties take him in and out of Thetford station, and according to him Mr Logan boarded the Cambridge train this afternoon, sir."

This time no reaction was visible, beyond a long cold stare which made Samson feel decidedly uncomfortable. Mr Franklin sat for a moment, and then said:

"I can't imagine what you think that has to do with anything – or with your going to London, or this nonsense about some emergency – "

"It's no use, sir – if you'll forgive me for saying so. I know when I'm being got out of the way." Samson's tone was gentle. "You've been cleaning your revolvers. And behaving rather strangely since last night, if I may mention it."

"What the blazes d'you mean – strangely?"

"You didn't sleep last night, sir, at Oxton. I noticed that, in passing. Then this morning, you took a very peculiar way home, sir, and you were on the look-out all the time, left and right – I didn't think much of it till we got home, and I saw you looking over the garden. What we used to call 'quartering ground', in the cavalry." Samson looked almost apologetic. "You've been doing the same thing, sir, all day, from the windows. I couldn't think what it meant, until I remembered that Mr Logan, sir, in the hall at Oxton."

"What about him?"

"He's a wrong 'un, sir. A very dangerous wrong 'un, or I'm no judge. And now you're cleaning your pistols, and trying to get me off the premises. Well, I put two and two together, sir, and the four they add up to is that you're expecting him back, sir. With deadly intent, sometime this week, and probably by night."

Mr Franklin stood up abruptly, walked across to the door, and then walked back, evidently undecided. Then he turned to face his servant.

"All right, Thomas. You've earned top marks. You're absolutely right." He paused. "All the more reason why I want you out of the way. This is a personal matter – strictly personal. It's got nothing to do with you, and I won't have you mixed up in it. Understand?"

"Certainly, sir," said Samson. "If I may take the liberty – I take it you've thought about the police, sir?"

"You take it right, Thomas – and they wouldn't be any help. At best, it would only postpone . . . and from what you tell me, there isn't time." He stood, calculating, and then said abruptly. "Anyway, Thomas, thanks for your offer. I appreciate it more than I can say. But I won't have it. You catch the London train tomorrow morning, you hear?"

"No, sir." Samson shook his head. "I'm not going."

Mr Franklin took a deep breath, and his jaw set in anger, but before he could speak Samson was going on: "It's no use, sir, as I said before. I don't know what's behind it, of course, and I'm not asking. But I know that man's been threatening you, and he's the kind that will carry out his threat – you think that yourself, sir, and you know him. Very well – I'm not saying this is the kind of work I expected when I took service with you, sir, but since it's happened, and there's no other way – I'm quite sure you've considered the police and that sort of thing very carefully, sir – then I suggest we use our heads and make the best use we can of our resources. I'm certainly not leaving you on your own, sir, and that's that. If you wish to give me notice, that's another matter, but you still won't get me out of this house for the next fortnight – not unless you go too, sir."

The quiet finality of it was not to be gainsaid, and Mr Franklin knew better than to try. But where anger or bluster would have been useless, common sense might prevail. He looked at the stocky, powerful figure, the blunt, calm face, the steady eyes, and nodded to a nearby chair.

"Sit down, Thomas." Samson sat, hands on knees, easily upright. "In the first place, it isn't a question of defending this house. I'm going to have to meet this man head-on; either he kills me or I kill him. There's no safety short of that. And I know him, how he works and fights, the deadly skill he has – believe me, it's something beyond your understanding. You don't know his kind, or his world – which means that you wouldn't be any help. In fact, you'd be more of a hindrance. I know you think – "

"Beg pardon, sir, but perhaps I know more than you imagine," said Samson. "I was in the light dragoons, in South Africa, during the Zulu troubles, and in both the Boer Wars. I'm more than competent with small arms, sir – "

"That's what I mean, Thomas," Mr Franklin interrupted. "I'm not talking about army training – "

"Neither am I, sir. Between enlistments I worked in the goldfields, and in Kimberley at the time of the diamond rush. I was a sergeant in the Cape Mounted Rifles, sir – perhaps you've heard of them. From what I understand, South Africa wasn't very different from your own ... er, Wild West, sir. I had quite a lot to do with persons like Mr Logan, sir. That's how I knew what he was, as soon as I laid eyes on him." He hesitated. "That's how I knew about you, sir, when we first met in London."

Mr Franklin stared. "How you knew about *me?*"

Samson cleared his throat diffidently. "I knew you had made your living out of doors, sir, that you were American, and that you weren't accustomed to wealth, if you'll pardon my saying so. Then, when you took me on down here – well, you'd bought a property very out of the way. And a few weeks ago, when we emptied your trunk to stow it away, I noticed your pistol-holsters were cut away round the trigger-guard. Very few people who use revolvers do that, sir." He raised his eyes to his employer's. "I'm not trying to sound smart, sir, But I wondered if something like this might not happen, eventually."

"Well, I'm damned!" said Mr Franklin, and laughed shortly. "You don't miss much. And we know you can add two and two. But in this case the four they make could be a crook – or a murderer, or worse. Couldn't they? For all you know, Logan may have the right on his side."

Samson shook his head. "I've seen him, sir, and I know you." He smiled and met his employer's eye squarely. "If it comes to that, sir, I might be a crook, or murderer, or worse – for all you know." He waited a moment, and then got to his feet. "Might I ask, sir, when you expect him to come back?"

This eminently practical question brought Mr Franklin back to his – or now, it seemed, to their – immediate predicament. Obviously there was no point in further academic discussion with Samson; he had an unexpected ally, and that was that, and the more he thought of it, the more reassuring it was. Even if Samson was less expert than he thought himself – and Mr Franklin decided that he wouldn't be prepared to bet on it – he would still improve the odds considerably. That being so, he could plan accordingly.

He crossed to the table, and opened the ordnance survey map he had been consulting earlier that day. "The carrier's boy says he caught the Cambridge train. That's in character – it looks as though he's leaving the district. All right – he'll ride for a few stops, maybe for a dozen miles, and then drop off when the train's moving – he's had a lot of practice, believe me. Then he'll circle across country, keeping well hidden; he'll wait until tomorrow to do that, since he doesn't know the territory and can't risk moving in the dark. By tomorrow afternoon he'll be around Castle Lancing, watching the house – but nobody'll know he's there. Then . . . " Mr Franklin turned away from the map and stood considering, his eyes half-closed; he was seeing Curry, holed up in the woods perhaps a couple of furlongs from the

273

house, on the side away from the village, watching as dusk came down, the dark figure crouched invisible under a bush, the bright eyes fixed in unblinking attention on the distant house and trees, the ears instinctively alert for any noise in the empty green around him.

"He knows I know he's coming – but he doesn't know that I have a good idea when he'll come. Until you told me he'd left Thetford today, I was figuring maybe two, even three days – he's the kind that would reckon it a good idea to try my nerves by waiting. But then he knows I know that, too – so he'll come sooner than he reckons I'll expect. Yes, tomorrow night, probably. He'll lie up until dark, and then move in – and by dawn he'll be lying up, snug and handy, within twenty yards of the house. Oh, he won't try to break in – he'll wait for hours, days if necessary, and never move above a foot, and the moment I show my head out of doors . . . one fast shot, maybe two. That's all he'll need. And then he'll be gone – into nowhere, pick up a moving train, and by the time the Norwich police or Scotland Yard have finished examining my corpse, he'll be in London, or on a boat, even."

He glanced at Samson, who was considering him gravely, and went on: "There's an outside chance he might try to get a long shot at me – if he got somewhere fairly close by tomorrow afternoon. But I doubt it. He won't have a rifle, and he wasn't much with one, anyway. A handgun is his weapon – and I doubt if even South Africa has anything better or faster. He's very, very good, Thomas; in fact, he's the best, and a split second is all he needs, anywhere up to thirty paces."

Samson said: "How should we tackle him, sir?"

"We won't," said Mr Franklin. "Or at least you won't. You stay indoors tomorrow, all day – and keep away from windows. Late afternoon, I'll go out to the stable, or on the front path, to let him have a look at me. Then inside again, and when it gets dark you light the study lamp. I'll be outside by then, but he won't have seen me this time. You douse the lamp around ten, and light my bedroom for half an hour. Then douse *that* light and come downstairs; take your post at the kitchen window, so you can watch the back yard. I'll be in the front garden, because that's where he'll come, if I know any-thing. And when he does, I'll be ready for him."

"And then, sir?"

"Then I'll kill him."

Samson may well have been on the point of saying "Very good, sir," but instead he gave the statement a moment's silent thought, and then said: "Is it possible that he might have taken up his position in the garden by tomorrow morning, sir?"

"Coming tonight, you mean? Now?" For a moment the possibility startled Mr Franklin, and he automatically glanced towards the drawn curtains. It promised to be a stormy night; the wind was already rising and sighing through the bare branches of the chestnuts round the house. In imagination he could picture the December dark before moonrise; the empty fields towards Thetford, the shadowy figure moving silently down the dripping hedgerows, patiently feeling each step through the night, skirting the copses, waiting in the ditches before flitting silently across the deserted roads, and so to the walls of Lancing Manor. Then the soft rustle over the wall, the gentle footfall in the damp grass, the dark shadow beneath the trees, eyes fixed on the dull crimson glow of the curtained study window, beyond which he and Samson were standing, invisible, waiting. How many miles? How many hours? He made a hasty calculation and shook his head. "That train left Thetford around five, didn't it?"

"Five-twelve, sir."

"Then he couldn't make it, not tonight – not through country he doesn't know, in the dark. Tomorrow night'll be the earliest. But we'll each keep a loaded Remington handy from now on, just in case. You know how to handle one?"

"Yes, sir."

"How well?"

Samson considered. "You wish me to keep guard at the kitchen window, sir. If I were to see Logan in the yard at any time, I should be confident of hitting him – even in the dark, sir. The moon is almost full, sir."

"Is it, though? Well, moon or not, don't let drive at this fellow unless you're dead certain of hitting him with your first shot, for you won't get a second chance. You understand?" He stared at Samson doubtfully. "In fact, if you do see him – don't shoot. Run quickly through the house, as fast as you can without making a noise, and strike a match in the front hall window – and blow it out as soon as you've struck it. I'll see it – and if he can bushwhack me after that, well, I'll deserve it."

They stood together in the silence of the study, listening to the gentle soughing of the wind, and the ticking of the clock on the mantelpiece. Mr Franklin said quietly:

"This is a crazy business. But it's happening." He took a deep

275

breath. "And I thought I was joking when I said our tranquil days were over. You're sure you want to be in it, Thomas?"

"Yes, thank you, sir."

"Don't thank me, man. It's I who thank you – but understand me: you keep under cover, and don't start trying to play Buffalo Bill. By the way, his name isn't Logan – or, at least, it isn't what he usually answers to. His real name's Kid Curry – ever hear of him?"

"I can't say I have, sir."

"No, well – he's got eight dead men to his credit that I know of, law officers, mostly, and not a dentist or school-teacher among 'em, if you know what I mean. And he likes killing people."

"I see, sir." The clock struck the first note of ten, and Samson glanced at it. "I notice you made very little of your supper, sir. Perhaps if I were to prepare some sandwiches – there is some rather good roast ham, and cold beef, sir. And a pot of coffee?"

"Good idea – make enough for two, and bring it all in here – you can regard yourself as on active service," he added, "so we'll mess together, whatever your social objections about mixing with me. Dammit all," said Mr Franklin, irritably, "you're all right, Thomas! And I'm . . . oh, well! But look here – don't you want to know what this is all about, even? Yes, I know you say you know me, and that you can tell Curry's a bad man – which he is, by God – but even so . . . you're putting your neck on the block, you realize that? Forty-eight hours from now there's an even chance I'll be dead, and if I know you, you'll try to do something about it, and that means there'll be two of us stiff. The least you're entitled to is an explan – "

"I'd rather not, sir. Really." Samson picked up the supper tray. "I shall bring the sandwiches in a few moments, sir."

They ate the sandwiches and drank the coffee by the fire, more or less in silence: there seemed to be very little to say. Then Mr Franklin brought down the Remingtons and a shotgun, which he intended to have to hand when the time came. "If there's one advantage I fancy against a guy like Curry, it's a nice spread of buckshot. Here, take one of the pistols and load her up." He handed a Remington to Samson, and watched critically while his servant broke the weapon, slid the glittering brass cartridges into the cylinder, and carefully closed it.

"Suppose the clock is Curry's head," said Mr Franklin, "Let's see you draw a bead on him."

Samson glanced at the clock and covered it with his pistol at hip-level. Mr Franklin nodded approvingly: he had fully expected to see the pistol extended at eye-level, possibly over a crooked elbow. "Good enough, Thomas. Now, you keep that piece next to you from now on. I pray to God you're not going to have to use it."

"Very good, sir. I've locked up, but I think that I shall go round again, to make sure everything is secure. You will be sleeping in your own room, sir? Very good, I shall keep to mine. In that way we shall have both ground and upper floor occupied. Good night, sir."

Yet it was another two hours before they finally said good night for the last time. Mr Franklin had no wish to turn in, and Samson seemed to be spinning out his duties in the kitchen, moving about in his apron, checking windows, turning down lights, putting things in cupboards, while Mr Franklin moved aimlessly about between study and hall, reluctant to settle in upstairs. Indeed, he was struggling to accustom himself to the reality of the situation, to attune his mind and reactions, in the cosy peace of Lancing Manor, to the violent necessity of that life out yonder, where the pistol, not the tweed jacket, had been the first article of wear for the well-dressed man; where the day's business had been struggle and danger and quite often wounding and death, not driving to Oxton for tea, or watching Peggy arrange flowers on a side-table, or strolling through the quiet village, stick in hand, exchanging salutations with Mrs Laker and the other country-folk who called him "Squire" now to his face. It was so difficult to recognise what was real, and what had been real, and reconcile the two – he had made the contrasts many times over the past two months, but always they had been worlds apart. Playing bridge with the King and Mrs Keppel, and facing the Kid across the greasy table at five-card stud; trying to flirt with Lady Helen, and hearing the whore yelling about her good manners in a Fort Worth hook-shop; good-timing with Pip at Monico's above the fashionable diners, and seeing the boys dance on the tables at the Bella Union; sitting in a Thetford tea-shop, and waiting out in Cheyenne for Deaf Charley Hanks to show; strolling on Piccadilly with morning-coat and gloves to take tea at the Ritz, or slogging up the muddy hill at Tonopah with the dead-weight of the dirt sledge and harness cutting into his shoulders; standing bare-headed in the soft rain of Lancing churchyard with the damp grass underfoot while they buried some rustic of the village and turned away sniffing and soft-voiced, and watching Dave Lant throw the last rock on to the pile that covered who-was-it with a mutter of "There, you poor ole bastard, that'll have to keep the dogs off you,"

277

before they swung into their saddles again in the heat of sweaty cotton and leather, dirty hands on the guns and bridles; playing truth or consequences in the stuffy, well-bred comfort of Sir Charles's drawing-room, and watching the chuck-a-luck cage spinning in the smoky atmosphere of a Casper saloon; petting with Peggy in the scented warmth before the fire, and shaking his head at the Spanish girl on the balcony outside old Davis's room; cucumber sandwiches at the Ritz and beef hash at Hole-in-the-Wall; following the King from dining-room to drawing-room and backing out of the jail in Deadwood with Curry hand-cuffed beside him and his gun trained on the glaring deputy; Mrs Keppel's dainty fingers and old Davis's cracked nails – it was no use trying to reconcile the two worlds.

And yet they were one now, because out there, through the damp dark, the old life – the old death – was approaching to run him down in his choicely-furnished bachelor residence in this peaceful corner of England, a bloody road agent was coming to violate the civilized seclusion of himself and the tidy, middle-aged man in the apron with his sleeves neatly rolled up as he polished a glass methodically and set it on a shelf in his pantry.

Finally Mr Franklin took himself another pot of coffee and went up to his room, but he did not get into bed. He stretched out, in shirt and trousers, drinking coffee and listening to the rising wind and the steady patter of rain on the roof. He heard the hall clock strike two, and the distant sound of Samson's bedroom door closing at the back of the ground-floor. He smoked one cigarette after another, and let his coffee go cold in the cup – was he mad, waiting like this, playing into Curry's hands, letting the old world make the rules? What was to prevent him from driving into Thetford early tomorrow, striding into the police station and telling them that Kid Curry, notorious desperado and gun-fighter, was prowling the fields of Norfolk with a six-shooter in his pocket and murder in his heart? "Curry, you say, sir. I see – would that be Curry with a 'y' sir, or an 'i-e'?" They would think he was a lunatic.

And there was another objection to official interference. "And why should this man Curry want to kill you, sir? You knew him in the United States, where he is a wanted murderer, did you? How did you come to know him, sir?" Inevitably, however discreetly he answered the questions – he could almost hear the patient, relentless voice of some Scotland Yard detective – in the end the telegraph would take the names of Curry and Franklin back across the Atlantic, to the

Pinkerton office, to Wells Fargo and U.P., to Denver and Laramie and Casper, to evoke uncomfortable replies. It was true there were no warrants or rewards attached to his name – but it was still known, to a score of peace officers in four states. There might be no witnesses now to come forward, certainly not at this distance, no evidence to detain him even for a second in any state of the Union, let alone England – but there would still be memories, circumstantial facts, gossip and rumours, and *they* could make an ugly cloud over his name, and Peggy's, and her family's. There was a headline in the Cheyenne paper, for whoever cared to look for it: "Two Killed In Street Shooting: O. C. Hanks Dead, Tracy Wounded In Duel With Franklin'; much could be made of that, and the death of an innocent bystander in the blast of Tracy's shotgun, even though Mr Franklin himself had been allowed to leave town with his guns on and his innocence pronounced. "Members of the notorious Wild Bunch . . . Hole-in-the-Wall thieves fall out . . . vendetta among the railroad brigands . . . " That was the brush he would be tarred with, fairly enough, if all the facts came out.

Which was why he must wait, and meet it in the old way, and the final act in the melodrama of the "railroad brigands" must be played out in the parish of Castle Lancing.

He stirred and blinked his eyes open to find that the lamp was burning down to the last of its oil. He must have been asleep, for his right arm was numb beneath him, and he had to use his left to lift it, swearing softly at the tingle of pins and needles. The last chime echoed dimly from downstairs – that must have been what woke him, and he pulled out his half-hunter for confirmation. Four o'clock. Stiffly he rolled off the bed – there was no sense in lying around half-dressed when he could be between the sheets. It sounded as though the wind had dropped; cautiously, and keeping close against the wall, he touched aside the edge of the curtain and glanced out and down, towards the rear of the house. The moon was up, bathing the side garden and bushes in white light and black shadow; the servants' quarters projected slightly from the main building, and he could see the dull glow behind the curtains of Samson's window. Mr Franklin gave a tired smile; he was not the only one waking, then. Well, Samson could make them another pot of coffee, and Mr Franklin was about to let the curtain drop when he froze suddenly, his breath stopping with a sob deep in his throat.

Far out, at the end of a hedgerow across the moonlit meadow –

had something moved? It was hard to tell in that silvery, unreal light – there, again, the shadow at the end of the hedge seemed to have wavered momentarily. His hand strayed automatically towards the lamp, and stopped – the last thing he must do was turn it out, or give any indication that he had seen . . . whatever it was he had seen. Moonlight could play odd tricks, but if his senses told him anything at all it was that something had stirred out yonder, beside the ditch and hedgerow which ran across his line of vision, perhaps three hundred yards away. He stared steadily, through the tiny gap between wall and curtain . . . it couldn't be, surely, so soon? And it was one hell of a coincidence that he had happened to glance out, just then . . . except that his instinct, which he had learned to trust, might have prompted him to do just that. He felt the hairs prickle on his neck as he realized that the distant hedge, running directly across his front, began in a tongue of the woodland – any stalker wishing to approach his house from the wood must surely come along the hedge, following it across the far side of the field to a smaller hedge which turned at right angles and came in towards the back of his property. His eyes never wavered from the distant gap – yes, there was something there, for certain, something living. How far off? Three hundred yards, maybe more – he had ample time to slip out of a window on the opposite side, and steal unseen to some hiding-place near the stables – and wait. And if he was wrong – if the movement there was a cow, or some nocturnal prowling animal – it would do him no harm to skulk in his grounds in the kind of conditions he could expect tomorrow night . . . Have to let Samson know, though . . .

There it was again! Something had definitely moved in the distant gap. Mr Franklin felt elation running through him as he slid away from the window, working his numbed right arm, picked up the Remington from the side-table, and slipped it into his waistband. He padded across the room in his stockinged feet, softly opened the door, and stepped on to the landing. The large windows of the upper floor were throwing moonlight across the landing and the empty, silent hall below as he turned towards the stairs and suddenly shrieked aloud for there not fifteen feet off and halfway up the stairs was Curry with his eyes glaring wildly in the moonlight and his teeth bared in a ghastly grin as his hand streaked out from beneath his coat and the Colt was whirling up to cover Mr Franklin while he gaped flat-footed with his yell echoing around him and his numbed right hand twitching feebly at his Remington until instinct sent him diving desperately sideways drawing left-handed and the thunderous boom-boom-boom of revolver-fire reverberated through the house. Something smashed resoundingly on the wall behind his head, the Remington kicked in his fist as he sprawled against the balusters, Curry's outstretched hand was flaming at him as the shots crashed together in one great explosion, but there was no agony of slugs tearing into him and suddenly Curry was screaming, his hands flung up and his eyes staring through the wreaths of powder-smoke, his thin body twisting horribly and turning to pitch headlong down the staircase, the Colt clattering from his hand and skidding away across the polished hall floor. The frail body smashed into the newel-post and lay there grotesquely, and Mr Franklin lunged forward on his belly to the top of the stairs, firing once, twice, into the twitching form, seeing his shots strike on the white shirt-front.

Mr Franklin scrambled up, his ears deafened by the cannonade, the stench of gunsmoke in his nostrils, and slid rather than ran down the stairs, his Remington out before him, thrust towards Curry's face. He stared at his fallen enemy, but the thin jaw was already hanging wide, a trickle of blood running from the corner, and the dark eyes already filmed in death. Suddenly the body seemed to crumple, and then it slid sideways to lie face down on the bottom step, and Mr Franklin saw the sodden bullet-holes between the shoulders, and was aware that Samson was standing opposite him, the other Remington still smoking in his hand.

"You . . . ?" His voice came out in a croak.

"I shot him behind just as you came out," said Samson. "And then again. You hit him yourself, I think, while he was shooting at you." He stooped over the body and rolled it off the step on to its back in the hall. Curry's whole front was sodden with blood; Mr Franklin thought he could see it pumping out of him beneath the soaked shirt. "Leaking like a sieve," said Samson.

"Christ!" said Mr Franklin. "He was in the house! In the house! How the hell did he . . . ?"

"Study window, sir, I fancy." Samson had recollected some of his calm; he was using the honorific again. "I heard him in the hall, so I came out quietly into the kitchen. I listened for about five minutes – he must have been getting his bearings, for it was after that I heard him at the foot of the stairs. I took a look out, and there he was, but I couldn't get a sure shot at him, sir, because of the bannisters, you understand. So I waited, while he moved up the staircase – very quietly he did it, sir, if you'd closed your eyes you wouldn't have heard a thing – and he was just getting to a spot where I'd have been able to draw a bead on him, sir, when your door opened and you stepped out. So I didn't wait, sir – I just jumped out and let him have it. For a moment I thought I was too late – you were right, sir, he's quick. Quicker than anyone I ever saw. We were all shooting at once, sir."

Samson's voice ran up into a breathless quaver, and he swallowed hard. For the first time Mr Franklin saw him shaken, small blame to him. He himself suddenly found his hands shaking uncontrollably. He sank into a sitting position on the stairs, and they stared at each other with the dead man between them.

"How the devil did he make it?" wondered Mr Franklin.

"It occurred to me that he might," said Samson. "You said, sir, he would try to come before you expected him. That's what he did, sir."

"We've got to get him out of here!" said Mr Franklin. "My God, the mess!" Curry's body was bleeding steadily, on to the polished boards of the hall; there was blood on the carpet of the stairs, and on the newel-post, and on Samson's sleeves.

"I'll get a blanket," said Samson. He was back in a moment, laying a blanket on the floor and rolling the body onto it, then in turn rolling the bundle on to a tarpaulin. Then he turned abruptly to Mr Franklin.

"We've got to make up our minds, sir," he said.

"What'd you mean?"

"Well, sir . . . what are we going to do with the . . . the body? It depends, you see. He was an armed house-breaker; we shot him. The police would accept that, sir – it would be manslaughter, but . . . "

"But why did we pump enough lead into him to sink a ship?" said Mr Franklin. "There's two of your shots, two of mine at least. And at least three people saw him at Oxton Hall. The police would ask a lot of questions – "

"Exactly, sir. I just mentioned it. On the other hand," Samson glanced at the tarpaulin-wrapped bundle, "I doubt very much if anyone would hear the shots, sir. We're a good way from the village, and it was all indoors. Nobody knows he was here – I don't suppose anyone in England knows who – "

"My God!" Mr Franklin came abruptly to his feet. "I'd forgotten – I saw someone moving, out beyond the meadow. I thought it was him, but it couldn't have been! He was already in the house!"

"An accomplice, sir?"

282

"No. No. He'd be alone – I'm certain of that. But we'd better make sure."

He ran swiftly upstairs, and went cautiously to the window. The moon was still bright, and across the meadow, near the gap, there were a couple of dark, bulky shapes moving slowly and at random about the field. Mr Franklin heaved a deep sigh and hurried down to the hall.

"Horses." He shook his head. "I forgot they were in the field – I tell you, Samson, I've been a pretty rattled man this last couple of nights. And I thought I had nerve!"

"Nothing wrong with your nerves, sir. You were very smart when the time came."

"If it hadn't been for you . . ." began Mr Franklin, and stopped. "All right, Thomas, I won't waste time over it. Thank you."

Samson nodded. "What I was saying, sir. If it would be inconvenient to go to the police – well, we don't need to, sir."

"I know. If we plant him somewhere quietly, then that's the end of it. It crossed my mind while I was still back at Oxton – assuming that he came, and I was faster than he was. I was going to put him – " he jerked his head towards the rear of the house " – out there somewheres."

"I wouldn't advise that, sir. Not on your own ground. You never know when – "

"Well, where, then? Dammit, we can't take him far."

"There's the marshy ground, sir, over the other side of the road. Up towards Lye Cottage, in the thicket on the far side of old Mrs Reeve's place – away from the village. Nobody ever goes there, and if we cross the road outside our own gate and go through the spinney, we can circle round to it. There's no houses that way – "

"But that's a good half-mile!"

"He doesn't weigh much, sir. And there's two of us. And it'll be easy ground to dig, and to cover any traces. But the main thing is, we won't run into anyone at this time of night. We could have it done before daybreak, sir."

Mr Franklin looked at the bundle, and at Samson kneeling beside it, and at the blood-stained floor and carpet, and at the fading moonlight shining in from the upstairs windows. He was steady enough now, after the shattering shock of the encounter, and thinking clearly. It was the only way, of course – by no stretch of the imagination could it be officially reported to the police, and if they were going to get rid

283

of Curry secretly, the sooner the better. Was there any virtue to waiting, and carrying him farther afield? – no, that only added to the risk, and anyway, he wanted that hateful thing out of the house as quickly as possible. Samson was watching him.

"Right," said Mr Franklin, "let's go."

At Samson's suggestion they bound the tarpaulin tightly with rope, and between them hefted it to the back door, carrying it slung between them. The moon was dying, and it was almost pitch-dark as they moved down the side of the house to the gate, and across the road to the empty field on the other side. Samson had picked up a couple of shovels from the stables, and they carried one apiece, trudging along the hedgerow towards the distant spinney. Every few hundred yards they changed hands, but Samson had been right – Curry was no great weight, and they were able to move quickly. They reached the spinney and skirted it to another hedge which led to the distant, marshy thicket beyond which was Lye Cottage. They were tired and sweating by the time they reached the thicket, which extended for about two hundred yards before it ended with the tall quickset hedge which marked the bottom of Mrs Reeve's jungle of a garden. They found a piece of flat, marshy ground among a tangle of rotting tree-stumps and brambles, and began to dig.

It took them about three-quarters of an hour, during which rain began to fall, but it did not hamper their labour. They dug hard, without much precaution for silence; Lye Cottage was more than two hundred yards off, with a tangle of undergrowth between, and the nearest cottage beyond it was a good quarter of a mile away. The soil was soft and easy, and once they were past the first tangle of roots they made good progress. Mr Franklin had undone the tarpaulin, on which they piled the spoil; when they had a narrow trench between four and five feet deep they unwrapped the body from its blanket, and Mr Franklin went quickly through the pockets of jacket and coat – a few papers, which he pocketed carefully, but he left the small change, pen-knife, watch and chain, and such articles. He had no desire to rifle Kid Curry's belongings. Then they rolled the body into the hole and filled it in; the surplus soil they cast broadside into the surrounding bushes. It was growing light as they finished, and the rain was descending in torrents; neither said so, but it occurred to them both that the rain was a blessing; it would help to obscure the traces of their work, and any bloodstains they had left on their way from the house would be quickly obliterated.

Finally, it was done. Samson quickly bundled up the tarpaulin, blanket, and ropes, Mr Franklin took the shovels, and they looked at each other, two exhausted, mud-splashed, soaking figures with the rain teeming down about them, clattering on the bushes and into the puddles around their feet, while the pale dawn began to steal through the thicket.

"Well," said Mr Franklin. "God rest him, I suppose."

"Amen," said Samson.

And he was gone. So far from Dodson, Missouri, so far from the Wyoming hills. No doubt, when he thought about it, the wicked little man had expected to die by violence, in the heat of a skirmish round an ambushed train, or in some frenzied shoot-out among the rearing horses outside a rifled bank, or strung up to a tree-limb by outraged citizens, or shot down in a gully by a *posse commitatus*, or in some brawl in alley or saloon. Never, in his wildest nightmare, could it have crossed his mind, or the minds of any of the hundreds who had feared and hunted him, that he would die by the hand of a butler in an apron in an English country house – and no one would ever know. Kid Curry was listed dead and buried at Glenwood Springs. Whatever those sturdy Norfolk ancestors of Mr Franklin's, or those sober Scottish emigrant forebears of Harvey Logan, could have foreseen, it could not have been this – two men shovelling another into the ground of Castle Lancing by night, and setting off silently in the rainy daybreak to go home. Nor would any of the Wild Bunch, or the Pinkertons, or the railroad bulls, ever have credited it. That, Mr Franklin reflected, was all in his favour.

They came back round by the spinney, having seen no one; the road running past Lancing Manor was empty in the early daylight. They put the blanket and tarpaulin in the stables, to be burned when occasion served, and went into the house. While Samson boiled water, and set to with mop and cloths and buckets to remove the ugly, congealed pool from the polished floor, and the stains from the newel-post and skirting board, Mr Franklin went up to the landing to survey the damage. Beyond his bedroom door lay a shattered vase, and low down in the plaster of the wall two bullet holes; there was a third in the polished planking close to the balusters, a great splintered furrow in the wood – the little bastard had got off three shots, then, as Mr Franklin dived, and they had all come within inches. Perhaps the Kid had not been the deadly shot of old; none out of three, even in that

285

light, was poor shooting for him – unless he already had one of Samson's bullets in him when he began to fire.

He checked the Kid's Colt, lying half under the big hall rug where it had slid away after he fell. Two chambers loaded, three discharged. He broke his own Remington; four spent chambers. Two he had certainly put into Curry after his fall – Samson reckoned he had scored another hit earlier, so one had missed. He checked the wall beyond where Curry had been standing; there was one hole, neatly drilled in the panelling.

"How many shots did you fire, Samson?"

Samsom, wringing out his cloths, said: "Three, sir," and picked up his Remington from the hall table to make sure. "Yes, three. The first two hit him, sir, I'm pretty certain."

They found a third hole, after a brief search, in the lintel of Mr Samson's door, and on the staircase itself, one slug, battered out of shape, which had presumably passed clean through the outlaw's body.

"We'll have to get rid of the stair carpet, sir." said Samson. "We'll never get the stains out. I can go into Norwich and get a matching piece of runner, and we can burn the old one. I'll plug and plaster the holes in the wall, and do a job with one of these patent fillers on the woodwork. In a day or two, no one will ever be able to guess what happened, sir. That's the floor done for now, but I'll go over it carefully again, with scrubbing brushes and polish."

They fell silent, thinking the same thing. It was probable that Curry's body was hidden forever, or at least for more generations than would worry either of them, and even if it was found years hence, there would be nothing to connect the skeleton with Lancing Manor. But the facts of scientific detection were well-known; bloodstains could be traced long after they had been made, and it was essential that there should be no tell-tale evidence of them on the floorboards or in the cracks between. The slugs buried in the walls and woodwork were safe enough, plaster and paint would see to that.

But there were other scars, and they both knew it. There was a common secret now, a common guilt – so far as guilt entered into it – and they would share it to their graves. It had to be spoken about, and Mr Franklin knew it had to be done now.

"I'm sorry, Thomas," he said. "You didn't deserve any of this. It wasn't fair, and I want you to know the full responsibility is mine. It was my quarrel, and whatever you did . . . well, that was my deed. As far as I'm concerned, you weren't in this fight tonight; I fired all those shots, and you didn't come on the scene till it was all over. In fact, you weren't here at all. Understand? We may have acted in self-defence, but we've hidden a body, and that will make it murder, in the law's eyes, if it ever comes out. Between ourselves – he was a bad man, and he got what he deserved. I'm no saint myself, but you may take my word for it."

Samson laid down his cloths and dried his hands on a rough towel. "I know that, sir. And I was here, and it happened exactly as it happened – if it should ever come out. But I think it's something that only you and I will ever know." He picked up Curry's gun from the table and held it out, butt first. "Do those marks mean what I think they mean, sir?"

There were eleven neat little nicks lightly carved on the gold tracery along the edge of the pearl handle. Mr Franklin nodded.

"They mean what you think," he said.

"Then I'll lose no sleep over it, sir," said Samson. "You'll be disposing of the pistol, of course. I'll clean the Remingtons, and get rid of the empty cases. In the meantime, may I suggest that you get out of your wet things and have a hot bath; I'll attend to the boiler and prepare some coffee and brandy."

There was much more that should have been said, of course. There was the not unimportant question of whether a master and servant who had been party to a homicide could, in the nature of things, continue in their relationship. It was a matter which might well have taxed the professional ethics of Mr Pride, although with his profound experience of such things, he would probably have said that it depended entirely on the inclinations of the parties involved. And he might well have been right, for it did not occur to either Mr Franklin or Samson for a very long time, and by then it was no longer worth bothering about.

287

14

Early in the year 1910 the Liberal Party won the General Election with a reduced majority, eighty labour exchanges at which unemployed workers could apply for jobs were opened, "By the light of the silvery moon" was established as the hit song of the moment, and a dead elm tree, succumbing to the January gales, fell in Lye Thicket, Castle Lancing, across the slight mound which marked the tomb of Harvey Logan, alias Kid Curry. Events both momentous and trivial, and remarkable in combination only because they were the principal things that Mr Franklin was forever after to associate with his marriage, at St James's Church, Piccadilly, to Miss Elizabeth Clayton, of Oxton Hall, Norfolk. He remembered the election because he could hardly help noticing it at the time, even although, as an alien, he had no vote, and was able to preserve an amiable neutrality in the face of Colonel and Mrs Dammit when they called to enlist his aid in the Conservative interest. He did, however, contribute an article to the jumble sale which Mrs Dammit was organizing to assist party funds – a very fine pearl-handled revolver with golden tracing (slightly scarred) round its butt, which raised the remarkable sum of £25 from a local sportsman, more than all the other items in the sale together. Mr Franklin presented the weapon on the kind of hare-brained impulse to which men are prone in the month before their weddings; there was nothing ghoulish about it; indeed, it seemed to him quite fitting that the gun which had earned so much hard money for Kid Curry, a private enterprise traditionalist if ever there was one, should, even at the last, be used to raise funds for the Conservative cause.

The eighty labour exchanges he was to remember because in the week before their marriage Peggy, glancing idly through the paper, noticed the announcement of their opening and remarked: "Oh, dear, Daddy won't be at all pleased; he says they're sure to be clearing-houses for agitators and Bolsheviks," which for some reason stuck in his mind; "By the light of the silvery moon", like the election, impressed itself on his memory by sheer repetition. And the elm tree he remembered because, after three weeks' determined avoidance of the place where they had buried Curry, he strolled over one afternoon to see that nothing had been disturbed, and only with difficulty recognized the untidy, muddied spot among the brambles with the newly-fallen elm across it.

They sailed from London on February 5 on their honeymoon cruise of the Caribbean, which was provisionally booked to last six weeks, at £4 a day for their de luxe stateroom on the port side, and in the event took three months. They extended it, by transferring to another ship, because neither of them had been so happy in their lives before, and Mr Franklin reflected that they were indeed fools who supposed that bliss could not be bought for hard cash, at least on a temporary basis. They cruised through the Antilles in a rapturous haze, intoxicated by blue water, golden sand, magnificent scenery, and each other's company, they rode on bamboo rafts down jungle rivers, shopped in colourful waterfront bazaars, drank strange sweet liqueurs in mountain distilleries, listened to amazing native bands playing throbbing and vaguely sinister music at midnight barbecues on tropical beaches, jaunted in open carriages on misty hill trails, danced after dinner in hotels from Port-au-Prince to Nassau, and made love ecstatically each evening on the mosquito-netted double bed beneath their stateroom window, open to the purple sky with its twinkling stars. Peggy got sunburned at Kingston, and Mr Franklin caught a peculiarly unpleasant stomach germ in Antigua, but these were small things in their West Indian idyll. And finally, on a pleasant May evening, they disembarked at Southampton to see a sad-faced urchin selling papers beside a black-bordered news bill, and Mr Franklin bought a newspaper with a cold feeling of disbelief, and read that portly old Mr Lancaster, who had offered him a glass of wine by the roadside and complained petulantly when he overbid, had died – the paper said it was sudden, but it seemed that many people, including the King himself, had expected it.

Mr Franklin found himself strangely affected by the news. Peggy's immediate reaction was to catch his arm and gasp: "Oh, poor old thing! And I said such beastly things about him that evening, over that awful dinner! Oh, I'm sorry!" It was a fairly typical response among the British on that day; Mr Franklin noticed an elderly woman in tears, being patted on the shoulder by an old man while she exclaimed: "Oh, dear! Oh, dear old Dad!" He did not feel regret so much for the man, whom he had liked well enough in their brief acquaintance, while being under no illusions about his faults, as for the passing of an institution; in his few months in Britain Mr Franklin had sensed an underlying confidence that while "dear old Dad" was there, all would be well. Mr Franklin had been close enough to guess that the royal influence on affairs was slight, and yet, so long as he had lived, with his reassuring, portly presence, his easy, human manners, and his aura of knowing, rather raffish shrewdness, Edward had been a symbol for his people; a wayward but steady, dissolute but decent old codger in the eyes of the populace, a royal John Bull with just a touch of that rascality so essential for popularity in a ruler of the island race. And now it had gone, and an age with it, and Mr Franklin shivered even in the warmth of the May evening.

They caught an evening train to London, and it was midnight when their taxi drew up outside the new house in Wilton Crescent. The lamps were twinkling on the pavements, with moths fluttering round the mantles, there were lights in the ground-floor windows, and Samson was throwing open the front door and sending down the footman to collect the luggage. One or two passers-by turned idly to look at the new arrivals, a policeman on the corner glanced incuriously in their direction. Mr Franklin handed Peggy from the taxi as Samson descended briskly to pay the driver, and to murmur "Welcome home, madam; welcome home sir." For a moment they stood in the summer dark; Mr Franklin could see through the front door the row of figures waiting in the hall – trust Samson to see that the whole new staff was on hand for the homecoming of the master and mistress – the starched aprons and caps, the curious faces looking out, the sombre warmth of the panelled hall in the glare of the electric light.

He glanced at Peggy and took her arm. She was smiling in delighted anticipation, and looking beautiful in her fur boa and broad-brimmed hat.

"Glad to be home, Mrs Franklin? I'd carry you over the threshold, but I doubt if Samson would approve."

"Glad to be home, darling," said Mrs Franklin, and they went up the steps to the house with Samson stepping sedately in their wake. As they passed through the door, and the waiting maids smiled and bobbed at them, Mr Franklin had an odd memory of resting his head on his valise that first night in the empty hall of the manor; that night he had gone to sleep in Castle Lancing; tonight he would fall asleep in London Town.

15

During the year 1910 Mr and Mrs Mark Franklin lived in Wilton Crescent, except for occasional visits to Castle Lancing, Oxton Hall, and a shooting box in Scotland. They were well received in polite society, were photographed for the illustrated papers (Mrs Franklin's striking beauty being especially noted at the famous "Black Ascot" meeting of that year), and were minor favourites with the fashionable columnists, who described them respectively as "distinguished-looking" and "lovely".

In that year which had seen the funeral of King Edward, there also died Florence Nightingale, Tolstoy, and Mary Baker Eddy. Season tickets were issued for the first time on the railways, Stravinsky produced The Firebird, *Jack Johnson knocked out James J. Jeffries, and the powers of the House of Lords were reduced.*

In 1911 King George V was crowned during one of the most brilliant summers in living memory, Amundsen reached the South Pole, suffragettes (including Lady Helen Cessford) continued to smash windows and set fire to pillar-boxes, the Mona Lisa *was stolen from the Louvre, Italy went to war with Turkey, the literary world enthused over the poetry of a stripling named Rupert Brooke, Society laughed politely at the cruel wit of "The Chronicles of Clovis", and the commonalty enjoyed "Sanders of the River". A gallant old gentleman saved a young woman from drowning and died himself as a result, and the country sang one of his best-loved songs, "He is an Englishman" in his memory; it was not inappropriate that as Gilbert died the feet of the younger generation were beginning to stir to the work of another great songwriter, and "Alexander's Ragtime Band" was heard in the land. The last great sunset of the Indian Empire began with the Delhi Durbar, the Kaiser promised that the German Navy would secure for the Fatherland "a place in the sun", and at the Palace Theatre Pavlova's partner dropped her, she struck him, the curtain was lowered, and a cinema film was shown instead. Mr and Mrs Franklin continued to live in Wilton Crescent.*

In 1912 the United States Marines landed in Cuba, there were strikes and riots in the London docks, the suffragettes succeeded in breaking a window at Number 10 Downing Street, Mr Lansbury protested about the forcible feeding of those who had been arrested and lost his seat in a by-election, the Titanic *went down in the Atlantic and both Oxford and Cambridge boats sank in the Boat Race on the Thames, "Alexander's Ragtime Band" was joined in the public repertoire by 'Oh, You Beautiful Doll", "When Irish Eyes are Smiling", and a swinging little song which a few years later was to become the anthem of a generation – "Tipperary". After several centuries of living by their wits, British members of Parliament realised that they had the power and lack of shame to vote themselves salaries, and did so, £400 a year, no less, cinema audiences were entranced by Sarah Bernhardt in the role of Good Queen Bess, Germany had over 4 million men under arms, and Britain fewer than a million, Woodrow Wilson was elected President of the U.S., and war broke out among certain obscure countries in the Balkans. Mr and Mrs Franklin continued to live in Wilton Crescent.*

In 1913 the suffragette campaign mounted, with bombs, arson, mass demonstrations, and the death of a woman who threw herself in front of the King's horse during the Derby; either despite or because of these things Mrs Pankhurst was sentenced for a bomb plot and the House of Commons threw out the women's franchise bill. The warring Balkan countries signed a peace treaty in May and began a second war in June, the Commons passed the Irish Home Rule bill, England beat Australia at cricket, and Mr and Mrs Franklin remained in residence at Wilton Crescent.

292

Part Two

16

It was as he was reaching for the marmalade that Mr Franklin realized what a creature of habit he had become. It stood where the maid had placed it, precisely six inches beyond his coffee cup and to the right of the toast rack, as it had stood for the past four years; Peggy never used it, having her own small pot of honey on the other side of the table, and Mr Franklin could have reached out, without taking his eyes from the morning paper, in the absolute certainty that the marmalade would be there. In fact, he was doing just that when the automatic nature of his action struck him, and he murmured aloud: "Phileas Fogg has nothing on me. One of these days they'll put strawberry jam there, and I'll think the sky has fallen in."

Peggy, deep in the illustrated magazines, said vaguely, "What?" and Mr Franklin sighed and spooned marmalade on to his plate.

"I was just remarking," he said, "that according to the paper his holiness the Pope doesn't care much for the tango. It says here that he prefers the furlana, a local Italian dance which he used to watch when he was a boy."

"Mm-m," said Peggy, frowning as she leafed over the pages, and then softly exclaiming "Ah!" and sitting back to stare at the page. Mr Franklin knew exactly what she was looking at, and studied her surreptitiously past the edge of his paper. It was a little less than a week since they had been for the first time in their lives to Buckingham Palace, to attend the opening Court of the year, at which young ladies, most of them single but one or two married, were presented formally to their majesties. Peggy had never been a debutante, and at twenty-three was rather past the usual age, but the circumstances had been exceptional. Two years earlier the leader of the Conservative Party, Mr Balfour, had been succeeded by the Scots-Canadian Bonar Law, with whom Sir Charles Clayton was closely acquainted, both politically and socially; Miss Bonar Law had been one of the debutantes due for presentation, and Mr Franklin did not doubt that Peggy's inclusion had been arranged through the influence of the new Tory leader. So they had driven out on a wet Friday evening, Peggy immaculate in white silk and diamonds, and betraying not a sign of nervousness; she had made her curtsey, and in so doing had made the final formal passage into polite society, and what was almost equally important, had been photographed by respectful attendant cameramen.

What she was looking at now was the result, in the society magazines, and it obviously pleased her. Not that an outsider would have guessed it; she looked almost bored as she studied the pages, and the tiny deprecating twist at the corner of the perfectly-shaped mouth was in evidence; it usually was nowadays, and Mr Franklin wondered if its presence had anything to do with his own feelings as he watched her. Four years ago the sight of her across the table, the angelic face with its superb complexion, framed by the high lace collar of her deshabille and the artful carelessness of her piled auburn hair, would have produced a reaction in him; it might have resulted in his sitting gazing at her in quiet wonder and deep content, or in his quickly locking the morning-room door and sweeping her up suddenly towards the couch – either way, it would have been different from the interest he was taking in her now, which was decidedly more clinical, and he wondered for the hundredth time if the change in him stemmed from the change in her, or vice versa, and how much that tiny curl of the lip was a symptom or a cause of that change. Certainly the Peggy of four years ago would not have studied her picture so coolly; she would have exclaimed: "Mark! Darling! It's in!" and flown round the table with the magazine, to throw her arms around his neck and laugh over his shoulder as he admired it. Now, after studying the page for a minute, she pushed the magazine aside without even drawing his attention to it, remarking only in passing: "I can't think what possessed Mavis Littleton to wear that awful antique shawl; it made her look like a grandmother," and turned to her correspondence.

In fact, Mr Franklin, first down to breakfast, had already seen the picture, and had shaken his head over it in silent admiration. Peggy had never looked so composedly stunning. And, to be fair, four years ago he would have gone straight upstairs again to show her the magazine at once; two years ago he would have drawn attention to it, with a kiss and congratulations, when she came down; now, he wasn't sure why, he left it for her to find. Of course, in some ways it was natural enough; honeymoons didn't last forever, and the enthusiasms of their first year had gradually ebbed away; at the same time, after the passing of that first heady rapture, somehow life had not settled into the placid, loving amiability he had expected – well, he had not known quite what to expect, but he had certainly not foreseen that four years of marriage would expose such marked differences in taste, in temperament, in purpose, and in outlook between them, and it was only when he looked the differences in the face, and studied them, that he realized their cause.

At first he had put it down to his own background, his strangeness in a strange land. But it had not been that; he had merged into England as easily as the young British immigrants he had known had merged into the United States – he thought of Cassidy's family, still talking with the thick accent of their native Lancashire, yet as American as the Americans of the frontier, and knew that he had adapted to England in precisely the same way. It had been a homecoming; any disenchantments he might feel were not so much those of the stranger, as of the travelled native. Even in small things he had acclimatized; he still occasionally said "Every time!" and "gotten" and "guess", but he was used to being taken for an Englishman by strangers, and these were the superficial things. Deep down, he was easy here; the drifting imperceptibly away from Peggy had been nothing to do with upbringing or background or culture.

Had there been a change in Peggy, then? After all, when they had met and married, she had been only nineteen, hardly more than a schoolgirl, and she had grown quickly into a leading society beauty, the wife of a wealthy man, sought after and admired – it would have been no wonder if she had become completely spoiled. But she had not; the level-headedness which had balanced the girlish impulses was still there, there was none of the wilfulness or pettishness which disfigured the behaviour of so many of her friends. No, the change in Peggy had been nothing more than the early maturing of a lovely, spirited girl into an even lovelier, spirited woman; the fault did not lie there.

It was, as he eventually concluded, the simple fact that he was almost sixteen years older than Peggy, entering middle age while she was still a young woman. He had pondered on the age difference, without too much disquiet, before they were married; any doubts he had had then dwelt on a vague thought, quite consciously sexual, that he would be an old man when she was still in her ardent prime, but he had dismissed it as being too far ahead to worry about. Now it was the least of his anxieties – paradoxically enough, it was when they made love that the disparity of years was most easily forgotten; Mr Franklin at forty was a healthy and vigorous animal who occasionally surprised himself, and it was in bed that he and Peggy came closer to recapturing that early, careless happiness. It was in the ordinary, everyday pursuit of life that they parted company, amiably enough, but inevitably and, he sometimes felt, irrevocably.

At first it had gone well enough. She was, he realized, a socialite; she loved to entertain and be entertained, to attend parties, to dance, to go on trips, to pay calls, to make the day a constant round of driving into Town, visiting shops and hairdressers, lunching with friends, hurrying to some afternoon function, giving or receiving tea, dressing for dinner, dining out or going to the theatre, dancing until after midnight – and being out next morning, fresh as a daisy, for the same activities all over again, apparently without cessation. To which he could have no reasonable objection, although he sometimes reflected wrily on her pre-marital remark that she was not one of the bright young things, really, and was looking forward to a fairly settled married life. Possibly she had believed it then; more probably their definitions were just different. For there was no doubt, he soon discovered, that they simply lived at a different pace; Peggy was in a higher gear than he was, and there was nothing either of them could do about it.

He had tried; during the first year at Wilton Crescent he had joined in everything – and been all too conscious of being out of it. For while he could make the effort to share her interests, he could not pretend to belong to her generation – the seemingly endless horde of young women, married and single, whom she had known at school, or in the nursery, or in Society (a word he was beginning to detest), and the young men who were their husbands or boy friends or Peggy's old playmates – Buster, who had been sick at the Lord Mayor's children's party when they were seven, or Jenny, who had fallen in the Round Pond, or Michael, who had given them all chicken pox over the Christmas hols – it was a well-laid basis for social acquaintance whose passwords were "Do you remember?" and "Oh, that time when . . .", and there was no true admittance for those who had not had the privilege of catching Michael's germs, or screaming with panic or delight when Jenny was immersed, or being present when Buster had vomited so memorably.

Ironically, what made him feel more of an outsider was the fact that he got on with their parents very comfortably. Dinner parties which demanded a cross-section of the generations he could always tolerate and often enjoy, but for the rest he found himself accompanying Peggy less and less frequently, or absenting himself when her young friends and Arthur's invaded the premises; if they did not interest him, it was equally plain that he did not interest them – except for the three young ladies, bosom friends of his wife's, who had tried to seduce him. He had dissuaded them, with no great difficulty; what astonished him was that they continued thereafter in Peggy's lively social circle as though nothing had happened. He wondered increasingly, as men approaching forty are inclined to do, what the world was coming to.

Unable to share in Peggy's activities, it was natural that, almost unconsciously, he should develop interests of his own. It was a casual conversation with Sir Charles, in which the baronet recalled his suggestion, at their first meeting, that Mr Franklin might eventually settle to an agricultural life in Norfolk, that opened up an opportunity in front of him. The Oxton estate, scraping along a little deeper into debt each year, was in urgent need of management; Sir Charles himself, though an intelligent and even gifted man (he had played an unobtrusive but important part in Lord Haldane's great military reorganization a few years before), was no farmer, and Arthur, now commissioned from Sandhurst and serving with his regiment in Ireland, was in no position to help. Would Sir Charles's new son-in-law consider taking matters in hand?

Mr Franklin had accepted, and was no way deterred by the discovery that the principal need of the Oxton estate was hard cash. He had enough and to spare, and Sir Charles was disarmingly candid about the situation, which was rather worse than the American had imagined. He had always known that the Claytons were not affluent; he had not realized that the estate was deeply mortgaged and that Sir Charles was desperately short of ready money even to keep it going. However, Mr Franklin could remedy that, and it was done without contract or signature, on the simple understanding that the hall and estate should pass to Peggy and her husband on the baronet's death. Sir Charles altered his will, Arthur agreed without hesitation, and that was that.

Nor was there any dispute over how Mr Franklin's capital should be employed; he and his father-in-law might not be farmers, but they shared a common love for horses; the establishment of a stud was simply a matter of purchase, of hiring a competent steward and studgroom and stable hands, of repair and equipment; within a year the

299

Oxton estate, from going to seed, was beginning to revive, and Sir Charles and Mr Franklin could indulge in dreams of a racing stable, when they had the business on a solid footing.

For the moment, if the enterprise was a powerful drain on Mr Franklin's funds, it kept him usefully if not strenuously employed, his time divided almost equally between London and Norfolk. At first he had half-hoped that he might wean Peggy away, at least a little, from her beloved social life, and indeed she did accompany him to begin with, but the country life bored her, and Mr Franklin concluded sadly that he probably bored her too. So their life fell into the half-together, half-apart pattern – which, Mr Franklin observed resignedly, seemed not unusual in Society – with himself spending ten days to a fortnight of every month at Oxton and Castle Lancing and Peggy pursuing her pleasures in Town or farther afield. He missed her unconscionably when they were apart, and concealed his hurt at the obvious fact that she did not particularly miss him.

It was not, he knew, an ideal basis for marriage, and sometimes it saddened him to think of her married to an old stick-in-the-mud (which was how he increasingly saw himself) when she could have had a young husband to share and heighten her pleasures, some Buster or Jeremy whose notion of living was to frolic at the 400 all night and have haddock and eggs for breakfast before dashing off to a weekend at Brighton or a week at Biarritz, or spend the day racing and the evening dancing the Boston and the one-step, with a midnight fancy-dress party to follow. On the other hand, she seemed perfectly happy with the present arrangement, and that saddened him most of all. At first he had consoled himself with the hope that her social delights would pall in time; now, after four years, he could not delude himself. They were drifting wider apart, until he felt sometimes that he was looking across the table at a beautiful stranger who regarded him much as she regarded warm weather – something which arrived occasionally, and was pleasant enough to have around, but would not be unduly missed when it went away.

Once or twice he had ventured, in a roundabout way, to talk about the estrangement which he knew was growing – even if it had led to a quarrel, he felt, it might have helped – but Peggy seemed to have no notion what he was talking about; the little curl would appear at the corner of her mouth, and she would turn the conversation with some light remark, or tease him playfully in a way that left him at a loss and feeling slightly stuffy. He found himself smiling ruefully at that, as he watched her now across the breakfast table, and she glanced up from her letters and saw him.

"What are you laughing at? Have I got honey on my nose?"

"No," said Mr Franklin, "I was just smiling contentedly at the thought that I have the most beautiful wife in London." Peggy raised her brows and managed to convey a curtsey while sitting down. "Well, thank *you*, kind sir," she said gravely. "You look extremely fine and proper yourself." She went back to her letters.

"And I was thinking how much I'm going to miss her these next few weeks," he added. "What time does your train leave?"

"Two o'clock."

"And when do you get into Paris?"

"Mm-m?" Peggy glanced up briefly. "Oh, in the evening some-time." She went on reading.

"And then on to Switzerland. Where is it again – Murren? Or Les Avants? There must be something about snow and ice that has an irresistible attraction for the British – even Shackleton's going back to the Antarctic. Who's all going to be there? Didn't you say something about Arthur joining you?"

"What? Oh, yes." Peggy put down her letter. "Yes, Arthur's coming over with his regimental team for the bob-sleigh at St Moritz. I expect we'll be there for a week or so. But it'll be Murren most of the time – the Stewarts are going to be there with a big party. I thought it might be a good thing if I had the car sent over, d'you mind? I could take the St Leger, and that would leave you the Landaulet in case you need it." They maintained two cars, although Mr Franklin, a horse-and-foot man, as he called himself, seldom used either; there was the smart St Leger Cabriolet which Peggy drove, and the more imposing Grenville Landaulet "for evening wear", as she put it, which required a chauffeur. There had been a Rover 12, too, but he rather thought Peggy had discarded it as not quite smart enough.

"Sure, take whichever car you like. It'll make you independent, so long as you take care. I imagine the Swiss roads are pretty icy, aren't they?"

"Oh, don't worry, I'll take chains. Perhaps you'd ask Samson to arrange the shipping. If it goes off tomorrow it should arrive at Murren a day or two after I do. And then hey for the snowbound slopes!" She smiled brightly and opened another letter, and Mr Franklin poured himself another cup of coffee. He had accompanied Peggy on her annual skiing holiday once, three years ago, and quite enjoyed it

– the skiing part, anyway, but that, he knew from experience, was only the pretext. The real reason for going to Switzerland was simply to obtain a change of scene for the social round; the people would be exactly the same, and the topics and gossip and party-throwing and driving up to Sophie's place for a midnight supper and curling by artificial light in the small hours and dancing at the new café on some bloody snowbound peak which Buster had discovered, absolutely divine – no, if he was a stick-in-the-mud, so be it, he had no desire to repeat the experience of being a stick-in-the-snow. That was his own choice, and it was utterly unfair of him to feel a little twinge of pique as he recalled the sequence over the years . . . 1911: "Oh, but Mark, darling, you *must* come! It'll be glorious fun, and we can go skating – well, I'll teach you, then – and ski-joring, which is when you have horses to pull you along on skis, it's marvellous, and we can spend nights up in these lovely wooden lodges on the mountains – just like your log-cabins, you know – and you can look out on the moonlight on the snow, and it's ever so cosy inside with blankets, and a log-fire, and just the two of us?" 1912: "Wouldn't you like to come, darling? No, well, if you'd rather not . . ." 1913: "I don't suppose you feel like coming, do you?" And now 1914, and it was taken for granted she'd go alone.

Well, it was entirely his own fault, but he couldn't stand the thought of the frantic gaiety and Poppy going off with this French count to Chamonix, well she says he's a count, and old Boodle getting stuck in a snowdrift, such fun, and this amazing Negro banjo-player at the Restaurant aux Fines Herbes who does the most terrific ragtime, and the Stewarts arranging sledge picnics, and Peggy swirling through it with endless energy while he contemplated the Alps over a cup of coffee and wondered what he was doing there. No, a few weeks at Castle Lancing, riding the lanes, seeing how the horses were doing at Oxton, listening to Sir Charles and his friends discussing the ruination of the country, perhaps dropping in for a drink at the Apple Tree, hearing the steward's views on field drainage – it might not be everyone's idea of a good time, but it would suit him.

He went back to his paper, and another instalment of those interminable stories which, if they could have been lifted into isolation in another time, would have been sensational, but which repetition had turned into the commonplace daily fare of the British public: a suffragette attempt to blow up a pillar-box at Westminster ending in a scuffle with police and four arrests; rumours of a great shipment of rifles and Mills bombs being successfully run from the Clyde into Ulster, where the Protestants were arming to fight against their incorporation in an independent Ireland; the possibility of a third Balkan war, and the likelihood of a rapprochement between Britain and Germany; rumblings of a plan among the unions to back any future demands by a general strike of all railwaymen, miners, and transport workers – it might have been last week's paper, or last month's, or even last year's; all these impending crises were part of the scenery, to be glanced at idly or impatiently before one turned to more interesting topics, such as Mr Orville Wright's invention of a stabilizer which would enable an aeroplane to fly itself while the pilot rested, or the reviews of the new spectacular musical *Hullo, Tango!* at the Hippodrome, or the forthcoming baseball tour of the American All-Star White Sox and the National League Giants. Then he became aware that Peggy was sitting staring at the wall, with a letter in her hand; he waited a moment, and then asked her if anything was the matter.

"It's from father – Arthur's talking about resigning his commission."

"What? Quit the Army?" Mr Franklin lowered his paper. "I thought he liked it."

"So did I. Well, he did, I mean – simply loved it. Until recently."

"You mean he's talked about resigning before? You never said anything about it."

"Maybe you weren't here. Oh, it didn't seem worth mentioning, anyway. Arthur just grumbled once or twice, and said that if certain things happened he might have to send in his papers – it was all vague, though, and I didn't pay much attention at first. But now he seems to be quite serious." Peggy pushed the letter away impatiently. "It's all this idiotic Irish business."

Mr Franklin frowned. "Why should he want to resign over that? I wouldn't have thought he cared all that much."

"Oh, yes." Peggy glanced at him sharply. "Mummy was Irish, you know."

"No, I didn't know." Mr Franklin was mildly surprised – not that there was any reason why the late Lady Clayton, whom he had hardly ever heard mentioned, shouldn't have been Irish, when you came right down to it. "But how does that affect Arthur's Army career?"

"Well, of course, Mummy's family were Protestant – Randalls, from County Clare, and terribly Loyalist, like most of the English-Irish. Her family took it awfully seriously – some ancestor Randall

303

fought at the Boyne or helped to close the gates at Londonderry, I can't remember which, but he got knighted by King William, or something like that. You've seen his sword – over the fireplace at Oxton. Arthur used to play with it, and he's always been terribly romantic, the ass, and been dead set against Home Rule, although I don't suppose he knows what it's all about. Lot of bally rot! Well, I suppose it isn't rot, really, but I don't see why he should get into a stew over it."

Mr Franklin, however, could see quite clearly. He knew, like every thinking person in Britain – which effectively excluded Peggy's circle – that the chance of civil war in Ireland was better than fifty-fifty. Mr Asquith's government, committed to Irish Home Rule, were in the process of putting a Bill through its final stages in Parliament, in the teeth of strenuous opposition from those Unionists who were determined that Protestant Ulster would remain part of Britain; Sir Edward Carson and his Loyalists were ready to fight to keep Ulster out of an independent Ireland, and for months the two sides, Protestant North and Catholic South, had been secretly arming and drilling for the day when negotiation finally failed. In the South the Citizen Army had been formed in response to the setting up of Carson's Ulster volunteers; if Peggy had ever looked beyond the fashion and society pages she would have seen the pictures of stern-faced men in bowler hats and bandoliers, and the iron profiles of Carson and Craig against the Union Jacks and "No Surrender" banners, or the news stories which estimated that 100,000 Southern Catholics were ready to take up the rifles trickling in from Germany and America. For any man in Britain who had Irish blood it was an issue not to be shirked; for a descendant of the Englishry, who had grown up playing with a sword used at Boyne Water, neutrality would be impossible.

"Well, with any luck Arthur's in the one place where he can keep out of it," said Mr Franklin, "and that's the British Army itself. Unless he has to fight the Home Rulers, and from what you say he won't mind that."

"Daddy says he thinks he might have to fight against the Unionists – the Protestants," said Peggy. "There have been stories about . . . oh, what a lot of rubbish it is! Anyway, he's talking about resigning, and – "

"That's haywire," said Mr Franklin decisively. "What – Asquith use the British Army against Ulster? Against the very people who want to keep it part of Britain? Don't you believe it."

Peggy looked at him doubtfully. "Well, I don't know. It's all boloney as far as I'm concerned, but Arthur's an absolute jughead on the subject; he really is – you think he's just a cheery great ox, but you've never seen him all worked up. If he says he's going to resign, he will. And that'll be that."

"Well, if he does, he does. It'll be a pity, though. What would he do? – I mean, I thought the Army was his whole life."

"I don't know, quite." Peggy chewed gently at her lower lip, hesitated, and then faced him across the table. "Look, Mark, I'd better say it, because if I'm in Switzerland I may not get a chance until . . . well, it might be too late. It's not too easy, though." She smiled ruefully at him and pulled a slight face. "I don't quite know how to put it, but nobody else can."

Mr Franklin was intrigued. If he knew Peggy at all, she was slightly embarrassed, and that, if not unprecedented, was at least unusual. "Go on," he said.

"Well," said Peggy, "in the first place, you've been terribly decent about Arthur."

Instinctively, he knew what was coming, and it was a relief. "Being decent about Arthur" meant only one thing in their vocabulary, and they seldom referred to it. When Arthur had been in his later terms at Sandhurst, the question of his regiment had come up, and Mr Franklin had received yet another intimation of the Clayton family's straitened circumstances – it had come at the time when he was already investing heavily in the rehabilitation of Oxton estate, and in financial terms the shock had been a slight one, out of all proportion to the importance which the Claytons themselves attached to the matter.

It had been a light remark of Peggy's about Arthur's graduation that led to the revelation. "The poor old thing had set his heart on the Lancers, but Daddy simply can't run to it. It's a shame, I suppose, because the 16th was Daddy's regiment, and his father's, and goodness knows how far back – they've all been cavalrymen. And poor old Bonzo's going to have to make do with some Line regiment – whatever that is – and hates the idea."

Naturally, Mr Franklin had shown proper concern, and had learned to his astonishment that even in these egalitarian days there were social and financial differences between British Army regiments which must stagger an ignorant colonial like himself. He could understand that cavalry were considered superior to infantry or artillery, but it came as news that the income necessary to support a young officer was infinitely greater for the mounted units than for the common-or-garden foot-sloggers. Pay, of course, went nowhere, and Sir Charles had long since known that his meagre assistance would not keep Arthur decently in anything beyond a foot regiment (and an unfashionable one at that); even so, he would find it necessary to sell land in order to raise the necessary capital – "it sounds like something out of Jack and the Beanstalk," said Peggy. "Selling Daisy the cow to equip young Arthur for the wars – in fact, to equip him for hunting and hacking about the polo fields."

It was not suggested for a moment that Mr Franklin should do anything about this regrettable state of affairs – financing Oxton estate was one thing, on a gentlemanly business basis, but he knew Sir Charles would have gone to the fire before soliciting assistance where his son's upkeep was concerned. Still, what was not asked could be volunteered, and what else could a decent son-in-law do, especially when he was known to be flush of cash, and already playing Pactolus for the family acres? Mr Franklin had said that something must be done, Peggy asked what, and he had replied: "We'll have to see that Arthur gets what he needs." She had protested, and a pretty debate had ensued; she had pointed out the impossibility of Arthur's accepting charity from his rich American brother-in-law, and Mr Franklin had said charity be damned, he could accept it from his own sister, couldn't he, and what was Mr Franklin's was Mrs Franklin's so where was the difficulty . . . ? The upshot was that a sum of money was placed in Peggy's name, for her personal disposal, and christened by her, with sisterly vulgarity, the A.B.W.G.P.F. (for "Arthur's Boozing, Wenching, and Garden Party Fund"), from which it was understood that an allowance would be paid to the aspiring subaltern; any question of eventual repayment was strictly a matter between Peggy and her brother, Mr Franklin and Sir Charles never so much as spoke to each other on the subject, and Arthur confined himself to saying, with much head-scratching and a crushing hand-clasp: "Mark, I just want to say . . . well, hang it, I know you know how much it meant to the guv'nor, and you're a bloody white man." Peggy did not weep, but she regarded Mr Franklin with slightly misty adoration at the time, which was 1911. Now, three years later, with Arthur comfortably situated as a lieutenant in the 16th Lancers in Ireland, and apparently intent on resigning the commission which Mr Franklin's tactfully-

306

placed funds had enabled him to maintain in proper style, she was looking slightly misty again.

"You've been terribly decent about Arthur," she repeated. "And I'm terribly grateful; so is he, and so, although he couldn't bear to say it, is Daddy – "

"Oh, nonsense," said Mr Franklin uncomfortably, but secretly well pleased; there is no sight so delightful to a man as a lovely woman's gratitude, and he was wondering how he could take advantage of it.

"The trouble is," continued Peggy, sitting forward with her hands clasped on the table-cloth, and looking serious, "that I know Arthur is really going to chuck it in – sisters always find these things out before anyone else, and Bonzo has always told me his troubles first. So I'm sorry, because it means it's all been wasted, really."

"No, it hasn't," said Mr Franklin. "Three years in the Army can't be a waste."

"It's been jolly expensive," said Peggy. "And now he has to find something else to do."

She paused, frowning, and Mr Franklin waited a moment before asking: "Has he said anything about that?"

"Not exactly." Peggy considered the alignment of a butter-knife thoughtfully. "Well, he's told me that he has ideas about starting up in business, but he hasn't told me the details. It's some scheme that he and one or two of his close friends have discussed, and they want to keep it to themselves at first, I suppose."

"I wouldn't have thought of Arthur as a business man," said Mr Franklin. "But after all – why not? He's got as many brains as most of the business men I've ever met. I guess he'd do all right."

"Yes," said Peggy. "I think he would, once he got started."

He knew perfectly well what they were leading up to, but it was as difficult for him to broach the matter as for Peggy, so he said nothing. Peggy realigned the butter-knife and then exclaimed:

"Oh, bother! Of course, the thing is, he needs money. And until he knows he can get it, he can't resign, and . . ." She shrugged and fluttered a hand impatiently and met her husband's eye. "So that's how it is, you see."

Mr Franklin folded his paper and dropped it on the floor, smiling at her.

"How's the Boozing, Wenching, and Garden Party Fund?"

"Pretty low, I'm afraid. Well, we knew it was only going to last a few years, didn't we? And it hasn't stretched quite as far . . ." Peggy

307

shifted in her chair impatiently. "I suppose prices go up for Army officers just as they do for everyone else, and when the old thing asked me – "

"How much is left?"

"Eight hundred. Oh, gosh, Mark, I'm sorry!"

Mr Franklin made a quick calculation; at that rate Arthur had been spending something over twelve hundred pounds a year from his sister's fund, which was about double what had been calculated. However, it would be unthinkable to inquire into it, and he was not much interested anyway.

"That's what it was for," he said. "How much does he need for his business venture?"

Peggy took a breath and looked him in the eye. "Do you mind if I put it another way? If I ask you a question?"

"Of course not. Go right ahead."

"You remember when this thing of Arthur's regiment first came up, years ago? We had all the argument about how he couldn't take your money, and that sort of thing . . . and we worked it out, about the Fund? You said then . . ." she hesitated. "Well, you said, if ever I wanted anything – that I just had to ask?" She suddenly shaded her eyes with her hand, staring at the table. "Oh, God, this sounds horrible – as though I'm putting a pistol to your head . . ."

"Oh, stop it!" Mr Franklin was laughing as he got up and moved quickly round the table to her. He put an arm round her shoulders, drawing her to him, kissing her cheek, and she nestled her head on his shoulder. "Come on – how much does this spendthrift ruffian want?"

"No!" said Peggy, lifting her head. "That's what I mean! It isn't what the big blister wants – I don't want you to think about that!" She was almost defiant, if moist-eyed. "It's I who am asking – not him. At least, that's the way I want it to be."

"All right, then," said Mr Franklin, and kissed her gently. "How much do you want? Not that it matters – so long as we've got it."

"It's rather a lot."

"Dammit, girl, I'm not a banker!" He was kneeling beside her chair now, and taking advantage of the situation by slipping his hand inside her gown and on to her bare breast, squeezing gently and stroking the nipple: Peggy gasped and opened her mouth quickly.

"Oh, don't, you rotter! That's not fair! Oh, no!" She squirmed in his grasp. "No, look, Mark, it's serious! It really is a lot. It's . . . well, it's ten thousand."

If it was far more than he had expected, he did not betray the fact by the slightest relaxation of his hand on her breast. He simply said: "Uh-huh" casually, as he slipped his free arm under her knees and lifted her bodily out of the chair. She was looking up at him apprehensively, so he kissed her long and lingeringly, and during the kiss and what inevitably followed on the morning-room sofa he was thinking confused thoughts about persuading her not to go to Switzerland, and revolting at the idea of making any such condition, and at the same time wondering if perhaps it might not occur to her without prompting. It wasn't fair to try to use the occasion to bring her back towards him; indeed, anything like that could be fatal – it was something best not even thought about, which was quite convenient, because Peggy with her arms round his neck, and her wonderful body naked in his embrace, was hardly an aid to rational consideration.

And afterwards he was careful not to exert the least pressure on her, although it trembled on the tip of his tongue once or twice – he realized how badly he wanted to have her to himself, living quietly, spending their time gently at Castle Lancing and Oxton, being together . . . but that was something that would have to come from her, of her own free will. And he realized, sadly, as they talked afterwards on the sofa, that the time was not yet. They murmured their endearments, and imperceptibly the endearments blended back into the discussion that had begun it all, and Peggy asked him very seriously if he was sure he didn't mind, and he protested that of course he didn't, and she sighed contentedly and stroked his face and kissed him, and when she murmured lazily that she could hardly be bothered to get dressed for her journey, his heart leaped for a moment, only to resume its normal pace when she added that she supposed she had better, because her maid still had oceans of packing to do, and they mustn't miss the afternoon train.

When she had gone upstairs, he went to his study and the desk in the window looking out on Wilton Crescent, and wrote a cheque for ten thousand pounds to Peggy. It was as he was appending his signature that an ugly, unworthy thought crossed his mind – how long was it since she had come down to breakfast in her negligée? He couldn't remember; she had often done so in the first year of their marriage, but over the last couple of years at least she had normally come down fully dressed and ready to go out as soon as breakfast was over. Of course, they had been up late last night, and there was nothing to take her out today before her train left – no reason why she shouldn't laze down informally ... but it was unusual. Or perhaps he just imagined that it was – what was he thinking, anyway? That she'd come down to seduce ten thousand pounds out of him? Ridiculous – and rotten even to let it cross his mind. He'd been the one who'd started the nonsense ... but that had followed on her confused, embarrassed attitude – if she had remained coolly practical it would never have occurred to him to lay a finger on her. In which case, would he have responded so readily to her request for what was one hell of a parcel of jack? Yes, he would. But, she wasn't stupid; she knew as well as any woman that a man making love is the softest touch in the world, and there was no harm in sweetening the process for him. Anyway, what was wrong with that, if she had – what would have been wrong with his using the occasion to try to win her back a little? But he had hesitated to do that – it would have been pretty mercenary in him, he felt. And he wouldn't have been comfortable if, for example, he had asked her to come down to Castle Lancing with him instead of Switzerland, and she had agreed; he would have felt that he had bought her agreement. The hell with it, anyway; he was wasting his time thinking a lot of inconsequential nonsense.

There was another aspect of the matter, which had occurred to him at the start. Ten thousand pounds was a great deal of money to entrust to Arthur, who had already gone through almost half that sum in social expenses. But as it was, it was officially being entrusted to Peggy – he knew what she was going to do with it, but that was her affair. What else could he have done, anyway? He couldn't have refused her. He knew how much Arthur meant to her – come to that, Mr Franklin liked the big idiot himself, and he wasn't such an idiot, either. He had brains, and charm, and boundless enthusiasm; the odds were that he'd make a go of whatever business he set his hand to – whatever it was. Yes ... Mr Franklin knew that by every law of common sense he ought to satisfy himself in detail about the sound-ness of Arthur's plans before he parted with a penny – but no, that was Peggy's business. He had promised *her* the ten thousand, and he must trust to her judgment; she had a good head on her shoulders.

However, while he might not hesitate to pass the cheque over to Peggy, it was still not something to be done without consulting the little bank-book in his desk, and seeing how he stood. The deposit account had been heavily drained by the Oxton outgoings, and there had been his investment – almost the bulk of his fortune – in brewery shares a couple of years ago. He didn't want to touch that, and with the new stables and paddock that they were to start that summer, it would be inadvisable to reduce the deposit account any further at present. He consulted his book: yes, it would be best to tap that cash reserve which had lain untouched for more than four years in Mr Evans's safe deposit . . . not by much, but just enough to cover his immediate outgoing; the interest on his shares would take care of their normal running expenses, which were not small. However, when he juggled all the pieces in his mind, the ship was cruising along, with no surplus, admittedly, but with no reefs ahead either.

He stared out of the window, his eyes seeing but not registering the governess walking on the opposite pavement, holding a little girl by the hand while ahead of them a small boy in a sailor suit was bowling his hoop. A nursemaid was pushing a perambulator in the opposite direction. It was dull, but dry, and a trifle foggy – not unlike the day he had first set foot in England. And since then he had become a landed gentleman, had married a beautiful lady and become curiously lonely, had sunk his money into a business venture which occupied his interest if not his enthusiasm, and – although it was a crude way of putting it, but there it was at the back of his mind – enabled a fine old English family to live in the style to which they presumably ought to be accustomed. In return, he had position, comfort, marriage, and a way of life which most men would have thought enviable – and which, if only he could draw Peggy closer to him, he would have thought close to perfection himself. As it was, it wasn't at all bad; it beat the hell out of grubbing in the mud at Tonopah, or riding herd on cold, dry nights on refractory cattle, or hiding out at Hole-in-the-Wall. He couldn't think of any better way he could have invested his pile, in the States, or in Europe, or anywhere else. No, he had done the thing that he had really wanted to do, although he had not been able to define it exactly – but it had something to do with going back to Castle Lancing, to his people's place, and putting his stake in the ground, and calling it his, and knowing it was there. It was a strange, atavistic thing which went far beyond the mere possession of Lancing Manor; it was belonging, and being one with something that surrounded him when he walked in the Lancing woods, or the meadows towards Thetford, or the old churchyard with its long-bow yews, or the cool musty dimness of the Apple Tree, or the chestnuts outside his window.

311

The door opened suddenly, and Peggy came in, dressed for the road in a smart velvet brocade trimmed at the sleeves and collar with white fur; there was a fur piping round the close-fitting hat, and she carried a muff in one hand.

"All ready for the snow," smiled Mr Franklin, rising. "But aren't you staying for lunch? I thought the train wasn't leaving until two."

"Didn't I tell you? I'm lunching with Maud Llewellyn, and we're catching the train together. Oh, what a rush! I'm late as it is – all your fault of course." She smiled at him and winked mischievously. "Now, I'll have to fly!" She put up her face to be kissed, and patted his cheek gently. "Now – you'll be good, and take care, and let me know how everything is at Oxton – oh, and give my love to Daddy!" She was sweeping towards the door, when he said:

"Here, hold on! You'd better drop this into the bank on your way." He held out the pink slip worth ten thousand pounds, and Peggy's eyes widened as she took it.

"Gosh!" She examined it reverently. "I say, it's an awful lot of money, isn't it?"

"A sizeable amount," said Mr Franklin, "so don't lose it. And for any sake, don't take it to Switzerland with you, or it's sure to go astray. Here – maybe you'd better let me keep it, until you've seen Arthur and found out exactly – "

"Don't worry – it goes into the bank this very minute!" Peggy tucked the slip into her bag, and came back towards him. Her eyes softened, and she put her hands on his shoulders. "You're really a darling, Mark – didn't I ever tell you?" Her lips opened on his for a moment, and then she was away, leaving him with a breath of perfume in his nostrils, and the feel of her soft waist in his hands.

He followed her into the hall, where the last of her cases was going out to the car. "As for me taking care – how about you?" he called after her. "Stay away from avalanches and precipices and French confidence artists!" Then she was gone, with a wave and a blown kiss, and the door closed, and he was wondering what he would do that afternoon, and evening, and in the days that would follow.

17

He had not intended going down to Castle Lancing until later in the week, but with Peggy gone the house seemed unusually empty, and he knew that another couple of days would bore him exceedingly. He had an early dinner and thought of going to the theatre, but there was nothing that attracted his fancy – there were the usual revues, but they were sure to be filled with topical gaiety and smartness, and after a couple of weeks in London, exposed occasionally to the noise of Peggy's friends, he felt he had had all the metropolitan sophistication he could take. *Parsifal*, now being performed outside Germany for the first time, in defiance of its late composer's wishes, was drawing the highbrow audiences and exciting the critics by the spectacular melancholy of its sets, but the mere thought of three hours' Teutonic bawling without benefit of plot filled him with horror. He had already seen *Great Catherine* at the Vaudeville, and while not certain that he entirely understood what Mr Shaw was talking about, had been amused by the dialogue and intrigued by the sight of an eighteenth-century English officer carrying pistols in his boots – that single touch had raised Shaw considerably in Mr Franklin's estimation.

He went early to bed, and on the following morning he and Samson caught the train down to Norfolk, arriving at Castle Lancing in mid-afternoon. It was snowing lightly, and by the time they had collected provisions from Mrs Laker, lighted fires in the main rooms at the Manor, and had an al fresco supper, Mr Franklin found his spirits reviving. He felt he was back at home, and took pleasure in walking round the house, looking into the rooms, seeing that all was as he had left it, taking comfort in the familiarity of it all. And as he always did, he paused on the stairs and let his eyes dwell on the patch in the plaster at the far end of the landing, barely noticeable now after several coats of distemper, where the jagged holes left by Curry's shots had been repaired four years ago – Samson had spent a fortnight in painstaking labour, digging the battered slugs out of the wall, and out of the scarred floor planks and panelling and door jamb, and then patching and planning, plugging and plastering, varnishing and polishing, with a patience and skill that would have done credit to an articled tradesman. Now, standing on the landing, Mr Franklin could run his fingers over the door jamb and wonder where the bullet-hole had been; when he glanced down into the hall he could not be certain of the exact spot where Curry's body had bled, and they had scraped and scrubbed so laboriously; the new stair carpet which had replaced the old stained one was now itself showing signs of wear. No physical trace remained of that distant desperate battle; if its memory lingered, at least it carried no shadows of regret or guilt or fear; it was just another incident, past and done with, and by the time he had returned to the study it had vanished from his mind.

During the evening he took a turn up to the Apple Tree and stood drink for Jake and the locals; he knew all their faces now, and Christian names, and how old their children were, and who had won the prize for the best marrow at the last Oxton agricultural show, and who was getting married; he was au fait with local politics and gossip, and could take an informed interest in the news that Thetford was going to pay its mayor the princely sum of £20 per annum to defray official expenses, or that Gower Estate had purchased new land over at East Harling. Some of the Apple Tree's customers were now his own employees, for the development at Oxton had meant new jobs, and a number of labourers at Castle Lancing had been ready to leave their billets to work for their Yankee squire – it no longer seemed strange to him to be addressed by that old world title; indeed, it would have surprised him to be called anything else.

He was at last part of Castle Lancing, and well content to be so. It had been a gradual acceptance, he now realized, although there had been a moment, just over a year ago, when the seal had been set on it. Old Bessie Reeve had died, full of years, and with the rest of the village, and some of her late husband's kinsfolk from other hamlets, he had attended her funeral in the Castle Lancing churchyard. At his request the vicar had allowed her to be buried near the headstones of which Johannes Franklinus's was one. Old Jake, in his capacity of sexton's assistant, had dug the actual grave, and found old bones as well as rusted clamps and unidentifiable scraps of rubbish – but as Thornhill said, the bones might have been anyone's. On a gusty November day they had placed the coffin of Elizabeth Franklin, later Reeve, in the earth beside her kinsfolk, and the vicar conducted the service and called the deceased Reeves by mistake, and dropped

314

his spectacles and lost the place with high-pitched apologies, while Thornhill muttered "Old fool! He'll be christening her in a minute!" at Mr Franklin's elbow.

And afterwards the odd thing had happened. As he was turning away from the grave into which Jake was starting to shovel the warm brown earth, Mr Franklin found himself confronted by Jack Prior, who had shaken his hand and muttered condolences, and after him everyone had come up and done the same thing, the women nodding and sniffing and the men looking askance and shaking his hand briefly. It had dawned on him then: they were condoling with him as Bessie Reeve's only living blood-relative, as a Franklin of Castle Lancing, as the head of the family to which she belonged. It had shaken him, and he had had to walk away alone afterwards, to stand among the yews and look out across the rainy fields, not trusting himself to speak, while Thornhill had watched him curiously from a distance, and old Jake had gasped and muttered as he plied his shovel and finally stamped down the turf. But from that moment Mr Franklin had realized that, whatever he had felt before about his homecoming, Castle Lancing had now recognized it, too.

It was strange, he thought as he walked back from the Apple Tree, that now, more than a year after Bessie's death, he was the one link left in Castle Lancing to those Franklins of the past. And it was possible that when Peggy settled down – he sighed and corrected the "when" to an "if", to be on the safe side – there would be other Franklins in the countryside, and all because he had come home after two and three quarter centuries.

Strangely enough, it was a topic which came up on the following day, when he drove over to Oxton to see Sir Charles, and view the progress of the Oxton stud. They watched the horses being exercised in the paddock, there was a new foal since his last visit, to be admired, a piece of field-drainage work to be examined, and time spent over the blueprints of the new stable buildings and grooms" accommodation which, when completed in the following year, would make Oxton the most up-to-date establishment of its kind in that part of the country. It was as they were walking back to the Hall for lunch that Sir Charles suddenly said:

"It's a great work; a very big business altogether. I like to think that it's going to be a splendid going concern for your descendants – our descendants – long after we're gone. I think it's an enterprise they'll have cause to be very proud of, Mark."

Mr Franklin murmured some commonplace of agreement, and found the keen, thin face turned towards him with what seemed to be a look of inquiry. Then he realized that what he had said was: "Oh, we'll see, I guess," and that Sir Charles had caught the note of resignation in his voice.

They walked on a few steps, and then the baronet said drily:

"Do I detect no great enthusiasm – should I say optimism? – at the thought of children and grandchildren? It's probably no business of mine . . . on second thoughts, it's very much business of mine, and we know each other well enough by now . . . am I right in thinking that Peggy has shown no inclination for a family?"

It was the first time he had ever mentioned the subject openly, and Mr Franklin considered how to answer. "We haven't discussed it a great deal."

"But I take it you'd like a family?"

Again Mr Franklin hesitated. "Yes. When the time comes, there's nothing I'd like better."

"Which means when Peggy wishes it," said Sir Charles. "And unless I mistake your tone, you have some doubts if she ever will. She has a tendency to follow her own course – always has." He mused for a moment. "And she's still young, and taken up with that smart set of hers. But she'll grow out of it, you know, in a year or two. And once you have a son and heir – or a daughter – you'll be astonished at the change it brings. I confess I'm an extremely interested party." He smiled and shook his head. "If I have an ambition left in life it's to lead a grandson's first pony along that bridle path yonder. That's where I was led, and my father in his time. Didn't know you had a sentimental father-in-law, did you? Seriously, though, Mark – I think I can guess some of the worries you've had where Peggy is concerned. But they'll pass, if you have patience – and I rather think patience is your long suit."

Over lunch Sir Charles continued to talk of his daughter, and reassuringly of the future, with particular reference to the heritage of Oxton Hall.

"These last few years I've reposed my hopes in Peggy and you – and your children – more than in Arthur. If he'd fallen heir to the place – well, it would have gone, and that would have been that. The days are past when a soldier can keep up a place like this, and Arthur'll be a soldier and nothing else, as long as he draws breath."

At this, Mr Franklin drew breath himself, rather sharply, while Sir Charles continued:

"But that's all right as long as you and Peggy are here. You'll make this place go as Arthur never could." He smiled whimsically. "I can content myself with the thought that he can devote himself to becoming a mutton-headed general."

Mr Franklin was not taking him in, however. He was reflecting that something, somewhere, was badly wrong, and for an instant he nearly blurted out the question which would either have led to a disturbing revelation, or to the elucidation of some astonishing misunderstanding, and until he had decided which was more likely it seemed best to go slowly.

"You think Arthur will stay in the Army?" he asked casually.

"I'd be surprised if he didn't," said Sir Charles, and poured Madeira into Mr Franklin's glass. "He's had an excellent start – thanks largely to you. I've never mentioned it to you, and you've never said anything to me – there really isn't anything to say, I suppose. But just because we have observed a ponderous delicacy on both sides is no reason why we should go on doing so for the rest of our lives. I know all about Peggy's ridiculous fund, as she calls it, and while one can subscribe to the fiction that it is she who has supported her brother – and so save ourselves the embarrassment of expressions of gratitude which would have been as painful to you as to me – well, talking as we have done today, on a more candid basis than hitherto, I can say it at last. You've done for me and mine something which I'd never have allowed any other man to do – couldn't ever have conceived of any other man doing. It's something that can't be repaid, so there's no point in discussing it further. But you know what I feel." Having delivered himself, Sir Charles sipped his Madeira critically and added: "No – I expect Arthur to do well in the Army. When the war comes – and it will, sometime in the next five years – he'll be able to show what he's made of. That will be his repayment – and his opportunity. I rose as high as colonel of a regiment, but I'll be surprised if he doesn't do better than that. He'll make a fighting soldier, and in war they leapfrog over the others."

This had given Mr Franklin time to phrase his next tentative inquiry. "You don't think there's any likelihood of his resigning then? – Peggy was saying the other day that you'd mentioned in a letter that Arthur had been thinking about it."

Sir Charles shook his head emphatically. "No. That's true enough,

317

that he did talk of it – but it's pure politics. Between ourselves, I have it from friends in the War Office that there's going to be a storm in the military teacup in Ireland. You know Carson and the Ulstermen are getting ready to fight against Home Rule, and since Home Rule is government policy, it follows that government are going to have to do something about them. If Carson won't see reason – and reason is about the last thing you can look for in a Scotch-Irish Protestant, although frankly I'm all for him in this instance – then the Army will have to make him. In other words, British troops will have to disarm the Ulster Volunteers."

"That's what Peggy said was in your letter – something like that, anyway."

"Quite so. But the Army won't do it, you see. It's officered by Protestants, mainly, who are dead against Ulster being coerced into Home Rule. They sympathize with Carson, and they'll tell the government politely to go to the devil before they'll take up arms against the Loyalists. Mutiny, in fact – "

"But no British government would be that crazy – "

"Right you are," said Sir Charles. "They'll stick a toe in the water first. Very shortly, officers serving in Ireland will be asked if they are prepared to serve in Ulster – for reasons to be specified later. They'll say 'no', to a man – that's certain. And then . . . they'll have to resign their commissions."

"So Arthur could be leaving the Army?" said Mr Franklin with an inward hope. Sir Charles smiled and shook his head.

"It might appear so – but no, he won't. You see what will happen when he and the others send in their papers, will be an almighty row – consternation in Whitehall, cries of 'Mutiny', leaders in *The Times*, questions in the House, all the usual rubbish – and then placatory sounds will emerge from Whitehall, there will be talk of a misunder-standing, perhaps even a hint of apology that such a question was put to honourable men – and the resignations will be withdrawn. So if Arthur resigns, it'll be for a few days at most."

"And just what," asked Mr Franklin, "will the government have gained by that? It sounds a damned dangerous game, for no good reason."

"There's an excellent reason. The Irish Nationalists will have been given public warning that the Army won't oppose Carson. If there's to be fighting to set up an independent Ireland, the Army won't do it for them. That will cause 'em to think – possibly moderate their

318

present attitude, give a better chance of a peaceful negotiated settlement. That's what Asquith is counting on, I imagine – a convincing demonstration to put the fear of death into the Irish extremists. I don't doubt he'll get it."

"Do the officers know about this – charade?"

"Certainly not. They'll resign without anyone telling 'em – that's predictable. And withdraw their resignations when the proper diplomatic apologies are made. No, the majority will be acting in perfect good faith." Sir Charles smiled. "But I daresay the more intelligent – among whom I count Arthur – will know exactly what's going on. He knows what's in the wind – so he talks loudly of resignation, even to me. But he knows it's just window-dressing, to show his superiors his heart's in the right place. No, you can count on one thing – Arthur will still be in the Army this time next year."

This was serious news to Mr Franklin, with his depleted cheque book in his pocket. Of course, Sir Charles might be wrong – Arthur might be serious about resigning. On the other hand, Sir Charles presumably knew his own son. In which case Arthur was either imposing on his sister, or Peggy was imposing . . . no, that was unthinkable. He spoke casually.

"Well, that's good news. From what Peggy said I thought Arthur was practically a civilian – in fact, I gathered he'd already made some plans for going into business – "

"Who, Arthur?" Sir Charles laughed outright. "Oh, that's coming it a bit strong, even for him! If he told Peggy that, he's indulging in some brotherly leg-pulling! Business! I'd hate to invest in any commercial venture of his!"

You and me both, Sir Charles, thought Mr Franklin grimly. Should he tell his father-in-law about the cheque? No – there must be an explanation, the obvious one being that Arthur *was* going to leave the Army. He couldn't swindle his sister out of ten thousand pounds – or Mr Franklin, and hope to get away with it. Equally impossible that Peggy had solicited the money in anything but perfect good faith. No, it must be genuine, and Sir Charles was being too clever by half in imputing Machiavellian motives to his son. Arthur would certainly be resigning – he might, indeed, be genuinely quitting so that there could be no possibility of his ever having to bear arms against his conscience. That made sense – but there was no point in sharing his conclusions with Sir Charles.

In the meantime, was there anything to be done? Should he write to Arthur, and find out exactly what was going on? No – he had given the money to Peggy, it was for her to handle any discussion there might be about it with her brother. He ought to get in touch with Peggy, then – should he go to Switzerland and see her? For a moment he was tempted, for more reasons than one – but he quickly put the thought aside. It must look as though he was tearing overseas out of alarm for his ten thousand pounds, and he wasn't going to have Peggy thinking that. He might mention it in a letter – but it wasn't the sort of thing that could easily be explained in writing. The best thing was to wait until she got back in three weeks' time, and discuss it then – if there was anything to discuss. For the more he thought about it the clearer it seemed that Arthur was going to resign, and that Sir Charles had been at fault in not taking him seriously.

On that thought he succeeded, if not in putting the matter from his mind (it is difficult to dismiss any problem with a ten thousand pound price tag attached to it), at least in subduing it for the time being. It was a casual train of coincidence and reminiscence, later that evening, that was to distract him entirely on to another subject, and that one to which he had barely given a thought in years.

He stayed to dine at Oxton, in company with a few of Sir Charles's neighbours who were now among Mr Franklin's closest acquaintances as well – Sir Peter ("Colonel Dammit") Stringer, Major Aldridge, and Mr Plowright, a retired Indian civil servant. It was, as always, a companionable occasion, with talk of farming and politics, and inevitably, since it was the depth of winter, of cricket – and for the hundredth time Mr Franklin gave up trying to understand the difference between a green wicket and a plumb wicket and a turning wicket and a sticky wicket and a fiery wicket, arcane matters which he knew had to be thrashed out before they actually got round to discussing the game itself. But they obviously knew what they were talking about, and as he watched them lazily through the haze of cigar smoke – Stringer puce and emphatic, Aldridge amiably reminiscent, Sir Charles precise and knowledgeable, Plowright aglow with enthusiasm – he reflected on the fascination there was in listening to experts on their chosen subject; even if one felt the sense of being an outside observer who understood only about half of what they were saying, there was something reassuring about listening to familiar voices, being admitted and accepted in their private world . . .

Starshine on the hill beneath them as they sat or crouched in the brush, looking down at the distant lights of the town, listening to the faint drift of music from the Number Ten saloon; the tiny, dimly-seen figures moving on the main street between the brightly-lit buildings, the occasional raucous voice of a reveller raised in drunken song. The five of them huddled in their coats against the night cold – Cassidy, Longbaugh, Carter, Kid Curry, and himself, waiting, whispering in the bitter dark.

"Dear old Deadwood. Sure has changed, though, hasn't it, Harry? How often we been in that old bank of theirs? Hell, you'd think they'd know by now to leave the door wide open. Wouldn't you, Harry?"

"Yeah. Remember how it used to be in the old days, Butch? Pinkerton men cat-footing around with their shotguns, peeking at all the little old ladies, in case it was you and me in poke bonnets?"

"Sure, Harry. They say there's a new Pinkerton man come out of Denver a couple of months ago. Name of Siringo. Comes from Texas, wears two guns, tied down, butts forward. Tod Carver reckons he's just about the fastest man around, this Siringo. You hear of him, Kid?"

"I heard of him. And I know how much I value Tod Carver's opinion – he reckons anything with a Texas accent and two guns is a mixture of Curly Bill and Wyatt Earp. I'll take care of Mister Goddam Siringo."

"You'll take care of him when he tries to take care of us. Not before. We don't go looking for trouble."

"What do we go looking for, Cassidy? What say we go down and look at that goddamn bank, huh? And never mind chewing the rag about some dandy Pinkerton gunslick while our asses freeze off with sitting here all night! What d'you say, Sundance?"

"I say always look out for anybody that wears his gun-butts turned forward. That's the old-timers' way, so they could spin their pieces out on one finger, real quick. Hickok used to do that, so they say. I guess this fellow Siringo must be real good." A pause. "They say he packs a derringer in his hat, too."

"He can pack his goddam pecker in his hat for all I care. Pinkerton men! We seen 'em before, haven't we? What's so great about this one? You tell me that, Butch."

"This one's smart, Kid. He uses his brains, and he ain't just a gun-slinger; he's a detective, a real one. They say McParland picked him special, to track us down and find out all about our plans, figure out just exactly what we'd do next, keep his ear on the ground."

"Oh, that's just bully! And what are our plans, Butch? To sit up here belly-aching until that goddam bank falls down with old age?"

"Take your time, Kid. I want someone to go down and look that bank over before we move in. Where's the new chum, Charley Carter? You there, Charley? Now I want you to slide down there, Charley, and take a good look, understand? Take a real good look – we've got all night. You take in that bank real close – then come on back. Off you go now, Charley; easy does it."

The stealthy scuffling as Carter stole down the slope in the starlight, his shadow dwindling into those other shadows beneath them; the silence as they waited, Cassidy watchful, Longbaugh whistling softly through his teeth, Curry squirming with impatience.

"For Chrissakes, Butch, why send him down? We know where the goddam bank is! Hell's bells, we ought to!"

"Sure, Kid. You know, I reckon it's true what Sundance says about wearing the butts forward – gives this tricky quick draw, or you can grab 'em by reaching across your body. They say old English Ben Thompson used to do that. I tried it myself a few times, but I kept dropping the goddam gun. That Siringo must be a likely enough fellow; I'd rather not tangle with him."

"Ah, ——Siringo! Who the hell cares about him! Just let him come within shot of me, that's all! Just let him!"

"You reckon, Kid? Say, now, why don't you just go on up the hill, see the horses are O.K.? We'll follow after; I reckon it's time we were riding out."

"Riding out? You gone crazy? What are you talking about – riding out? What about the goddam bank?"

"Oh, we're going to find us a bank, Kid, but not the one in Deadwood. There's a real pretty bank over in Winnemucca, Nevada. I thought we might try that."

"Nevada? What the hell's the matter with you, Cassidy? Haven't we been planning this Deadwood job for weeks, every ——ing last detail, and the ——ing thing's sitting there, down the hill, waiting to be busted? You hear this crazy bastard, Mark? What the hell d'you mean by it, Cassidy?"

"I mean we're going to Winnemucca. Take that bank instead. The hell with Deadwood. I'm tired just looking at it."

"Why, you loco son-of-a-bitch! What did we ride all this way from Powder Springs for? Hey, Butch, come back here! Listen – what about Charley Carter down there? We gotta wait for him."

"Oh, never mind him, Kid. You ready, Mark? Sundance? Come on, let's high-tail it out of here!"

"Goddamn you, Cassidy! Wherever we're going, how the hell is Carter gonna catch us up, if he don't know where we're headed?"

322

"I don't want him catching us up. Not never."

"Why the hell not? You are *goddamn crazy! He's a good man!"*

"Bet your life he is. But it just happens his name ain't Carter. It's Siringo. Now will you get up that goddam hill, Kid?"

". . . but the genius of Hirst is that every ball looks the same – wrist action, delivery, flight, absolutely identical. Only they're not – nine or ten, perhaps, and then the eleventh comes through that fraction faster, or pitches that inch shorter – and you're gone. Medium-pace bowling raised to the realm of fine art. Mark, I don't believe you understand a word we're saying!"

Laughter round the table brought him back from the starlit slope, from the chill Dakota dark to the warm dining-room, from the shadowy figures hurrying and blaspheming through the brush to the flushed smiling faces of his friends. He smiled and made his apologies, and Colonel Dammit clapped his shoulder as they rose from the table.

"We should apologize – talking religion with no thought for the stranger within our gates. But you won't be properly acclimatized, you know, till you know what a yorker is. Why not let me take you to the Gentlemen and Players match this summer – start your education properly?"

"It's a deal," said Mr Franklin, "if you'll come with me to watch the White Sox play the Giants. It's time you assimilated some colonial culture, too, you know." But the choleric sportsman refused to believe there were any such teams.

And afterwards, when the others had gone, and Mr Franklin and Sir Charles were sharing a last nightcap before the fire, the American remarked idly on the train of thought that had been in his mind after dinner. "They're good men, those. I was thinking, through there – comparing them with a bunch of fellows I used to know out West. Very different – and yet very like, too, in some ways. Good friends to have, I guess; good neighbours."

"They don't come much better," said Sir Charles comfortably. "I must say, it's pleased me to see how you've settled in among them, Mark; quite a compliment – to you and to them. Yes, they're good neighbours." He stared into the fire and added casually: "Which reminds me – ever see Lacy these days?"

Mr Franklin was mildly startled. "Frank Lacy? No – at least, never to talk to. If we happen to catch sight of each other in Thetford High Street we keep right on going. Why?"

Sir Charles was silent for a moment. "It's a pity," he said at last. "Oh, not that I blame you. He behaved quite scandalously over that tenant of yours . . . Mrs Reeve, wasn't it? Nasty business, that." He pondered. "Still, it's a while ago now. I was just thinking, at dinner – you get on so well with everyone hereabout; they accept you absolutely as one of themselves . . . it seems a pity you and Lacy are still at odds. Well, it's better to have friends than enemies next door, isn't it?"

"Lacy's friendship," said Mr Franklin, "would be no great bargain from where I'm sitting."

"He's not the most likeable of creatures," Sir Charles admitted, "or the neighbour one would choose. Still, there he is, and you're going to have to live with him for many years, I hope. It might be no bad thing . . . if you buried the hatchet."

"In my skull, if he had his way." Mr Franklin glanced curiously at the baronet. "Sounds as though you've changed your mind about him."

"Not at all. I showed him the door four years ago, and in the same circumstances I'd show it him again. But – I tell myself that it's water under the bridge, and my reason for keeping him at arm's length disappeared when you married Peggy – "

"He did his best to queer that, too," said Mr Franklin, recalling his eavesdropping in the passage that Christmas Day.

"– but I'm really thinking of your own interests, Mark. After all, like him or not, Lacy's a big man in the county. To put it at its lowest, it might do our business here no harm – some day – to be on good relations . . . you know what I mean?"

"It's a beautiful thought," said Mr Franklin without enthusiasm. "But somehow I don't see him ever forgetting the shellacking I gave him that night the King was here – or my crossing him over Lye Cottage."

"That's exactly what I meant," said Sir Charles. "Lye Cottage. Why not sell it to him, Mark?"

Mr Franklin had been lounging back comfortably; his head came up sharply.

"How's that?"

"Sell him the cottage. Is there any reason why you shouldn't – now? The old woman's dead, and the place has been standing empty. You don't need it – do you? It would be a splendid gesture."

"Has he asked you about this?"

324

"Not directly, no. But Blake has dropped hints about it; apparently they have a scheme to build model farm cottages down the Lye side, for estate workers – an admirable thing, by the sound of it, and would certainly benefit the village. And say this for Lacy, he's done wonders in farming development, and seems to be heart-set on this scheme. But even that's probably not his main reason."

"What is it, then?"

"Pride, Mark. It's something you've denied him. He's locked horns with you – and lost. If you've a nature like his – "

"Being a spoiled, arrogant pup, you mean?"

"No doubt. But if you're Lacy, a thing like Lye Cottage can become an obsession – especially when the man who's got it is the man who knocked you down and stole your girl – which is how he regards you. But . . . well, I know Frank, warts and all; he's an odd bird. A few coals of fire might well alter his whole attitude to you – and much more important, you'd have done the decent thing, and everyone would know it, and think the better of you. And that matters – in the county, among the sort of men who were here tonight. You gain credit by it – face."

There was a silence while Mr Franklin contemplated the ceiling. Then he smiled at Sir Charles, shaking his head.

"You're a persuasive advocate, father-in-law. But the fact is – and we both know it – that Lacy's the kind of skunk who doesn't deserve favours, so why should I go out of my way to do him one?"

"Not for his sake, I agree absolutely. But I was thinking of your own, really. Your own eventual peace of mind, perhaps. Your children, possibly – his, if he has any. It isn't good to carry a feud."

"You'd be surprised how lightly I've carried this one," said Mr Franklin. He mused for a moment. "I don't know. It goes against the grain . . . But you really think I ought to sell?"

"Yes. I've no doubt of it."

"Well," said Mr Franklin. "I'll tell you what I'll do. I don't want Lye Cottage, personally, and while I haven't got five cents' worth of use for Lacy, I don't mind all that much if he gets it. But I *do* mind about Castle Lancing. His model cottages sound fine, and if his plans will help the village then I'm for them, every time. But I want to satisfy myself on that score, first. If they look good . . ." he shrugged and gave his father-in-law a resigned smile ". . . then fine. He can have Lye Cottage. Is that fair?"

Sir Charles, knowing his man, was well satisfied; if he had known precisely what was in Mr Franklin's mind he might have been less so. For the American was sincere in his determination that the general good of Castle Lancing should be decisive, and it was in his mind that the best way of testing that would be to canvass opinion in the village itself – a notion which would have struck Sir Charles as setting a dangerously communistic precedent. In the event, Mr Franklin did not make general soundings; a casual mention of the possible sale, to old Jake and Jack Prior over a pint in the Apple Tree, was enough to convince him that the exercise would be neither rewarding nor, by local standards, even fitting. Jake contemplated his beer with the air of Asquith pondering the Home Rule bill, and observed that that there Lye Cottage thing was a thing, right enough; yeah, it was a thing, all right. Prior simply nodded and said nothing.

Slightly puzzled, and vaguely irritated, Mr Franklin loafed up to Thornhill's place to seek advice; here at least it was uncompromising.

"I wouldn't give that swine Lacy the time of day," said the don. "The brute's a total outsider – the type who gave the Middle Ages a bad name. Can't you just see him roasting witches and hanging peasants and ravishing milkmaids? Have some beer. However, I wouldn't let that stop me from selling him something he wanted – and seeing he paid through the nose for it. Trouble with you is you're an altruist, which is a rare bird in this country. Last one was Sir Thomas More – although I'm by no means sure he wasn't an ecstatic old hypocrite underneath. That by the way . . . no, I can't see it would do anything but good to have model dwellings down that side of the village; old world charm's all very well, but it doesn't hold a candle to decent drainage."

"The villagers didn't seem to mind much," said Mr Franklin, and recounted his experience at the Apple Tree. Thornhill stared at him.

"By George, I always knew you were eccentric. What did you expect 'em to say? 'Well, now, we'll have to think about that – can't have you disposing of your personal property just as you see fit.' What did you think it had to do with them?"

"Well, it's their village – "

"Is it? I understood that it was owned by the Dean and Chapter, and Lord Lacy, and Franklin, and Thornhill – they're the chaps with title deeds. Everyone else just rents. Of course they weren't going to offer an opinion on a private transaction between you and Lacy. I daresay it looks different to American eyes – your history has given you this sense of common good based on democratic decision. Absolutely

326

necessary for survival on a dangerous frontier. But the communal sense here, while just as strong, is rather different; it's based on individual – and I mean individual – right within the law, and minding one's own business. A man's private acts – so long as they're legal – are simply nobody else's concern. He can offend the community as much as he likes, provided he stays within the law. Mind you," added Thornhill, "someone will pretty soon get a law passed, prohibiting him, but that's beside the point. It's all a question of privacy, really. More beer?"

"They surprised me," admitted Mr Franklin. "I thought they'd be interested."

"Oh, they're interested, all right. But that doesn't mean they feel qualified to judge your affairs, any more than they'd think you qualified to judge theirs. Try telling Jake how to dig a grave sometime. Mind you, he might be prepared to consider what *you* said – but he wouldn't pay the slightest heed to me."

"How d'you mean?"

"My dear chap, you're the squire! Don't you see? Dear me, no wonder they stood in stony silence at the pub." Thornhill drank his beer meditatively. "Anyway, don't go asking the women at Laker's shop what they think, or we'll have a bloody revolution. They think you're cranky enough as it is."

Mr Franklin decided there were things about England he had still to learn, but at least he was satisfied that if he sold Lye Cottage to Lord Lacy it was unlikely that the villagers of Castle Lancing would burn him in effigy on the village green. So he gave his final agreement to Sir Charles, and a couple of days later Major Blake's smart Lanchester rolled up the drive at Castle Lancing, to decant the agent of Gower Estate, who came bearing the necessary documents and an air of genial satisfaction. Of the painful scene in his office four years earlier not a word was said; the Major was all brisk good nature and business, accepting Mr Franklin's offer of whisky and soda, expressing gratifying professional interest in the *charro* saddle in the hall – very different from the camel saddles of his own days in the Sudan – and commending in flowing terms the progress of the Oxton Hall stud, which he had been shown by Sir Charles.

Mr Franklin returned the compliments by expressing polite interest in Gower Estate's plans for Castle Lancing. There were to be between a dozen and twenty model homes, the Major told him; work would begin in late spring or early summer, and those villagers employed by

327

the estate might expect to be into their new homes by the year end. His lordship, who was abroad at the moment, would be gratified beyond measure when he learned how unexpectedly his hopes had been realized; the Major would be writing to inform him at once. On this cordial note Major Blake handed over a cheque for £200, and took his leave, his motor-horn honking as he rolled down the drive. To Mr Franklin it sounded almost like a note of triumph, and he chided himself for being unduly sensitive.

Shortly thereafter, on the eve of his return to London, he received a letter from Peggy, announcing that she was extending her Swiss holiday for another fortnight. It was a gossipy, affectionate letter, and while he was disappointed that she was not coming home, it cheered him to read her happily malicious witticisms at the expense of her fellow-guests – this, he decided, was the ideal way of keeping in touch with the social scene. She had skied, skated, ski-jored, and gone down the Sanloup bob-sleigh run at Les Avants " – which Arthur, the great show-off, says is just baby stuff, and not to be compared with the Cresta! Brothers are the limit!! The big stiff has gone back now to Ireland. Oh, your old admirer Poppy Davenport has sprained her ankle skiing, and sits on the terrace all day whimpering at me and devouring chocs. Personally I think the skis broke under her weight . . ."

No other word of Arthur or his impending resignation; Mr Franklin had, however, read with close interest an article in *The Times* which seemed delicately to foreshadow the kind of Army crisis which Sir Charles had predicted. He had also telephoned his London banker and learned that the cheque given to Peggy had, as he expected, been cashed. Well, there was nothing to be done except wait until she got home and he could discover exactly what was happening; in the meantime, he decided to return to London as originally planned, in case she cut short her holiday after all.

He caught the train at Thetford next day and had to wait an hour at Cambridge for a connection. While he was pacing the platform, huddled in his greatcoat against the March wind, a news bill caught his eye: "Ireland: new sensation"; he bought a paper and took it into the waiting room to read: the main story was the Prime Minister's announcement of a plan whereby Ireland would be granted Home Rule, but that the northern counties of Ulster would have the right, if they chose, to remain outside an independent Ireland for six years, at the end of which time they would be incorporated into the new self-governing state; what the purpose of this elephantine compromise could be was not clear, since it was obviously unwelcome to both sides. Irish National opinion was hostile, since much could happen in six years; Ulster's feelings were aptly summed up by the picture in the paper of the tight-lipped and jut-jawed Carson, and his reply to the Premier: "We don't want sentence of death with stay of execution for six years." Elsewhere he was quoted as saying: "Give us a clean cut, or come and fight us."

To the paper's leader writer it was apparent that Mr Asquith was shirking the issue in the most cowardly fashion; if he could get his compromise accepted temporarily, it was not to be doubted that within the six years he would find himself out of office and the ticking bomb of Ireland could be hastily passed to his successor. The immediate outlook was desperate, for if Ulster remained intransigent the government would have no choice but to send in the Army to seize key points, stations, ports, and ammunition depots throughout the province. And Ulster would resist.

Mr Franklin read the news soberly; suddenly Sir Charles's optimism about his son's future began to seem pathetically unjustified. Arthur wouldn't fight in Ulster for Asquith's policy – not if what Peggy had said was true about his Loyalist sympathies; if the Army was sent in he would have no option but to resign, and for good. So he would probably need his ten thousand pounds for his civilian business, whatever it might be. And in the meantime Ireland would be going up in smoke.

He climbed into his compartment and discarded the paper for an illustrated magazine. There were photographs of members of the Irish Citizens" Army being addressed by a Sinn Fein orator, and of Ulster Volunteers practising on a firing range "somewhere in County Tyrone". Elsewhere there were pictures of Mexican firing squads executing ragged men in bare feet and sombreros, and of Pancho Villa, whose rebels were alleged to have shot a British subject. The new Roman stripes were expected to be the dominating influence in Spring fashions. Bombardier Billy Wells had knocked out Bandsman Blake in four rounds at the Palladium. Mr Franklin leafed idly over the pages until his eye was caught by a heading: "Winter Sports Supplement" and pictures of skaters and skiers enjoying the season at the Alpine resorts. He saw a name he knew in a caption, and turned the pages with renewed interest – there might be a picture of Peggy. He glanced quickly at the figures in the photographs, men in Alpine hats and knickerbockers, ladies in scarves and ankle-length skirts, balancing precariously on skates, poised, smiling, on skis, or wrapped up in fur rugs in the backs of horse-sleighs. There were the names she had mentioned: Murren, Les Avants, St Moritz, the Village Run – but no picture of Peggy that he could see. He was laying aside the magazine when a figure in a group of skaters caught his attention; he felt a start of surprise and then his eye went down to the caption:

". . . among those enjoying the ice at Murren with Sir Cecil and Lady Stewart's party was Lord Lacy, of Gower Castle, Norfolk . . ."

18

In the weekend of March 20, 1914, almost all the officers of the two cavalry regiments of the Third Brigade stationed at the Curragh Camp, in Ireland, resigned their commissions. At their head was General Gough, commanding the brigade, and among them was Arthur Clayton, subaltern, of the 16th Lancers. The Curragh Mutiny, as it came to be called, had begun, and Britain was faced with a crisis for which there was no precedent in her history. Soldiers, even whole regiments, had mutinied before, but what amounted to a mass defection of officers was something unknown and undreamed of. Suddenly the question which had not been asked for more than two centuries was being heard: what if the Army refuses to obey the government?

Mr Franklin read the news in his *Times* which, in view of the grave national emergency, had been reduced in price to one penny. It was, he reflected, a typically British reaction: when disaster threatens, do the unlikely. In fact, *The Times*'s patriotic gesture had preceded the Curragh Mutiny by two days, and there were those wags who suggested that the cavalry officers had resigned in protest against this cheapening of a national institution; at the same time, however, came warning that the railwaymen and their employers were unlikely to agree on wage demands, that a national rail strike, and possibly a general strike, could well follow, and that it was not impossible that the workers, following the example of the Ulster Volunteers, would take up arms. Mr Lloyd George, never at a loss for a telling phrase, described the Army crisis as the most desperate since the days of the Stuarts – a majority of his audience could probably not have said, off-hand, when the days of the Stuarts were, but they were left in no doubt that in his opinion the very existence of representative government was in danger.

It did not appear to disturb them unduly. To Mr Franklin the most remarkable feature of the crisis was the almost total lack of public interest it aroused. The more popular papers preferred the story of the French Minister's wife who, incensed by *Le Figaro's* criticism of her husband, had entered the editor's office and shot him dead; prominence was also given to pictures of scantily-dressed revellers frolicking with purple balloons at the Chelsea Art Club Ball. From what *The Times* said, Mr Franklin would have expected the name Curragh to be on every lip, but the people of London gave no sign that they had even heard of the place; that Saturday afternoon, as he walked along Oxford Street, the news boys were chanting their usual raucous slogans: "All the racing! Big winner! All the football! Final results! Getcha papers! Football final!" And from the way the buyers scanned the back pages under the flickering lamps it became evident that they were more interested in Arsenal and Tottenham Hotspur than in the historic convulsion of their armed forces.

He turned into Bond Street, threading his way briskly through the late afternoon shoppers, wondering whether he should stop at Claridge's for some tea, or make his way home to Wilton Crescent. Peggy was not due until next week, and the house would be quiet; he would be glad when she got home. That picture of Lacy in the magazine had upset him; it was ironic to think that while he had been allowing himself to be persuaded into doing the fellow a good turn, Lacy had been living it up in Switzerland, and undoubtedly in close proximity to Peggy. Knowing Lacy, Mr Franklin had no doubt that he would make himself a complete pest where she was concerned; he was one of the Stewart party, and Peggy had been going to spend time with them, so it was beyond doubt that they'd be thrown together; without a husband along to shoulder Lacy off, she'd probably have difficulty avoiding and getting rid of him; he'd force his attentions on her at every opportunity, and no doubt the kind of scene he had overheard in the passage at Oxton Hall would be played over again.

He found himself striding out unusually quickly, swinging his stick; he accidentally jostled a passer-by and pulled up, apologizing. This wouldn't do – it wasn't the thought that Lacy would make a nuisance of himself that was bothering him – Peggy could handle that sort of thing with one hand tied. If she wanted to. That was it. At the back of his mind – no, right at the front of his mind, ever since he'd seen the picture, was the ugly suspicion that it wasn't chance that Lacy was at the same ski-resort; that the whole thing was preconcerted, that she and Lacy were . . . he found himself looking into the dimly-reflecting glass of a shop window, and was glad that nobody could see his face. What the hell was he thinking of? Peggy was all wool and a yard wide, he knew she was – and still the foul, dishonourable thought was there. Well, it was bound to be; even while he knew it wasn't true, it was a thought that would have occurred to a saint, faced with that kind of unexpected coincidence.

They were not coherent thoughts that went through his mind; just a repetition of fleeting things that he had been unconsciously juggling with ever since he'd seen that picture. He was a middle-aged fool with a beautiful young wife; Lacy was an unscrupulous lecher who had been besotted with her and probably still was; on the other hand, Peggy was a faithful and loving wife, and if she'd had any lingering affection for Lacy it must surely have shown itself in the past four years – but it hadn't, had it? No, she detested the fellow – he'd heard her tell Lacy to go to hell back at Oxton, he could recall that conversation almost word for word . . . had any of the things she'd said that day been capable of any other interpretation than the obvious one? Might she not be flattered to find Lacy still tagging after her? But even if she was, wasn't a woman entitled to be pleased if an old flame tried to scorch her? Had Peggy known Lacy was going to be in Switzerland? Suppose she had – she was still a faithful and loving wife, and he was a jealous middle-aged idiot . . .

And so on, jumbling in his brain, and for the most part creating a firm impression of reassurance – and yet the slight, nagging doubt . . . no, it wasn't doubt, even. He knew it was all right, and when the unworthy phantoms arose the best thing was to look them in the face with commonsense and decency and dismiss them. It was coincidence, and Peggy would deal with Lacy if he got out of step. And his jealousy was just that – because Lacy was in Switzerland and he wasn't; because Lacy could see her and he couldn't.

He felt better, as he'd felt better every time the thoughts had gone through his mind and been resolved; he turned away from the shop window, walking at a gentler pace. It was half-dusk, and Bond Street was beginning to take on that misty, enchanted look that the West End of London wore at evening before the days of neon lights, when the streets had that pearly radiance which was the compensation for its ugly stepfather, the pea-soup fog. The lights seemed to hang like magic lanterns against the fading silvery-blue of the sky; the air, for March, was mild and dry, and the bustle of the pavements and the crowded narrow street was leisurely. The horse-cabs and the cars rolled past, and he was glancing idly at them as he strolled down towards the Brook Street corner when a voice suddenly called sharply, close by, and he turned to look.

333

"Hey! Hullo! Mr American! Yoo-hoo!"

There was a car parked at the kerb, with its hood down, and a woman was waving from the driving-seat. Mr Franklin automatically glanced behind him to see whom she was waving at.

"It's me! Mr American! Hullo!"

There was no doubt she was waving at him, and no doubt that she was blonde and smart and extremely attractive; for a moment Mr Franklin thought he was being solicited, until it occurred to him that the light ladies of the West End were not in the habit of accosting prospective customers from Sheffield Simplex sports cars, and certainly not at the tops of their voices. And then the strange phrase "Mr American" triggered his memory, and he was looking with disbelief into the laughing, dimpled face with the pert nose and the sparkling blue eyes – with that curious squint – and the blonde curls peeping out modishly from under the smart little hat, and the years rolled away in an instant.

"Pip!" he exclaimed. "Well, I'm darned! It's you, Pip!"

"Well, of course it's me! Who'd you think it was? Florrie Ford? Well, come on – hop in!"

She was pushing the passenger door open with a gloved hand, and holding the hand out to him. He shook it, laughing, and she cocked her head gaily and said: "Well, if it isn't Mr Mark J. Franklin from Way Out West! Climb aboard, partner!"

"All right – " He was about to step into the car when he realized the motor wasn't running. "Don't you need a crank, though? I'd better – "

"Crank, nothing! I've got a self-starter! In you get, Mr American!"

He swung himself into the passenger seat and pulled the door to. At that moment a policeman blew his whistle, waving peremptorily, and Pip called out: "Right you are, Arthur! I'm coming!" She pressed the self-starter, the motor purred into life, and she swung deftly out from the kerb, causing the constable to step back hastily; she managed to spin the wheel, change gear, and flutter her fingers at the policeman all in one rapid movement, and then they were roaring down Bond Street.

"This is amazing!" exclaimed Mr Franklin. "Pip! Where on earth – "

"Hold on a sec!" Pip applied the brake just in time to avoid collision with a Rolls Royce, called "And the same to you, Percy!" to an

334

indignant chauffeur, and inched her way expertly between a horse-cab and a van. "Men drivers!" she said. "The frozen limit!"

"Where are we going?" laughed Mr Franklin.

"Wherever you like," said Pip. She turned a radiant smile towards him. "Gosh, it's good to see you! It's been years!" She was having to shout above the noise of the traffic and the roar of her own sporting engine; Mr Franklin saw the Brook Street turn just ahead and pointed to it, calling: "Claridge's!"

"Whoops!" said Pip, and executed a neat turn in front of an oncoming taxi, which honked indignantly. "Claridge's, eh? That's what I like to hear! Hold on, then, we'll be there in half a jiff!" She clashed the gears alarmingly, made unladylike noises, revved the engine with a roar which startled a passing horse, and brought them gliding smoothly to a halt outside the unobtrusive front of the famous hotel. Mr Franklin got out of the passenger door and was going round to the offside, but Pip was out before him, clicking briskly to the pavement in her hobble skirt and addressing the approaching door-man.

"Look after her, Basil, all right? Don't let the Brook Street kids climb on the bonnet, and don't play with the horn."

And the doorman was smiling ingratiatingly and saying: "Certainly, Miss Delys, I'll take care of it."

"You still have your old way with doormen, porters, and waiters," said Mr Franklin admiringly, as she preceded him into the hotel. "If that had been me, he'd have told me to park somewhere else."

" 'Course he would," said Pip. "If he didn't, there wouldn't be room for musical comedy actresses in their sports models, would there? Eight hundred and eighty quid that little beauty cost – isn't she swell?" She turned to admire the Sheffield nestling expensively beside the pavement. " 'Course, it would have been cheaper without the self-starter, but if you're going to make a splash, make it in style, that's what I say. Here, but this is lovely!" She glowed at Mr Franklin. "You know, you haven't changed a bit! I knew you the minute I saw you, sauntering along like Gilbert the Filbert, as if you'd owned London all your life. Where have you been keeping yourself? Have you been away? Back to America?"

"Let's have some tea," suggested Mr Franklin, smiling. "If musical comedy actresses take anything so common, that is."

"Musical comedy actresses take anything they can get. Tea – and dinner. Where you going to take me this evening?"

335

"Tea first," said Mr Franklin, and guided her into the lounge. They found a quiet corner, Mr Franklin nodded to a waiter, and then he and Pip looked at each other, and laughed.

"Mr American," she said.

"Miss Pip Delys of the *Folies Satire*," said Mr Franklin, "and looking lovelier than ever." Which was no more than the truth; the pretty oval face was as fresh and youthful as he remembered it, if more artfully made up, and he had noted with amusement how the male heads had turned at the sight of the perfect hour-glass figure when she crossed the lounge. She was the same jaunty, cheerful gamine who had pounced on him that night outside the stage door four years ago; if there was a change it was that she dressed now with a greater sophistication than the soubrette of twenty. The tiny hat with its little aigret was a Paris model, and the afternoon dress of black silk with the striking white front panel in the skirt, if cut a good deal tighter than fashion demanded – trust Pip for that – was probably from Worth. The small handbag was black crocodile, matching the neat shoes with their ankle-ribbons just visible beneath the hobble skirt. Mr Franklin surveyed her and shook his head in admiration.

"All right!" said Pip, feigning indignation. "I've put on six and a half pounds, if you want to know. Well, seven. Does it show? – 'cos if it doesn't, it's meant to." She giggled. "If I bend down in this dress, it splits. But I've grown an inch taller, too."

"Well, however much you've grown, it looks great on you, Pip. How've you been – and where have you been?"

"Where have I been?" Pip looked at him in disbelief. "I like that! Where have you been, you mean! I've been on the stage, right here in the West End, like a good hard-working girl! Don't you ever go to the theatre?"

Mr Franklin confessed that he did go, but usually to plays; revues he saw only occasionally. "But I did see you again, once, just about a year after we met – that was in a show, but I'm afraid I don't remember what it was called – "

"*Monte Carlo Millie? The Bride Wore Tights? Birds of a Feather?* Let's see – that'd be three years ago – gracious, has it been that long? What was I in about then, after the *Folies* closed? *Paris Vanities?* No, that was later . . ."

"I just don't know – but you had a solo number, *Bessie in the Bustle* – "

"Oh, that old thing!" Pip clapped her hands. "That was the 'Broad-

336

way memories' finale from *Good Old New York*! Me with my corset
and parasol and all the chorus boys dressed as great big females?
That's the one!" And she hummed: " 'Wait till you see Bessie in the
bustle, she's got a figure like Lilian Russell". Very Victorian that
was. And you saw it – well, you might have come round afterwards!
Why didn't you?"

"Well, tell you the truth, I was with a party, and it included my
wife – "

"You never! You got married!" Pip squeaked and regarded him
with delight. "Well, you sly Yankee, you! Oh, I'm glad! Who is she,
and what's she like, and when did it happen?"

The waiter was deftly setting out the tea things, and when he had
gone and Pip was pouring, Mr Franklin said:

"It happened about six months after you and I met, and her name's
Peggy, and she's . . . very nice."

"Is she a stunner? I'll bet she is. Trust you to pick a looker. Is she
a blonde, or a brunette, or red-head? Is she tall? Here, is she a
theatrical?"

"No, she's not a theatrical," laughed Mr Franklin. "She's a . . .
a . . ."

"She's a lady," said Pip, wisely mischievous. "I know. I'll bet she's
as well-bred as all get-out, isn't she, and wore a big bow when she
was a little girl, and had a nursemaid, and went to school for young
ladies, and talks about 'Mummy and Daddy', and clapped her hands
for Tinker Bell when the little perisher was dying of poison? No,
here, I'm a cat – but I'm as jealous as sin, of course." She twinkled
at him as she passed his cup. "Congratulations, anyway. And her
name's Peggy. Well, that's – " Pip suddenly checked in the act of
pouring hot water, her lips parted. "Hey! Peggy? Franklin? She isn't
the Mrs Peggy Franklin, surely? Well, she must be!"

"I don't know about *the*," said Mr Franklin. "But she's certainly
Mrs Peggy Franklin. Don't tell me you know her?"

"I don't *know* her, but I know about her – seen her at the big
parties, and her picture in the glossies. Why, she's one of the bright
young things – she's society!" Pip looked at him with reverence. "And
she's your trouble and strife? Well! No wonder you look like the cat
that swallowed the canary! And I asked if she was a stunner! She's
gorgeous, that's what she is! Didn't she get her picture painted, a
while back – what was it called? 'A Study in Silk', by what's-his-
name?"

337

"Lavery? That's right. I think it's going on show at an exhibition sometime this year. Where did you see it?"

"Oh, I get about in the art world, too, you know," said Pip mysteriously. "But here – you can't half pick 'em, can't you? I looked at that picture, and just went green! Straight up. And, of course, she's at parties, like I say, and in the smart spots – here, I've never seen you with her, though?"

"No, well, I find the Society whirl a bit . . . of a whirl," said Mr Franklin, and Pip blinked and there was just an instant's pause before she said: "Smoked salmon sandwiches, goody! Here, they give you them thin-cut, don't they? Just as well, when you have to watch your figure." And she patted her hip complacently.

"And you're a settled married man," she went on gaily. "That's lovely. Any kids? No? Well, I'm not even married yet, you won't be surprised to hear, although it looked a near thing about a year ago." She sighed. "Well-spruced he was, too, and making a mint out of bicycle tyres or car hoods or something – actually, it was through him I got the car, although I finished up paying for it in the long run. Men! I thought we were all set, and then," Pip bit moodily at her sandwich, "the big stiff went off to France or Germany or somewhere, and next thing I knew his business had gone splat and the broker's men were round trying to get the car off me. So I had to stump up." She grimaced and selected another sandwich daintily, holding it limply and looking wistfully across the room. "That's life, though, isn't it? Mind you, it's good for trade, the car is; makes a good impression."

"In the theatre? On managers, you mean?"

Pip chuckled. "No, silly! Actresses don't have cars – not unless they're the top-drawer kind, in the big plays. Heavens, you don't think you can run a motor on what they pay in revue and music-hall? Well, if you get to the top, like Marie, it's different, but I haven't." She smiled ruefully. "'Member, that night at Monico's – or was it the Troc? No, Monico's, that's right – anyway, I told you I had the face and the figure and the cheek, but it all depended on whether I'd got 'it', whatever 'it' is? Well, I guess I didn't have 'it', so there. Still, I've been working steady, into another show as I was out of one, and paying the rent regular, thank you, and a bit over – but I've never got above second principal, and Dandini and Alice Fitzwarren in the pantos. I'd have given it up, I s'pose, but I love it – the theatre, I mean. But you can't just stick at second spot all your life, can you, singing, 'Boiled beef and carrots' and 'Knocked 'em in the Old Kent

Road' and swinging your bum – beg pardon, your sit-upon – every time the big drummer goes boo-boom?" She looked at him in appeal. "I mean, can you?"

"I shouldn't have thought so," said Mr Franklin. "Of course, I haven't given the matter much – "

"Well, you can't," said Pip seriously. "And you're looking at my rotten squint again."

"I'm doing no such thing!" protested Mr Franklin. "As a matter of fact, I was looking at the little ornament in your hat, and wondering what it was."

"What, my little snail? D'you like him? He's from France! Here, I'll show you," and Pip reached up to unpin the tiny brooch from the aigret. "Must mind and not disturb my expensive kwa-foor." She grimaced as she deliberately over-pronounced the word. "There, isn't he cute?"

Mr Franklin examined the snail with proper admiration. It was a beautifully-fashioned piece of work, the shell in pale gold, the snail itself in silver, with tiny stones set in the miniature horns.

"All the rage in Paris, but nobody wears 'em over here, much, 'cos they're too creepy-crawly, they say. Actually, it's because they cost the earth – they're real little diamonds, you know. Oh!" Pip suddenly put up a hand to her mouth, and stared at him wide-eyed. "What on earth must you think? Chattering away, and I've never even said a word about those deevy things you sent me! I couldn't believe it! They were so beautiful! And the expense – what on earth did you do it for? I mean, I was just joking, that night, when I said any old diamond bracelet would do, and then those gorgeous jewels – I thought you must be a loony! I still think so!"

She regarded him solemnly, and to his embarrassment he saw that the blue eyes were moist; he looked away, round the spacious lounge, with its muted conversation at the low tables, the gentle tinkle of cups, and the tail-coated waiters moving softly to and fro.

"I don't know," he said. "I just felt like it. I couldn't ever remember such a happy evening, not in my whole life – so it seemed . . . well, I just wanted to, that's all."

"Oh," said Pip, "that's the nicest thing. It really is." She sighed deeply, with her whole body, and a gentleman at a nearby table who happened to be looking in her direction knocked over his cup in agitation. "Anyway, I don't know how to say 'thank you', but I do. Thanks ever so much, Mr American." She reached across and patted his hand, and giggled again. "Here, though, you'll never know what a rumpus it caused back-stage! The girls were fairly curled up with envy, and no one knew who you were, and the manager said I ought to send 'em back, 'cos you could see with half an eye how dear they were, and he said it was fishy. I got quite anxious – so I took 'em to be valued, at a proper jewellers in Covent Garden, and when he told me what they were worth – well, you could have knocked me over. I wear 'em now on special occasions – if I'm doing a star turn at parties, or in cabarets, I do a good deal of that sort of thing nowadays, and when anyone asks me where I got 'em, I just say: 'That's the loot from the Deadwood Gulch stagecoach, given me by Texas Tommy himself.' " She chuckled. "More tea?"

"Thanks. I'm glad you liked them." He remembered at the time the thought had been in his mind that if ever Pip's stage career hit a rocky patch, the pearl necklace with its diamond cluster might come in useful. That, plainly, had not happened; she might not have attained the top of the theatrical ladder, but she was obviously doing extremely well as second principal and with her party and cabaret turns – even so, he wouldn't have thought that would have supplied the expensive sports car, the Worth dress, the jewelled snail, and the general opulence of Pip's appearance. There was an obvious explanation, but somehow it didn't suit her. He was curious.

"What exactly are you doing now, Pip?"

"Well." Her eyes gleamed at the prospect of discussing her favourite topic. "Let's see – I came out of *Keep Smiling* at the Alhambra last month, didn't you see it? You did? Well, remember the big staircase scene that was the high spot of the show, with everyone on stage, and the girl in red feathers – that was me! 'Course, you wouldn't recognize me, not in all that lot, it was like Piccadilly Circus, and I had a couple of speciality spots, but I was wearing a mask in one of 'em and a Chinese make-up in the other. It was a good show, but five months is a long enough run for anybody, so I chucked it. I could have got into *Hullo, Tango* at the Hippodrome, but it would have been the same old thing all over again, wouldn't it, and Oscar Ashe offered me a part in *Kismet* which is due to open next month at the Globe – they say it's done huge business in Australia, you know – and it paid well, but all it amounted to was being the target girl, so I didn't take it, and – "

"The target girl? That sounds dangerous."

"You might be right, you never know," chuckled Pip. "The target

340

girl's the one in the big revues who gives the customers something to look at while the principals are singing their duets – you know, there's always a nice-looking one, a little apart from the rest, who just sits there looking dreamy, usually in gauze, and you watch her. That's the target girl. Well, it's all right, and a lot of second and third principals like it, 'cos the money's good – but I like doing my numbers and chaffing the audience to join in the chorus, not sitting round the harem catching my death of cold with a jewel stuck in my belly-button. Oh, stop me, I'm vulgar, aren't I? Anyway, I turned it down, and went back to my other work. It pays better, and it's a nice break from the stage – although I always go back to the shows, after a bit."

Mr Franklin said nothing, but possibly he studied his plate in rather too casual a manner, for the quick-witted Pip immediately read his mind, and gave an exaggerated squeak of indignation.

"Ooh! Here! You don't think I mean . . . Really! You men! Talk about nasty minds! You only think about one thing, and jump to wicked conclusions – "

"I never said a word," protested Mr Franklin.

"No, but you thought a good few. 'Drives a sports car, does she? Jewellery from Paris, eh? Got a line of work that pays better than the theatre, well, well, who'd have thought it? How shocking!' That's what you were thinking, and don't pretend you weren't. The idea!" Pip sniffed righteously, and then bubbled with laughter. "Can you see me on the Prom at the Empire, giving the nuts the glad eye over my feather boa? 'Hello, darling' " – she dropped her voice into a cavernous contralto drawl – " 'would you care to view the Oriental exhibits in my flat in Glasshouse Street?' I'd die laughing! Anyway, that's a mug's game, and I'm legitimate. Always have been, always will be. Besides, I'm too good-looking to waste myself on that – squint or no squint. And that's what you need in my line – looks."

"All right, I apologize," said Mr Franklin, "although I haven't anything to apologize for, because I know you're legitimate, as you call it, and I never thought otherwise. What is this line, then? – it obviously pays better than the theatre."

"I'm a model," said Pip proudly. "And I mean a real model – not a mannequin, although I do commercial work, too – haven't you seen the Scrubb's ammonia girl, in all the magazines? That's me – but you might not recognize me, because the artist takes out the squint, of course. But you must have seen the ads!"

341

"Sure I have. Yes, I guess she does look like you, but the painter makes you rather more . . . well . . ."

"Wholesome?" Pip put her tongue in her cheek. "Not quait so common? I know. Well, what d'you expect when you're modelling for ammonia – 'the key to cleanliness. Try it in your bath.'" They don't say *what* you should try in your bath, but that's the point. Lewd men like you look at my picture, and get naughty ideas, and go out and buy ammonia. That's modern advertising for you. All I do is get drawn with lions and pekes and parrots and Japanese kimonos and barrister's wigs."

"Astonishing," said Mr Franklin. "Well, I feel I ought to buy some Scrubb's ammonia, to further the good work."

"You'd be surprised how many letters they get, asking who the girl in the picture is," said Pip. "But not as many as they do for my other ad., which is for Mademoiselle Merlain's bust developer, the new French method, no creams or ointments, write to our address in Oxford Street. It's shocking, really," said Pip virtuously. "I never knew how many men look at the advertisements in ladies' magazines. Disgusting, I call it."

"I don't recall seeing that particular advertisement," said Mr Franklin.

"No, well you can't miss it, if you do see it," giggled Pip. "But that's the commercial stuff. You know your Peggy's been painted by a proper artist? Well," said Pip proudly, "so have I. What is more," she went on, tossing her head, "I am going to be hung at the Royal Academy – twice. What d'you think of that?"

"I think that's extraordinary," said Mr Franklin, "and worthy of that dinner you were talking about. If such an exclusive model will honour a humble member of the public with her company, that is."

Pip beamed, and then frowned. "Thanks very much, and I'd love to," she said. "But you're a married man now, you know. Ought you to be taking models out to dinner? What would your wife say?"

"I can't think she'd object," said Mr Franklin. "Especially since she'll be eating dinner herself this evening somewhere in Switzerland, and I can't believe she'll be eating it alone."

Pip looked at him, thoughtfully, and it might have been his imagination but for an instant the pretty, animated face looked almost sad. Then she brightened and sat up.

"Right-ho, then. Dinner for two. Got a fiver on you, have you?" She collapsed with laughter. "Remember that night at Monico's, when

342

I asked if you wanted to go dutch?" She sighed happily. "That was a lovely evening."

"Yes, it was. Would you like to go back to Monico's?"

Pip pursed her lips. "No, I think I'd like somewhere else, if you don't mind." She smiled at him across the table. "Dinner."

"That's right," said Mr Franklin. "Dinner."

They decided eventually on the Trocadero, and since they would both have to change, Pip drove Mr Franklin back to Wilton Crescent before going on to her own flat in Bloomsbury, where she had removed from Chelsea. The drive was an entertaining experience, if alarming; Pip's method of travel was to go as fast as possible, with constant racing of the engine, hammering of gears, and squealing of brakes, talking incessantly, until she had driven herself into a hopeless tangle with other vehicles and blocked the traffic, when she would come to a sudden halt and trust to wide-eyed innocence, fluttering lashes, and parted lips to see her through. Mr Franklin was astonished at the success of this technique; twice threateningly advancing constables were melted into avuncular tolerance, and other vehicles made to retreat to let the Sheffield through; once, in a particularly bad jam at the Piccadilly end of Bolton Street, she half got out of the car in agitation, and the display of shapely calf and ankle elicited sympathetic whistles and stentorian roars to an unoffending taxi-driver to get his rattletrap aht the wye an' let the pore little gel through. Another outraged motorist, impervious apparently to female charm, became abusive, and received in return a stream of music-hall ribaldry, delivered in her most affectedly ladylike voice, which sent him back red-faced and shaken behind his own wheel, and caused Mr Franklin to sink as low as possible in his seat and shield his face with his hat.

He was happy to reach Wilton Crescent in one piece, and as she roared away with a wave and cry of: "See you eight-thirty, chief!" it struck him what a dramatic change there seemed to have been, even in his few years in England. At their last meeting he had taken her home in a horse-drawn cab, and she had looked, to all intents, very little different from those beauties of the Victorian theatre whose pictures had adorned the saloons of his young manhood; now, in her smartly-tailored day dress and ridiculously tiny Paris hat, she stamped on the clutch and spun her wheel and honked her horn and zoomed away in a cloud of petrol fumes. Less than five years, and yet already that first night was like a relic from a past age; in hard terms, it had probably been little different, and yet somehow it seemed more

343

leisurely and ordered and stable, and now a new roaring modern age was upon them, and it could never be the same again.

It was a relief to discover when they met for dinner that one thing which had not changed was Pip's appetite; her capacity for oysters, foie gras, truffles, and sweets of glutinous kind remained as generous as ever, she addressed the waiter indiscriminately as "Marcel", "Fritz", or "Jake" and coaxed second helpings from him with a beck and a wink as though it were a shared conspiracy to defraud Mr Franklin or the management or both, she appraised the Veuve Clicquot coolly and advised Marcel (or Jake) to stick it well down the bucket, she chattered incessantly, and yet managed to find time for eating and ensuring that nothing that happened in the crowded restaurant escaped her attention and comment. He could have closed his eyes and imagined himself back at the Monico again – but he would have had to close his eyes, for to look at her was to be reminded of how great a change five years had made.

Knowing her, Mr Franklin had expected her to arrive at the Trocadero dressed in the height of theatrical extravagance; he discovered that the sophistication which he had noticed in her during the afternoon was emphasized in her evening dress. Where all around there were exotically feathered and tiaraed heads, and even one or two powdered according to the Paris fad, Pip wore her blonde locks neatly swept up and unadorned; where other ladies used a profusion of frills and lace and wispy chiffons, she wore a simple French evening gown of grey velvet, admittedly tight and smoothly-fitted, but of a plain elegance which proclaimed its expense, and contrived to make the competition look like carnival finery. It was not even unusually low cut, which did surprise him, knowing her particular vanity; he remarked on the subdued splendour of her appearance, and Pip sipped her champagne and winked.

"Pile on the frills and ribbons when you're twenty," she remarked, "but when you're twenty-four and look as much like a tart or a flapper as I do, then discretion's the thing, my dear – especially when it looks twice as fetchy as all the skimpy gauzes and silks. Besides, if Mr Mark Franklin, of Wilton Crescent, Belgravia, a respectable married gentleman, is to be seen dining out at a fashionable restaurant with a companion not his wife, it's as well if she looks summat like a lady, and not a tarrarraboomdeeay with bells on. Oi, Ginger," she added in a low voice to the passing waiter, "got any nuts and olives, have you?"

344

They toasted her forthcoming appearance at the Royal Academy, and Pip became confidential. "It isn't definitely fixed yet, you see, 'cos the Hanging Committee or whatever they're called have to decide what gets shown and what doesn't. But my two pictures are as near a stone-ginger cert. as any can be – both well-known painters, see, so they're sure to get picked. And they're lovely pictures, both of 'em – not 'cos I'm in them, I mean, but because they're good; they really are."

"Are they portraits?"

"No-o, not really," said Pip. "There's one which is very classical, called Carthage, and it's by this lovely Italian gentleman, Mr Matania – you'll see his drawings in the magazines. Ever so kind and polite, he is, and draws like a dream. This is a Roman picture, and there's two of us, me and another girl, and we've been captured by corsairs, or we're going to be, I'm not sure which, and I'm lying face down on a bed, in the altogether. So you couldn't say it was a portrait, exactly. And the other picture is me in a field in a bit of gauze, with the wind blowing, and it's called 'Summer Zephyr', I think – something like that. You can see my face in that one, so it's more of a portrait, I suppose."

"Well, that's really something, Pip," said Mr Franklin. "Being hung at the Royal Academy – that's fame. It's more than that; it's immortality, because hundreds of years from now people'll be looking at those pictures, and thinking, that's a real pretty girl."

"You think so?" Pip looked pleased, and sighed. "Only thing is, I won't be able to wink back at 'em and give 'em sass over the footlights. I daresay it's nice having people like your picture centuries after, but it isn't the same as a real live audience."

"Don't tell that to an artist, whatever you do," laughed Mr Franklin. "Anyway, when those pictures go up, I'm going to insist on a personally conducted tour of the gallery. Is it a date?"

"All right!" said Pip, delighted. "Opening day, the model herself will show you round. Here," she added, "you don't think the suffragettes will have a go at 'em, do you?"

"At your pictures? Heavens above, why should they?"

"Didn't you see what they did to that picture of Venus, in the National Gallery?" said Pip anxiously. "Made a hell of a mess of it, they did, just last month."

"Oh, the Rokeby Venus, by Velasquez. Yes, I read about that. But that's an old master, Pip – something famous and valuable, which is why they picked it. I'm not belittling your pictures, but I don't see any reason why the suffragettes should take a hatchet to them."

"Don't you, though?" said Pip darkly. "Well, I do. The picture they smashed was a nude, wasn't it, and you know why? Because these silly cows think that nude pictures of women are degrading – I read that in the paper. So they give 'em the axe and the acid. Well, those pictures of mine are about as nude as you can get, and if one of those mouldy old bags lays a finger on them, God help her." Pip scowled fiercely at her champagne glass. "Women's suffrage! They give me a pain!"

"I can't say I've any sympathy with defacing pictures – even less than I have with bombing politicians' houses and shouting at trains," said Mr Franklin. "But the cause isn't a bad one, is it? Don't you want the vote?"

"Come off it," said Pip. "What good's the vote to me – or anyone else, for that matter? It means you get a chance every few years to vote for one or other of a pair of boobies that they've picked before-hand. That's just bully, isn't it? It doesn't mean because you've got a vote that you can *do* anything, does it? 'Course it doesn't. Anyway – I'll tell you something. If Mr Asquith or Mr Lloyd George was to come in here now, and address the restaurant, how many votes d'you think he could swing? Precious few. But – " she raised a small finger and tapped her upturned nose in what she imagined was a gesture of conspiratorial cunning " – give me the platform for five minutes, with a good drummer and a spotlight man who knows his stuff, and I could have every man-jack in the place voting for the Kaiser. D'you believe me?"

"Every time," confessed Mr Franklin. "I think women will have to get the vote, if only so that you can enter politics."

"Fat chance," said Pip. "I wouldn't waste my time. I've got no use for these female agitators. You know why they do it – and why they go about defacing pictures? It's jealousy, that's all. Look at 'em – ugliest set of old hags you ever saw. That's what's wrong with them. They rant on about women being slaves to men – you can see the Maharajah of Astrakhan wanting that lot in his harem, can't you? They haven't got the thing that doesn't just make women equal to men, but makes 'em superior, and they know it, and it makes 'em sour and warped."

"What haven't they got, Pip?"

"I dunno what you'd call it," said Pip seriously, "but it's what any woman's got – unless she really looks Godawful. It's being able to make men do what you want, I suppose. I can. So can your Peggy. And even more – it's being able to get men to do what the men want to do, but maybe don't know it. Even Godawful-looking women can do it, if they set their minds to it, instead of blowing up pillar-boxes and scratching policemen's faces. I'd flog those bitches," said Pip relentlessly. "I really would. Anyway, all this talk about equality's bunkum. There's things you can do that I can't – but I'd like to see you on the Hippodrome stage, second house Monday night, with the pit full of drunk sailors and the conductor's lost his music. Or let Mrs Ruddy Pankhurst try it, and I hope she gets a hole in her tights."

"Have some more champagne," said Mr Franklin, "or a liqueur. I hadn't realized what an anti-suffragette you were. By the way, they don't all look Godawful – I know one who's rather handsome."

"You would," said Pip cynically. "Well, you can tell her from me she's wasting her chances – if she's got looks she should use 'em, and be thankful, 'stead of yapping on about women's slavery. What do they know about it, anyway? Most of 'em are ladies, you'll notice, and never did a hand's turn in their lives, swanking about in their hundred-guinea sealskin coats, and bully-ragging poor little tweeny maids who don't earn in a year what those . . . those old cows spend on a couple of dinners. They make me mad, honest! Sorry, I got worked up. I'll have a kummel, please."

She brooded, her pretty face overcast, and looked darkly at the surrounding tables, as though in the hope of surprising Mrs Pankhurst demanding women's rights. "Slavery! Huh! I'd like to show 'em. Look here – what d'you think of this?" And to Mr Franklin's amazement she opened her mouth, leaned towards him, and put out her tongue. She made a muffled noise, realized she couldn't talk with her tongue out, withdrew it and said: "Take a good look at it – notice anything?" She protruded it gently between her teeth.

Mr Franklin took a quick look to see if anyone was noticing, and said hastily:

"It's a very pretty little tongue. You have lovely teeth, too – "

"Never mind my teeth. Notice anything odd about the tip of my tongue?"

"No . . . wait, though, it's shiny – as though it had been polished. That's strange."

"You bet your life it's strange," said Pip. "It's been polished all right – you know how? When I was seven years old, I was licking

347

labels in a sweatshop for a penny an hour. Thirty gross of labels a day – know how many that is, six days a week, for two years? That's more than two and a half million labels – and I licked every one of 'em. That's why my tongue's got a polished tip – and always will have. That's nothing – it doesn't hurt, it won't kill me, it's not disfigurement. But I remember it – every time I clean my teeth. And they talk about slavery!"

Mr Franklin sat silent for a moment. "I thought that was illegal – sweated labour. Especially for children."

" 'Course it's illegal," said Pip, and took a delicate sip at her liqueur. "But if there's ten of you living in one room, like we were in Seven Dials, with one tap and one privy in the street, and Dad out of work – which he was for four years, until he got the fish-barrow, and nothing to live on, it doesn't matter whether it's legal or not, does it? We were meant to go to school – so we did, my sisters and me, but we had to work too, on the sly – 'part-timers', they called us. If we stopped off school, the attendance officer was down on poor old Dad like a ton of bricks – he got jailed over it, twice. So we did it evenings, mostly – I can taste them labels yet. I've never licked one since, not even to seal an envelope or put on a stamp. My little sister died of it, I reckon, though they said it was consumption. Poor little soul – day she died, all she was worried about was missing the old Queen's jubilee procession."

"And you got out of it, in the end," said Mr Franklin. "You're quite a girl, Pip."

"It wasn't my fault I got out," said Pip. "I was lucky – bar the squint, I was the beauty of the family. At least, I had the figure, even when I was fifteen. I say a prayer of thanks each night that I didn't finish up on the game, like those poor little swine on the 'Dilly or the Empire Prom – and they're the cream of the crop, the five-pound jobs. You ought to see some of the others." She shivered. "It was the Salvation Army gave me my chance – I used to bang my little tambourine round the pubs and sing 'Come and join us', and a scout told me to go and see Mr Edwardes – dear old Gaiety George. He was square, and he recommended me – I told you how I lied about my age, didn't I? They knew, the managers, but they were decent and didn't let on. And I didn't have to audition on an office couch with the blinds down, either – they weren't that sort. So I got started – and it was just blind luck, and what makes me so wild about these Women's Rights people is that if they had their way, I'd be an old woman this minute, worn out like Ma; I'd be in Seven Dials, scrubbing steps and waiting to die. I had my woman's looks – nothing else. Suppose I'd been flat-chested or skinny-legged? Lot of good the vote would have been to me, wouldn't it?"

She took an angry sip at her kummel, and then suddenly threw off her gloom like a cloak and twinkled at Mr Franklin.

"Here, I'm sorry! I'm just a pain in the neck! Going on about hard times, and Christmas Day in the workhouse, and we're meant to be celebrating. I dunno what got into me – yes, I do, though, it's those old bags slashing pictures of girls like me – wonder if your Rokeby Venus model was worried about the vote? Not half, I'll bet! Anyway, I'm here, and we're having a good time, and none of my family's going short, I can tell you. And if I thought they were going to, I'd take that job in *Kismet* tomorrow, or go back to the chorus, two shows a night, and high-kick my backside off six nights a week – and if I got tired and fed up, know what I'd do? Go to the nearest looking-glass and stick my tongue out."

She finished her liqueur and looked round the restaurant, listening to the hum of conversation and drinking in the scene. "This is a dead-and-alive hole, this is, and we both need cheering up after Miss Delys's lecture on the Rights of Woman. Tell you what – how'd you like to come to a supper club? I don't feel like going home yet, and you deserve some fun after listening to me. I'm a member at the Lotus, and we can have a dance, and a late meal, and drink all night if we feel like it. What about it?"

"It's your celebration party," said Mr Franklin. "I don't know about the late supper, though – "

"Garn, the dinner's just the hors-d'oeuvres," said Pip happily. "A few two-steps, and some ragtime, a couple of snorts, and you'll be ready for poached turbot before one o'clock. Pay the bill, Mr American, and you can have the cocktails and late supper on me!"

The Lotus Club was in Knightsbridge, one of that spreading number of all-night establishments catering for a generation of pleasure-seekers to whom time meant very little now that the ever-present motor car could whirl them from one end of the metropolis to the other in a matter of minutes, and who were in the grip of the latest dancing craze which, perhaps more than anything else, had wrought the great change in manners and style and spirit which Mr Franklin had pondered on earlier that evening. The genteel ballroom exercises of waltz and polka had been invaded from across the Atlantic

349

by the more intricate and intimate patterns of the Boston, the one and two steps, and that extraordinary fusion of the classical and the abandoned, improvised originally by dockers on the Buenos Aires waterfront, and now such a passion with the smart set that it had become a national joke – the tango.

Mr Franklin knew them, and had been able to hold his own on those occasions when he had accompanied Peggy to dances and parties, but like everyone else in Europe who was not stone-deaf he was aware that even these new rages were becoming old hat, not just with the ordinary public but also at the exclusive dances which were something of a mania with fashionable hostesses that year, from four to six-thirty every evening, and which were threatening to sweep away for ever that sacred ritual of polite society, afternoon tea. Even the latest sensation, the fox-trot, was positively sedate beside some of the rag-time rhythms which had come blaring out of the West, to be insistently amplified by every gramophone and dance orchestra in the land, and convince the older generation that Babylon and Sodom were come again. The spectacle of young men and women (some of the latter quite obviously unencumbered by corsets) quivering and gyrating wildly to the insistent beat of Negro music, with its suggestion of the bordello and the jungle, was a scandalous symptom of the new decadence – but what could one expect of a society in which even Bishops could be seen smoking in public?

Mr Franklin paid off the taxi outside the Lotus Club, while Pip tapped her feet to the muted, lively strains emerging from the brightly-lit doorway where well-built, battered young men in incongruous dinner jackets were checking the credentials of those going in. Mr Franklin took her arm and was making for the door when a late news bill caught his eye: "Ulster: Latest Threat"; he bought a paper and while Pip, cheerfully impatient, peered past his shoulder, scanned the front page to see if the news had anything to do with Arthur and the Curragh. But on that topic there was nothing that he did not already know; the latest threat had to do with an incident off the Scottish coast in which a suspected gun-runner had slipped past a Royal Navy destroyer; it was alleged that rifle-shots had been exchanged, and a cartoon on the front page commented scathingly that if a Navy which had just been the recipient of the unprecedented expenditure of £48 million could not hold up a tramp steamer manned by Carson's volunteers, what could it hope to accomplish against the might of the German High Seas Fleet? Mr Churchill was depicted in sailor suit, playing with toy ships in the Round Pond, while behind his back Sir Edward Carson armed with a club labelled "Illegal arms shipments", was shown belabouring a ragged and tearful urchin representing Ireland.

"Come on, what is it, then?" demanded Pip, skipping urgently at his elbow. "Oh, blinking Irishmen again! Who cares? Let's get inside!"

The Lotus Club came as a pleasant surprise to Mr Franklin. It was bright and commodious and as well-appointed as a first-class restaurant – which in fact is what it was. There was a large dining-room upstairs which would have done credit to an exclusive hotel, where anything from a large dinner to a substantial breakfast could be had, and downstairs was the dancing-floor, surrounded by tables to which waiters and waitresses kept up a running service from the well-stocked bar. A large orchestra was going full blast at one end, with a cheerful black pounding the piano, and rasping out "Oh, You Beautiful Doll" in accompaniment to a trio of girl dancers on the stage, one dressed in black face as a golliwog, another as a pierrot, and the third in the frilly costume and exaggeratedly long lashes of a baby doll. They jerked gaily as though to the directions of an invisible puppet-master, and as the number reached its climax to a thunder of applause, all three bowed mechanically and squealed: "Mummy, I'm going to be thick!" before skipping off.

"That's Jessie Mount, in the pierrot rig – with me in *Keep Smilin'*," said Pip, as a waiter showed them to a table. "And Rosie Sweet in the golliwog get-up. She used to be my stand-in at the *Folies*. Nice pay to be picked up in these places." She glanced round the crowded room, waving to friends. "Let's start off with a cocktail, shall we?" She clicked her fingers to a waiter. "No, no, Mr American – you keep your wallet to yourself. This is on me. Anyway, you can't pay, 'cos you're not a member, see? Two John Collins, Charley, and don't go easy on the gin." She surveyed the dance-floor, which was filling up for a fox-trot. "Nice crowd, aren't they? Not what you expected, I'll bet!"

Mr Franklin was forced to agree; he had been prepared to find the Lotus a rather shabby den, run by suspicious-looking characters, but the men and women crowding the dance-floors were all in evening dress, and plainly perfectly respectable members of the upper-middle and middle classes. " 'Course, it's not as toney as the Four Hundred, but it's pretty good; plenty of society people come here – I think I've seen your Peggy, once or twice. Come on – let's dance!"

351

They threaded their way among the couples on the floor to the smooth rhythm of the orchestra; Mr Franklin was hesitant at first, having fox-trotted only a few times with Peggy, but Pip was an expert and made him feel a far better dancer than he was. He experienced a rather guilty pleasure at the contact of the soft, supple body in its smooth velvet, and the drift of perfume from the blonde head just below his chin – but it was a guilt that came not only from the sensual pleasure of holding her but from the realization that he was enjoying himself. When he had been out with Peggy, at balls or tea dances, the steps on the floor had been a mechanical ritual for them; they had not been there to dance, but to be part of the social scene, to see and be seen, to keep abreast, and the real business of the evening had been the chatter and exchange with the other guests. But Pip danced *with* him, and her non-stop talk had none of the social affectation and dreary predictability of Mayfair and Belgravia – as they returned to their table she was describing, with animation, how she had been caught in a police speed trap on the way to Brighton – he found himself laughing at her account of how she had found herself in the dock, and how the elderly magistrate had blushed because she had insisted on kissing the book after taking the oath, although he had explained that it was no longer necessary.

"I gave it a great big juicy smacker, just to tease him, and everyone in court laughed, and that made him go redder than ever," she explained. "But he was all right – let me off with a warning and said it would be ten bob next time." Why could he listen to her nonsense quite happily, when the upper-class trivia of the smart set so bored him? Was it because one had to do with a real, earthy world, where interesting things happened, and the other was artificial and based on conventions which seemed shallow and manners which seemed false? Humbling thought, was he just finding his own level? The gulf between Hole-in-the-Wall and Wilton Crescent was limitless, but in five minutes Pip would have been at home in the Bella Union or the front parlours of those little settlements of his youth – more at home in the Bella Union, admittedly, sassing the hairy miners and chaffing the waiters, but of the same clay as those frontier folk from whom he came, or of the peasantry of Castle Lancing, for that matter. Peggy's was a different world.

"All right, come on out of it!" Pip was shaking her blonde head merrily at him across the table. "You're deep in thought, aren't you – and that's cheek, if you like, when you're being wined and dined

352

by a star of the musical stage who is also one of the most sought-after models in London. Doesn't show proper respect for Scrubb's ammonia if you ask me. Or are you thinking about your Peggy? Wouldn't blame you if you were." She sighed. "That's the trouble with squinty-eyed little bits of fluff like me – we can't compare with the real lookers. And there's far too many of 'em about these days – I don't mean just in society, like your missus, but in the business. Look at Marie Lohr, and that Gladys Cooper – it's rotten anyone's as beautiful as that. Have you seen *My Lady's Dress*, where she's a mannequin, and stabs the manager with a pair of scissors through the curtain? – no, of course you haven't, I was forgetting, it's still in rehearsal. Wait'll they see Gladys doing her stuff, though – that'll put Mr Bernard Shaw back in the basket, however many swear words he sticks in his plays. Have you heard about the new one – Pig-something-or-other?"

"No, I didn't know he had a new play coming out. I saw *Great Catherine*, though – "

"Opens next month, all about a flower-girl and this chap teaches her to be a lady, and she shocks everyone by saying 'bloody'. " Pip giggled. "Isn't it daft? I mean, everybody swears, and you hear far worse every day, but just 'cos it's in a play they think the Lord Chamberlain'll ban it. Stupid old bastard. If him and the rozzers spent more time keeping little girls off the game, and pinching white-slavers, it'd be more useful. Here, I'm getting hungry again – what about another dance and then some supper?"

So they danced, and Mr Franklin toyed with a little scrambled egg in the dining-room while Pip set about a rump steak with chipped potatoes and discoursed, between mouthfuls, about the contrast between the high moral tone demanded of the public stage, and the licence accorded to anything which could be dignified under the heading of art. "I mean, it's all right for every Tom, Dick, and Harry to gape at me with nothing on at the Royal Academy, but if it was on the stage I'd finish up in Holloway. Odd, isn't it. I suppose one's education and the other's dirty. Ah, well."

They went back upstairs and watched a girl in Red Indian costume and headdress singing, "The Pipes of Pan", a comedian who, curiously enough, seemed to have laundered his material for the supper-club audience, and when the cabaret was finished, danced some of the less strenuous numbers. But Mr Franklin could sense that Pip was missing joining in the more energetic jazz dances; she sat with parted lips and tapping feet as the couples threw themselves about, and he was not surprised when, towards the finish of a one-step, she guided him through the dancers to the platform, and slipped away for a whispered word with the black pianist. He listened, teeth gleaming in a great grin, and when the dance finished he struck a dramatic chord, clapped his hands to the orchestra with a chant of "And-a-one-two-three-four!" yelled "Hit it, honey!" to Pip, and swung into a crashing ragtime number.

Pip, from the platform, winked at Mr Franklin while the dancers began to stamp, clapped her hands, swayed in time to the music, and in a voice astonishingly strong and clear for her small body, gave tongue:

> Everybody's doin' it, doin' it, doin' it!
> Everybody's doin' it, doin' it, doin' it!
> See that ragtime couple over there,
> Watch them throw their shoulders in the air . . .

Around Mr Franklin the dancers were clapping and chanting with her, the room began to swing to the heady, insistent beat, the Negro pianist pounded ecstatically, standing up and bouncing as he hit the keys, Pip threw back her head and punched her fists in the air to emphasize the words:

> It's a bear, it's a bear, it's a bear – oh!

Mr Franklin gingerly edged his way to the side of the crowded floor, out of the shuffling, stamping, chanting throng, but keeping his eye on Pip's impromptu performance. He was no authority on ragtime, or even on stage presentation, but he did not have to be to see how skilled she was, how practised her style, how complete her control of her audience. Hips swinging, shoulders shrugging, she swayed along the front of the stage, coaxing the dancers to even greater exertions, then retreated, laughing and clapping, beckoning them to follow, then teasing them by dropping her voice to a throaty whisper:

> It's a bear, it's a bear, it's a bear – ooo-ooh . . .

and finally strutting forward again to finish on a magnificent, full-throated flourish, arms flung high above her head:

Everybody's doin' it,
Everybody's doin' it,
Everybody's doin' it – now!

The applause was thunderous as she took her bow, blowing kisses,
planting one on the gleaming black pate of the pianist, and then
skipping quickly off, shaking her head with delight at the enthusiastic
cries of "Encore! More! More!" Mr Franklin applauded her as she
sank breathless into her chair and seized on the cocktail which he
had thoughtfully provided.

"Phew! I needed that! That got 'em going, though, didn't it? What
d'you think, then – has the little girl got a future in show business?"

"You're tremendous!" he said, laughing. "I thought you said you
didn't have 'it', whatever 'it' is. They seem to think you've got it, all
right."

"They're half-sloshed," said Pip elegantly. "Putting a number over
here's one thing, but there's more to it than that. Hullo, here's Mario
on his way – oh, lord, I should have known better! Here, let's be off
while the going's good!"

She beckoned urgently to Mr Franklin, who got to his feet just as
a beaming and delighted Italian bustled up to their table.

"Peep! Oh, leetle Peep! You were wonderful! What about an
encore, eh? Another chorus – see, they love it! Or the boil" beef and
carrots, maybe? Please, Peep, my darling!"

He drew back her chair, chuckling and making sounds of entreaty,
waving and nodding to the orchestra, but Pip shook her head playfully,
patting his cheek and retreating.

"Not on your life, Mario! Gee, the cheek of it! I'm a member here,
aren't I? And you want me to keep your show going free! You want
to hire yourself a good rag singer, that's what you want to do, ducky!"

"Oh, Peep!" The manager spread his hands, stricken. "Who sings
ragtime as well as you? Oh, just one encore! Plee-z, Peep, for Mario!"

"See my manager!" laughed Pip, shaking her head firmly. "No
tickee, no ruddy washee, see? If you're lucky I might look in again
next week and give your patrons a boost. But no more tonight, darling.
We're off!"

"I give you free subscreeption – no?" The manager smiled coax-
ingly. "Ah, Peep, you are cruel. Never mind, I love you, leetle
sweetheart!" He bowed over her hand and kissed it resoundingly.
"Good-night, darling, good-night, sair!" And he bowed them away

from their table, Pip glowing with her small triumph, and Mr Franklin smiling at her obvious pleasure.

To his surprise, when he looked at his watch, it was nearly one o'clock. He took her back to Bloomsbury in a taxi and saw her into the hallway of her ground-floor flat. She opened her door with her key and said: "Like a cup of coffee? And I mean coffee – no hanky-panky, mind."

"I like that!" said Mr Franklin. "Who took advantage of my back-woods ignorance that night at the Monico?"

"That was different," said Pip indignantly. "You weren't a respectable married man then."

So he sat decorously on the couch in her cheerful little living-room, hung with the posters of her shows, and photographs of scenes from musicals, while she prepared coffee in the tiny kitchen. There were pictures of Pip herself, ranging from a chorus group in which she could be seen, looking very small and pale in a lace bonnet and parasol, obviously at the beginning of her career, to a large hand-coloured photograph over the fireplace, in which she stood pertly posed in tricorne hat, brief embroidered tunic, tights and high heels, with a riding switch tucked under one arm, and a lace handkerchief negligently flourished.

"That's me as Dandini," she explained, as they sipped their coffee. "You know, in Cinderella. What, you've never seen a panto? You haven't lived, my lad. Dandini's the Prince's mate, who goes round trying the glass slipper on the girls – nice little part, and all you need is legs and impudence."

"You love it, don't you?" he smiled. "Well, I hope it keeps fine for you, Pip, because you deserve it. I hope nothing comes along to spoil it for you."

"My, that's solemn!" Pip grimaced. "What should spoil it?"

"I don't know. Nothing, I guess. It's just – oh, you read nothing but crisis in the papers, and suffragettes, and strikers, and war scares, and then you see all those people enjoying themselves, having great fun . . . but it's kind of frenzied, somehow, as though everyone were trying to cram as much as they can into the time that's left to them. Maybe it's the ragtime, and I'm getting old." He laughed. "I guess it's just the same in every age, and people like me get sour and feel it can't last."

"You're not sour!" said Pip. "I never met anybody less sour than you. But you're sad, aren't you – as if you were disappointed? Hasn't England been the way you thought it would be?"

He thought of Castle Lancing, and Peggy, and Samson, and Pip, and said at length: "It's been better – most of it. Not everything, but most things. I'd just like to see it last, that's all."

"Don't you worry about that," said Pip confidently. "We always have lasted, haven't we? Gee, don't tell me about changes – I've seen plenty in my time. So you just get used to 'em, and make the best of it. If there's a war, in Ireland or somewhere – well, it'll get over, I reckon, and there's nothing you and me can do about it. But I don't reckon there will be – I mean, there hasn't been a real war for ever so long, has there? Not like the ones they told us about at school – Napoleon and the Light Brigade and that sort of thing." She smiled and shook her head. "I won a prize book at school, *Our Indian Sisters*, for reciting that at the Christmas concert – 'Half a league, half a league, half a league onward'. Good poem, that – and the first engagement I ever got anything for. Knocked 'em cold in the front stalls, took a couple of curtains, and did the last verse of 'Gunga Din' as an encore. Six years old I was, and they damned near had to use the hook to get me off."

They talked for another quarter of an hour, and then Mr Franklin said he must go. Pip saw him to the door, they thanked each other for the evening, and she laid a hand on his shoulder.

"You're a gent, Mr American, d'you know that?" she said. "Your Peggy's a lucky girl."

"I don't know about that – what makes you think so?"

"Never mind," said Pip, mysteriously, and then added: "All right, then – I'll tell you. You didn't spoil the evening, the way most men would – married or not. By trying it on, I mean."

"Don't think I wouldn't like to," said Mr Franklin.

"Don't think I wouldn't, either," said Pip. "But I'm glad you didn't." She slid her arms up round his neck and kissed him gently but firmly on the mouth, and he kissed her gently back and said, in a bass voice:

"You don't have to if you don't want to, you know."

"Oh, get out before I put you on the street!" giggled Pip, pushing him over the threshold. "Here, mind and give us the office about the Royal Academy – it's in May. And I'll show you works of art." She gave him a wave. "Chin-chin."

357

He walked out to the street, turning west, and never noticed the taxi which pulled away from the kerb opposite and trundled past him towards Russell Square.

19

A few days later the nation learned to its relief that the Curragh Mutiny was over. Mr Asquith announced to an attentive Parliament that there was no question of using the Army against the Ulster Loyalists, the officers who had resigned withdrew their resignations, and there was rejoicing in the Protestant North, and among all opponents of Irish Home Rule, at what they interpreted as a climb-down by the Government.

One person who did not rejoice was Mr Franklin, scanning the papers in vain for any mention of exceptions among the officers who had withdrawn their resignations. As it stood, it looked as though Arthur must be back in the Army again, in which case there was the delicate matter of ten thousand pounds of Mr Franklin's hard-won fortune floating about unaccounted for. He waited a day or two, partly because Peggy's arrival back from Switzerland was imminent, and partly in the hope of receiving word from Sir Charles, or from Arthur himself, that the heir to the Clayton baronetcy was, indeed, a civilian after all. Then, since nothing happened, he wrote to Sir Charles at Oxton Hall, seeking news, but making no mention of the funds provided for Arthur's business career.

By way of reply he received a visit from Sir Charles himself, who had arrived in London ostensibly to get his hair cut at his favourite establishment in St James's, but in fact, Mr Franklin guessed, to discuss the recent sensation with cronies at his clubs and the War Office. He called at Wilton Crescent after lunch, apparently in excellent spirits, although he expressed disappointment at finding his daughter still absent.

"You're having a long spell as a grass widower," he said, and Mr Franklin nodded, offered refreshment, and asked if Sir Charles had got his letter.

"Yes, indeed, it arrived before I left. It surprised me a little, because I had assumed Peggy was at home – you didn't mention she was still away – and that Arthur would have been in touch with her before he went off."

"Went off? Didn't he go back to the Army, then?"

Sir Charles smiled thinly. "Oh, yes, he went back. But I gather he was one of the last to withdraw his resignation, with a great show of reluctance – he even suggested to his commanding officer that it might be as well if he were given extended leave – the implication being that if the Government even looked like going back on their word, he'd slap in his papers again. He seems to have played the firebrand rather strongly, and his C.O. wisely decided he'd be better out of the way for a couple of months. So the young scoundrel has got himself a pleasant holiday out of it – and impressed his seniors that he's a man of staunch Loyalist sympathies. No bad thing these days. I just hope he doesn't overdo it; he's a shrewd child, but one wouldn't want him to give his chiefs the impression that he's too clever by half."

No, thought Mr Franklin, we wouldn't want that to happen. Aloud he asked: "How do you know all this? – there haven't been any details in the press, of course."

Sir Charles raised his fine brows. "Why, from Arthur himself. He came over to Oxton the day before yesterday – as soon as he'd got leave. Stayed overnight and was off yesterday morning – came up to Town in fact. I assumed he would look in on you on his way to the Continent."

"No," said Mr Franklin, "he didn't call here."

"Ah, well, I expect he wanted to catch the boat and didn't have time." Sir Charles smiled indulgently. "I'm afraid the younger generation are too much for me – here one moment and off like lightning the next. I can't help wondering if Arthur found some pressing attraction in Switzerland while he was over there with his regimental sports team, and is now off hotfoot to make sure no one else cuts him out. It won't surprise me in the least if he turns up with some French charmer or Germanic ice maiden on his arm, and informs me that this is to be my new daughter-in-law. Peggy didn't hint at anything like that in her letters?"

Mr Franklin shook his head. "Just said that Arthur had been and gone with his bob-sleigh outfit." He must make absolutely certain that there was no misunderstanding. "So there's absolutely no possibility now that Arthur will be leaving the Army?"

"None that I can see. The Home Rule Bill goes through in about six weeks, I fancy, so if there's to be another Curragh Mutiny it will have to be before then. And our intelligent Arthur has made sure that he'll be well out of the way."

"I see. Yes, he seems to have extricated himself pretty neatly. I'm glad – from what Peggy said it seemed certain he was going to resign for keeps. She didn't have any doubts about it."

"You surprise me," said Sir Charles. "I've never doubted the exact opposite. And Arthur and Peggy usually have no secrets from each other. Of course, as I think I said once before, it's quite possible that he's simply been pulling her leg, and she took it seriously."

Mr Franklin made a noncommittal noise, and wondered again what the reaction would be if he told Sir Charles that the leg-pull had cost him ten thousand pounds. Stark disbelief, probably – and thereafter an ugly family crisis. No, it was not fair to precipitate that before Peggy – or Arthur, more probably – had been given a chance to explain.

The opportunity came two days later, after Sir Charles had returned to the country, when Peggy came sweeping in from Switzerland, bright-eyed and glowing with the pale suntan acquired on the ski slopes, embraced Mr Franklin with enthusiasm, leaned back in his arms to laugh at him with sheer pleasure, and then kissed him long and contentedly before collapsing into a chair with cries of happy exhaustion. It had been hectic, but tremendous fun, he should have been there, what had he been doing while she was away, had he missed her because she had missed him, she was absolutely fagged out but it was wonderful to be home again, she had skied and skated every day, the Stewarts were the most fearful old fusspots, Poppy Davenport had made a complete idiot of herself over a Finnish ski instructor who hardly spoke a word of English but was six feet five inches tall which had excited Poppy because he was probably the only man in Switzerland capable of carrying her off in his arms, she (Peggy) had gone bob-sleighing several times and won the ladies' prize on the Village Run, a handsome cup which was in her trunk – and that reminded her, she had something for him . . .

Mr Franklin was only too pleased to let the happy spate of words pour out of her, content to sit smiling with pleasure at the sight of the slender, graceful body half-reclining on the couch, and the beautiful face full of laughing animation. He was advancing to kiss her again when she remembered what she had brought him; they clung together for a moment, and then she was off to the hall, to return presently with a small packet which she presented to him, while she placed a forefinger beneath her chin and dropped him a sweeping curtsey.

He took it in one hand and encircled her waist with the other.

"You don't have to bring me presents," he said, laughing. "Just bring yourself – that's all the present I want." He emphasized the point by kissing her again, squeezing her bottom with the embracing hand until she wriggled free.

"Open it, then! Carefully – it's quite fragile."

He undid the wrapping, and gasped in admiration at the contents – a beautifully-fashioned gold watch with a gold chain and clasp to fit round the wrist. He had seen them, of course, but it had never occurred to him to wear one himself – they were still rare enough to be curiosities.

"But, Peggy, darling – that's magnificent! I've never seen anything like it!"

"It's Swiss," said Peggy, pleased. "Here – let me put it on for you." She fastened the clasp round his wrist, kissed him on the cheek, and said: "A present for a good boy from Geneva. Are there any letters for me?"

"On the hall table. But Peggy, this is a wonderful present ... " She was out of the room before he had finished the sentence, and when she returned and he was continuing to exclaim over the watch, she was already deep in the first letter from the bundle in her hand.

"It's from Grace Shaw – in Rome ... do you really like it, darling? I hoped you would. I'm so glad. Grace and Ralph have been in Venice – coming home on April the fifth – will I go to Wales with them for a week-end ... don't know about that, Grace, my pet, I don't think I could stand Ralph for more than two hours at a stretch, especially in Wales. And there's the Talbots' dance in aid of the sick kids – I'm sure that's the second week in April, so bad luck, Grace ... " She slit open another envelope. "Mark, darling, could you ring for some tea? I'm dying of thirst ... "

He resigned himself with good-humoured patience to wait until she had waded through her correspondence – this was the breath of life, and there would be no coherent conversation from her until she had satisfied herself that the London world still spun on its social axis. Fortunately, it never took very long; a quick glance at each letter, a brief summary aloud of sender's name and contents for his benefit, with her own frequently pungent comment, was the normal procedure; as she went through it, he wondered how to broach the subject of

362

Arthur – he was reluctant to disturb the pleasure of her homecoming, but if, as seemed likely, Arthur was up to something without his sister's knowledge, she would not thank her husband for keeping it from her any longer than was necessary. Still he hesitated – he looked across at the lovely face intent on the letter in her hand, and felt a surge of affection; he admired his new watch – it gave him inordinate pleasure to think of her carefully considering her choice in some Geneva jewellers, weighing what would please him best.

Peggy laid aside the last letter with a sigh of relief, and reached for the tea-cup which the maid had set down at her elbow. "That's that," she exclaimed. "Now, then – what's been happening while I've been away?"

"Not too much. Your father was up a couple of days ago – he'd had Arthur at Oxton en route for the continent. You didn't run across him on you way home?"

"Arthur? On the continent?" She looked at him in surprise. "What on earth's he doing there?"

"On leave, apparently. Didn't you hear about all the excitement there's been in the Army in Ireland?"

"Oh, yes – Cecil Stewart said something about it. People resigning, or something. Why, what about that?"

"Well, Arthur was one of them – just as you said he would be. He resigned his commission – and then a week later he withdrew his resignation, like all the others, when the Government satisfied them that they wouldn't have to fight in Ulster."

Peggy hesitated, and then shook her head. "Sorry – I don't understand. You say Arthur resigned – and then went back? Why on earth should he do that?"

"That's what I'd like to know. Your father seemed to think it was natural enough – but I gather he never thought Arthur was serious about resigning in the first place. And yet Arthur convinced you that he *was* going to resign – didn't he?"

Again the momentary hesitation, and then Peggy said: "That's certainly what he told me – at least, it was the impression I got."

The delicate hedge sent a cold chill through Mr Franklin, but he deliberately kept his side of the conversation casual, almost uninterested.

"Me, too – from what you told me. I mean, he was pretty serious about going into business. He must have meant to resign, when he spoke to you."

363

"Yes." Peggy was sitting up now, frowning. "I can't think what he's playing at. Did he explain to Daddy at all?"

"Sure – your father is under the impression that the whole thing was a political exercise. But then – " he paused, keeping his eyes fixed on her profile " – your father doesn't know that Arthur got ten thousand pounds from you on the understanding that he was definitely going to quit the Army."

"Good lord!" She turned to stare at him, her eyes widening. "Oh – but that's silly! I mean – I'm sure he was going to resign. If he hasn't, or if he's changed his mind – well, there has to be some good reason, doesn't there?" She stood up, apparently in alarm, and he noticed that she was clasping her hands nervously. "He told me – I mean he was positive he was going to resign – that's what he said – and that's why he needed the cash . . . "

"That's the impression you got? How definite was he?"

"Oh . . . oh, absolutely definite. He was going to resign and go into business! Mark, if he hasn't – well, I'm sure that something must have happened – he must have changed his mind, or something – "

"But surely he'd have let us know? We were both expecting his resignation, and he gives it, and then withdraws it. Surely the first thing he'd do, when he's had all that money from you, would be to let you know what's happening. But he hasn't even written to you, or left a message. He's just gone off to the continent without saying a word."

"Perhaps . . . I don't know." Peggy seemed to be at a loss – more at a loss than he would have expected. Knowing her, he would have guessed that after an initial blank astonishment she would have been angrily inquiring of no one in particular what the blazes Arthur thought he was doing; anger at her brother's irresponsibility would have seemed more natural than her present nervous bewilderment.

"Perhaps," Peggy suddenly said, "perhaps he was going to resign, but wanted to do it quietly . . . or something. And then this thing at the Curragh – " he noticed that her mention of the Curragh by name seemed to argue a closer knowledge of the incident than she had displayed a few moments ago " – perhaps when it blew up, and he had to resign with all the others, and then they went back, perhaps he felt he had to, too, and means to resign later on . . . "

"The reason he and they resigned was exactly the reason he gave you for resigning," said Mr Franklin. "I can't see any reason why he shouldn't stick to it."

"No – no, neither can I. I just don't understand it, Mark. God, he's an idiot! Oh, but there must be some good reason for it! I'm sure there is!"

He had been looking down, frowning, as she spoke; when he raised his head suddenly, he thought he caught an odd look in her eye – was it apprehension? Not anxiety about Arthur and whatever mystery lay behind his conduct, but anxiety about what Mr Franklin himself was thinking? There was something slightly unnatural about her attitude, but he could not put his finger on it. He only knew that Peggy, who carried frankness to the point of fault, and had never had an instant's hesitation in saying exactly what she thought, was now, for some reason, not telling him everything that was in her mind. So he took another way, with rather more guile than he would ever have believed himself capable of. For he did not meet her eye, as she might have expected him to do if she herself was under suspicion; instead he frowned heavily at the inkstand on his desk, as though thoroughly puzzled.

"It doesn't make sense. I don't get it. Did he ever say what kind of business he had in mind? – that could give us a clue, perhaps."

"No." Peggy shook her head. "No. He didn't."

It was then that Mr Franklin knew for certain that she was not only concealing something, but lying. Peggy had a hard head, she was eminently practical, she would never have dreamed of entrusting ten thousand pounds to Arthur without wanting to know every last detail about his schemes. Even if she had not known what they were at the time she herself got the money from Mr Franklin, she would have made absolutely sure she knew them before letting a penny into Arthur's hands. It simply wasn't in her nature to do otherwise. And yet now she was telling him that she had passed the money across without asking Arthur what it was for. No – that was simply not possible. It was, in fact, utterly ridiculous. Therefore she knew – or suspected – what the money was for, and was trying to conceal that knowledge from him. Mr Franklin felt slightly sick – it was so utterly unlike her that he shrank from believing it. Peggy was honest, if anyone in the world was honest – what on earth could make her dissemble with him? It must be something huge. Or perhaps he was wrong, perhaps he was jumping to conclusions. There was one way of making certain.

He looked up at her. "He didn't tell you – when you gave him the cheque?"

"But I didn't give it to him – I banked it, in the A.W.B.G.P. Fund."

"Didn't you mention it to him, though, when you saw him in Switzerland?"

"No – I didn't think about it. But, Mark, I'm sure it's all right – Arthur wouldn't do anything silly. If he's going to resign, he'll tell us what it's for – and if he isn't, why, he'll just give it back. He can't do anything else!"

She was asking him – she was pleading with him, he felt, not to push it any further. And he had not been mistaken: she was dissembling, trying to deceive him. If she had been honest – if she had, in an entirely uncharacteristic moment of carelessness, been so rash as to pay the cheque into the A.W.B.G.P. Fund without satisfying herself beforehand that Arthur's scheme was sound, her first instinct now would have been to seize the telephone and check with the bank to see if Arthur had drawn the money out. And if he had, she would have been after him like a tigress. But she wasn't doing that – she knew the cheque had been cashed, and she knew why, and she wasn't telling him.

Well, that was that. Was there some dime-novel explanation why Arthur had to have money – gambling debts, or making off with the regimental funds, or something? Nonsense – if that had been so, Peggy would have laid it on the line to him. A chilling thought struck him – was it for herself she had needed the money, and did Arthur not, in fact, figure in it at all? Whatever the answer, he couldn't ask her – if he examined his mind, he didn't really want to know what the answer was. He forced himself to look up at her, and smile, and shrug his shoulders; she was pale, and he wondered if he imagined that she looked relieved for a split second.

"Well," he said as lightly as he could. "We know what Arthur's like, don't we?" He shook his head in assumed mock despair. "I'm quite sure it's all right – I just wish the big chucklehead had told you what he was doing. Chances are he's changed his mind about resigning, and in all the excitement at the Curragh he's forgotten all about the money. I guess we ought to find out from him – your father probably knows where he's gone on the continent, and we can get in touch with him. I wouldn't be surprised if the money's in his pants pocket."

There was no doubt now of the relief in her face. And that, too, was sure proof. If her conscience had been clear, and Mr Franklin had said what he had just said, she would have looked at him as though he was mad, and assured him that if he was prepared to shrug it off, she wasn't, and she would have an explanation out of Arthur or know the reason why. But now the troubled, anxious look left her face, and she said:

"Yes – Daddy will know where he is, and we can find out. I just don't know – it's not like Arthur. He must have . . . well, he must have changed his mind, or there's some other explanation. I'm . . . I'm so sorry, Mark."

He found he could not look at her, and made a play of opening his desk drawer as though in search of something.

"Sorry, nothing. It's Brother Arthur who ought to be sorry, racketing off to Europe without a word to either of us. We'll make him sit up and take notice, though."

There was a silence, and then she said, with an emphasis that was almost defiant: "I'm positive it must be all right. It's just Arthur being completely thoughtless, the oaf." And then she added: "It's such an awful lot of money."

She was, he decided, like most straightforward people, an extremely bad actor; quite unused to dissembling, she did not know how to do it, but said mechanically the phrases which she supposed fitted the part.

"I'm not worried about the money," he said. And it was true. He would gladly have thrown ten thousand pounds on the fire to avoid the whole incident, to be spared the knowledge that Peggy was deceiving him. And to avoid the unhappiness that she surely must be feeling – oh, she must have some reason, and it must be a good reason. She was straight, and she wouldn't lie unless she had to. That was the thing he had to remember, that whatever dishonesty was being forced on her by circumstances that he couldn't imagine, underneath she was one hundred per cent. Whatever she was doing she was almost certainly doing for Arthur, and he couldn't blame her for that.

Honesty and straight dealing were ticklish things anyway. People didn't say everything that was in their minds, and was *suggestio falsi* any worse than *suppressio veri*? He would not tell Peggy, for example, that a week ago he had held Pip in his arms, when they kissed goodnight, and felt sensual, unfaithful pleasure in it – who knew but that, if Pip had been willing, he might not have been unfaithful in fact? No – he knew he would not; at the same time, it was something he was keeping from Peggy, and however innocent and trivial it was, it was best it should be so kept. Could he blame her, then, for keeping something from him, if it seemed good to her to do so? And in the scale of married trust, money secrets were surely the least important.

"I'm not worried about the money," he repeated. "But I *am* worried about seeing you look unhappy. Forget it – I'll find out from your father exactly where the big hunk has gone, and then we'll see what he's up to."

But Sir Charles, when approached, was little help. Arthur had spoken of visiting Germany; indeed, Sir Charles thought he remembered the Hamburg boat being mentioned. But where in the Fatherland he was to be found was anyone's guess; he had taken wandering continental holidays before, drifting where the spirit moved him, so unless he chose to write home while he was away there would be nothing for it but to wait until he turned up after a couple of months. Which was unsatisfactory, and yet in a way Mr Franklin welcomed it. Better to leave things as they were, at least for the time being, than have Peggy made miserable – and he had a shrewd idea that the secret concealed was better than the secret revealed. He did not want to see Peggy forced into a position where she had to admit to something which, whatever Mr Franklin thought about it, would almost surely lower Peggy in her own self-esteem, would make her feel that she was smaller in his eyes. Anyway, the whole thing might be perfectly harmless – or he might have misread Peggy entirely and been doing her a great injustice. And if in the end he finished up ten thousand pounds (dear God, that was fifty thousand dollars!) poorer . . . well, if it spared unhappiness, it was cheap at the price.

So he let it lie, and was cheered to see Peggy going on her way undisturbed; by next day, in fact, she seemed to have forgotten the matter, or else had decided not to mention it again. By the week-end she was back in her London routine of calls, parties, dances, teas, and Mr Franklin, determined to do all in his power to improve their relationship, stifled his dislike of polite society, and squired her about whenever the opportunity arose. To his delighted surprise, she seemed pleased, and April that year now and then approached the happiness of a second honeymoon; they went to the theatre (and heard the stunned silence followed by the shocked buzz and stifled giggles which greeted Miss Doolittle's first public rendering of "Not bloody likely!" in what one critic described as Mr Shaw's sanguinary play), they went to numerous tea dances, and even gave one themselves in the garden behind their Wilton Crescent home, with boards on the lawn and covered trellis overhead; they rode together in the Park and dined out several times on their own, apart from attending dinner parties.

And in the meantime more and more news filled the papers of Volunteers massing and drilling in Ulster, as the time for the third reading of the Irish Home Rule Bill in May drew nearer, and while the gaiety of the London scene seemed brighter than ever, and long hours of sunshine gave promise of a brilliant summer ahead, in Cabinet rooms and newspaper offices and Ministry corridors there was an air of tension growing as men realized that the time was approaching when the Lambeg drums would thunder and the flags of white horse and red hand would take the breeze in Ulster, and the ranks of the stern-faced men would close as the gates of Derry had closed two and a half centuries earlier. Two and a half centuries in recorded time, yesterday in the minds of the Scotch-Irish who saw their freedom threatened and were ready to die in its defence. "A clean break or come and fight us"; no one could doubt that Carson meant exactly that, and that unless some compromise was reached at the eleventh hour, there would be civil war.

The blow, when it came, fell on Belfast Lough one night in late April, and on Wilton Crescent the following evening.

They were quietly at home for once, in deference to Sir Charles, who was staying with them on his monthly visit to Town; dinner over, the three of them were in the billiard room, Peggy and Mr Franklin playing bagatelle while the baronet stretched himself comfortably in a chair beside the scoreboard, and shook his head as his daughter, who was uncommonly good at the game, tinkled the bright metals balls into the 500, 1000, and Replay pens.

"Now we see how the young matrons of Belgravia beguile their time," he remarked. "You should keep her on a tight rein, Mark. If she ran up this kind of score in a public hall she would be arrested."

"Just for that, I'll give you fifty up at billiards presently," said Peggy, intent on a shot. "At a penny a point – that should teach you." She pushed her cue, watched the ball curve round the long slate board, rebound from pin to pin, and finally settle in the 2000 cup. "Now then, Mark, let's see you beat that." She took a cup of coffee from the tray which Samson had just brought in, and sauntered to the open French windows, looking out at the dusky garden. "What a gorgeous evening! It's like summer already. Coming for a stroll in the garden, Mark?"

"Hold on," said Mr Franklin, concentrating on the bagatelle cue.

"I'm going to make three figures or die in the attempt." Sir Charles, lounging in his chair, had picked up the evening paper which Samson had brought with the coffee, and was scanning it idly; they heard him give a soft whistle of astonishment.

"Well! That's the cat among the pigeons with a vengeance!"

"Essex beaten by an innings again?" wondered Peggy, from her position by the window.

"Rather more than that. Listen to this." Sir Charles read aloud: " 'In the hours of darkness a merchant ship, the *Fanny*, ran the naval blockade off Belfast Lough, and landed the largest cargo of illicit arms ever seen in Ireland. It is estimated' " – his voice altered in astonishment '— that fifty thousand rifles and three million rounds of ammunition were put ashore from the vessel, which was manned by Ulster Volunteers.' " He lowered the paper. "That is almost incredible. A rifle and sixty rounds of ammunition for each of fifty thousand men – why, it's enough for an army! Well, if anyone thought Carson was bluffing, they know better now. He can start his war whenever he likes – and win it, too, so far as the Irish Nationalists are concerned."

"Or lay a hand of aces on the conference table," said Mr Franklin, his eyes on the bagatelle board.

"Indeed he can. And the Navy seem to have known all about this arms ship, but simply let it through. Well, well – first Curragh, and now the senior service show their hand – they won't stir a finger against Carson, either."

"So Mr Asquith is going to have to think again," said Mr Franklin, laying down his cue. "Fifteen hundred, Peggy; I admit your female superiority."

"Good heavens!" Sir Charles was intent on the paper. "No – I can't take that. Listen: 'The rifles are of the latest Mauser pattern, and it is reliably reported that they were recently purchased in Germany by Loyalist agents, who received every assistance from the German government. A German diplomatist of rank is said to be arriving in Belfast shortly, and is expected to confer with Loyalist leaders.' "

Peggy set down her coffee cup on the table by the window. "Coming, Mark? It'll be too chilly in a moment."

"Well, we know Carson is capable of almost anything, but that's not to be believed." Sir Charles was still with his paper. "Nothing could injure him more than to drag a foreign power into the Irish question – and Germany, of all countries! It's unthinkable – inviting

370

the Kaiser into a British quarrel? Not that he wouldn't love to stir up mischief for us, but Carson couldn't be so foolish, surely. German arms, German diplomats!"

Mr Franklin picked up a coffee cup and was carrying it across to join Peggy. "It doesn't sound likely," he said. "If the guns happen to be German, that could give rise to all kinds of wild rumours, but it doesn't mean they were supplied *by* Germany. I imagine you could buy Mausers anywhere." He stopped halfway to take a sip of his coffee.

"These came from Germany, all right," said Sir Charles. "The report says the ship sailed from Hamburg. Well, if that's true, and Carson is supping with that particular devil, he'd better look for an outsize spoon . . . "

But Mr Franklin never heard the end of the sentence. He was standing like a man frozen, the cup poised above its saucer, staring at his wife, stunned by the thought that was beating in his mind. It was impossible – but one look at Peggy's face told him it was true. She was standing stock-still by the French windows, watching him; her eyes were open with apprehension, and the colour had left her cheeks. For a moment they stared at each other in silence, and then she turned abruptly and went into the garden. Mr Franklin remained still for a few seconds longer; then he carefully set down his cup, and said in a quiet, conversational voice:

"I think I'll just join Peggy in the garden."

"Forgive me if I don't come, too." Sir Charles smiled up from his paper, but Mr Franklin was already out of the room.

She was beside the conservatory, turned to face him; he stopped short in front of her.

"Hamburg," he said. "You knew, didn't you? That's where Arthur's gone – that's where ten thousand pounds has gone! To buy guns for the Ulster rebels!"

She looked at him steadily, apparently composed; she certainly did not look guilty – if anything, there was an assurance in the lift of her head that was almost defiant.

"Yes," she said. "I knew. I'm sorry about it, Mark." But there was no contrition in her voice.

"Sorry?" For a moment he was at a loss for words. "How long have you known? Did you know before you went to Switzerland – when you told me that cock-and-bull nonsense about Arthur's quitting the Army, and needing capital? Did you know then?"

"Yes, I knew then. But it wasn't cock-and-bull, at the time. He thought he would have to resign. It was only after Curragh that he decided it would be more useful if he stayed on in the Army. But it wouldn't have made any difference about the money, anyway; that was in Germany a week after you gave it to me."

The cold calmness of it took his breath away. He stood facing her, and she saw him look as she had not seen him since the first moment of their meeting, when he had faced the huntsman across the trapped fox, and she had seen that blaze in his eyes, and known this was a dangerous man. But she stood her ground, while he controlled his anger, and when he spoke his voice was deliberately soft.

"Why the hell didn't you tell me? Why did you have to cheat it out of me? If you wanted the money, why in God's name didn't you tell me what it was for? Peggy! I'm your husband, aren't I?"

It was hardly the reaction she had expected from him, and she, in her turn, was taken aback: her voice faltered a little.

"Arthur," she began, and hesitated. "Arthur said we couldn't take the risk of your refusing. We had to make sure. There was no other way of doing it."

"No other way except to lie to me, and trick the money out of me, like ... like ... " He stopped, struggling to keep his temper. If he was closer to losing it than he could remember, it had nothing to do with the money, but with the fact that she had felt it necessary to lie to him, to use her sex to pluck him like some bunco artist's moll. "Spinning me that bill of goods about not knowing the details, and Arthur's friends wanting to keep it secret – by God, they wanted to keep it secret! And you knew! I can't believe it, Peggy! Giving me that little-girl stuff, and doing your Delilah in your negligée! Dammit, couldn't you have come straight out? Why should you think I wouldn't give it you, if you asked fair and square?"

Anger on her face was followed by surprise, and then doubt hardening into certainty. "You wouldn't have. I knew you wouldn't. I've heard you talk about Ireland, when it's been mentioned. It means nothing to you, you've no interest in either side." The little curl of the lip was showing at the corner of her mouth. "You wouldn't have given ten thousand pounds, to me or anyone else, to smuggle contraband guns to the Volunteers. I don't believe it."

It dawned on him that she was perfectly sincere, and the irony of it shook him. She had complete trust in his honesty; in her eyes he was the hundred per cent. straightforward American of the novels

372

and cartoons, the law-abiding pillar of rectitude and integrity who would never stoop beneath his own steadfast Republican ideals. That was how she saw him, and all the more so because they were of different generations; that was how he must seem to her – and why not? That was what he had been for the past five years; for all she knew, it was how he had always been. She had no way of knowing that the man she had married was an ex-Hole-in-the-Wall gunslick, a rider of the Wild Bunch, the man who had broken Kid Curry out of Deadwood jail and outshot Deaf Charley Hanks on the Cheyenne boardwalk. He had taken extreme care that no one should ever know, to bury the wild youngster who had followed the happy-go-lucky Cassidy in escapades that had seemed more like high-spirited games than the crimes they were. That was all behind him – except for the one horrific moment when Curry had come back like a ghost from another century – and she had never guessed. It would have been comic, if it had not led to this, but he was still too angry to see the irony of it.

"I wouldn't, wouldn't I? You're right, I don't care about Ireland, except as any man cares who'd rather see people live at peace than killing each other. But I do care about you – about us! Didn't that occur to you? And if you wanted something – wanted it bad enough to lie and deceive me – don't you think I'd have given it you? For heaven's sakes, people drop pennies in collecting boxes every day for Free Ireland and the Citizens' Army and Carson's Volunteers and the Empire Fund, don't they? Did you think because it was ten thousand pounds, I'd be a piker? Sure, I know nothing about Ireland, or the rights and wrongs. But you do, apparently, and Arthur goes around like King William incarnate, and your father says he sympathizes with Carson – well, what made you think I wouldn't? If you believe in the ... the cause, or whatever it is, that much – don't you think I would have been for it? Just because it was your cause?"

He might have expected remorse or contrition when she realized that she could have attained her end straightforwardly, but hardly the cold, unemotional expression on the beautiful face.

"There was no reason why I should believe that," she said. "It's a crime, in the eyes of the law. Why should I think you'd lend yourself to it – even for me? Anyway, most Americans' sympathies lie on the other side, don't they?"

"Most Americans?" The flatly-stated assumption was a gall to his subconscious Anglo-Saxon pride. "What d'you think I am, Peggy?

Some shanty Mick from Boston who sleeps with his hat on? What has being American got to do with it, anyway? I'm the man you married – the man you're supposed to love and trust! And what you're saying is that you didn't believe I'd give you the money, didn't believe I'd help you if you asked me – so you just went about cold-blooded to swindle it out of me! Is that it?"

He thought he saw her flinch, but when she spoke again her voice was steady.

"If you choose to regard it so . . . I've said there was no other way, and that we could not risk making a mistake. I didn't like doing it – swindling, as you call it – "

"Well what else is it?"

"Very well, you married a swindler. Now you know. I have told you that I'm sorry – I certainly did not like deceiving you." She managed to convey that what she had disliked was not any offence against him, but the violating of her own principles. "And if, as you say, it was unnecessary, then that doubles the regret – "

"Peggy!" He came a step closer. "For God's sake! Anyone listening to this would think you were the injured party! I'm the one who has been deceived – but all I'm asking is why? You knew I loved you, that I'd do anything for you, give you anything within reason – "

"That's just it, isn't it? I assumed that you would not think this within reason. Apparently I was wrong – very well, I was mistaken. That being so, I had to swindle you – "

"Oh, drop that! It's just a word – "

"An appropriate one, as you've pointed out. It happens that I didn't do it lightly; indeed, I nearly didn't do it at all." There were tears in her eyes suddenly, and instinctively he reached towards her, but she stepped back against the glass of the conservatory. "But there was no other way."

"Did it matter all that much?" He shook his head. "More than our marriage?"

"It mattered to Arthur. It mattered to me. Perhaps you don't understand how much these things can matter. You probably think Sir Edward Carson is a fanatic, that freedom of religion and law are unimportant – "

"Of course I don't! But I never guessed that you . . . that you . . . well, took it to heart like this. I didn't know, Peggy. That day, when you first talked about Arthur resigning, you said Irish politics made you sick, or something like that; you talked as if he was the firebrand and that you . . . well, that you didn't care – "

"I was out to deceive and swindle, remember," she said, and before the blank hostility he felt suddenly baffled and sick. First, the full realization that she had gone about, methodically and coldly, to cajole money out of him, and now the discovery, when she was confronted with it, that any remorse she might feel was certainly not for him. Indeed, she was blaming him for being the witness of her dishonesty, and blaming him with a bitterness that he could not understand.

"If only you'd told me." In his bewilderment he tried to be fair, to decide what his reaction would have been. "Yes, I'd have tried to talk you out of it, I guess, tried to . . . to convince you that buying guns for Irishmen to kill each other doesn't help anybody – "

"The money was not for the guns – they'd been purchased long ago, for considerably more than ten thousand pounds. It was to charter the ship – there was no money left."

"Ship or guns, it's all the same! All right, I'd have tried to stall you, to talk you out of it, I suppose . . . but if you'd really wanted it, if it meant that much to you . . . if you think I wouldn't have given it you – then you're wrong, Peggy. I'd have given it you, just as I'd give you anything I've got."

He was obviously sincere, and a little of the hardness left her face. "I've told you – I didn't know that."

"Couldn't you have trusted me? Taken a chance? Dammit, you must have known you couldn't get away with it, that I'd find out – "

"We did get away with it. That was why I couldn't take the risk. We had to get away with it. You were bound to find out, in the end, I knew that – but by then it would be done, and whatever you said would be too late."

Again the matter-of-fact certainty of it left him helpless. This was a new Peggy, and yet a Peggy he had always half-known was there, underneath the beauty and the boundless high spirits – a calm, determined, and in the long run, quite ruthless young woman who knew what she wanted and would get it, whatever the cost. If she counted it as cost – but she must; he had seen the tears in her eyes a moment ago.

"You knew I'd find out – didn't you stop to think what would happen then? What it might do to us – to our marriage? What you've done – whatever name you give it, swindling, or deceiving, or . . . I don't know – can you do that to someone you love?"

375

He was watching her for some sign of softening, for anything except this impersonal composure. She looked at him for a moment, and then away.

"I don't know, Mark. What has it done – to you? I know it has left you ten thousand pounds poorer – "

"You know that's got nothing to do with it! I just don't understand you. You've done this, and I can even see why you did it – if I'd known it was so important . . . but I never had the chance to know. You didn't tell me, because you say you couldn't be sure I'd agree. All right, I can appreciate that – although why you had to regard me as some kind of Victorian ogre instead of as a husband who's devoted to you . . . don't you understand, Peggy, I love you? You could ask me for anything." He shook his head. "But you didn't know. So it's done – and naturally I was shocked by it. But what I don't understand is . . . " He searched her face, looking for any flicker of softness or affection " . . . is the way you are now. I don't know what it is – whether you're ashamed, or resentful at the way it's come out, or whether you just don't care." She said nothing, so he went on: "I guess you thought this . . . cause, this ship, was more important to you than I. Was it? I guess it must have been."

She turned to look at him again, and shook her head. "I didn't look at it in that way. I'm sorry if it has shocked you, or caused you distress, and if you find my attitude now . . . strange, then I'm sorry for that as well. What else should I say, Mark? That I regret what I've done? That I wouldn't do it again? But I would, you see. At least I'm honest that far. Or am I supposed to ask to be forgiven, like a good little girl?" The hard look was about her mouth again, the little sneering curl that he hated to see. "I'm sorry, but that isn't my way."

He drew himself up a little, considering her. "What is your way, then? Just to forget about it – all right. Just to regard me as someone who's around to be . . . tolerated? And used when you want to use him? But not to be trusted?"

She looked at him for a long moment, very intently, without expression, and he found himself realizing, with a sudden pang, how beautiful she was, and how great the gulf was between them. At last she spoke, quietly and deliberately:

"What is your own way, Mark? Just to forget about it? All right. Just to regard me as someone who's around to be . . . tolerated. And used – when you want to use her. But not to be trusted."

They were facing each other in the silence that followed when there was a creak at the French windows, and Sir Charles's voice was heard:

"What about that fifty-up at billiards, young woman? Or are you two going to stand out there spooning all night? You must be freezing."

"Coming, Daddy." Peggy turned away and walked quickly towards the shaft of light from the window. "Have you got the balls set up? I expect twenty start, you know – didn't I mention it? Oh, come, if it's a penny a point . . . "

Mr Franklin stood by the conservatory, looking at his new wristwatch, remembering the smiling girl who had given it to him, and thinking of the other girl he had encountered tonight. He was numbed; it had been like stepping on a stair that wasn't there. The money, Arthur's resignation, the arms ship, all seemed vague details in a puzzle that didn't matter; all that mattered was that pale, lovely face in the dusk, with the auburn halo of hair, looking at him with the appraising impersonality it might have bestowed on a total stranger, showing no contrition, no guilt, above all, no feeling. If she had raged, or burst into tears, or begged his forgiveness, or argued to justify herself – he could have understood all those, and dealt with them, and he knew it would have ended with him comforting her, and assuring her that the money didn't matter, and all the rest of it. For what he had said was true – he would have done anything for her. And she could have played on that, if she had wanted to.

But she didn't want to. The way she had looked, and spoken, had been clinical, almost. Had all the rest, all the past been just a sham? Certainly their marriage had not been all he had wished, but he had been content to be in love with her, and had supposed her content, too; they had been happy enough, after their fashion. He had known he was not very necessary – or not often necessary – to her ordinary life, but he had never doubted that she needed him, as he needed her, in the deepest sense, which was based on love. But if tonight had told him anything, it was that he had been mistaken. Peggy did not need him, and probably never had.

Except, apparently, in one way. The thought was born of pain, and frustration, and anger, and no doubt a generous measure of self-pity. But if the emotions were unworthy, that was no reason to disregard the thought itself. He had been extremely necessary where money was concerned. Peggy herself had been enabled to live in high style which her father could never have provided, to have everything she wanted, to cut a splendid figure in society; her brother had been

377

maintained in a fashionable regiment; her father's estate had been rescued from bankruptcy – the great Clayton revival had been financed entirely by him. Two of the family – he could acquit Sir Charles – had even been able to take up gun-running on the money he had sweated out of the Tonopah mud. Jesus, the English landed gentry! No wonder they'd taken over a quarter of the globe. The words ran through his mind even while he told himself that he was being despicable . . . and yet the thought was there, the question he had thrust resolutely aside when the matter of Arthur's allowance had arisen, when Peggy had stated her wish to live in Belgravia, when Sir Charles had agreed to the metamorphosis of Oxton estate. It was an ugly question, and all the uglier because he knew the answer beyond a shadow of doubt.

If the American who had so ridiculously got a fox trapped in his lunch-basket, had subsequently proved to be of moderate means, would he have been quite so welcome at Oxton Hall? Would the daughter of the house have taken such an interest in him? Would the father have encouraged his attentions, and congratulated him so warmly as a son-in-law? Would Peggy have been so concerned to see that his room was comfortable that night of the blizzard?

They were not new questions, but they had not troubled him before, because he was a realist. Old Man Clayton had seen him coming – very well. So had Peggy – very well. Arthur had been damned glad he'd come – very well. You can only get it where it is. That had been true for him, too – he had got a beautiful wife, a comfortable acceptance in a new land, a high place in its society (which, by the way, had been opened to him by someone rather more exalted than the Claytons, to wit, Edward Rex et Imperator). Still, she had been a beautiful, and he supposed, loving wife to the good. But, in those terms, she hadn't kept the bargain; she had demonstrated as much tonight.

Unless that *was* the bargain, in her terms – to be a beautiful decoration, companion, concubine, hostess, mistress of his household. Was that what she had been saying when she had repeated his own words: "What is your own way, Mark?" Perhaps he had expected too much, in expecting more. Perhaps, from the standpoint of her youth, she gave all that she thought necessary. And considered herself entitled to plunder him deceitfully at the same time.

Well, he was the last person on God's earth who was entitled to object to that. He had plundered in his time. On the other hand, he'd never promised to love, honour, and obey the Union Pacific Railroad or the Farmer's Bank. He had never smiled lovingly at them, or breathed his affection in their ear, or lain in their arms under a tropic moon, or moaned with passion in their embrace, or brought them gold watches from Switzerland, or straightened their necktie, or smiled with pride beside them in Buckingham Palace, or walked hand in hand with them slowly through the fallen wet leaves at Castle Lancing.

Oh, God, Peggy, he thought. It was no use telling himself he was unjust – that he, too, was a deceiver who had married a girl with never a word to her that he had been an outlaw, a criminal, even a killer (not a murderer; Deaf Charley had reached first). To conceal all that had been a kindness. He could have forgiven her if she had robbed him, swindled him, cleaned out his pockets while he slept – if only she had done it in the determination that he would never know. But she had deceived him in the certain knowledge that it would be discovered; that had not troubled her. If she had hesitated, it had been for the thought of her own derogation, not for what it might do to their marriage. To that she was indifferent.

He walked back to the French windows, and into the billiard room. Whatever he felt, he could keep his face as well as anyone, even a Clayton. Sir Charles turned to smile at him and nod ruefully towards the table, where Peggy was placing her ball in the "D" and appraising the red and white.

"She needs five more," said Sir Charles. "I blush to admit that I am eighteen behind, and that she is playing without a start."

They watched as she settled her white, lined up the cue, and played a slow cannon, nudging the red up the cushion. Then she came round the table, stretched across from the middle pocket, and with extreme care cut the red deftly into the top bag. Sir Charles laughed and exclaimed, Peggy bowed, and then looked across the table at Mr Franklin and said: "Care for a game, Mark?"

Her eyes were serene, her voice was cheerfully casual, there was even a little smile on her lips.

"You'll get little joy out of it, I can tell you," said Sir Charles to Mr Franklin, counting out his coppers. "One and eleven, you little shark." He handed the money to his daughter, who slipped it into her evening bag.

"Well, Mark?" She took up her cue again. "Shall we play? We might as well."

He looked across the table at her thoughtfully, while Sir Charles,

suspecting nothing, chuckled and settled himself to watch. Mr Franklin turned and took a cue from the rack.

"Why not?" he said.

20

On the first of May London was charmed by the sight of omnibuses lit by electricity for the first time; one or two people complained that it was too bright and garish, but for the most part pedestrians were happy to turn and stare as the jewelled monsters rumbled past, their interiors bathed in the cold, white light, a brilliant reminder that this was the scientific twentieth century in which technical wonders were becoming commonplace. A few traditionalists might shake their heads and wonder where all this material progress was leading, and whether the good old values and institutions were not in danger of being lost in the dazzling glare of the new age; but even they were cheered when His Majesty the King, attending a notoriously plebeian occasion, the Football Association Challenge Cup Final between Burnley and Liverpool at Crystal Palace, was greeted with thunderous acclamation by the commonalty. More – after His Majesty had presented the Cup to the victorious Burnley team, their captain had called for three cheers for the sovereign, the teams had given them with enthusiasm, and the whole vast mob had then sung "God Save the King". Lighted buses, jazz music, and disgusting pictures at the Royal Academy notwithstanding, England was England still.

And while those who had read the prophetic novels of Mr Wells might wonder sometimes if the march of technology – symbolized by that masterpiece of marine engineering, the great floating palace, the *Aquitania*, which was about to make her maiden voyage – might not prove to have a less happy side to it, they were in a minority. They did not include Mr Franklin, whose literary nourishment that month was taken from the pages of the new romantic seller, *The Gates of Doom*, by Mr Sabatini. Mr Franklin would not have considered himself a romantic, but like most people encountering the deceptively austere Anglo-Italian's work for the first time, he found himself helplessly ensnared by the story, and with nothing for it but to read to the end. It was about a young Jacobite agent who gambled at cards for the right to woo a great heiress – he intended to apply her vast fortune in the Jacobite interest, but of course he finished up falling in love with the girl, and there were mistaken identities and escapes and the hero survived a Tyburn hanging, and Mr Franklin finished it at a sitting and missed his dinner in consequence.

It was, he supposed, an unlikely story in retrospect, and yet he had accepted it unhesitatingly as he read – a tribute to the gifts of the writer. Anyway, what was unlikely? No one knew better than he did that truth had a brutal habit of beggaring fiction – if ever he doubted that, there were patched bullet-holes in the walls at Lancing Manor to remind him. What struck him, as he closed the book, was how simple and soluble had seemed the romantic problems of the principals in the story – with his own marital difficulties ever present even as he read, it seemed to him that Captain Harry Gaynor had had a relatively easy passage in winning the heart of the heroine, despite misunderstandings, unhappy appearances, Bow Street Runners, hangmen, moneylenders, and treacherous rivals. They were trifles compared with the unimagined, intangible barriers that could come between a man and a woman in reality – or so it seemed to him as he slipped the book back on to its shelf in his study and contemplated his position for the hundredth time.

Peggy had gone down to Cornwall, to spend a week yachting with friends, leaving him to try to make sense of the days that had elapsed since their confrontation in the garden. He had determined, as they played billiards that evening, to let things be; eventually it must right itself, she must say something, matters could not rest forever as they had been left. It had been a wary, artificial, anxious time for him, waiting to see ... what? Some change in her, some sign that she wanted to be reconciled, some crumbling of that outward composure that would give him the opportunity to reach her again. But nothing happened. Peggy seemed determined to behave as though nothing *had* happened, as though no crisis in their relationship had been reached, and in the face of that implacable serenity he felt himself helpless. She was civil, pleasant, cheerful even, as attentive as she had ever been to him; she went about her social round, filled her engagements, chatted about them to him, greeted him amiably at meals, kissed him goodbye when she went out, and pecked his cheek when she came home; to all outward appearance things were exactly as they had been before that miserable night.

He told himself that she couldn't keep up the pretence for long, but as the days passed he began to realize that he was wrong; that she simply did not care. She was capable of carrying on as though nothing was changed, because for her nothing, in any deep sense, was changed. He only realized it after, in a desperate attempt to break the barrier down, he had made love to her – and discovered that for her there was no barrier to break. She had responded, to his amazement and joy, warmly at first and then with passion, but when it was over, and he had tried to talk about the things that must be talked about, she had simply looked at him impassively and said: "No. Don't talk about that, Mark. Leave things as they are," and he saw with hopeless clarity that there was no point in trying to touch her, since there was nothing in her to be touched, and nothing to be done except meet her on her own terms.

So the outward appearance was maintained, with an inward despair on his part, but with apparent serenity on hers. And curiously, it was not difficult to keep up the masquerade, probably because for her it was no masquerade at all; for the sake of surface harmony, Mr Franklin must be the actor. The alternative would have been to sulk in silence, which was not only alien to his nature, but would not, he knew, have produced the slightest change in her attitude. As things were, he was at least not constantly reminded of her indifference.

Heroes of romance, Mr Franklin reflected, faced no such strange situations, such uneasy relationships. Or, if they did, they hid their emotions under an imperturbable mask – which made him smile, since it was precisely what he was doing himself.

He stayed in Wilton Crescent when Peggy went down to Cornwall, because it happened to be the week in which he had promised to accompany Pip to the Royal Academy; it crossed his mind to mention the visit to Peggy, to see what reaction, if any, it provoked. Complete lack of interest, probably; worse still, she might assume that he was clumsily trying to make her jealous; worst of all, he admitted to himself, that would have been precisely what he was trying to do. And, in the circumstances, it would have been a pathetic attempt.

He took Pip to lunch at the Criterion, and they visited the gallery in the afternoon, among a fashionable crowd trying to convey an understanding of art, and an artistic crowd trying to convey a contempt for fashion. Neither succeeded, to their own mortification and the delight of Mr Bernard Shaw, who enjoyed the distinction of being both fashionable and artistic and quite plainly knew it, as he prowled among the paintings, stopping abruptly every now and then to straighten up to his commanding height and frown appraisingly at some particular canvas. However, since he confined himself to the two observations, "Remarkable!" and "Extraordinary!" no one had the slightest idea what his opinion was, as Mr Franklin remarked to Pip.

" 'Course not," said Pip, scornfully. "That's his stock in trade – look at his bloody plays, if you'll pardon the expression."

She had dressed in keeping with the occasion and her part in it; her costume was of pale rose and white silk in the fashionable Roman stripes, with a Medici collar; her blonde hair, worn in long ringlets, hung to her shoulders from beneath a tiny circular cap on the back of her head. "Classical innocence," she said, when Mr Franklin commended her appearance. "If you're a model you can either be bold and statuesque, or else look as though you took your mother with you to the studio to keep these randy artists at a safe distance. Now, let's go slowly, as though we're interested in the other pictures, too."

They joined the throng round the painting which was destined to become the most memorable, perhaps, of all that year's Academy: Dollman's dramatic canvas of Captain Oates setting out into the blizzard from the tent in which Scott's expedition were dying in the Antarctic waste. Everyone present knew the story – how Oates knowing that provisions were exhausted, had said "I'm just going outside", and had deliberately walked away to certain death so that the others might have a better chance of life. It followed that the picture was viewed with considerable respect – as it deserved to be, since it was also an extremely good painting.

"I think it's just lovely," said Pip. "Don't you? It makes me shiver just to look at it – all the snow and the black and him huddled up as if he was freezing." A critique which could hardly have been bettered by Mr Shaw himself, although he would probably not have sniffed and applied a tiny lace handkerchief to his eyes as he said it. "It's rotten sad, though, isn't it?" she added. "Him being so gallant, and it didn't do a ha'porth of good; they all froze to death anyway, poor perishers." Mr Franklin had no doubt that her emotion was genuine, although it also served to attract attention.

Pip's artistic soul was even more profoundly stirred, though in a noticeably less sentimental direction, by the other major attraction of the exhibition, the Hon. J. Collier's controversial painting "Clytemnestra". This depicted Agamemnon's adulterous and murderous queen as a strikingly handsome Amazon of impressive development, naked to the waist and glowering brazenly out at the viewers. The ladies among them coughed delicately and looked askance; the gentlemen frowned intently in a vain attempt to suggest that their interest was purely academic; a man in a clerical collar murmured that it was remarkable how the viewer's eye was inevitably attracted to the blood-stained sword in Clytemnestra's hand.

"If that's where his eye's attracted there's something wrong with him," muttered Pip darkly, her personal pride stirred as she surveyed her rival's generous proportions. "Disgusting, I call it. Anyway, if Mr Matania had painted me that way, they wouldn't be gawping at this, I can tell you. I may not be six feet tall with shoulders like a house side, but I've got better – "

Mr Franklin coughed hastily and the clergyman said nervously that it was remarkable that the artist had not included in the picture the queen's lover, Aegisthus; he felt the composition would have been enhanced by the addition of another, er, human figure.

"Well, there wouldn't have been all that much room, would there?" remarked Pip in a distinct undertone. "Anyway, I hate to think what he'd have done with a male model – "

Mr Franklin took her by the arm and steered her firmly away.

"I think we ought to look at your pictures now," he said, and Pip glowed with pride and led him to the fine canvas in which she was displayed with provocative decorum, lying prone and nude on a couch, awaiting abduction by Punic pirates. She surveyed her likeness with a sigh of profound satisfaction, glanced shyly at the considerable group of viewers who were admiring the work, and confided to Mr Franklin:

"They always slept bare in Roman days, you see, because it was warm. It's a pity, I suppose, that you can't see my face, but that's not the point, really, is it?"

Mr Franklin said soberly that he imagined not, and Pip explained that had her face been visible, it would have been necessary for it to register terror, which would have robbed the painting of its resigned pathos. "It's better to be all cowering and helpless, don't you think? I mean, you can do that with your body much more expressively. I reckon I've put on about an inch round the hips, though. D'you like it?"

"It's beautiful, Pip. He's a fine artist."

"You don't think it matters that you can't see my face?"

"No – it's better that it's turned away for a subject like this. Of course, it's a waste of a lovely face," he added gallantly. "But you're perfectly recognisable."

385

"Cheek!" said Pip, and they went to view her other painting, a strikingly different study, in which she was shown dancing across a field towards the viewer, clad in a few discreetly diaphanous wisps, with tiny sprites lending support. It was, Mr Franklin decided, of considerably less merit than the Matania, and yet he looked at it with immensely greater pleasure – for it *was* Pip, laughing gaily out of the painting, teasing with a happy abandon that made him want to smile as he looked at it; the artist, evidently setting out with the intention of glorifying the female figure for its own sake, and no doubt brightening calendars and chocolate boxes as well, had ended by capturing all her vivacity and spirit and sheer good nature. If the man in the clerical collar had been present, he might have accurately observed that the eye was drawn to the face, bright and pretty and – Pip.

"Of course, my hair isn't quite as dark as that, but it's not bad otherwise," said Pip critically. "And it isn't art, really, is it? – but I think I like it. It's a jolly sort of picture."

"I don't think I ever realized before what a nice girl you are," said Mr Franklin. "If it was for sale, I'd buy it."

"You wouldn't!" Pip was not given to blushing, but she went slightly pink with pleasure. "You really like it! Oh, I'm glad! I don't know that I should be – 'cos it's a bit commercial, you know, and cheeky – but if you think it's that nice, well, it means it's come off, doesn't it?"

She went on to tell him how long it had taken, and how she had had to pose holding onto a hall-stand, with one foot propped up on a chair and an electric fan blowing to keep her muslin draperies flowing properly – "Talk about freeze! Poor Captain Oates wasn't in it. But if you really like it, then I reckon it was worth it."

They lingered a few moments in front of the painting, and to Pip's delight a lady among the spectators recognized her and approached to ask if she was indeed the model. Mr Franklin was intrigued to observe that Pip received this with a demure politeness that stopped just short of reproaching the questioner with a breach of good taste; yes, she had posed for the painting, and also for the study by Mr Matania across the hall; her vocation, however, was the theatre, and modelling was an occasional obligement in the interests of pure art. Did she paint herself? Pip replied gravely that she had not exhibited personally – not at the Academy, and had the lady remarked the fine picture of Captain Oates, an exquisite blending of the dramatic and harmonic that satisfied the canons of both in an artistic whole? Mr

Franklin thought he recognized the description from a review in one of the papers, but the lady was deeply impressed.

By this time a small group had gathered to eavesdrop politely and view the centre of attraction with respectful admiration; Pip, whom Mr Franklin would have expected to blossom like the rose, appeared coolly unaware of the minor sensation she was creating, and presently, with a gentle smile at the lady, she took Mr Franklin's arm and passed sedately on; only when they had turned a corner did she stop to nudge him in the ribs, giggle exultantly, and exclaim: "What about that, then? Honest, I ought to get a percentage!"

They strolled about the gallery, revisiting the Matania which Pip, her identity now satisfactorily established, viewed with a cold appraisal, inviting Mr Franklin's attention, in an aside which was audible to the interested and attentive spectators, to the subtle shading of the draperies in an obscure corner of the painting; she even insisted that they view the area under discussion from close range, with the result that when they passed on, there was a general movement towards the lower left-hand corner of Mr Matania's canvas, and much peering and nodding and appreciative whispering about tone and line.

"You ought to be horse-whipped," said Mr Franklin quietly, and Pip looked serenely ahead and whispered: "Garn, it makes their day! By the time they're ready for tea they'll feel proper educated."

They were sauntering idly past the paintings, and Mr Franklin was on the point of suggesting that they seek some tea themselves, for the crowds in the gallery were now thinning out, when his eye was caught by two women standing by one of the largest canvasses in the hall, a scene from medieval mythology showing a boyish Galahad reverently contemplating what appeared to be a large electric light bulb in the recesses of a forest grove, with celestial nymphs lurking in the thickets. It was by an eminent English artist, and if anything more prestigious if less popular than Clytemnestra and Captain Oates. It was the smaller lady who first attracted Mr Franklin's attention; she was quite old, rather eccentrically dressed in a rusty coat and a most unbecoming black beret, and carrying a large leather satchel; he had an impression of flowing grey hair and bright, hard eyes in a strained face which glanced sharply round as her companion spoke to her. The taller lady was fashionably turned out in a maroon three-piece suit trimmed with dark fur, and wearing a stylish toque with a sweeping feather. Something about her was familiar, and then she half-turned, and he recognized Lady Helen Cessford.

387

"Why, there's someone I know," he said automatically, and Pip made a rapid survey and commented: "Oh, society – and brought her charwoman along, by the looks of it." And he was just wondering whether to approach and make himself known, when it happened.

The older lady stepped up to the Galahad picture, facing it, and Lady Helen moved swiftly out to a spot in the very centre of the gallery. She glanced quickly both ways, drew herself up, and in a voice that rang through the entire hall, declaimed:

"Ten days ago the House of Lords rejected the bill for women's enfranchisement! Without regard for justice, for decency, or for common sense, these selfish and arrogant men decreed that women must remain inferior beings, slaves without a voice in the land that dares to call itself the citadel of liberty – "

Every head was turned in her direction, every eye in the main gallery was staring at the tall slim figure, one arm raised as though in denunciation as she pealed out her message. All except Mr Franklin – he was heading, with rapid strides, for the little old lady before the picture. A large man, turning to stare at Lady Helen, bumped into him; they blundered against each other, and in that moment over the large man's shoulder Mr Franklin saw the little old lady whip something that looked like a butcher's cleaver from her satchel and slash viciously at the painting. He shouldered the large man aside and ran, but Lady Helen darted in front of him, thrusting at him with the folded parasol she carried. Instinctively he fell back, and then a small pink and white fury flew past him, squealing with indignation.

"Stop it! Stop it, you wicked old hag! Police!" Pip rushed at the little old lady, but she was too late. Two slashes of the cleaver had cut a large strip from the centre of the canvas and it was hanging out horribly from the frame; another sideways slash and it was almost severed, and the little old lady, grim-faced, having completed the mutilation of Galahad, was striking at random at the rest of the canvas. Pip snatched at the cleaver and screamed as it narrowly missed her hand; she grappled with the little woman and they went down in a welter of skirts and kicking legs. Mr Franklin parried a sweep from Lady Helen's parasol and wrenched it from her hand; she recognized him, and for a moment he thought she would launch herself at him. But one quick glance at the vandalized painting told her that the work was done; she shot him a glance of triumph and shouted:

"Women of Britain! How long – "

A burly attendant seized her round the waist from behind and

388

dragged her back. The gallery was in uproar, people shouting and hurrying to the scene, Pip was half-sitting up on the floor, her hand holding on her cap, while the little old lady was being pulled to her feet by an attendant and one of the male spectators. The cleaver lay where she had dropped it before the picture. Someone was blowing a whistle, voices were demanding that the police be summoned, the large man was shouting: "Suffragettes! Damned suffragettes! Damn them all!", a thin woman stood staring at the mutilated canvas in horror, screamed, and fell over in a faint.

Mr Franklin helped Pip to her feet. "Are you all right, Pip? She didn't catch you with that axe, did she?" She shook her head, her eyes blazing, and actually flourished her small fist at the little old lady, who was being held, grey-faced, in the grip of the attendant.

"You – you bad, bad old woman!" Pip stamped her foot. "Look what you've done! You're a heathen! You're a . . . a murderer! I hope they feed you forcible, you old trot!"

Elsewhere the woman who had fainted was having a bottle of smelling-salts waved under her nose, an attendant was lifting up the great torn lump of canvas and aimlessly looking at the huge rent in the painting as though wondering if he could fit it back in place; murmurs of shock and outrage were heard as people crowded round to view the damage; Lady Helen was sitting on a couch against the gallery wall, pale-faced and resolute, with the heavy hand of an attendant on her shoulder, while another man in uniform tried to restrain the threatening crowd clustered round her.

"You're a disgrace to your sex! A damned disgrace!" The large man's voice trumpeted over the rest.

"They should be publicly whipped!" This was the lady who had spoken to Pip earlier. "Whipped at the cart-tail! They're worse than street-walkers!"

The little old lady suddenly burst into tears, burying her face in her hands. The attendant guided her to the seat beside Lady Helen, who put an arm round her shoulders.

"Oh, yes, you can bawl now!" cried the large man. "You've shown how fit creatures like you are to have the vote!"

Mr Franklin held Pip's elbow as she straightened her dress; he could feel that she was trembling violently. She looked from the shattered canvas to the frail figure of the little woman crouched against Lady Helen, the beret pathetically askew, a thin hand over her face to hide her sobbing. Pip stared helplessly at Mr Franklin; two uniformed policemen were pushing their way through the crowd, ordering every-one to keep back and move along.

One of them took charge of the two suffragettes while the other demanded the names of eye-witnesses. There was a clamour of volun-teers until the large man claimed attention. "I saw everything, con-stable. That is the culprit – " he pointed dramatically at the little woman whose sobbing could now be heard distinctly in the compara-tive quiet. "The other one is her accomplice." Lady Helen regarded him with icy contempt, and turned to whisper to her companion, who was clinging to her arm, her face hidden against Lady Helen's shoulder.

"This plucky young lady," the large man was continuing loudly, "tried to prevent the crime, and might well have been seriously injured." He indicated Pip and Mr Franklin. "The gentleman also attempted to intervene, and was assaulted by that woman. In my opinion, they might both be charged with assault with a deadly weapon – "

"Hear, hear!" said a voice, and there was a murmur of approval. "I can testify on oath that the woman with the cleaver tried to use it against this young lady," said the large man with relish. "A murderous assault, unprovoked – "

"Oh, give it a rest!" snapped Pip. She looked in despair from the huddled form of the suffragette to the indignant face of the large man. "You talk a lot; I didn't see you doing anything."

"Well!" said the large man. "Well! On my word!"

"If you don't mind, sir." The constable scribbled in his notebook and turned to Mr Franklin. "May I have your name, sir, and the young lady's?" Mr Franklin produced his card. "And this is Miss Priscilla Delys." Pip gave her address, the constable nodded and closed his book, and addressed the crowd. "Now, please, everyone move along. Don't block the gallery. Move along, please."

Two attendants were already shrouding the mutilated picture in a white sheet; there was a sudden storm of hissing, and Mr Franklin saw that the other policeman was shepherding Lady Helen and the little woman, who was being helped by an attendant, out of the gallery. "Oh, Gawd!" said Pip. "The silly old faggot! What she have to do it for? What good's she think she's done?"

"Excuse me." A small, sharp-eyed man was at Pip's elbow, a notebook in his hand. "Miss Delys? I'm from the *Star*. Would you be Miss Delys of *Keep Smiling*? And do I understand that you also posed for two of the paintings on show in the Academy? Oh, that's great, Miss Delys . . ."

Others swarmed around, and Mr Franklin discarded the notion of trying to get Pip quietly out of the gallery. For one thing, she seemed ready enough to answer the reporter's questions; no doubt she had weighed up quickly that the publicity could do nothing but good, and she had a living to make. Certainly one of the Royal Academy's models risking life and limb to defend a painting would make splendid copy, and he guessed it would lose nothing in the telling. He stood aside, waiting, while the babble of questions went on; the attendants were erecting a little roped fence round the shrouded picture; several frock-coated gentlemen who were presumably Academicians were lifting the sheet to survey the damage.

"What would you have felt, Miss Delys, if one of your own pictures had been defaced? Is it true that she ran at you with the hatchet and that you disarmed her? What are your plans now that you've left *Keep Smiling*, Miss Delys? Have you any ambition to appear in films, Miss Delys? What are your views on votes for women? . . ."

At last they were finished, with profuse thanks and much lifting of hats, and Pip was free to be escorted from the gallery. "Sorry," she said to Mr Franklin, "but you can't say 'no' to the press. I hate to admit it, but this afternoon could be worth more than top billing in a hit show. They ask the daftest questions, though." She signed wearily. "God, but I'm tired. Could we go and sit down somewhere?"

He hailed a taxi, and in a few minutes they were installed in a hotel lounge, and the heroine of the Royal Academy was restoring herself with gin and Italian. "You think we'll have to give evidence?" she asked, and Mr Franklin shook his head.

"Probably not. They usually plead guilty – after all, they're not trying to get away with anything; they want the world to know what they've done."

"I suppose so," Pip sipped her drink and shivered. "Wasn't it awful? I mean, you read about things like that, but you don't know what it's like till you see it. Did you see that old girl's face? – she was like a mad thing, hacking and tearing at that picture like she wanted to kill someone! It might have been my pictures – " her eyes dilated at Mr Franklin. "God's truth – you remember me saying, suppose they tried to damage one of mine?" She shook her head helplessly. "What's wrong with women like that? And then afterwards, she was crying like a baby! Honest, I know it's crazy, but I felt downright

391

sorry for her." Her pretty face hardened. "Not for your society madam, though. Flinty-faced sow! Notice another thing – she did all the spouting, but it was the poor old bag that carried the hatchet! I'd give evidence against your snooty piece, twice over!" She glanced curiously at Mr Franklin. "You know her well?"

"Not very. We've met socially." He sighed. "But I have a feeling she won't be attending many functions for quite some time now."

"I wouldn't be too sure," said Pip cynically. "Somehow I can't picture her scrubbing floors in Holloway. Mark my words, she put the old girl up to it – got her to do the dirty work, and – "

"Now, we don't know that, Pip."

"You may not, but I wasn't born yesterday. The poor old biddy'll draw a stretch, but you wait and see if Lady Mayfair doesn't get off with a fine. Daddy'll have a word with Lord Muck at the club, and somehow word'll trickle down to the beak, and he'll give your girl a hell of a lecture and take a hundred quid off her – but it won't be bread and skilly for her, no fears. They know how to look after themselves, that lot do."

"You're wrong, Pip – they want to get arrested and jailed. I've seen Lady Helen Cessford in action, I tell you. She won't be looking for any special privileges, and I'm quite sure she'll get none."

He spoke a little more brusquely than usual, and Pip gave him a knowing look over the top of her glass.

"Oh, Lady Helen, eh? Worried about her, are you? Well, I suppose she's not bad-looking; put a saddle and bridle on her and stick her in the 2.30 at Newmarket –"

"I'm not specially worried about her, except . . ." He shrugged; he would have found it difficult to describe his thoughts about Lady Helen. "While I hate what she does, I guess I have a respect for her – because she believes in what she's doing, and won't shirk the consequences. And I admit I don't like to think of her . . ."

"Going through the mill, with wardresses shouting 'Left-right-pick-'em-up!' after her? All right for the old girl, but not fitting that a nice-looking lady should be treated common, and her an aristocrat, too!" Pip sniffed scornfully. "Don't you fret! Anyway, you wouldn't respect her half as much if she was fat-legged and flat-chested. Men!" She shook her head. "No – it's the old 'un I'm sorry for, 'cos even if she did get the vote it wouldn't do her a ha'porth of good – she'd still be fetching and carrying, doing what she was told, whether it was smashing pictures or washing dishes, while your Lady Snoot sat upstairs and rang the bell. Going to buy us another gin, then?"

"Sheer naked female jealousy," said Mr Franklin, but after he had taken Pip back to Bloomsbury he gave serious thought to what lay ahead for the two suffragettes. Criminal charges, obviously; possibly a trial in which he might have the distasteful task of giving evidence. Would the police be able to say yet whether that was likely? Probably not – but he could always ask. On the spur of the moment he redirected his taxi, and they turned east, threading their way through the narrow streets towards Covent Garden.

The great central police station was quiet at that hour of the evening; only one customer was being dealt with by the desk sergeant, but as Mr Franklin approached the counter he became aware that several uniformed constables were listening to the exchange with covert amusement.

"I'm sorry, sir," the sergeant was saying with that heavy emphasis which is the verbal expression of the majesty of the British law, "but there's absolutely nothing I can do. No communication with prisoners, except for authorized legal representatives. I'm very sorry, sir."

"Authorized fiddlesticks!" said the customer, and Mr Franklin examined him sharply. There was no doubt about it: the massive, ancient frame, the lined and mottled countenance, the splendid white moustaches, the rakishly-tilted top hat and the beautifully-cut, if well-outmoded evening cloak, signified only one person, and that was Lady Helen Cessford's great-uncle, the garrulous pursuer of between-floors maids – he was announcing himself this very moment.

"I'm General Sir Harry Flashman, and it's my great-niece I want to see! I don't know you, sergeant – you're since my time.Where's Sergeant O'Rourke? Or what's his name – Billingham? Bellingham? Chap who used to raid the knocking shops out West. Oh, God, that would be forty years ago. Wait, though! Fields? Saw his name in print t'other day – Inspector Fields! I'll see him – wheel him out, there's a good fellow!"

"You know the Inspector, sir – er, General?" The sergeant looked respectful. "Well, he's about, I think –"

" 'Course I don't know him. But I suspect he's the son of old Paddy Fields, used to be a super in A Division – before your time. Pinched me for breach of the peace, public nuisance, and causing an obstruction. Year of the Great Exhibition. Paddy was a constable then –

splendid chap, great friend. So drum up this new fellow, and I'll have a word with him."

Faced by this commanding and eccentric antiquity, the sergeant despatched a constable for the inspector, and the General turned to stare about and observe that the old place had changed considerably. His eye fell on Mr Franklin, and narrowed.

"Know you," he said accusingly. "But you're not a bobby – too well-dressed. Army? No-o, too clever for that. Haven't got the sneaky look of a politician, either, and I doubt if I owe you money, or I'd recognize you. Well, dammit, who are you?"

Mr Franklin reintroduced himself. "We met at Sandringham, you may remember, General."

"To be sure we did." The General thumped his cane on the floor with satisfaction. "Hellish place – and probably no better now that Bertie's gone. New chap looks like a muff – haven't met him. Royalty's going down, of course – not that they were ever up to much. Know who was on the throne when I made my entry to this vale of tears? George the Fourth – Prinny! What d'ye think of that, hey? You youngsters – " he waved his cane at the constables " – never heard of Prinny, I don't suppose. But then, you're not ninety-two," he added with satisfaction, "and probably never will be, because you won't look after yourselves as I have done. *Mens sana in corpore sano* as they used to tell us at Rugby, and if you believe that you'll believe anything." He grinned wickedly, and Mr Franklin reflected that whatever the General's recipe for sprightly longevity, it seemed to work. His face might be an artist's nightmare, but his dark eyes were bright, and he carried himself with the vigour of an active sixty.

"Franklin – yes. American, Nebraska, made a pile in silver." The old man twinkled shrewdly. "And in other things, I don't doubt. Yes – you were slavering over that peacocky little great-niece of mine at Sandringham. Aha! Is that what brings you here? Same errand as mine? You know she's in the jug, don't you? Silly little baggage! Some rumpus at the Royal Academy – well, it's original, hand her that. When I heard about it, I thought 'Well, bigod, that's one ken they never slung you out of.'" Odd place to start a turn-up; don't even serve drink there, I believe." He wagged his great white head. "Any odds, she's inside, the dear little half-wit, and – ah, you Inspector Fields, are you?"

A steady-looking man of middle age, in plain clothes, had come through the barrier, running a quick eye over the General and Mr Franklin.

"You Paddy Fields' boy? Used to be straw-boss in A Division?"

"Er . . . yes, sir. What can I do for you?"

"Your father," said the General loudly, shaking the Inspector's hand, "was an excellent and honest man, and a credit to his calling. Firm, courteous, upright and intelligent. Diligent in inquiry, steadfast in apprehension, tolerant in prosecution. It was a pleasure to have dealings with him, and I should know," added the General, "since I've been collared by half the traps between Maidstone and Manila. You look like him. You shake hands like him – good, firm grip. British. Tell me," went on the General in a quieter tone, but with great earnestness, "you're an inspector. Why not a chief – or a superintendent? Hey?"

"Well, sir . . ." The inspector hesitated, at a loss. "I don't know that – "

"Don't say it!" said the General grimly. "It's always the way. Get a good man and authority'll do its damndest to keep him back. Jealousy and corruption rife – as they always have been. Your father had the same trouble. Damnable, absolutely damnable. Too many blasted Army castoffs at the top of the force, no doubt. Never mind, they can't live forever. And you're Paddy Fields' son! Well, well! It's a pleasure to make your acquaintance. But I tell you what it is," the General lowered his voice confidentially. "There's this foolish great-niece of mine, Lady Helen Cessford, and I'm most anxious to see her – matters to arrange, like bail and so forth, legal representation, get this trumped-up nonsense settled. Fields is the man, says I; no point in dealing with underlings when a word with him will open the door – "

"I'm sorry, sir." The startled inspector managed to get a word in. "But the lady's in Holloway. She was charged here, but she was taken to the suffragette wing, as they call it, and – "

"Holloway? But that's near Tottenham Court Road, isn't it? Practically in Yorkshire, good God! Can't you get her back?"

"I'm sorry, sir. She'll be there till committal proceedings, and then . . . well, from what I've heard, sir, it's not unlikely she'll be sent for trial – "

"Don't you believe it," said the General. "Whole thing's a fabrication. I can see I shall have to consult my solicitors." He fixed the inspector with an eagle eye. "And you're sure you can't get her down here – for any consideration?"

Any emphasis laid on the last three words might have been purely imaginary. The inspector repeated, apologetically, that there was nothing he could do, and for a moment Mr Franklin thought the General would explode. But he merely breathed deeply, blew out his cheeks, shook hands again with Fields, and said he supposed that the committal would take place at the police station.

"Because anything you can do for Lady Helen," he said, "will be regarded as a particular favour to me. I know I can rely on you – Paddy Fields' boy, eh? Very good, inspector, I'm delighted to have met you. A very good night to you." And he made his exit with dignity. Mr Franklin, realizing that he had nothing to stay for, followed, and was in time to see the General hurl his cane into the gutter.

"Useless little squirt!" he exclaimed. "Mind you, I needn't have expected better. His father was a toad, and would have shopped his own mother for a sovereign." He glared at Mr Franklin. "But it's always as well to butter the bogies, you know. Fields, eh? I'll send him a half-dozen of whisky presently – never know when he'll come in handy. Not that it'll be any help to young Button, if they make this charge stick. You heard she smashed some damned daub at the Academy?"

"I was there," said Mr Franklin. "Indeed, I'm very much afraid I'll be a leading witness."

"You don't say?" The General regarded him with interest. "Well, I'll be damned. Did she do it?"

"She was what I think you'd call an accessory. Another woman actually cut the picture."

"And you saw it all?" The General considered. "That might be very fortunate. Ye-es. Will you dine with me, my boy? Of course, of course you will. Let's see, now . . . where, that's the point? United Service, but they kicked me out . . . White's? Full of damned Tories, and they keep sending me bills – don't know how I ever got into the place, anyway. Travellers isn't bad, but I'm not sure I'm a member. Was that the place they wouldn't let me take in that exotic dancer, what's-her-name – it may have been the Savage, though – "

Mr Franklin mentioned that he was a member of the Athenaeum; perhaps the General would care to . . .

"That's a frightful pub," said Sir Harry gloomily. "Jumped-up schoolmasters and bloody bishops. Won't do your standing any good to take me there – still, if you're game, I am. Don't let me fall asleep, though, because if I wake up there in that long room of theirs I'll think I'm dead and waiting in some ante-room to the Day of Judgement."

Mr Franklin reassured him, and they took a cab to the famous club, where Sir Harry stared round the imposing hall and remarked that things weren't what they had once been. "Saw Palmerston fall down that staircase – the whole damned way from top to bottom. Tight as a fiddler's bitch. Finished up wrapped round that pillar there. Can't see Asquith doing that, somehow. Rotten prime minister. D'you know, I presented him with a school prize once? Must be fifty years ago – ugly little swot he was then, and hasn't improved over the years. Mind you, Balfour wouldn't have been any better – 'Pretty Fanny', they used to call him. Only good thing I knew about him was that he taught Asquith how to ride a bicycle. Argued some kind of capacity, I suppose – I'd as soon try to teach a whale to play the fiddle."

With the General keeping up a steady fire of comment and reminiscence, they reached the dining-room, where Sir Harry astonished his host by confining himself to three plates of different soups followed by a pudding and cheese and biscuits – "innards haven't been right since the Crimea – not painful, you understand, but I must take care or I'm seized shockingly with wind. Inconvenient." However, he evidently observed no restrictions where liquor was concerned; he drank whatever was set before him with relish, but Mr Franklin noticed that it had no visible effect on his wits. He cross-examined keenly on the scene at the Royal Academy, and when he had wrung every particle of information from the American he sat back and stroked his great whiskers.

"Bad – but might be worse," he observed. "Button didn't actually wield the hatchet; that's good. Yes, if she's well defended, she might just slide out of it. Can't escape a conviction, but at least she should avoid the worst possible consequences."

"Do you think she'll want to?" asked Mr Franklin, and the General considered him.

"She's seen the inside of Holloway now," he said. "I know she's set on being a martyr – they all are, these idiot women – but it's surprising how the clang of those iron doors and the sight of those gruesome faces can change one's mind, even a mind as stiff as hers. I've had more cell doors shut on me than I care to remember, and there wasn't one I wouldn't have sold my soul to open again. A night or two in there may take some of the starch out of her – and, if it doesn't, well, we shall have to see what can be done."

"I don't see that anything can be done," said Mr Franklin, "if she's determined to take her medicine."

"Don't you? Well, let me tell you that it depends on whether they want to give her the medicine, d'you see? It's politics, Franklin. You mayn't remember, but when this suffragette nonsense started, there was a case not unlike this one – two women, one a commoner, one a Lady Something, were arrested. And the lady was far more leniently treated by the courts. There was a tremendous howl from the public, and from the suffragettes who wanted to show that rank meant nothing to them, and that the duchesses among 'em wanted to take their gruel just like the sluts. That's past history." The General tapped the table. "But it's worth remembering. What's the position now? I'll tell you. The government are sick to death with suffragettes, sick to death of martyrs, sick to death of the Cat and Mouse Act whereby women are let out of jail and can be brought back to finish their sentences as the government pleases. The last thing they want is an eminent martyr. The Pankhursts are bad enough, but Lady Helen Cessford? No, they don't want her. She's too damned well-connected, she'll attract attention, she'll give the suffragettes a splendid boost if she's put inside and forcibly fed and goes on hunger-strike. No, they don't want her. And, by God," said the General ferociously, glaring at Mr Franklin and screwing up his napkin in a great claw-like hand, "they're not going to get her! I haven't bled for this damned country so that it can send my great-niece to a felon's cell for helping to cut up some lousy daub by some penniless pimp in a Bloomsbury garret! I'll bet it was a rotten painting, wasn't it? You saw it – wasn't it something that should have been burned before it was exhibited? Hey?"

"I'm no judge, but I don't think it was a masterpiece, exactly," confessed Mr Franklin. "But surely that's not the point – "

"I knew it!" said the General. "A piece of glorified wallpaper! None of these modern bastards can paint. Not like Wollen – ever see his 'Last Stand of the Forty-fourth at Gandamack'? That's painting, if you like. Not that it looked a dam' bit like the real thing – I *saw* the real thing, back in '42, so I should know. But it was a decentish picture. Turner, too – he could paint ... 'The Fighting Temeraire' going up the Thames to the knackers, eh? That sunset! And the whole sky and river bathed in white fire with the shadows creeping, and the smoky little tug pulling the old fighting giant to her last berth, and

398

the bells ringing for the last time – " He hunched forward over the table, and to Mr Franklin's alarm began to croak:

> Now the sunset breezes shiver,
> And she's fading down the river,
> But in England's song forever,
> She's the Fighting Temeraire.

"That's the way we all go – the old hulks!" The General tugged angrily at his moustache. "You can ruin yourself being battered and chased and shot at half your life, and fighting like hell on behalf of a lot of damned lick-spittles who infest cesspits like the Athenaeum Club where they put too much damned salt in the damned consommé and try to poison people with curried turtle soup that would make a Bengali privy cleaner sick – not that I ever fought except when I couldn't avoid it, but any man's a bloody fool who does otherwise – and what d'you get for it at the end of the day?" His voice was rising steadily, and his eye was glaring horribly. "I'll tell you what you get – a set of tinware and a few meaningless titles and a pension that won't keep your blasted dog in bones, and your niece, a lady of quality, expressing her proper contempt for a worthless travesty of a picture by some mountebank whom you wouldn't pay to distemper a kitchen ceiling, may be haled into a police court, subjected to the degradation of a public trial – "

Mr Franklin felt his sleeve gently tugged, and a steward's voice hissed discreetly into his ear: "Would you mind asking your guest to lower his voice a trifle, sir? I'm rather afraid he may disturb the members." He scuttled quickly away, and Mr Franklin turned back desperately to try to stem the tide.

"I've a damned good mind," blared the General, "to take my V.C. and all the rest of my *ferblanterie*, and throw 'em over Buckingham Palace gate! Show my contempt for what society has come to! In my youth, if a lady of quality had expressed her opinion – as she has a perfect right to do – d'you think she'd have been dragged before a magistrate? Certainly not! She'd have been sent down to the country for a rest, her father would have brought the damned painting, her brother would have horse-whipped the artist, and that'd have been that! But this blasted Liberal lot have ruined our way of life completely. I foresaw it – I told that ass Gladstone as much, in the lavatory of this very club – no, it wasn't, either, it was the Reform, I remember.

Good billiard table they have in the Reform – slept on it on Mafeking night. Better club than this, too – " he glared round the dining-room. "They don't have a chef at the Reform who served his apprenticeship in some confounded Siberian salt-mine!" His voice dropped suddenly to a normal conversational tone. "Shall we go to the smoking-room, my boy? I fancy a soothing glass of port, I think."

Mr Franklin was only too glad to make his escape. He preceded the General, aware of the indignant stares directed at them from the tables, but when they got outside Sir Harry laid a hand on his arm.

"Forgive me, Franklin. I can't resist the temptation to stir those damned monkeys up – and believe it or not, I may have done our little girl a spot of good." He winked; so Beelzebub might have winked at Lucifer. "Fine set of snobs we have here, and Tories, and so-called authorities who hate modern art. Think I'm joking? Not I, my son. And I learned a thing or two from our Russian friends – confuse, alarm, bewilder. If you haven't got a good case, it's worth more than a dishonest juryman. Come on."

Mr Franklin, feeling not a little confused, alarmed and bewildered himself, settled his guest in a distant corner of the drawing-room, and prayed there would be no further outbursts. But to his astonishment the General had turned into a model guest, and a most entertaining one. He talked at large about the American West, of which he obviously had an exhaustive knowledge, described his part in the Battle of Little Big Horn in graphic detail, and threw in an entertaining memoir of President Lincoln for good measure.

"Good lawyer. Damned good lawyer. Rather have him in my corner than Carson or Smith or any of 'em – pity his people emigrated. He'd have been the best Lord Chief Justice, or Lord Chancellor, this country ever saw. Strange, isn't it, that some remote ancestor may have first seen the light in our Courts of Justice? Oh yes – the name Lincoln, you know – well, it's possible his people came from Lincoln, but just as likely one of 'em was a foundling. They used to abandon unwanted infants in the Inns of Court, Lincoln's and Gray's. So half the folk you meet called Gray or Lincoln are liable to be the descendants of those foundlings. Temple, too. I told Abe about that, and he just said he was glad his ancestors had chosen such a respectable place to be abandoned in, when you thought of the spots they might have lit on. He was a decent fellow – far too decent for politics. He wouldn't have lasted, you know, after the war. Men like him never do; people decide they're too clever, and besides, they feel obliged to 'em, and no electorate likes that. No, you'd have got rid of him, if Booth hadn't."

It was nearly midnight when they left the club, and Mr Franklin dropped the General at his house in Berkeley Square. The old man sat in silence for a moment before descending, and said:

"Have to keep Button out of jail somehow. Not easy, because if they turn her loose the little shrew's just liable to set fire to Lloyd George, or break a stained-glass window, in order to martyr herself properly. Unless Holloway's taught her a lesson already. I don't know." He turned his livid face on Mr Franklin. "If it comes to trial, you'll give your evidence – intelligently, I've no doubt. In the meantime I'll see what I can do. I thank you for the dinner – it wasn't your fault. I'd apologize for shaming you in the Athenaeum, but the sooner you're out of that awful hole, the better. If they turf you out, come to me, I'll put you up for a decent place – Madame Desirée's, off the Haymarket, or a Chinese establishment I know down in Pennyfields." He chuckled hoarsely and climbed stiffly out, and Mr Franklin watched the stalwart figure march slowly and carefully across the pavement. He waited until the door had been opened, heard the General say: "Hollo, Shadwell, her ladyship still awake? No? Well, why don't you and I go out and pick up a couple of girls and have a bath in Trafalgar Square fountain? No? You've no spunk, Shadwell – all right, malted milk and brandy, as usual . . ."

Mr Franklin shook his head ruefully, and directed the taxi to Wilton Crescent.

401

21

In June the builders' strike which had begun in January became a national lock-out, London theatregoers had the choice of Chaliapin in *Boris Godunov*, John MacCormack in *Rigoletto*, or Massine and Fokine in the Russian ballet, Britain beat the United States at polo (an event which brought Mr Franklin nostalgic memories of his first rail journey in England), fighting took place in Vera Cruz, the Archduke Francis Ferdinand of Austria prepared to make a visit to Sarajevo, Mrs Mark Franklin's portrait by Lavery was greatly admired in a showing of that eminent artist's work at the Grosvenor Gallery, a new French government was formed, and Britain and Germany reached an agreement on the Bagdad Railway question. Other notable events of the month were the opening of the new revue, *Pip, Squeak!*, starring Miss Priscilla Delys, whose story blazoned across the popular press had inspired an opportunist impresario to strike while her celebrity was hot, and the trial of Lady Helen Cessford, of Cessford Castle, Northumberland, and Curzon Street, and Millicent Shore, of Alma Street, Highgate, before a judge and jury. The charges were of malicious damage and assault with a deadly weapon (against the prisoner Shore), and aiding and abetting the malicious damage and common assault (against the prisoner Cessford). The trial was necessary because while both defendants admitted the malicious damage charges, both pleaded not guilty to the assaults.

It was not an event to which Mr Franklin found himself looking forward with any pleasure at all. When, at the committal proceedings (in which he had not been required to appear), the defendants had entered their pleas and reserved their defences, the police had taken a statement from him and warned him to hold himself in readiness as a witness for the prosecution. He was going to have to testify against Lady Helen, which was bad enough; what might have made it infinitely worse was a deliberate and diabolically cunning attempt by General Sir Harry Flashman to compromise Mr Franklin's standing as a witness. He had sent round a note to Wilton Crescent inviting the

American to lunch at the Oriental Club (one of the institutions at which, presumably, he remained a member in good standing). Mr Franklin had been on the point of accepting when he had received an agitated telephone call from his solicitor commanding him in no uncertain terms to stay away from the lunch engagement and, as he valued his reputation, the General himself.

It transpired that Sir Harry, labouring with the assistance of a disreputable private detective on his great-niece's behalf, had tracked down a witness to the Royal Academy outrage who was, it appeared, prepared to give evidence favourable to the accused. So far so good, but he had then conceived the notion of taking the witness to lunch, and inviting Mr Franklin also, to talk the affair over in a friendly manner. He had known perfectly well that such a meeting of opposing witnesses with a relative of the accused presiding, could not fail to discredit the testimony of both, when it became known – as of course it would. Sir Harry could be relied on to see to that. Fortunately the private detective took fright, and spoke to the defence's solicitor, who lost no time in getting in touch with the firm who advised Mr Franklin. A scandal was averted, and Sir Harry, taxed with his behaviour by indignant lawyers – principally his own, a sorely-tried and ready-witted practitioner in Wine Office Court – claimed total innocence of any attempt to pervert the course of justice. On being assured that he might easily have been prosecuted for conspiracy, the old soldier had remarked scornfully: "Let 'em try to put a ninety-two-year-old hero of Balaclava in the Scrubs if they dare. There'd be a revolution." And there that particular aspect of the case had rested, with not a few sighs of relief.

It remained that Mr Franklin would have to testify, and quite apart from the distaste which he felt for the task, he was also uncomfortably aware that it must emerge that he had been at the Royal Academy in company with Pip, who would also be appearing as a witness. And while there was, on the face of it, nothing untoward about their visiting an art gallery together, he knew from bitter experience what the sharp tongues of Belgravia and Mayfair could be relied on to make of it. If Pip had been from his own social class, no one would have given it a thought; his own wife was constantly being attended by young males of the smart set in which she moved, with probably no more than the normal malicious sniping which was the common currency of that society. But Pip was a well-known star of vulgar revue and musical comedy, as well as an artist's model, and Mr Franklin was bound to

403

concede that her appearance and style were not immediately suggestive of chastity and a high moral tone. The fact that their relationship was innocent, and that Pip had strict views on the sanctity of the marriage tie, would be accepted by nobody within sneering distance of Eaton Place; they would place only one construction on the association of a respectable married resident of Wilton Crescent (whose wife, my dear, is seldom seen in his company in Society) with a spectacularly earthy blonde who exhibited herself indecorously on the stage and even more indecorously in the artist's studio.

Where Peggy was concerned his unease was not that she would believe the sly tattling of her cronies, whose minds she knew as well as he did, but that she might be wounded by it, and pardonably annoyed with him for having exposed her to it. And if he pointed out to her gently that she was constantly in the company of young men of her own circle, she could reasonably reply that there was a difference between that and her being seen, say, in the company of a muscular young professional pugilist at Premierland – or, for that matter, at the Royal Academy where he had posed for a nude study of Hercules. Mr Franklin realized that he had been indiscreet, not to say downright oblivious . . . and yet it had happened so gradually and innocently that only now was he aware of the possible implications. Well, the gossips would make of it what they wanted, and there was no help for it.

Peggy had come back from Cornwall as outwardly calm and amiable as when she left; the artificial surface normality of their relationship continued, and although she had read of the Royal Academy affair, her only remark on learning that he had been involved as an eye-witness and would have to give evidence, was: "Bad luck that you happened to be there – anything to do with courts is a crashing bore, isn't it? This Cessford woman must be a lunatic." He had reminded her that he had met Lady Helen at Sandringham four years before, and that she had slapped his face even earlier outside the Waldorf Hotel; Peggy, without looking up from her paper, had simply observed: "That's the trouble nowadays; society's full of cranks. You meet some apparently normal person at a tea dance and the next thing you know they're waving a banner in Trafalgar Square or going into a convent. Hilda Tredenham's brother is working on the railway somewhere, and has actually become a trade union delegate, and the Fleming boy – you remember, we met him at the Conroys, last Christmas? Well, he's joined the Foreign Legion."

Time was, Mr Franklin reflected, that Peggy would have demanded full details of the Royal Academy fracas, with a minute recapitulation of his Waldorf encounter with Lady Helen, and a rehearsal of everything he recollected about her at Sandringham, down to such details as her clothing, conversation, and what she ate at breakfast. Things had changed; she now seemed politely indifferent, and infinitely more concerned with her own personal affairs, even when they were together. For a moment he wondered if it was worth making the effort, to try to break through the invisible barrier, to dismiss the whole Arthur business as of no account, and re-establish that happy intimacy of minds that they had known before the gradual drifting apart, before Arthur and his damned silly political plots – but he knew that Peggy would not welcome it, that she preferred things as they were, and that the preference was based on her genuine indifference to him – and that in turn was an inevitable result of the disparity in their ages, and so on, and so on through the thoughts that he had rehearsed a thousand times before.

Nothing more was said of the impending trial until the night before it took place, when it happened that he and Peggy were making one of their rare excursions out together. The occasion was the Anglo-American Peace Ball at the Albert Hall; not only was it one of the highlights of the season, which Peggy would have attended anyway, but it was sponsored by the United States Embassy, and Mr Franklin, as an American of some slight standing in the West End community, felt he could hardly avoid it. On their drive to the Albert Hall he made some remark about his attendance in court the following morning, and Peggy, glancing out at the passing traffic as their car sped down the Mall, inquired idly:

"Do you think they'll get away with it?"

He looked at her in some surprise. "Who? Lady Helen Cessford and the other one? They can't get away with damaging the picture – they've admitted it."

"No – the other charges. She hit you with her umbrella, didn't she? I must say she seems to be an extremely violent woman. And someone was telling me that this girl who tried to stop the suffragette with the hatchet was jolly lucky not to be badly injured."

"I'll be surprised if they can make it stick," said Mr Franklin. "The women weren't there to commit assault – I daresay in the dust-up you could say that anything like a push or a blow *could* constitute an assault. But they weren't trying to injure anyone."

"But Helen Cessford did hit you?"

405

"Hardly. She tried to, but I caught her parasol, and she let it go."

"You do live, don't you? She didn't try to hit you at Sandringham, I suppose?" There was the ghost of a smile on Peggy's lips.

"She wasn't being a suffragette at Sandringham."

"No, I imagine she has decided views about the propriety of brawling in some places but not in others. One doesn't assault guests of royalty, but the common herd are fair game. You must be confusing for her, popping up in unlikely places. Equally, it must be difficult for you – not knowing whether to say 'How do you do, Lady Helen', or duck." Peggy laughed softly.

"I haven't met her all that often," said Mr Franklin, "and only once on what you would call formal terms."

"What was she like then?" asked Peggy. "I've met her here and there, at parties – not that she seems to mix a great deal – one feels that she prefers the company of horses and servants, when she isn't making a fool of herself in public. Does she condescend to those beneath her lofty station?"

"You've probably seen more of her than I have. I'd say she's probably not the warmest personality I've met. But it's difficult to say – the suffragette is always pretty much in evidence."

"Hiding the sweet and fragile nature underneath." He watched her dim reflection in the glass behind the driver's head, and saw the upward curl at the corner of her mouth. "It'll be interesting to see whether she plays the grand dame in front of a judge and jury – I wouldn't be surprised."

"Are you going to be there to see?"

"Good heavens, no! Nobody's going – if she puts herself outside the pale the best thing to do is ignore her."

"I'd have thought," said Mr Franklin, "that Hilda Tredenham, or Poppy Davenport, would have been too overcome with curiosity to keep away. Belgravia must be coming to a pretty pass if good taste is spoiling their appetite for scandal."

"Oh, you'll find it hasn't quite done that," laughed Peggy. "You can expect a minor deluge of invitations in the next week, I expect – all the eager hostesses in search of the gory details."

"Then they can expect a minor deluge of polite refusals," said Mr Franklin. "They'll have to be content with the papers."

"Spoil-sport! The papers may tell them what the accused wore, and whether she looked 'composed' or 'penitent' or 'distraught', but they'll expect you to tell them exactly how you gave your evidence, and how La Cessford took it, and whether she regarded you with distaste or well-bred contempt or aristocratic loathing, like the heroines of the women's novels." Peggy seemed to enjoy the prospect. "What will you say, by the way – in court, I mean?"

"My evidence? I'll tell 'em what happened."

"Oh, you know what I mean! Obviously it depends on you – about the assault charge. If you say she was trying to thump you, she's a goner; if you say she wasn't, I suppose she might get off."

The thought had been in Mr Franklin's mind for days, but it had not occurred to him that others, like Peggy, would have reached the same conclusion – that Lady Helen's fate, on that charge at least, rested with him.

"I doubt that very much," he said slowly. "I'm not the only witness."

"But you were the object of her attack – of the brutal assault on an innocent bystander! I mean – you took her parasol away from her – because she was trying to poke your eye out with it, or because you thought it might come on to rain?" Peggy turned to laugh at him. "It all depends how you put it, doesn't it?"

"And that could depend on what I'm asked," said Mr Franklin, as the taxi drew up outside the Albert Hall.

"I think," said Peggy, gathering her skirts together, "that you're going to be chivalrous. Poppy Davenport doesn't. She thinks you're the kind of brute who'll be quite happy to swear la belle Hélène into a deep, dank cell – you tried to throw *her* into the corridor at Oxton, she says, which shows what you're capable of."

"Anyone who could throw Poppy any distance would have to be a bigger and better man than I am," said Mr Franklin, as he handed her down. "And she has a very vivid imagination."

Neither of them mentioned the subject again during the ball, or on the way home, and in the morning Peggy decided to have breakfast in bed, so that Mr Franklin was left to his own thoughts and the morning paper downstairs. If the approaching trial, or Peggy's remarks about it, were troubling his mind, it did not diminish his appetite; he ate a steak and two fried eggs, called a taxi, and was at the court in excellent time. There he was conducted to the room set aside for witnesses; the large man who had been so vociferous at the Royal Academy was already there, and they exchanged nods, with furtive glances at the attendant constable to make sure that even such a cursory greeting did not amount to collusion. Three uniformed minions of the gallery were also present, and there presently arrived, in succession, the lady who had spoken to Pip, and who smiled timidly at Mr Franklin and thereafter sat in nervous immobility with a handkerchief pressed to her nose; an imposing gentleman in morning coat and resplendent top hat, with an orchid in his buttonhole and a faintly Bohemian air, who proved to be the President of the Royal Academy; and finally, with a bustling of helpful constables and setting of chairs, the leading lady of *Pip, Squeak!*, smiling demurely in appreciation of all this attention, inclining her head graciously to the President, who made her a bow both austere and artistic, ignoring the large man, who went pink, and taking her seat opposite Mr Franklin, on whom she bestowed, unseen by the other waiting witnesses, a wink that would have taxed the facial muscles of a circus clown. Otherwise, she was on her best behaviour, modestly attired in a pale grey dress of such simple elegance that the lady with the handkerchief could not tear her eyes from it, and her golden hair neatly contained under one of the severely expensive new German hats with the smallest of aigrets. The room was now almost full; plainly if the truth failed to emerge in court it would not be for lack of testimony. Mr Franklin sat patiently, noting how the eyes of the constable at the door would range casually round the room and inevitably alight on Pip's profile, and how she, in turn, was restraining her natural inclination to cross her legs and display her ankles. Obviously she was impressed by the solemnity of the occasion.

It came as a shock when the door opened and a voice said: "Mr Mark Franklin", and a moment later he was in the great, dark-panelled court-room, aware of a wigged judge behind the elevated bench, a double row of nondescript faces which must be the jury, men in wigs and black robes before him, and General Flashman, a hulking figure at the back of the public benches, sitting chin on fist with his mane of white hair shining like a beacon. And there was Lady Helen Cessford, gazing coldly before her as he took the oath, with the small woman looking wan and old, beside her in the railed dock. Policemen bare-headed at the doors, his own voice saying "So help me God" and adding his name and address, and then one of the men in wig and robe turning to address him.

"Mr Franklin, I believe you were present at the Royal Academy's exhibition on the afternoon of May 18th?"

"Yes, sir, I was."

"Before I ask you to describe what took place there at approximately 3.30 p.m., I wish to ask a question which you may think strange, but which I put to you, in the form in which I put it, with the agreement of my learned friends and with the leave of his lordship." The barrister paused. "In the gallery, at any time during the afternoon, did you see any person known to you – I do not mean a friend or acquaintance, but a person who might be thought well-known, and in the public eye?"

Mr Franklin was puzzled, and asked for the question to be repeated, which it was, with the deliberation of assumed weariness, as though counsel were addressing a deaf Irishman or a backward child. He considered it in some bewilderment.

"I can't think that I did, sir. Unless you mean Lady Helen Cessford?"

There were exclamations from the seated barristers, looks of irritation, and a sigh from the barrister on his feet.

"No, Mr Franklin – a prominent public personality, someone who I daresay might be considered a celebrity?"

Mr Franklin was beginning a mystified apology when the judge intervened, "Perhaps I may be able to assist the witness, Mr Sullivan?" Obsequious murmurs from the barrister, whereafter the judge contemplated his stomach in an attitude of prayer and asked:

"Did you see a tall person, an author of plays?"

The light dawned. "Oh, Mr Shaw. Yes, sir – my lord, I saw him. Mr George Bernard Shaw."

The judge nodded benignly, the barrister expressed his gratitude, and turned again to Mr Franklin.

"You saw Mr Bernard Shaw. What was he doing?"

"He was looking at the pictures," said Mr Franklin, thanking God for an opportunity to tell the truth with confidence at last.

"At the pictures. Yes. Anything more than that? Tell us what he did."

"Well, sir," said Mr Franklin, "he walked up and down, looking at various pictures. Er . . . with great interest, it appeared to me. I didn't watch him closely, of course, but that was . . . about . . . what he did."

"Did you hear him speak to anyone?"

Mr Franklin replied carefully. "Not *to* anyone – but he made one or two observations, I believe."

"Can you tell us what they were?"

"Well, I believe he looked at the picture of Captain Oates and – "

"Captain who?" asked the judge.

"Oates, m'lud. Witness is referring to the picture of Captain Oates in the snow, at which Mr Shaw was looking."

"Ah, Oates. The explorer. I see. Mr Shaw was looking at that picture. Go on."

"Well, sir," said Mr Franklin, "he looked at the picture of Captain Oates, and – "

"Are you an American?" asked the judge suddenly.

"Yes, sir," said Mr Franklin, startled.

"I see," said the judge. "I beg your pardon, Mr Sullivan. Do go on."

"Thank you, m'lud. Mr Shaw looked at the picture of Captain Oates, and . . . ?" The barrister invited Mr Franklin to continue.

"And he said," began Mr Franklin, feeling slightly desperate. "No, he didn't. I'm sorry, my lord. It wasn't at Captain Oates's picture that he said it – it was at another one. I do apologise; it was at another picture that he said – what he said. He didn't say anything about Captain Oates. I'm sure of that." He stopped, appalled at the thought of perjury narrowly avoided.

"I see," said the judge thoughtfully. "He said nothing at Captain Oates's picture. At what picture did he say something?"

Mr Franklin was aware that his palms were sweating. "It was at the picture of the . . . the Greek lady . . . the Greek queen, I believe she was."

"Clytemnestra?" said the barrister helpfully.

"That's the one," said Mr Franklin, relieved. "Yes – Clytemnestra."

"Indeed," said the judge. "Clit-*em*-nestra – that, as I recall, is the pronunciation we were taught, Mr Sullivan. Queen to Agamemnon, whom she betrayed and murdered on his return from Troy?"

"As your lordship pleases," said the barrister. "What," he added hastily before anyone else could get in, "did Mr Shaw say about that picture?"

"He said 'Remarkable', sir." Mr Franklin spoke with confidence.

"I see. And what other observations did he make?"

"I believe I heard him say 'Extraordinary'," said Mr Franklin, and went on quickly: "But I don't remember at which picture he said it."

"I see. These were critical appraisals, would you say?"

"Yes, sir. Just his opinions – spoken musingly." Mr Franklin felt rather proud of that, and the barrister brightened.

"Did you hear him say anything else? To any other person?"

"No, sir."

"Think carefully, Mr Franklin." The barrister looked earnest. "You are positive that he spoke to no one else, that you are aware of? He did not, for example, address either of the defendants?"

Mention of the defendants took Mr Franklin momentarily aback; what did they have to do with it when George Bernard Shaw was plainly in peril of his life unless Mr Franklin's evidence was believed? Then he remembered: the defendants were on trial, and this bewildering nonsense about Mr Shaw was ... was ... well, he did not know what it was, but at least he could answer the question.

"Good gracious, no, sir! He never – I mean I never saw him near them. Indeed," said Mr Franklin, cudgelling his memory, "I had not seen Mr Shaw in the gallery for some time – when the ... ladies ... that is, the defendants – when I first saw them. I would have thought that Mr Bernard Shaw had left the gallery by then."

"Why should you have thought that?" snapped the barrister, quickly.

"Well, sir, he had the air of a man – when I last noticed him – he looked as though he was about to leave. He looked, if you ask me," Mr Franklin said diffidently, "like a man who'd seen all he wanted to see."

There was a murmur of laughter in the court, and a voice that might have been General Flashman's muttered: "Shaw isn't the fool he looks."

"Silence!" cried someone, and the barrister went on doggedly:

"So, Mr Franklin – do you have any reason whatsoever to connect the presence of Mr George Bernard Shaw in the gallery with the events which later took place there? The events with which we are concerned today?"

Precisely which events they *were* concerned with had been becoming less clear to Mr Franklin as time went on, but now he saw where the barrister was headed, and it shocked him.

"Certainly not, sir. None at all." And for no sane reason that he could have given, he added: "Mr Shaw didn't show any disapproval of the picture that was defaced."

Laughter in court was promptly hushed by the constables; the barrister glared at Mr Franklin as though suspecting him of levity.

"Well, Mr Sullivan," said the judge, and addressed the barrister in a mumble in which could be heard: "no need to hear further ... unusual procedure ... oh, quite, harmful rumours ... reputation ...

411

plainly demonstrated . . . no question of implication whatsoever . . . perfectly satisfactory . . . Mr Lees? Sir Huntly? Mr Stratton? Very good . . . obliged . . ." at the end of which Mr Sullivan gathered up his papers, bowed to the bench, murmured, and strode from the court, leaving Mr Franklin a trifle dazed, but under the impression that his testimony thus far had been of service to Mr Bernard Shaw, which, since he had enjoyed portions of the man's plays (although not *The Shewing Up of Blanco Posnet*) was quite an agreeable sensation.

It was not, however, the principal reason why he had been called to court, as he was now reminded. Another barrister, Mr Lees, now rose and invited Mr Franklin to describe what had taken place at or about 3.30 p.m. in the vicinity of the painting "Vision of the Stainless Knight".

Since he had rehearsed what he would say, this presented no great difficulty. He must have told it concisely and well, for counsel did not interrupt, although the seated ones scribbled busily. He described how Lady Helen Cessford had denounced the House of Lords" decision, how Millicent Shore had then attacked the painting with what appeared to be a butcher's cleaver, how he had tried to intervene but had been blocked by a spectator, and how Pip had prevented Shore from continuing the destruction of the picture. At this point Mr Lees intervened.

"You hastened forward when you saw the picture being mutilated, but someone was in your way. Who was that?"

"I don't know his name. A tall man – I believe he is among the witnesses. It was quite accidental."

"Meanwhile Miss Delys had run forward and was grappling with the defendant Shore. What did you do then?"

"I pushed past the tall man, to try to help Miss Delys."

"And did you?"

"No, I didn't reach her."

"Why not?"

Mr Franklin had no wish to make the case against Lady Helen blacker than it was, but he knew that hedging would probably do just that.

"Lady Helen Cessford was in the way."

"Ah. She was blocking your path – with the intention of preventing your reaching the painting and helping Miss Delys, who was trying to save it from destruction?"

Before he could answer a tall barrister with a large hawk nose was on his feet. "M'lud, the witness can hardly know what the intentions of my client were."

"He could judge from her actions, however," said Lees promptly. "Did the defendant Cessford, in your opinion, intentionally block your path?"

"I believe she did – yes." That could do no damage that had not already been done by her own plea of guilty to aiding and abetting the attack on the picture.

"Did she attempt to prevent you by force? Did she simply impede you, or did she offer to strike you?"

This was the vital question and he had to answer carefully. "She was holding a parasol, in such a way that I might have run onto it. I grabbed it from her, and she drew back and shouted some slogan. Then the attendant caught hold of her and pulled her away."

"Did she not attempt to strike you with the parasol?"

Mr Franklin permitted himself the hint of a smile. "I can't say what she might have done if there had been more time. As it was, things happened very quickly. I saw the parasol in her hands, and without thinking, I suppose, snatched it away from her. She certainly didn't attempt to recover it; indeed, she took a step away."

It was as far as he could go, in honesty. Mr Lees's lips tightened. "Other witnesses will say that they saw her strike violently at you with the parasol – at your head. If that were so, you must surely have been aware of it?"

"It happened very quickly, sir, as I said. As I was moving towards her, she may have raised the parasol, drawing it back from me. I don't know. Then I was very close to her, and I wrenched the parasol away – "

"So presumably you thought she was going to strike you? Other people say they saw her actually swing the parasol at your face."

"I can't speak for them," said Mr Franklin firmly. "I know she certainly did not hit me, with that or anything else. Whatever she intended, I had the parasol away from her too fast for her to do anything. She was blocking my way, and I wanted to get past her quickly."

It was fairly plain that Mr Lees was not going to get the admission he wanted. He paused and changed his ground.

"But she has struck you, on a previous occasion, has she not?"

He had not expected it, but Mr Franklin did not hesitate.

"Yes, sir. In September, 1909, she was selling suffragette literature outside the Waldorf Hotel. I was new to the country then, and I'm afraid I unintentionally offended her. She slapped my face, after I had declined to buy her papers."

There was a buzz in the court, and on the press bench there was a sudden outburst of shorthand.

"I see. So whatever her behaviour at the Royal Academy, you knew she was given to violence – she had indeed assaulted you on a previous occasion?"

"Yes, sir. Possibly that was why I moved so nimbly in the gallery."

There was a ripple of laughter from the public benches. Mr Lees looked hard at the witness, but said nothing. To his left, Mr Franklin could feel Lady Helen watching him; he glanced towards her, and she looked away, her face expressionless. Mr Lees changed his tack again.

"During all this nimble activity on your part, in which you disarmed the defendant of her parasol for no reason, since you had no cause, apparently, to suppose she was going to strike you with it – " Mr Franklin made a mental note that one shouldn't assume that one had ever got the better of an English barrister " – while you were engaged in this unnecessary exercise, did you have leisure to observe what was happening to Miss Delys?"

"I saw her grapple with the woman with the hatchet and they fell down on the floor."

"She grappled with the defendant Shore, who had the hatchet, and was wielding it. Did Shore attempt to strike Miss Delys with the hatchet?"

"Not that I saw. No."

Mr Lees sat down, and the hawk-nosed barrister arose and looked blandly at Mr Franklin, as man to man.

"Mr Franklin, you have told us what happened at the Royal Academy, very fairly, I believe. And at the prompting of my learned friend, you have described how Lady Helen Cessford assaulted you outside the Waldorf Hotel." No mincing of words, straightforward stuff. "I wonder would you tell the jury precisely why she slapped your face on that occasion." His smile was sympathetic.

"As I said, I was new to England. I was foolish enough to make a joke about . . . about the sale of suffragette papers. Lady Helen was offended."

"I see. But I gather that you were not so violently assaulted that

414

you took grave exception to it? There was no question of a charge – anything of that nature?"

"It wouldn't have crossed my mind," said Mr Franklin, but he forebore to mention the policeman.

"So – we have heard of two of your encounters with my client. But I understand that you have met her on other occasions also?"

"We've met socially – yes."

"Where, Mr Franklin?"

"At Sandringham House, Norfolk."

There was an instant murmur in the court, and counsel repeated: "Yes, at Sandringham – "

"Where, Sir Huntly?" said the judge.

"Sandringham House, m'lud, the – "

"Where's that?" demanded the judge.

"In Norfolk, m'lud."

"Ah. Norfolk. Very well."

Sir Huntly sighed, and said loudly: "You met at Sandringham, where you were the guests of his late Majesty King Edward, and of Queen Alexandra?"

"Yes, sir. Christmas, 1909."

"So you know my client well?"

"Not well, sir. We're acquainted."

"But you conversed with her – talked in friendly terms? The customary exchanges between fellow guests."

"Yes. sir."

"I see. But you are not close friends, although both of you were honoured by the friendship of their majesties." Having established that, for what he conceived it to be worth in the eyes of a middle-class jury who presumably loved a lord (and equally, a lady), Sir Huntly reluctantly turned to weightier matters. "Mr Franklin, I will not trespass further on your time, or on the time of the gentlemen of the jury. We have heard you tell my learned friend of the unhappy events which befell at the Royal Academy. I believe these gentlemen will agree with me – " Sir Huntly invited the jury into intellectual fellowship " – that you gave your evidence with admirable clarity and good sense. Nothing could be fairer. I will confine myself to one question, the all-important question to my client. She is charged with assault – upon you. Mr Franklin, did she assault you?"

"No, sir."

"Thank you, Mr Franklin."

415

Sir Huntly smiled and sat down. Mr Lees smiled and stood up.

"One last question on my side. She did not assault you, you say. You may not be entirely clear on the legal meaning of assault. Did she *offer* to strike you?"

"By offer," said Mr Franklin slowly, "you mean did she intend – "

"No, not precisely. Did she make as though to strike you – was she on the point of striking you?"

"M'lud," interposed Sir Huntly with weary tolerance, "I do believe the witness has already answered the question to the very best of his ability – "

"Indeed, Sir Huntly. I am inclined to agree, Mr Lees, that you covered the point thoroughly in your examination."

"As your lordship pleases." Mr Lees bowed. "I had thought that the witness had *avoided* answering the question to the best of his ability. But if I may touch on a point raised by my learned friend." He turned to the witness box. "Mr Franklin, you have told us that while you are not a close friend, especially, of the defendant Cessford, you are acquainted with her on social terms – Sandringham, and so forth. You are both accustomed to move in the highest station of society?"

Mr Franklin was far from sure that Lady Helen would be flattered by the association, but he replied carefully: "Yes, sir."

"I see. Now, despite the fact that she has assaulted you once, and – " Mr Lees paused for effect " – shall we say for the moment has rather strenuously impeded you (it will be for the jury to decide whether a stronger term is applicable) in the present instance – despite this, and the fact that you say –" there was just the barest emphasis on the two words "– that there is no special intimacy between you, am I right in suggesting that your feelings towards her are those natural from a gentleman towards a lady in that exalted circle to which you both belong?"

Not quite how Mr Franklin would have put it, but he could only say: "I hope so, sir," and trust it didn't sound too pompous.

"From a gentleman to a lady," continued Mr Lees, "in distress?"

"I don't quite follow," said Mr Franklin, and Mr Lees shrugged expressively.

"The lady is in the dock, Mr Franklin. A distressing position, you will allow. And I am sure you feel keenly for her in that unhappy situation, do you not?"

"I'm sorry to see her there, of course."

"Of course. You feel that natural sympathy – chivalry might not be too strong a term —which a man of sensibility must feel for her. The more so since you both move in a class," Mr Lees went on relentlessly, "which must view her predicament with peculiar abhorrence, and would do anything consistent with honour to alleviate it?"

Mr Franklin, pressed, gave as neutral a reply as possible. "Very well, sir."

Mr Lees became brusquely frank. "Come, come, sir – can you deny that it has been most painful to you to give evidence today? That while you have given it, as you believe, truthfully, your sense of loyalty to one of your own kind has revolted at the thought that your words might tell against her? That you have felt obliged to give her the benefit of every doubt?" Mr Lees threw back his head. "Can you deny that you would most gladly see Lady Helen Cessford acquitted of the charge on which you have done your best to defend her?"

Sir Huntly's protests, drowned by Mr Lees' peroration, broke through in an indignant squawk, the judge rebuked the prosecution, Mr Lees apologized and withdrew the question, the jury looked knowingly from witness to defendant, and the former member of the Wild Bunch, saddled with the ideals and principles which Mr Lees had so generously thrust upon him, was allowed to stand down. He took a seat on the public benches, at a safe distance from General Flashman, who had viewed the prosecutor's performance with the approving eye of a connoisseur of the art of humbug.

Miss Priscilla Delys was called, and tripped demurely to the witness box, where she took the oath in a breathless little voice which Mr Franklin guessed had been carefully rehearsed. The judge told her gently to speak up a little, Miss Delys turned in the box to regard him with unbounded awe, and his lordship smiled paternally. Mr Lees elicited from her that she was a revue artiste, witness implying by her tone and manner that the decorum of her stage performance would have done credit to a morality play; she had also appeared in musical comedy and pantomime, and was a professional artist's model –

"What did you play in pantomime?" asked the judge with kindly interest.

"Dandini, my lord," said Pip gravely, and the judge said, "Ah, yes, in *Cinderella*, I think," and nodded wisely. Pip gave him her first shy smile, and then agreed carefully with Mr Lees that she had been at the Royal Academy on May 18. Alone? No, she had been accompanied by Mr Franklin, the first witness – the jury regarded him with respect-

417

ful envy while Mr Franklin sighed inwardly; his own evidence had not been quite so specific. Mr Lees invited her to describe what had taken place, and Pip drew herself up, took a deep breath which caused the jury to become even more attentive, and complied.

She did it extremely well, in a quiet, modulated voice, without smiling; while looking quite astonishingly pretty she seemed to be entirely unaware of the fact, which was as unlike Pip as Mr Franklin could imagine. Modesty, he decided, was obviously her watchword of the day.

"Now, you saw the defendant Shore begin to deface the picture, you say. Tell us about that."

"Well, my lord, I was so shocked that for a moment I couldn't move, and then Mr Franklin ran forward to try to stop her, but someone bumped into him, you see, and – "

"Speak to the jury, not to me," said the judge, not without regret.

"Oh, I beg your pardon. Well, then, when I saw her hacking at the painting, I called out to her to stop, but she just went on cutting at it, and it was shocking to see, so I just ran at her and tried to catch hold of her hand, but I – "

"The hand that was wielding the cleaver?" asked Mr Lees.

"What? Oh, yes, but I couldn't catch it, and it nearly hit me – "

"What did? The cleaver?"

"Yes. It just missed my fingers." Pip held up a small grey-gloved hand, and even Mr Lees winced. "So I pushed at her, and she fell over, and I tumbled on top of her, and we landed on the floor."

"And then what did you do?"

"Well, nothing, you see. I just wanted to stop her spoiling the picture, and when she fell, of course, that stopped her. It was a dreadful mess, with a great piece of canvas hanging down. I couldn't bear to look at it."

Don't overdo it, thought Mr Franklin, but Pip had weighed her audience to a nicety, and although not a soul in court realized it, she had calculated carefully how to give her evidence with the maximum of credit to herself and the minimum of damage to Millicent Shore. At the moment she had the jury furrowing their brows in sympathy, and Mr Lees was nodding solemnly.

"I see. Now, Miss Delys, there is a point on which I want you to answer very carefully indeed. When you tried to stop the defendant striking the picture, you say you tried to catch her hand, and the cleaver just missed you." Mr Lees signed to a constable who picked up the cleaver from the clerk's table and passed it to him. Mr Lees weighed it in his hand, and turned it so that the ugly, glittering blade caught the light.

"Is this the weapon, Miss Delys?" Pip nodded, wide-eyed. "I don't wish to distress you, but I'm sure you are aware that it could have injured you very seriously."

Pip said in a small voice: "I didn't think of that," and the jury would have laid down their collective life for her.

"Well, that does you great credit. But tell me – you came at her from the side, and caught at her hand. Was she in the act of striking the picture?"

"Yes, sir. She had her hand up, like this – " Pip raised her hand above shoulder level " – and as she struck, I grabbed and missed."

"I see. Did the cleaver then strike the picture?"

Pip frowned. "No, sir, it missed, too. It went sort of sideways, but it didn't hit anything."

"It went sideways. It went towards you, in fact?"

"Well – sort of, yes."

"Miss Delys, I know it is difficult for you to say exactly, because in a struggle of that kind everything is confused, but is it possible that the cleaver was aimed *at* you?"

Pip might have been expected to widen her eyes and look like a stricken fawn, but she reacted quite otherwise. She shook her head firmly and said: "Oh, no. It wasn't, I'm sure."

"Well," said Mr Lees, hiding his disappointment, "you may not like to think it was aimed at you, but some of the people watching will say they believe it was. Are you certain you were in a position to judge?"

"Oh, yes," said Pip confidently. "You see, she was trying to hit the picture – she never even saw me until I grabbed at her, just as she was letting fly. She's very small, you know, and my snatching at her spoiled her aim and put her off balance, so that the axe thing missed the picture. But it was just an accident that it swung near my hand, which was stretched out. I know she wasn't trying to hit me, because she wasn't looking at me, you see; when she started to swing the thing, she didn't even know I was there, I'm sure."

It was comprehensive, and Mr Lees may have wondered sadly what he had done to deserve such articulately unco-operative witnesses. However, he had not earned his silk for nothing, and he was an even more practised public performer than Pip herself; he made one or

419

two further attempts, in a disarmingly gentle manner, to induce her to admit that the cleaver might have been aimed at her, and then said:

"I've no doubt, Miss Delys, that you were considerably upset by the incident, and it reflects great credit on you that you acted as promptly and bravely as you did. Many young ladies would have been quite incapable of moving – I believe one woman at the scene fainted, did she not? Well, well. But you were not at all flustered when you tried to stop the defendant Shore? Were you?"

Pip hesitated. "No, sir. Shocked, at first, when I saw what she was up to – "

"But when you ran to stop her, you knew exactly what you were doing?"

"Ye-es, sir," Pip frowned doubtfully.

"I mean, you were not panicky, at all? Quite collected?"

It would not have been in Pip's character to look suspicious, so she looked serious instead.

"Oh, yes. Perfectly collected, really."

"Good." Mr Lees appeared satisfied. He smiled at her. "Tell me, Miss Delys, had you any special reason for visiting the exhibition that day?" Before she could answer, Mr Lees chuckled genially, "I think you did, didn't you?"

"Oh . . . oh, yes." Pip smiled back at him.

"You had modelled for two of the other paintings at the Academy, isn't that so? One of them by Signor Matania. Quite a distinction, to have your likeness hung twice at one Royal Academy."

"Yes, sir." Pip could not conceal her pride. "Mr Matania's 'Carthage', and 'Summer Zephyr'. "

The judge roused himself. "Two pictures? Of you, Miss er-um . . . ? Was that correct, Mr Lees?"

Mr Lees said it was, and the judge asked what were the names again, and Mr Lees told him, and the judge made a note and said that was remarkable, thereby joining critical hands with Mr Bernard Shaw. Mr Lees smiled at the happy witness.

"You must have been relieved, that *they* were not attacked," he said casually. Pip's face fell at once. "Did the thought occur to you, Miss Delys?"

"Yes, I remember it did. I remember saying to Mr Franklin – after that other one, of Venus, you know – "

"Ah, yes, the Rokeby Venus."

420

"Well, when the suffragettes smashed it, I hoped they wouldn't touch mine, of course."

"Oh, so it was in your mind *before* you went to the Royal Academy?"

"Yes – I suppose so. It had been, but I wasn't really worrying. "Why?" asked Pip, frowning.

"I think perhaps you were worrying, Miss Delys. I think the thought was in your mind, and you were very relieved to see that your paintings were all right, and then – " Mr Lees suddenly leaned forward " – when you saw Shore suddenly attack the Vision painting, with horrid violence, you were momentarily appalled. It might just as easily have been one of your paintings – the Matania perhaps? Didn't that flash through your mind? Didn't it?"

"I don't know." Pip was momentarily taken aback by the barrister's sudden vehemence. She shot a nervous glance at the judge. "It might have – I don't think I – "

"I'm sure it did! In your mind's eye you saw your own painting being defaced, and you were shocked, frightfully shocked, and you lost your head and rushed blindly forward, without really thinking, and tried to stop her. You weren't quite sure what you were doing, were you?"

"Of course I was!" said Pip. She stared angrily at Mr Lees. "I wanted to stop her hacking the painting – it didn't matter whose it was!"

"Didn't it? Are you quite certain? Didn't you think: 'That's my painting – the lovely nude by Mr Matania – I've got to save it!'" Isn't that what you thought? And didn't everything suddenly swim round you, and the next thing you knew you were being helped to your feet?"

To Mr Franklin's astonishment, and that of everyone else in the court, Pip said nothing. She was looking pale, and angry; Mr Lees shook his head sadly.

"That's what you told the press, you know." He held up a clipping. " 'For a moment I was petrified. Then I thought "That's my painting – the lovely nude by Mr Matania – I've got save it". And everything swam round me, and I didn't know where I was, and I think I ran forward, but all I could see was my picture being cut to pieces by that awful axe, and then everything went black, and next thing I knew they were helping me to my feet.' "

Mr Lees laid down the clipping. "From the *Star* of May 19. There are similar quotations in the other papers. I think that's the truth, isn't

421

it, Miss Delys? I don't believe you really remember what happened – and you're in no position to say whether the cleaver was aimed at you or not."

"That's not true," Pip spoke quite steadily, making no attempt to revert to her role of ingenue. "What I've said here is on oath, and it's what happened. What's in the papers – well, they make up anything. I can't remember every word I said to them, at the time, but I know what I've said here today is gospel." She looked at the judge. "She didn't try to hit me with the axe. She was just hitting the painting. That's the truth, my lord."

The judge nodded solemnly, and looked at Mr Lees, who sat down. Sir Huntly said nothing, since this aspect of the case was no concern of his, but Mr Stratton arose and did what he could on behalf of his client, Millicent Shore. But beyond getting Pip to restate that her evidence was true, and the account in the papers a mixture of romantic fiction and distortion, he accomplished little. The jury, who had hung on Pip's every word at first, looked uncertain; their admiration of the fair witness's charms might be undiminished, but their faith in her memory was visibly shaken. After all, it was in the papers . . . they hated Mr Lees, but they could not fail to be impressed by him.

The judge, whatever he may have thought of Pip's reliability as a witness, was in no doubt of what was fitting. "You are an extremely plucky young lady," he told her when she stood down. "If all your sex acted with such selfless disregard, and with such a proper concern for the public good, we should not be trying this deplorable case today." Pip managed a polite smile in reply, but Mr Franklin could see she was inwardly boiling.

"I'll never trust a bloody reporter again!" she exploded, when they were seated in the corner booth of a public house during the luncheon recess. "Why won't I learn to keep my mouth shut? They egg you on to say such damfool things, and you never think . . . my stars, I ought to know better. And that slimy shark of a lawyer, leading me on, and then making me out to be some hysterical cow that doesn't know what she's doing! Makes you feel such an awful fool!"

"I know," said Mr Franklin. "The same gentleman thoroughly convinced the jury that I'm the biggest liar that ever took the oath – oh, a very honourable liar, to be sure, but . . ."

"And I haven't done that poor old soul a bit of good!" said Pip bitterly. "It's so unfair! All right, she slashed the picture, and she's a wicked old faggot, but I think she's barmy, anyway. And she looked so frail and old, and that oily villain of a lawyer'll shop her all the way to Holloway and back. It's not right – she never *thought* of taking a swipe at me!"

"I'm quite sure she didn't," said Mr Franklin. "But I'm very much afraid the jury will end up believing she did." He was thinking of the large man's evidence which was still to come, and the event justified him.

The large man was named Miller, a stockbroker of Ealing who testified with confidence and a fine sense of outrage. This did no great harm to Lady Helen's defence; witness's evidence of how she had "thrust viciously" and "slashed violently" with her parasol at Mr Franklin was effectively countered when Sir Huntly produced the parasol itself, weighing the frilly little article in his palm, and then placing it open over his shoulder. The jury laughed, and looked sceptical when Mr Miller declared huffily that the ferrule might easily have taken Mr Franklin's eye out. But the stockbroker hammered a convincing nail in Millicent Shore's coffin: he was positive she had aimed a blow of the cleaver at Miss Delys, directly and deliberately, and no cross-examination could shake him. He had seen what he had seen, and that was that.

Even so, the evidence seemed evenly-balanced until the appearance of Mrs Jennifer Redcliffe, the lady who had spoken to Pip earlier on the fateful afternoon. Dabbing constantly at her nose with a handkerchief, Mrs Redcliffe described with agitation how Shore had undoubtedly aimed her final blow at the actress's hand.

"She tried to *chop* at her," said Mrs Redcliffe in shocked tones. "She tried to chop at her arm. It was a dreadful wicked thing! I expected to see the little girl – " at this Pip gave a suppressed snort " – appallingly injured. That fearful weapon missed her by a fraction – the merest fraction." Mrs Redcliffe shuddered, and dabbed vigorously.

Mr Stratton made the mistake of suggesting that Pip, who had given contrary evidence, was surely in a position to know best; he received a crushing retort.

"How could she?" demanded Mrs Redcliffe indignantly. "She was distraught, trying to restrain that . . . that wicked woman! I am sure she may not believe herself that such a callous attack was made on her – she could not conceive of it! She has womanly instinct, and no doubt even feels pity for her . . . her assailant. Misguided pity." Mrs Redcliffe sniffed rendingly. "She is the most sweet and delicate creature imaginable." The sweet and delicate creature squirmed and muttered "Oh, Christ!", and Mrs Redcliffe struck a final telling blow by describing Pip's wild entreaties, as she called them, which indicated the overwrought condition of the heroine.

The remaining witnesses had little to add. One attendant testified that Lady Helen had not resisted arrest; another described the state of the vandalised painting, and the gashes in the wall behind, which suggested that Shore had struck with the strength of frenzy. The President of the Academy testified tactfully that the defaced picture's value was not to be calculated in financial terms; when the judge suggested that the Academy might consider covering its paintings with unbreakable glass, the President winced and replied that quite apart from the matter of cost, the viewing of works of art through glass was an affront to the sensibilities; his additional aside that one might as well wash one's feet with one's socks on was fortunately lost in the judge's observation that he had some pictures at home – quite good pictures, he believed – and they had glass on them. The President looked as though he wasn't in the least surprised, and thereafter stood down.

There being no defence witnesses, the judge reminded the accused that they had the choice of remaining silent, or making an unsworn statement, or of giving evidence on oath subject to cross-examination. At this Sir Huntly went into earnest whispered consultation with his client and her solicitor. General Flashman sat forward attentively watching. Lady Helen was seen to speak forcibly in a low tone. Sir Huntly made soothing gestures, and finally Lady Helen, whose expression suggested both impatience and suspicion, gave an irritated little shrug and withdrew from the consultation. Sir Huntly announced that his client had no statement to make, and Mr Stratton called Millicent Shore to the witness box.

She took the oath in a surprisingly strong voice, although her hand was seen to be trembling on the edge of the box. She agreed that she had no regrets about the mutilation of the picture, but denied absolutely that she had tried to injure the young woman who had attempted to restrain her; indeed, she most sincerely begged the young lady's pardon – at which Pip was seen to shake her head in distressed acknowledgement. Mr Stratton pointed out that several witnesses had given an exactly opposite account, and Millicent Shore became pathetically vehement. She would never do such a thing; it was a wicked lie to suggest that she had tried to hurt a fellow-creature. At this point she burst into tears, and a wardress was allowed to attend her, which consisted of seating her on a chair in the box and laying a hand on her shoulder. After a moment the accused dried her eyes and repeated her denial in a shaking voice.

"Why should I wish to injure her? It's not true!" She had her head down, and her words were punctuated by sobs. "Her hand may have been there, but I didn't try to hit it! I did not. I never struck at her! She knows I did not – she's told you!" She raised a ravaged face to stare round the court; her white hair straggled untidily from beneath her shabby hat, and her face was a picture of grief. "Why don't you believe her? I swear I didn't try to hurt her! I wouldn't for the world!"

"Of course she didn't!" This was Pip, indignantly audible. "Why don't you let her alone?"

There were admonitory murmurs, and the judge, more in gentle reproof than anger, warned the interruptor that she must be silent or she would be removed from the court. Pip, pale but mutinous, was subsiding, when suddenly Lady Helen Cessford stood up in the dock and announced in a loud, firm voice:

"I wish to be called as a witness."

Sir Huntly flapped up like a startled eagle, the judge ordered Lady Helen to be seated. Sir Huntly whispered to her urgently, and presently she sat down with evident reluctance. Mr Stratton resumed his examination, but beyond her repeated assertion that she was innocent of any attempt to injure Pip, delivered in a tearful voice with much shaking of her lowered head, he got little more from Millicent Shore. To Mr Franklin it appeared that there was a sense of sympathy in the court for the pathetic figure in the box; the jury were looking uncomfortable, and there were even a few muttered murmurs from the public benches. And then Mr Lees got to his feet.

He stood in silence until the witness's sobbing had subsided, and began his cross-examination in a quiet, patient voice, asking about the choice of the cleaver to mutilate the picture. Whose cleaver was it? The accused's; she used it for chopping kindling. Had Lady Helen suggested its employment? No. But Lady Helen must have approved it, surely? Witness could not remember; she rather thought Lady Helen had said it would do; something like that. Mr Lees then wondered why Millicent Shore, rather than the younger and stronger Lady Helen, had undertaken to make the attack on the picture. No reply. Mr Lees continued quietly:

"Did Lady Helen tell you to make the attack?"

425

"I don't remember."

"I think you do. Did she not instruct you to destroy the picture?"

There was a long pause, and then Millicent Shore lifted her head and spoke clearly.

"No, she didn't. It was agreed."

"Agreed." Mr Lees paused. "Very well. Now tell me – when you struck the picture . . . what was in your mind?"

Millicent Shore hesitated. Then: "To destroy it."

"And did you? You struck three blows, I understand. Did that deface it to your satisfaction?"

It was the first hint of an edge to his examination, but Millicent Shore seemed not to notice.

"I had no opportunity . . . to strike again. I was thrown down and they took hold of me."

"Would you have struck further blows – if you could?"

"I might have done." She was more composed now, with her head up. She pushed aside a tendril of hair from her face.

"Why?" Mr Lees's voice was sharp. "You had effectively ruined it. You had cut a great piece right out of the canvas – destroying forever the work on which someone who had never done you the least harm, had expended so much love and labour. Why strike again?" Millicent Shore's mouth had begun to quiver, and without waiting for an answer Mr Lees went harshly on: "But when Miss Delys caught at your hand, you *did* strike again, didn't you?"

"At the painting – yes."

"Oh? You didn't hit it, though, did you? You came much closer to hitting Miss Delys."

"I didn't mean to!" Suddenly the tears began again. "I didn't try to hit her! I struck at the p-picture!"

"Quite deliberately? You were calm and collected, were you?"

"I was hitting at the painting!"

"You wanted to hit it again?"

"Yes – I've told you – "

"Yes! But Miss Delys got in your way, didn't she? She tried to stop you, and you didn't want to be stopped!"

"I . . . I don't know what you mean . . ."

"Yes, you do! You were slashing at the painting with all your might, intent on destroying it – that was the one thought in your mind, remember? And suddenly someone intervenes – " Mr Lees's voice

426

was rising " – before your work of destruction was complete – but you went on striking, with maniac strength, didn't you?"

"I didn't strike at her!" Millicent Shore was weeping steadily now. "I was hitting at the painting – "

"Yes, until a hand reached out between you and the picture, and you went on slashing callously, with furious disregard for whoever was getting in your way – "

"I didn't! It's not so! I didn't!"

"Then why strike at all? When you saw her hand, why not drop the cleaver? You'd done your beastly work – why continue the blow that almost severed a young girl's fingers? Why turn the fury of your blow on her?"

"I didn't! I didn't! It's a lie!"

"Witnesses saw you do that very thing! They say that only by merciful chance was she not terribly mutilated – "

"No! No! No!" Millicent Shore's face was in her hands, she was rocking in her seat. "I wouldn't have hurt her for – "

"How touching!" sneered Mr Lees. "You would not have hurt her, but you slashed madly at her with a cleaver, and came within an ace of shearing her fingers – of crippling an innocent girl for life! I put it to you that in your fury you would have slashed at anything that came in your way – "

"No! No! I wouldn't! That's a wicked – "

" – that in your evil, spiteful rage at the frustration of your crime, you were ready to mutilate without pity, to hack blindly at anyone who – "

"I would have hacked at you!" It came out in a tortured shriek, from a contorted face, and was followed instantly by a flood of sobbing; she beat her hand feebly on the edge of the box and sank back, holding her face and wailing, while the court sat shocked. Mr Lees stood for a moment, took up his pen, replaced the cap, and sat down.

Mr Stratton did what he could. When her hysteria had passed, he was able by painful persuasion to extract a halting, almost incoherent apology from his client. She was sorry – it came out in a whisper – very sorry: she had not meant what she said to the gentleman. Finally, she had not tried to strike Miss Delys.

Stratton sat down, and Millicent Shore was helped back to the dock, whimpering softly. Lady Helen did not look at her, but sat bolt upright while Sir Huntly rose unwillingly.

"My client wishes to make an unsworn statement, m'lud."

427

The court buzzed as she came to her feet. General Flashman stroked his chin, Sir Huntly looked apprehensive, Lady Helen spoke dispassionately to the wall above the judge's head.

"I wish to state that I take full responsibility for the events at the Royal Academy. The reason why Miss Shore and not I attacked the painting was that we had agreed that I should distract attention by calling out to the persons in the gallery. The suggestion that she attacked anyone is utterly ridiculous and malicious – "

The judge intervened sternly to remind her that she might speak on her own behalf only; also, that since what she said was not open to cross-examination, it would have corresponding weight with the court.

"Very well, I was the instigator of the attack on the painting, and acted as one with Miss Shore in every respect. Whatever guilt attaches to her, attaches to me equally, in the eyes of the law and of the cruel and unjust society we are fighting against. That is all." She sat down.

The addresses to the jury were predictable. Mr Lees used his ironic gift lavishly in dealing with Lady Helen's gentle birth, high principles and lofty connections, reminding the jury that they were not medieval peasants who need quail before the imperious glance of a lord's daughter. (The jury assumed the look of sturdy yeomen, and glanced surreptitiously at the dock, but nobility's imperious glance was levelled indifferently at the opposite wall.) A paragon of society, Mr Lees continued, with a penchant for violence, who admitted a previous assault and might be thought likely to use a parasol as freely as she would, in a previous incarnation, doubtless have used a horsewhip. Bowing to Sir Huntly's indignant interruption, Mr Lees passed on imperturbably to suggest that between Mr Franklin's gallant evasions and Mr Miller's impartial testimony there was an obvious choice, and he could rely on the jury's good sense to make it.

In the case of Shore, however, he could see no choice at all. The evidence was all too dreadfully clear, and the accused herself had provided the most damning of it: they had seen for themselves her reaction in the grip of passion. Mr Lees touched indulgently on Pip's understandably suspect memory, and movingly on her fragile beauty which might have been so foully disfigured. He cautioned the jury not to be unduly moved by Shore's present pathetic appearance, "which might move your pity if you did not recall how little pity she showed when she swung that horrid cleaver at a tender girl. She shed no tears then."

Mr Stratton laboured manfully on the point that Pip herself denied the charge against his client; he reminded the jury of the well-known question of reasonable doubt, and drew attention to the accused's age, frailty, and obvious repugnance at the charge. In Mr Franklin's view, he made only a middling best of a fairly bad case – unlike Sir Huntly, who knew well how to make the best of his, by skilfully contrasting the charge against Shore with that against Lady Helen, and pointing up the triviality of the latter. He dwelt flatteringly on Mr Franklin's intelligence, integrity, and reliability, implied with masterly innuendo that Ealing stockbrokers were perhaps not the most impartial witnesses where the aristocracy was concerned, and concluded that a jury of such shrewd perception (here he looked knowingly at the bovine faces of the twelve good men and true) could hardly suppose that an honourable lady – for however they might deplore her political views, she *was* a lady – would freely admit to abetting the destruction of a valuable painting, and at the same time demean herself by lying about a mere slap with a parasol.

The judge's summing-up was a revelation to Mr Franklin. He had supposed his lordship asleep for much of the trial; even during his waking moments he had looked and sounded rather like something out of Gilbert and Sullivan. Now, like many before and since, Mr Franklin received a humbling surprise as he listened to a brisk, lucid, and comprehensive account of the evidence, with brief dissertations on the legal definition of assault, and on the delicacy of deciding between conflicting witnesses. This last, the judge emphasized, was of crucial importance, especially where accused and principal witness were in agreement against the testimony of other bystanders, as happened in both cases here. It was for the jury to weigh this, and perhaps to remember the old sporting adage that the onlooker sees most of the game.

"In other words, you and me don't know what we're talking about," observed Pip shrewdly to Mr Franklin as they waited in the corridor outside the court. When the jury retired they adjourned to the pub, where the sight of Mr Lees and Mr Stratton, in their wigs and gowns, discussing cricket scores with a uniformed police inspector, had so moved Pip's indignation that she had insisted on returning to the court building. There, the most interesting spectacle was General Flashman conversing aside with two large and capable-looking men in blue serge suits; Mr Franklin wondered vaguely who they were.

"Think they'll get off?" asked Pip, for the twentieth time. "You'd

429

reckon they would, wouldn't you, after what we said? Not that I care, honestly, about that snooty bitch Cessford, but if they send the old girl down it'll be just . . . just damned nonsense, that's what! I *know* she didn't mean it! Look, tell you what – you heard me, and I heard you. Tell me what *you'd* do, about my one, if you were on the jury, and I'll tell you what I'd do about yours."

Mr Franklin considered. "I'd believe your evidence. I'd reckon Miller was too prejudiced against suffragettes to be reliable – and Mrs Redcliffe can't see anything except that cleaver just missing your hand. If we were in Scotland, where they have the in-between verdict, I'd say 'not proven''. As we're in England – well, I'd acquit, I guess. But it would be a pretty close thing. What about Lady Helen?"

"Well," said Pip slowly, "I'd convict her – and that's not being catty or jealous just 'cos she's got a good figure and tons of style. She'd make a good second lead —you know, stately-proud, like the wife in *Ideal Husband*, or a principal boy, if she didn't look more likely to neigh than sing – "

"She's on trial for assault, not auditioning for *Puss-in-Boots*," said Mr Franklin. "Why would you convict?"

"Because it's plain as a pikestaff she tried to land you one. Well, she did, didn't she? And everyone can see you fancy her quite a bit – even those clods on the jury. Now, don't deny it," Pip added, with amusement, "because that *will* be perjury. I don't mean you're biting your nails over her, but she fascinates you a bit. So I reckon the jury'll believe Miller rather than you."

"Well, I'll be damned!" said Mr Franklin.

"You'd be a mug if you didn't fancy her," said Pip cheerfully. "I mean, she's not bad – and she's a marquess's daughter. Men!" She shook her head and giggled. "Here, isn't the judge a little pet? I'll have to get the Dandini part again this Christmas, if only for his sake. Hello – what's happening?"

There was a general bustle towards the court; Mr Lees hurried in, straightening his wig, constables appeared, Sir Huntly strode through majestically, and Pip and Mr Franklin made their way inside to the benches. General Flashman took his stand in the aisle, eyeing the jury as they filed back; the two burly men had disappeared. The court settled once the judge had seated himself, and the clerk rose and asked the jury if they had reached their verdicts, and were they the verdicts of them all? The foreman said they were, the prisoners were

430

instructed to rise, and there was a tense hush as the clerk asked for the verdict on Millicent Shore.

"Guilty, my lord."

Pip gasped and put her hands to her mouth, turning a white face to Mr Franklin. "They can't! She didn't!" The murmur of the court was stilled again as the verdict was called for on Lady Helen Cessford.

"Not guilty, my lord."

This time the murmur was louder, there was a hiss from somewhere on the public benches, the clerk glared furiously round, and there were cries of "Order! Silence!" Mr Franklin's eyes were fixed in fascination on the dock; Millicent Shore was leaning forward with both hands on the rail, her head down; Lady Helen was bolt upright, her face white and furious. As the noise subsided her voice rang out across the court:

"I wish to change my plea! I wish to plead guilty to the charge of assault! I – "

This time there was no stilling the uproar. Noise seemed to be coming from every direction except the press table, where the reporters were scribbling furiously, one eye on the court and the other on their shorthand. Sir Huntly had risen and was falling over things in his efforts to get to the dock, the judge was staring scandalized, the clerk was demanding silence and order.

"The defendant will be quiet. This is most improper." The judge admonished Lady Helen in shocked tones. "Your plea has been taken, and the verdict given. You must be silent. In a moment you will have an opportunity to speak." For a second it looked as though Lady Helen was about to answer back in no uncertain voice, but with Sir Huntly restraining her in dumb show she eventually put her lips together and waited, obviously biding her time. Order was restored, the judge conferred with the clerk, and then addressed the dock.

"Prisoners at the bar, you have pleaded guilty, the defendant Shore to the charge of malicious damage, the defendant Cessford to the charge of aiding and abetting that damage. You have heard the verdicts of the jury on the further charges of assault. Have you anything to say before sentence is passed upon you? Shore?"

Millicent Shore shook her lowered head; she was trembling violently, but suddenly she seemed to master herself and raised her tear-stained face.

"I am so sorry . . . that the young lady . . ." The whispered voice trailed away. Then: "I did not try to hurt her; I did not. I ask her

431

pardon with all my heart . . ." She relapsed into sobs, and the wardress came to support her.

"Cessford?"

Lady Helen took hold of the dock rail, and the court braced itself. Sir Huntly was screwed round in his seat, glowering at her.

"If I am not to be allowed to change my plea," she said, in a surprisingly quiet voice, "and if my admission of the assault carries no weight, then that is a matter for the court – and for the country, who can judge of the way in which justice is dispensed in its name. That I can be pronounced innocent, where Miss Shore, in the face of clear evidence to the contrary, is found guilty, is nothing less than a travesty of justice. In all that took place at the Royal Academy, I am as guilty as she; no, I will not call it guilt, since what we did was forced on us by the blind stupidity, prejudice, and cruelty of the shoddy and unworthy men who abuse the trust – "

A thunderous banging from the clerk's table interrupted her. The judge said calmly: "You are permitted to make a statement; that does not give you licence to indulge in vulgar abuse. It does not become you, and it will not help you. If you have anything to say, you must say it in proper terms."

"Then," said Lady Helen, "I have nothing to say except to protest against the corrupt and unjust laws which have placed us where we are, to express my disgust with the proceedings of this court, and to assure you that I am glad that we did what we did, and that I shall do as much again when the opportunity arises. I shall continue to use any weapons in my – "

"That will do," said the judge. "The court will not listen to political harangue." He looked at the barristers inquiringly, there was a shaking of heads, the judge pondered his notes for a moment and then looked up.

"Millicent Shore, you have pleaded guilty to a most shocking act of vandalism. Wantonly and callously you have destroyed a valuable work of art, for no reason except the furtherance of your political views. It is not for me to comment on those views, but it is my duty, by passing sentence, to express the abhorrence of society at the way in which you have misguidedly sought to promote them, and to give warning to others who may be tempted to commit similar outrages. On the charge of malicious damage you will go to prison for a period of eighteen months. You have also been convicted of a far more serious offence – assault with a deadly weapon on the person of a young woman, an assault which I cannot regard but as a most vicious and cruel attack; it is no fault of yours that the victim was not seriously maimed, and I should be failing in my duty if I did not pass on you a sentence appropriate to the wickedness of your offence." The judge paused. "However, in view of the fact that by providential chance no actual bodily harm was done, of your advanced years, and of the contrition which you expressed – which I believe to be genuine – the sentence will be the most lenient that can be passed in the circumstances. You will go to prison for three years, the sentences to run concurrently."

Millicent Shore fainted. The wardress caught her as she fell, tried for a moment to support her on the seat, and then, with the help of a constable, carried her down the hidden stair leading from the dock. The judge turned to Lady Helen, who stood erect and white-faced, waiting. Mr Franklin might have been mistaken, but he sensed almost an air of triumph about her, as though, having heard the kind of sentence that was being passed, she was looking forward to her own. She was the instigator, she had expressed defiance, not contrition, she had admitted – belatedly – the assault.

"Helen Cessford, you have pleaded guilty to aiding and abetting a most scandalous act of vandalism, and you have told this court that you assume full responsibility for the acts committed by the prisoner Shore. That you acted in concert I fully believe, and I find your conduct the more deplorable in that you have shown, by your demeanour in this court, a brazen lack of regard for the consequences of your behaviour. And your case is the more distressing in that you have had the privilege of upbringing and refining influence in that class of society to which, above all others, the public is accustomed to look for patterns of duty, honour, and high principle."

"That's what he thinks," muttered Pip derisively.

"Nevertheless," the judge continued, "I am bound to take into account that you were the second, and not the author, of the outrage, and that your behaviour was not aggravated by the kind of savagery against an innocent bystander of which your accomplice has been found guilty. In view of this, and of the fact that your age and station are such as may encourage reformation, and that the salutary effect of this experience may serve to curb a temperament which I believe is wilful rather than corrupt, I am inclined to deal leniently with you." There was an exclamation from Lady Helen, but the judge went on: "I will impose a fine of £500. You will also compensate the artist and

433

the Royal Academy for the damage done – Sir Huntly, you will be good enough to consult in the appropriate quarters in that respect – and you will be bound over to be of good behaviour for two years."

He got to his feet, the clerk cried: "The court will rise!", and the murmur of astonishment from the public benches was half-drowned by the rustle as everyone stood up. But the hissing was heard distinctly now, and in the dock Lady Helen, from chalk-white, had turned crimson.

"No!" she cried. "No! I will not accept this! I will not be set free! I demand to be punished with Millicent Shore!"

The judge, half out of his seat, regarded her for a moment.

"If there is any further outburst I will hold you in contempt of court. You are not – "

"Then hold me in contempt! I *am* in contempt, of you and of this miserable apology for a court of justice! This is a conspiracy to deal leniently with me while persecuting Miss Shore! To discredit our movement and – "

"Sir Huntly, will you restrain your client, and instruct her that this court has no intention of assisting her foolish pursuit of martyrdom." The judge said it quietly, and turned through the little door in the panelling beside his seat. Lady Helen's strident shout followed him.

"This is criminal! Hold me in contempt! I will not be silenced!" She was blazing with rage, her knuckles white on the rail of the dock. "Come back, you coward!" She struck out angrily as a constable tried to lay a hand on her arm, and suddenly two men appeared at the back of the dock; Mr Franklin recognized them as the ones who had been talking to General Flashman. The first gripped Lady Helen's elbows with practised ease, and with one swift movement had swung her round bodily and virtually lifted her from the dock. "Let me go! I demand to be – " What she demanded was abruptly cut off; Mr Franklin guessed that the second man had clapped a hand across her mouth. And suddenly she had disappeared down the hidden stair, leaving a babble of consternation in the court, and a rush from the press table for the exits. Pip turned to Mr Franklin in anger and exultation.

"What did I tell you? They fixed it! It's a bloody carve-up! The old girl goes down, and her ladyship walks out free as a bird! British justice, they call it!" She was trembling with indignation. "Of all the rotten tricks!"

Mr Franklin took her arm; he had not been unduly surprised by the verdicts, or by the sentence on Millicent Shore; Lady Helen he felt had got off lightly, but what had startled him had been the court's obvious determination to ignore her outbursts from the dock. "Come along," he said. "Just be thankful it's over, and let's go and have a quiet drink somewhere."

But they were not to be permitted to escape so easily. In the corridor there were reporters waiting for Pip – had she been shocked by the verdict on Millicent Shore? Did she still stick to her story? Would she be going to visit Shore in prison? Did she expect the publicity to have any effect on the success of her revue *Pip, Squeak*? Had the trial been an ordeal for her . . .?

"Right," said Pip with determination. "You want a statement, boys? I'll give you one!"

"Pip, be careful," Mr Franklin was beginning, but Pip cut him short.

"Don't you worry – if they won't touch precious Lady Helen for contempt, let's see 'em try to touch me. Anyway, it's a free country, isn't it?" She turned to the group of reporters, and Mr Franklin was preparing to wait resignedly when he felt himself touched on the arm. To his astonishment, it was one of the large men who had spirited Lady Helen from the dock.

"Beg pardon, sir. A message from General Flashman, and could he have a word with you?"

In view of Sir Harry's recent attempt to compromise him, an interview with that eccentric old scoundrel was the last thing Mr Franklin wanted. He was on the point of refusing when the man added:

"He says it's most urgent, sir – and he'd be deeply obliged to you. He's got a car waiting, sir."

Mr Franklin hesitated, but Pip was now obviously well launched into her views on the British judicial system, no doubt with asides on the future of her theatrical career. So he nodded, and followed the man out of the far door, where General Flashman was waiting beside a closed motor, eyeing with some amusement the small crowd which was being kept back by a couple of uniformed constables.

There was a buzz of excitement as Mr Franklin appeared, which surprised him. "That's him!" called someone, and then the General was preceding him stiffly into the car, he was being ushered aboard, the door closed, and as the car roared away into the traffic he found himself staring at Lady Helen Cessford.

435

22

She was pale, and quite plainly furious, but she said nothing, her hand drumming on the arm-rest as her great-uncle settled his huge bulk beside her, grinned at Mr Franklin, and observed:

"Well, that's over, and all's well that ends well. Eh, Button?"

His great-niece took a deep breath, shot Mr Franklin a baleful look, and turned on her relative.

"This is your doing. Well, I hope you are pleased! You have made a fool of me, disgraced me in the eyes of my friends, done irreparable damage to . . . to our cause – and I suppose you expect me to thank you for it! Well, I shall never forgive you – never!" She turned to stare fixedly out of the window, containing her anger. "I shall never forgive you!" she repeated, and the General winked across at Mr Franklin.

"Wait till you read my will, Button," he remarked cheerfully. "You'll feel warmer towards me then, I dare say. Come along, you silly girl!" He patted her knee, and she started away as though he had leprosy. "I haven't made a fool of you – you've been doing that yourself, for years. And who are these friends you're worried about? A pack of mildewed old maids who've never had a man to keep 'em warm, and have gone sour in consequence. And what's your cause – the vote! Pah! I've done you a good turn, that's all."

His great-niece looked ready to burst. "A good turn! When Millicent Shore goes to prison for three years – and I go free! You know what they will say? That there is one law for the rich and powerful, and another for the poor and feeble! The very injustice our movement is dedicated to – "

"Well, if that's what they say, they're quite right, and you can thank God for it," said Sir Harry. "Now, look here, Button. I've kept you out of jail – I had a few friends of mine, and – "

"And you expect me to be grateful! I feel shame – nothing but shame!"

"Very good," said Sir Harry equably. "It's a dam' sight better feeling shame between linen sheets in Curzon Street than feeling virtuous on a blanket in Holloway, let me tell you. And if you don't think so tonight, or in a week's time, even, you can take my word for it you'd certainly feel it before six months of prison was out. Anyway, there's no help for it; you ain't going to jail, and that's that. So you can make the best of it."

"Am I not!" His great-niece turned on him passionately. "Oh, we shall see! You think you've been so clever, so shrewd, the wise old soldier – well, you will find out otherwise! I shall *force* them to arrest me, I shall – "

"You can try till you're blue in the face," said Sir Harry calmly. "Look here, you little fool, d'you think I was born yesterday? You think you'll smash another painting, or lead a charge in Trafalgar Square, or blow up Westminster, or tear off Asquith's breeches in public? Very well – you do it. And then what? Arrest, trial, publicity, ringing speeches from the dock, martyrdom in the forcible feeding wing – the gallant Lady Helen Cessford victimised by the brutal masculine society which treats women as slaves? That's your style, ain't it?" He turned in his seat to look at Lady Helen, who glared at him in silence.

"No, no, Button, don't you believe it. Oh, you can commit your outrages and be arrested – and you know what will happen then? An eminent poultice-walloper from Harley Street, with some bearded German quack in tow, will come to look at you, and talk very gently to you, and go off in a corner and whisper, and we'll have a little chat with a pal of mine who's a chum of the Home Secretary – and they'll take you off to a quiet little spot in the country, with nice parkland and excellent nursing, and good books to read, and when you're feeling better, and promise not to smash pictures any more – why, you'll come home again. See? And then you can say what you like – and of course no one will believe for one minute that you were crazy, but they'll believe, as you say, that there's one way of treating a suffragette who's a scrubwoman, like that old trot Shore, and another of treating a peer's daughter. And they'll be right," he added complacently.

"You wouldn't dare! You ... you ... you unspeakable man! You ..." Words failed her, and Sir Harry shook his head.

"I would, though. It wouldn't be difficult, you know. Look at your father – the fellow's half-witted, and all the world knows it. Thank God you take after your mother. And if you think it's an awful thing, well, I've seen more of the world than you, Button – and I won't have you ruin your life for some half-baked crank notion that thinks the way to get votes for women is to bomb railway trains. Don't you see it's the last thing that can work – no government, not even that weak-kneed rabble of Asquith's, dare give in to terror and vandalism? Anyway, they'll have a dam' sight more important thing to think of shortly, with this next war that the country's spoiling for." Sir Harry snorted derisively. "Look at 'em – legions of bloodthirsty lunatics drilling in Ireland, workers within an ace of a general strike – dammit, even you women have got the fighting fever, with your smashing and bombing and shooting up locomotives. Any fool can see it'll end in civil war – or more likely our tackling the Kaiser when he takes a slap at Russia or France, which he's itching to do. Your votes are going to look small beer, Button – which is why you're sure to get 'em in the end, and much good they'll do you. But war or not, you'll get 'em all the faster if you lie low and work away quietly. Ain't that right, Franklin?"

Mr Franklin, who had been silent through this remarkable conversation, found Lady Helen's cold stare turned on him, and felt no wish to get embroiled.

"It's not my business, Sir Harry. Personally, whatever Lady Helen may think, I'm thankful she's free. I'm only sorry the other woman was so . . . unlucky. But I don't understand what I'm doing here. You wanted me urgently, I believe."

"Yes." Sir Harry nodded. "Not to talk to, though. I wanted the mob to be edified by the sight of the acquitted noblewoman driving off with the leading prosecution witness. Makes it look all the worse, you see – like a put-up job, which is sure to spread discontent among the suffragettes. All sorts of dear little women from Hackney Wick will think twice about rioting in Whitehall if they know they'll finish up on bread and gruel while their more privileged sisters walk off with a fine. Oh, I know they jailed Pankhurst, and all that – but this case will cause a fair stir among our middle-class females who are busy making bombs in their kitchens. See if it doesn't. I'm surprised," said Sir Harry thoughtfully, "that the Government didn't think of it long ago."

His great-niece was regarding him with unmixed loathing.

"And you . . . you exposed me to the shame of that? To my becoming a target of odium and contempt – "

"Oh, Button, haven't you a grain of sense? No one'll think the worse of you for a minute. The judge, the judiciary, the powers of Whitehall and Westminster – they're the ones who'll take any odium that's going. They're used to it. It makes no difference to them. The public will sneer and scoff and say that 'they' have done it again – but who's 'they'? No one knows. I don't even know myself – but I know if I drop a word in an ear here and there that something pops out at t'other end – like a £500 fine instead of a year's picking oakum. I suppose," he added regretfully, "that I'll have to find the £500 – but I'm shot if I'll fork out more than a tenner for that bloody atrocious office calendar that your friend cut up."

"Are you saying," said Mr Franklin grimly, "that that trial was rigged?"

"You're a bigger ass than I thought you were, if you believe that," said Sir Harry. "Of course it wasn't. It didn't have to be. This isn't America, where you have to slip a thousand dollars to a congressman or a judge to get things done. You're a new country; things ain't settled yet. But here – things aren't rigged. Look at Button – her father's a lord, connected to God knows who. She's my great-niece, and I'm half-Paget, and my sister-in-law married a Rothschild, and among the lot of us I dare say we're connected with half the criminal upper classes – you don't 'rig' things, because you don't have to. There's a sort of atmospheric pressure that causes things to go properly and fittingly. Button couldn't go to jail unless her family washed their hands of her – which they would, like a shot, if it was murder or high treason. But smashing pictures? Hardly. And it isn't rigging, you see. You couldn't rig a British judge and jury nowadays, not if you tried."

There was a short silence, and Mr Franklin became aware that they had driven past Nelson's Column for the second time; evidently the car was pursuing a circle.

"So there it is," said Sir Harry. "And the result is I'm a few hundred quid out of pocket, and my great-niece, who is one of the idols of my eye – I'm singularly blessed, Franklin, in that among all my grand-daughters and great-nieces, there isn't one that wouldn't grace a beauty chorus – my great-niece, I repeat, loathes me for being a corrupt and venal old scoundrel who has, in her misguided view, disgraced her. It don't matter – I'd sooner she loathed me than that she came out of Holloway two years hence, drawn and ugly and old before her time, with the warp of prison woven into her soul."

"And Millicent Shore?" Lady Helen turned on him. "What about

439

her? What will Holloway do to that poor woman, old and feeble and miserable, with – "

"Millicent Shore isn't my grand-niece," said Sir Harry. "And that is her bad luck. If she was, she'd be in this car this minute, and you'd be getting fitted out with prison drawers and chemise." He sighed heavily. "Tap the glass, will you, Franklin, and tell the driver Berkeley Square. Your great-aunt Elspeth has your room ready, Button; you can stay with us for a day or two."

"I prefer to go home," said Lady Helen icily. "If you will explain to Aunt Elspeth that I – "

"Shan't do anything of the sort," said Sir Harry. "Do it yourself, if you like – but I shall tell you something, for the good of your health, young Button, because my temper is rapidly beginning to fray." He turned his great satyr face in her direction. "Or rather, I won't tell you anything, I'll ask you two questions. And if you can answer 'em with a straight face, looking me in the eye – why, you're even more of a hard-barked young bitch than I think you are." He glared at his great-niece, and then asked:

"You're truly concerned about that poor old woman, ain't you? It wrings your heart to think of her sleeping on a plank bed and living off slops and working her old bones into an early grave, doesn't it?"

Lady Helen stared back at him levelly; after a moment she said in a low, hard voice: "You know very well it does."

"Very good," said Sir Harry. "Then tell me, Button – why didn't you swing that cleaver yourself?"

Lady Helen started, but her glance did not falter. She continued to stare at him, and Mr Franklin could hear her breathing. But she said nothing, and after a moment Sir Harry sat back in the corner of the car. "God, I'm tired," he said. "Hate court-rooms – always have. Remember one, back in New Orleans – slaving-ship court of inquiry, and I came so close to perjury I wake up in a sweat about it still. Now *that* was a rigged affair, if you like, young Franklin." He chuckled. "But it all ended happy, with no one the worse; even the little yellow girls from the . . ." He coughed and glanced towards his niece, who had turned away and was staring out of the cab window.

They rode in silence for a few moments, passing the Nelson monument again, and Mr Franklin realized that he had not obeyed Sir Harry's injunction to direct the driver to Berkeley Square. He glanced at Lady Helen, wondering if he should ask if she wished to go instead to Curzon Street, and at that moment an audible snore erupted from the General's corner of the cab. He was leaning back, his great head sunk forward on his chest, his hat tilted over his eyes, breathing stertorously; one great mottled hand lay palm down on the seat beside him; Mr Franklin could see the shiny white streak of a wound running from wrist to little finger, and there was the star-shaped scar of what might have been an old bullet-hole in the loose flesh between thumb and forefinger. He shivered; he had looked Sir Harry up in *Who's Who* and read incredulously through the succinct list of campaigns and decorations – that gnarled old man sleeping there had seen Custer ride into the broken bluffs above the Little Big Horn, and fought hand-to-hand with Afghan tribesmen more than seventy years ago; he had ridden into the guns at Balaclava and seen the ranks form for Pickett's charge at Gettysburg; he had known Wellington and Lincoln – and now he was snoring gently in the corner of a motor car in the busy heart of modern London, and all the glory and horror and fear and bloodshed were small, dimly-remembered things of no account, and when he woke his one concern would not be the fate of nations or armies or his own life in the hazard, but the welfare of one wilful young woman whom he was trying to save from her own folly, in his strange, unscrupulous way.

Lady Helen had heard the snore, too, and turned to look. For a moment her face was expressionless; she seemed to be unaware that Mr Franklin was watching her, and then she sighed quietly and glanced across at him.

"Would you tell the driver Berkeley Square, please?" Mr Franklin tapped on the glass and passed on the order, and when he looked again Lady Helen was watching her great-uncle with an expression close to resignation. She reached sideways and let her gloved fingers rest on the great brown hand, and the General's snoring checked before resuming its deep even note. His cane was resting against his knees, and in danger of slipping; Mr Franklin laid it more securely against the seat.

"He is over ninety, you know," said Lady Helen, and Mr Franklin said yes, he knew.

"One forgets, sometimes," said Lady Helen. "He doesn't behave at all like a very old man – he remembers everything, and his brain is so alert and active. Did you know, that only fourteen years ago, he was staying at the Residency in Peking, when it was attacked in the Boxer Rising, and he took charge of the artillery belonging to your American contingent, and commanded it all through the siege? He

441

was seventy-eight then. And when the Residency was relieved, the officer in charge of the American Marines said he would write to the President to ask for some special decoration for him, and Uncle Harry laughed and asked one of the Marines to give him his hat, and then he put it on and said: 'That'll do better than a medal', and off he went." She pressed the old man's hand, and Mr Franklin saw there were tears in her eyes. "We're very proud of him, of course."

"I guess you must be."

"Although he is a quite dreadful person, really. He is absolutely selfish and dishonest and quite shameless. He has a shocking reputation – and deserves it. Just a few years ago he had to leave Sandringham in disgrace." She had apparently forgotten that Mr Franklin had been there. "How Aunt Elspeth has endured him ... do you know that next year they will have been married for seventy-five years? It seems incredible ... she is ninety years old, and a darling. So is he, I suppose – and yet sometimes I feel that I hate him more than anyone I've ever known; you would not believe how mean and deceitful he can be – even with people he loves. Today, for example."

She was talking as much to herself as to him, her eyes on the old man's sleeping face, but now she seemed to realize Mr Franklin's presence, and withdrew her hand from the General's.

"I beg your pardon." She gave a little frown, and for the first time in his experience she seemed slightly embarrassed. "I think I must be rather tired, too."

"I'm sure you must be; that was a dreadful ordeal ... in the court."

Lady Helen took a deep breath. "Yes," she said. "I am very angry, when I think of that. And of what he ... did."

"What did he do, really? I know what he said – but d'you suppose it made so much difference?"

"He kept me out of prison." She looked directly at Mr Franklin and then away again. "Oh, yes, what he said is true – influence counts for everything, and it can be very subtly directed. And he did it for what he conceives to be my own good – that is why I can hate him so much, sometimes. It is as though he were the embodiment of everything that we are struggling against – the belief that we have no minds and souls of our own, that we aren't fit to find our own way, to be independent, to rule ourselves, instead of always being the meek, stupid, obedient ... oh, why should I be saying this to you? It is no concern of yours."

"I don't think," said Mr Franklin, "that you are meek or stupid –

442

or especially obedient." He smiled at her. "And I doubt if your great-uncle does, either."

She regarded him coldly. "No, I'm not – and the very tone in which you recognize it, and the way in which you smile as you say it, is in itself a reminder of the fact that a woman who is not meek and stupid and obedient is . . . oh, some kind of freak."

"I'm sorry. I'd no intention of suggesting that."

"I know. I beg your pardon. I'm afraid you must find me extremely tiresome. I have been a great deal of trouble to you, haven't I? But for me, you would not have had to give evidence in court – and my great-uncle would not have had the chance to use you, as he has just done. Perhaps you realize now how unscrupulous he can be."

"It's been no trouble. I'm just sorry for the whole thing. And I don't know that he's all that unscrupulous, is he? I know he talks a good deal, but – "

"You're thinking of his threat to have me put into some exclusive madhouse if I don't behave?" Lady Helen gave a bitter little laugh. "Don't think he wouldn't, if it was to keep me out of prison. Oh, he would – and he could do it, too – nothing distasteful, just a pleasant country retreat that I could leave whenever I promised to do as I was told. I see you don't believe it."

"Well, it's a little hard to – "

"I had a cousin, a young man who was causing his parents distress because he had some trouble with a woman – a barmaid in some low place in London . . ." Lady Helen shrugged in a way which would have caused Mr Lees to reflect on the attitudes of the aristocracy. "He wanted to marry her, his parents wished to avoid a scandal, and somehow the matter was mentioned to Uncle Harry. He invited my cousin to dinner – at one of his clubs, I believe. The young man woke up on a whaling ship bound for the Antarctic, and was away for two years. That is perfectly true. My great-uncle is an extremely resourceful and dangerous person; you should understand that."

Mr Franklin digested this in silence; it was crossing his mind that dangerous was a word that could reasonably have been applied to the entire family, from what he had seen of the great-niece. Suddenly Lady Helen said:

"As you know, I wish now that I had been convicted of the assault charge today. I pleaded not guilty only because I was certain that Millicent Shore and I must both be acquitted, and when she was not . . . I should have pleaded guilty in the first place, of course, but my solicitors advised against it. And it seemed such a trivial and demeaning charge . . ." She made a little impatient gesture. "But I feel obliged to thank you for the way in which you gave your evidence. I realize that you were trying to be considerate – although why you should have been I can't imagine."

She was looking a question, and he found it difficult to answer.

"I don't know that there was any reason except that I didn't want to see you convicted. And – it wasn't much of an assault, was it?"

The car, which had been threading slowly through the late afternoon traffic, was drawing into Berkeley Square. Lady Helen looked at Sir Harry; he was still sleeping peacefully, with rhythmic snoring. She leaned forward and tapped the glass.

"Not here. Curzon Street." To Mr Franklin she said: "So that odious barrister was right – chivalry. I suppose both you and he regard that as a proper attitude to women?"

Mr Franklin considered her. "You allow men to open doors for you, I guess. Women's rights notwithstanding."

"Courtesy is one thing. Coming close to giving false evidence is rather different, don't you think? Especially since our relations had hardly been friendly. The Waldorf Hotel – and I seem to remember we had a rather disagreeable conversation not long after – "

"At Sandringham. When your great-uncle left early."

"Was that the time? Ah, yes. You were trying to flirt with me, as I recall."

"I was trying to be amiable, probably. But if you're trying to get me to admit that I was attracted by you, you're perfectly right. And so possibly my evidence – however I gave it – may have been slightly biased. And if that's an offence against the rights and dignity of women, I apologise."

"Why? Do you think that because a woman believes in women's rights, she ceases to be a woman?"

"I've no idea, Lady Helen. I don't know enough about women."

"Are you married, Mr Franklin?"

"Yes. I wasn't when we met at Sandringham."

"Does your wife believe in women's rights?"

"She's not a suffragette, if that's what you mean."

"Would you have married her if she had been?"

"Shouldn't the question be, would she have married me?"

"Suffragettes *do* marry, Mr Franklin – many of them. They are not some strange species, whatever the gutter press and political bigots

444

may say about them." Lady Helen glanced out at the passing traffic. "And some simply prefer to live with the man, or men, of their choice, rather than submit to the legal slavery of marriage. But perhaps your wife does not regard it in that light?"

Mr Franklin thought of Peggy, and smiled. "I don't think she feels enslaved. I hope not, anyway."

"Most men would probably give the same answer. But she is bound to you nonetheless. You take it for granted that she is docile and faithful. And you – are you faithful to her?" Lady Helen glanced at him with a faint smile. "Or does the question shock you?"

Mr Franklin hesitated. "No – it doesn't shock me. I guess I'm old-fashioned enough to find it unexpected, though."

"From a suffragette? We prefer the term suffragist, by the way."

"I didn't know. But – yes, I'm faithful."

"And Miss Delys?"

Mr Franklin smiled. "I see that being a suffragist doesn't deprive a lady of her sense of scandal. No, Miss Delys is an old friend – in the conventional sense. Not a mistress."

"Many wives would rather that their husbands had a mistress than an old friend in the conventional sense," said Lady Helen. "I think I should myself – but then, I am not married. And I believe my views are what are called advanced."

The car had turned into Curzon Street, and was drawing up outside a house near the Park Lane end. Lady Helen glanced at the General, still noisily asleep in his corner.

"Would you care to accompany my great-uncle back to Berkeley Square?" she asked Mr Franklin. She paused and looked at him directly. "Or if that is out of your way, his driver will deliver him safely."

"It's no trouble," said Mr Franklin. He got out of the car and handed Lady Helen down to the pavement.

"Then good-night, Mr Franklin." The cool eyes met his again as she extended a gloved hand. "Or, more probably, good-bye."

"I hope not," said Mr Franklin courteously, taking her hand. "Good-night, Lady Helen."

He watched her mount the short flight of steps and let herself in, and turned back to the car. "Berkeley Square," he told the driver, and settled into the seat Lady Helen had vacated; the car drew away from the pavement.

"It wasn't a whaler," said the General's voice. "It was an Atlantic

445

tramp, but the young fool jumped ship somewhere in South America and got himself crimped." He pushed back his hat and regarded Mr Franklin dyspeptically. "Don't you care for Button, then?"

Mr Franklin struggled for speech. "I thought you were – "

"Asleep? Don't be an ass. I started snoring tactfully because I'd touched the poor little chit on the raw with a question she couldn't answer. Silly of me, but when she starts playing the *grande dame* and refusing to stay the night when she knows dam' well her great-aunt is fretting to death about her – well," confessed the ageing warrior, "she gets me riled peculiar, as your countrymen say. I shouldn't have asked her that, though – bad thing to let a woman know you've sniffed out her guilty secret. Mind you, it was as plain as the nose on your face."

"What was?" Mr Franklin was perplexed. "What shouldn't you have asked her?"

"Why she didn't cut up the painting with her own fair hands, if she's so all-fired set on playing the diehard suffragette? Instead of egging on that pathetic old harridan to do it. Of course, she couldn't look me in the face and answer." He rolled a bright and bloodshot eye at Mr Franklin. "Could she?"

"I don't know what you're talking about, General."

"My God, you're dense. And from Nebraska, too. She's my great-niece, ain't she? You don't think she'd do the dirty deed herself if she could get some simpleton to do it for her? Of course, she won't care to admit it, even to herself, but it's true, just the same. I know my own kind."

"I don't believe that for a moment," said Mr Franklin. "Why, she *wanted* to share the blame – you heard her – she'd have gone to prison like a shot."

"Yes, I heard her," said Sir Harry. "Heard myself, in similar situations – when I reckoned it was safe. Oh, she's a bit of an ecstatic martyr, no doubt, our Button – as long as it don't go too far. And she may rage and rail at me for smoothing her path out of trouble, but she's not too sorry I did, I'll be bound. Not that she isn't sincere in her beliefs, and all this dam' nonsense about women's rights, and so forth. But you'll notice it's she who's loose, and Shore who's doing time. My conniving, if you like – but I wonder if Button would have been quite so ready to assist in outrages, and plead guilty, and damn the judge's eyes, if she hadn't known that Uncle Harry was on hand, pulling the strings? Eh? And you'll also notice that she pleaded not guilty to the assault business – if she'd been convicted on that, she'd have been in real peril of going to chokey, for all my efforts. No, she's sincere enough – ain't we all? – but like the rest of us she doesn't want to pay too high a price for it."

Mr Franklin sat a moment silent. "I don't think you know your own great-niece very well," he said. "You're doing her a great injustice."

"Am I though?" The General grunted. "Well, I'm not the only one. She's a damned sight madder at you this minute than she is at me." The General surveyed him curiously. "Didn't you want to go to bed with her?"

Mr Franklin regarded him in disgust and wonder. "You're talking about the lady who is your own great-niece – "

"So I am, but that doesn't mean she's any different from all the rest of them. Heavens above, you could have been snug on the sofa in Curzon Street this minute if you'd had your wits about you. Don't you know a plain invitation when you hear one?" The General shook his great head in disgust. "You young fellows nowadays beat me. Just because Button looks down her haughty nose at you as though you're dirt, doesn't mean she hasn't got a healthy appetite. She came as near as she could to telling you, short of dragging you out of the car and upstairs. Would have done her a world of good, too, after the trying day she's had." The General sighed moodily. "In fact, one of the reasons I brought you along from court, and then obligingly dropped off to sleep, was so that you and she could size one another up, and . . . well, I knew back at Sandringham that you fancied each other rather above half. Still . . . " Sir Harry shrugged in resignation at the younger generation's lack of enterprise. "Poor little Button. I hate to think of her being disappointed."

"One thing becomes clear," said Mr Franklin grimly, "and that is that every word she said about you is true."

"What, about being deceitful and dishonest and rotten to the core, you mean? Of course it's true," said Sir Harry comfortably. "Though why you should complain, when I was doing my best to help you into the saddle – " A thought seemed to strike him. "Of course, if you're assigned to that little blonde bouncer you had in tow at the court, I can understand – "

"I should have thought you overheard, while you were asleep," said Mr Franklin caustically, "that Miss Delys is only a friend, that I'm married, and strange as it may seem to you, I'm faithful to my wife."

"You don't say!" The General seemed genuinely surprised. "Well,

447

I'm blessed!" He gave Mr Franklin a curious look. "You a Baptist, or something like that? Ah, well." He ruminated on this, shaking his head. "It's a shame you don't fancy Button, though, because she's taken quite a shine to you. Can't say I blame you, mind – she's the kind I'd love and leave in the deuce of a hurry. What's your own wife like? Good-looking? Bound to be – you're not the kind who'd settle for plain Jane. Like to meet her sometimes. Ah, here we are."

The car had turned into Berkeley Square, and as it drew into the kerb Sir Harry heaved himself painfully up, grunting, but restrained Mr Franklin as the latter made to help him out. "Stay where you are – car can take you home. Well, thank'ee my son, for helping Button out – even if you did miss your chance this evening. You'll regret it some day – I always do, when I think back to the wasted opportunities of youth. Give me a call, any time you feel like standing me a dinner, and I'll tell you a few tales about the old days."

He climbed out on to the pavement and shouted to the driver: "Take the gentleman wherever he wants to go, Wilkins or Jackson or whatever the hell your name is, and pick me up tomorrow at ten-forty-five sharp. Lady Flashman's going shopping at eleven, and if you don't have me off and out of danger before that, I'll stop your grog."

He turned back to the open door. "Well, good-night to you, young Franklin. Yes, give me a call one of these days. Perhaps you can tell me a few tales, instead. You're an interesting chap, you know." The grotesquely-mottled old face with its flowing whiskers wore a curious, knowing expression. "Knew it the first time I saw you. Yes. You've got gunfighter's eyes."

And that, thought Mr Franklin, as he drove back to Wilton Crescent was a most odd, and vaguely unsettling, thing for anyone to say. But then, Sir Harry was an odd and vaguely unsettling person – so, for that matter, was his great-niece, and Mr Franklin had quite enough masculine vanity to wonder if the cunning old gentleman's reading of her character, and of her supposed *tendre* for Mr Franklin himself, was correct. It seemed unlikely – he doubted if Lady Helen was amorously inclined towards anyone, and yet, when he thought back over their conversation, and tried to recall her expression and manner on the drive to Curzon Street, and the cool, direct glance of the fine eyes – of course, these emancipated women believed in free love and socialism and all manner of strange things, if rumour was to be believed. And, he admitted it, she was an attractive woman – formi-

448

dable, yes, undoubtedly, and any man who became entangled with her had better be of a nature as resolute and implacable as her own. But that was no concern of his, not now. Perhaps, four years ago at Sandringham – if Sir Harry had not indulged in pinching maids' bottoms, and so led to his great-niece's early departure . . .

Mr Franklin dismissed his speculations, and as the car idled at a crossing, waiting to be waved on by the traffic constable, he bought an evening paper from a passing vendor. Yes, there were the morning's court proceedings, on an inside page – with a picture of Pip and a column of her evidence; his own contribution occupied about a sixth of that space, he was glad to see. The verdict and sentence had obviously come too late for the edition, but they would certainly be on the front pages in the morning. He glanced at the stop press, but there was nothing there except cricket scores, racing results, and an item headed "Outrage in the Balkans". Mr Franklin folded the paper and yawned as the car sped on to Wilton Crescent.

23

Rather more space was given on the following morning to the latest Balkan atrocity, which Mr Franklin noted briefly was concerned with the murder by students of an Austrian princeling and his wife; it was quite overshadowed, however, by what one sheet described as "the Cessford Scandal". Even the serious papers devoted columns to it in their Law Reports, and the cheap press had a field day, with pictures, graphic accounts, interviews, and scathing leaderettes on the double standard of justice which appeared to have been applied. Samson had brought to the breakfast table as many of the daily journals as could be got from the local newsagent's, and Mr Franklin and Peggy scanned them with interest.

Many carried studio portraits of Lady Helen looking disdainful and splendid in her debutante finery, and another of her in coronation dress, when she had been in attendance on royalty; she was also shown leaving court on the arm of her great-uncle, who appeared to be trying to brain a reporter with his cane while Lady Helen stared calmly to her front. There were pictures of Pip, theatrical and otherwise, and a long interview in which she tempered justice with mercy by describing the conviction of Millicent Shore as a downright scandal, and referring to the judge as "a sweet old dear, a real pet".

Peggy read the reports with some amusement. "You seem to have done quite proud by Lady Helen," she told Mr Franklin. "I hope she appreciates that but for your evidence she probably wouldn't be a free woman this morning. Did you see her afterwards?"

"Yes, briefly – but I doubt if she's very appreciative. For one thing, she wants to be a martyr, and for another, I doubt if she cares to feel under an obligation to anybody."

"I shouldn't imagine so." Peggy was studying a pictorial display which contrasted Millicent Shore, looking drab and haggard, with the debutante study of Lady Helen, under the heading "Gruel . . . and caviare". "Gosh, she looks a stuck-up piece. The kind who always had beautifully-made and spotless clothes for dancing lessons at school, and couldn't add two and two. The Delys girl looks nice, though." She giggled. "I should think the ha'penny rags will be selling well to the Pall Mall clubs today – most of them have got the Matania picture of her. Lovely figure – Lady Helen probably won't care for that, either. I see she's billed as the star attraction – Pip Delys, not Lady Helen – at the Savoy do next week; it doesn't take the charities long to hop on the roundabout, does it?"

"Which Savoy do is that?" wondered Mr Franklin. He was a little astonished; Peggy seemed not in the least curious about his association with Pip, which must have come as news to her and, in the circumstances, he supposed would at least have aroused her interest, if nothing more. But she obviously thought nothing of it; if he detected a hint of feminine jealousy at all, it was in her references to Lady Helen.

"The midnight ball, silly," said Peggy. "You know, for the National Institute for the Blind. We're going with the Stewarts – it's the great attraction of the season, and everyone's going to be there. Well, your friend Pip is to be one of the top turns in the cabaret – I suppose they signed her up as soon as they saw the early editions yesterday; perhaps earlier. Lots of the leading theatricals are going to be there, as well as the whole of society. You bought us ticket ages ago."

"Did I?" said Mr Franklin; he seemed to remember something of the sort, from that happy period before the arms-running. In that moment, it came on him again like a physical blow: this isn't real – that awful business between us, and here we are chatting cheerfully about midnight parties as though nothing had happened. He tried to order his thoughts, and said:

"Well, it sounds like a big affair. I suppose we won't get home till morning."

"If then," said Peggy. "It's fancy dress, you know," and Mr Franklin lowered his paper in dismay.

"You know I've never been to a fancy-dress ball in my life," he was beginning.

"Oh, come on," said Peggy, "you went to the Peace Ball just a fortnight ago."

"Sure, in plain clothes, like a lot of other people. But I'm not dressing up like a . . . a Roman emperor or a Chinese mandarin, not for anything."

"You don't have to," said Peggy brightly. "I've been thinking about

451

it. I knew you'd kick at the idea of fancy dress, so I hit on just the costume for you."

"Go on," said Mr Franklin heavily. "And if it's Pierrot, the answer's 'no'. "

"Not Pierrot," said Peggy. "Something far more exciting than that."
"Well?"

"You've still got those American pistols, and that cartridge belt, down at Lancing, haven't you? And that lovely old hat, with the big brim – what do they call them? Wideawakes. And your boots. Well – any theatrical costume shop could get you a shirt and breeches or whatever is right, or the woolly trousers and those big handkerchiefs for round your neck. You can go as Deadwood Dick. It won't be fancy dress at all, really – since it's what you must have worn in America."

Into his mind, for no reason, came the picture of Sir Harry's suffused face and knowing look. "You've got gunfighter's eyes." Dead-wood Dick – that was the name that would spring to Peggy's lips as it did to everyone's when the West was mentioned. The romantic figure, the frontiersman, the man with the six-shooters, which no one ever bothered to think of in its unromantic reality. Cassidy and Deaf Charley and Big Ben Kilpatrick. He sat looking at her across the top of his paper.

"Well, it's perfect, isn't it? And so much better, because you've got the real things. I remember that old cartridge belt, full of those shiny brass bullets – it would be splendid. D'you know," she added, as she picked up her paper, "I've never seen you as you must have looked when you were roughing it. Well, of course I haven't. But I'm sure it would suit you. I'm going as something Marie Antoinettish – you know, the big silk gown, and a wig and a mask and a fan. What d'you think?"

"Oh, you'll look fine – that's proper fancy dress," said Mr Franklin. "I'm not sure about the Western rig, though – "

"Now don't be difficult," said Peggy. "You can't go in tails – no one else will. And your objection has always been to dressing up like a guy. Well, this won't be dressing up – it'll just be putting on your old clothes. We'll get you a proper fringed shirt, like Buffalo Bill, and Samson can polish up those boots with the high heels – "

"All the gear is down at Lancing, though."

"Well, Samson can collect it in a day, easily. And the ball isn't till

452

next week. So you needn't start trying to make excuses – unless you really want to go as Pierrot."

After all, he thought, why not? It was the easiest sort of fancy dress, if he had to wear one. It would be kind of odd, though, after so many years – even back before Tonopah and the diggings, before the cattle-drives, back fifteen years to Hole-in-the-Wall and waiting in that eating-house in Cheyenne – it was Cheyenne, wasn't it, not Casper? – watching Tracy across the street. And he would wear it at the Savoy Hotel, among the bright young things and the bright old things, among the cavaliers and pirates and dancing-girls and Maid Marions and the circus clowns. Pierrots, certainly. There was something crazy about it, but comic, too.

"All right," he said. "Deadwood Dick."

He gave it little thought in the next few days, as June turned into July, and the brief sensation of the Cessford trial vanished from the papers and the public mind. A brief paragraph in one of the last stories on the subject mentioned that Lady Helen Cessford had retired to her father's country seat – the journalist did not fail to remark in passing that Millicent Shore was then completing her first week in the stone tomb of Holloway, with only one hundred and fifty-five weeks to go, in none of which was she likely to visit Biarritz or Nice, or enjoy even a morsel of foie gras or overripe pheasant. But it was the last squib on the subject, a mere afterthought to the story of the next suffragette outrage, in which a hammer was taken to Millais' portrait of Thomas Carlyle. There were wits who suggested that this could only improve the sepulchral features of the sage of Ecclefechan and Chelsea, and one even proposed that when the perpetrator was sentenced, her punishment should be rendered more severe by imprisoning her, not in Holloway, but in the Royal Academy.

The public were, in fact, tired of suffragettes; there was fresher sensation in the trial of Madame Caillaux in Paris – she who had taken a pistol to the editor of *Figaro* with fatal effect – and in the arrival in England of another French notable, the handsome and charming M. Carpentier, who was due to fight Gunboat Smith for the world cruiser-weight title, an occasion which promised to attract to Olympia not only the sporting fraternity, but the flower of society as well. Wimbledon was breaking out again, the sun was shining brilliantly, Ireland might be an impending crisis but there was no doubt that it was also a thundering bore, and only the more sober readers, or the chronic pessimists, paid any attention to the vaguely

453

disquieting news from Eastern Europe, where Austria was expressing indignation at the assassination of her Archduke. Mr Lloyd George quieted the anxieties of that small section of the public which was listening by talking of a rapprochement between Britain and Germany, it was emphasized that in the highly unlikely event of any crisis in Europe, Britain was under no commitment to France, and that Persia was a far more pressing question anyway, since Britain's oil interests in that country were vital to the maintenance of her huge petrol-driven Dreadnought fleet.

And on the evening of the Fourth of July, which struck him as appropriate, Mr Franklin eased on his well-worn but highly-polished boots, buckled the cartridge belt with its glittering brass rounds (specially burnished by an excited kitchen-maid) round his waist, tied the holsters down to his thighs, put on the old broad-brimmed Stetson on which Samson had spent at least two hours' brushing, picked up his Remingtons, checked that their cylinders were empty, slipped them into the holsters – and looked at himself in the mirror.

His immediate reaction was that it was ridiculous. His sensations were precisely those that he had felt almost five years before when he had stood in the Waldorf Hotel, surveying with revolted disbelief his first full suit of white tie and tails. And then, as now, Samson was at his elbow, glancing critically at his reflection; Mr Franklin gave a snort of derisive amusement and turned on his tall heels, rested his thumbs in his belt, and said to his valet:

"All right, go ahead – what are you going to find to straighten about this lot?"

Samson shook his head with gentle gravity. "I'm afraid, sir, that I can be of no assistance. The breeches are cut for service rather than style, and the hat . . . " Words failed him about the hat. "Perhaps I might refold the neckerchief – "

"You leave it alone," said Mr Franklin. "I want it nice and sloppy so that when shame overcomes me I can slip it up over my face, like a dime-novel desperado." He looked at himself again, and decided that it might have been worse; it was gratifying that the broad belt with its heavy brass buckle was only one notch farther on than it had been all those years ago – an inch on the waist wasn't bad, between thirty-five and forty. But it was still a shock to see that outlandish figure, tall and straight enough, but so out of keeping with the Indian carpet and electric light and modern furniture – and the weight of the weapons on the hips seemed enormous. Had he ever carried them without noticing? He slipped his hand on to the polished butt of the left-hand gun, drew it and spun it deftly on his forefinger before sliding it back into the holster. It was an automatic movement, like straightening his tie or flicking a speck of dust from his sleeve; he had performed it without conscious thought, and he realised that Samson was watching him. They looked at each other for a moment in the glass.

"Yes," said Mr Franklin quietly, and knew they were both remembering the same thing.

"I'll have to practise walking in these damned boots," he said. "At least I can thank Mrs Keppel that I don't have spurs to worry about – I could see my wife thanking me if I put one of those rowels through her dress. Heavens above, Samson, I'm never going to be able to dance in these!"

They were debating this important point when sounds from the landing announced that Peggy had completed her transformation into a lady of the *ancien régime*, and Mr Franklin stalked out to look, and have his breath taken away. She looked incredibly beautiful in her high powdered wig, sparkling with little paste jewels, and the delicate pink embroidered gown, with its huge sweeping skirt; her body seemed to emerge from it like some perfect statue, white-shouldered and slender-necked, with the angel face above it, touched with a tiny black beauty spot high on one cheek. She fluttered her fan and sank into an elaborate curtsey, murmuring, "Serviteur, monsieur"; Mr Franklin, equally in character, touched his forefinger to the brim of his hat and said gravely, "Evenin', ma'am." At which Peggy's maid went into peals of laughter, and even Samson deigned to smile.

Mr Franklin rode in the front seat of the car, for the simple reason that there was room in the back only for Peggy and her spreading finery. They went by way of Grosvenor Square, where the Stewarts lived; it was a considerable consolation to Mr Franklin, as he got out to help Lady Stewart into her own automobile, after the obligatory squeal of recognition had been exchanged between her and the temporarily imprisoned Peggy, that she was attired either as Boadicea or Lady Macbeth, he couldn't be sure which, and that Sir Cecil, who was tall and slender almost to vanishing point, had unwisely decided to impersonate Sandow the Strong Man, in leopard skin and grotesquelywrinkled tights. A fringed shirt of imitation buckskin might be bad enough, but at least he didn't look like *that*. And while they waited for other members of the party to emerge, and Sir Cecil could

455

only clutch his huge cardboard dumb-bell and gawk foolishly while pretending not to notice the amused stares of passers-by, Mr Franklin could lounge against the side of the limousine with his ankles crossed, striking a match on his boot-sole and lighting a cigarette with his hat tilted over his eyes, as to the manner born.

The Strand was choked with late-night traffic as they drove along, and turned into the glittering entrance of the Savoy, which had been transformed for the great occasion. Crowds of sight-seers were being held back by lines of uniformed police as the guests and celebrities arrived; there were oohs and ahs at every fresh extravagance of costume, as maharajahs, highwaymen, Columbines, gladiators, Cleopatras, Cossacks, and ballerinas crowded into the great foyer, each testifying to the steel-nerved resolution of the British upper classes in the face of disaster – for nothing, in Mr Franklin's opinion, could have been more catastrophic than the appearance which some of them presented. Sir Cecil Stewart in his leopard skin and knobbly knees was grace itself compared with the spectacle of an angular and elderly gentleman in horn-rimmed glasses who had chosen to impersonate Nero in the briefest of tunics and an enormous laurel wreath, or the sheer monstrosity of an obese dowager who had clothed herself in wisps of gossamer as Scheherazade. "Do yer dance, Salome!" pursued her as she waddled hastily through the great doors, and there were raucous requests to Nero to "sing us a song, guv!" However the commonalty were cheered by the appearance of the younger society ladies as Bacchanals and nymphs, and there was thunderous applause for a daring young gentleman who made his stately entrance on foot from the Strand, in full fig as Charles II, with a buxom Nell Gwynn on his arm, and even a pack of spaniels trailing at his heels.

Downstairs the noise at the gaily decorated supper tables was deafening; the Stewart party were comfortably ensconced in a corner, Peggy contrived to eat, talk with unbounded vivacity, and preserve her spectacular appearance in spite of the fact that she was seated next to a whiskered Neptune whose enormous trident was a danger to anyone within six feet of him, Mr Franklin resisted gallantly the efforts of a Greek goddess to disarm him of his revolvers so that she could click them at her companions, champagne and Hock flowed in impressive quantities, delicacies of every variety were consumed by the hundredweight, conversation rose to shouting pitch, the orchestra played manfully in spite of the fact that not a note was audible, and it became evident that the guests who had paid exorbitantly for their tickets on behalf of the nation's blind, were going to have their money's worth. Mr Franklin's chief interest was to see if any dancing would, in fact, take place; he suspected that the combination of elaborate costumes and strong drink would lead to some remarkable evolutions when the programme began, and he was not disappointed.

Upstairs the management of the Savoy had risen to the occasion. The entire foyer, restaurant, Parisian café and Winter Garden had been turned into one gigantic ballroom by the expedient of flooring them with parquet for the occasion, and taking down all the removable screens and furniture. There were three orchestras, playing in relays, and sometimes, it seemed to Mr Franklin, in unison, even if the tunes were different. He would, he knew, have the grandfather of all headaches in the morning, not from champagne, of which he had partaken sparingly, but from the sheer noise and press and thunderous activity around him. In the meantime, he was rather enjoying himself; he waltzed with Peggy, in spite of the proportions of her skirt and his own high-heeled boots, they sat out a polka which would have been physically impossible for them, and made bets with each other who would subside in an exhausted heap first, Neptune or the gamely-puffing Scheherazade; then he bought her handfuls of raffle tickets, and they waltzed again – it was, they discovered, about the only dance which their costumes would permit, although they tried a tango which ended with Peggy having a fit of the giggles and his helping her, laughing, back to their side-table.

There followed a grand parade past the stage which had been erected between two of the orchestras and draped with patriotic red, white and blue silks, where the dance committee and judges sat to judge the costumes. Peggy, to her intense delight, won a prize in the historical section (ladies); the Emperor Nero, on the other hand, was mortified to receive an award in the comic section (gentlemen), explaining loudly that his garb had been carefully copied from a genuine Roman frieze. More dancing, and the cabaret, followed. Mr Harry Lauder to rapturous applause and enthusiastic vocal support with the choruses, roamed in the gloaming and hailed Caledonia, Mr Peter Dawson silenced all competition with "A policeman's lot" in a voice that boomed like a great bronze bell, Fokina danced the dying swan, and Miss Pip Delys, sparkling in an entirely silver costume of leotard, tights, and feathers, sang and pirouetted before a chorus line of energetic young men in "Oh, you beautiful doll". As an encore she joined Mr Lauder in "Stop your tickling, Jock", in which she did

457

her level best to steal the limelight from one who had learned that particular business long before she was born, but who tolerantly refrained from proving it. The artistes then joined in a patriotic finale of "Rule, Britannia"; it occurred to Mr Franklin, watching Pip as she stood glittering and obviously bursting with delight between the kilted Mr Lauder and the imposing Mr Dawson, that this, for the former third lead of the *Folies Satire*, was probably the greatest moment of her theatrical career; the applause thundered to a climax, and the performers bowed and left the stage to join in the dancing or seek refreshment at the buffets.

Traffic in that direction was heavy, the waiters having abandoned all attempt at service in the chaotically-crowded ballroom; Sir Cecil Stewart, having broken his cardboard dumb-bell pounding it on the table in an attempt to order further magnums of champagne, led his party en masse to the nearest bar, where they struggled to attract the attention of the hard-pressed servers. Mr Franklin used his command-ing presence to clear a way for Peggy and the other ladies, who clustered at the buffet chattering expectantly while Sir Cecil bleated: "Pink champagne! I say, you fellows, what about some pink cham-pagne?" and the barmen strained and sweated in the deafening din. Mr Franklin, with Peggy in front of him and Greek goddesses hem-ming him in on either side, heard a familiar squeal of laughter from the direction of the crowded dance-floor, and turned to see Pip with a glass of bubbly in one hand while with the other she expertly fended off the attentions of Neptune, whose eye had been taken by her silvery fish-netted thighs and had attempted a friendly pinch.

"I'm king o' the sea – hic – an' you look like a lovely little mermaid!" explained the amorous monarch, to which Pip responded with "Leave off, you silly old goat!" as she slipped nimbly away from his embrace. In the next moment she was face to face with Mr Franklin, shrilling with delight: "There you are! I spotted you in the parade! Well, don't you look bully!" She drew a bead with her forefinger, clicked her tongue, and winked at him. "The man from Cactus Gulch, or wher-ever it was! What did you think of the show? Was I all right? Stop it, you stupid get, or I'll lose my temper!" This last was addressed to Neptune, who was trying to prod her with his trident, while around them the guests, attracted by the appearance of one of the star turns of the cabaret, laughed and egged him on. Pip, having diverted the drunken thrust of the trident, and evidently unaware of the attention directed at her, thrust her torso forward at Mr Franklin, laughing proudly, and tapping at the jewellery round her neck.

"And see – what d'you think of that, Mr American? I'm wearing your sparklers – always do on special occasions! Don't they look lovely, then?"

The words rang out clearly, even in the noise round the buffet, and as Pip uttered them Mr Franklin was aware of Peggy at his elbow. Pip was leaning forward, her face alight, one silver-gloved hand holding up for his inspection the pearl and diamond necklace on which, in his extravagant euphoria, he had spent so recklessly five years ago, and Peggy was registering with interest the information that her husband had bestowed on this glittering soubrette a trinket which even an unpractised eye – and Peggy's was by no means unpractised – must have valued at some hundreds of pounds.

The implications dawned on Pip as quickly as they did on Mr Franklin. Her smile vanished as though wiped from her face as she realized who was the beautifully Marie Antoinette appraising her from Mr Franklin's side; it said something for her self-control that she did not express her dismay in one of those rich oaths which the ladies of the *Folies Satire* had been wont to address to enthusiastic members of the audience when they tried to clamber over the footlights. But she gasped and her eyes widened in alarm – Mr Franklin noticed irrelevantly that her squint seemed to become momentarily more pronounced, possibly with the shock; then, actress that she was, Pip had recovered, smiled at Peggy, and extended her hand.

"You're Mrs Franklin," she said. "I've seen you at parties, and wanted ever so much to meet you. I'm Pip Delys – how d'you do?"

It would not have astonished Mr Franklin if his wife had turned on her heel and walked away; indeed, for a split second he was wondering how she would manage it in that enormous skirt through a crowd of people. But instead Peggy was shaking hands and saying: "How do you do, Miss Delys? I must congratulate you on your splendid performance – quite the high spot of the evening."

"Oh – thanks!" It obviously crossed Pip's mind for an instant that the compliment was double-edged, but she went lightly on: "It's a lot easier when you've got acts like Harry and Peter either side of you. Anyway, I've been wanting to congratulate *you* for a long time."

"Oh?" Peggy glanced at Mr Franklin. "Whatever for?"

"On the way you look," said Pip bluntly. "I think you're the most beautiful woman in London. You know that picture of you – the

Lavery one? I just stood and gaped at it the other day at Grosvenor Gallery. I really did – it just takes your breath away, you know what I mean?"

"Well, how kind of you to say so." Peggy's manner was perfectly easy. "Praise indeed, from someone who has been hung twice at the Royal Academy."

"It wasn't me that was hung," said Pip. "It was Signor Matania."

Mr Franklin was aware that Lady Stewart, the Greek goddesses, and several other ladies in the party were digesting every word, and that Lady Stewart's eyes were intently examining Pip's necklace; he could sense the busy clicking in her ladyship's mind as words, facts, and inferences were docketed against the time when they would be needed for gossip. But now Sir Cecil was plunging in heartily, making some ponderously gallant joke about how beastly it was to talk of "hanging" beautiful gels, and insisting that Pip should join their party. Mr Franklin silently cursed him for an insensitive idiot, and was astonished when Pip accepted, laughing as she held up her glass to be refilled from one of the magnums which the knight had managed to obtain from the buffet. But he was more astonished still when, after they had trooped back to their table, he became aware that Peggy and Pip appeared to be conversing amiably on the other side of the large table; they were separated by Neptune, but since he had relapsed into a semi-comatose condition they were able to talk across him without difficulty.

It was not, from that point on, the most cheerful party that Mr Franklin could recall. Of all the infernal luck – that Pip should have identified that necklace as his gift, in front of Peggy and half the tattlers of Mayfair; even the most charitable of gossips could not be blamed for drawing the obvious conclusion, false though it was. What must Peggy be thinking? But strangely enough Peggy seemed to be thinking nothing at all; when the dancing recommenced, and she had been led ponderously round the floor by Sir Cecil, who sang an accompaniment to the music as he circled unsteadily in his leopard-skin, she stopped behind Mr Franklin's chair and whispered: "Let's have the next dance." And when he took her on to the floor, she talked and laughed cheerfully and teased him for being so quiet; Mr Franklin wondered if he was hearing aright. Was it possible that she had misunderstood Pip's remark about the necklace, or perhaps not even caught it at all? He felt he must broach the subject, and explain, but the Savoy ballroom was hardly the place, and she seemed to be enjoying the party thoroughly; they danced together twice again, and when towards dawn the lights were lowered, and they took the floor for the last waltz, with Mr Lauder and Mr Dawson singing "Auld Lang Syne" in deep-chested accompaniment, she nestled close against him in apparent content. It was a puzzled Mr Franklin who sat down to the final event of the party, which was breakfast in the lower restaurant; despite the fact that the ball had now been in progress for over eight hours, and enough liquor had been consumed to float the new *Aquitania*, Sir Cecil's group seemed to have lost none of their zest for enjoyment; even Neptune had got his second wind, and Peggy herself was as vivacious as ever, clapping her hands and laughing gaily as she joined in bursting the coloured balloons which descended in showers from the ceiling at the conclusion to the breakfast. And when they emerged into the sunlight of the London morning, the extravagant costumes looking strangely tawdry by day, she made room for Mr Franklin in the back of the car, pulling her voluminous skirt to one side.

"It doesn't matter if it gets a bit rumpled now," she sighed, settling into a corner of the seat. "Gosh, what a splendid party! Wasn't it marvellous?"

"Did you enjoy it?" asked Mr Franklin mechanically.

"Of course! It was easily the best this season. Didn't you?"

"Er, yes . . . I guess so."

"Your cowboy costume was an immense success. I told you it would be, didn't I? And I won a prize for my Marie Antoinette," said Peggy contentedly. "That was rather a score, don't you think?"

"Well, you deserved to. You looked wonderful."

"Oh, it's a pretty costume, but I'm glad it came off so well. Wasn't that nice of Pip Delys?"

Mr Franklin braced himself. He had not spoken to Pip after their first encounter, and she had left the party during breakfast, pleading the need for some sleep before a matinée of her show, and including him in a general good-bye wave to the whole table. "Wasn't what nice?"

"To say what she did – about my being the most beautiful woman in London. All rot, of course, but it was jolly nice of her just the same. I like her – and she's a marvellous artiste. One of these bubbly people who can put it across; she had the audience eating out of her hand." Peggy yawned. "Golly, I'm tired. I could sleep for a year."

461

"Peggy." He considered his words carefully. "About Pip, and that necklace. I want to explain."

"What, the pearl and diamond thing? I thought it suited her perfectly – just right for that kind of blonde looks." Peggy sounded sleepy. "And that heart shape would be the sort of thing she would like – I don't mean that it's vulgar, but that it suits, exactly . . ."

"I wanted to tell – "

"You're awfully good at that sort of thing, for a man. Those emerald earrings you gave me were perfect. Other things, too – d'you remember —?" She stifled another little yawn " – there was that housemaid we had who left to get married – the dumpy one, Tilly, wasn't it? – and we chose a locket for her. You picked the right one. You've got a taste in these things."

He glanced at her sharply, looking for the sarcastic curl at the corner of her mouth, but it wasn't there; she seemed perfectly casual, snuggled in her corner, chatting drowsily with her eyes almost closed.

"I didn't want you to misunderstand," he said. "Especially with those other women there – Lady Stewart, and so on, because I've no doubt they misunderstood – oh, they'd be happy to. And Pip blurting out the way she – "

"I should think she blurts a good deal, doesn't she?" Incredibly, she sounded amused. "It wasn't terribly discreet of her."

"It was damned unfortunate, but I guess she didn't mean – well, to cause any misunderstanding."

"Well, she didn't." Peggy's voice was still drowsy, but now she gave a sudden squeak of excitement and sat up, looking eagerly out of the window. They were passing through Trafalgar Square, which was already heavy with traffic and pedestrians in the morning sunshine, but what had attracted her attention was a group in fancy dress, obviously early leavers from the Savoy party, who were clustered round one of the fountains in altercation with two helmeted policemen. One of the revellers, a statuesque young woman who had won a prize in the ladies' section (classical) as Minerva, was bathing in the fountain, despite the attempts of a constable to get her out, while the others were arguing and getting in the way, to the delight of a gathering crowd. "Oh, look, Mark! It's Jessie Freeman – and Jinks! Heavens, they'll get themselves arrested! Oh, the asses!" Peggy rapped on the glass partition. "Stop, Ernest! Let's see what – "

"Drive on, Ernest!" said Mr Franklin, and as Peggy's laughter turned to disappointment, he tried to recall her to the matter in hand.

462

"Of course she did – cause misunderstanding, I mean. There she was, with an expensive necklace I'd given her – what on earth were people like Sarah Stewart going to think – "

"What? Oh, Jessie – they've got her out! Why, she'll be pinched for indecency!" Peggy, giggling, was staring out of the back window, but as the car swung towards the Mall and her view was cut off, she turned to meet Mr Franklin's look. "Well, they won't think anything they don't think already, will they?"

"What d'you mean?" He stared at her, appalled.

"About Pip Delys? Why, that she's your – " Peggy fluttered her fingers " – little side-show."

"Good God!"

"Well, naturally," said Peggy, looking at him almost with curiosity. "After all, she is."

"She's nothing of the goddam sort!"

Peggy continued to look at him, and then sat back in her corner with a little shrug. And now the tiny curl was there on her lip, along with a look of mild surprise in her eyes.

"Well," she said, "it doesn't matter. But if she's wearing your necklace, which must be worth at least a couple of hundred – "

"That's exactly what I mean! That's what those women'll think, having the kind of minds they've got, and I – "

"Well, you can't very well blame them, can you?"

" – and I just want you to know that I gave Pip that necklace long ago – five years ago, before I'd even met you. Matter of fact it was only the second day I was in London."

"Well," said Peggy, "she must have been extremely accommodating on the first day."

Mr Franklin sighed. "Very well, I've never pretended I was a saint before I met you. But I do want you to understand that I've been a faithful husband since, and that the conclusions which charitable ladies like Sarah Stewart will undoubtedly have drawn from Pip's – well, unfortunate remarks last night, are – well, they're the wrong ones, d'you see?"

"Oh, come off it, Mark!" The tiny curl was a scornful smile now. "It's hardly just a conclusion drawn from 'Pip's unfortunate remark', is it? Not when you take her about Town, and visit her in the middle of the night – "

"What?" He was incredulous. "What did you say? When did I visit her in the middle of the night?"

"*I* don't know," Peggy shrugged carelessly. "Anyway, it doesn't matter – "

"What do you mean, it doesn't matter? Of course it matters, if you think I've got a mistress that I go sneaking off to in the middle of the night! Who the blazes told you that?"

Peggy seemed mildly amused, which stunned him as much as her allegation had done. "Oh, someone or other. It may have been Sarah – no, it was Poppy, I remember. When we were in Switzerland – she got a letter from Jeremy – you know, Jeremy Paton-Streeter? He'd seen you with your Pip at a night-club somewhere, and afterwards, like the little toad he is, he and his chums followed you to her flat and waited to see you come out in the small hours. That's just the kind of scandal they love, of course. So it was hardly news tonight, you see – "

"My God," said Mr Franklin quietly. Indeed he had gone with Pip to her Bloomsbury flat, and they had drunk coffee for half an hour – yes, it probably had been after midnight. And, for a man who had never accounted himself stupid, it had been a remarkably foolish thing to do, knowing what gossip could make of it. But it had never crossed his mind that anyone would know, or notice – he ought to have been aware that the Lotus Club on any night would probably contain at least one person who knew him, and if it happened to be the kind of little creeping Jesus that Jeremy was well known to be . . . and on top of that, the Royal Academy business, showing Pip and himself together, and then last night at the Savoy party . . .

"My God," he said again. "What else could you think?"

He turned to look at her, and found her regarding him without any apparent emotion except – yes, there was no doubt of it – a gently amused curiosity. There was the tiny cynical touch to the mouth, but the perfect face beneath the silver Marie Antoinette wig was serene; there was no hostility in her eyes, not even displeasure. And that was baffling. Dispassionately considered, the evidence was damning, and yet unless he was entirely mistaken, Peggy simply didn't mind. And now her words confirmed it.

"Anyway, what does it matter? I mean, I'm sorry if it upsets you that I know, because it needn't. As a matter of fact, from the way you've spoken of her, during that Cessford woman's trial, I thought perhaps you knew that I knew. About Pip Delys, I mean. But if you didn't . . . well, really, there's no reason to fret about it now – "

"No reason to fret? You think – you've been thinking for God knows how long, that I've been keeping an actress as a mistress – and there's no reason to *fret?*"

"Well, hardly – I mean, it's not so unusual, is it? And we've hardly been cooing love-birds for the past year or two, have we?" Her tone was mild, almost pleasant. "Oh, now and then – but it's not exactly been one long blissful honeymoon, has it? I mean, if you'd bolted off to the Gaiety stage door the day after we were married, or even in the first year, I daresay I'd have been rather miffed, but we're quite an old married couple now. And we've gone our different ways – I know you don't like Society much, and it's been a bit of a bore for you. In fact, I felt quite cheered up, in a way, when Poppy told me – and this Pip seemed rather a nice person, and not the kind who'd cause fuss. Did you really think I would mind?"

Mr Franklin found himself staring out of the window at the red-jacketed Guardsmen before the Buckingham Palace railings, vaguely aware that they were halted in heavy traffic at the head of the Mall. It was as though he had been physically stunned; he could remember precisely the same sensation when he had been clubbed in a saloon, and for minutes afterwards had been able to move only feebly, his thoughts scattered and incoherent, words forming only with immense difficulty.

"You would mind?" he said slowly, echoing her last words.

"Why should I? Oh, perhaps I thought you were a little indiscreet – you gave the gossips a good deal of rope, didn't you? I can't say I exactly enjoy having people like Sarah and Poppy asking me if I've been to the Royal Academy lately to enjoy the view, but – " she shrugged " – that was just embarrassing bad luck, wasn't it? I hope I've never embarrassed you."

If anything could have been calculated to shock him out of his momentary stupefaction, it was that last remark, with all its implication.

"Embarrassed *me*? You? How could you?"

She regarded him levelly for a moment, and then frowned, and gave a little laugh.

"You know, Mark, I don't think this is an awfully clever conversation, really. Do you? We've been going along perfectly pleasantly, but I gather from your expression that we shan't much longer if we don't talk about something else. You seem to think I ought to mind about Pip Delys – and if you mean that I ought to mind about her

465

floating about in public thrusting your presents in everyone's face, I'm inclined to agree – but as to her being your mistress – "

"She isn't. I've never had a mistress. Since we were married – "

"Very well. If you say she isn't, then she isn't." Her shrug was eloquent of sceptical indifference. "I don't mind. And if she were, I wouldn't mind – I certainly would mind having to listen to a lot of boring protestations or confessional stuff, though. After all, it's none of my business – "

"Are you crazy?" It came out in a harsh bark. "We're married, aren't we? Anything we do is the other's business! Of course it's your business!"

"My business is what I choose to make my business," said Peggy calmly, but for the first time there was an edge to her voice. "And if I say that I am not concerned with what you do in your private life, then that is my affair. I certainly don't wish to have it thrust upon me. By the same token, I don't see why . . . " She stopped, impatiently. "Oh, never mind. It's all so stupid, this sort of talk."

There was a pause, and then he said: "You don't see why I should concern myself . . . about your private life? Is that what you were going to say."

"Yes." She sounded irritated. "My own life is my own life, just as yours is." She gave a weary little sigh. "Really, I do think we ought to let well alone. I didn't invite you to tell me about the Delys woman, or explain anything, or deny anything. We go on all right, don't we? Well, then, let sleeping dogs lie." And being Peggy, with her own bizarre sense of humour, she could not resist adding: "And sleeping bitches."

The traffic had begun to move slowly round the side of the palace, and looking across past her he saw only the blank grey wall of the grounds with its barbed-wire crest. He did not know quite what he felt – not anger, not amazement, because as he looked at the perfect, pale profile, like some Watteau painting with its silver coiffure and beauty patch, he knew instinctively and beyond any doubt that their conversation had really only confirmed what he should have realized all along, or for the last few months, anyway. Certainly ever since that nightmare of the ten thousand pounds and the arms-running. What had she said then? "Leave it alone, Mark. Don't talk about it." Something like that – as though there were things that should never be discussed, never disinterred, and if they were, should be pushed back out of sight, and forgotten, or at least a pretence maintained that they were forgotten. He had thought then that he was seeing another, unique Peggy – a Peggy he was prepared to believe was passionately devoted, all unsuspected by him, to a political cause, or at least to her brother's cause, and while he had been terribly hurt by her lack of trust in him, and by her dishonesty, he had understood, or thought he had a glimmer of understanding, of why she had acted as she had. In a way, he had even respected her for it, in spite of the ruthlessness she had shown – he had seen enough of hard cases and hard natures to appreciate that sometimes the only way was the cold-blooded calculating, brutal way, and damn the consequences. It was not his own nature, and never had been, but he could understand it in another.

He might have known that the totally selfish practicality of such a nature would not be confined to one thing alone; it would always be there, unseen for most of the time, but still there, to be used when occasion demanded. And it seemed that their marriage demanded it, so far as she was concerned. They had gone their separate ways, and while that had disappointed him, and he had hoped things might right themselves, he had always assumed that there was a limit to how far they could divert from each other. But it seemed he had been wrong – Peggy didn't care. She didn't mind if he had a mistress, if he was unfaithful; she didn't even mind knowing about it, as long as it remained unspoken, something that would not disturb the surface harmony of their shared existence. And obviously she expected him to concede as much to her. There were husbands and wives who did, he knew there were, he had seen them, plenty of them, in the society in which he lived now. In which Peggy had always lived, in which she had been brought up. He had seen it, after all, on the very first day of his admittance to this world – the obese and pouchy Edward, with his publicly acknowledged mistress sitting on the rug at his feet with her husband waiting complacently in the wings; it had been taken for granted by everyone – dammit, the Queen and Mrs Keppel had even been good friends.

But it had never occurred to him that Peggy and he could be partners in such a marriage. A marriage of convenience conducted according to the unspoken but well-understood code of the place and time. It had never occurred to him to doubt Peggy, to wonder if, in the half-separate lives they led, in that other life in which she moved and played and enjoyed herself without him, there might not be someone else, someone younger, even some others – no, that wasn't true: he *had* wondered, in dark moments, more than once, and had

467

pushed it away violently, as an unworthy thought. There came back to him now the memory of a picture in an illustrated magazine only a few months ago which had stabbed him with jealous doubt, and remembering it in a sudden surge of feeling he involuntarily said aloud:

"Frank Lacy." And automatically he turned to look again at Peggy.

He saw her stiffen, and for an instant there was a touch of colour on her cheek, and then she was pale again as she stared at him in angry contempt.

"Are you intent on behaving like a complete boor?" She controlled herself with a visible effort, taking a deep breath and when she spoke again it was in the impatiently despairing tone of one dealing with an obtuse child. "Oh, really, Mark! I can't think what's the matter with you. Haven't you any sense? Just because that stupid little slut comes prancing up squealing about what you've given her – and a ridiculous waste of money, if you ask me, but that's no concern of mine – we have to have this . . . this fatuous and distasteful nonsense. I don't want to talk about it, do you understand? And if you'd a grain of intelligence – to say nothing of good taste – you wouldn't either."

For the first time in his life that he could remember, Mr Franklin's voice shook a little.

"Is it Lacy, then?"

Peggy sat in silence a moment and then said coolly: "I really can't imagine what right on earth you think you've got to ask me that. After all, he hasn't come bouncing up to me in the middle of a Savoy party shouting 'Look, here's the night-dress you left in my hotel room at Lugano'. And if I told you I was a goody-goody meek little wife, would you be content with that? No, of course you wouldn't. You would want to be reassured, and told over and over again, until we were both bored to death, knowing it was all nonsense anyway, but pretending it wasn't – and I'd have to listen to endless explanations about how you'd been squiring that little tart all over the place for the pleasure of hearing her views on Aristotle, and spending all night at her flat singing madrigals together!" Peggy gave a snort that ill became Marie Antoinette. "Really, I never thought you were a hypocrite, or that you could be stupid enough to think that I was. I suppose you think I ought to have swooned away at the Savoy tonight, or swept out in a jealous fury? Can't you see that's the last thing . . . oh, hell." Peggy sank back wearily into her corner, and if she continued to sound even less like Marie Antoinette, her fancy-dress costumier

468

might at least have been gratified to see that she was fanning herself in a languidly petulant eighteenth-century manner. "Why you should think that the fact that I didn't – that I behaved like a normal civilized being, and did my level best to save us both embarrassment in what I realized was just a damned unlucky accident – why you should think that gives you the right to behave like some bloody Pantaloon in a comedy, beats me."

He had been sitting with his eyes closed, absorbing the hardest mental shock of his life; as he opened them the car was turning into Wilton Crescent. Peggy said:

"I've never asked you questions, and I never expected you to ask me any, either. I assumed that that was understood. Since I've obviously been mistaken, I suppose I ought to have played the injured wife and all the rest of it, but I didn't, because I'm not. And you're certainly not in a position to play the injured husband, are you? I mean, to be honest – "

"Honest?" The word was jerked out of him, incredulously. "You can talk about honesty – after what you've just been saying?" Anger boiled up in him. "And after the way you cheated – " He broke off, biting it back.

Peggy stopped fanning herself. "What? Oh, I see. We're going to have that ten thousand dragged up again. Very well. No, that was bloody dishonest, on my part, but only because there was no other way. Or so I thought. Well, I was wrong. I admit it, and I admit that dishonesty. And I asked you to let it alone, you may remember. Just as I asked you to let things alone a little while ago, but of course you wouldn't, and what good has it done? It's all so silly and pointless, and it just makes you miserable, and causes a lot of . . . of tiresome bother." She sighed wearily. "It's all so boring."

The car had drawn up at their front door, and he was sitting listening to her last words echoing in his mind, as last words will, while the chauffeur turned the motor off and prepared to get out to open the door. Abruptly Mr Franklin leaned forward and slid open the glass partition.

"I've forgotten my keys, Ernest. Go up and ring for Samson to open the front door, will you? We'll come up in a moment." And when the man had gone he asked:

"Would you mind telling me – how long have you and Lacy . . . ?"

Peggy, gathering up her skirts to leave the car, paused and looked at him.

469

"You want to crucify yourself thoroughly, don't you?" she said. "Oh, Mark! Does it matter? I don't know – two years, perhaps. Why? It was long before I knew about you and Pip Delys, if that's what's bothering you." She sat forward, preparing to rise. "I think we'd better go in. I've had enough soul-searching for one morning, and I'd rather like to go to bed."

He had had a vague, slender hope that her affair with Lacy might have been a retaliation; that it might not have taken place before she heard the false but circumstantial gossip about Pip. At least he could have understood it then. And now it led inevitably to another question which he did not want to ask, but he heard his voice forming the words without conscious volition.

"Was Lacy . . . the only . . . ?"

"Oh, Mark, really!" There was the well-known little curl of the lip. "Don't you think we've had a little too much of this ill-mannered inquisition? Pip Delys is enough for me – and I got that without asking for it. Now, I'm beginning to feel rather conspicuous, so if you wouldn't mind opening the door . . . "

But there was a final question that he had to ask, however much unhappiness it caused – it did not seem that it could possibly cause any more, whatever the answer. He looked at her for a long moment and then said:

"Why did you marry me, Peggy?"

It took her by surprise, but she answered readily enough.

"Why, because I liked you, of course. Why else would I marry you?" She looked at him curiously, her eyes searching his face, as though trying to fathom what lay behind the question. "If you really want to know, and if it will put an end to all this cross-examination, I'll tell you exactly. I liked you, and enjoyed being with you, and talking to you, and looking at you, and making love with you, and . . . just having you there." She gave a little shrug, and it seemed to him that her expression softened. "All sorts of things. Being proud of you – you're a very handsome man, you know. And kind and strong and rather . . . mysterious. I'm making you sound like a lady novelist's hero, aren't I? Completely house-trained. But . . . I just liked you. Don't you see?"

He was silent, watching her, and then she frowned and gave a little irritated sigh. "That's why I so hate all this tedious raking over . . . over things that don't matter a bit, really. And it just spoils everything to talk about them, because they don't make any difference. Not to me, anyway. Oh, I know they're meant to – all this Victorian stuff and pretence, but they needn't, unless you get all stupid and serious and acting shocked. Look, I know we're different in some ways – everyone is. Well, you're much older than I am, but what about it? I don't like you any less – and I really don't mind about Pip Delys. And you mustn't mind about . . . well, I mean, it's got nothing to do with us, has it? When we're together, it's such good fun, the two of us, as long as we don't have silly jealousies and sulks about things that aren't important." She shook her head, and the little twist of mockery touched her smile. "Anyway, you're a jolly good catch, and I hope you think I am, too." She patted his hand smartly, leaned across, and kissed him on the cheek. "There – and that wasn't for Ernest's benefit, either. Oh, don't look so serious, silly! Come on, and let's see if Samson's got a snack for us before bed. I'm ready to drop!"

He got out and held the door, suddenly conscious of the strange figure he must cut in his fringed shirt and six-guns in the full glare of the morning sunlight. And yet that was no more unreal than the knowledge that Peggy had had a lover for years, and suspected him of infidelity himself, and had just kissed him blithely on the cheek and patted his hand and assured him it didn't matter anyway.

He followed her automatically up the steps, and Samson was on post at the front door.

"Good morning, sir. Good morning, madam. I trust you enjoyed the party. Two gentlemen are here to see you, sir. I informed them that you would wish to go to bed immediately, but they said that their business was urgent, so I showed them into the morning-room. A Mr Crawford, sir."

"Don't know him," said Mr Franklin. "All right, Samson."

"They mentioned Mrs Franklin also, sir." Samson paused for a moment. "Shall I bring tea in for you, sir?"

"Yes – yes, Samson, please do." He glanced at Peggy, but she was obviously no wiser than he was. "Better make it tea for four."

He opened the morning-room door for Peggy to pass ahead of him, and then followed himself. Two men were standing by the window, and turned as they entered. One was a tall, wiry man with sandy side-whiskers, a long nose, and a sleepy expression; he was clad in ill-fitting tweeds and carried an ancient ulster over his arm. The other was stout and burly, with a neat black moustache, wearing a plain

471

blue suit; Mr Franklin guessed what he was even before the taller one spoke.

"Mr Franklin? Good morning to you. Mrs Franklin, I apologize for this early intrusion. My name is Crawford – Chief Inspector Crawford, of Scotland Yard. This is my colleague, Sergeant Green." He had a soft Scottish accent and a courteous, slightly magisterial manner; Mr Franklin gained the impression that Mr Crawford despised idle folk who gallivanted at fancy-dress balls until ten in the morning. "I'll try not to take up too much of your time," he added.

"I hope not, too," said Mr Franklin. "We're rather tired." He set a chair for Peggy. "Won't you sit down, inspector? What can we do for you?"

Inspector Crawford sat, crossed his long legs, regarded first Peggy and then Mr Franklin with a bright blue eye, and asked:

"I wonder if either of you know a gentleman named Mr Harvey Logan?"

472

24

It was fortunate for Mr Franklin that his head was turned away as he looked for a chair for himself; in fact he was reaching for one at the dining-table, and the movement concealed the involuntary start that he gave at the mention of the name. He had a second's grace in which to brace himself, so that he was able to pull the chair out, place it beside Peggy's, and assume an expression of incomprehension.

"Logan, did you say?" He sat down, his heart racing, and frowned as though in recollection. "I seem to recall having known one or two people called that . . . Scotch, isn't it? What was the first name again?"

He was playing for time, waiting to see if Peggy showed any reaction; she had been there, at Oxton Hall, but the name might easily have slipped her memory. In which case . . .

"Aye, but this isn't a Scotsman – or we believe not," said Mr Crawford. "Harvey Logan."

"Wait – Mark!" Peggy said suddenly. "Wasn't that the name of the little man who came to Oxton – you remember, the Christmas before we were married? The American who – "

"Of course!" Mr Franklin cursed her memory inwardly, but he had no choice but to agree promptly. "That's right, Harvey Logan. A fellow I'd known in America, inspector – I'm American myself, you know."

"I'm aware," said Crawford. "Did you know him well – in America, Mr Franklin?"

"Not to say well," said Mr Franklin. "Our paths crossed once or twice; we were acquainted." He met the inspector's eyes. "Why – what about him?"

"And he called on you at Oxton – that would be Oxton Hall, Mrs Franklin's former home in Norfolk," said Crawford, ignoring the question. He seemed a well-informed inspector; Mr Franklin could feel his stomach muscles tightening. "What Christmas was that – before you were married, I think you said, Mrs Franklin?"

"Why, yes," said Peggy, and glanced at Mr Franklin. "That was

473

1909 – and it was on Christmas Day. I remember distinctly – we asked him to stay to supper, didn't we, Mark?"

"That's right," said Mr Franklin.

"Could you tell me," said Crawford, "precisely in what circumstances he called upon you?" His sleepy blue eyes included both of them.

"He came to see me," said Mr Franklin. "But I'm not quite sure I understand why you're asking – "

"If you'll bear with me a moment," said Crawford, "I'll explain presently. Why did he come to see you, Mr Franklin, can you tell me?"

"Why, certainly. I'd known him in America, as I said, and he was across in England – on business, he said, but I don't know what it was – and having found out I was in the neighbourhood, he dropped by."

"Just so." Crawford nodded. "A social call – I imagine he would stay an hour or two, then?"

"About an hour, I guess," Mr Franklin shrugged. "I don't remember exactly. He didn't stay to supper, as I recall."

"No, he didn't," said Peggy.

"And he gave you no hint of his business in England?" The blue eyes looked impassively at Mr Franklin. "Uh-huh. D'ye happen to remember, Mr Franklin, what you and he talked about?"

Mr Franklin frowned as though searching his memory. "It's a long time . . . I guess we talked about the States, and that sort of thing – you know, places we'd met – "

"Where had you met – in America?"

"Oh, out West. I was a miner, and a cattleman – we'd met in Colorado, Wyoming, I guess. But I hadn't known him that well, you see."

"And there was nothing of special significance that you spoke about that evening?"

Mr Franklin shook his head. "He asked how I was getting along – we exchanged news, you know how it is. We hadn't seen each other in nearly ten years – matter of fact, I didn't even recognize him at first."

"I see." Crawford's glance travelled to Peggy. "Mrs Franklin – do you recall anything about this Mr Logan? What he looked like, for example." The inspector gave a slight smile. "Ladies are often more observant than us men."

"Nothing particular," said Peggy. "I remember he looked a little – well, threadbare. Not awfully well-dressed – or well-fed, for that matter. He was a skinny little chap, wasn't he Mark? I thought – " She stopped, glancing at her husband.

"Go on, Mrs Franklin."

"Well, I was going to say, I thought he was a scrounger. You know, he looked rather down on his luck, and I wondered if that was why he'd called on Mark."

"Ah, yes." The blue eyes travelled back to Mr Franklin. "Was that your impression, too, Mr Franklin?"

"He didn't look too well-off." Mr Franklin paused. "I gave him a few pounds, now that I think of it – as my wife says, he looked down on his luck."

"Do you happen to remember how many pounds, Mr Franklin? In sovereigns?"

Since he had given Logan no money at all, Mr Franklin quickly calculated a likely amount. "I think it was five pounds – but, really inspector, I'm not certain. And I feel entitled to ask what these questions have to do with my wife and myself. I'm sure she's very tired – "

"I'll not detain you a moment longer than I must," said Crawford. "So he left you, with five pounds or thereabouts – did he say where he was going?"

"No, he didn't. But I had the impression he was catching a train to London."

"But he had said nothing of his business in England. Curious, that. You didn't inquire of him, Mr Franklin?"

"Not directly. I think he said something about looking up some relatives, or friends – something like that. He was quite vague about it."

There was a momentary interruption caused by the entrance of the maid with a tea-tray. Mr Franklin was relieved that Samson had not brought it himself: the mention of Logan's name in his butler's presence might just have caused even that imperturbable individual to react, and Mr Franklin had an idea that Inspector Crawford, for all his sleepy eyes and gentle manner, was not the kind who would have missed any significance that might attach to a clumsily rattled teaspoon, much less a laden tray descending at his feet. At a sign from Peggy the maid dispensed tea, which Mr Crawford received with a murmured "Thank'ee, thank'ee"; he spooned sugar liberally into his

475

cup, sipped, bobbed his head at Peggy and said "Very acceptable indeed, ma'am," before setting his cup on a side-table and resuming his inquiries.

"So you have no precise notion – indeed, no notion at all – of what he was doing in England, of where he had been immediately before calling upon you, or where he was bound. Not a communicative man, then, Mr Harvey Logan?"

"Not very, I'm afraid," said Mr Franklin. "Or if he did say anything like that, I've forgotten it."

"He said he'd been in banking, in the United States," said Peggy. "I remember he mentioned that, just as he was leaving."

"Indeed?" Crawford sipped at his tea again. "Banking, eh? That's most interesting. Did he make any other remark at that time, Mrs Franklin?"

"I don't remember," said Peggy thoughtfully. "Something about not seeing us again, I think – no, he said he might, very briefly. Something like that. But he didn't."

"No? And have either of you seen him since that Christmas Day of 1909 – what time of day did he leave you, by the way?"

"In the evening," said Peggy. "About eight o'clock, wasn't it, Mark?"

"Of course, you had asked him to stay to supper. Have you seen him since?"

They said "no" simultaneously.

"Or heard of him at all?"

"Not a word," said Mr Franklin, and Peggy shook her head.

Crawford glanced at Green, who produced a notebook, and the inspector asked:

"I'd be obliged if you could give me, between you, as accurate a description as you can of this Harvey Logan." He looked at Mr Franklin. "If you, sir, would begin, I've no doubt Mrs Franklin can recollect some details also."

"Well," said Mr Franklin, concentrating on the Logan of 1909, and not the Kid Curry of earlier years, "he'd be about five feet seven, I guess, slight build, thin features, kind of sandy hair, going back a little. His eyes were dark – "

"And very bright," said Peggy. "Like a bird's."

"His clothes were shabby, dark-coloured. He had on an old topcoat, and I think he had a hat. A billycock, wasn't it?" he asked Peggy.

"I'm not sure. But he wasn't wearing shoes – I remember seeing they were boots. I noticed because they were cracked."

"Very good," said Crawford. "Did you notice if he was wearing a watch and chain? No? Aye, well, it's a while ago." He nodded, and in the same quiet conversational voice asked: "Did you see – or did you get the impression – that he was armed?"

Mr Franklin felt as though a block of ice had been laid against his spine. Peggy was looking blankly astonished, and he hoped his own expression matched hers.

"Armed? Lord, inspector, why should he be?"

"Did you get any such impression?" asked Crawford.

"No, certainly not. That's an extraordinary question, inspector."

"He may well have been an extraordinary man, Mr Franklin," said Crawford drily. "Well – I think that covers about everything. I apologise again for taking up so much of your time. You've been very helpful." The blue eyes were amiable as they moved from Peggy to Mr Franklin. "There is nothing else you can recollect that might be of value – either of his visit to Oxton Hall, or in your case, sir, about your knowledge of him in America?"

Mr Franklin shook his head slowly. His mouth was dry, and he felt desperately in need of something stronger than tea. He wondered if there was anything harmless that he could volunteer that might help to satisfy this inquisitive policeman – but it was an insignificant wonder beside the enormous question of why they were asking about Logan at all. How the devil had they found out he had been to Oxton, and why should that be of the slightest interest anyway? He could mean nothing to them – and he'd been safely underground for five years now. The American law agencies had crossed him off their books ten years ago –

"Nothing, Mr Franklin?" Crawford was shaking his head. "Aye, well. There's one point on which I'd appreciate a wee bit of help, though – you knew him in Colorado and Wyoming, you said. What did you know of him – or where, if you can tax your memory that far, did you meet him?"

This was potentially dangerous ground, in view of his own American past, but he had to put a good frank face on it.

"That's difficult, inspector." He smiled ruefully. "I moved around a great deal – mining, ranching, and so on. We met in Denver, Colorado, I'm certain – I was going off to the silver diggings at a place called Tonopah – and Logan was in a group of us discussing the strike there had been there. I don't know what his interest was. Then I met him another couple of places – " he tried to think of places he had never been with Logan " – but I'm not sure where. Possibly Carson City, or Laramie, if those names mean anything to you. Come to think of it," he improvised, "he might have been working in a bank in Denver. But out West isn't like here, you know – you drift into people, and half the time you never know who or what they are. He was just like hundreds of others that I ran into one time or another."

"I understand," said Crawford. For a moment it seemed that he was about to ask something else, but if so he changed his mind. "Aye, well. So." He pulled at his large nose. "Then, if there's nothing more you can tell us about this man – nothing that you think might be of interest . . . ?" The blue eyes were as bland and open as an infant's; their very innocence alarmed Mr Franklin as no menacing stare could have done. What the hell was Crawford after? Well, now was the time to find out. Like good, law-abiding citizens he and Peggy had answered all these mysterious questions, and now that the interview was plainly drawing to an end, it was only natural that as good, law-abiding citizens they should want to know the purpose of the interrogation.

"Nothing I can think of, inspector," he said. "But perhaps if we knew the purpose of your questions . . . I don't want to pry into police business, but I'd very much like to be told what this is all about, and what's so important about this fellow Logan."

Crawford nodded. "Of course, I promised to explain, did I not? Forgive me – knowing you were both weary, I hesitated to keep you any longer. Aye, you're entitled to know, if you wish. It's a curious business – most curious. You have a property not far from Oxton, I believe, Mr Franklin? Lancing Manor, in the village of Castle Lancing?"

Mr Franklin had been prepared for anything from the moment Logan's name was mentioned, and he managed to keep his face unmoved, and meet the inspector's glance. But it was a herculean effort, and he had deliberately to refrain from clenching his hands visibly; he could feel a suffocating grip inside his chest. Fortunately Peggy spoke before he did.

"Yes, it's our country house."

"Is that the only property you have in the village?"

He had to volunteer it; concealment could have been fatal, now that he guessed what was coming.

"It's the only property I have there now," he said steadily. "A few months ago I sold a cottage that I owned in another part of the village. Just a little place where an old relative – " he forced a smile " – a very distant relative of mine, used to live. She died some time back, and I had no further use for it."

"That would be Lye Cottage, would it not? Occupied until the year before last by a Mrs Reeve?"

"That's the place. I sold it to a neighbour – a Lord Lacy, who runs an outfit called Gower Estate. He wanted it for agricultural development." God, he thought, Lacy – and with a rush came back the whole miserable, unbelievable conversation with Peggy in the car, driven out by the advent of Crawford and this new crisis. Within an hour his marriage had been ruined, and Kid Curry had come back to haunt him again – and Crawford was nodding agreement.

"That accords with what we've learned. Agricultural development, as you say. I take it you haven't been down to Castle Lancing for some time?"

"Not for more than a couple of months, no."

"Then you'll not be aware that Lye Cottage has been cleared away, for building purposes?"

"I knew it was going to be. But what's this got to do with – "

"I said it was a curious business, Mr Franklin," said Crawford quietly. "And it's a wee bit complicated, too. A very singular affair – and you'll see why I've been asking so many singular questions. As I say, Lye Cottage has been pulled down, and the ground thereabouts cleared for building work which the Gower Estate has in hand. Cottages for farm workers are to be erected, I understand, of the very latest kind. Well, it appears that labourers were at work digging a trench for drainage or piped water – something of the sort – and they came on an extraordinary thing." The blue eyes seemed to be unblinking, hypnotic to his imagination. "They found the remains of a body – a man's body, a skeleton. It was at some depth, and they supposed it had been there perhaps for generations – until one of them noticed that among the bones – I beg your pardon, Mrs Franklin, I don't wish to distress you – "

"No, no," said Peggy. She was intent on the inspector. "Please go on."

"Very good. Among the bones, then, they noticed a watch and

479

chain. Now, they were Irish labourers – " Crawford's expression nicely reflected Scotland's opinion of its fellow-Celts " – and no doubt they would have pocketed it and said nothing, but by unusual good luck a constable from Thetford arrived on the scene at the very moment of discovery. He was there about the disappearance of some poultry, and had naturally gone immediately to investigate among these Irish navvies. So there he was, just as the watch was in the hand of the man who had that minute picked it up, and the gang of them clustered round a half-buried skeleton."

Crawford paused, possibly for dramatic effect, and looked from Mr Franklin to Peggy and back again.

"The constable immediately took possession of the watch, and noticed it was gold; he opened it, and there was the owner's name, with an inscription. It said: 'Presented on the occasion of his twenty-first birthday, June the third, 1886, by grateful friends of his family, to Harvey Logan, Esq.' "

"Good heavens!" Peggy exclaimed. "Oh, how dreadful! That poor little man!"

"My God!" said Mr Franklin quietly. He was back in the rainy dark, in the Lye thicket, rummaging hurriedly through the dead man's pockets, removing papers – papers, for God's sake, that would have rotted in a few weeks, but leaving the pen-knife, the coins, and the watch which he had forgotten until this minute. It had never occurred to him that Logan's body would ever be found, or that any of the articles left would give a clue to his identity. His only thought had been to get the dead thing shovelled under – and now Crawford was pausing in his tale, watching them.

"But how . . . " Mr Franklin began. "Are you sure, inspector – that it's the same man? I mean – how on earth could he have gotten there?"

"How indeed?" said Crawford.

"Could he have wandered – and collapsed, or something?" said Peggy. "Oh, Mark, how awful!"

"No, Mrs Franklin," said Crawford, "he had been buried. The remains were approximately five feet below the surface. However, as I was telling you. The constable, on seeing the inscription, realized at once that the skeleton he was looking at had been a living man at least as recently as the year 1886, and that this was no ancient grave. He's a smart boy, yon," added the inspector approvingly, "and acted with an intelligence rare in a country constable – aye, or some greatly his senior that I could name, but that's by the way. He ordered the navvies off the site, under strict instructions to say nothing of the matter, and remained on guard while their foreman brought help from Thetford. The result was that the site was closed, Lord Lacy's agent informed, and the navvies whisked off the next day to work in another county. Oh, some word got out about a curious discovery, but nothing more. Lord Lacy's agent observed complete discretion, and I doubt if there's a soul even in Castle Lancing that knows what was found by Lye Cottage. In consequence, when the Norfolk constabulary brought us in, we were able to go to work unhindered – " Crawford did not quite lick his lips in satisfaction, but he came close to it " – and that's something rare in a murder investigation."

"Murder?" Mr Franklin looked suitably horrified, and Peggy gasped and put a hand to her mouth.

"Aye, murder," said Crawford. "It was to be assumed, from the fact that the body had patently been hidden within the last thirty years. And there were other indications that confirmed the assumption beyond doubt. The science of criminal investigation," he continued with some complacency, "is a great deal further advanced than even the readers of Sherlock Holmes might think. For example, our examiners were able to determine that the body had been in the earth not less than three, and not more than seven years. Your Mr Harvey Logan was last seen alive – by you, at least – four years and seven months ago. A watch bearing his name is found in the grave, and the description which you have given me, of a man about five feet seven inches tall, of slight build, corresponds satisfactorily with the Bertillon measurements of the skeleton. I am afraid," said Crawford deliberately, "that the man who walked out of Oxton Hall that Christmas Day, is the man who was subsequently murdered not more than eighteen months later, and whose body was found as I have described." The inspector paused. "I wonder, Mrs Franklin, if I could impose on you for another cup of your excellent tea? No, no – please don't ring for any more – what is in the pot will do admirably."

He waited while Peggy refilled his cup, and Mr Franklin sat calculating the odds. They'd found Logan, they knew he'd been murdered at or presumably near Castle Lancing. What else did they know – God, he himself had mentioned Colorado and Wyoming! That was enough to set them on the trail – a telegraph to Denver would tell them who Logan really was ... except that Kid Curry was officially dead in – where was it? Glenwood, or some name like that, ten years

481

ago. That would puzzle them. But in any event, there was nothing to connect Mark Franklin, Esq., of Castle Lancing, with Curry's criminal past in the States. Nothing to suggest that Mark Franklin had ever seen Curry again after that night at Oxton Hall. Then . . . what the hell were they doing here, talking to him? What did they know, or suspect? Was this sleepy-looking bastard Crawford playing some elaborate game of cat-and-mouse, or just pursuing some routine inquiry?

He fought down the thoughts, and the temptation to demand of Crawford why they were here. What would an innocent, respectable citizen say? How would he look?

"But who could have done such a thing?" If his voice sounded strained and shocked, that was natural enough. "I can't believe it!" He shook his head in bewilderment. "I mean – he couldn't have been murdered by . . . by robbers, surely? He didn't look . . . well, he didn't seem to have five cents to rub together – did he, Peggy?"

"He would have the five pounds or thereabouts that you gave him, Mr Franklin," Crawford reminded him. "Unless, that is, he had spent it in the meantime. We have no way of knowing how long elapsed between his leaving Oxton and his death. The fact that there was nothing but a few coppers in the grave suggests that he had spent it – for if murderers robbed him, why did they leave a fine gold watch? No, robbery seems unlikely. And yet – to spend five pounds takes a wee while, and our inquiries so far have turned up no traces of the man after he left Oxton Hall. If he remained in the vicinity, as seems likely in view of where his body was found, it's odd that no one remembers him – Americans aren't that common in those parts. And that he *was* an American was something we quickly established – and which you've confirmed this morning. The watch was made in Philadelphia; the coppers in the grave included an American cent coin; the boots – or what remained of them – were of American manufacture; that was established from the heel-plates. So you can understand," continued Crawford mildly, "why our investigations have led us to you, Mr Franklin. As the only American residing – or occasionally residing – in the vicinity, you were a natural subject of inquiry – if you'll forgive the expression."

"I see. Of course." Mr Franklin saw all too clearly. They didn't know who Logan really was – yet. But they might find out. And if they did, with the help of the American lawmen, what else would they find? There was no reason why they should ever stumble across any

482

trace in America of Mark Franklin – as he'd reminded the Kid, there were no posters, no rewards, no files on him. There was no earthly reason why Crawford should connect him with Logan's death, beyond the fact that they were both Americans, and the grave had been found within half a mile of Lancing Manor. But what did that signify? As long as his own American past remained hidden, there were no grounds even for suspicion, much less proof. The fact that he'd admitted knowing Logan in America meant nothing – thousands of respectable people must have known him, without even suspecting what he was...

"And now that I learn that you were acquainted with him in the United States, you can appreciate my anxiety to learn anything at all that you knew of him there – anything that might afford us some further clue, or suggest a line of inquiry." The blue eyes were placid, interested.

"I'm trying to think, inspector – but it's tough to know what I could tell you that might help. I still can't get over the shock of this . . . this dreadful business. To think that this poor fellow's been . . . murdered, you say, and buried on my property, goodness knows how long – "

"Not on your property, Mr Franklin. Did I not make it clear? No, possibly not; I beg your pardon." Crawford's eyes showed a flicker that might have been annoyance – or disappointment. "The grave was not in the ground of Lye Cottage, but in a thicket nearby."

"Oh, I see. I'm sorry, I misunderstood."

"Not at all, I may have misled you." Crawford paused, and gently fingered his long nose reflectively. "However, if nothing comes to your mind at the moment . . . perhaps if you recollect any wee thing – no matter what – you'd be good enough to give me a call at the Yard? Criminal Investigation Department will find me, or Sergeant Green here. In the meanwhile, you've been most helpful, both of you." He rose and smiled at Peggy. "I can see Mrs Franklin's ready for sleep, and I apologize again for imposing on your time." He gathered up his ulster, and the sergeant rose behind him.

"You'll bear in mind, Mr Franklin, that the nub of the question for us is a simple one," Crawford added. He pursed his lips and contemplated the carpet. "Why would any person – here, or in America, or anywhere at all – wish to do this man Logan to death? That's the clincher." He shook his head and smiled ruefully at Mr Franklin. "It always is, in this kind of case. Give us the motive, and we'll give you the man."

483

It was casually said, the kind of quietly philosophical remark with which Inspector Crawford had no doubt terminated a hundred similar interviews. It might have been a normal reminder to stimulate the memory of a possibly helpful witness. Or it might have been an invitation to someone of whom Inspector Crawford knew, or suspected, a great deal more than he had admitted – in which case bland silence would in itself be a damning admission. Suppose Crawford already knew all about Mark Franklin of Hole-in-the-Wall? But he simply couldn't – it was not possible. And in that confidence Mr Franklin was able to shrug regretfully and say:

"I'll certainly give it some thought, inspector, but I'm afraid it won't be of much help to you. As I said, I didn't know the man all that well – hardly at all, really. Certainly not enough to know why anyone should want to shoot him."

He was turning to the door as he said it, and his hand was on the knob when Crawford's voice said quietly behind him.

"Did I say he'd been shot? Surely not, did I?"

Mr Franklin's heart gave a sickening lurch, but he turned the knob and opened the door, looking round as he did so, trying to sound natural.

"Didn't you? I don't remember. I guess I just assumed it, then. Wasn't he shot, inspector?"

"Aye – as a matter of fact he was." Crawford was regarding him with interest, Green stolidly, and Peggy, near the inspector's side, was looking from him to Mr Franklin with only mild curiosity. "What made you think that that was so, Mr Franklin?"

"I really don't know, inspector." He forced a wry smile. "Probably just that if you've been brought up in the Western states, as I was, when you hear someone has died violently, you assume it was from a gunshot. I'm afraid that used to happen all too often."

"Aye, so I believe," said the inspector, but he made no move to pass through the door that Mr Franklin was now holding open. He glanced at Peggy, and then at Mr Franklin, and seemed to be debating something in his mind. Finally he came to a conclusion. "Aye, he was shot. Fractures in the rib-cage of the skeleton are consistent with gunshot wounds, but what put our examiners' diagnosis beyond doubt was the presence in the grave of three metal objects, much misshapen, but still easily identifiable as spent bullets from a revolving pistol of heavy calibre." The inspector's tone was brisk and matter-of-fact. His glance went from Mr Franklin's face to his waist, and his gesture was casual.

"A pistol similar to those you're wearing, Mr Franklin. Not uncommon, of course, but not commonplace. Are those your own, or were they hired for the costume ball?"

"What about you, Mark? Had enough?" On the table, his pair of kings, an eight, an ace – and another ace in the hole. Across the table, two pairs visible, and an opponent ready to go all the way while the others threw in and old Davis sweated and groaned and seemed to be on the verge of apoplexy. "Had enough, Mark? Why don't you quit? I got you licked, little boy!'

That had been for money. Now it was for life.

"What d'you say, Franklin? I can't hear you! Talk up, goddamn it – if you got anything to say!" Deaf Charley Hanks with his back to the hitching-rail, his thumbs hooked into his belt where the big Navy Colt was thrust into the band of his britches, his shaven head cocked to catch the words. Behind him Tracy on the boardwalk with the shotgun cradled, feet clattering as the onlookers scampered for cover, the shrieks and cries of alarm, his own ears trying to shut out the sounds and his eyes fixed on those big hands – and a half-eye for Tracy as well. His own voice? "I've nothing to say to you, Charley, except I'm here if you want me. It's up to you. If you don't want me, go on inside with your prairie-dog there." "Want you, you son-of-a-bitch? Why would I want you? You're no-account!" The ugly peasant face twisted in the well-known grin, the head turned in the permanent attitude of the deaf man. "I don't want you, Franklin – not till I'm ready! And when I'm ready, in my own good time. I'll pay you out, like any other fresh young squirt! But you won't be here, if you know what's good for you! And you know what's good for you – running like hell away from O. C. Hanks! So git – and when I feel like it I'll come settle you!" And knowing that all he had to do was stand his ground, with his life in the balance, and wait for Deaf Charley to do what he had promised to do.

And he had stood his ground, and Deaf Charley had made his move, and his nerve had not failed him, just as it had not failed him at the poker table. Now it was for his life again, and the opponent this time had all his cards in the hole, none showing, and the opponent himself, with his long nose and sleepy eyes and avuncular manner and gentle

485

voice was a damned sight more dangerous than any Kid Curry or Deaf Charley Hanks, heeled or not. If he was an opponent – he *must* be – and yet Mr Franklin could still not be entirely sure. There was no absolute certainty yet that Crawford had even a hand or a stake to get into the game.

"No, they're my own guns," he said easily, as any innocent, law-abiding citizen might have done. "They're Remingtons – my wife thought they might add an authentic touch for the fancy-dress party."

"Indeed," said Crawford. "May I see one of them, Mr Franklin?"

Again only mild curiosity – and what innocent man could object to that? Mr Franklin put his finger inside the right-hand trigger guard and drew the pistol, and by sheer force of habit spun it so that the barrel lay in his hand and the butt was towards the inspector. And he heard Peggy's sudden gasp, and saw her eyes widen with shock, and knew that the careless, practised gesture had suddenly brought home to her the possible implication of everything that had been said in that room. Logan dead from revolver fire, buried within a half-mile of Lancing Manor, Logan an acquaintance of Mark Franklin who handled a six-shooter with such familiar ease. And it was utterly impossible that Crawford should not have drawn the same inference – certainly in the course of the interview, possibly long before it began. Depending on how much Crawford already knew, or suspected. But the inspector was taking the gun imperturbably, examining the cylinder, turning it in his hand.

"A fine weapon," he said. "Aye, and dangerous. Are those live rounds that I see in your belt, Mr Franklin?"

"Yes, inspector. They're live shells – but don't worry. I take good care with them."

"I'm glad to hear it," said Crawford, and held the Remington out to him. "Aye," he added, "it would be just such a gun that killed Curry."

It was meant to stun, to strike inside his guard and make him betray himself. And if it had been said a few minutes earlier, it might have succeeded. But by now Mr Franklin was alert and ready, and while the name went through him like an electric shock, the shock did not show. In a way, he felt almost relieved, for now the game was on, and Crawford had shown his first card at last, having held back as long as he could in the hope that Mr Franklin would incriminate himself either by word or by silence. And Mr Franklin liked to think he had done neither, and if there was one thing sure it was that he wasn't going to be bluffed by any sandy-whiskered Scotch wiseacre with a long nose. He took the gun without comment, slipped it into its holster, and stood back to let Crawford pass into the hall. The inspector frowned.

"Did ye hear what I said, Mr Franklin?" He must be slightly put out; his accent had broadened suddenly.

"I'm sorry," said Mr Franklin innocently. "What was that?"

"I said it would be just such a gun that killed – Curry. Perhaps you didn't know that Logan also went under that name – in the United States?"

If he lied, did Crawford know enough already to prove him a liar? And if Crawford did not know enough, could he ferret it out, with the help of the American authorities? Possibly – in which case the lie could be damning circumstantial evidence. If he told the truth, admitted that he had known Logan was Kid Curry – what then? Why hadn't he admitted it already? Either way, it began to look as though there was a fair chance that his American history was going to come out, for what it was worth. The past that he had hidden from everyone, that he had thought was done with until the moment when he had seen Kid Curry standing there just inside the doorway of Oxton Hall, the past that he had thought was dead and buried with Curry in the Lye thicket. The past that could still be traced, by just such a bloodhound as Crawford, back all the way to Hole-in-the-Wall, and the U.P. hold-ups, and Deadwood jail, and Deaf Charley Hanks in the street at Cheyenne, and Cassidy and the Sundance Kid and the Wild Bunch. Not traced with certainty, and they couldn't pin a thing on him under American law – but if enough of it, or the suspicion of it, came out, what could Crawford make of it in connection with the body in Lye thicket? What would a jury make of it all? But it all depended on how much Crawford knew – or could discover. And as he stood, poker-faced, considering the inspector's question and how to answer, the decision was made for him.

"Mark!" It was Peggy, her voice sharp with bewilderment, fear in her eyes. "What is he talking about? What does he mean?"

"I'm not quite sure, Peggy," said Mr Franklin. "Just what do you mean, inspector?"

"I was merely asking, Mr Franklin," said Crawford quietly, "whether you were aware that Harvey Logan also went under the name of Curry?" He glanced at Peggy. "But it's of no great importance, for the moment, anyway. I wonder . . . perhaps we might continue this conversation at some later time that's convenient to you? Would you be able to spare me an hour at the Yard this afternoon? I could send a car for you – and we needn't trouble Mrs Franklin."

If it was said out of consideration for Peggy – which Mr Franklin doubted – it was plainly too late in the day. Her face showed that she knew there was something badly, dangerously wrong, that there had been a sinister purpose behind all these questions that she had not understood. And whatever was coming now, she could not be shielded from it – if the old past was going to come out, she would have to know it. And why not? Was it any worse than the truth he had learned from her in the car that morning? By her own curious standards of morality, of which he had received such stunning proof, what had he to be ashamed of? How did infidelity rate in the scale beside a bank raid or blowing a boxcar? It would be interesting to find out. As for Crawford – whether he was merely groping in the dark, or knew the whole past already, or part of it, or could find it all out – let him make what he could of it. He might think he had a full hand, but let him try to play it – there were two jokers, Franklin and Samson, and unless ultimately he could break them, he might as well go back to catching street bookies.

"I've no objection to continuing the conversation here and how, inspector," he said. "In fact, I'd prefer it. I don't really care to visit Scotland Yard."

Crawford glanced again at Peggy, hesitated, and then said slowly: "I think it might be better, Mr Franklin."

But Mr Franklin shook his head, and then to his astonishment Peggy took two quick steps forward and stood beside him, her hand slipping into his, clutching it tightly. Her face was frightened, but her mouth was tight-set and determined. For a moment he was puzzled, and then he understood, and looked at Crawford.

"Right now, inspector."

If Crawford was sure of his ground, if the worst was going to happen, he would know it now. Crawford would arrest him, or take him into custody, or use whatever device the law allowed him. But if he wasn't sure, he would just have to make do on Mr Franklin's terms. The sleepy eyes considered him for a moment, and then Crawford said:

"As you please. I merely wished to spare Mrs Franklin any possible distress. However . . . perhaps she had better sit down."

Mr Franklin nodded, and Peggy allowed him to guide her back to her chair; he remained standing beside her. Crawford, after a moment's hesitation, resumed his seat. "Well, Mr Franklin?"

"You asked if I knew that Logan sometimes called himself Curry. Yes, I did."

"Indeed?" Crawford raised his sandy eyebrows. "Why did you not tell me that earlier?"

"You didn't ask me it earlier. And it didn't occur to me."

Crawford's lips tightened. "Did you also know that in America he was wanted for robbery and murder?"

Peggy gasped, and Mr Franklin reached down and took her hand. "Yes, I did. Show me anyone west of Kansas City who didn't."

"But again – you didn't mention it earlier, when I asked for any information about him?"

"I assumed you knew it, inspector – but that for reasons of your own, you weren't letting on that you knew it." Mr Franklin's tone was quietly civil. "I don't care for people to play games with me – and when they do, I'm liable to play games with them."

Crawford looked at him coldly. "I take it you're aware that withholding information relating to a crime is a serious offence?"

"I didn't know that, no. But crimes which this man Curry may or may not have committed in the United States don't fall within your jurisdiction, surely?"

Crawford gave him a long hard stare. "A crime committed in this country does," he said deliberately. "Very well, Mr Franklin. You knew this man was a dangerous, wanted criminal, you had been told that he had been found murdered in close proximity to your own home – but you decided not to divulge to me what you know about him. Is that not strange conduct for a respectable citizen?"

There was a slight emphasis on the last two words, but Mr Franklin smiled slightly as he replied.

"Not when you consider the circumstances, perhaps. When Kid Curry – that was his professional name, as you know – called on me at Oxton Hall five years ago, I knew all about him. But I didn't tell my wife – then my fiancée – or her family, who or what he was. Maybe you can understand why. Although my association with this man Curry was of the slightest, and entirely innocent, he wasn't the kind of acquaintance one boasts about. I was newly arrived from America in those days – perhaps I was foolish, but it seemed to me inadvisable for anyone to know, and perhaps draw wrong conclusions

489

from the fact, that I was on nodding terms with a crook. Can you understand that?"

"Possibly." Crawford was sceptical. "You're ready enough to admit it now – and you've deliberately chosen to do so in Mrs Franklin's presence."

"We've been married five years, inspector – an engaged couple are perhaps more sensitive. But I'd gladly have spared her the knowledge now, if your own questioning hadn't alarmed her, and made it obvious that she'd have to find out anyway."

"I see. And, knowing Curry for what he was five years ago, you didn't then think it your duty to advise the British police that a dangerous criminal was in their midst?"

"I knew he was a reputed criminal, yes – and also that he'd served his sentence, as I understood. No, I didn't conceive it my duty – also, I've given you reasons why I was reluctant to own acquaintance with him, even to the police. I haven't formed such a high opinion of their discretion today to make me think I was wrong to say nothing five years ago."

Crawford sat back and surveyed him in some perplexity, and when he spoke it was in a tone of reproach. "D'you know, Mr Franklin, you astonish me? I find your attitude high-handed, sir – even offensive. And yet you know that I am here to investigate a most serious matter."

"A matter which happens to have nothing to do with me. However, I've answered your questions with the same candour and openness that you have used in putting them to me." His tone was quiet and level. "But I don't care for innuendo, or to have my wife alarmed. Perhaps I'm a little impatient, but if you have anything to say that really concerns me, I'd be obliged if you'd say it."

"Very well, Mr Franklin." There was a distinct flush on the inspector's cheek, and his nose twitched. "Very well, I'll do that. And I'll be as frank with you as you've just been with me. Ye may not like it."

Mr Franklin said nothing, and after a moment's bleak pause the inspector produced a notebook. "You'll have gathered," he said, "that since the discovery of the body of Logan, or Curry, we have been in touch with police in the United States. A very lengthy exchange by telegraph, at considerable expense, but well worth it, I may say. The New York force referred us to Denver, Colorado, and we addressed a long series of questions to the Pinkerton office in that city. A remarkable organization, the Pinkertons, for which we at the Yard have the highest regard – Pinkerton himself being a Glasgow man.

490

However – " the inspector recalled himself from the affectionate digression "we received in reply a long cable which answered all our questions. There are Pinkerton operatives with fine long memories – particularly a Mr J. P. McParland. Does the name mean anything to you, Mr Franklin?"

"James McParland. Yes, I've heard of him."

"The recollection is mutual." Crawford's flash of ill temper had left him; he was looking almost benevolent. "However, first things first. He furnished us with a full dossier on Logan, alias Curry, and his associates, a gang of desperadoes calling themselves 'The Wild Bunch', who terrorized the railroads and banks in several states round about the end of the last century. Their leader was one – " Crawford consulted his notebook " – Robert Parker, alias Butch Cassidy, since reported dead. Various others of the group are also dead, or imprisoned, or have disappeared. Some of the names may be familiar to you – Kilpatrick, Lant, Longbaugh, Tracy, Linley . . . " He paused. "Hanks," he said, and looked inquiringly at Mr Franklin before reading on: "Carver, Lee, Chancellor . . . and many others which you may have forgotten." He closed the book, and his sleepy eyes were serious, almost compassionate. "But I hardly have to remind you that among the list of names of the Wild Bunch is that of Mark Franklin."

Peggy gave a little cry, and Mr Franklin sat down beside her and tightened his clasp on her hand.

"Don't worry, honey," he said, "it's all right." He tried to smile reassuringly into the white face, ghostly and beautiful under the ridiculous Marie Antoinette wig, her eyes wide, staring at him. "You haven't heard it all yet. Wait till the inspector's finished. Go on, Mr Crawford – what did they tell you about Mark Franklin?"

"Just that; what I've told you. That he was a member of this gang of hold-up men."

"Nothing more? Didn't you ask for full particulars – knowing as you did that there was an American named Mark Franklin living at Castle Lancing?"

"I did."

"And did nobody," asked Mr Franklin quietly, "offer to prove anything? You say McParland, or the Pinkertons, told you Mark Franklin was a member of the Wild Bunch. What's their evidence? What charges have they against him? What crimes do they allege he committed? What records have they got on him? You must have asked them all of that, surely?"

Crawford hesitated, but only for a second. "They have never brought charges, nor did they furnish evidence of specific crimes. No. But they have information based on common knowledge that Franklin was a member of the gang."

"Information based on common knowledge?" Mr Franklin asked mildly. "And if McParland told you that Teddy Roosevelt was a member of the Wild Bunch, you'd believe that, would you? Did they tell you what this Franklin looked like? Have they even seen him? Have they anyone to swear to him?"

"No, Mr Franklin, they have not," said Crawford soberly. "Nor is it necessary that they should. I have no interest whatsoever in what can or cannot be proved against this man Franklin on American soil. But I am entitled to be interested in the common report that a Mark Franklin was a member of this gang, and consorted with Kid Curry, and in the fact that a Mark Franklin, formerly of Colorado and Wyoming, now lives in a Norfolk village within a mile of the hidden grave where Kid Curry's murdered body has been found. I am further entitled, in the course of my duties, to question this Mark Franklin of Castle Lancing, and put to him certain facts. You would concede me that?"

Mr Franklin glanced at Peggy. She was still pale, but her face was composed, and although her hand was trembling she had not taken it from his. He nodded to Crawford. "If you've anything that isn't rumour or supposition, I'll listen to it."

"Thank you," said Crawford. "There is, in fact, only one categoric entry for Mark Franklin in the Pinkerton files – and it does not specify a crime. Or not, at least, what passes for a crime under the criminal code of the state of Wyoming." His tone suggested that in his opinion the criminal code of the state of Wyoming was in need of drastic revision. "It is of a hearing before a justice of the peace in the town of . . . " He had opened his notebook again, and was frowning at the page. " . . . in the town of . . . Chay-enny–"

"Cheyenne," said Mr Franklin helpfully.

"I thank you. The entry is from a newspaper cutting, describing the arraignment – which seems to have been remarkably brief – of one Mark Franklin for the manslaughter of Camilla Hanks, alias O. C. Hanks, alias Charles Jones, alias Deaf Charley. According to the evidence then given, Franklin shot Hanks dead, but was immediately acquitted on the testimony of eye-witnesses that he acted in self-defence, the man Hanks having fired first." Crawford closed his

492

notebook, and looked solemnly at Mr Franklin. "There is a description of the acquitted person which I am in a position to say tallies closely with that of Mr Mark Franklin of Castle Lancing. And the acquitted man is also reported – I emphasize the word reported – to have been a former member of the so-called Wild Bunch. No witnesses may be available to testify to that, but I understand that there are still many people in Cheyenne who could, at need, come forward to identify the man who killed Camilla Hanks."

Mr Franklin sat quite still for a moment, and then he let go of Peggy's hand and stood up slowly. He paced to the window and stood looking out into the sunshine of Wilton Crescent.

"That won't be necessary," he said. "I killed Deaf Charley Hanks. And, as you say, I was acquitted on the ground of self-defence. I don't have any regrets about it, either, inspector, because he was a mean fellow, and he had it coming to him. And if I hadn't killed him, he'd have killed me." He was addressing Peggy rather than Crawford, but now he turned from the window and looked directly at the inspector.

"But that's all you know about me – except what you may find in Nevada newspapers about the great silver strike at Tonopah, and how an old man called Davis and I struck the big vein. For the rest, you'll have to look at the English society papers over the past few years. But as to these stories about the Wild Bunch – " he shook his head contemptuously " – they're neither here nor there. Rumour and gossip, and neither you nor any soul on earth can prove otherwise. And if you try I'll hit you with the biggest action for slander you ever saw." He came back to stand beside Peggy's chair, and laid a hand on her shoulder. "So there it is, inspector, so far as I'm concerned."

Crawford regarded him gravely. "No doubt, Mr Franklin. But there remains the matter of the murder of Harvey Logan, alias Kid Curry, which is what concerns me – "

"But it doesn't concern me, inspector," said Mr Franklin. "The last time I saw that man alive was when he walked out the front door of Oxton Hall on Christmas Day, 1909. Where he went, I don't know. How he got in the ground at Lye Cottage, I don't know. Who shot him – if he was shot, as you say – I don't know. I don't even know if the body in that grave *is* Kid Curry – and neither do you." Crawford's head came up sharply. "All you know is he was wearing Harvey Logan's watch, and was about the same build, and had American heel-plates on his boots. But you don't know that he was Kid Curry

493

– in fact, I'd say there's a considerable body of opinion to swear he wasn't. They'll tell you Kid Curry died more than ten years back, somewhere in Colorado – "

"How did you know that?" The sleepy eyes were narrow.

"I was in or around Colorado at that time, remember. Maybe they'll change their minds, after your discovery, but I wouldn't bank on it. They're mighty jealous about their dead outlaws in those parts."

There was a long silence, and then Crawford said patiently:

"Mr Franklin, you have admitted to me that you knew the man Logan, or Curry, and that you met and talked with him in England in 1909. You have further admitted to me that you are a practised hand with a revolver, and that you have killed a man in public fight. Curry's body is found, within a few hundred yards of your house in Norfolk, dead of revolver shot wounds. There is suggestion – we'll call it no more than that, even – that you were at one time his companion in crime. Would you not say, in the face of that great body of evidence, that you have much to explain?"

"No, I wouldn't," said Mr Franklin. "It's circumstantial evidence, if that, and you know it. I don't have to explain anything."

"I think you do," said Crawford. "Circumstantial or not, a jury may well agree with me. Come now, Mr Franklin – you're not so simple as to ask me to believe that all this evidence is pure coincidence?"

"I'm not asking you to believe anything. Believe whatever you like. It's what you can prove that matters."

"So it is – and among other things I can prove that you've consistently evaded my questions and concealed information, that – "

"There isn't a single direct question on a specific subject that you've asked today that I haven't answered," Mr Franklin interrupted. "If you doubt it, ask your sergeant to check his notes. Vague inquiries about 'anything helpful I might recollect' don't mean a thing." He became curt. "You're wasting your time. If you think you've got a case, bring it."

Crawford's lips came together in a tight line; the flush was back on his cheeks, and his eyes were no longer sleepy as he got to his feet.

"I put it to you that you wilfully shot and murdered Harvey Logan, alias Kid Curry, and that you made away with his body and buried – "

"Prove it," said Mr Franklin.

"Do you deny it?"

"Of course I deny it. And if you try to show otherwise I'll have half of Middle Temple and Lincoln's Inn tearing your case to pieces before you can even get it written out."

"Ye think so?"

"I know so. But if you think different, go ahead and arrest me – and take the consequences."

For a moment he thought Crawford would do it, as they faced each other in the quiet morning-room, with Green looming at his superior's elbow, and Peggy tense and white-faced in her chair beside Mr Franklin. For a full ten seconds the inspector stared at him, and then he said with quiet deliberation:

"In my opinion, there is a case to answer – "

"If that was your opinion," said Mr Franklin, "you'd have come here with a warrant in your pocket."

The inspector held his gaze, and then thoughtfully stroked his long nose.

"Aye, well," he said, "we'll see. But we both know what we both know – do we not, Mr Franklin? And there's an old saying with which ye may be familiar. 'Murder will out'. "

"I doubt if that's evidence, either," said Mr Franklin.

Crawford turned to pick up his ulster. "You'll be hearing from us presently," he said. "In the meantime, you'll kindly inform us if you have any intention of leaving London – "

"I won't inform you of anything at all, inspector," said Mr Franklin quietly. "I don't have to."

Crawford put his coat over his arm, and made a brief inclination of his head to Peggy.

"I regret any inconvenience we may have caused you, Mrs Franklin," he said. "Good morning." And without another glance at Mr Franklin he left, in reasonably good order, followed by the stolid sergeant. They heard the front door close behind them, and then they were alone in the morning-room, Marie Antoinette and Deadwood Dick.

Peggy was motionless in her chair, staring in front of her. Mr Franklin closed the door to the hall and stood until she turned to look at him. She was still pale, but she no longer looked frightened.

"So now you know," he said quietly.

"Was it true?"

"About the Wild Bunch? About the desperado Mark Franklin who raided banks and blew up trains? Yes, it's true. And a good deal more

495

that Jim McParland never got to hear about, much less Inspector Crawford." His voice was flat and tired. "You married a badman, Peggy. A reformed badman, if you like, but still a badman. I guess it's easy to reform when you've hit the big bonanza – although I'd gone straight before that. And I thought it was all over and done with, and neither you nor anyone else would ever know. I wouldn't have married you otherwise."

"Was it true – about Logan?"

He hesitated for only a moment. "Yes, that's true, too."

She did not flinch. "You murdered him?"

"No. I killed him, but it wasn't murder, whatever the law calls it. I killed him just as I killed Deaf Charley Hanks that the inspector told you about. In self-defence. That night at Oxton, Curry put it to me straight: he wanted half a million dollars – or my life. There was no point going to the police. For one thing, all the Wild Bunch stuff would probably have come out – anyway, I knew the Kid, and police or not, it was going to be one or other of us. So . . ."

"But where did it happen? When – "

"It doesn't matter. The less you know about it, the better. But you can take my word for it – if you think my word's worth taking any more – that it happened as I said. He tried to kill me, but I got him first. It may seem a vain, unimportant point to you, but I'd like you to believe that it was fair."

"Of course I believe you." She sounded almost surprised. "I'd always believe you."

"Even – after all this?"

"Why not? It was a dreadful shock – I didn't know what that awful man was driving at . . . and then when you showed him your pistol . . ." Her voice began to shudder violently, and then suddenly she was on her feet and flying round the table to throw herself against him, clinging to him in a frenzy, sobbing against his chest. "Oh, Mark! Oh, Mark! I was so frightened! So frightened!" She began to cry passionately, while he held her, and then the fit passed, and she began to take deep breaths, and after a moment she pushed gently away from him, mopping at her eyes and blinking. Her trembling subsided, and then she said: "God, I'm an awful fool! I'm . . . sorry . . . I don't usually get hysterical, do I? But for a moment there, when it came like a thunderbolt . . . when he seemed to be accusing you of murder . . . I was so terrified." She shook her head. "I'm all right now."

"You didn't act terrified. First thing you did was to stand alongside me. That was when I thought – what the hell, let him say what he's got to say. I didn't even know how much he knew about me – but I knew you were going to have to know it all, whether he did or not. I'm glad you did – I don't know why, but I am."

"Can he prove anything?" The powder on her cheeks was streaked, and her eyes were still moist, but she was composed again. "He seemed to think he had a good case."

"He hasn't got a case at all. Oh, he knows I did it, all right. As surely as if I'd handed him a signed confession. But short of a signed confession he hasn't a hope, and he knows it. He'll keep trying for a while, but he won't find any evidence, because there isn't any to find. I'll be a marked man for the rest of my time in England – but I've always been that, anyway."

"The rest of your time in England?" Her eyes opened wide. "What d'you mean?"

"I don't really know, Peggy. I don't really know." He sighed and rubbed his fingers wearily up and down his brow. "It's all . . . I don't know. But I don't see how it can – go on, do you? Twelve hours ago – I don't say it was all . . . peaches and cream, but it was getting by, somehow. Now – all of a sudden, you find you're married to a criminal and a killer – and I . . . " He looked away, and then back again, "I find out I've been sharing you with Lacy, and . . . " He shook his head hopelessly. "Quite a Fourth of July, one way and another. The night of the Savoy Ball in aid of the blind. Something appropriate about that."

Peggy waited for a moment and then said: "Does it matter so very much?"

"Matter?" He was incredulous. "You keep saying, does it matter, and that you don't mind! How can't it matter? For five years you think you've been living with a decent, honest, ordinary man – and in a moment you discover he's a crook and a gunslick and God knows what else, and Scotland Yard are after him for murder! Are you saying that doesn't matter?"

"It would matter if they could arrest you for it," said Peggy dispassionately. "Of course it would. But you don't seem to think they can. Are you quite sure of that, Mark?"

He stared at her in disbelief, and in the disorder of his thoughts the line of least resistance seemed to be to answer her question.

"Yes, I'm sure. Cast-iron sure. Crawford might as well retire now.

497

But that's the least of it. You know it's true, and I know you know it! And you ask if it matters?"

"Well," said Peggy, "it doesn't matter to me. Possibly it should, but it doesn't. If they can't touch you – that's the important thing. As to all this nonsense about the Wild Bunch – well, that was a long time ago, wasn't it? And I heard that creature who was here just now saying – well, admitting, anyway – that they couldn't prove anything about it. Anyway, I didn't marry a gunman or a crook – I married you. And it doesn't make any difference to me who you've shot, or anything – don't you see? You're not a criminal, and even if you were, you'd still be my husband. As long as you're safe, and we're all right, the rest is unimportant. It would be awful if there was a scandal, but I don't see how there can be. If this Curry business, or Logan, or whatever he's called, is a spent egg – " the schoolgirl slang gave her words the final bizarre ring in his ears " – then the other thing, this Western outlaw stuff, doesn't matter a bit. Even if it came out, it can't be proved. A lot of people," she added, "would think it was rather fun."

"Christ!" said Mr Franklin, and looked out of the window. Peggy continued to consider him, and then she said: "So when you talk about things not being able to go on, and hint about leaving England – because I've discovered that you're a killer and a criminal, as you call yourself . . . well, if that's all that's bothering you, it needn't. It just doesn't matter – I'm sorry if you dislike my using the expression, but it just doesn't."

She stopped and waited, and after a moment, without looking at her, he said: "Maybe it matters to me, though."

"It needn't, Mark," she said. "If that's all there is – and if you're not just using all this police stuff and your lawless past as a gallant excuse. Pretending that that's why it can't go on, as you put it." She waited again and then said: "But it isn't that, really, is it? It's Frank Lacy. And it's me, too. You've found out that I'm not what you thought I was, haven't you? Or perhaps you guessed, but tried not to see it – or to let me know that you saw it. But you're not being quite fair, Mark, are you? After all, there's Pip Delys on your side."

She said it in a reasonable, unreproachful voice, and he looked at her in heavy silence for a moment. Then he said:

"No. There isn't. I was Pip Delys's lover – once – before I met you. Since then, there's been nothing. All the rest of it, since – Jeremy's gossip, and the jewels, and that sort of thing – that's what our friend Crawford would call circumstantial evidence, but it just happens to be false. Just as the other circumstantial evidence, about Curry, happens to be true. But I guess you can believe me, about Pip. After all, if I'll admit murder – legal murder – to you, I'd hardly deny adultery."

"Wouldn't you, though?" said Peggy sceptically. "I should think most husbands would sooner admit murder than adultery to their wives. After all, the murder wouldn't be something done against their wives, would it?" She looked at him, searching the grey eyes. "But I do believe you – you're not the kind to lie about it. I'm sorry."

"Sorry?"

"It would be easier if she was your mistress – for you, I mean." Peggy sounded despondent. "You wouldn't mind – well, you couldn't, could you? – about Frank. As it is . . . " She sighed in utter weariness. "Oh, hell, what a mess it is! I should have kept my mouth shut. Look," she added suddenly, "is it because it happened to be Frank? If it had been someone else, would that have made it any . . . " she shrugged ". . . any different?"

"I don't know . . . was there anyone else?"

"One or two," said Peggy frankly. "Why not say so – since we're having all this confessional stuff? I'm the scarlet woman anyway, aren't I? Oh, I'm sorry, Mark, if it's all an additional wound to your sensibilities, but you might have known from the beginning! I suppose it's all my fault," she went on. "After all, I realized how different we were, when we first met – I knew it at that first dinner party, when the King was there, and we talked about Mrs Keppel, d'you remember? I realized we just didn't see things the same way. But I suppose I forgot, later, or thought that it didn't matter. I still don't think it does, but you do. And that's that. You're a bit of a Puritan, in your way, aren't you? In spite of having been a desperado, and robbing trains, and holding people up, which you seem to think I ought to find shocking." She gave her weary, crooked little smile. "I don't – I can imagine you shouting 'Stand and deliver!'" without any difficulty. But you can't understand me nearly as easily. I suppose it's . . . backwoods morality, or something. What you think is important. That's the difference between us. I want a drink," she added. "A large hot toddy, and then bed. God, what a rotten night! I must look like a survivor from the Titanic! Would you mind ringing, Mark?"

Automatically he went to the bell, while Peggy surveyed herself with murmurs of dismay in her handbag mirror and effected running

499

repairs. Samson came and Mr Franklin gave him the order mechanically – only when the butler had gone did he recall that other urgent
matter and left the room quickly, overtaking Samson in the kitchen
passage and motioning him in silence out to the sunlit back lawn,
under the trees. There, face to face, Mr Franklin spoke rapidly in a
low voice that would not carry to the house.

"They found Curry's body. Those two men were from the Yard.
They know all about it – they accused me of murder, and I told 'em
to go to hell. And they went." He was in complete control of himself;
he was master of this situation, he felt, if not of anything else. "They
can't prove a thing, Samson – not one solitary dam' thing, and they
know it. They'll be back, though – they won't let up, not until they
realize it's hopeless, which it is, as long as we clam up and don't say
a thing."

The butler was nodding. He had gone white at Mr Franklin's first
words, and glanced automatically towards the house, but he was
obviously not going to panic.

"That's the thing to remember. They can prove nothing as long as
we keep quiet. They don't know you were in it – they don't even
suspect it. And they won't, as long as you keep your mouth shut.
They'll come back, though – and they're bound to question you. All
right – the last time you saw Curry – the only time – was in the hall
at Oxton. To you he was a man called Logan – nothing else. You
gathered he was an American acquaintance of mine, but that's all. I
never mentioned him to you again, and you never saw or heard of
him again. Understand?" He stared intently into Samson's eyes. "Get
that – nothing ever happened at Lancing Manor. And don't get any
foolish ideas about sharing the blame with me, because that's the
worst thing you could do. If you stick your head in the noose, you
stick mine along with it. Remember that. Silence – and no one can
ever touch either of us."

Samson's colour had returned. "Very good, sir. May I ask – how
much does Mrs Franklin know?"

"She knows I did it. I told her, after they'd gone. Hell, it was as
plain as a pikestaff. But she doesn't know where, or when, or anything
like that. And she doesn't know about you. Nobody does. So let's get
the hell out of here before someone looks out of a window."

They went back to the house, and Mr Franklin returned to the
morning-room. Peggy was sitting by the table, apparently calm;
nothing was said until Samson had brought the hot toddy, made with

500

milk and honey. If anything were needed to reassure Mr Franklin about his servant's steadiness, it was the calm voice in which Samson suggested to Peggy that he could take the toddy to her bedroom if she wished, and his polite smile when she said: "No, thank you, Samson, I'll have it here." At the same time, Samson was appraising her, too; he was probably relieved to see that her hand and voice were steady, and to conclude that there was no danger of indiscretion where she was concerned.

Mr Franklin's toddy stood untasted on the table; Peggy sipped hers quietly for a few moments and then said: "Is it no go, Mark?" She lowered the glass between her hands and looked at him. "Am I too far beyond the pale, with my wicked ways and lack of morals and heartless indifference to principles? Is that it?"

Oddly enough, he realized, she was not being sarcastic. She was asking a plain question, and it was not easy to return a plain answer.

"I don't think you've come to the right shop for morals, have you?" he said, with a faint stirring of the old, gently sardonic Mr Franklin. "And I'm not exactly an authority on principles, either." He shook his head. "I can't judge anybody, Peggy, least of all you – "

"You're doing it, though, aren't you?" she broke in. "By gum, aren't you just! The only commandment that matters is whichever one it is – I can't remember the numbers – about thou shalt not commit adultery. Talk about damning sins you have no mind to – "

"Who said I didn't have a mind to?" asked Mr Franklin. "I only said I didn't in fact. If Pip had been what you think she is – "

"Well, that's better," said Peggy. "I was beginning to think I was married to Praise-God Barebones. And it was only her spotless virtue that saved you? D'you know," she went on, "I'm beginning to conceive a poisonous dislike of Miss Pip Bloody Delys. She's just too good to be true." She sipped at her toddy. "Posturing little slut."

"I doubt if she'd make much claim to virtue," said Mr Franklin.

"Well, that makes two of us," said Peggy. "You don't seem to be too fortunate in the women you associate with, do you? You should have made a bid for Lady Helen Cessford when you had the chance. Now, there's a woman of principle for you." She finished her toddy and stood up. "Well, at long last I am going to bed. Coming?"

He took the words at no more than their conventional face value until he realized that she was looking at him very steadily, with that mocking expression in her eyes and the little curl to her lip that had never failed to excite him, even when it repelled. He shook his head.

"Not just now. There are some things I ought to do."

"Oh, come on, Mark!" She held out a hand towards him. "It doesn't matter. None of it matters!"

"Doesn't it?" He came slowly round the table, looking down at her, considering that remarkable beauty, and what he knew went with it. "Peggy, tell me something. What *does* matter to you?"

At his tone she dropped her hand, but her expression did not change for more than a second. When she spoke her voice was matter-of-fact.

"All right, Mark, I'll tell you," she said. "Precious little. Enjoying my life, minding my own business, and not being a bore. On those terms, I'm prepared to be pleasant, and helpful, and cheerful and all the rest of it. What I said in the car was absolutely true. I like you, Mark, and always have. You're a damned attractive man, and great fun when you want to be. Thanks to you I have a marvellous time – most of it, anyway – and I couldn't have had it without you. Oh, well, I could, I daresay, because I'm not exactly plain Jane, but not with anyone I liked as well as you. I won't be a hypocrite and say I'd have married you if you'd been penniless, because you know darned well I wouldn't. I'd have made love with you, though, because I like you. But I don't like you enough to change, and I never shall. I'm what I am, and perfectly content – and if that's good enough for you, I think we can go on having a very happy and comfortable life, separately and together, as the mood takes us. If it's not good enough for you – well, it's just too bad. And now I'm going to bed."

She turned abruptly and walked gracefully to the door, the great embroidered skirt seeming to glide across the carpet. There she stopped and turned, as though on an afterthought.

"Another thing you ought to know. I've done very well out of you, and so has my family. In return for that you've got me – as I am, no better, no worse. I may not measure up to your notions of morality and principle, but if Inspector Crawford were to come stamping in this minute with his warrant, and enough evidence to hang you ten times over, I'd be exactly where I was when I thought he was liable to do just that. So there you have it. And if, after all this, you're prepared to accept things as they are, no one will be more delighted than I. But if you don't . . . ." she put her hand on the door-knob " . . .

then you ought to know that I shan't mind in the least. I really don't care one way or the other whether you go or stay. To coin a phrase, it just doesn't matter."

She went out and closed the door behind her.

25

In the next few days the fashionable topic of the hour was the splendid Venetian Masque held in Hyde Park, with gondolas on the water of the Serpentine, elaborate mock-ups of the Bridge of Sighs, music by Scarlatti, and all that was best in Mayfair and Belgravia re-living the splendours of the Serene Republic on an evening which was stubbornly foggy, unromantic, and English. However, the guests were made of that stern stuff which had been tempered in the windy chill of Henley, the torrential downpours of Ascot, and innumerable hunt balls; the masked ladies in their dominoes clung with stoic languor to the arms of their Casanovas, many of whom were thankful for the long woollen underwear beneath their thin silk breeches, and the evening was voted a huge success.

The same could hardly be said of the next event which drew Society by the hundreds to the great stadium at Olympia for the world title fight between Gunboat Smith of Britain and the dashing idol of the boulevards, M. Carpentier. It was estimated that never before had so many ladies, resplendent in evening finery, graced a prize-fight; Mrs Peggy Franklin was admired by many, and only the uncharitable among her friends drew attention to the fact that her escort was not her husband – not that there was anything unusual in that on past performance, but his absence from her side had gained an added significance for the gossips since the widely-whispered contretemps with that Delys woman at the Savoy Ball. However, Peggy's gaiety and high spirits were undiminished; like every female there, she hoped to see the handsome Frenchman exercise his undoubted grace and brilliance at the expense of the stolid Smith, and was bitterly disappointed when the contest ended in the sixth round, the hapless Gunboat inadvertently hitting his opponent when he was down, and being ignominiously disqualified. A sad anti-climax, not only for the ladies but for their escorts, who had privately hoped that the gorgeous Georges would get his flashing Gallic grin wiped off his face in no uncertain manner.

But disappointing though these social events might be, they were still infinitely more interesting topics of conversation than the pictures which had come through of the arrest in Sarajevo of Prinzip, the young fanatic who had, by a ridiculous freak of chance, been able to murder the Austrian archduke and his wife; few people did more than glance at the photographs of the bare-headed youth being hustled away by police and troops in kilts and fezzes. Austria might be making threatening noises towards Serbia, but Mr Lloyd George had publicly announced Britain's preoccupation with home affairs (especially Ireland), re-emphasized her desire not to be embroiled in foreign disputes, and called for disarmament.

Mr Franklin was faced with a similar call on a more personal level. Inspector Crawford had returned to Wilton Crescent, with a request to be allowed to examine the Remington revolvers, which was promptly refused. There was talk of warrants, and while the inspector retired to consider his next move, Mr Franklin took himself off to his solicitor, and laid before him those facts which were known to the police. Counsel's opinion was sought, and Mr Franklin found it highly reassuring.

There was not, counsel decided, a case to answer – no witnesses, no positive identification, no motive, and nothing concrete to link Mr Franklin to the crime, however extraordinary the circumstances might appear. As to the revolvers, counsel was advised (by a military friend at his club, in fact) that forensic science had still not devised a reliable method of identifying soft metal bullets with the weapon which fired them; even so, Mr Franklin should only surrender his weapons on production of a search warrant. "And if Crawford tries for a warrant on this evidence," counsel remarked privately to Mr Franklin's solicitor, "he won't get it. If he *doesn't* try, he's throwing in the towel, like a sensible bobby, and your American can sleep peacefully at nights." No warrant was forthcoming, but whether Mr Franklin slept peacefully or not no one in London could have said, for he was no longer there.

He had gone back to Castle Lancing, alone, to try to think, or rather to try to rediscover his bearings after the traumatic upheavals of the few hours following the Savoy Ball. He left without seeing Peggy; Samson understood that his master would probably be down in Norfolk for a week or two, but no definite date had been fixed for his return. This conformed to the pattern of the past few years, and

505

Mrs Franklin continued with her round of social engagements as usual.

Castle Lancing noted that the squire was back, but paid even less attention than usual, having other exciting matters on its collective mind. The redevelopment work which had started and then been mysteriously halted in the Lye Cottage area had recommenced; a new gang of Irish navvies was encamped beyond the thicket, and the laying of foundations of the model cottages was proceeding apace. The more nervous villagers locked their doors at night, sharing as they did Inspector Crawford's prejudice where Irishmen were concerned, but in fact the labourers proved to be inoffensive guests; they were quiet and respectful in their dealings with the local people, showed no inclination to rob hen-roosts or sleep in the horse-trough, and in their resorts to the Apple Tree were affable and reasonably sober. And since they and the bricklayers from Thetford brought additional trade in their wake, and an invigorating bustle to the village, many of whose inhabitants were looking forward to occupying the new cottages, it could be said that Castle Lancing generally considered itself blessed in the change. The vicar, who was stubbornly Low Church, might have reservations about the temporary influx of Roman Catholics, and Thornhill might inveigh at the motor lorries which brought what he called their insufferable stench to the main street, but they were eccentric exceptions.

All this Mr Franklin learned, whether he would or no, from the indefatigable Jake, who naturally gravitated to Lancing Manor as soon as its owner was in residence. It occurred to Jake that Mr Franklin was more preoccupied and taciturn than usual, but since this merely afforded the ancient an even greater opportunity to talk unchecked, he was glad enough to accept it.

"Wouldn't know where ole Bessie Reeve's cottage was, the way things is now," he said, having waylaid Mr Franklin on the front drive. "Them Paddies is making short work of the new houses, ain't they just. You'll 'ave been over for a look, sir, I expect."

"Yes," said Mr Franklin. He had taken a walk to Lye, wondering what Inspector Crawford would have thought about the miscreant returning to the scene of the crime, and had been astonished at the progress made. Of the old cottage there was no sign, even its garden and surrounding hedge were gone, and the thicket itself consisted of only a few outlying trees. Across the levelled land there now stretched an orderly row of concrete foundations with the beginnings of their

506

brick walls already in place, and gangs of men with picks, shovels, trowels, and barrows swarming busily on the site, watched by a bowler-hatted foreman who stood discussing blue-prints with the builder outside the temporary wooden office. As nearly as Mr Franklin could estimate from memory, the main concrete-mixer was parked on the spot where the bones of Kid Curry had lain undisturbed for five years – and would have lain forever if he had not allowed Sir Charles to persuade him to sell Lye Cottage to Lacy. That was the truly wonderful irony – that by doing his enemy a reluctant favour, he had put his own life in jeopardy. Strange that it had never crossed his mind that Lacy's building operations might well uncover Curry's grave; four years of confident security should not have blunted his sense of self-preservation so badly, but they had. No thought of danger had been in his mind when he had listened to Sir Charles . . . "I'm not asking you to do it for Lacy's sake, but for your own. Coals of fire . . . " And what he had done "for his own sake" had almost put his head in the noose; Lacy, who had sworn vengeance on him years ago, would never realize how close he had come to the ultimate revenge. But then, Lacy had already had sweet revenge enough, with Peggy; he had paid off his scores with interest. Mr Franklin wondered idly if she had had anything to do with her father's plea to him to sell Lye Cottage; if, at her lover's prompting, she had put the idea into the old man's head, and all unwittingly brought her husband into deadly danger. If so, it had been doubly ironic. Coals of fire, all right.

It would all have been vastly amusing to Kid Curry, Mr Franklin decided, if he had only been alive to appreciate it. He had wondered, as he turned away from the activity of the Lye building site, what they had done with the Kid's inopportune remains, and what unlikely grave now housed the former scourge of the Union Pacific and farmers' banks. What with Glenwood Springs, Lye Thicket, and the new spot, wherever it was, Curry must be about the buriedest man on record, which was a consoling thought, in its way.

" 'Course, the work was held up there a couple o' weeks," observed Jake, settling himself into his favourite resting position on his spade. "Yeah, Major Blake an' the police closed it up, packed off the navvies an' all. They say as summat was found under the old thicket – Mr Thornhill was sure it was treasure trove, and was all for a crowner's inquest, in case it was archi-malogical, but they warned him off. 'Ad a copper on it day an' night, they did, wi'' a red lamp, for nigh on a fortnight. Then they opened the site up again, an' that were that."

"Did anyone find out what it was?" Mr Franklin could not help asking, and Jake grinned and spat.

"No one ever learned official-like," said he, "but there was some as said it was a body. A ole skeleting, as 'adn't been buried proper. Well, it must ha' been summat like that, or why was the coppers askin' so many questions? 'Ad anyone seen a little stranger, might ha' been an American, 'angin' round the village four or five years ago? Well, I knew who they meant – it were that little bugger as came askin' for you the winter afore the ole King died. Yeah, that was him, right enough, I reckoned. But who it was they found in the ground – if they found anyone, like – I dunno."

Mr Franklin said nothing, and Jake, having considered putting his spade to the use its makers had intended, and changed his mind, added reflectively:

"Anyways, they was askin' all over, the coppers was. 'Course, they asked me. 'There's on'y one American 'ereabouts, or ever 'as been,' says I, "an' that's the squire. Why don't you ask 'im?',' I says. Maybe they did ask you, I dunno. They asked everyone else, an' precious little good it done 'em. Who're they, anyway, to come stickin' their noses into Castle Lancin' business? What's buried in our ground is our affair, I reckon." Jake chuckled. "Jack Prior gave 'em a proper answer, when this 'tec come in the Apple Tree, wantin' to know about you. 'Mr Franklin lives in Lancin' Manor,' says 'e. 'You want to know about him, you go an' knock on his front door,' says Jack. 'I did, an' 'e ain't there,' says the 'tec. 'Then you better wait till 'e comes back, 'adn't you?' says Jack. 'I'm seekin' information,' says the 'tec. 'Well, you got all I can give you, so bugger off,' says Jack. 'Mind your lip,' says the 'tec. 'I understand as this Mr Franklin ain't a local man, is that right?' I thought Jack was goin' to clock him. 'Not local?', says 'e. 'You go up the church, look at the stones, see whether 'e's local or not.' Maybe the 'tec went up there, I dunno. Maybe 'e asked you, I dunno," said Jake, and stuck his spade in the soil, at last, reluctantly. "Bloody cheek them coppers 'as got."

Little was seen of Mr Franklin in the village; he did not visit the Apple Tree, and beyond an occasional call at Mrs Laker's shop he kept to the Manor grounds, minding his own affairs as he had always done. Thornhill looked in once, for tea, and they discussed local gossip briefly, and the Irish question at some length; the news was that the King had taken the extraordinary step of convening a conference of all the leading parties, Government, Irish Nationalist, and Ulstermen, at Buckingham Palace, in a last desperate attempt to avert civil war. By comparison the news that at the other end of Europe Austria was virtually demanding a total surrender of Serbian independence, was of small account.

"These damned Irish," said Thornhill, "will have us all at each other's throats before they're finished. The old King was right: 'For God's sake, let 'em have home rule for Ireland, then perhaps we can have home rule for England.' No fool, your friend Edward. I just hope they get these Mick workmen away from Castle Lancing before the shooting starts – we had our civil war in the 1640s, and we're not quite ready for another just yet."

But the only other visitor to Lancing Manor arrived on the following day; he was waiting on the front drive when Mr Franklin came back from a solitary walk along the Oxton Road. It was fairly late in the evening, and for a moment, as he checked at the unexpected sight of a large man in tweeds sauntering before his front door, Mr Franklin did not recognize him in the fading light. And then the big man turned, and he saw that it was Arthur Clayton.

"Hullo, Mark," he said, and stood jauntily embarrassed while Mr Franklin returned his greeting and invited him inside. They crossed the hall to the study, and Arthur fidgeted while Mr Franklin poured whisky without undue haste and asked him how he was.

"Oh, I'm fine. Fine." Arthur grinned nervously, the glass lost in his enormous fist, and then thrust his free hand through his hair and said:

"Look, Mark, I can't apologize, can I? I mean, I've diddled you out of ten thousand quid, and the only excuse I can offer is that I didn't do it for myself. I can't even offer to pay it back some day, because I'll never have it – and if I did, I'd be bound to send it after the first lot. So – it was a cad's trick, if you like – but there was no other place to get it. And without it, there'd have been no ship, no arms for our people to defend themselves when – well, when the war starts. As it will, within the next few weeks. Here's how." He raised his glass and drank.

"You think it's going to start, then?" said Mr Franklin. "I thought Devlin and Carson and Asquith were meeting at the palace to make sure it didn't."

"They don't have a hope," said Arthur flatly. "Even Carson couldn't stop it now. We're not going to be part of a 'free Ireland', and that's all about it." The boyish nervousness had left him abruptly;

509

the young face was hard. Then he realized what he had come for, and some of his half-humorous uneasiness returned.

"Anyway, I can't apologize. I just wish it hadn't been you – because you've been so decent, for one thing, and because you're . . . well, *you*, don't you know? But I wanted to explain why – "

"You don't have to," said Mr Franklin. "I got it all from Peggy. As I said to her – you might have asked me. That's all."

"I know. Peg told me," Arthur took another gulp at his drink. "We thought we couldn't – that you'd refuse. I wouldn't have blamed you if you had – it's not your fight, after all, is it? But that's not the point." He put down his glass and avoided Mr Franklin's eye. "I saw Peg last night."

He hesitated, and Mr Franklin filled the gap by asking how she was.

"Oh, full of beans, as usual – off to some giddy bunfight somewhere – the Berkeley, I think. You know Peg – the brightest of the bright young things." Arthur paused unhappily. "Look, Mark – I gather all isn't well between you . . . is that right?"

Mr Franklin considered him, and asked: "What makes you think that?"

"Well, that proves it, doesn't it? If all was well, you'd say so." Arthur shrugged. "Oh, just Peggy, you know. I asked how you were – how you'd taken the ten thousand business, and she said, fairly grim, but you hadn't had apoplexy. But when I quizzed her a bit more she said you'd gone off, and she didn't know when you'd come back." He paused and scratched his head. "If ever. That knocked me over, I confess. Then she said you'd had an unholy row the other week, and . . . look, old fellow, this isn't hellish easy for me. But have you?"

"I don't know that you'd call it an unholy row," said Mr Franklin. "But let's say certain . . . differences have arisen." He took Arthur's glass and refilled it. "But I don't think Peggy minds too much, somehow."

Arthur took his glass gloomily. "I know what you mean. It was the same when we were kids; she'd just go her own sweet way, and damn what anybody thought or said. Got a hide like a bloody hippo, our Peg. Cheers." He drank and then said: "That's what I came to see you about, anyway. You and Peg. Look, Mark – if it's about the ten thousand, I just wanted you to know it wasn't her fault. It was my idea to get it from you, with all that boloney about leaving the Army and going into business – it was bloody unprincipled, and one part of me is as ashamed as hell. But I had to do it. And Peg was dead against it, at first. She said flat that she couldn't do that to you – that you'd been damned generous to her, and to me, and Father . . . all that sort of thing. Which I knew, of course. But I told her there was no choice, it was you or nothing."

Arthur emptied his glass and stood staring moodily at the carpet. "So in the end, she agreed. She said to leave it to her – she said she couldn't ask you for it, but she'd get it somehow. Knowing Peg, I imagined she'd vamp it out of you, but I didn't ask her. Anyway, she got it – but what I'm trying to explain, Mark, is that it wasn't her fault, d'you see? I put her up to it – and I felt utterly rotten about it, anyway. But if I thought that it had . . . well, busted you and Peg . . . Oh, Jesus, Mark, I'm sorry! I really am!"

He stood looking large and contrite on Mr Franklin's rug, watching anxiously to see how his host was taking it. Unemotionally, so far as Arthur could see. Mr Franklin was leaning against his desk, arms folded, his own glass neglected on the table.

"You can set your mind at rest, Arthur," he said. "The business of the money certainly drove in a middling-sized wedge, but not what you'd call a fatal one. Looked at objectively, I'd say it was as dirty a trick as even I have ever heard of, and I'm still not too happy about having been on the receiving end of it. Still, I guess political crimes are held to be in a higher class than ordinary sneak-thieving, so . . . the money side of it doesn't matter, anyway. Ten thousand isn't that important."

Arthur's fair face had flushed while Mr Franklin was speaking, but at this he looked solemn. "Ten thousand's a hell of a lot of money," he said. "And if it had broken you and Peggy up . . . well, I wouldn't have been surprised, I suppose. I'm glad it didn't, though." And being Arthur, his natural curiosity prompted him to ask: "What has – I mean, if anything has, and Peg isn't just being dramatic?"

Mr Franklin looked at him thoughtfully. "I don't wish to sound unfriendly or ungrateful for your interest, Arthur," he said. "But I don't really think that my relations with your sister are any of your business."

To his surprise, Arthur looked neither angry nor hurt. Indeed, he seemed impressed, rather. "By gum, she's really got into your midst, hasn't she?" he said. "Mind you, I can see how she would. Oh, well . . . I just hope it isn't anything serious, that's all." He took another rumple at his fair hair and asked: "Seen Father, have you, since you've been down?"

"Not as yet," said Mr Franklin, and could not refrain from adding: "My conversations with members of the Clayton family don't seem to have been over-profitable of late. I'm not hurrying out of my way to start any new ones."

Arthur stared at him glumly, hands in pockets. "No . . . I suppose not. And I don't seem to have made things any better, do I? Look – is it Peg carrying on?" Meeting Mr Franklin's cold stare, he added hurriedly: "I mean – oh, she's a silly little bitch! But . . . well . . . she's not a bad kid, really – "

"Arthur," said Mr Franklin quietly, "right now you're not exactly on the first page of my good books, if you know what I mean. Don't make it any worse. Did Peggy ask you to come here?"

"Good God, no!" Mr Franklin believed him, and felt a stab of disappointment. "Lord, Peggy would never do that – you know what she's like. Proud as Lucifer."

"Yes," said Mr Franklin. "That's never apparently stopped one Clayton from doing another's dirty work, though, has it? No," he added, "I'll except your father. He's been straight. Like another drink?"

Arthur shook his head. "No, thanks. Mark . . . " He stopped and then shrugged hopelessly. "Look, I know you must feel bitter about – "

"I don't feel in the least bitter," said Mr Franklin. "But I confess I do feel tired. And more than a little . . . disturbed. Have you had any supper?"

"No, I just caught the afternoon train down, but – "

"Then we'd better get you some, and you can bunk down here for the night."

"Oh, that's all right – no, I'd better get over to Oxton and see the guv'nor. I'm going up to Town tomorrow, catching the night boat to Dublin. My leave's up on Monday, and I'll have to be back at the Curragh."

"I'd forgotten you've been on leave." He switched his mind away from his own preoccupations. "Are you going to stay in the Army, then – what about when the civil war breaks out?"

"Yes, I'm staying. I don't know what's going to happen; maybe there'll be another mutiny – maybe the Army'll go over to Carson, even. Some regiments, anyway."

"You'd do that?"

"Yes."

Mr Franklin frowned. "I know you take this thing pretty seriously, Arthur – in fact, if anyone's had striking proof of it, I guess I have. But – I don't quite know your regulations, but aren't you bound by oath? Aren't you the King's man?"

"Ulster's a damned sight more loyal to the King than that Fenian rabble who want a separate Ireland," said Arthur, and again that hard look was on his face. "Just because Asquith's ready to sell out doesn't mean a thing. The Army's the King's, not the government's."

"Well, I can't argue with you about that – British constitutional niceties are over the head of an ignorant colonial. But wouldn't it be . . . better to see if you can't find a peaceful way out first?"

"It's been tried, hasn't it? I imagine they're trying now, at Buck House. But they'll fail." Arthur shook his head. "Anyway, I'd better be getting along . . ." He looked at his brother-in-law with his rueful Arthur-ish grin. "Oh, God, old son – I am sorry. I don't mean about the cash – but about you and Peg. I hope it comes out all right. I'll be honest," he added thoughtfully, "I think it would be hell being married to her – some of the time, anyway. Because there's no doing anything with her. But it could be a hell of a lot of fun, too, I should think."

"Because she's not a bad kid?" wondered Mr Franklin.

"Well, she's not. Bloody good-looking, too. And she likes you, you know – she really does. Anyway, I hope it comes out right." He hesitated, and then held out his hand. "So-long, Mark."

Mr Franklin looked at the hand, and glanced at Arthur, who looked inquiringly whimsical. Mr Franklin shrugged.

"I guess I can't refuse to shake with any man who's got as much sheer hard neck as you have, Arthur," he said, and took his brother-in-law's hand. They went to the front door together, Mr Franklin offered to run him to Oxton, and Arthur said he'd get a lift from the village. Mr Franklin watched the big figure striding down his drive in the dusk, turning to wave before the trees hid him from sight.

That was on a Friday. On the next day the papers carried the news that the Buckingham Palace negotiations between the contending Irish elements and the government had broken down irretrievably; most of the papers plainly regarded this as the gravest possible news, although one or two were beginning to follow the lead set by *The Times* of the previous day and wonder if perhaps Austria's policy towards Serbia

513

did not present an equally serious threat to the general peace. But by Monday foreign affairs had receded into the background again before the alarming news from Dublin.

On the Sunday Irish Nationalism had demonstrated visibly that it was preparing to meet the storm gathering in the north. A former clerk in the House of Commons, thriller-writer and Boer War veteran named Erskine Childers, a devoted supporter of Home Rule though of staunch Unionist stock on his mother's side, brought his yacht *Asgard* into Howth, five miles from Dublin, with an estimated 25,000 rifles for the Southern cause. Irish Volunteers unloaded the rifles, which were quickly dispersed on lorries before a British regiment from Dublin could arrive on the scene. The soldiers scattered the Nationalists, and having failed to intercept the smuggled rifles, marched back to Dublin, reviled and stoned by the mob who assumed, after the manner of most demonstrators, that discipline would prevent retaliation.

Unfortunately, they were wrong. Where a south country regiment would have gritted its teeth and endured the jeers and even the missiles which severely injured several soldiers, the King's Own Scottish Borderers were made of more volatile material. As their march reached Bachelor's Walk, by the Liffey, the hail of brickbats increased, the commander of the contingent, Major Haig, was struck five times, and the Scots lost their tempers. Without orders, some of the soldiers opened fire on their tormentors, and although their officers managed to stop the shooting almost immediately, when the smoke had cleared there were three of the crowd dead on the ground, and more than thirty wounded.

The reverberations of those shots rolled all over Ireland, where there was natural indignation at this breach of the civilian's inalienable right to assault troops with impunity, and into Britain, where there was some dismay that a line regiment had so far broken its discipline as to fire on a technically unarmed mob. There was universal sympathy for the dead, and for a fourth victim, one of the wounded who died in hospital next day, although in his case sympathy was modified west of the Irish Sea when it was learned that although in plain clothes he was a British Army officer named Arthur Clayton.

Mr Franklin received the stunning news in a note from Oxton Hall on Wednesday morning, and half an hour later, having hurried over from Castle Lancing, heard it from the lips of Sir Charles himself, standing in front of the great fireplace where five years ago King Edward had warned Mr Franklin to avoid the haddock at breakfast.

"I can't imagine what he was doing there. He went across on the night boat, and I suppose got word of this business of the arms coming in, and went out to see what was happening. He wasn't with the troops, apparently – he must have been among the spectators, and when those fools opened fire . . . "

The tragic irony of it sickened Mr Franklin. Arthur, the so unlikely Unionist fanatic, shot down by British troops, falling among those whom he regarded as his bitterest enemies. Arthur, the cheerful and honourable good companion, who had lied and cheated and been ready to sacrifice his own sister's happiness, for all he knew, in the cause of Loyalism. It was heart-breaking, but Mr Franklin's sympathy was all for the haggard old man, fighting to keep the emotion from showing in a face that had aged ten years.

"I always hated this damned Irish business – hated it like the poison it is." He was speaking quietly, but with an underlying force that shook him physically. "Even when it seemed harmless enough, old tales for children that they learned from their mother. God rest her. I'm only thankful that she didn't live to suffer this. I don't know how Arthur ever came to believe so passionately in . . . in this Loyalist thing. Peggy, too, I suppose, although not like Arthur." He raised his eyes, bright with grief and agony, to Mr Franklin's. "It seems so . . . impossible. Arthur was an Englishman, like me – and yet I suppose – I suppose he was Irish, too. There was a part of him that I knew nothing about. I suppose a father can never know more than half of his child."

There was nothing for Mr Franklin to say. Comfort, he knew, was seldom of any use even when the bereaved was in a highly emotional state, and Sir Charles Clayton was not emotional. Whatever he felt, he was expressing it calmly and sanely; if his face was ravaged and he had to clasp his hands together to prevent their trembling, he was still in control of himself. Mr Franklin knew that those few short sentences were the closest he would ever come to hearing Sir Charles's inner thoughts, that they were his class and kind's equivalent of the *coronach* or the sackcloth. They were being spoken now, to him, not only because he was the first person to whom they could have been spoken, but also because a man will speak to his son-in-law with a greater openness than he will use even to his own flesh and blood.

515

"Won't you sit down, sir?" was all he could find to say, and Sir Charles shook his head.

"No. If I sit down, I won't get up – and I'll have to be in Thetford in the next hour for the train. I'll catch the night mail from Liverpool and be in Dublin tomorrow."

"I'll come with you," said Mr Franklin.

"No. No, thank you, Mark." Sir Charles took a deep breath. "I'll be better alone. It's good of you, but you must look after Peggy. When the telegram came this morning – it came from Gough himself – I spoke on the telephone with your man Samson. It was he who told me you were at Lancing. But Peggy wasn't at home – went out to one of her parties last night, and hadn't returned. I'll telephone again before I go, and if she hasn't come back by then, perhaps you . . . "

"I'll go up to Town, and we can come across and join you in Dublin."

"No – I'd rather you didn't." Sir Charles hesitated, and then looked Mr Franklin in the eye, and his glance was defensive, almost hostile. "The way in which this thing has happened . . . it will be better if only I'm there when they . . . at the service, I mean." Even to Mr Franklin, whom he liked and trusted better than any man living, now, Sir Charles was painfully reluctant to say what was in his mind. To him, to the soldier and the father of a soldier, there was something almost shameful in the manner of Arthur's death – shot in a squalid riot, accidentally, by his own comrades-in-arms. It was not such a death as he could ever have envisaged. That Arthur must have been a mere bystander was beside the point; his presence there had not been military, it had been partisan and political, and Sir Charles was tormented by the knowledge.

"I suppose they'll bury him at the Curragh. They won't want any fuss. Gough's an old friend of mine – he'll see that things are properly . . . properly looked after." For a terrible moment Mr Franklin thought that Sir Charles would break down, but after a moment he went on steadily enough:

"You and Peggy should stay in London – or down here, or at Castle Lancing. I should be back by the end of the week."

One of the servants came into the hall, carrying two suitcases, which he set down by the door. Sir Charles spoke, and his voice was harsh.

"I said I wanted the large case – the brown one. Take one of those back and put its things in the brown case. The brown one. And don't lock it. I'll attend to it down here."

When the servant had gone, Sir Charles turned and glanced above the fireplace to where the great brass-hilted broadsword hung on its nails over the mantel. Abruptly he reached up to unhook it, but the thin wire which supported the scabbard was too tightly wound round the nails; he tugged sharply, and at the third tug the wire snapped. He turned with the weapon in his hands, looking down at the scabbard, black with age, and at the hilt, its leather grip cracked and discoloured. From tang to ferrule it must have measured over a yard, but no doubt the large brown suitcase would accommodate it. Sir Charles rested it against a chair beside the fireplace.

"It can go into the ground with him," he said.

When he left Oxton Hall, Peggy had still not returned to Wilton Crescent, and the business of breaking the news of her brother's death would devolve on Mr Franklin. It was a task he would have shrunk from at any time, but ten times more so since the Savoy Ball, with all its attendant shocks and miseries which had left him in a confusion that was still, he realized, unresolved in his mind. But there was nothing for it, and an hour after Sir Charles had left Thetford to catch the connection that would take him across country to Liverpool, Mr Franklin boarded the train to London. Before he left he telephoned Samson, and gave instructions that nothing should be said to Peggy until he got there.

But when he arrived at Wilton Crescent, it was to find a grim-faced Samson, as nearly flustered as Mr Franklin had ever seen him, with the news that Peggy had returned and left again within an hour, for Ireland.

"I very much regret it, sir, but when Sir Charles telephoned the first time, it seems that somehow Mrs Franklin's personal maid overheard my conversation – and learned of Mr Clayton's death. As you know, sir, she had been with the family since Mrs Franklin was a child; consequently, when Mrs Franklin came in this morning, she found Polly in tears, and learned the sad news from her. I am extremely sorry, sir. I told Mrs Franklin that you would be arriving, but she said she must go at once. She left to catch the Fishguard train a little under an hour ago." Samson hesitated before adding the suggestion: "I could have a telegram dispatched to meet the train at Fishguard if you wish, sir."

No, thought Mr Franklin, let her go. Whatever Sir Charles felt,

517

Peggy would want to be there. He knew how strong the tie between brother and sister had been – perhaps knew it better than Sir Charles himself. And the old man would be none the worse of Peggy's presence; nor would it cause the least embarrassment. Mr Franklin did not know General Gough, but he was quite sure, like Sir Charles, that everything would be looked after properly.

There was no point in going to Ireland himself, however; that would have been an intrusion. Nor could he go back to Castle Lancing; whatever his and Peggy's feelings, he ought to be at Wilton Crescent when she returned.

So he stayed in London, in that last week of July – the week which began not unlike so many other weeks, with the kind of domestic crisis that was now a familiar part of British experience, with rumours and fears and warnings of the kind that everyone took for granted, and of which they could say that they were no different from what their parents and even distant ancestors must have known. That fairly ordinary week, with its sunny weather promising well for the August Bank Holiday week-end, when Londoners would relax at the seaside, or picnic in the country, or take the children to the Zoo, the well-to-do planning motor trips to the Downs or weekends at Eastbourne, and the Cockneys dreaming of jellied eels and deck chairs and pints of old and mild and sand between the toes at Clacton or Southend. The week like so many others, that generations would look back on with a kind of disbelief and wonder, because it belonged to a world that no one would ever see again, the last ray of a setting sun that had risen in some misty, historic time before anyone could remember, and had shone brightly over a gradually changing but still comfortingly consistent scene, and was now about to go down at last. And what everyone would remember was how calm and untroubled it had been, with no possible hint of how the gears of time were about to change for millions of ordinary folk, clashing into a new and frightening revolution as the human race rushed suddenly forward into a new dark age. But in that week nobody knew. Nobody could possibly know.

In that week the Stock Exchange fell, recovered, and fell again between Tuesday and Friday, when the Exchange closed. Consols went down to 71, their lowest ever, Bank rate doubled to 8 per cent. and then rose to 10 per cent. For suddenly in mid-week even happy, sunny Britain was aware of a cloud thundering up into the sky beyond the eastern horizon, like a genie of smoke towering out of its opened bottle. On Wednesday came the news that Austrian troops were over the Serbian frontier, and Belgrade – unknown to the many, a name to some, a place on the map which school lessons hardly touched, to the informed – was being bombarded. It was still little enough; the foreigners were at it again, and good luck to them. Serbia had appealed to Russia for help almost a week earlier, and now Austrian troops were reported to be massing on the Russian frontier as the great useless bear began to stir; would there be war in the East? Possibly, but that was nothing new, and diplomacy would win the day in the end – but in the meantime, beyond the careless multitudes preparing for the holiday, there were officials at Westminster and Whitehall, and anxious men in the clubs who were heard to remark that *if – if*, mind you – it came to the bit, we would fight, although God forbid we didn't want to, and probably wouldn't have to, because the Germans didn't want to, either, and was it true that Berlin had given a private undertaking that in the event of war (which was highly unlikely, of course) they would have no claim on French, Dutch, or Belgian territory? Well, that would let us out, surely – I don't know; they say Grey's rejected it; I'm more alarmed, let me tell you, about this Irish business – they say there have been outbreaks in Dublin. Oh, well, that was to be expected, after Howth – but to get back to the point, I'd think the Tsar had more sense, wouldn't you?

But in the coast towns there were seamen, and even North Sea passengers, who had seen an ominous sight – the grey squadrons ploughing northwards through the sea mist, the endless columns of the most colossal naval power in history, the racing destroyers to the fore, the powerful cruisers, the stately and massive battle wagons, the Dreadnoughts, and in the pubs and at street corners from the Cinque Ports to Aberdeen the word was heard: "The Fleet's gone to Scapa." Yet even that was reassuring, too, for it was a reminder that Britannia was on the waves again, the indestructible English wall, and the trawler and lobstermen from the Dogger to the Forth could watch the mighty shapes dwindle into the fog and take comfort from the knowledge that there was no force on salt water that could threaten the lighted shoreline of their homes and harbours.

Mr Franklin, in Wilton Crescent, thanked God that he hadn't been induced to buy Consols, and wondered if Peggy and her father would be back by the week-end.

On the Thursday it was learned in the high places, and filtered through the lofty hall of the Reform and the hushed chambers of the Athenaeum, that Germany had demanded that Russia should cease

519

mobilizing her forces. Trust that damned idiot of a Kaiser to start throwing his weight about. Pompous little ass. Well, when you've got four million men under arms, presumably you think you can rattle your sabre. No doubt – what are the French going to do about it, though?

Then on the Friday, when it was realized that a financial crisis at least was suddenly impending, the word went round that old Rothschild had headed a deputation of bankers and City men calling on the Chancellor, Lloyd George, with an appeal that, whatever happened on the Continent, Britain should remain neutral; it was understood that the Chancellor was firmly opposed to war . . . oh, no doubt, but I heard that that firebrand Churchill is spoiling for a fight. Indeed, but it's what Grey and Asquith think that matters, wouldn't you say? – I mean, everyone knows what young Winston's like. What about Rothschild and his lot, then? – I don't know, but I shouldn't mind betting there's a German-Jewish banking conspiracy at work both here and in Berlin. Well, that'd be a blessing for once – they're the last ones who want to see everything go up in smoke. Is it true about the run on gold? Well, I heard they're going to print bank-notes. What on earth for? Well, my dear chap, for the simple reason that there's only enough gold in the cellar to meet five per cent. of the commercial paper. And they tell me the bank-notes are going to be boosted as being "as good as gold" while Lloyd George puts his head in a bucket and wonders what to do next. And I heard there was a meeting and someone suggested a moratorium, and Lloyd George didn't even know what a blasted moratorium was. Fact . . .

Mr Franklin listened to the small talk, and wondered with slight unease if the eagles and sovereigns in his safe deposit box were such a sound investment after all. He had no real inkling of what the financial scuttlebutt was all about, anyway, and he had no time to waste speculating on what seemed to be happening in Europe. Possibly Peggy would be back by the week-end, and he was not sure what he was going to do about that.

That Friday night the excursion trains steamed out of the brightly-lit stations, the shop shutters went up, fathers and mothers spread the wages on the kitchen table and calculated how much could be set aside for fun at the seaside, excited children were told to get out of the way of the packing and get upstairs or there won't be any holiday or ice-cream or Punch and Judy, and if you don't put them spades and buckets down I'll . . . the pubs did splendid business, society gave a great sigh as it settled down to dinner at the Trocadero and Monico's and agreed that it had been a jolly good season, really, queues a quarter of a mile long stood in cheerful patience watching the buskers and waiting to get into the second house of *Pip, Squeak!*, and inside the huge, stuffy, smoke-filled theatre, a packed audience roared its applause as a radiant Miss Delys stamped her high-heeled boots, clapped her hands, and with a thunderous accompaniment from the big drum, led the multitude in the new popular chant invented by Saki which was running round the city like wildfire:

> Cousin Teresa takes out Caesar,
> Fido, Jack, and the big *Bor-zoi!*

Stamp-stamp from the strutting principal, and boom-boom from the drummer, on the last two syllables. "All right, everyone – let's have it again!" And in Plymouth and Deal, in Yarmouth and Grimsby, in Dundee and Peterhead, in Oban and Douglas and Cardigan Bay, holiday visitors noted idly as they strolled in the dusk that there were unusual numbers of fishing vessels lying at the quays, but of the fishermen themselves hardly a sign. And at the stations the men in blue jerseys and reefers and sea-boots were kissing wives and girls good-bye and boarding the trains with their canvas hold-alls on their shoulders, for all over the island the reserve of the great fleet was mustering in response to urgent signals from the Admiralty. Whatever happened elsewhere, by Sunday every British seaman, regular or civilian, would be at his station, ready for war.

Still, for the majority of the nation, there was no real sense that the peace was about to be disturbed until the appearance, on the Saturday, of armed sentries at such strategic points as railway stations and level crossings. That, with the news in the day's papers that Russian and Austrian mobilization had become general, and that Germany had issued a stern demand to France to stay neutral in the event of eastern hostilities, finally brought home, even to the least interested, that something was seriously wrong, and that this time the crisis might not blow over. Mr Franklin, walking by way of Piccadilly and Trafalgar Square to the Strand, after digesting the foreign news with his breakfast, was struck by the air of normality and calm of the crowds who, as usual, thronged the great thoroughfares; at first he assumed that they did not understand the gravity of the events that were convulsing the chancelleries of Europe, including their own, that

521

they did not fully appreciate that within a few days they might be at war with the most powerful enemy they had ever faced, whose troops outnumbered their own by six to one, and were as great as those of Britain and France combined, that they might face invasion, or the unguessed terror of attack from the air. He did not, himself, expect these things to happen; it was difficult to believe, on this fine morning, that already at the other end of the continent men and women were dying under gunfire, or that the peaceful air of England might be shattered by bombs and high explosives, that battles might be fought in her streets and enemy armies march across her fields. Extremely unlikely – but even so, he would have expected the remote possibility to produce some effect on popular behaviour. Not panic, or even gloom; after five years he knew them better than that – but at least gravity, sober and concerned discussion, a diminution of the happy, careless bustle he saw all around him, perhaps even an eager congregation outside the great newspaper offices to hear the latest news. There might have been expected just a little reduction in the city's normal high spirits.

But there was no sign that the news was even being taken seriously, which at first suggested ignorance, or stupidity, or bravado. But it soon became evident to Mr Franklin that the crossing-sweepers on the Strand, the old ladies puffing on to buses with their parcels, the shop assistants and cab drivers, the men propping up the saloon bars, knew quite as well as he did what was in the news, and what it might portend; their attitude to it, however, seemed to be either genuinely nonchalant or simply flippant.

Of course, this was supposedly in the national character; it was proverbial that the Englishman displayed emotion only when faced by some truly earth-shaking crisis, like a cricket match, or the ill-treatment of an animal, or a rise in the price of beer; for such trivia as death, destruction, and national catastrophe he was supposed to reserve an indifference bordering on insanity. Drake had not played bowls before the Armada battle for nothing. But even with Mr Franklin's close experience of his adopted country, it only began to occur to him on that first Saturday of August, 1914, that perhaps the international joke might not be a joke at all; that the famous imperturbability, so beloved of cartoonists and humorous journalists, might not be assumed, but based on a stolid realism and common sense, not untinged by macabre humour, which was neatly summed up for him in a Fleet Street bar where he stopped in for refreshment.

522

"I 'eard," said a Jewish cab-driver, "as the Germans 'ave declared war on Russia."

" 'Ave they, though?" said a burly labourer. "Goin' to be bloody cold for 'em, then."

"Reckon, we'll be in it, too," said a small Cockney in a cloth cap. "The Fleet's at sea, an' my bruvver-in-law's been called up – 'e's an Army reservist. Another 'alf-and-'alf, Gladys!

"All depends on the Frogs," he added. "An' that's a bloody 'orrid thought, if you ask me."

"Why does it?" asked the Jew.

"Well, if the Germans fight the Russians, they'll 'ave a slap at the Frogs an' all, won't they?" said the Cockney. "That's wot it says in the *Mail*. An' if they 'ave a slap at the Frogs, we'll 'ave to 'elp the Frogs."

"Though why the 'ell we should, beats me," said the labourer. "Bastards wouldn't lift a finger for us."

"It's the balance o' power," said the Cockney. "Can't 'ave the Germans conquerin' France, can you?"

"Couldn't I? Just you watch me, mate. But I reckon," added the labourer, "the Germans won't rest easy till they've 'ad a go at us. Stupid sods. The Kaiser's got this 'Igh Seas Fleet, see, an' he wants to bring us dahn a peg or two."

"The Navy'll sort 'im out," remarked the Jew. "There's a German lives over me – third-floor front. Nice feller; plays the accordion."

"Well, just you watch 'im, Izzy, 'cos as soon as the war starts 'e'll be over your missus an' all," said the labourer. "Wot you 'avin'?"

"Same again, ta," said the Jew. "Still, there's nothin' to be done abaht it, is there? I mean, if the war starts."

"It depends on Belgium," said the Cockney. "But if it does start, it'll be a 'ell of a business. I don't reckon the Army'll be big enough – my bruvver-in-law reckons we'll all 'ave to go."

"Does 'e, now?" said the labourer. " 'E must be a right ray o' sunshine, your bleedin' bruvver-in-law. Mind you, I don't mind meself. I wouldn't mind flattenin' a few o' the buggers – an' a few o' their frauleins, an' all. Be a nice change from the missus."

"It's a question o' colonies, too, of course," said the Cockney. "The *Mail* reckons the Germans want to 'ave some more in Africa, same as we've got. An' the Frogs."

"I don't see that," said the Jew. "They don't need 'em, do they? I mean, we've always 'ad 'em, 'aven't we? For a long time, anyway.

Dunno abaht the Frogs. Anyway, I don't reckon the Germans would look after the niggers proper – I mean, they 'aven't the experience, 'ave they? Not like us."

"Well, we've got the Empire," conceded the Cockney. "That's the point. The *Mail* reckons the Kaiser wants one, too."

"Well, 'e's too bloody late in the day, isn't he?" said the labourer. "If 'e wanted one, he shoulda been fightin' for one, like we was, wiv Kitchener and Gordon an' them. An' Wellin'ton, I expect," he added. "An' Nelson, an' them."

"My Dad was in the Soo-dan," said the Cockney. " 'E liked it."

" 'E would, wouldn't 'e – bein' yore Dad?" said the labourer. "Right bloodthirsty lot, yore family – yore bleedin' Dad, an' yore bleedin' bruvver-in-law. I can see we'll 'ave to turn *you* loose on the Kaiser, first thing."

"I wouldn't mind," said the Cockney. "Always fancied bein' in the Buffs. My Dad was in the Buffs. Wot's everybody avin', then?" They gave their orders, and the Jew said:

"I reckon it'll 'appen. I reckon we'll all finish up fightin' the Germans."

"Well, it won't be this arternoon," observed the labourer. "Good 'ealth. Nor tomorrow, neither. I fancy the Guards, meself. Grenadiers, I think – always fancied them, at Troopin' the Colour, an' that. Talkin' abaht yore Dad, I 'ad a great-uncle in the cavalry – aht in India. 'E settled aht there – married an Indian bint an' got a job on the railway. Mind you, 'e 'ad 'is share first, of booze an' crumpet – an' scrappin' with the niggers on the frontier. Kind of life that'd appeal to me." He sipped his pint reflectively. "D'you know – I just 'ope the bleedin' Germans start it. Straight, I do."

"Well, I don't mind," said the Jew. "I'm sick o' the cabs, I can tell you. I've just abaht 'ad me bellyful o' them. But if I get the chance, it's goin' to be the Rifle Brigade."

"Why the Rifle Brigade?" asked the labourer. "Wot's special abaht them?"

"No buttons to clean," said the Jew. "All black buttons, no brass. An' they learn you sharp-shootin'. I wouldn't mind bein' a sharp-shooter, meself."

"It depends on Russia, too, of course," said the Cockney. "But I reckon it'll 'appen."

They drank for a moment in silence, and then the labourer said thoughtfully:

"Well, like I said, it won't be this arternoon. Kaiser can't 'ave got his bags packed yet. Time enough when 'e 'as."

"I just 'ope it isn't over afore I can get in," said the Cockney. "They reckon it won't last long – the *Mail* reckons that."

"Always did fancy soldierin'," said the Jew. "Nice change from the cabs. Good grub, an' all – an' a chance to travel. Drink up, an' let's 'ave another."

"Don't mind if I do," said the Cockney. " 'Course, it might not mean travellin' – not very far."

" 'Ow d'you mean?" said the labourer.

"Well, suppose the Germans was to invade? Suppose the war was – 'ere?"

"Don't talk bloody silly – 'ow could it? The Navy'd blow 'em to kingdom come afore they'd bought their steamer tickets, 'ardly!"

"That's right," said the Jew. "I remember, at school, they told us wot some ole Admiral said, in the ole days, when we was fightin' Napoleon or somebody. 'E says: 'I do not say that they cannot come. I say only that they cannot come by sea.' That's wot 'e said."

"Stands to reason," said the labourer. "Course they can't come by sea – an' we're surrounded by the bloody stuff, ain't we? There y'are, then."

"An' they couldn't beat the Navy," said the Jew.

"Mebbe not," said the Cockney. "But the Germans 'as nearly as many ships as we've got, 'cording to the *Mail*. Orlright, orlright – I know they're not as good, an' that, but our Fleet's gotta be spread out all round the British Isles, 'asn't it? An' it seems to me, if the Germans was to come sudden like, wiv all their ships, say at night, they might easy land a 'ell of a great big army somewhere, an' they got ten times more soldiers than we 'ave, an – "

His exposition was drowned by derisive cries. "An' wot'd 'appen to the German Navy, then? Fat lot there'd be left of it by that time." The labourer grinned scornfully.

"Wouldn't matter, would it? – not if they 'ad a million men landed, an' marchin' on London?" said the Cockney.

"A million?" said the Jew. "They ain't got that many."

"They got four an' a *'arf* million, mate," said the Cockney. "Don't you bloody worry. An' airships, wiv bombs." He drank with satisfaction. "It sez so in the *Mail*."

" 'Oo prints the bleedin' *Mail*?" demanded the labourer. "The bleedin' Kaiser?" But he scowled thoughtfully nonetheless.

525

"Mind you," added the Cockney, "if they did land, I'm not saying they'd win."

"No," said the Jew. "There's that."

They considered the implications of a German invasion, and then the labourer eased himself off his stool and went to look out of the window. He came back, shaking his head.

"Wot is it, then?" asked the Cockney.

"Jus' lookin'," said the labourer. "Not a sign o' the bleedin' Kaiser. 'Oo's round is it, then?"

Mr Franklin, who had some experience of violent action, wondered later if they would discuss the matter so lightly if the call to arms ever came. It was easy enough to talk in a pub – yet their talk, flippant though it was, had been far from foolish or uninformed. No, they would talk just the same if war did come, and they were forced to meet it personally; they were essentially practical – and quite probably spoiling for a fight, too, as General Flashman had predicted. They were ordinary enough men, but then the ordinary men of England had always demonstrated a great partiality and aptitude for warfare, in spite of the civilizing mission of which the nation was so proud. It had just been pub talk, of course, about something they thought unlikely to happen – something they rather regretted might not happen.

Why should he suddenly remember Samson accepting the Remington that night at Lancing? The thoughtful nod, the outward calm that now, he realized, had masked a secret excitement. He could think of Samson, silent in the dark of the house, listening for the stealthy raising of a window, watching as Curry's dim figure crossed the hall and flitted silently up the stairs. Or Jack Prior, stolid and reserved, but secretly terribly proud. Or the policeman who had almost arrested Lady Helen outside the Waldorf, calm, purposeful and deliberate. Or Lacy, even – suddenly turning to charge him like a wild bull that night at Oxton. Or the man in the steeple-hat and the woman in the apron, whom he had seen in his mind's eye setting out from Castle Lancing in the long ago. Or Fisher with his bull-dog face, Churchill the dangerous placid cherub, old General Flashman, the dying eagle – or Lady Helen with her striking profile, waiting eagerly for her sentence – or Peggy, stepping suddenly beside him and taking his hand in front of Crawford . . . but he did not want to think of Peggy, even though she was never out of his mind. It was a strange train of thought that had brought him back to her, from three Londoners in a pub looking forward to war. But all his thoughts came back to her eventually – would she come home this week-end?

She did not come on Sunday – the day that England heard that Germany had declared war on Russia, had crossed the frontiers of Luxembourg, and had demanded passage through Belgium. Berlin had concluded an alliance with Turkey, France was mobilizing and appealing to Britain to stand by her, to guard her northern shore from the naked menace of the German fleet. The little German ambassador, Lichnowsky, a familiar figure with his white sun-hat and cane, had called on Grey, the Foreign Secretary, and wept as he implored Britain to keep out of the war. Even Ireland was forgotten now; the rumour ran that both North and South would call a truce to their differences in the face of the common danger.

And still people wondered if it could be true – if after all the generations of peace, the ninety-nine years since Britain had been involved in a general European war, after all the crises and alarms and alliances and ententes and threats and notes and incidents and diplomacies of a century, the fighting time had come again. No one could tell; no one knew what telegrams were flying between London and Paris and Berlin and Vienna, what fears and doubts and hopes were being expressed in the offices of power, in the throne and cabinet rooms. But a strange belief was beginning to grip the people, a sense that had nothing to do with the visible evidence, that the thing had happened at last, unforeseen and inexplicable, and there could only be one way in the end. Even on that warm, tranquil Sunday, as the governesses led their befrocked charges through Kensington Gardens and the engines of the great fleet throbbed off the Orkneys, as the crowds basked on the beaches and the Uhlans trotted through the lanes and fields towards Belgium, as grave-faced men stared uneasily at each other in Whitehall and Mr Franklin sat in the garden and wondered where Peggy was and tried to concentrate unsuccessfully on a new book called *Dubliners*, as the millions of the French army stood to arms and the Kaiser assured his intimates that it was absurd to think that England would ever take the field against her fellow-Teutons – even then, before Mr Kipling had written his unforgettable line or coined the terrible nickname that would last for generations, everyone in England knew. The Hun was at the gate.

That this sense was shared by the government was seen on Monday, when the nation continued to relax in the Bank Holiday sunshine, and the Foreign Secretary told a packed and attentive House of

527

Commons that the British fleet would give all protection in its power to the northern coast of France. It was as simple as that: Britain would permit no one to make war in her Narrow Seas. Even more ominous, if more carefully-worded, was his further statement that Britain was interested in the independence of Belgium; by Tuesday afternoon it was common knowledge that Britain had demanded a categoric assurance from Berlin, to be delivered before midnight, that Belgian neutrality would be respected. But no one now believed that it would be; the Kaiser would not climb down. In a few hours the fever, which had started slowly and gradually gripped the national body, broke. It was going to be war. The holiday crowds in boaters and summer frocks began to converge, as drawn by some mystical magnet, on the Mall and the other streets leading to Buckingham Palace, people left their homes and began to stare about them in excitement and with strange exhilaration, and at Cessford Castle Lady Helen sat down and wrote, in her strong bold hand, a letter to the Home Secretary in which she assured him that, if war should come, she and all those on whom she could prevail in the suffrage movement – and she had no doubt that even the most militant of its leaders would share her views – would suspend their campaign for the duration of the emergency. Further, she urged that a general amnesty should be declared, and that all those suffragettes now in prison should be pardoned and released at once; in return she and they would place themselves at the country's disposal for whatever war work they could be given.

Still there was no word from Peggy or Sir Charles. Mr Franklin, restless in Wilton Crescent, finally accepted an invitation which had been made three times during the past week, which he had consistently refused, once by letter and twice through Samson on the telephone. However, when it came a fourth time on the Tuesday afternoon, he finally thought, why not? It would serve to take his mind off his own affairs, and it might even be interesting to hear the views of one who probably knew more of war than any man then living.

"Very well," he told Samson, "tell General Flashman I'll dine with him, but not at his club, or mine." He had no intention of risking another Athenaeum scene in any place where he might be recognized. He named an obscure Hungarian restaurant off Knightsbridge where he and Peggy had dined once or twice over the years, and said he would be there at eight o'clock. If Peggy had not come home before then, he could reasonably assume that she would not arrive that day.

In the event it was nearer to nine than eight when he kept his appointment; the eastern end of Knightsbridge was so crowded with traffic and pedestrians as a result of the war excitement that he had to take to the side-streets, and so eventually won to the cool, dark-panelled refuge of his restaurant, where he found his host ensconced in a corner, looking like a lecherous Old Testament prophet in evening dress and decorations, drinking bull's blood and trying to converse in what might have been a Balkan language with a buxom waitress in native costume.

"You don't know the Hungarian for bosom?" he was saying. "Well, you ought to, of all people . . . here, I'll show you – ah, there you are, Yankee, arriving inopportunely as usual." He watched the stout waitress go off giggling, and called after her: "And we don't want any damned gypsy fiddling, either, d'you hear? Balok soup and goulash, and another bottle of this red rubbish." His bright and bloodshot glance looked over Mr Franklin. "Gunfighter's eyes," he remarked, and poured wine into his guest's glass.

It had occurred to Mr Franklin, as he made his way through the packed streets, that he had been inconsiderate in suggesting such an out-of-the-way restaurant – after all, the old man was in his nineties, and it must be a great ordeal to have to make his way, even being driven, through all the bustle of London on the brink of hostilities. But a glance across the table reassured him – one foot in the grave he might have, and shockingly ravaged he might look, but Sir Harry appeared to be in no need of consideration. His flushed satyr face was grinning contentedly, his glossy white whiskers and mane shone in the lamplight, which glinted on the mass of bronze and silver and gold miniatures on his breast, and on the orders which hung on ribbons over his massive shoulders. He caught Mr Franklin's glance, and grinned even more broadly.

"Sporting my tin, as you see," he drawled hoarsely. "In the public interest. At a time like this it gives the mob confidence to be reminded of who I am, and that I'm too damned old to mismanage any more campaigns for 'em. Quite an impressive display, ain't they? That's the V.C., that shabby little chap at the beginning – and that's your own Congressional medal down there, among the foreign stuff. Ten bucks a year I still get for that – Sam Grant must be turning in his grave." He raised his glass. "Here's to Sam – when in doubt, have a drink. And that's the Bath, of course – but that's the one I'm proudest of." He touched a gilded archangel surrounded by sunbeams which depended on a violet-coloured ribbon to his snowy shirt front. "That's

529

the San Serafino Order of Purity and Truth, Third Class – and I got that for rogering the wife of the president-elect under her husband's bed at the height of the revolution. However, we're not here to talk politics. How've you been?"

Mr Franklin replied non-committally, and asked the General what he thought of the war situation. The old man shrugged.

"Contemptible – but of course it always is. We should stay out, and to hell with Belgium. After all, it's stretching things to say we're committed to 'em, and we'd be doing 'em a favour – and the Frogs, too."

"By not protecting them, you mean? I don't quite see that."

"You wouldn't – because like most idiots you think of war as being between states – coloured blobs on the map. You think if we can keep Belgium green, or whatever colour it is, instead of Prussian blue, then hurrah for everyone. But war ain't between coloured blobs – it's between people. You know what people are, I suppose? – chaps in trousers, and women in skirts, and kids in small clothes." The General took a pull at his wine and grimaced. "I wish to God that someone would tell the Hungarians that their wine would be greatly improved if they didn't eat the grapes first. Anyway, imagine yourself a Belgian – in Liege, say. Along come the Prussians, and invade you. What about it? – a few cars commandeered, a shop or two looted, half a dozen girls knocked up, a provost marshal installed, and the storm's passed. Fierce fighting with the Frogs, who squeal like hell because Britain refuses to help, the Germans reach Paris, peace concluded, and that's that. And there you are, getting on with your garden in Liege. But – " the General wagged a bony finger. "Suppose Britain helps – sends forces to aid little Belgium – and the Frogs – against the Teuton horde? What then? Belgian resistance is stiffened, the Frogs manage to stop the invaders, a hell of a war is waged all over Belgium and north-east France, and after God knows how much slaughter and destruction the Germans are beat – or not, as the case may be. How's Liege doing? I'll tell you – it's a bloody shambles. You're lying mangled in your cabbage patch, your wife's had her legs blown off, your daughters have been raped, and your house is a mass of rubble. You're a lot better off for British intervention, ain't you?" He sat back, grinning sardonically.

"By that reckoning," said Mr Franklin, "no one would ever stand up to a brute or a bully."

" 'Course they would – when it was worth while. You don't remember the war of 1870 – when these same Germans marched on Paris. Smallish war – but suppose we'd been helping the Frogs then? It wouldn't have been over half as quick, and God knows how many folk would have died who are still happily going about their business in Alsace and Lorraine. Same thing today – we should simply tell the Kaiser that if his fleet puts its nose out of the Baltic we'll send it to the bottom – that satisfies the Frogs, up to a point, since it guarantees their northern coast, it satisfies the Kaiser who'll swallow his pride for the sake of keeping us out of the war, and it saves his pretty little ships as well. And five years from now, Liege will be doing rather well – whether it's got a German provostmarshal still or not. And that won't matter a damn, to people whose main concern is eating, drinking, fornicating, making money, and seeing their children grow up safe and healthy."

"It's a point of view," said Mr Franklin, "I suppose. Sounds strange coming from a man with all that – " and he indicated the glittering medals on Sir Harry's chest.

"How the hell d'you suppose I've survived to wear all these?" croaked the ancient warrior. "Not by rushing to the aid of the poor little Belgiques when I can't do 'em a blessed bit of good, you may be sure. Not by prolonging the agony." He beamed as the waitress brought their soup, and gave her a wink. "Ain't she a little darling, though? Ah me, that's the only thing I regret about growing old – the poor thing'll never know what she missed. I considered," he went on, "writing a letter to *The Times* about it – not about her, about the war – but they'd not have printed it, and if they had, people would have said my brain had softened."

"Is there any hope it may not happen?" wondered Mr Franklin, and the General shook his head, inhaling the stewy soup noisily.

"No – Grey and Asquith haven't the stature. No politician could talk the country out of it now – Palmerston might have, but ironically enough he probably wouldn't want to. Not that he was a warmonger, you know – but he'd see it's what the country wants, and let 'em have it. Maybe Grey and Asquith see that too. I only wish," the General added, "that when it happens, I could take all the asses who'll be waving flags and cheering and crowding the recruiting office – take 'em all by one collective arm, and say: 'Now then, Jack, you know what you're cheering for? You're cheering at the prospect of having a soft-nosed bullet fired into your pelvis, shattering the bone and spreading it in splinters all through your intestines, and dying in agony

531

two days later – or, if you're really unlucky, surviving for a lifetime of pain, unable to walk, a burden to everyone, and a dam' nuisance to the country that will pay you a pension you can't live off. That, Jack,' I'd tell 'em, 'is what you're cheering for.' I'd probably be locked up." The General finished his soup and sat back, sighing. "Not bad stuff, that – kept me going on my second honeymoon, which was with a German Crown Princess. Lovely gel, with the appetite of a demented rabbit. Didn't care for soup, as I remember. No, one of my aides used to prepare it for me with his own hands. Splendid amateur cook, and the best man with a sabre I ever knew – frightful scoundrel. Threw him over a cliff in the end."

He drowned this wistful reminiscence with a hearty gulp of wine, shuddered with distaste, and went on: "I'd also like to remind our jingo-drunk public that they haven't the least notion what a war with modern weapons will be like and the only fellows who can even guess are your American survivors from places like Antietam and Shiloh – that's the only *real* war there's been in a hundred years." The General pointed an accusing spoon at Mr Franklin. "Know how many men went down at Gettysburg? Fifty thousand – and if I hadn't moved damned lively I'd have been one of 'em. Well, how many Gettysburgs d'you think it will take to settle a scrap between the kind of forces under arms in Europe today? I don't know – perhaps a month of it would make everyone cry quits, but knowing the sort of clowns who'll be in command – who are *always* in command – I take leave to doubt it." He rumbled volcanically for a moment, and then remarked cheerfully: "Aye, well, this is one bloody mess they won't get me into. God, I've been lucky!"

Having thus reminded himself of the United States, he began questioning Mr Franklin about his past, over the goulash, and received guarded replies, which seemed to give him quiet amusement. At length he said: "You don't fool me, my son. I don't know anything about you, but if you've lived all your life on the windy side of the law, I'm a Dutchman. No offence, and if you don't want to talk about it, I quite understand. Pity, though; I'd hoped to spend an evening listening for once. So let's talk about women instead. How's your captivating wife?"

Mr Franklin explained that she was abroad, visiting friends, and the General nodded sympathetically. "Mm-mh. I heard there'd been a *petite scandale* – my wife, who has ears like a Gilzai scout, picked something up on her last raid on Belgravia. 'Mr and Mrs F——, of

W— Crescent, have not been seen together since their meeting at the Savoy Ball with the exquisite . . . ah, but we must not be indiscreet, my dears, although it is whispered that Mr F— has been showing an unwonted interest in *objets d'art* lately'. " The General sniffed. "That sort of thing. Pity. The decline of duelling has ruined more private lives than I care to think of – in my young day nobody'd have dared to tittle-tattle the way they do now. Horse-whipping journalists has gone out too. Which reminds me of darling Lola – Montez, you know. Thrashed editors just to keep in training . . ."

He prattled entertainingly through the meal, and then said: "What say we have a look at the Palace – see how the many-headed are celebrating the opening of the temple of Janus? Charming meal, my dear," he said as the waitress presented the bill, "and I only regret that infirmity prevents me from inviting you out to express my gratitude in the old-fashioned way. Have a couple of quid instead and give us a hug." He rose stiffly to his feet, slipped a hand round her hips, and gave her a playful squeeze. "By jove, there's good stuff there. Come on, Franklin."

Sir Harry's open landau was waiting with its driver at the kerb. The old soldier, having adjusted his top hat and cloak, surveyed the congested thoroughfare and remarked that it looked like Taiping Rebellion.

"I'm afraid we'll never get near the Palace," said Mr Franklin, whereupon the General gave him a pitying glance and told him to get into the car. He then sent the driver for a mounted policeman whom he had spotted nearby.

"Now then, sergeant," he said, "I'm Brigadier-General Sir Harry Flashman – ah, you know me? Well, now, that's quite all right, sergeant – Rooney, d'you say? I'm delighted to meet you. The thing is, I have to get to the Palace – War Office stuff, you understand – must be there within the hour. Do you think you could clear a way? Perhaps some of your admirable chaps would precede my car . . . bless my soul, when I was four years old you hadn't even been invented! Astonishing, isn't it? Thank you, Rooney – what's your address? Get it down, Franklin. I shan't forget you, sergeant . . . "

"I shan't, either," he remarked as he climbed in beside Mr Franklin. "Bottle of the best for Sergeant Rooney, and a scarf for his missus . . . always pays. Ah, here we go."

It took the better part of an hour for the car, moving slowly with

Sergeant Rooney and a couple of constables ahead parting the crowds, to complete its journey. But their exhortations, the good humour of the people, and the sight of the General's chestful of decorations as well as his imposing appearance, had the desired effect, and eventually the car inched its way to the edge of the packed throng which filled the great space at the head of the Mall, pressing against the Palace railings. Here even Sergeant Rooney's efforts failed.

"I'm sorry, sir!" He was leaning down from his horse, shouting above the deafening roar of the crowd. "I can't get you any farther without more men! I'll 'ave to push through meself to the gates an' get a file of soldiers!"

"My dear fellow, what a splendid suggestion!" Sir Harry waved him on. "We shall sit tight here!" He watched the sergeant pushing his mount gently into the crowd, and nodded approvingly to Mr Franklin. "Smart chap, that. I'll make it two bottles."

"But you don't want to go into the Palace, surely?" said Mr Franklin.

"It's imperative," said the veteran coolly. "There's certainly nowhere else around here where I can answer a call of nature in comfort. In the meantime, I suggest we struggle up and sit on the top of this seat – we'll see better from there."

Mr Franklin helped him, to the accompaniment of oaths and groans in several languages, until they had their feet on the back seat and were perched on the hood.

"Now, there's a sight for you," said Sir Harry.

As far as they could see, they were surrounded by a vast expanse of faces, white in the glare of the tall lamps, surging and moving in a huge human lake from the tall railings to the Mall and the trees and gardens beyond. From it there rose a continuous rumbling roar, filling the warm night above them with its volume; every face was turned towards the Palace itself, far back beyond the railings, and the floodlit balcony above the central arch. There was a growing rhythm to the noise, vague at first, then gradually shaping itself into a chant, while the crowd swayed and stamped in unison: "King! . . . the King! We . . . want . . . the King! We . . . want . . . the King!" The chant grew to a thunder, rolling over the packed throng of heads, beating and echoing against the walls of the Palace, and then suddenly swelling into a great shout as the balcony window blazed with added light, and the two tiny figures appeared, like distant marionettes, coming forward to the stone balustrade draped with the royal arms, waving to the huge sea of humanity in front of them – the small dark figure, barely recognizable, and the taller white one at his side. The crowd was too tight-packed to wave or throw up hats, but the roar continued to swell up, blending itself into a mighty chorus of the National Anthem.

Mr Franklin sat spellbound. All around him they were singing, singing with an intoxicated fervour that was frightening in its power and volume, the human music beating in deafening waves around him until he had to put his hands to his ears. Beside him the General was leaning forward, hands on knees, bareheaded, and Mr Franklin had a glimpse of that eagle silhouette, brooding over the singing multitude like some great spirit of arms; he was not singing, just staring about him with a fierce intensity, and Mr Franklin realized that the old man was imprinting sight and sound in his memory – just as he must have imprinted so many amazing scenes from his astonishing past – Britain's past. The General nudged him, and pointed, smiling grimly, and Mr Franklin looked down; close beside the car there was a young man in a boater and blazer, staring fixedly ahead at the balcony, singing blindly in that surge of patriotic elation, his arm clasping a girl in a flowered hat, only her eyes were closed, and her cheeks were wet with tears, but she was singing, too.

> Oh . . . Lord . . . our . . . God . . . arise!
> Sca . . . tter . . . our . . . en . . . emies
> And . . . make . . . them . . . fall!

It thundered on, the majestic, insistent roar, culminating in another ear-splitting shout at the finish, the crowd chanting out the tremendous triple cheer of the old battle-cry that the Roman legions had heard as the hordes of half-naked, indigo-stained savages had hurled themselves against the shield wall. "Hip . . . hip . . . hip . . . hooray! Hip . . . hip . . . hip . . . hooray!" No doubt somewhere in the enormous mob some sturdy traditionalists were chanting "hurrah!", but there was no doubt that the hoorays had it. And as the cheering died away, and the noise subsided to a mere deafening baying, Mr Franklin saw that about twenty yards ahead of the car's bonnet a double file of red-coated Guardsmen in their great bearskin hats, white-slinged rifles held high, were gradually pushing the people aside, with infinite care, and a lane was opening up before them, with Sergeant Rooney pacing his horse along it, waving the crowd to stay back.

Mr Franklin helped the bemedalled veteran back to his seat, having to pause as the crowd gave another good-natured cheer for the white-whiskered old codger, whoever he was, and Sir Harry waved his hat and sank back panting against the cushions. With the aid of those pressed against the car, the hood was brought forward, and with the din comparatively cut off, Sir Harry sighed deeply and remarked:

"And they'll be singing just as loud beneath the lime trees and along the Wilhelmstrasse. The Marseillaise will be taking some stick, too, I fancy, on the Seine bridges. Wouldn't mind hearing that – fine sound . . . wasted on the Frogs, of course. About the only ones who won't be singing are the best singers of the lot – the Russians. Most of them won't realize there's a war on until someone sticks a bayonet in them, and anyway, I don't suppose they know the words. Everybody singing . . . everybody off to war. Not you, though – Uncle Sam'll stay out, I daresay, as long as he can. Quite right, too!" He glanced out of the mica window at the press of bodies round the car. "Poor devils. Aye, poor old *me* – they'll live longer than I will, most of 'em. But I can't complain. I've had a good innings – this'll be the last outbreak of war I'll see, and for once I shan't be going. Went to South Africa, you know – just as a tourist, during the Boer business. Interesting. But not this time – unless Kitchener asks me along as a guest." He snorted with laughter at the thought. "He'll be the man they'll send for, you'll see. Middling general – we could do worse. Now where the hell have those soldiers got to? Trust the Guards to lose their way!"

A sudden, odd thought struck Mr Franklin, and it seemed doubly odd that it had only just occurred to him.

"D'you think England'll win the war?"

"Ask them," said the General, and jerked his thumb at the window, grinning. Then he considered, the eyes narrowing in the flushed, ancient face. "Probably – yes, on balance, we ought to win. Germany can lick Russia, but not Britain and France together. But they'll take a lot of beating, if it's a fight to the finish. Yes, I'd say we were odds on to win – not that it matters all that much."

Mr Franklin stared at him in astonishment. "You can't mean that – it doesn't make sense!"

Sir Harry turned to look at him, and then glanced out of the window again.

"It isn't important whether you win or lose," he said, "so long as

536

you survive. So long as your people survive. And that's the only good reason for fighting that anyone ever invented. The survival of your people and race and kind. That's the only victory that matters."

A scarlet tunic appeared at the window, and a face beneath a bearskin stooped and peered. "Not before time," growled Sir Harry. "The amount of liquor that's occupied my bladder in ninety years has rendered it a rather perished article."

Mr Franklin felt slightly anxious. "What are you going to say when we get inside?"

"Who knows? The Lord will provide," said Sir Harry placidly. "They can't throw an old man into the street, now, can they? Not," he touched his medals, "with all this."

"Well, if you don't mind," said Mr Franklin, "I feel I ought to get out here." This old gentleman, he told himself yet again, was decidedly unsafe. "I hope you don't think I'm running out – "

"I do," said the veteran promptly. "And I commend you for it. First sign of exceptional character I've detected in you. But you're missing a great chance, you know." He tapped Mr Franklin on the knee. "The first man I ever rode through those gates with was the Duke of Wellington, seventy-two years ago. Wouldn't you like to be the last?"

Mr Franklin hesitated. He was amused, and astonished, and a little touched. He looked into the mischievous, grinning old face, and then he shook his head.

"I think you ought to ride in alone," he said gently. "And with the hood back."

He reached across and shook the old man's hand, and then managed to push his way out of the car. The Guardsmen had succeeded in clearing the crowd from round the car, and a long aisle between the people ran fairly clear to the gates; police were moving in it, ushering them to keep it clear. At a word from Mr Franklin the hood was removed, and with the General leaning back comfortably in one corner the car rolled slowly forward. The crowd had begun to sing again, willing the King and Queen to come out on the balcony; as the car pulled away, Sir Harry was waving to him with his crooked grin; the crowd jostled forward into the space where the car had been, but Mr Franklin, craning, could see over their heads. With policemen half-running on either side, and Sergeant Rooney pacing ahead on his horse, the car was moving into the opened gates held back by the red-coated Guardsmen; the singing was thundering up in full-

537

throated ecstatic chorus, and he could just glimpse the great white head above the back seat and Sir Harry's raised hand solemnly waving in time to the music:

> Land ... of ... hope ... and ... glory!
> Moth ... er ... of ... the ... free!
> How ... can we ... extol ... thee,
> Who ... are ... bo-orn of thee!

The car was lost to sight as it turned through the gates and made towards the Palace, even as the lights on the balcony came up again and royalty reappeared. The singing swelled to a triumphant climax; Mr Franklin could imagine the monarch glimpsing the car with its eccentric occupant as it sped across the open space before the Palace – what in God's name was the old villain going to say when he got inside and the Palace minions discovered he was an entirely unauthorized visitor bent only on relieving himself? Mr Franklin could not guess – but he had no doubt Sir Harry would think of something. He'd had a lot of practice.

It took Mr Franklin some time to push his way out of the crowd into the less congested environs of the Mall. He glanced back from a distance at the floodlit Palace, and the swarming mass before it; they were singing "Rule, Britannia!" now, the stirring strains floating on the midnight air beneath the trees. Up by Admiralty Arch the crowds were thick again, but here the people were standing in small groups, laughing and talking as they listened to the distant sound. There were ladies in evening dress and girls in frocks, men in tails and young fellows in open necks and blazers, a couple of sailors in their bell-bottoms and flat white caps, a news vendor offering his papers, a policeman sauntering majestically, pausing by one of the groups.

"That's right, miss," Mr Franklin heard him say. "I understand it's official that no satis-factory answer 'as been received to the government's hultimattum to Germany. Yes, sir, that means we are at war – now, if you'll please to pass along, ladies and gentlemen ... move along, please ... "

So that was it. War. Mr Franklin thought about the labourer, and the Jew, and the Cockney, and wondered what they were doing. And Peggy – would there be any word from her tomorrow? In the small hours he made his way through the busy, laughing, bustling streets, gay with the heady news of conflict about to begin, and came home past the lighted windows of Belgravia to Wilton Crescent.

26

Royal Hibernian Hotel
Dawson Street
Dublin

Dear Mark,

Daddy tells me that you've been holding the fort at Wilton Crescent while we've been over here, so I thought I should let you know that I shan't be coming back to London immediately. Susan Dean and Basil have asked me to spend a few days with them in Westmorland – as you know, Basil's brother John is at the Curragh, and when they heard from him that I was there with Daddy they sent the invitation through him, which was kind. And after that it would hardly be worth while coming up to Town again, as I promised to go to Scotland with the Stewarts for the "Glorious Twelfth", which always means . . .

Mr Franklin paused in the doorway of the morning-room to turn the page. He had torn open the envelope as soon as he recognized Peggy's hand-writing, reading the first page as he crossed the hall. He moved aside to let the maid pass in with his coffee, and as she set it beside his place he went on reading.

. . . at least two weeks – I expect I'll be with them at Knockinsh until the twentieth or thereabouts, and then go over to the Cheshires' place near Crieff – I can never remember what it's called, something frightful in Gaelic, but you christened it Whisky Slide when we were there a few years ago, remember? They asked if you'd be coming, and so did Cecil Stewart. And there's the usual open invitation from Tommy Appin, who will be having all the big guns. So I shan't be darkening the doors of Wilton Crescent until September at the earliest, and probably only for a flying visit then, because dear Cecil was hinting heavily, as you know, about the Mediterranean – he's been dying to play Captain Kidd on his yacht ever since last autumn

when I was with them at Antibes. I suppose all this war nonsense may put the kibosh on his cruising, but I hope not.

Mr Franklin reached his chair and sat down. He poured himself a cup of coffee, and was preparing to take up the next page when the maid asked, "Mrs Fields said to ask what you'd like, sir – kidneys and bacon or a chop? Or she thought you might care for some kedgeree, sir?"

He became aware that she was regarding him with slight apprehension, and had to shake himself mentally and ask her to repeat her question, while he forced himself to pay attention. This was Ellen, the parlour maid, the little jolly one who was being courted by Constable Atkinson; she was standing there in her starched cap and apron, with the tray held flat against her in the approved style, asking him what he wanted for breakfast. "No, thanks, Ellen – nothing . . . just some toast, perhaps. Oh, it's here, . . . tell Mrs Fields." She tripped out and he went back to the letter.

So would you ask Polly to bring my trunk up on the ninth, and wait at the Station Hotel in Perth? She'll know what to bring me for the moors and so on. Tell her I'll be all right until then – I've got enough things for Westmorland, and I shall be arriving at Perth on the tenth with the Stewarts and going on to Knockinsh the same day.

Daddy has gone across to Galway to stay with an old friend of his for a few weeks – he's rather used up, and says he couldn't bear Oxton just now, which is understandable.

Could you tell Polly to bring my red jewel case? I don't think she'd better be entrusted with the blue one from the safe – unless you're coming to Knockinsh, in which case perhaps you wouldn't mind bringing it with you.

Fondest love,
Peggy.

Mr Franklin read the letter through carefully a second time, and then sat looking thoughtfully before him while his coffee went cold and untasted. So there it was, as plainly as though she had written it: "We can go on or not, as you please, but it will be on my terms as far as I'm concerned. And on your terms as far as you're concerned. If that suits you, fine – if it doesn't, equally fine." It was more or less what she had said to him on that morning after the Savoy Ball, and she was saying it again now to let him know that nothing had been changed by Arthur's death – to which she had not referred directly in her short letter.

He could see her reasoning, or thought he could. If she had returned from Ireland to Wilton Crescent, and he had been there, he must have tried to comfort her, or at least sympathize in husbandly fashion, over her brother. And she did not want that; it would have blurred the lines of difference between them, perhaps led to the appearance of reconciliation of the fearful problem with which he had been confronted after the Savoy Ball. But the problem would have remained unresolved, or would have had to be thrashed out again without getting any nearer a solution. She was simply restating what they already knew, to let him know that outside, temporary, and necessarily sentimental considerations, like Arthur's tragedy, were not to be weighed in balancing the main issue, which was whether he would accept her terms for living, for marriage, or not. He was not deceived by the fact that she had not mentioned Arthur in the letter – he knew her well enough to understand that her feelings, her shock, and her grief would be things that she would not willingly share with anyone else, but that however serene a face she presented she would still be experiencing them underneath. In that respect, it was not as callous a letter as it might have appeared to a third party. It was, in fact, an eminently practical letter, carefully phrased to let him see what the position was, and leave the decision to him. She was making no plea, no recommendation, no statement of feeling one way or the other; she had carefully avoided any word or sentence that might disturb the delicate balance – "... unless you're coming to Knockinsh..." "... they asked if you'd be coming... " Cool, guarded, realistic Peggy.

When he came to think of it, the letter was not unlike half a dozen similar notes she had dashed off to him on occasions in the past, when she had changed plans at some country house or other – "Bobbie and Madge say why don't you meet us at Newmarket?" or "Tom was asking if you'd feel like a spot of fishing – we don't expect to be coming back from Wales until next week, anyway." But this time the circumstances were different; it was quite literally make or break, and they both knew it.

In the meantime, it was the morning of August the fifth, and if Polly was to assemble her mistress's extensive wardrobe for the grouse moors, picnics, social calling, and, of course, the evenings, and no doubt foray through Bond Street for various cosmetic impedimenta, in time to catch the overnight train on the eighth, she might as well start now. He rang for her, passed on Peggy's instructions, and ordered hot coffee while he lit a cigarette and glanced at the morning paper. It was only after several minutes, when he realized that he had skimmed the main news page, which was devoted entirely to the war, and got half-way through a theatre review – Montague Love in *Grumpy* – without taking in a word, that he pushed the paper aside and rang for Samson.

"Mrs Franklin's in Westmorland for a few days, staying with friends – doesn't feel like coming back to Town so soon after . . . her brother, you know. Then she'll be going up to Scotland for the Twelfth – I've told Polly, and she's getting everything together."

"I see, sir." The square, impassive face displayed no more interest than usual. "Will you be going to Scotland, also, sir?"

"I haven't made up my mind yet, Thomas. Mrs Franklin's going to be up there until well into September, so there's no desperate hurry. I think I'll probably go down to Lancing at the week-end. So you can start thinking about packing – for yourself as well."

Afterwards he went for a walk in the Park, and watched the unusual sight of ammunition wagons rumbling past under the trees, their khaki-clad drivers sweating in the hot sunshine as they cracked their whips and encouraged the heavy horses pulling the long tarpaulin-covered carts. He walked on, following his feet along Piccadilly to the Circus, and observed the constables marshalling the crowd of men who were besieging a recruiting office which had opened near the corner of Regent Street. Men in their twenties, obviously in high spirits as they allowed themselves to be shepherded into line by the constables, all under the benevolent eye of an imposing warrant-officer with three stripes and a crown on his arm, a broad red sash, and a magnificent waxed moustache.

"All in good time, gentlemen!" he was saying. "This is one shop where you'll find the customer is always right – provided he's the right customer. Single file, gentlemen, and we'll have you enlisted before you can say Jack Robinson."

"And you won't be calling us gentlemen then, Fatty!" sang out a voice from the queue.

"That I won't," agreed the warrant-officer, with a genial chuckle. "And you won't be calling me Fatty, neither." He winked at Mr Franklin and added: "If you wouldn't mind moving along a little,

543

please, sir – the photographers would like to take a picture. Unless you'd care to join the queue? Always room for one more."

Mr Franklin stood aside; two men were erecting a camera tripod on the edge of the pavement, and the waiting queue was arranging itself to be snapped – men smiling with unabashed pleasure, others self-consciously, some presenting impassive profiles as though this was a great performance about nothing, a few mugging shamelessly for the camera and being nudged playfully by their companions, those at the back craning on tiptoe so that they would get into the picture. Young men in jackets and open necks, working men in overalls, a bus conductor in his peaked cap, a drayman from one of the Piccadilly pubs in his apron, an obvious "knut" in tight collar and rakish hat and spats, leaning nonchalantly on his stick, clerks in their humdrum suits, noisy Cockneys in boaters, a stout man in well-cut tweeds – passers-by were stopping, smiling, to watch; the warrant-officer, cane beneath his arm, drawn up as smartly as his portliness permitted, posed with a proudly proprietorial air.

"All still! Smile, please! Stea-dy . . . all smiling now." A flash and a puff and a cheer from the crowd, and the queue relaxed, laughing and well pleased. At that moment there was the rumble of a charabanc drawing up at the kerb, and a squeaking of brakes, followed by female cries and greetings as a horde of young women descended and advanced on the queue; they were all unusually pretty and strikingly-dressed, and the thickening crowd pressed forward to look, while the would-be recruits grinned broadly and called out invitations. The photographers shouted, the police asked everyone to keep back, please, the girls attached themselves to the young men in the queue, and then there was a spatter of applause as a field officer in Sam Browne, red tabs, and gleaming riding boots appeared, handing down from the charabanc the guest of honour, the former third lead of the *Folies Satire*, now the reigning star of Shaftesbury Avenue and glittering attraction of the smash-hit revue, *Pip, Squeak!*, none other than "that delightful celebrity, Miss Pip Delys, who with the young ladies of her company has kindly, and I may say, most patriotically, come to assist us in the worthy and – ah – noble cause, of . . . of . . . er, recruiting."

Loud applause, a flashing smile and curtsey from the beautiful principal, who had chosen to appear for the occasion in her Lilian Russell costume, crimson spangled Victorian gown, huge feathered hat, and long parasol which, when unfurled, proved to be a Union

544

Jack. The field officer beamed and clapped his elegantly-gloved hands, the warrant-officer stamped and saluted with a flourish, the photographers shouted hoarsely for order, the chorus girls squealed and chattered with the grinning young men, and the pictures were taken. First Miss Delys was photographed in front of the queue with the field officer on one arm and a Chelsea Pensioner in his red coat on the other – as a tourist attraction he was almost as used to cameras as she was. Then the warrant-officer was persuaded to step bashfully forward, removing his cheese-cutter cap to reveal martially short hair apparently gummed down into a permanent cow's-lick; Pip cuddled him fondly while the crowd roared approval, the warrant-officer beamed and posed, the field officer smiled indulgently at this breach of discipline, and the flash recorded it for posterity.

Pip then took charge herself, organizing a group photograph. She indicated the drayman. "We'll have you, you great big handsome brute – " Laughter and cheering as the drayman obligingly flexed his massive biceps " – and you, too, Algy." Pip beckoned to the knut, who coloured slightly, but allowed himself to be drawn forward on her right arm while the drayman took the left. Two of the girls flanked them, with the field officer and warrant-officer next, and finally two more of the chorus on the outside. All then linked arms and smiled, the photographers went through professional contortions, and when the picture had been taken the entire company of *Pip, Squeak!* set themselves to accost young men passing by and invite them into the recruiting office, those who accepted being warmly but decorously kissed for the benefit of the camera.

Mr Franklin, watching from a distance, found himself confronted by a pretty red-head with a little Union Jack on a pin. "Won't you enlist?" she cried gaily, catching his lapel, and when he smiled back and shook his head she only pouted for a moment before launching herself at the next young male, who allowed himself to be borne off on her arm. However, the incident started a train of thought in Mr Franklin's mind which led him eventually to the American Embassy, where he sought out one of the senior staff whom he knew and asked him a question.

"Well, the plain fact of the matter, Mr Franklin, is that for American citizens in England, the war just doesn't make any difference. We're a neutral country – a very friendly neutral country, of course – but neutral, and our citizens here are in exactly the same position they've always been. You've been here five years, you have property here? So

545

– none of that's affected by the fact that Britain's at war with Germany. You have exactly the same rights and protections here that you've always had, both from the United Kingdom and the United States. You can buy, sell, come, go, do what you please – just as you've always done. Nothing's changed. Quite a few people have been in here the last couple of days, just like you, and that's what we tell 'em. Why – did you have any special thoughts in mind?"

"No, none at all."

"I just wondered there for a moment if you were thinking of joining the British Army – one or two fellows have asked about that."

"It hadn't occurred to me."

"No, well, no reason why it should – and I'm afraid when these chaps asked it took me aback a little." The embassy man smiled wrily. "Matter of fact, I didn't know what to tell them. I've an idea there's some prohibition on foreign enlistment of U.S. nationals, but we have nothing in our regulations here, so we've had to ask Washington. On the other hand, one of the older men here had some recollection of certain special provisions where Americans desirous of entering British service are concerned – I believe there's a regiment that used to be called the Royal Americans back in colonial days, and there's some loophole to do with them, he thinks. The King's Royal Rifle Corps they're called nowadays – apparently they figure in 'The Last of the Mohicans'. " He laughed and declaimed. " 'Forward, gallant Sixtieth!' Anyway, we'll see what Washington says. I advised the young fellows to hold their horses, reminded them they were officially neutrals, and that it might not be quite fitting for an American to get mixed up in the British Army. Know what one of 'em said to me? He said: 'George Washington and Daniel Boone got mixed up in it, didn't they?' Read me the deuce of a lecture about the retreat from Fort Ticonderoga or somewhere. Well, sir, I told him he was wasting his ardour." He shook his head, becoming confidential. "I told him that between ourselves it's highly unlikely that this war will last out the year, and the British Army is going to be in no need of foreign recruits – they'll have more of their own than they can handle."

Mr Franklin, recalling the throng at the recruiting office, agreed that this was probably so.

"In fact, though," the embassy man went on, "most of the inquiries I've had have been in the other direction. 'Can I go home?' and 'Can I take my assets with me?' That's what I've been getting asked – to which the answer is, sure, any time you like. Mind you, if anyone wants to take bullion with him he'd be advised to do it pretty quickly, because a friend in the F.O. tells me that an embargo on gold is inevitable. That's understandable – but as I tell 'em, what difference does it make, when credit transfers will still hold good? I tell 'em not to worry, anyway; it's sure to be a short war, and one thing you can bank on is that whoever loses, it won't be England."

Which was reassuring until, remembering General Flashman's thoughts on national anthems two nights earlier, Mr Franklin wondered if perhaps U.S. embassies in Berlin, Paris, St Petersburg, and Vienna might not be saying much the same thing about Germany, France, Russia, and Austria. And no doubt just as convincingly – one had only to think of the armed might of Germany, of the sheer ponderous strength of her four million fighting men, to ask oneself if such a colossus could conceivably be defeated. On the other hand, he had only to recall the naval review he had seen at Spithead, the sea covered with those huge splendid ships, or the solid marching ranks that he remembered at the Coronation, or the Olympia displays. Germany was taking on the strongest, biggest empire the world had ever seen, richer and more powerful than any nation on earth, because she was many nations. For some reason the association brought to mind a face that he had hardly seen in five years, vividly remembered from Sandringham – the young Churchill with his hands on his hips, head thrust forward, in the billiard-room. "Money and power – they're what *count*." And now Churchill himself was wielding that power, as master of the Royal Navy, with the limitless wealth of Britain to back him up. Mr Franklin wondered if, great as it was, it would be sufficient.

They travelled down to Castle Lancing on the Friday, from a St Pancras that seemed to contain more Germans, Frenchmen, Belgians, and other assorted continentals than Englishmen. These were the foreign reservists leaving by the trainload to rejoin their national armies, nor did it strike anyone as odd that they should be allowed to do so. War, as far as Europeans were concerned in 1914, was still a word that conjured up pictures of colourful uniforms and massed regiments, of jingling cavalry and infantry in red coats, of trumpets and banners and manoeuvres, Wellington and Napoleon in their cocked hats, bearded Highlanders in kilts, Polish lancers in winged helmets, Frenchmen in blue greatcoats, Guardsmen in bearskins. And the conventions that went with the visions still held good; it would have been an affront to fair play to take advantage of a foreigner's presence in one's country to intern him, enemy though he might be. In a sense it would have been to make a deserter of him; war was still a chivalrous business in the summer of '14.

So the small, alert Frenchman in his spats courteously made way for the large German in his homburg when they arrived simultaneously at the ticket-window, and the German acknowledged it with a stiff bow and said: "Danke." A few months later they might meet again in a special kind of living hell which neither of them could even remotely envisage, where a smiling countryside had been churned into a waste of mud and tangled wire and poisonous stagnant shell-holes and the air was alive with exploding death and the stink of rotten corpses. But for the moment they used each other with formal politeness, pretending not to notice their different nationalities. And together they stood watching a regiment of British troops entraining, the Frenchman with eager interest, the German with deep thought, and when a contingent of English nurses went by in their long blue coats and wimples, they both raised their hats, the German stolidly, the Frenchman with a smile.

Even so early, the railways were beginning to feel the strain of war. Mr Franklin found himself standing all the way to Cambridge in a first-class corridor that seemed to be full of young officers; only on the Norwich line was he at last able to find a seat. Yet even here, from the train window, he caught an occasional glimpse of a convoy of lorries on the road, or of a khaki-clad regiment marching along in column of fours, with a mounted colonel at its head.

Castle Lancing was busy, but that at least was with the civilian bustle of the new housing at Lye; of the war there was no sign. They settled in at the Manor, and for the first two or three days Mr Franklin busied himself with the stud at Oxton Hall. They knew it would be some time before Sir Charles returned, but all seemed to be well and flourishing; the head groom was a steady man, expert in his business, and Mr Franklin felt as he drove away from Oxton on the third day that there was at least one area of his affairs which was in good hands.

Thereafter he began to behave in a way which caused Samson surprise and not a little concern. Samson was shrewd, and he had some inkling that all was not exactly as it should be where his employer's marital relations were concerned; even so, Mr Franklin worried him. For he had become quiet again, in a way which Samson remembered from the beginning of their association; the butler would occasionally surprise him standing alone in the hall or the study or the garden, lost in thought; and he spent a considerable amount of his time in long walks along the surrounding roads and byways. Once he walked as far as Oxton, and another time to Thetford; he had always, Samson knew, been one for healthy exercise, but that seemed excessive. He wondered what his master was brooding about, and felt that it boded no good.

Mr Franklin, in fact, was saying good-bye. He was not saying it to anyone, but he was saying it to places that he had grown to know and love. He was saying it to the shades of the Babes in the Wood and their wicked uncle in the cool solitude of Wayland, and to the pleasant, dusty Thetford road, along which another English American named Tom Paine had set out a hundred and fifty years earlier; he was saying it to the bridge where Mr Lancaster had sat puffing morosely at his cigar while a beautiful woman with green eyes laughed as she searched the map for West Walsham, and to the narrow lane where a fox had invaded his luncheon basket and his heart had stopped at the sight of an angel face beneath a black bowler hat; he was saying it to the musty, dim interior of the Apple Tree, where he stood again and bought pints for the garrulous, bright-eyed Jake and the burly Jack Prior, and rejoiced with them over the fine new cottage into which Jack and his family would be settling on the Lye model estate before the year-end; he was saying it to the bridle path by Oxton where he had talked with Sir Charles and ridden with Peggy, and to the chest-nuts and beeches which shaded his home; and he was saying it to that home itself, to the panelled hall where he had stretched out on the bare boards on that first night in his rough blanket and said: "We're back," to the comfortable furniture with which he had filled the study and dining-room and drawing-room (and felt such quiet pride), to the graceful curved staircase where it had been such a pleasure to walk, with the ice-smooth polished banister beneath his hand, where on that terrible night he had sprawled, blasting shots at Curry for his very life, where his enemy's blood had run on the boards and the shots had ripped into panel and plaster. And to the old stables and the apples and the ivy-covered walls and the broad gravel drive and the flower-beds which old Jake had laboured to keep free – well, fairly free – of intruding weeds.

But most of all he was saying it in the old churchyard of Castle Lancing, to the great yew trees and the square tower and the lichened stones warm in the afternoon sun as they had been on that first evening five years ago, when he had sat drowsy with October beer and muttered snatches from Grey's *Elegy* and the Harfleur speech. To the thick green grass among the tombs, and to the tombs themselves, from the fine new one of timeless polished granite which he had caused to be set up, bearing the words

ELIZABETH FRANKLIN REEVE

(so that everyone should know it was a Franklin born who lay there), to the ancient weathered stone propped against the church wall with its thin, spidery inscription: "Johannes Fran .. in .., obit 1599." And to those imagined people on the road away, so very long ago, who had travelled so far and so well, so that he might travel back, and in the way of things, set out again. For he was going, and he could not really tell why; it was not that he was restless, or drawn like his ancestors by the horizon, or tired of his surroundings, or longing for the places of childhood – this was the place of childhood, far more than the Nebraska farm he could hardly remember, this was the place where the "free-born landholder, not of noble blood" had begun it in the unknown past, and where the generations of yeomen had tilled their land and planted their seed and courted their wives and watched their children grow, and in their time taken the terrible seven-foot staves cut from the hearts of these black twisted trees and gone out to the vineyards of Bordeaux and the passes of Spain in their country's quarrel, and perhaps to Shrewsbury and Barnet and Bannockburn and Halidon Hill, and certainly to Edgehill and Naseby and Marston Moor – and to the long road of the pilgrims, across the western sea to the place which in their homesick longing they had called New England. His people, and in a dim, half-understood way he had felt he was realizing some great hope by coming home again, and now it was over, with the hope unfulfilled, and he could not tell why. He wanted to stay, God knew but he wanted to stay, and yet there seemed to be nothing now to stay for.

Perhaps he had been fooling himself from the start, with some sentimental dream which, after all, was no substitute for life itself. A dream was not a purpose, and a purpose was what he had lacked all along. Happy marriage to Peggy, the raising of a family – these would have supplied it. Even the protection of Bessie Reeve had been a purpose, in its little way, while it had lasted. But for the rest, it had been without a future or a goal – maybe it was his evil luck that he had looked for West Walsham that day, and been deluded by the glimpse he had had of the artificial, useless world which surrounded the King, and which seemed important only because it gave itself importance. He had despised it for the shallow, vicious façade that it was, without values, without honesty, without worth – and yet it had shaped his acceptance of the way of life which he had drifted into with Peggy. He had been as helpless as any fish out of water, knowing nothing in this new old world, and he had been content to drift, and not see that he was drifting; no code or experience from the wild past of Hole-in-the-Wall or Tonopah could have helped him, in an atmosphere as different as that of another planet. In fact, he had been looking for the impossible; it was not his world, and he knew it. He had been a misfit, a pretender, and a fool. He did not belong . . . and yet, as he looked at the old stones in the churchyard, and across the green meadows and hedges and woodland in the evening haze, he knew that he belonged in a sense that went deeper than mere living and walking and sleeping on the surface of the land. If this was not home, the birthplace and the native soil, then there was no home anywhere.

It was difficult enough to bid good-bye even to the inanimate things, it was impossible where people were concerned. Five years in England might have added an ease to Mr Franklin's conversations and a polish to his manner, but it had also awakened in him emotions which he had not suspected, and it had not eroded his natural reserve and taciturnity. He could no more have walked into Mrs Laker's shop to bid his adieus, or into the Apple Tree to say farewell to Jake and Jack Prior, than he could have struck the Queen; his soul shuddered at the thought. He would, once he was away, write brief letters of thanks for friendship and service, but that was another matter; that he owed to his sense of simple courtesy as much as to anything. But say good-bye in the flesh to anyone in Castle Lancing he could not.

The one exception was Thornhill. Perhaps because he had been the first with whom he had conversed on level, easy terms, perhaps because he was the first who had truly welcomed him to the village and made him feel that it was home, perhaps simply because he was Thornhill, the unfailingly kind, eccentric, helpful friend with whom no ceremony had ever been necessary, or would be now, Mr Franklin felt that he was different. With Thornhill there would be no embarrassment, no fuss, no stilted phrases of regret; it would more likely be "Close the door after you, old fellow, and – hold on, pop that letter into Mrs Laker's for me as you go, will you?" It was, as it turned out, something like that.

"You're leaving?" Thornhill turned in surprise from among his welter of books, knocked one over, and upset a cup of forgotten cocoa on his papers. "God damn and blast, what was that doing there? Well," he looked at Mr Franklin over his spectacles, "that was a short stay, wasn't it?"

"It's been five years, almost to the day."

"And what's five years?" Thornhill was looking for a cloth, couldn't find one, used the front of his jersey in a desultory way, and gave up. "In three centuries, my dear chap, it's absolutely damn all. Well, I'm sorry – going anywhere special?"

"States, maybe – or Canada. I'm not sure yet."

"Coming back?"

"I doubt it."

"Well, there it is," said Thornhill. "It'll seem odd without you. Mind you, the damned place has changed so much lately, I don't know whether I'm coming or going myself. Do you know I saw a beastly mechanic the other day, actually filling up the front of his motor lorry with water from the horse-trough? 'Has it come to this, Thornhill?' I asked myself. 'Yes, by God, it has; the Philistines are upon thee,' I added. Disgusting brute. Anyway, I thought the bloody things ran on petrol, or oil, or some filthy chemicals or other. And they call it progress!"

"I feel responsible for that," said Mr Franklin. "If I hadn't sold Lye Cottage to Lacy it would never have happened."

"If it hadn't been for you," said Thornhill, "it would have happened sooner than it did. You saved us for a couple of years from the helots and 'the march of the mind'. Good old Thomas Love Peacock. Let's drink to him – I've got some beer in the sink." And when he had filled two glasses and soaked the front of his trousers and cursed, he said: "To dear old T.L.P., and to your departure, or safe arrival elsewhere, or something. Anyway, although I hate to admit it, the model cottage thing may not turn out at all badly – I thought, Lacy being the swine and bounder that he is, that he'd raze the whole village to the ground and turn it into a factory for producing mechanical dung. In fact, they'll probably be jolly good homes, instead of the hovels some of the poor souls are living in now. And it'll mean more work, I daresay."

"I hope so. I'd like the village to . . . to do well – as well as it's

552

been doing for a few hundred years, anyway." He hesitated. "There's something I want to do, Geoffrey, and I'm not sure how. I'd like to give something to the village. Nothing that anyone would know about, you understand, although it would have to involve money. You know those old parish registers and books and rolls and things – all the documents in the vestry, the records? I want to make sure they're safe, for all time – I want them copied and bound, every darned page, and either the copies or the originals deposited somewhere safe. Maybe if the originals could go to a museum – unless you and the vicar thought it fitting they stay where they've always been, in which case I'd want proper cabinets to store them in at the church – and the copies could go somewhere like your old college at Cambridge . . ."

"Bloody marvellous!" cried Thornhill, and took a deep swig at his beer. "Now that is common sense. Yes – yes, most decidedly, that is an excellent idea!"

"You'd have to oversee the whole thing, of course. No one else could do it. But I'd leave money for all expenses, with the bank in Thetford – I guess maybe a thousand pounds would cover it, and anything over could be used for the church fabric, and the graves, and so on – "

"Don't give money to me, for God's sake!" cried Thornhill in genuine alarm. "I'd lose it, or throw it out with the rubbish, or have a sudden mad fit and put it on a horse for the Grand National! Do you know," he added meditatively, "I've never backed a horse in my life, or even seen a race? Strange . . ."

"I'll leave it with the bank manager, and you can just send him the bills for copying and printing and the rest of it," Mr Franklin promised him, and once reassured Thornhill waxed enthusiastic, and gloated at the thought of researches catalogued and indexed and published, and all neatly stored and preserved. Mr Franklin mentally decided to make it two thousand, and after a little more talk stood up to take his leave.

"Thanks for everything," he said, as they shook hands. "For old Matthew and Jezebel, as well as myself."

"My dear chap! It's I who thank you! What a splendid idea! Yes, the old college would be the place for the copy, I think, and the originals here . . . properly bound and impregnated against death-watch beetle and careless louts like me. I'll see it done, don't you fret. And you'll drop us a line, to let me know where you are, and how you're faring? Excellent! You're not saying good-bye in the village? Quite, quite, I'll let the vicar and curate know that you'll be writing to them; in the meantime I'll hint that you've decamped with a gypsy woman to Barbados, or somewhere. Mind how you go, now . . ."

Mr Franklin walked quickly down the little path, and into the lane, and was almost out of sight when Thornhill's window crashed open and his bald head and spectacles appeared.

"And a copy to the Library of Congress!" he roared, waving, and then Mr Franklin was round the corner.

It was now late August, and while he had been much occupied with his own affairs, Mr Franklin had been following closely the news of the war which dominated the papers collected from Mrs Laker's each lunchtime. Even the illustrated journals were heavy with photographs and artists" impressions from France – British and French troops fraternising self-consciously outside estaminets, a Lowland regiment landing in France, German military police patrolling the streets of Liege with mastiffs on leads, diagrams showing how the blast of zeppelin bombs could be expected to spread, and how to reinforce houses against it, sketches of refugees with handcarts and farm animals crowding the roads of Belgium, photographs of the correct way to wind bandages or adjust splints – even the women's pages carried "war fashions" and the "military look".

The hard news was not good. Everywhere the Germans seemed to be making headway. They had taken Liege on August the tenth and Brussels by the twentieth; "gallant little Belgium" was beyond protection if not beyond rescue – and Mr Franklin remembered with misgivings Sir Harry's prediction. On the day that he said good-bye to Thornhill, news came in of a decisive German victory in the east, where the Russians were beaten at Tannenberg, and an ominous name was beginning to occupy the headlines from the Western Front – Mons. Then the Germans were over the Meuse, taking Lille and threatening Amiens, the French and British were falling back after heavy fighting at Namur, and Lord Kitchener was predicting a war that would last three years at least. Mr Franklin put aside the papers, and turned to his desk to perform the task that he had been shirking for a fortnight, the writing of a letter to Peggy.

It was easier than he had expected. Following the precedent that she had set, he said he would not be coming to Scotland for the grouse-shooting, and added that he was leaving England. He was instructing his lawyers and bankers, and ensuring that ample funds

554

were left whose interest would not only maintain her (he did not say "in the style to which you are accustomed," although that was what he meant) but also their establishment in Wilton Crescent, which was on an annual rent, and at Castle Lancing, which would remain in his name for the time being, although she would have its use. There was a capital sum which would cover the development at Oxton Hall, which he assumed would be showing a profit in a few years anyway, if it continued to be competently handled. In short, neither she nor Sir Charles would notice any difference financially.

Mr Franklin laid down his pen and read over what he had written. What he was doing, in effect, was simply getting up and going, leaving behind the three-quarters of his fortune whose interest would be necessary to keep up those things to which he had committed himself in England – those things which depended on him, even though he was leaving them and would not see them again. Provision for Peggy, for her father, for the houses and the land. He had no heart for accountings or settlements; he was leaving what was needful to maintain things as they were; what remained, including the bulk of the fifty thousand in Mr Evans's safe deposit, he would transfer back to the United States in due course. It was more than enough for him; he wanted as little trouble as could be in making his break with England, which was one reason why he had not yet put Lancing Manor on the market; another reason, he admitted to himself, was that he still found it hard to bear the thought of parting from it.

He picked up his pen again, and sat for a good two hours staring at the paper while he considered how to phrase the last sentence – something that would be good-bye without saying good-bye. In the end he simply wrote: "Take care. All my love. Mark." He read it through, sealed it in an envelope addressed to her, and put it in his pocket to leave at Wilton Crescent before he sailed. Eventually he would write also to Sir Charles, but that would be a more difficult letter, only to be composed at careful leisure.

There remained Samson, to whose future he had already devoted some thought, and whom he summoned to his study on the last day of that fateful August, the day on which the news arrived of the fall of Amiens, and of the German preparations for an assault across a river of which few in England had ever heard – the Marne. Mr Franklin folded up his paper and stood before the fireplace.

"I'm leaving England, Thomas," he said. "Going away for good. To the United States, at first, I think – after that, I'm not sure. I'm sorry I haven't been able to give you more advance warning, but that won't make any difference to your situation." He paused, watching the square figure and the steady, expressionless face. Finally Samson spoke, and his words, to Mr Franklin, were about what he had expected.

"I'm sorry to hear that, sir. When will you be going?"

"To London, in the next couple of days – as soon as we can get cleared up here. I'd like you to pack up all my clothing here, and then go ahead to Wilton Crescent and do the same there. A couple of trunks should do it, and you can send them up to Liverpool by rail for the *Aquitania* – I'll catch her week-end sailing. I'll follow you up to town, and go north myself on Friday."

"I see, sir." Samson considered this, and then asked: "Will Mrs Franklin be meeting you at Liverpool, sir?"

"No, Thomas. I'll be going alone."

"Very good, sir." Samson's face reflected no more concern than if he had been told that Mrs Franklin would not be going to the theatre that evening. "And do you wish me to accompany you?"

It was said in precisely the same tone of polite inquiry as his previous questions, and it took Mr Franklin by surprise. But he replied evenly:

"No, thank you, Thomas. As I said, I'll be going on my own."

Samson nodded. "Very good, sir. I take it you have not yet reserved a berth on the ship, sir? Then I shall telegraph this afternoon; perhaps I had better reserve a compartment on the train also, and a room at the Adelphi on Friday night. With the war, the trains tend to be rather crowded. I shall start packing now, sir."

"Thank you, Thomas," said Mr Franklin, and so accustomed was he to their normal formality that the servant was half-way to the door before the unreality of the situation came home to him.

"What the hell!" exclaimed Mr Franklin. "Dammit, Thomas, where are you going? Hold on – there are things I want to tell you . . ." Samson stopped, and Mr Franklin stared at him helplessly for a moment and then said: "Don't stand there looking like . . . like a valet. Sit down, for God's sake!"

Samson said nothing, but obediently sat on the nearest chair, and waited.

"Tell you the truth," confessed Mr Franklin, "I don't quite know what I have to tell you – except that I'm going, and that means – well, it means that I shan't need . . . but Mrs Franklin will be delighted to

556

have you stay on at Wilton Crescent, I'm certain of that – if you wish it." He was by no means sure that either Peggy or Samson would want it, but he had to make the offer.

"I think not, sir, thank you," said Samson quietly. "May I ask, sir, if your departure has anything to do with the discovery of the man Curry's body?"

"No, not a thing – not in any way that affects the police. We're clear there, as I told you. No, I'm just . . . going. That's all. And whether you stay at Wilton Crescent or not, I'm writing to Mr Pride – I'll give you a copy of the letter, and you'll see it's the most glowing testimonial anyone could wish for." He hesitated. "At that, it can't say a tenth of the things I want to say, or express the . . . the gratitude and sense of obligation I feel for you. Nothing can ever do that."

He stopped, not in embarrassment, but because he had said what he wanted, and he knew that with Samson there was no need to say more.

"That's very kind of you, sir," said Samson. "The feeling is entirely mutual, I assure you. I have enjoyed the last five years more than any I've spent in service; I'm just sorry it has to end."

"So am I."

After a moment Samson said: "However, it is not entirely unexpected, sir. I have been wondering in the past few weeks if you were contemplating a return to the United States. What with that, and the war, I have been thinking about my own position – "

"You don't miss a damned thing, do you?" Mr Franklin smiled and shook his head. "What have you been thinking?"

"That, with the war, I might return to the services, sir."

"The Army?" Mr Franklin looked doubtful. "Will they take you back? I mean . . ." he hesitated tactfully. "Isn't there an age difficulty? Would they –?"

"Not in the regular forces, sir, no. But I had a letter only last week, sir – from an old friend from Africa. A gentleman called Selous – we were in Mashonaland together, sir, and the Matabele war. He's over sixty, but he tells me he has approached the authorities – he's rather well-thought of in official circles, you see – suggesting that they might consider forming a corps of older men, sir, who wouldn't be acceptable for the Army, but might be of some use in the field by virtue of . . . of experience. He was kind enough to think of me, I'm just fifty-five, you see, and the kind of person he's looking for."

Mr Franklin was intrigued. "What's his idea, exactly?"

557

"Well, sir, he's an elephant hunter to trade – what they call a white hunter. In fact, he's the best. I imagine you know a book called *King Solomon's Mines*, sir?"

"Sure. By Rider Haggard."

"Yes, sir. Well, Mr Selous *is* Allan Quartermain – Mr Haggard based that character on him. He's the best shot and scout in Africa, I should think. And his notion is that when the campaign begins between ourselves in Kenya and the enemy in German East, it might be useful to have an irregular force of people who know the country and are used to roughing it – the Legion of Frontiersmen, he's thinking of calling it. He thought it might suit someone like me – and he's written to some other friends, hunters mostly. One or two people from your own country, as well – former Rough Riders, and that sort of person. He thinks we might cause the Germans some embarrassment, sir."

"Embarrassment," said Mr Franklin. "I see." Recalling the embarrassment of Kid Curry, he considered the potential of a group of veterans like Samson, ex-service for the most part, versed in the ways of bush and frontier, too old for regular military duty, but infinitely wise in the arts of living off hard country, trekking, foraging, scouting, back-tracking and dry-gulching, irregular adventurers and soldiers of fortune who knew the wild ways of the earth – the Empire must be full of them, eager for one last fling on the frontiers of danger, one last chance of active service. How Cassidy would have jumped at it . . . for that matter Mr Selous could have enlisted the whole Wild Bunch, with mutual satisfaction and no questions asked. Yes, he thought, such a Legion might very probably embarrass the Germans.

"So I think I shall accept his invitation, sir," said Samson.

"Well, I wish you luck," said Mr Franklin. "And I think Selous can count himself a very fortunate man to get you. I'm sure he does, too. However, the war'll be over one of these days, so I'll send my letter to Mr Pride just the same."

"Thank you very much, sir."

"There's another thing." Mr Franklin paused. "You may object to this, but frankly, Thomas, I don't care whether you do or not. There's an account in your name at Drummond's Bank, with five thousand – "

"That's quite unnecessary, sir."

"– with five thousand pounds in it, whether you want it or not. And it would be there," Mr Franklin added, "even if the events which took place out on that staircase at Christmas five years ago had never happened. I want you to understand that, and I don't want any protests or discussion. The money's there, and it'll stay there. It's the only tangible way I can express my appreciation for years of help and friendship. So I don't want to hear any more about it. Now," he said briskly, making for his desk, "you'd better start the packing. Thank you, Thomas."

However, it occurred to Mr Franklin two days later, when Samson was leaving to catch the train at Thetford with the bulk of his master's luggage, that there was another gift which might, in the not-too-distant future, prove infinitely more useful than money. The trunks had gone out to the carrier's cart, and Samson, bowler-hatted and with his coat over his arm, was crossing the hall when Mr Franklin called him into the study again.

"I don't know what kind of hardware the Legion of Frontiersmen are going to carry, but something tells me this won't be out of place." He opened his desk drawer and brought out one of the Remingtons, with a box of cartridges, and held it out.

Samson for once was taken aback. "I couldn't take that, sir – it would never do to break the pair. And they were your father's, weren't they?"

"He'd be glad for you to have one of them. I know that," said Mr Franklin. "I'd like to keep the other, though."

"Well," said Samson, and hesitated again, and then he took the Remington, and weighed it thoughtfully in his hand.

"That was quite a night, wasn't it" said Mr Franklin quietly.

"Yes," said Samson. "It was."

"There's twenty rounds in the packet – but you'll be able to get others easily enough."

"Yes, sir, I expect so." Samson looked at him. "I appreciate this, sir, very much indeed. It's a beautiful weapon."

"For somebody who knows how to use it." He watched while Samson stowed the Remington carefully in his attaché case. "Oh, and put this with it." He handed Samson a letter. "It's a copy of what I've written to Mr Pride – you'll probably just get plain embarrassed reading it – professional excellence, trustworthiness, loyalty . . . all the usual things, but they happen to be true. I'd like to be able to add a post-script stating that '. . . in addition to carrying out his duties to complete satisfaction, the bearer also went up against Kid Curry in the dark, gun against gun, and came out on his feet.'" One or two of

559

your future employers might appreciate it, but then again, it might fall into the wrong hands."

Mr Franklin himself travelled up the following day, having packed his few remaining personal effects. He stood for a few moments in the hall, glancing round; all the furniture, the rugs, the curtains, the pictures, were his own additions, bought since he came to England – the only thing out of place was the big *charro* saddle, mounted on its stand in a corner. He looked at it for a moment and then thought, let it stay, and went out and locked the door for the last time. The horse and trap were in the drive, and he wheeled out of the gates beneath the beeches and chestnuts and drove up the road without a backward glance.

It was as he was bowling through the village that he suddenly remembered something and drew up outside the Apple Tree and went in. There were a few of the locals enjoying a liquid lunch, and Mr Herbert was on duty at the bar, under the horse brasses.

"I just remembered, I forgot to turn off the stop-cock," said Mr Franklin. "Would you mind asking Jake to attend to it? Thanks." Normally, on such an occasion, he would have left a half-crown to be passed to to his aged retainer, but not this time; Jake, like all the others who had rendered services during his time in Castle Lancing, would receive an unexpected honorarium in due course, via Mr Franklin's lawyer in Thetford. He was turning away when he almost bumped into a young man coming into the pub – a stalwart youth in new khaki, whose face was familiar. Mr Franklin halted.

"Why, Tommy Marsh!" He started in surprise, while the soldier grinned broadly. "What on earth – you're never in the Army!"

He had seen the boy very occasionally over the years; presumably he had been working farther afield, and Mr Franklin had barely noticed the gradual change from the cheeky urchin who had drawn attention to his deplorably unarmed condition that first night in Castle Lancing.

"You can't be old enough!" he exclaimed.

"I am, though," said Tommy. "I'm eighteen – bin in the Terriers this last year, nigh on. I'm goin' into camp tomorrow."

"Well, I'm blessed!" Mr Franklin shook his head, smiling. "Well, you look swell, Tommy. What does your mother say?"

"Ah, she don't mind," said the boy. "It's the old man I got to worry about – 'e wants to know why I ain't joinin' the Navy, like 'e did. Yeah – so I says: 'Look, gaffer, my territorial battalion's a Norfolk

560

Regiment battalion, an' the Norfolks was the first marines in the ole days, an' that's as close to the Navy as any respectable man wants to get, ain't it?' " Tommy laughed, and the locals grinned, and Mr Franklin demanded a pint of Mr Herbert's best for the recruit. He hesitated at a further thought that crossed his mind, and then decided, the blazes with it, and extracted a five-pound note from his wallet.

"You keep that by you, Tommy – for when rations are short or you need something warm," he said, and Tommy beamed widely and nodded.

"Say, thanks," he said, as they shook hands. "Thanks very much, squire." It was the use of the last word that assured Mr Franklin that he had done the right thing; well, there'd be another squire in Castle Lancing presently, once he had got well away and could order his lawyer to dispose of the Manor without his personally having to go through the painful rigmarole of estate agents and prospective buyers. Unless Peggy wanted it kept on, which wasn't likely. And when the time came, and he gave the word, and alien inhabitants moved in, he would not know who they were, or what they were doing to the old house. It would be better so.

He arrived in London in the late afternoon to find that Samson had everything in readiness for the next day's journey to Liverpool; a stateroom had been reserved on the *Aquitania*, a room at the Adelphi, and a first-class single on the afternoon train. His effects had gone ahead, variously labelled wanted on voyage or otherwise, and a large suitcase would serve until he got on board. All was arranged; his tickets were on his bedside table. In the meantime he had an evening ahead of him, and it seemed only appropriate to have a last look at London.

And yet he hesitated. Now that the decision was well taken, and he was calm and quiet in his mind, not unduly depressed, but merely subdued, he had no desire to go out into all the bustle and noise and glitter and activity. It would only remind him of things he would rather forget, things that were going to be put behind him now; he would be sure to compare it with the first breath-taking exciting night, when the taxi-driver had driven him to the Embankment, and he had been engulfed in the wonder of the enchanted city – and Lady Helen had slapped his face outside the Waldorf. And then on the next night there had been the theatre, and his chance encounter with Pip in that grimy alley by the stage-door, and the wilting bunch of flowers in his hand, and her blonde curls glinting under the lamp, and that mischievous inviting smile, and then the dazzling luxury of Monico's and . . . the rest of it.

It had all been so fresh and new and inviting then, and he had still been dreaming, in his quiet way. It would be different now. He had turned over in his mind the idea of seeing Pip again – perhaps getting a seat for *Pip, Squeak!* and calling round on her afterwards, but that would have been too much like playing the gramophone record backwards, and he knew it would just have meant discussing his departure, and the reasons for it, and Pip was far too shrewd not to have linked herself with his break-up with Peggy . . . no, it would not have done. So he had a quiet dinner at home, and sat up and read *Beasts and Superbeasts* – it was at least funny, which made it a welcome change from *Dubliners*, and yet after a few stories he realized that it was somehow uncomfortably close to home. Saki's images of the England that he knew all too well, and which were delighting and convulsing polite society that month were such a brilliantly accurate reflection of part of his own experience, of all that he had found to dislike and despise, of the very things that he felt had betrayed his own vague hopes, that he had to close the book and lay it aside.

It was all in there – all the affectation, and snobbery, and brittle emptiness, all the cruelty and shallowness and false values, dissected by a master surgeon who inspected it idly, turned it over contemptuously, and then discarded it with the flick of an epigram. Peggy seemed to be on every page – clever, unscrupulous, beautiful, selfish, and heartless. She could have doubled for any one of the author's sophisticated little bitches; the young men who inhabited her circle were so many Clovises; their amusements, their pursuits, their arrogant, self-satisfied, callous manners, even the smart cross-talk in which they conversed, or put the upstart or the underling in his place, seemed to echo so much that he heard in the dining- and drawing-rooms of the West End. He had to admire the skill with which Saki could hold them up to themselves and make them like it – he wondered idly what such a writer could be like, and decided he was probably the complete opposite of the things he described; for one thing, he'd be a deal too intelligent to resemble the people he used as his models.

And after all, they were only stories, written for fun, and if they touched raw nerves in him that was his own fault and his own bad luck. And that was only a part, a very small part, of England, like the charmed vicious circle he had seen round King Edward. There was

562

another England, too, the England of those three men he had heard talking in the Fleet Street pub, good-humoured and basically decent and ordinary, or the England of Pip, with its vulgar earthy honesty and cheerful vitality, or the England of Thornhill and Jake and Jack Prior and Tommy Marsh, that he had grown truly to love, and that he felt he had become a part of – perhaps had always been a part of – in his own way.

He caught the Liverpool train from Euston the following afternoon. He had simply shaken hands with Samson and said good-bye, and been whirled away in his taxi through Mayfair and across Oxford Street, to a station that was thronged with troops in khaki, fresh-faced young men in peaked caps and boots and tightly-wrapped puttees, with haversacks slung on their hips, rolled blankets over their big packs, and snub-nosed rifles in their hands. They waited cheerfully in raucous groups, cigarettes pasted on to their lips, chaffing the girls and yelling their catch-phrases; the civilians smiled indulgently as they hurried past to their trains, harassed sergeants strode to and fro in an endless quest for missing men, or their superior officers, or orders about what to do next, or information, and ended up blaspheming at station officials, or fate, or the misfortunes of war, while their insolent charges cried encouragement. Mr Franklin passed by a news bill proclaiming: "French Government Leaves Paris", and found his first-class carriage; a porter heaved his bag on to the rack, three other gentlemen glanced up with the vaguely hostile silence of the British railway traveller, and returned to their newspapers, and Mr Franklin took his corner seat. He was thankful that Samson had managed to book him a place (facing the engine, trust Samson), for the platform had been a mass of troops and travellers struggling for seats in the second and third class compartments.

Two of the gentlemen in the compartment evidently knew each other intimately, since they exchanged several sentences in the fifteen minutes before the train departed.

"I see the Germans have crossed the Marne," said one, and there was a long pause before his companion replied: "According to this report, they'll be in Rheims by tomorrow." Silence fell again, and Mr Franklin studied the steam hissing up past the carriage window. Then the first man observed:

"The Russians have changed the name of St Petersburg to Petrograd."

"What for?"

563

"Doesn't say. Possibly in the hope that the Germans will mistake it for somewhere else." They both laughed, and the second one said:

"Be interesting to see if the French decide to change the name of Paris. I must say it seems to me the height of irresponsibility to move the government to Bordeaux – damn it, they couldn't have gone any farther without being in the sea."

"Best place for 'em," said the first.

"Doesn't display much confidence on their part, anyway," said the other. "It's tantamount to admitting that they expect the Germans to take Paris in the next few weeks – the very sort of scuttle that could easily breed panic."

"Well, thank God we've got the Navy. By the way we're being pushed back from Mons, we're going to need it."

On this comforting thought they relapsed into silence, and presently the train started off, chugging north through the endless grey buildings and warehouses and serried rows of grimy roofs. Mr Franklin looked out at them with unseeing eyes, while the wheels thundered their metallic rhythm, and occasionally a paper rustled in the compartment. He was lost in thought as the train rattled on, and the city gave way to the countryside, with its flat green meadows and hedgerows and occasional woodland; he did not notice the names of the stations as they sped by, for his eyes and ears were elsewhere, looking and listening at the memories of five long years.

"You want to go down there, sir? Paradise Street? Take us oot o' the road to the Adelphi, like." The Liverpool cabby, his face astonished and disappointed, at this fare who wasn't interested in where Mr Gladstone had been born . . .

". . . if anyone had suggested to me that an American polo team could come over here and open our eyes to the game, well . . ." The white-whiskered old buffer in the train south. "Give me a call if you feel like a week-end's shooting. The Turf Club . . ."

". . . a copy of the Englishwoman. *Will you please buy it and support the cause of women's rights?" Those splendid hazel eyes in the long handsome face with its generous mouth and imperious nose. "Now, then, miss, please to move along, you're annoying this gentleman . . ."*

"Plain grey in spats, I think . . . I'll look back in a couple of hours . . . very passable, sir." Samson's face reflected in the glass. "I've known frauds, sir, and gentlemen . . . I've even known some Americans . . . will there be anything else, sir . . . ?"

"Have you got five quid? You're sure – 'cos if you're not, we could go dutch – that's fifty-fifty." Pip's face, pretty and earnest, with the slight squint in the happy blue eyes. "I'm sorry . . . I'm dead common, aren't I?" The splendid milk-white body soft in his hands, the red lips pursing impudently at him. "Go and bolt the door. I want to enjoy myself . . . Goodnight, Mr American . . . Boiled beef and carrots . . ."

"Good God! You've come back . . . after all these generations . . . Look – Johannes Franklinus . . ." The thin lettering in the flickering matchlight . . . "Welcome home . . ."

"Break the dam' thing open!" . . . "Come on, Jarvie!" . . . "Please sir, may we have our fox back?" The angel face, the red mouth touched with that mocking little smile. ". . . this is the King's Highway, I reckon . . ."

Mrs Keppel's perfume, her jewelled wrist on the table, Soveral's veiled eyes, the bearded pouchy face opposite him. "Very good, partner. Let us go, indeed. I trust I have . . . ah, spread them to your satisfaction." "Double six hearts." "Redouble" . . . green eyes smiling, hesitant . . . the ace of diamonds going down . . .

"You like land, Mr Franklin?" "We call it country . . ."

"What are you doing?" "Well, I'm living here . . ."

". . . we're not one of the invitations you're determined to refuse . . . ?" The soft lips opening beneath his own, the half-closed eyes. "Don't do that too often, or you'll find yourself married before you know it . . ."

"Ar, my name wor Franklin." The old, wrinkled face, and the skinny claw-like hand in his. "You're . . . Franklin?" The earth on the coffin, Jack Prior's handshake crushing his fingers, the steady grey eyes in the broad weathered face. Bessie Reeve Franklin. The rain on the wet green grass in Castle Lancing churchyard.

"So that you could flirt over the teacups, perhaps? It would be a waste of time." The chilly smile . . . : "The stuffed dates are delicious . . ." Churchill's cheerful grin: "America and England – it's the hope of the world; the only hope . . ."

"This year you'll make your first snowman . . ." The glowing warmth of the fire in the darkened room, and Peggy in his arms, her head cradled beneath his chin . . . the perfume of her in his bed, the sleepy lust in her eyes. "We could go on doing this forever . . ." The passionate body against his beneath the mosquito net under the Caribbean night sky.

"Lichfield! Change for Birmingham, Nottingham, and Derby! Lichfield!" The cry of the porter roused him; another platform crowded with people, and again the inevitable khaki figures among them; feet shuffling in the corridor, a carriage door slamming, and the shrill whistle, the swirl of steam, and they were gliding on again. One of the passengers yawned and folded his hands across his ample stomach, closing his eyes; Mr Franklin sat in his corner and watched the telegraph posts flying past.

"... hope I don't intrude. My name's Logan. I understand there's a Mr Franklin staying..." The bright dark eyes, the tea cakes and scones disappearing under the straggling moustache. "You're fixed kind of pretty here, Mark... I want exactly one half of everything you've got... you've got nothing when you're dead..."

"I'm certainly not leaving you on your own, sir. If you wish to give me notice, that's another matter... Perhaps if I was to prepare some sandwiches – there is some rather good roast ham..." The wind sighing outside the house, movement by the hedge in the distant moonlight, the soft-footed walk to his bedroom door, working his numb hand, opening the door – then the wild glaring eyes, the booming crash of shots, the little twisted figure soaked in blood... "You were right, sir, he's quick." The hiss of falling rain, the mud sucking at his feet, the blanket-wrapped bundle thumping into the grave, the pale dawn over Lye Thicket.

"Am I right in thinking that Peggy has shown no strong inclination for a family?" Sir Charles's keen, thin face turned towards him. "If I've an ambition, it's to lead a grandson's first pony along the bridle-path yonder..."

"... among those enjoying the ice at Murren... Lord Lacy of Gower Castle, Norfolk..."

"And you're a settled married man? Why, you sly Yankee, you!" Pip strutting and swaying across the stage at the Lotus Club. "See that ragtime couple over there? Watch them throw their shoulders in the air..." The tip of her tongue, hard and polished from the sweatshop. "Hasn't England been the way you thought it would be...?... Good-night, Mr American..."

"He was going to resign! Mark, if he hasn't – something must have happened... oh, but there must be some good reason for it!" Peggy's hands twisting, her eyes pleading with him not to ask...

"The report says that the ship sailed from Hamburg..." Then the ice-cold, beautiful face in the twilight. "I'm sorry about it, Mark... I was out to deceive and swindle, remember...?" "... Shall we play? We might as well."

Shattered canvas at the Royal Academy, and a frail little woman sobbing

566

with her beret askew . . . "Did she not attempt to strike you with the parasol?
Did Shore attempt to strike Miss Delys with the hatchet?" . . . "You will
go to prison for three years . . ." Lady Helen white and furious in the dock.
"No! No! I will not accept this!" . . . and her voice suddenly gentle in the
cab, as the old man snored in the corner. ". . . he asked one of the Marines
to give him his hat – 'That'll do better than a medal.' We're very proud of
him, of course . . . absolutely selfish and dishonest and quite shameless . . ."

He must have been dozing; a hand was tugging gently at his sleeve;
one of the other passengers was leaning towards him. ". . . I was
just asking if you had any objection to these soldiers sharing our
compartment? The rest of the train is full, you see."

The door to the corridor was open, and Mr Franklin saw the khaki
tunics, the diced glengarry caps, the dark tartan of the kilts. One of
the soldiers had his arm in a sling; the other, his foot swathed in
bandages, was leaning on a crutch. At once he understood – they
must be wounded from France, and with the train packed to the
seams his companions had obviously invited them in; the sanctity of
first class could go by the board for the nation's heroes.

"You don't mind?" the man was asking.

"Good heavens, no! Certainly not." Mr Franklin hastened to make
room, and the two soldiers were helped in and seated, grinning
bashfully. "Och, ta verra much, sir. Ye're a toff, so ye are." The man
with the crutch, small, sharp-faced, and wiry, sank down gratefully
beside Mr Franklin. His companion, large and sandy-haired, with a
huge barrel chest and massive red knees beneath his kilt, sat opposite,
bringing with him a strong odour of antiseptic and damp serge.
"Thank you, shentlemen," he said, and Mr Franklin was astonished
at the soft, almost effeminate cadence of the voice issuing from that
rugged presence.

"Are you quite comfortable?" inquired the big man's neighbour, a
round-faced businessman, and the little soldier echoed the question:
"Ye a'right, big fellah?" The large Highlander nodded and said:
"She's fine, thank you kindly."

As the train pulled out the round-faced man inquired: "Were you
at Mons?"

"Aye, right enough," said the little soldier. "No' much o' a place.
Sure an' it wisnae, big yin?" The larger soldier nodded and said
nothing.

"Were you wounded there?"

"Naw. Le Cateau." The little man glanced at his foot, and at the passengers, and being a Glaswegian, decided to elaborate. "It wis a shell-burst that Ah stopped – most o' oor casualties wis shell-fire, ye see. Ah never thocht they had that many guns in the Germany Airmy – sure that's right, big fellah?" He chuckled at his friend. "Bastard guns 'a ower the place, so they wis. Sure an' they wis, eh?"

Mr Franklin had heard many Scottish accents in five years in England, but the noise issuing from the small soldier was something new to him – a rapid, slurred guttural croak of which he could make out only a word here and there. From the expressions of the three other passengers he gathered that they were almost equally at a loss; fortunately the large soldier seemed to sense it too, for after a moment he remarked at large, in that mild, accentless voice:

"The Cherman artillery is fery accurate."

"As accurate as ours, do you think?" asked one of the gentleman, and the soldiers looked at one another.

"Ah dae ken aboot that," said the small one, and then grinned cheerfully. "Mind you, Ah hivnae been hit by oor guns, so it's hard tae say." When the laughter had subsided he went on: "But their snipers isnae much good, sure an' they're no", big fellah? Sure they couldnae hit a barn door if they wis inside, hey?"

The large soldier considered this. "I don't know but what you're right," he said. "But their artillery is nott bad. Nott bad at all."

"Were you wounded by artillery?" asked another passenger.

"No." The big soldier paused. "No," he said again.

"How were you wounded, then?"

The big Highlander reflected and then said gently: "It wass a bayonet. Aye. A Cherman put his bayonet in my arm."

"Good heavens!" exclaimed the round-faced man, and there were murmurs of shocked concern. The small soldier cocked a bright eye.

"Tell themm wehre you pit *your* bayonet, big yin." He winked at the passengers. "It's no a sair arm that German's got. Ah'll tell ye. Fact, he's no feelin' any pain at a" – is he, big fellah? Go on – tell them!"

The passengers, intent on gory details, looked expectant, but the big soldier merely thought for a moment and said "Aye." He reminded Mr Franklin of an unusually docile steer; there was the same quiet, ruminative air about him, a heavy delicacy in the way he adjusted the bandage on his slung arm with a hand that looked as though it could have tied knots in a poker. But he was not prepared to talk about himself, evidently, and the passengers turned their questions on the smaller man. How were conditions in the line? Were the rations and comforts adequate? Were the people of France and Belgium friendly to the British Expeditionary Force? How was the morale of the troops? They clearly wanted to ask what prospect there was of the German advance being checked, but hesitated to do so. The Glaswegian was voluble in his answers, his interrogators straining visibly to comprehend, while the big Highlander listened in benevolent silence; once his mild blue eye met the American's, and Mr Franklin wondered if there was just a glimmer of patronising amusement in it – for his garrulous companion, for these eagerly inquiring civilians, for his own situation as an early casualty of the war who could be stared at with something like reverence and ushered into a first-class carriage – it would be different later, the big man might well have been thinking; they're all curiosity and morbid interest now, but they'll have enough of wounded soldiers by and by. And reading that glance, Mr Franklin's thoughts went back to that other soldier who had been in his mind when the train stopped at Crewe.

"He is a quite dreadful person, really." The tears in Lady Helen's eyes . . . "He kept me out of prison. Oh, yes – influence counts for everything . . . Are you faithful to your wife? . . . Would you care to accompany my great-uncle back to Berkeley Square? Or if that is out of your way . . ." The level impersonal glance, the gloved finger-tips touching his . . . "Didn't you want to go to bed with her?" The knowing, evil old face. "You've got gunfighter's eyes . . ."

Gunfighter's eyes . . . the Remingtons on his hips . . . Peggy as Marie Antoinette . . . Pip in glittering silver, the hysterical laughter and strident music of the Savoy . . . and then that hideous car ride home . . . "Pip Delys, our little side-show . . . if I told you I was a goody-goody meek little wife, would you be content with that? . . . I've never asked you questions and I never expected you to ask me any, either . . . I don't mind – and you mustn't mind either . . . you're a jolly good catch . . ."

Crawford's sleepy eyes . . . "A pistol similar to those you're wearing . . . I put it to you that you wilfully shot and murdered Harvey Logan . . ." Peggy's hand slipping into his. "It just doesn't matter . . . I'm the scarlet woman anyway, aren't I? . . . you might have known . . . I won't be a hypocrite and say I'd have married you if you'd been penniless – I'd have made love with you, though, because I like you . . . I've done well out of you . . . I really don't care one way or the other . . . it just doesn't matter . . ."

Well, if it didn't matter to her – then nothing much mattered, not to him. It had been coming apart, gradually, and then that morning it had all fallen to pieces with a vengeance, and he had realized that it had all been a dream with a bad ending. Nothing had seemed quite real since then – even the coming of the war had been more a disquieting distraction than a tragedy; it did not affect him. And it should not – that had been his mistake, five years ago; he had allowed himself to become affected. He who had been self-sufficient, solitary, dependent on no one, had become entrapped, imperceptibly but surely.

There had been so many things to weave their different spells: the bustling, glittering, magic city which had opened its doors to him and his money-belt; the cheerful, sensual, friendly Pip; the romance of antiquity and coming home enhanced by the warmth of England's welcome – not only the spurious friendship of King and court, but the honest kindliness of folk like Thornhill and Jack Prior; the peace of a quiet haven after wild adventuring; the loyalty of a man like Samson which went to the limit and beyond; the growing knowledge of what wealth could mean, and the vaunting feeling of power that went with that knowledge, whether it was exercised in spending hundreds on a diamond necklace, or thousands on fine houses, or just a few pounds to secure Bessie Reeve forever; the curious, exciting attraction of such a woman as Lady Helen, belonging to a world to which he had suddenly found himself able to aspire – even that dreadful old satyr, her great-uncle, had exercised a strange charm of his own, with all his unabashed, even boasted, faults and vices.

But that was true of even the worst that he had found in England; it had still worked its mysterious attraction, so that whatever he had recognised as good or bad, worthy or corrupt, admirable or detestable, had held his imagination still, above all with that abiding atavistic magnetism of earth and air and sky and wood and water, working on him as on some modern Anteas.

Even with Peggy. It was impossible to disentangle his feelings for her from his feelings for England – so much beauty, so much warmth, so much love, so much coldness and cynicism and bitter disappointment. They were as one in his mind, and the disillusioned longing remained, for England and for her. And he was leaving them, a good deal poorer than he had come; he had paid a high rent for a short five years. And he was going probably no wiser; certainly less certain of anything except the knowledge that something of him would always stay.

"Do you expect to be going back to the front?" one of the passengers was asking, and the Glasgow soldier was shaking his head emphatically.

"Nae fears. It'll be a couple o' months afore my foot's better, an' it'll a' be ower by then. It cannae last – it'll be ower by Christmas – that's what they're sayin'. Eh, big yin?"

"The German army," the round-faced man asked carefully. "Is it as . . . ah, powerful . . . as we've been led to believe?"

The Glaswegian shrugged. "Ah dae ken. There's an awfy lot o' them. Sure there is, big fellah? See, at Le Cateau, there was far more o' them than of us, an' they just kept pushing us back, an' back, until the fellahs wis so tired, they couldnae retreat nae mair. Sure an' they couldnae?" He looked to his friend for confirmation. "So we jist had tae stop, becuz we couldnae march nae further. Aye, we stopped in a wood. An' it wis there we stopped the Germans. That's where the big fellah here got his arm wounded. An' Ah caught my shell a wee bit after." He frowned and shook his head. "We lost a lot o' fellahs at Le Cateau."

It was a name that Mr Franklin thought he remembered from the papers, but without details. The public had still to learn about Le Cateau, and how a British Corps, too exhausted to retire farther, had turned in its tracks and with that machine-gun-like rapid rifle fire which was to become a fearsome legend in German memory, had halted attack after attack – as they had done at Mons where, in the words of a German general, his army had been "shot flat" by the aimed volleys of the Lee Enfields. But it was easy enough to envisage the tattered remains in the wood, too tired to retreat, but not too tired to fight until they had recovered the strength to stagger up again on the road from Belgium. The bandages were a reminder of what General Flashman had said – wars were not between coloured blobs on the map, but between people. Suddenly the war was very close, and there was silence in the compartment until the round-faced man burst out angrily:

"It's disgraceful! Why weren't you properly supported? Weren't there any – " he gestured helplessly " – any reinforcements?"

The small soldier laughed uncertainly. "Ah dae ken. Ah didnae see any – sure an' we didnae, big yin?"

"It's damnable!" said the round-faced man angrily. "I don't know what the government's thinking of – or the general staff. Sending in a token force, ill-prepared, just to satisfy the French! Typical mismanagement by the politicians, I don't doubt. What about the French?" he asked. "How are they behaving?" He was plainly ready to believe the worst, but he was disappointed by the inevitable reply.

"Ah dae ken. We didnae see many French; they were nae in oor sector, like. No' many Belgians, either – except the refugees. There wis an awfy lot o' them on the Le Cateau road, tryin' tae get awa' frae the war, poor souls. Sure they wis, big yin?"

The big Highlander broke his silence. "Aye," he said.

"Hellish, yon, though," said the small man. "Auld wives an' bairns, an' wimmen, an' gran'faithers, wi' a' their gear piled on cairts an' barrows and prams – onything at a'. Jist whit they could carry, an' a' fleein' as fast as they could. Ah doot a lot o' them wullnae get far." He shook his bullet head. "Hellish, so it wis."

There was silence for a moment, and then one of the other gentlemen said hesitantly: "Is it true, d'you think, that the Germans have been behaving . . . behaving badly – to civilians, I mean? One hears stories . . ." He looked round doubtfully. "Of course, one can't tell whether they're true or not – "

"I heard they turned the dogs on them in Lille," said the round-faced man fiercely. "Simply turned the dogs on the people – those damned great shepherd dogs. Like wolves. I won't disbelieve it until it's proved otherwise. Did you hear about that?" he demanded of the small soldier, who looked uncertain.

"Och, ye ken whit they say. Ye aye get that sort o' story. Ah dae ken. Whit aboot that, big fellah? Is the Germans bein' hard on the folk?"

Appealed to directly, the large Highlander stirred. "There wass much devass-tation about Le Cateau," he admitted. "Farms and houses burning, and the beasts aall killed. But I don't know about atrocities. I've seen none."

"The reports tell a different story," said the round-faced man grimly. "And we probably don't know the half of it. A man I spoke to the other day had heard of entire villages wiped out, old and young alike – civilians, you understand. And, the women . . ." He drew in his breath. "The rape of Belgium may be a more terribly apt description than we realize. I don't doubt it – the German, the Hun . . ." he added in disgust, "is capable of anything."

"And the advance – the German advance, I mean, is going on?"

One of the others had finally decided to ask the question. "You saw no signs of their being checked?"

The small soldier looked uneasy. "Aye, weel – they were still advancin' – or we were still retreatin', onywye – when the big fellah an' me came oot. Sure an' they wis, big yin?" He looked at the silent Highlander, who nodded.

"Aye, well," said the small man doggedly, "they're sayin' it'll be ower afore the New Year."

There was another silence, and then the round-faced man said ominously: "So we know what France can expect." His silence invited them to picture that country overrun by hordes of bestial Teutons intent on pillage, rape, and destruction.

"Thank God for the Channel," said his friend. "And the Navy."

Mr Franklin remembered the men in the Fleet Street pub; they too had put their faith in the Navy. But now the prospect of war in their own countryside and homes was that much closer, and perhaps they were beginning to ask themselves if all was as secure as they imagined. A British Army – an admittedly small army, it was true – was being driven back, step by step; even the huge French military machine, supposedly the equal of any, seemed powerless to stop the onward sweep of the German advance. Of course, the Navy was a different matter – but if the war went on and on, who knew how the balance of power and chance would turn? Like the men in Fleet Street, they were thinking of German armies in the fields of Kent and Sussex, and pondering the horrid rumours that were seeping out of Belgium as that country was trampled under the jackboots.

Mr Franklin was sceptical about the atrocity stories; he imagined they were inevitable in any war, and that even the slightest irregularity would make ready fuel for propaganda. He could guess the origin of the tale of dogs turned on the helpless inhabitants of Lille – he had seen the sketch in one of the papers of German military police patrolling the city with shepherd dogs on leashes. But there might be something in the rumours, of course – no doubt rapes and murders had taken place in Belgium – and even the sober imaginations in that carriage could conjure up pictures of jackboots in the Strand, and field-grey uniforms and coal-scuttle helmets on guard at the House of Commons. It was impossible to take seriously – and yet that England should suffer the fate which Sir Harry had graphically sketched for Belgium, and which the round-faced man at least believed

573

she was even now undergoing, was not beyond the bounds of possibility.

And plainly his companions in the carriage, from their solemn silence, had less difficulty in envisaging it now than they would have done a few weeks ago. Germans in London . . . strutting through Trafalgar Square, gazing up at Nelson's column, ejecting beefeaters from the Tower, swaggering in the restaurants and bars, commandeering the taxis . . . occupying the boxes at *Pip, Squeak*!, ogling the principal, calling with haughty politeness at Wilton Crescent and demanding billets, establishing command posts in Lady Helen's flat in Curzon Street, rounding up suspected persons, crushing all resistance mercilessly, taking over the administration of the greatest city on earth, imposing their own Prussian rule, invading its society . . . how would Peggy and society – but Peggy and society would be long gone by then, he was fairly sure of that. Unless Peggy decided to take her own independent line, as was always possible. If any woman in England was capable of dying in a ditch, literally fighting for her country, she was. Germans at Oxton? Germans at Castle Lancing? No, it was all too far-fetched – or had they thought that in Lille and Amiens, too?

"Ah, well," said one of the passengers consolingly, "our wars always start with disasters and end with victories, don't they?" He looked round hopefully.

"One of these days," said the round-faced man sternly, "the exception is going to prove that rule. We can't go muddling on forever – especially against people as active and unscrupulous as the Germans."

"Well, their push can't last indefinitely," protested the other. "They're bound to run out of steam. What d'you say, Jock?" He addressed the small soldier. "By Christmas, eh?"

The small soldier shrugged and made one of his curious guttural noises. "Aye, I daresay. Eh, big yin?"

"Well, we all very much hope so," said the optimistic man heartily. "And then you fellows can all get back to your wives and families and . . . and that sort of thing. And if it *is* all over by then, it will be because ordinary chaps like you have been so *extra*ordinary, and – and have done your stuff, so . . . so gallantly." He evidently realized that he was sounding pompous, for he looked round the compartment as though challenging contradiction. "I'm sure we're all very proud of you," he added. "Very proud indeed."

There was a murmur of agreement, and the optimistic passenger, taking encouragement from this, rushed impulsively to destruction.

"And grateful," he announced, looking meaningly at his companions and producing his wallet.

"I'm sure you'll understand the . . . ah, spirit in which we would all like to express our appreciation," he went on, burrowing into his wallet's interior while the round-faced man glared and Mr Franklin felt his toes begin to curl. "I'm sure there must be some comforts which you would like to procure, and I'm equally sure that . . . ah, a shilling day, if that's what it is, doesn't go very far, I mean to say." He looked up beaming, with notes in his hand. "I – that is, we – would be honoured if you would . . ."

His voice trailed off as he saw the expression of the others. The round-faced man was looking thunderous, the third passenger was reaching uncertainly towards his pocket, Mr Franklin was studying the luggage rack, and the little Glasgow man was grinning uneasily. The big Highlander glanced at the hand holding out the bank-notes, and then at the passenger himself.

"I'm thinking," he said gravely, "that you would be better giving it to the Belgians."

The passenger gulped, and went red, and obviously wished that the floor would swallow him and his kind, pathetically misguided, intentions. Then he muttered, "Of course, of course," restored his money to his wallet, picked up his newspaper, glanced at it, glanced at the others, and finally stared miserably out of the window. Mr Franklin felt sorry for him, and deeply embarrassed and apologetic towards the big Highlander. He wasn't so sure about the Glasgow man, who was looking distinctly doleful, and probably thirsty. But it was the big man who was attracting Mr Franklin's interest; to cover the uneasy silence, but also because there was something in the other's quiet, patient attitude that demanded a question, he spoke for the first time.

"Do you think you'll be going back to France?"

The Highlander turned placid eyes on him, considering. Then: "Aye," he said. "Like enough."

The passenger who had offered the money turned suddenly. "Look here," he began, "I didn't – " And then fell silent.

Mr Franklin was still watching the Highlander.

"You don't think it'll be over by Christmas, do you?" he said, and it was more of a statement than a question.

"I don't know," said the Highlander carefully. "It'll be over for some."

575

There was a troop train preparing to leave from an adjoining platform when Mr Franklin descended at Lime Street. A large crowd
had assembled to see it off, pressing forward dangerously close to the
carriages; every window was down, with khaki figures leaning out to
embrace or shake hands with friends and relatives; handkerchiefs
were fluttering, hats waving, eyes being dried, and frantic guards and
porters vainly trying to clear a space down the edge of the platform
as the whistles blew. The troops themselves were singing lustily,
drowning out the last goodbyes.

> And I can no longer stay!
> Hark! I hear the bugles calling,
> Good-bye, Dolly Grey!

The two wounded soldiers were getting off; Mr Franklin helped the
Glasgow man, who was still inexpert in the use of his crutch. A pretty
nurse came forward to take charge of them: "Private McGuigan?
Private Gunn? Here you are, then!" The Glaswegian promptly
attached himself to her arm, beaming gallantly, while the large Highlander nodded shyly, and then they set off up the platform, with the
nurse laughing and talking between them, as the troop train drew
away.

Mr Franklin made his way to the station entrance, carrying his
suitcase; it was too short a distance to the Adelphi to be worth a cab,
and he set off to walk in the gathering dusk. There was another crowd
outside the station, and another regiment swinging down the street,
bound for the trains. They were singing the inevitable "Tipperary";
he watched as they marched by, the lamplight gleaming on the brass
buttons and on the rearing horse insignia in their caps – they were
the darlings of Merseyside, the King's Liverpool going down to the
war.

> Goodbye, Piccadilly!
> Farewell, Leicester Square!
> It's a long, long way to Tipperary,
> But my heart's right there!

They halted with a thunderous crash of ammunition boots at the
station entrance, and to the accompaniment of thunderous bellowing
of orders began to file off to the platforms; the band struck up again,

and the crowd began to sing the regimental march, the jaunty little jingle that the King's had learned in the North American backwoods a hundred and fifty years earlier, when the fame of "The School for Scandal" first crossed the sea.

> Here's to the maiden of bashful fifteen,
> Here's to the widow of fifty,
> Here's to the flaunting, extravagant quean,
> And here's to the housewife that's thrifty.

Mr Franklin watched the flushed, smiling faces beneath the peaked caps as they filed past, and wondered if it would, after all, be over by Christmas. One soldier did not think so – except for some, and that "some" might well include the wounded Highlander himself. Of course, a humble private could hardly be an authority on a question which neither Kitchener nor the Kaiser could have answered – still, he had been there, and they had not, and his words carried a chilling implication. Over for some. Over for how many of the young men going by, and for how many others? Over, perhaps, for Samson and his Legion of eccentric elderly Frontiersmen; over for Tommy Marsh in his new uniform; over for the Cockney in the Fleet Street pub, the Jewish cabby, and the burly labourer; over for the Haymarket drayman and the knut with the spats and cane who had posed self-consciously to be photographed with the star of *Pip, Squeak!* – but then, it was quite possible that they might never be needed, any of them; it might be quickly over after all.

And if it was not – then it might drag on for years and years, with incalculable effects. It might be "over" not only for the men he had been thinking about, but for men who were still boys at this minute, for men who had at present no thought of war. How many more might Pip and her chorus see off for the stout recruiting sergeant? It might yet be that she would see off some man of her own – if not a husband, at least a lover; perhaps more than one. So the war might yet come to Pip in a way she almost certainly did not imagine. As he walked across to the Adelphi a thought struck him – a thought so bizarre that he stopped in his stride. Yet it was entirely possible – probable, even. Lacy might go to the war – what would that mean to Peggy? Would it mean anything at all? Yes, of course it would – if it had been himself, and not Lacy, it would have meant something – for a while, at least. Not something that she couldn't handle, being

577

Peggy, but something just the same. And Lady Helen – there might be someone for her, too; a lover, perhaps, or if the war lasted long enough, maybe a husband.

How would they be, if it did come to them in that way – how would they be when the crowd sang "Tipperary" and *their* men went away, whoever they were? Lady Helen would be calm and outwardly serene, whatever she felt; her man might guess at her feelings, but he would never see them, as she waved good-bye and went off purposefully to do whatever task she had set herself to do.

Pip? She would give her beloved an absolute orgy of herself, burst into tears at the moment of parting, sob for a couple of hours after he had gone, and be on stage bubbling and radiant for the evening performance. And then she would cry herself to sleep.

Peggy? She would be vivacious and laughing, making the parting as carefree as she knew how, full of optimism and gaiety, with perhaps a few tears at the last moment, if it was someone she liked. And afterwards – she would decide that she might as well enjoy herself while the light lasted, and she would have no difficulty in doing it.

All these things might easily happen – if the war lasted, it would come to them all, whether the Germans invaded or not. It would come in a way which even the mighty Royal Navy could not prevent, reaching its dark fingers into every corner of the land – it would come to the castle and the croft, the grimy back street and the upland farm. It would come to Castle Lancing, to Oxton Hall, to Thetford High Street, to Gower Castle. Wherever an eager young man, or a thoughtful young man, or a frightened young man, or a careless young man went away, leaving an emptiness behind – the war would be there, scarring the people and the land with an invisible wound. For, if it lasted, it would not be like other wars – how many Gettysburgs and Shilohs would Europe endure? They might be fought here, too – and the casualties might well be as terrible. No shot in the civil strife of Ireland had been heard in Oxton Hall, but he had seen a victim there, a victim scarred and crippled for what remained of life. So it would be with the new war, and nothing that was English, or of England, could escape it.

It was a different porter at the Adelphi desk, but he was still an Irishman, inevitably.

"The *Aquitania*, sir? Yes, indeed – Mr Franklin, is it?" The porter consulted his embarkation list. "Ah, yes – Cabin 43. I have the receipts for your baggage here, sir – the trunks themselves are in the

Customs shed. Sailing at ten o'clock, sir, boarding not later than nine-thirty. Indeed, I shall have you called in good time, Mr Franklin. Eight o'clock – early morning coffee and *The Times*. Very good, sir. Boy – show Mr Franklin to 212."

It was a room identical, so far as he could remember, with the one he had occupied five years ago – five years almost to the night. He stood looking about him, remembering how it had been then, how last thing before going to bed he had checked through his trunk – the trunk that was lying with its hinge now broken beyond repair, in some cupboard at Wilton Crescent. His new trunks, much better articles, were down at the Customs shed, and the contents of that old trunk were dispersed among them – the hat, the boots (but without spurs), the books, Shakespeare and the rest, the slicker, the old tin cup. Everything but the saddle, which at this moment would be standing in the silent shadows of Lancing Manor. And the remaining Remington in his suitcase.

Idly he opened the case and lifted out the top articles, until he came to the gun underneath. It sat in his hand, silver, immaculate, as it had done five years ago. He spun the cylinder, checked that it was empty, and put the revolver back carefully in the case. That was what he had done five years ago, the night he came to England, never guessing that a day would come when he would do exactly the same thing over again, only this time he would be going away.

Strange, how he had retraced his steps, perhaps to the very room. Then, he had spent part of the evening studying maps, looking eagerly for the names of places he had yet to see – conjuring them up, imagining them. He couldn't remember his visions, because now he knew the real thing, knew it so well that he could close his eyes and see every detail of it again. And it was all behind him, and tomorrow he would say goodbye to Paradise Street, and a chapter of his life would be over. The English chapter. He could ask himself if it had been worth while – in financial terms, it certainly had not, he thought ruefully; in other terms, he had no idea. It was not a question of worth while, anyway; it had happened, and it had ended.

He undressed slowly, like a man who is very tired, and climbed into bed. For a few moments he lay, staring up at the ceiling, the grey eyes far away, and then he was asleep in Liverpool again.

579

27

Superintendent Griffin came down to the landing-stage on that wet September Saturday to see the *Aquitania* sail. It was no longer part of his job; since his promotion a year ago, the business of being on hand for the berthing and leaving of the great liners had passed to his subordinates, Inspector Welland, Sergeant Murphy, and others. For them to run the expert eyes of the detective department over the arriving and departing passengers, to check the lists for any names that might have been brought to their attention by the police of Halifax or New York, to watch for the odd cases, the suspicious signs, the luggage or clothing or expression that might be out of the ordinary, to scan the faces in the queues at the Customs tables or the gangplank, but for the most part simply to be on hand, while Superintendent Griffin sat at his office desk and thanked God for the warm coal fire at his back.

But this morning he had descended from Olympus. Welland had influenza, and Murphy had gone two weeks ago to join his regiment. And, he admitted, as he paced the quay in his greatcoat, slapping his gloved hands together and keeping under the shelter of the shed, it was not unpleasant to be back in his old manor again, listening to the gulls scream as they wheeled above the dirty yellow water, watching the tugs chuffing by, turning to cast an eye at the orderly bustle of the sheds, or gazing up at the towering iron side of the great ship at the quay – she was, Griffin had to allow grudgingly, a beauty; he was something of a *Mauretania* loyalist, but when he had gone over the new ship in the summer, on the eve of her maiden voyage, he had had to acknowledge that the *Aquitania*, with her lofty lounges and spacious cabins and magnificent stairways, was the nearest thing to a floating palace he had ever seen.

Even Murphy had admired her – Murphy, who affected to despise any means of locomotion that was not aerial. He wondered if Murphy would realize his ambition of flying in the war; he had enthused to Griffin about the lethal possibilities of aeroplanes in a way which had made the Superintendent shudder. As if flying in peacetime wasn't offence enough to providence, Murphy had waxed rhapsodic about preposterous and ghastly schemes for raining high explosives on hostile cities, and machines that would carry riflemen to pour down fire on enemy troops. Bloody horrible, Griffin had told him, and Murphy had said, never mind, he would see. Well, no doubt he would; Superintendent Griffin, as staunch a conservative as even a police officer can be, had no illusions about so-called scientific progress. The war would accelerate the production of murderous machinery, and no doubt bring forth all sorts of new devil's devices for the slaughter of mankind, and it went without saying that some of them would be airborne. He only hoped that Murphy would come through it safely – not just because he had a deep affection for the lad, although that was the main reason, but because he had shaped into a first-class police officer whom the force could ill spare. Well worth his sergeant's stripes. Make inspector one of these days, if absence at this damned war didn't cost him too much seniority.

It was typical of fate's irony, mused the Superintendent, that a fine young fellow like Murphy, with his pretty little wife and chubby six-month-old son, an honest, hard-working pillar of the community doing a valuable job, should be off to the Army, risking his life in a senseless bicker between stupid, selfish and incompetent statesmen, while the criminal scum of Merseyside were left all that much freer by his absence to batten on the public. If Lloyd Griffin were running things, there would be a regulation positively forbidding police officers to enlist, and a conscription law to sweep into the forces every rascal who had anything above a misdemeanour on his record. Let the jailbirds fill a pit in France; let them practise their villainies on the Germans – why, the Germans might do the same thing, to everyone's advantage. A happy vision rose before Superintendent Griffin, of vast armies of criminals destroying each other on some foreign field, while the law-abiding prospered at home.

Alas, it would never happen – but in the meantime he could at least make life as difficult as possible for the evil-doers. Griffin wandered casually past one of the lines which was forming at the foot of a gangplank, caught the eye of Constable Foster, the plainclothes man who was his colleague for the morning, and stepped into an office doorway out of the general view. In a moment Foster joined him.

"Clipper McCarthy's hanging about the second-class plank," said Griffin, and the constable looked vacant.

"Clipper who, sir?" he asked, and Griffin sighed.

"Clipper McCarthy," he said patiently, "has a real bad habit of putting his grubby little hand in other people's pockets and removing their valuables, see? How long you been off the uniform beat, boy?"

"Three months, sir."

"And you don't know Clipper yet? Don't you look at the sheets, then? How d'you think you're going to do a worthwhile job if you can't spot the wrong 'uns? And how you going to spot the wrong 'uns if you don't study the sheets to see what they look like?" Griffin shook his great head. "Now, Clipper is a weedy little runt in a mole-hair jacket and cloth cap, and he's sizing up a likely mark this minute at the far gangway. So just you go and keep him under observation, wait till he makes his dip, and then try the quality of his collar, see?" And Griffin humorously rubbed forefinger and thumb together. "Wait – boy! Take off your hat, and carry it. We don't want Clipper to think you're a policeman, do we?"

Constable Foster removed his hat and turned away, only mildly resentful. Sarcastic old bastard. But nobody's fool, either – Welland and Murphy would never have thought to tell him to take off his tile. They didn't call him Griff the Copper for nothing, and Constable Foster infinitely preferred the Superintendent's gentle irony to Sergeant Murphy's irritating habit of making him turn his back to a crowd and describe the appearance and mannerisms of some suspect they'd had under observation – that was a real pig's trick. Foster spotted the mole-hair jacket hovering close to the passenger line, and with his bowler in his hand sauntered off at an angle and lurked nonchalantly.

Superintendent Griffin resumed his progress and paused near an iron shed-pillar to observe the smaller, better-dressed queue which was forming at the first-class gangplank. There were only half the people, but ten times the amount of small luggage that there was at the second-class, with a small army of stewards and cabin boys bustling among the piled bags and cases under the guidance of valets and ladies" maids, each jealously seeing that his or her employer's effects were carefully taken aboard.

"Watch what you're doing there! Those are his lordship's optical instruments!" A sharp-faced gentleman's gentleman in a wing collar and regulation bowler prodded with his umbrella at a cabin boy who was shouldering a small leather case. "Take particular care of them – and place them in Cabin 28 directly, d'you hear?" He chivvied the boy like an agitated hen, and Superintendent Griffin abruptly stopped his casual survey, frowned, smiled, and then moved slowly forward towards a stout and familiar back near the foot of the gangplank.

"Good morning, my lord," he said quietly, and the man turned. He was a large, prosperous gentleman in a fur coat, with a bland fleshy face that might have belonged to a captain of industry or a minor statesman. He started slightly at the sight of Griffin, and then smiled with over-hearty assurance as he returned the greeting.

"Why, good morning, inspector!"

"Superintendent."

"Indeed? Then I congratulate you."

"I'll bet you do," said Griffin amiably. His eyes moved from the man to the bold-eyed brunette beside him; she avoided the policeman's glance and adjusted her sable wrap disdainfully. "A little business trip to the States – my lord?"

"No – no, just pleasure, superintendent. A short holiday for my niece and myself."

"I see." Griffin eyed the brunette sceptically. "What happened to that other niece of yours – Lady Hilda, wasn't it? Or was she your daughter?" He watched the cabin boy carrying the leather box up the gangway. "And optical instruments – well. Come in little packs of fifty-two, do they, with kings and queens and jacks on 'em?"

The fleshy man looked uneasy. "Have a heart," he muttered, out of the corner of his mouth. "The ship isn't on your patch – and I'm not breaking any law – "

"You will be, the way you play," said Griffin, and turned away without another word, to draw the Chief Steward aside at the foot of the gangplank and warn him that his first-class passengers included "Reader" Monk, alias Monte Carlo Monk, alias Dutch Monty, alias Lord Whatever-it-was, cardsharp and confidence man extraordinary, and scourge of the luxury liners. There was nothing the Superintendent could do about him, officially, but if the Chief Steward could ensure that his lordship's little leather case, which no doubt contained the tools of his trade, to wit, stacked decks, readers, clips, springs, strippers, hold-outs, and the like, somehow failed to turn up in his cabin, he would be saving the other passengers considerable expense and annoyance.

Having done his good deed, Griffin ignored the sullen glare of the

583

frustrated swindler, tipped his hat courteously to the disconcerted niece, and glanced at the other passengers. A middle-aged woman and her maid, the latter carrying a little wicker cage containing a beribboned kitten; two fairly obvious businessmen in fur-collared coats, chuckling over a joke, the flushed red faces creased with mirth; an elderly female in a wheelchair pushed by a liveried coachman, with a maid and companion either side of her; a tall man, dark-featured, with thoughtful eyes and a black moustache lightly flecked with grey.

The Superintendent knew at once that he had seen the man before, but that was all. English, by the look of him, well-dressed with that simplicity which bespoke Savile Row or thereabouts. Not one of the Superintendent's clients, just someone he had seen some time or other, perhaps years ago, possibly embarking or landing. Probably not a businessman, not quite austere enough to be military, didn't have the air of a professional man, either. More like a gentleman of leisure. Age about forty, travelling without a servant, evidently, since he was carrying his own suitcase – might be a rich sportsman; there was a hint of strength, of the out-of-doors, that didn't quite go with the expensive broadcloth and tilted homburg and quiet air of city money.

". . . and I shall be able to have Kitty in the cabin with me, shan't I? Her feeding is so important, you know, and she has never been to sea before, have you, Kitty?" The middle-aged woman smiled fondly as she tickled the cat through the bars of its wicker cage.

"Certainly, madam. The quarantine people will wish to examine her in New York, you understand. Cabin 22, steward, port side. A pleasant voyage, madam. Good morning, sir."

The tall man with the suitcase was at the foot of the gangway, standing patiently while the Chief Steward ran a finger down his list and produced a cabin card.

"Cabin 43, sir. Starboard side. Boy – Cabin 43. A pleasant voyage, sir. Good morning, madam."

The tall passenger, having taken his card and thanked the Chief Steward, turned and looked back at the crowded sheds and quayside. He stood for a long moment, just looking, tapping the card against his thumb, while the cabin boy hovered beside him, waiting to take his suitcase. Griffin transferred his attention to the next passenger, the elderly lady in the wheel-chair with her attendants, and then to Monty the cardsharp and his popsy, who had entered into talk with the two businessmen; they were raising their hats gallantly to the smiling lady, who was adjusting her veil and looking fetching as Monty performed the introductions. "... my niece, Lady Cynthia ... how do you do? ... such a jolly voyage!" You'll learn, you poor bastards, thought Griffin, and turned away, sauntering towards the other gangplanks.

Constable Foster was in the office doorway. Clipper McCarthy had attempted no dip – indeed, the only money he appeared to have gone off with had been a shilling tip bestowed on him by a stout woman whose bags he had carried.

"Sure she's still got her purse?" grunted Griffin sceptically. "He must have spotted you, boy."

"No, he didn't," protested Foster. "Never even looked at me."

"Then he certainly spotted you," said the Superintendent heavily. He shook his head at the crestfallen constable. "No wonder – you look more like a flatfoot than I do, even." He patted Foster on the shoulder. "Come on, boyo – I'll buy you a cup of tea." There were only a few passengers still waiting at the foot of the gangways now, as the two policemen went in towards the coffee stall.

Later, they came out on the quayside again to watch the huge *Aquitania* as she churned out into midstream, the sirens shrilling, the tugs fussing about her, the water thrashing into yellow oily surge under her stern,

"Fine ship, so she is," commented Griffin, contemplating the great liner with satisfaction. "A fine ship." As they were turning to go, he noticed that on the edge of the quay, where the first-class gangway was now lying neglected under its tarpaulins, there was a small pile of two or three trunks and cases which had not gone aboard; a porter was loading them on to his handcart, trundling it up towards the sheds. As he passed the two policemen he paused to steady one of the trunks which was in danger of slipping; Superintendent Griffin automatically glanced at the labels – they said "*Aquitania*. New York," but someone had scored out the words with a heavy blue pencil and written new directions. Griffin noticed the owner's name, but after five years "M. J. Franklin" touched no chord in his memory.

He watched incuriously as the porter wheeled the cart away, through the echoing shed, towards Riverside Station and the London train.

Also by George MacDonald Fraser
in Harvill Paperback

THE STEEL BONNETS

THE STORY OF THE ANGLO-SCOTTISH
BORDER REIVERS

"If Jesus Christ were emongest them, they would deceave him," it was said of the Border reivers, the rustlers, outlaws and gangsters who terrorized the Anglo-Scottish frontier of four hundred years ago. Theirs is an almost forgotten chapter of British history, preserved largely in folk-tales and ballads. It is the story of the great raiding families – Armstrongs, Elliots, Grahams, Johnstones, Maxwells, Scotts, Kerrs, Nixons and others – of the outlaw bands and broken men, the "hot trod" pursuits, and the great battles of English and Scottish armies across the Marches. *The Steel Bonnets* tells their true story for the first time and in its historical context – how the reivers ran their raids and operated their system of blackmail and terrorism, and how the March Wardens, operating the unique Border law, fought the great lawless community.

"A splendid book, both scholarly and readable, accurate and alive"
HUGH TREVOR-ROPER

Harvill Paperbacks are published by Harvill,
an Imprint of HarperCollins*Publishers*